From Brenda + Terry March 2003.

THE STARS LOOK DOWN

By the same author:

HATTER'S CASTLE

THREE LOVES

GRAND CANARY

THE CITADEL

THE KEYS OF THE KINGDOM

THE GREEN YEARS

THE SPANISH GARDENER

THE MINSTREL BOY

LADY WITH CARNATIONS

THE STARS LOOK DOWN

by

A. J. CRONIN

LONDON
VICTOR GOLLANCZ LTD
1984

First published 1935
This edition 1984

British Library Cataloguing in Publication Data
Cronin, A. J.
The stars look down.
I. Title
823'.912[F] PR6005.R68
ISBN 0-575-03433-5

NOTE

All the characters in this book are imaginary, and no reference is intended to any person, living or dead.

Printed in Great Britain by
Biddles Ltd, Guildford, Surrey

CONTENTS

BOOK I

I

WHEN Martha awoke it was still dark and bitter cold. The wind, pouring across the North Sea, struck freezingly through the cracks which old subsidences had opened in the two-roomed house. Waves pounded distantly. The rest was silence.

She lay quite still in the kitchen bed, holding herself rigidly away from Robert whose coughing and restlessness had fitfully broken the night. For a minute she reflected, sternly facing the new day, choking down the bitterness she felt against him. Then with an effort she got up.

Her bare feet felt the stone floor like ice. She struggled into her clothes quickly, with the active movements of a powerful woman not yet forty. Yet when she had dressed, the exertion left her panting. She was not hungry now—for some queer reason the worst of her hunger had gone days before—but she was sick, deathly sick. Dragging herself to the sink she turned on the tap. No water came. The pipe was frozen.

She lost herself momentarily, stood with her calloused hand pressed against her swollen side staring through the window towards the hesitant dawn. Miners' rows beneath her, stretching dimly, row upon row. To the right the blackness of Sleescale town, the harbour beyond with one cold light and then the colder sea. To the left the stark outline of Neptune No. 17's headgear rising like a gallows against the pale east sky, dominating the town, the harbour and the sea.

The furrow deepened on Martha's brow. Three months now the strike had gone on. At the misery of it she turned abruptly from the window and began to get the fire alight. It was difficult. She had only the damp driftwood that Sammy had gathered the day before and some duff, the worst kind of dross, fetched in by Hughie off the pit-tip. It maddened her that she, Martha Fenwick, always used to fine silkstone coal, to a real collier's fire, should be forced to potch with duff. But at last she had it going. She went through the back door, smashed the new ice on the water-butt with one resentful blow, filled the kettle, came back and set it to boil.

The kettle was a long time. But when it boiled she filled a cup and sat crouched before the fire clasping the cup with both hands, sipping it slowly. The scalding water warmed her, sent vague currents of life through her numbed body. It was not so good as tea; no, no, nothing like tea; but for all that it was good, she felt herself "coming to." The flames darting about the green wood illuminated a bit of old newspaper, torn from her kindling, lying on the pipeclayed hearth. *Mr. Keir Hardie asked in the House of Commons whether, since the destitution is as great as ever in the North, the Government proposes a measure to enable the education authorities to take steps to feed destitute children. The answer given was that the Government did not intend to give authorities power to feed destitute children.* Still sipping her hot water she read it idly. Her face, gaunt as bone, showed nothing, neither interest nor resentment; nothing. It was inscrutable like death.

Suddenly she turned. Yes. He was awake, lying upon his side, his cheek on his palm, in the familiar way, watching her. Instantly all the bitterness surged over her again. Everything, everything, everything—him. Then he began to cough, she knew he had been holding it for fear of her. It was not a racking cough, but a deep, gentle, experienced cough. It was an intimate cough. In fact the cough was himself, not unkindly, possessing him almost benignly. It filled his mouth with a vast quantity of phlegm. Raising himself upon his elbow he spat upon the square of *Tit-Bits*. He seemed always to be cutting these squares from *Tit-Bits*, cutting them carefully, painstakingly, with her old bone-handled potato knife. He had a stock of them, never ran out. He would spit upon the little square, contemplate the result, fold and burn it . . . burn it with a sort of optimism. When he was in bed he dropped the little packets over the edge . . . burned them when he got up.

She felt a sudden hatred of him and the cough that was he, but she rose, refilled the cup with hot water and handed it to him. He took it in silence.

It was lighter. The clock had been the first thing pawned, the temple marble clock her father had won for bowling—a fine man her father and a real champion at pot-stour bowls!—but she judged the time about seven o'clock. She twisted one of David's stockings round her neck, pulled on a man's cloth cap which was now her own, then got into her shabby black cloth coat. That, at least, was something, her coat. She was not a shawl-woman. Never. She was respectable, was, and would be, in spite of everything. All her life . . . respectable.

Without speaking, without looking at him, she went out, the front door this time. Bracing her figure to the bitter wind she set off down Cowpen Street, the steep slant leading to the town. It was colder outside, terribly cold. The Terraces were deserted, not a soul in sight. She passed the Salutation, passed Middlerig, passed the deserted steps of the Institute, covered with frozen spittle, the spume of past debate. The side wall was chalked, *Mass meeting at three.* Charley Gowlan the check-weigher had wrote that—the big boozy waster.

She shivered and tried to hasten her pace. But she could not go faster. The child within her, still without life, lay heavy as lead, pulling, dragging, bending her down. To be like this; at such a time! Three grown sons; David, the youngest, nearly fifteen; and then to be caught. She clenched her hands. Indignation boiled within her. Him, again, coming home in liquor, silently, doggedly, in liquor, to have his will of her.

In the town most of the shops were shut. Many of them would not open. Not even the Co-op., where credit, strained to the uttermost, was finally exhausted. What did it matter, anyway, she had one red two-penny token in her purse; that would buy her plenty, wouldn't it ? Not Masters either—for two days he had been shuttered, glutted with pledges, her own good things among them, his three brass balls dangling without promise. Not Murchison, nor Dobbs, nor Bates. They were all shut, all frightened, dead frightened of trouble.

She turned the corner into Lamb Street, crossed the road opposite Ramage's, went down the narrow Scut to the slaughter-house. As she approached, her face brightened. Hob was there, sweeping the concrete yard, sweeping in his shirt-sleeves and leather apron.

" Anything this morning, Hob ? " Her voice was quiet and she stood quiet, waiting until he should notice her.

He had noticed her all along, but still kept his head down, slushing the water with his brush. Steam rose from his wet red arms. She did not mind. Hob was all right, Hob *knew* her, Hob would do what he could. She waited.

" You haven't a bit left-ower, Hob ? " She was not asking much, an unwanted piece, a piece of the lights or pluck, usually thrown out as offal.

He stopped at last, not looking at her, surly because he must refuse.

" Aw've nowt in the place."

She looked at him.

" No ? "

He shook his head.

" Not nowt! Ramage made us kill six a'clock last night and cart everything te the shop. He must ov heard aw was handin' out nap bones. Near blew my head off! "

She drew in her lips. So Ramage had stopped their chance of soup, of a scanty liver-fry. She looked worried. Hob was slashing viciously with the brush.

She walked away, thinking, hastening gradually, back through the Scut, along Lamb Street to the harbour. One glance was enough. She stopped short while the wind billowed her skirt, dismay at last flooding her pinched face. Not a chance of a herring even; though she had brought herself to the point of asking the Macers' charity. The *Annie Macer* lay with the other boats, lined behind the stubby breakwater, nets snug, untouched. The weather, she thought, heavily, letting her gaze shift to the dirty churning waves beyond. None of the boats had been out.

Martha turned slowly and began, droopingly, to go back. More people in the streets now, the town bestirring, a few carts clattering over the cobbles. Harkness of Bethel Street School went by, a little man with a pointed beard, gold-rimmed glasses and a warm overcoat; some rope-work girls in clogs; a clerk to the Council Offices hurrying, blowing on his hands. They all avoided her, studiously, avoided her eye. They did not know her. But they did know she was from the Terraces, part of the trouble, the blight that had lain upon the town these last three months. Her feet dragged as she began to climb the hill.

Outside Teasdale's bakery, a horse and van stood loading bread for delivery. Dan Teasdale, the son, hurried in and out with a big basket on his arm, loaded with new-baked loaves. As she came abreast the shop the hot sweet scent of the new bread rose from the basement bakehouse, and caught her by the throat. Instinctively she paused. She could have swooned with desire for the bread. At that moment Dan came out with another basketful. He saw her, saw the ravening in her face. He paled; a kind of horror clouded his eyes. Without thinking, he took a loaf and thrust it into her hands.

She said nothing, not a word, but a mist of gratitude, the nearest she ever got to tears, danced before her as she continued up Cowpen Street into Sebastopol Row. She liked Dan, a decent lad who was working for his ticket at the Neptune, but now, since the strike, was helping his father, driving the van, delivering the bread; he often spoke to Davey. Breathing a little fast from the climb, she laid her hand upon the door of her house.

" Mrs. Kinch's Alice has the congestion." Hannah Brace, her next-door neighbour, stopped her on the way in.

Martha nodded: all that week the children of the Terraces had been going down with pneumonia.

" I'll look round later, tell Mrs. Kinch," she said and entered her own house.

They were up and dressed, the four of them, Robert and her three sons, gathered round the fire; but as usual her eyes fell first on Sammy. He smiled at her, that ready, tight-lipped grin which sent his deep-set blue eyes right out of sight beneath his nobby forehead. There was an infinite hardihood behind Sam's grin. He was only nineteen, already a hewer in the Neptune, Martha's eldest son, her favourite.

" Eh, look," Sam winked at David. " Look what yer mother has been and gone and done. She's been and gone and done and pinched a loaf for ye."

In his corner Davey smiled dutifully: a thin, quiet white-faced boy with a long, serious, stubborn face. His shoulder-blades stuck out as he stooped over the fire; his big dark eyes looked inquisitive usually, but they were less inquisitive now. He was fourteen years of age, horse-putter in the Neptune, Paradise section, nine hours each day underground bank to bank, now on strike and rather peckish.

" What do ye think about it, lads ? " Sam went on. " Here's your uncle Sammy trainin' for the living-skeleton act. Loses ten stone a fortnight, doin' the Hints for Stout Ladies, doin' the cure for cor*pul*ency. And then wor mother walks in wi' a banquet. Hard lines on Sammy, eh, Hughie lad ? "

Martha drew down her dark brows at him.

" You're lucky to be getting it." And she began to slice the loaf.

They all watched her, fascinated; even Hughie looked up from cobbling a patch on his old football boots, and it took a lot to take Hughie's mind off football. Hughie was mad on football, centre forward —at seventeen, mind you—of the local Sleescale team when not hand-putting in the Paradise section of the Neptune. Hughie did not answer Sam. Hughie never had much to say, silent, even more silent than his silent father. But Hughie looked at the loaf.

" Pardon *me*, mother," Sammy jumped up and took the plate. " Whatever in the world wor I thinkin' ov te forget my manners. Allow me, said the Duke, in his magnificent uniform ov the Tyneside Hussars." He offered the plate to his father.

Robert took a slice. He looked at it, then at Martha.

" Did this come from the Guardians ? If it did I'm not wantin' it."

She looked back at him.

He said in a defeated voice:

" I'm asking you if this bread came from the Guardians ? "

She still looked at him, still thinking of his madness in flinging their savings into the strike. She said:

" No."

Sammy stepped in with loud cheerfulness.

" What in all the world does it matter, wor all goin' te eat it I suspect." He met his father's eyes with the same hardy cheerfulness. " Ye needna look that way, dad. All gud things come te an end. And aw'm not bleedin' well sorry. Aw want te be workin'. Not sittin' about handless like, waitin' for mother te fetch in wor bait." He turned to Davey: " Here, count, have a doormat—do. Don't hesitate. Believe me, they'll only be chucked out."

Martha snatched back the plate from his hand.

" Aw don't like that kind of fun, Sammy. You oughtna te mock good food."

She frowned upon him heavily. But she gave him the biggest slice, And serving Hughie next, she kept the smallest to herself

II

Ten o'clock. David took up his cap, slipped out, and sauntered along the unevenly sunk pavement of Inkerman Row. All the miners' rows in Sleescale were named after the glorious victories of the Crimea. The top row, David's row, was Inkerman; the next Alma; the one below Sebastopol; and the lowest of all, Joe's row, was Balaclava. David was on his way to Joe's house now, to see " if Joe was comin' out."

The wind had fallen, the sun broke through unexpectedly. Though dazzled, not quite used to it, the brilliant profusion of sunshine was beautiful to David. In winter, when he was working, often he did not see real sunlight for days on end. Dark in the morning when he went down; dark at night when he came up.

But to-day, though cold, was bright, flooding his being with a strange brightness, reminding him oddly of those rare occasions when his father took him fishing up the Wansbeck. Away from darkness and pit dirt, green hazel woods, a ripple of clean water——

" Look, dad, look! " as a clump of early primroses yielded themselves to his excited eye.

He turned the corner of Balaclava Row.

Like the other rows, Balaclava stretched for a bad five hundred yards —a reach of grimed stone houses sooty black in colour, but daubed and seamed with clumsy veins of white where mortar had been added to fill the larger and more recent cracks. The square chimneys, broken and uneven, looked drunken; the long line of roofs undulated from subsidences, like a wavy sea; the yards were palinged with decayed railway sleepers, broken stubs and rusty corrugated iron, backed by heaps of slag and pit-waste. Each yard had its closet and each closet had its pail. An iron pail. The closets stood like sentry-boxes, between the rows, and at the end of the rows was a huddle of home-made outhouses, built on lumpy ground beside a span of naked rail tracks. Neptune No. 17 stood up near the middle, with the hummocky drab of the Snook behind. The Snook was all waste land, cracked and puddled and seamed with the old Neptune workings that went back one hundred years. The old Scupperhole yawned in the Snook. All of it had to do with pits. The far flat background was all pit chimneys, pit heaps, pit-head gear, pit everything. A string of washing flapping its vivid blues and scarlets against the dreary pattern of dirt caught the eye like an affront. That string of washing gave to the picture a grim, perverted beauty.

David knew it all and he did not like it much. He liked it less now. Over the long line of dreary back-to-back dwellings there hung an air of apathy and defeat. Some colliers—Slogger Leeming, Keeker Howe, Bob Ogle and a few others that made up the gambling school in ordinary times—squatted upon their hunkers against the wall. They were not schoolin' now, they had no coppers for schoolin', they were just crookin' their houghs. They squatted in silence. Bob Ogle, marrow in the Paradise foreshift, stroking the narrow head of his whippet bitch, nodded to Davey. Slogger Leeming said:

" How, then, Davey ? "

David said:

" How, again, Slogger ? "

The others looked at him curiously, identifying him with Robert, his father, who had brought them out. They saw a pale-faced boy dressed in a shoddy suit he had out-grown, a cotton muffler and heavy pit clogs because his boots were in pawn, with hair that needed cutting, thin wrists and work-big hands.

He felt their scrutiny upon him, and sustained it calmly as, with his chin thrust well out, he walked towards Number 19, which was Joe's house. Above the doorway of No. 19 was a notice irregularly painted: *Agent Flyaway Cycles. Undertaking. Boards kept.* David went in.

Joe and his dad, Charley Gowlan, were at breakfast: a china bowl was on the wooden table full of cold pot pie, a big brown teapot stood beside it a tin of condensed milk punched open, and a raggedly hacked loaf. The clutter of the table was unbelievable; the whole house—two rooms joined by a perpendicular ladder—was cluttered. Dirt, disorder, food in plenty, a roaring fire, clothes flung everywhere, dishes unwashed, the smell of living, beer, grease, sweat, a dirty blousy comfort.

" Hulloh, lad. how are ye this mornin' ? " Charley Gowlan, with his night-shirt tucked into his trousers, his galluses hanging loose over his fat stomach, his bare feet in carpet slippers, shoved a big bit of meat into his big mouth. He waved the knife in his big red fist and nodded agreeably to David. Charley was always agreeable: never anything but friendly, ay, a matey beggor, Big Charley Gowlan, the checkweigher at the Neptune. Well in with the men; well in with Barras. Willing to turn his hand to anything, from housekeeping—since his wife was dead these three years—back to rabbit dodging or salmon poaching up the Coquet.

David sat down and watched Joe and Charley eat. They ate with infinite relish: Joe's young jaws champed methodically, Charley smacked his fat lips as he knifed out the rich jellied gravy from the pot pie. David couldn't help himself; his teeth watered painfully, a thin trickle of saliva ran into his mouth. Suddenly, when they were nearly done, Charley paused, as at an afterthought, in his knifing at the bowl.

" Would ye like te scrape the pot, lad ? "

David shook his head: something in him made him refuse. He smiled.

" I've had my breakfast."

" Ah, weel. If ye've had yor bait." Charley's small eyes twinkled slyly in his big red face. He finished the dish. " An' how does yor feyther take it now we're like to be beat ? "

" I don't know."

Charley licked his knife and sighed contentedly.

" A heap o' trouble it's been. Aw diddent want it. Heddon diddent want it. There's none ov us wanted it. Meykin' trouble ower backskins and a happenny ton raise. Aw said from the start it was no gud."

David looked at Charley. Charley was the men's checkweigher, a lodge official, and well in with Heddon the Union agent from Tynecastle. Charley knew it wasn't just the backskins, nor the halfpenny rise. He said thoughtfully:

" There's a lot of water in Scupper Flats."

" Watter! " Charley smiled: a broad omniscient smile. His work never took him inbye; he checked his tubs upon the surface as they came screeching to the bank. He could afford to be omniscient. " The Paradise always was a wet beggor. Watter's been there mony a day. An' Scupper Flats is like to be no worse than the rest o't. Yor feyther's not feared ov a drop watter, is he ? "

Conscious of Charley's slow grin, David sat hard upon his indignation. He said indifferently:

" He's worked in it twenty-five years, he oughtn't to be feared of it."

" That's reet, that's reet, aw know all aboot it. Stick up for yor dad. If you doan't then God knows who will. Aw think none the worse ov ye for it. Yor a canny lad." He belched wind loudly, scliffed over to his seat by the fire, yawned, stretched himself and began to fill his blackened clay.

Joe and David went out.

" He don't have to go in the Paradise! " Joe remarked irreverently the moment the door had banged. " The old beggor, it would do him a power of good to stand in the wet places like I have to."

" It isn't only the wet, Joe," David persisted. " You know what my dad says."

" I know, I know! I'm sick of hearin' it an' so are the rest of the lads, Davey. Yor dad has got notions about Scupper Flats. He thinks he knows the whole shoot! "

David said warmly:

" He knows a lot, let me tell you. He didn't start it for fun."

Joe said:

" Naw! But some of the lads did. They was sick of workin' in water and thought it was fun for to stop. Now they've had that much bloddy fun they'd give their navels for to start in again, ay, even if the Flats were roofed with water."

" Well! Let them start in again."

Joe said sourly:

" They're goin' to start, bet your bloddy life, you wait till the meetin' at three. But don't get up on your hind legs. I'm as sick of it as you are. I'm sick of the whole bloddy pit anyhow. I'm goin' to slip my hook first chance I get. I'm not goin' to be stuck in this sheugh all my days. I want to get some brass and see a bit of life."

David remained silent, troubled and indignant, feeling that life was going all against him. He wanted to get out of the Neptune too—but not Joe's way. He remembered that occasion when Joe had run away before and been brought back, blubbering, by Roddam, the police sergeant, to be soundly leathered by his father.

They walked on without speaking, Joe swaggering a little, throwing his weight about, his hands in his pockets. He was a finely built lad, two years older than David, with square shoulders, a straight back, thick curly black hair and small alert brown eyes. Joe was extremely good-looking in a physical way. And Joe knew it. His glance was full of self-assurance, the very tilt of his cap dashing, conceited, aggressive. Presently he resumed:

" Ye've got to have money if you want to have sport. And will you ever make money in the pit? Not on your bloddy soul. Not big money, you won't. Well, I want to have sport. And I want big money. I'm goin' places. You're lucky, you are. You're goin' to Tynecassel, maybe. Your dad wants you to go to college, that's another of his notions, like. But I've got to look out for myself. And I'm goin' to look out for myself. See! That's how to do it. Get there first or somebody'll get there afore ye." He suddenly shut off his bluster and slapped David heartily upon the back. He smiled at him, a genial, affable smile. When Joe chose, none could be more genial, more affable—a geniality which warmed the heart, an affability which radiated from Joe's handsome brown eyes and revealed him as a prince of good fellows.

" Come on, now, to the boat, Davey, we'll set a shoreline, then we'll row out and see what we can pick up."

By this time they had passed down Quay Street and reached the shore. They dropped over the sea wall on to the hard sand below. A high range of dunes matted with coarse grass and salt-stung rushes lay behind them. David liked the dunes. On barfe-Saturdays in the summer, when they had come outbye from the Neptune and his dad had gone with the marrows in his set to split up at the Salutation, David would be amongst the rushes, all alone, listening to the sound of the lark, dropping his book to search for the tiny soaring speck against the bright blue sky. He felt that he would like to lie down there now. His head was giddy again, the thick slice of new bread which he had eaten so ravenously lay like lead in his stomach. But Joe was already at the breakwater.

They climbed the breakwater and reached the harbour. There, in the slack scummy water, some lads from the Terraces were fishing for coal. With an old pail, knocked full of holes, fixed to a pole, they were dredging for lumps which had fallen off the barges in working times. Deprived of the fortnightly allowance from the pit, they were scraping in the mud for fuel which would otherwise have been forgotten. Joe looked at them with secret contempt. He paused, his legs planted wide apart, hands still bulging his trouser pockets. He despised them. His cellar was full of good coal pinched off the pit head, he had pinched it himself, the best in the heap. His belly was full of food, good food, Charley, his dad, had looked after that. There was only one way to do it. Take things, go for them, get them, not stand shivering and half-starved, scratching about in the feeble hope that something would take a soft-hearted jump and come tumbling in your bucket.

" How do, Joe, lad," Ned Softley, the weak-witted trapper in the Paradise, called out, propitiating. His long nose was red, his undersized skimpy frame shuddered spasmodically from cold. He laughed vaguely. " Got a fag, Joe, hinny ? Aw'm dyin' for a smoke."

" Curse it, Ned, lad . . ." Joe's sympathy was instant and magnificent. " If this isn't my last! " He pulled a fag from behind his ear, considered it sadly, and lit it with the friendliest regret. But once Ned's back was turned, Joe grinned. Naturally Joe had a full packet of Woodbines in his pocket. But was Joe going to let Ned know that ? Not on your life! Still grinning he turned to David when a shout made him swing round again.

It was Ned's shout, a loud protesting wail. He had filled his sack, or near enough, after three hours' work in the biting wind and had made to shoulder it for home. But Jake Wicks was there before him. Jake, a burly lout of seventeen, had been waiting calmly to appropriate Ned's coal. He picked up the sack and with a pugnacious stare at the others coolly sauntered down the harbour.

A roar of laughter went up from the crowd of lads. God, could you beat it! Jake pinching Softley's duff, walking away with it easy as you like, while Ned screamed and whimpered after him like a lunatic. It was the epitome of humour—Joe's laugh was louder than any.

But David did not laugh. His face had turned quite pale.

" He can't take that coal," he muttered. " It's Softley's coal. Softley worked for it."

" I'd like to see who'd stop him." Joe choked with his own amusement, " Oh, Gor, look at Softley's mug, just take a look at it . . ."

Young Wicks advanced along the jetty, easily carrying the sack, followed by the weeping Softley and a ragged, derisive crowd.

" It's my duff," Softley kept whimpering, while the tears ran down his cheeks. " Aw mucked for it, aw did, for my mam te hev a fire . . ."

David clenched his fists and took a side step right in the path of Wicks. Jake drew up suddenly.

" Hello," he said, " what's like the matter with you ? "

" That's Ned's duff you've got," David said from between his teeth. " You can't take it this way. It's not fair. It's not right."

" Holy Gee! " Jake said blankly. " And who'll stop me like ? "

" I will."

Everybody stopped laughing. Jake carefully put down the sack.

" You will ? "

David jerked his head affirmatively. He could not speak now, his whole being was so tense with indignation. He boiled at the injustice of Jake's action. Wicks was almost a man, he smoked, swore and drank like a man, he was a foot taller and two stones heavier than David. But David didn't care. Nothing mattered, nothing, except that Wicks should be stopped from victimising Softley.

Wicks held out his two fists, one on top of the other.

"Knock down the blocks," he taunted. It was the traditional invitation to fight.

David took one look at Jake's full pimply face surmounted by its bush of tow-coloured hair. Everything was defined and vivid. He could see the blackheads in Jake's unhealthy skin, a tiny stye coming on his left eyelid. Then like a flash he knocked Jake's fists down and smashed his right fist hard into Jake's nose.

It was a lovely blow. Jake's nose flattened visibly and spurted a stream of blood. The crowd roared and a thrill of fierce exhilaration shot up David's spine.

Jake retreated, shook his head like a dog, then came in wildly, swinging his arms like flails.

At the same moment someone on the fringe of the crowd gave a warning shout.

"Look out lads, here's Wept comin'."

David hesitated, half-turned his head and took Jake's fist full on his temple. All at once the scene receded mysteriously, he felt giddy, he fancied for an instant he was going down the pit shaft, so sudden was the darkness that rushed upon him, so loud the ringing in his ears. Then he fainted.

The crowd took one look at David, then scattered hastily. Even Ned Softley hurried away. But he had his coal now.

Meanwhile Wept came up. He had been walking along the shore, contemplating the thin ebb and flow of the furthest waves upon the sand. Jesus Wept was very fond of the sea. Every year he took ten days out of the Neptune and spent them at Whitley Bay quietly walking up and down the front between boards bearing his favourite text: *Jesus wept for the sins of the world.* The same text was painted in gold letters outside his little house, which was why, though his own name was Clem Dickery, he was known as Wept or, less commonly, Jesus Wept. Although he was a collier Wept did not live in the Terraces. His wife, Susan Dickery, kept the small homemade mutton pie shop at the end of Lamb Street and the Dickerys lived above the shop. Susan favoured a more violent text. It was: *Prepare to meet thy God.* She had it printed upon all her paper bags, which gave rise to the saying in Sleescale: Eat Dickery's pies and prepare to meet thy God. But the pies were very good. David liked the pies. And he liked Clem Dickery. Wept was a quiet little fanatic. And he was at least sincere.

When David came round, dazedly opening his eyes, Wept was bending over him, slapping the palms of his hands, watching him with a certain melancholy solicitude.

" I'm right enough, now," David said, raising himself upon his elbow weakly.

Wept, with remarkable restraint, made no reference to the fight. Instead he said:

" When did ye eat food last ? "

" This morning. I had my breakfast."

" Can ye stand up ? "

David got to his feet, holding on to Wept's arm, swaying unsteadily, trying to smile it off.

Wept looked at him darkly. He always went directly for the truth. He said:

" Yor weak for want ov food. Come away wi' me to my house." Still supporting David he led him slowly over the sands, across the dunes, and into his house in Lamb Street.

In the kitchen of Wept's house David sat down by the table. It was in this room that Wept held his " kitchen meetings." From the walls highly coloured allegories flamed: The Last Trumpet, The Judgment Seat, The Broad and Narrow Paths. A great many angels were in the pictures, upbearing sexless blond figures in spotless garments to the blare of golden trumpets. Light blazed upon the angels. But there was darkness too, wherein, amidst the ruins of Corinthian columns, the beasts of darkness roared, and harried the massed hordes that trembled upon the abyss.

Hung from the mantelpiece were strings of dried herbs and seaweeds. Wept knew all the simples, gathered them assiduously in their season by the hedgerows and amongst the rocks. He stood by the fire now, brewing some camomile tea in a small marled tea-pot. Finally he poured out a cup and offered it to David. Then without a word he went out of the room.

David drank the infusion. It was bitter, but aromatic and steaming hot. It warmed him, comforted him and strengthened him, caused him to forget all about the fight, made him feel hungry. At that the door opened and Wept came in again followed by his wife. She was oddly like him, a small neat woman, dressed all in black, quiet, restrained in movement, with that same composed intentness of expression. Without speaking she put a plate before David. On the plate were two new-baked mutton pies. From a little blue enamel jug she poured some hot gravy over each pie.

" Eat them slow," she observed calmly. Then she drew back to where her husband stood. They both studied him as, after a moment's hesitation, he began to eat.

The pies were delicious, the gravy rich and savoury. He finished the first to the last crumb; then, looking up suddenly, caught their serious eyes still fixed upon him. In a solemn undertone Wept quoted: " I will nourish you and your little ones; and he comforted and spake kindly unto them."

David tried to smile his gratitude; but something, the unexpectedness of this kindness he had received, caught him by the throat. He hated it in himself but he could not help it. A terrible rush of feeling came upon him, the memory of what he had been through, of what they had all been through in these last three months. He felt the horror of it: the scrimping, the pawning, the latent bitterness between his parents, his mother's anger, his father's obstinacy. He was only fourteen. Yesterday he had eaten a turnip taken from Liddle's Farm. In this rich and beautiful world he had gone like a beast to the field and taken a turnip to appease his hunger.

He supported his head on his thin hand. A sudden passionate aspiration rose in him to do something . . . something . . . something to prevent all this. Something to uplift and heal humanity. He must do it. He would do it. A tear dropped from his eye and mingled with the gravy of the mutton pie. Upon the walls the angels blew their trumpets. Shamefaced, David blew his nose.

III

HALF-PAST one; and lunch at the Law almost over. Sitting up straight, with his bare knees under the white damask and his boots barely touching the deep red Axminster, Arthur continued to importune his father with loving, troubled eyes. The concealed tension in the air, the sense of crisis, dismayed, almost paralysed him. As was always the case in the face of an emotional crisis, his appetite was gone, even the pretence of eating made him sick. He knew that the men were meeting to-day, his father's men who ought to have been working honestly and faithfully in his father's pit. He knew that everything hinged upon the meeting, whether the men would go back or this awful strike go on. A little shiver of anxiety went through him at the thought; his eyes burned with loyalty towards his father.

He was waiting, too, for the invitation to accompany his father to Tynecastle, he had been waiting since ten o'clock that morning when he had heard the order given to Bartley to have the dog-cart ready. But the usual invitation did not come. His father was going to Tynecastle, going to Todd's, and he, Arthur, was not going with him. It was very hard to bear.

At the table a certain amount of calm conversation went on, conducted and dominated by his father. During the entire period of the strike this calm conversation had been maintained. Always on quite irrelevant subjects—the Choral Union's next performance of the *Messiah* maybe, or how mother's new medicine was suiting her, or how fresh the flowers on grandma's grave had kept—and always calm, perfectly calm. Richard Barras was a calm man. Everything he did exhibited inflexible control. He sat at the head of his table, with iron serenity, as though the three months' strike at his Neptune colliery were the merest quibble. He sat very straight in his big chair—that was why Arthur sat straight too—eating cheese, celery of his own growing and bath oliver biscuits. It was plain food, the whole lunch was plain, Barras would have nothing but the plainest dishes—he liked regularity, too—thin sliced beef, cold ham, a joint of mutton, in their turn. He despised richness and show upon the table. He permitted neither. He ate almost abstractedly, compressing his lips which were narrow, and of a good colour, crunching the celery with his sound teeth. He was not a big man, but he had a fine chest, thick arms and big hands. He conveyed a powerful sense of physical vitality. His complexion was florid, his neck so short and muscular his head seemed sunk in the barrel of his chest. His iron-grey head was closely cut, his cheek-bones prominent, his eyes unusually penetrating and well defined. He had a northern look about him not exactly rugged but solid, hard. A man of firm conviction and sound evangelical belief, a Liberal, a strong sabbatarian, who held family evening prayers, gave readings from the Scripture which often made Arthur cry, and was not afraid to own that he had written hymns in his youth. There was nothing that Barras was afraid to own. As he sat there, against the yellow varnished background of the large American organ which—from his love of Handel—he had built into the dining-room at a great expense, he radiated his own spiritual integrity. Arthur often felt this radiation. He loved his father. To Arthur his father was absolute, he was like God.

" Come, Arthur, eat your pudding, dear," Aunt Carrie, chiding him gently, recalled his perplexed eyes to his plate. St. George's pudding, made up of cake-ends, the burnt pieces, which he detested. But he struggled with it, hoping his father would notice and approve. Hilda had finished already, was staring straight ahead with her dark, forbidding expression. Grace, smiling and artless, was enjoying a secret happiness with herself.

" Shall you be home for tea, Richard ? " Aunt Carrie asked respectfully.

" Yes! At five o'clock." The voice was concise and self-controlled.

" Yes, Richard."

" You might ask Harriet if she has any commissions for me, to-day."

" Yes, Richard."

Aunt Carrie inclined her head. She always showed a glad passion of obedience towards Richard; and in any case her head was usually inclined. She carried it to one side in token of her submission; submission to everybody and to everything; but chiefly to her lot in life. She knew her position, did Aunt Caroline Wandless. Though she was of a good Northumberland family, a county family, she did not presume upon it. She never presumed, not even upon the fact that she was Richard's sister-in-law. She looked after the children, gave them lessons every forenoon in the schoolroom, sat up with them when they were sick, waited hand and foot on Harriet, prepared delicacies, did the flowers, darned socks, knitted comforters and turned over the dirty linen of the household, all with an air of genteel subservience. Five years before, when Harriet took to her bed, Aunt Carrie had come to the Law, to make herself useful as she had always done on the occasions of Harriet's confinements. At forty, with a thickening figure, a pale plump face, a brow creased by a slightly worried frown and neutral untidy hair, she was still making herself useful. She must have had innumerable opportunities to assert herself. But she had never forgotten that she was a dependant, she had acquired the little tricks of the dependant. She kept a tea-pot in her own room and a private store of biscuits; while the others were talking, she would slip out of a room silently, as though deciding suddenly she was not wanted; in public she spoke with marked correctness to the servants, but in private she would talk to them agreeably, even familiarly, with pleasant propitiating ways: Now, Ann, would you care to have this blouse? Look, it's hardly worn, child . . . She had a little money of her own: about one hundred pounds a year from Consols. She dressed always in the same shade of grey. She limped slightly from a carriage accident in her youth and there was a vague inference, wholly untrue, that she had, at the same time, been badly treated by a gentleman. She was extremely fond of hot baths and took one every night of her life. Her horror was that she might be found using the bathroom when Richard required it. Occasionally this gave her nightmare, from which she awoke pale and sweating, convinced that Richard had *seen* her in the bath.

Barras surveyed the table. No one was eating.

"Will you take a biscuit, Arthur?" he inquired firmly, with his hand on the silver lid of the squat glass barrel.

"No, thank you, father." Arthur swallowed tremulously.

Richard filled his glass with water, held it for a moment with a steady hand. The water seemed more clear, more cold because he held it. He drank slowly.

Silence. Richard rose and went out of the room.

Arthur almost burst into tears. Why, why was his father not taking him to Tynecastle, on to-day of all days, when he wanted to be near him? Why was he not taking him to Todd's? His father obviously had business with Adam Todd, who was a mining engineer, his father's oldest friend; but that didn't matter, he could have taken him, surely, and let him play with Hetty. With a swelling heart he hung about the hall, which Aunt Carrie always referred to as the vestibule, staring at the pattern of black and white tiles, staring at his father's lovely pictures on the walls, hoping against hope. Hilda had gone straight upstairs, marching to her room with a book. But it didn't matter. There was never much feeling between Hilda and himself. She was too abrupt, severe, unreasonably passionate; she appeared always to be struggling within herself, struggling against something unseen. Though she was only seventeen, three months ago, just before the strike began, she had put her hair up. That removed her further than ever. He felt that Hilda was not lovable. She was not good-looking either. She was harsh, with an air of despising everything. She had an olive skin. She did not smell nice.

While he stood in the hall, Grace came down from the schoolroom with an apple in her hand.

" Let's go and see Boxer," she begged. " Do let's go, Arthur."

He gazed down at Grace. She was eleven years of age, a year younger, a foot shorter than himself. He envied Grace her happiness. Grace had the happiest disposition. She was a sweet, lovely, dreadfully untidy child. The crock-comb pushed lop-sidedly through her soft fair hair gave her little face a comic look of wonder. Her big blue eyes radiated an artless innocence. Even Hilda loved Grace. He had seen her, after the most violent display of temper, catch hold of Grace and hug her passionately.

Arthur considered: should he go with Grace, or should he not? He wanted to go, yet didn't want to go. He could not make up his mind, it was always painful for him to make up his mind. He wavered. At last he shook his head.

" You go," he said sombrely. " I'm worried about the strike."

" Are you, Arthur? " she asked wonderingly.

He nodded; and the feeling that he was denying himself the pleasure of seeing the pony munch the apple made him even sadder than before.

When Grace had gone he stood listening. At last his father came downstairs. He carried a flat black leather case under his arm, but he took no notice of Arthur whatever, he went straight into the waiting dog-cart and was driven away.

Arthur was humiliated, broken-hearted, crushed. It was not that he minded missing Tynecastle, nor yet that he minded missing Todd's. Hetty was nice, of course; he liked her long silky plaits, her bright smile, the warm feel of her when, as she sometimes did, she flung her arms round him and asked him to buy her chocolate cream with his Saturday sixpence. Oh yes, he liked Hetty, he would marry her, no doubt, when he grew up. He liked her brother, too, Alan Todd; and he liked old man Todd—as Alan called his father—with his ragged, tobacco-stained moustache, the little yellow spots on his eyes and his funny scent of cloves and something else. But it did not in the least upset him not to see them. What upset him, ravaged him, tortured and killed him was this neglect—this miserable neglect from his own father.

Perhaps he wasn't worth noticing, perhaps that really was the trouble. He was so small for his age and, he supposed, not very strong—he had heard Aunt Carrie several times: Arthur is *delicate*! Though Hilda had been to school in Harrogate and Grace was going soon, he, Arthur, would not go to school. He had so few friends, too, it was extraordinary how few people came to the Law. He was morbidly aware of himself as shy, sensitive, lonely. Being fair, he blushed easily, which often made him wish the ground would swallow him. He longed with all his soul for the time when he would be working with his father in the Neptune. At sixteen he would start, learning the practical side; then some classes, his certificate; and finally the wonderful day when he went into partnership with his father. Ah, that was a day to live for.

And meanwhile, with tears smarting in his eyes, he wandered aimlessly through the front door. The grounds of the Law lay before him, a fine span of lawn with a laburnum in the middle, then a paddock sloping to the dene. Two belts of trees lay upon either side, cutting off all that was unbeautiful in the view. Actually the house stood quite close to Sleescale, upon the law or hill which gave the place its name. Yet it might have been a hundred miles away for all that was seen of pit chimneys and pit dirt. It was a good stone house, square fronted, with a portico in the Georgian style, a later addition built out behind, and a big conservatory attached. The front of the house was covered by smartly clipped ivy. Though it was completely unostentatious—how Richard hated ostentation!—everything was in the most spotless order: the lawn shaven, its edges cut as by a knife, not a weed marring the long red blaze drive. There was a great deal of white paint about, the best white paint, on gates, palings, the window sashes and woodwork of the glass house. Richard liked it so; and though he kept only one man—Bartley—there were always plenty willing to come up from the Neptune to " crible for the mester."

Arthur's woebegone gaze travelled down the pleasant prospect. Should he go down to Grace ? He thought yes, at first, then he thought no. Desolate, he couldn't make up his mind. Then, as usual, he left it, wandering away from the decision, wandering back into the hall. Absently, he stared at the pictures upon the walls, these pictures on which his father set such store. Every year his father would buy a picture, sometimes two, through Vincent, the big art dealer in Tynecastle, spending what seemed to Arthur—whose ears absorbed the last detail of his father's conversation—incredible sums. Yet consciously Arthur approved this action of his father, as he approved all his father's actions, and he approved his father's taste as well. Yes, they really were lovely pictures, large canvases, superbly coloured. Stone, Orchardson, Watts,

Leighton, Holman Hunt, oh, Holman Hunt especially. Arthur knew the names. Knew that these—as his father said—would be the old masters of the future. One in particular, *The Garden Lovers*, entranced him with its sweetness, it was so lovely it gave him a queer pain, a kind of longing, low down in his stomach.

Arthur frowned, hesitated, looking up and down the hall. He wanted to think, to puzzle things out about this awful strike, his father's strange and preoccupied departure for Todd's. Turning, he went along the passage and into the lavatory. He locked himself in. Here, at last, he was safe.

The lavatory was his retreat; the place where no one could disturb him, where he took his troubles some days and on others gave himself to his dreams. The lavatory was a lovely place to dream in. It reminded him, somehow, of a church, a cathedral aisle, for it was a tall room with a cold churchy smell and a varnished wallpaper made up of little gothic arches, he got a feeling here like when he looked at *The Garden Lovers*.

Arthur let down the oblong varnished cover and seated himself with his head in his palms and elbows on his knees. He felt, suddenly, an extra pang of anxiety and stress. Overpowered by a desire for consolation, he shut his eyes tight. With that fervour which often took him, dear God, he prayed, make the strike end to-day, make all the men go back to work for my father, make them see their mistake, dear God, you know, dear God, how good my father is, I love him, dear God, and I love You too, make the men do right like he does and don't let them strike any more. and let me hurry up and be with my father in the Neptune quick for Jesus' sake, amen.

IV

RICHARD BARRAS returned at five o'clock to find Armstrong and Hudspeth were waiting for him. He arrived, with cold unhurried precision, frowning slightly, bringing the stern pulse of his personality into the house, to find them sitting on two hall chairs, side by side, staring at the floor in silence. Aunt Carrie in a flutter of uncertainty had put them there. George Armstrong was, of course, the viewer of the Neptune and would have gone ordinarily to the smoking-room. But Hudspeth was only the underviewer who had once been merely the overman, and he had, moreover, been with the safety-men, had come straight out the pit with dirty boots, wet knickerbockers, stick and leather cap complete. Impossible to admit him to sully Richard's room. Altogether a difficult situation for Aunt Carrie; she had compromised by leaving them in the *vestibule*.

At the sight of the two men Richard's expression did not change. He had expected them. But through the cold weight of his inflexibility a faint gleam momentarily irradiated his eye, then was instantly suppressed. Armstrong and Hudspeth rose. A short silence.

" Well ? " Richard asked.

Armstrong nodded emotionally.

" It's done with, thank God."

Richard received the news without a sign, as though the faint break in Armstrong's voice was repugnant to him. He remained erect, veiled within himself, apart. At length he stirred, made a gesture with his hand and led the way into the dining-room. He went to the sideboard, an enormous oak piece of Dutch origin carved in baroque taste with the heads of smiling children, and poured whisky into two glasses, then he pulled the bell, ordered tea upon a tray for himself. Ann brought it immediately.

The three men drank standing—Hudspeth put his tot away neat at one stolid swallow, Armstrong took his with a lot of soda in quick, nervous gulps. He was a nervous man, George Armstrong, a man who seemed always to live upon his nerves. He worried a great deal, was upset by trifles, lost his temper easily with the men but got through a vast amount of work by the sheer nervous intensity of his application. A medium-sized man going bald on the top, with rather a drawn face and pouches under his eyes, he was, in spite of his irritability, quite popular in the town. He had a good baritone voice and sang at the Masonic concerts. He was married, with five children, felt his responsibilities acutely and was, in his soul, desperately afraid of losing his job. Now he excused his nervous hand with his short deprecatory laugh.

" Before God I'm not sorry it's over, Mr. Barras, the whole stupid business. It's been a pretty rough time for all of us. I'd rather work a year double shift than go through these three months again."

Barras ignored all this. He said:

" How did it end ? "

" They had a meeting at the Institute. Fenwick spoke but they wouldn't listen to him. Next Gowlan, you know Charley Gowlan, the checkweigher, he got up and said there was nothing for it but to start. Then Heddon let loose on them. He'd come in special from Tynecastle. He didn't mince his meat. Not on your life, Mr. Barras. Told them they'd no right to have come out without Union support. Said the Federation disowned the whole business. Called them a pack of confounded fools, only saving your presence, Mr. Barras, he used a different word for trying to run things on their own. Then they voted. Eight hundred odd in favour of starting. Seven against."

There was a pause.

" And what then ? " Barras said.

" They came up to the office, a crowd of them—Heddon, Gowlan, Ogle, Howe and Dinning, and pretty small they looked, I can tell you. They asked for you. But I told them what you'd said, that you'd see none of them till they'd started in again. So Gowlan made a speech, he's not a bad sort, for all he's a boozer. Said they were beat and knew it. Heddon came on then with the usual Union claptrap, made a song and dance about taking the case to Harry Nugent in Parliament, but that was just to save his own face. To cut it short, they're whacked, they've asked to start in on the fore shift to-morrow. I said we'd see you, sir, and let them know your answer by six."

Richard finished his tea.

" So they want to start. I see," he said. He appeared to regard the situation as interesting, and to review it without emotion. Three months ago he had secured the Parsons contract for coking coal. These contracts were precious, they were rare and very hard to get. With the contract in his pocket he had begun operations, driving into the Scupper Flats district of the Paradise and starting to strip the Dyke of its special coking coal, the only coking coal remaining in the Neptune.

Then the men had walked out on him, in spite of him, in spite of their Union. The contract was not in his pocket now, it was in the fire. He had forfeited the contract. He had lost twenty thousand pounds.

The pale smile fixed upon his lips seemed to say, interesting, upon my soul!

Armstrong said:

" Shall I post the notices then, Mr. Barras ? "

Richard compressed his lips, let his eye dwell upon the obsequious Armstrong with sudden distaste.

" Yes," he said coldly. " Let them start in to-morrow."

Armstrong sighed with relief, he moved instinctively towards the door. But Hudspeth, whose obtuse mind dealt only with the obvious, stood twisting his cap in his hands.

" What about Fenwick ? " he asked. " Has he to be started ? "

Barras said:

" That remains with Fenwick."

" And the other pump ? " went on Hudspeth laboriously. He was a big dull-looking fellow with a long upper lip and a heavy, sallow face.

Richard moved restively.

" What other pump ? "

" The hogger-pump you spoke about three months back, the day the lads came out. It ud take a lot of that water out Scupper Flats. Take it quicker, I mean, leave less muck for to stand in . . ."

Cold as ice, Richard said:

" You are sadly mistaken if you think I am proceeding in Scupper Flats. That coking coal must await another contract."

" Whatever you say, sir." Hudspeth's earthy face coloured deeply.

" That's all, then," Barras said in his clear, reasonable voice. " You might let it be known that I'm glad for the men's sakes they're going back. All that unnecessary hardship in the town has been abominable."

" I'll certainly do that, Mr. Barras," agreed Armstrong.

Barras was silent; and as there appeared nothing more to be said Armstrong and Hudspeth left the house.

For a moment Barras remained with his back to the fire, thinking; then he locked away the whisky in the sideboard, picked up two lumps of sugar which had fallen on the tray and methodically replaced them in the sugar basin. It hurt him to see untidiness, to think even of a lump of sugar being wasted. At the Law *nothing* must be wasted, he could not stand it. Especially in small ways this was manifest. Matches he habitually stinted. He would use a pencil to its last bare inch. Lights must be turned out regularly, soap ends pressed into the new cake, hot water husbanded, even the fire banked with a modicum of dross. The sound of breaking china drove the blood to his head. Aunt Carrie's chief virtue, in his eyes, was the rigour of her housekeeping.

He stood quietly, examining his white, well-cared-for hands. Then he opened the door, and slowly ascended the stairs. He did not see Arthur, whose upturned anxious face made a tremulous white moon in the semi-darkness of the hall. He entered his wife's room.

" Harriet! "

" Yes, Richard! "

She was sitting up in bed with three pillows behind and a bed rest in front, crocheting. She had three pillows because someone had said three pillows were best. And she crocheted because young Dr. Lewis, her newest doctor, had prescribed it for her nerves. But now she paused, her eyes raised to his. Her eyes had thick black eyebrows above and very brown skin underneath, the pigmented skin of the complete neurotic. She smiled, rather apologetically, and touched her glossy hair, which lay undone, framing her sallow face.

" You don't mind, Richard ? I had one of my bad headaches. I had to make Caroline give my scalp a little brush this afternoon." And she smiled again—her suffering invalid smile, the sad smile of the invalid, a confirmed invalid. She suffered from her back, her stomach, her nerves. From time to time she had the most prostrating headaches for which toilet vinegar was useless, for which everything was useless but Caroline's gentle brushing of her head. On these occasions Aunt Carrie would stand for an hour on end gently, soothingly brushing Harriet's head with long slow strokes. No one had been able to get to the root of Harriet's trouble. Not really. She had exhausted Drs. Riddel, Scott and Proctor, the doctors of Sleescale; she had seen half the specialists in Tynecastle, she had turned in despair to a nature healer, a homeopathist, a herbalist, an electrical physicist who swathed her in the most marvellous magnetic belts. Each of the quacks had started by being wonderful, *the man at last,* as Harriet said; and each had sadly proved himself—like Riddel, Scott, Proctor and the Tynecastle specialists—to be a fool. Not that Harriet despaired. She had her own case in hand, she read persistently, perseveringly, patiently, a great many books upon the subject of her own complaints. Useless, alas! All, all useless. It was not that Harriet did not try. She had tried every medicine under the sun, her room was surrounded by bottles, dozens of bottles, tonics, sedatives, liniments, alleviatives, antispasmodics, everything—all the physic that had been prescribed for her in the past five years. It could at least be said of Harriet that she never threw a bottle away. Some of the bottles had only one dose out of them—Harriet had such experience that after even one spoonful she could say: " Put it away. I *know* it'll do me no good." The bottle was put on the shelf.

It was terrible. But Harriet was very patient. She was confined to bed. Yet she ate very well. At times, indeed, she ate magnificently, that was part of her trouble, her stomach it must be, she had such gas. She was amiable, though, she had never been known to disagree with her husband, but was always docile, yielding, sympathetic. She shirked none of the more intimate wifely duties. She was there: in bed. She had a big white body, and an air of sanctity. She conveyed the strange impression of being like a cow. But she was very pious. Perhaps she was a sacred cow.

Barras looked at her as from a long way off. How exactly did he regard her? At the moment it was impossible to say.

" Is your headache better now? "

" Yes, Richard, it is a little better. Not gone, but a little better. After Caroline had done brushing my hair I made her pour me a little of that valerian mixture young Dr. Lewis gave me. I think it helped."

" I meant to bring you some grapes from Tynecastle but I forgot."

" Thank you, Richard." Amazing how often Richard forgot those grapes; but the intention was there. " You went to Todd's, of course."

His expression stiffened ever so slightly. Arthur, still busy with his enigma, should have seen that look.

" Yes, I went there. They are all well, Hetty looking prettier than ever, full of her birthday; she's thirteen next week." He broke off, turned towards the door. " By the way, the strike's broken. The men start in to-morrow."

Her small mouth made the letter O; she placed her hand protectively against her flannelette swathed heart.

" Oh, Richard, I'm so glad. Why didn't you tell me at once? That's splendid, such a relief."

He paused, the door half open. He said:

" You may expect me to-night." Then he went out.

" Yes, Richard."

Harriet lay on her back, the pleased surprise still lingering upon her face. Then she took a slip of paper and a silver pencil with a small cairngorm set at the end. She wrote neatly: " Remember tell Dr. Lewis heart gave a great thump when Richard delivered good news." She paused, meditatively, then underlined the word great. Finally she took up her work and began placidly to crochet.

V

It was quite dark as Armstrong and Hudspeth came through the big white gates of the Law and entered the avenue of tall beech trees—known locally as Sluice Dene—which led towards Hedley Road and the town. They walked some distance apart, and in silence, for neither cared much for the other; but at last Hudspeth, smarting under the snub he had received, ground out bitterly:

" He makes a man feel like dirt on times. He's a cold devil right enough. I cannot make him out. I cannot make him out no how."

Armstrong smiled to himself in the darkness. He despised Hudspeth secretly as a man of no education, a man who had worked his way up, succeeding more through doggedness than actual merit; he was often irritated, humiliated even, by the other's bluntness and physical assertiveness; it was pleasant to see him humiliated in his turn.

" How d'you mean ? " He pretended not to understand.

" What I damwell say," said Hudspeth disagreeably.

Armstrong said:

" He knows what he's about."

" Ay, he knows his job. And God help us if we didn't know ours. He'd not spare us. He's that perfect himself he'd have no mercy whatever. Did you hear him, too ? " He paused, mimicking Barras bitterly, " All the unnecessary hardship in the town. Good Christ, that was funny."

" No, no," Armstrong said quickly. " He meant that."

" Meant it like hell! He's the meanest devil in Sleescale and that's saying something. He's just flaming inside over losing his contract. And I'll tell you another thing since I'm about it. I'm damned glad we're shot of Scupper Flats. Though I've kept my trap shut I've been feeling pretty near Fenwick's way about that bloody water."

Armstrong darted a sharp, disapproving glance at Hudspeth:

" That's no way to talk, man."

There was a short silence, then, sulkily, Hudspeth declared:

" It's a sheugh of a place, anyhow."

But Armstrong said nothing. They tramped on in silence, down Hedley Road, and into Cowpen Street past the Terraces. As they drew near the corner a blare of light and a hubbub of voices from the Salutation made both men turn their heads. Armstrong remarked, with an obvious desire to change the subject:

" They've a full house to-night."

" Ay, and a tight one," Hudspeth answered, still sulking. " Amour has started tick again. The first time he's had the slate out for a fortnight."

Not speaking any more they went on to post the notices.

VI

BACK in the Salutation the row increased. The pub was full jammed to suffocation, swirling with smoke, words, bright lights and the fumes of beer. Bert Amour stood behind the bar in his shirt-sleeves with the big chalked slate—the tally of men and drinks—slung on the wall beside him. Bert was a knowing one: for the last two weeks in the face of curses and entreaties he had refused all credit; but now, with pay-Saturday a near-by certainty, he had re-established himself at a stroke. The bar was open; and payment deferred.

" Fill them up, Bert, lad." Charley Gowlan thumped hard with his pint pot and called for another round. Charley was not drunk, he was never really drunk, he became saturated like a sponge, he sweated and took on the pallid look of veal, but no one had ever seen him wholly soused. Some of the crowd about him were well lit-up, however—Tally Brown, old Reedy and Slogger Leeming in particular. The Slogger was quite wildly drunk. He was a rough lot, the Slogger, with a red, bashed-in face, a flat nose and one blue-white cauliflower ear. He had been a boxer in his youth, and had fought in the St. James's Hall under the captivating title of the Pitboy Wonder; but drink and other things had burned him out; he was back once more in the pit—no longer a pitboy and no longer a wonder; with nothing to show for the prowess of those golden days but a hot good nature, a vicious left swing and the sadly battered face.

Always the unofficial toastmaster in the pub, Charley Gowlan rapped on the table again; he was displeased at the lack of levity in the company, he wanted the old cosy sociability of the Salutation to be re-established. He remarked:

" We've had to put up wi' plenty in the last three months. Come on, lads, wor not downhearted. It's a poor heart that niver rejoices." His pig-like gaze beamed over the company, seeking the familiar lush approval. But they were all too sick and surly to approve. Instead he caught Robert Fenwick's eye fixed sardonically upon his. Robert stood in his usual place, the far corner by the bar, drinking steadily, as though nothing held much interest for him now.

Gowlan raised his pot.

" Drink up, Robert, mon. Ye might as well get wet inside te-night. Ye'll be wet enough outside te-morrow."

Robert appeared to study Gowlan's beery face with singular detachment. He said:

" We'll all be wet enough some day."

The company shouted:

" Shut up yer face, Robert."

" Be quiet, mon. Ye had yer say at the meetin'."

" We've heerd ower much about that these last three months."

A film of sadness, of weariness came upon Robert's face, he looked back at them with defeated eyes.

" All right, lads. Have it yer own way. I'll say nowt more."

Gowlan grinned slyly:

" If yer feared to go down the Paradise why doan't ye say so ? "

Slogger Leeming said:

" Shut up yer face, Gowlan. Yer nowt but a blatterin' woman. Robert here's my marrow. See! He hews fair an' addles fair. He knows more about the bloddy pit than y' know about yer own mickey."

There was a silence while the crowd held its breath, hoping there might be a fight. But no, Charley never fought, he merely grinned beerily. The tension lapsed into disappointment.

Then the door swung open. Will Kinch came into the pub and elbowed his way uncertainly to the bar.

" Stand us a pint, Bert, for God's sake, I feel I could do wi' it."

Interest reawakened, and was focused upon Will.

" How, then! what's the matter with ye, Will ? "

Will pushed the lank hair back from his brow, gripped the pot and faced them shakily.

" There's plenty the matter wi' me, lads." He spat as though to cleanse his mouth of dirt. Then with a rush: " My Alice is badly, lads, she's got the pneumonia. The missus wanted her to have a drop hough tea. I went down to Ramage's a quarter hour since. Ramage hissel' was standin' there, ahint the counter, big fat belly an' all. ' Mister Ramage,' I says perfectly civil, ' will ye gie us a small end o' hough for my little lass that's badly an' aw'll pay ye pay-Saturday for certain.' " Here Will's lips went pale; he began to tremble all over his body. But he clenched his teeth and forced himself to go on. " Weel, lads, he looked me up an' down, then down an' up. ' I'll give ye no hough,' he says, jest like that. ' Aw, come, Mister Ramage,' I says upset like. ' Spare us a little end piece, the lock-oot's ower, pay-Saturday's come a fortnight certain, I'll pay ye then as God's my maker.' " Pause. " He said nowt for a bit, lads, but jest gien me that look. Then he says, like he were speakin' to a dog, 'I'll give ye nothin', not even a rib of bone. Yer a disgrace te the town, you an' yer lot. Ye walk out on your work for nowt, then come cadgin' to decent fowks for charity. Get out of my shop afore a have ye thrown out.'" Pause. "So aw jest got out, lads."

Dead silence had come upon the company while Will spoke; and he finished in a mortal stillness. Bob Ogle moved first.

"By God!" he groaned. "That's too much."

Then Slogger jumped up, half-tight.

"It is too much," he shouted, "we'll not put up wi't."

Everybody started talking at once; an uproar. Slogger was on his feet, shouldering drunkenly through the crowd.

"I'll not lie down under this, lads. I'll see that bastard Ramage for mysel'. Come on, Will. Ye'll have the best for the lass and not a measly end o' hough." He caught hold of Kinch affectionately and dragged him to the door. The others surged round, followed, supported them. The pub cleared in a minute. It was a miracle : no "time, gentlemen, please" had ever cleared that bar so quickly. Full one minute—empty the next. Robert alone waited, watching the astounded Amour with his sad, disillusioned eyes. He had another drink. But at last he went, too.

Outside, the crowd was swelled by a score of the younger men, the corner lads, the hangers on. They had no idea what it meant, but they scented excitement, trouble, a fight—since Slogger was laying his weight about. They marched in a body down Cowpen Street. Young Joe Gowlan shoved his way into the thick of it.

Round the corner they went and into Lamb Street, but when they got to Ramage's a check awaited them. Ramage's was shut. The big shop, closed for the night, was blank, unlit, presenting nothing but a cold iron-shuttered front and the name above: James Ramage—Flesher. Not even a window to smash!

Balked. Slogger let out a howl. The drink was in his blood; and his blood was up. He wasn't done, no, by God, he wasn't. There were other shops, here, next door to Ramage, shops without shutters, Bates, for instance, and Murchison, the licensed grocer's, which had nothing but a plain bar and padlocked door.

Slogger let out another yell.

"We're not beat, lads, we'll take Murchison's instead." He made a run at the door, raised his heavy boot, smashed hard on the lock. At the same time somebody from the back of the crowd threw a brick. The brick shattered the window of the shop. That did it: the crash of the glass gave the signal to loot.

They swarmed round the door, beat it down, burst into the shop. Most of them were drunk and all of them had not seen proper food for weeks. Tally Brown seized a ham and shoved it under his arm; old Reedy grabbed at some tins of fruit; Slogger, his maudlin sympathy for Will Kinch's Alice completely forgotten, knocked in the bung of a barrel of beer. Some women from the Quay, attracted by the noise, pressed in behind the men and began in a panic to snatch at anything: pickles, sauce, soap, it didn't matter so long as it was something, they were too terrified to look, they simply snatched feverishly and thrust what they took below their shawls. The street lamp outside threw a cold clear light upon them.

It was Joe Gowlan who thought of the till, Joe had no use for the grub—like his dad he was too well fed—but Joe could use that till.

Falling on his hands and knees he squirmed between the legs of the pushing men, crawled round behind the counter, and found the cash drawer. Unlocked! Gloating over old Murchison's carelessness, Joe slipped his hand into the smooth bowl, his fingers clutched at the silver in the bowl, a good round fistful, and slid it easily into his pocket. Then, rising to his feet, he darted through the door and took to his heels.

As Joe came out of the shop Robert entered it. At least, he stood on the threshold, the uneasiness upon his face turning slowly to dismay.

" What are ye doing, lads ? " His tone was pleading: the pathos of this misdirected violence hurt him. " Ye'll get in trouble ower this."

Nobody took the slightest notice of him. He raised his voice.

" Stop it, ye fools. Can't ye see it's the worst thing ye could do. Nobody'll have any pity on us now. Stop. I tell ye, stop."

No one stopped.

A spasm came over Robert's face. He made to push into the crowd, but just then a sound behind caused him to swing round full in the lamplight. The police: Roddam from the Quay-side beat and the new sergeant from the station.

" Fenwick! " Roddam shouted instantly in recognition and laid his hands on Robert.

At that shout a louder shout went up from those inside:

" The cops! Get out, lads, it's the cops." And an avalanche of living, inextricably mingled forms disgorged itself through the door. Roddam and the sergeant made no attempt to stop the avalanche. They stood rather stupidly and let it go past them; then, still holding Robert, Roddam entered the shop.

" Here's another, sergeant," Roddam said in sudden exultation.

Amongst the desolation of the looted shop, swaying helplessly astride the beer barrel, sat Slogger Leeming. He held to the bung-hole with one blissful finger. He was blind to the world.

The sergeant looked at Slogger, the shop, then at Robert.

" This is serious," he said in a hard, official voice. " You're Fenwick. The man who started the strike."

Robert returned his look steadily. Robert said:

" I did nothing."

The sergeant said:

" Of course you did nothing."

Robert opened his lips to explain; saw suddenly the hopelessness of it all. He said nothing. He submitted. He was taken with the Slogger to the cells.

VII

Five days later, at four o'clock in the afternoon, Joe Gowlan strolled easily along the Scottswood Road of Tynecastle, making scrutiny of those windows which displayed the card APARTMENTS. Tynecastle, that keen bustling city of the North, full of movement and clamour and brisk grey colour, echoing to the clang of trams, the clatter of feet, the beat of ship-yard hammers, had engulfed Joe graciously. Joe's eyes had always been turned towards Tynecastle—it was only eighteen miles from his native town—as a place of possibilities and adventure. Joe looked well, a bright-complexioned, curly-haired young man with his boots dazzlingly brushed and a cheerful air of knowing his way about. But for all his shiny look Joe was broke. Since he had run away from home, the two pounds in silver, stolen from Murchison's till, had been pleasantly dissipated in a style more sophisticated than Joe's untarnished aspect might have suggested. Joe had seen the gallery of the Empire Music Hall, the inside of Lowe's bar, and other places. Joe had bought beer, cigarettes and the most captivating blue postcards. And now, his last sixpence honourably spent in a wash, a brush and a shine, Joe was looking for a decent lodging.

Down the Scottswood Road he went, past the wide iron pens of the cattle-market, past the Duke of Cumberland, past Plummer Street and Elswick East Terrace. The day was dull but dry, the streets pulsed pleasantly, on the railway lower down an incoming train whistled importantly, and was answered by the deep chord of a steamer's siren as she warped out in the Tyne below. Joe had a stimulating sense of life around him and within him he felt the world like a great big football at his feet and lustily prepared to boot it.

Beyond Plummer Street Joe paused outside a house which bore the sign, *Lodging House: Good Beds: Men Only.* He contemplated the house thoughtfully but, with a faint negation of his curly head, sauntered on. A moment later a girl, walking quickly in the same direction, came abreast of him and then passed by. Joe's eyes glistened; his whole body stiffened. She was a neat little piece right enough, small feet and ankles, trim waist, smart hips, and her head in the air like a queen. His gaze lingered enviously, followed her as she crossed the road, skipped up the steps and briskly let herself into 117A Scottswood Road. Fascinated, Joe stopped and moistened his lips which had gone rather dry. In the window of

117A Scottswood Road was a card which said APARTMENTS. "By gum!" Joe said. He buttoned up his jacket and, crossing without hesitation, he rang the bell.

It was she who came to the door, made, by the removal of her hat, suddenly more intimate to him. She was even nicer than he had thought: about sixteen, maybe, with a small nose, clear grey eyes and a waxen complexion into which her recent walk had whipped a fresh colour. Her ears were very small and close to the side of her head. Her mouth was the nicest though, he told himself. It was a big mouth, not deeply red, but very soft with an entrancing little membrane to the upper lip.

"Well," she asked sharply.

Joe smiled at her modestly, lowered his eyes, took off his cap and twisted it in his hands. No one could register homely virtue better than Joe: he did it to perfection.

"Excuse me, miss, but I was lookin' for lodgings."

She did not smile back at him; her lip curled, she considered him distastefully. Jenny Sunley did not like her mother to keep lodgers: not even the single lodger whom the spare top back accommodated. She thought it low, and "lowness" was to Jenny the unpardonable sin.

She smoothed her blouse, put her hands upon her neat shiny belt, and said with a certain arrogance:

"I suppose you better come in."

Stepping reverently he followed her into the narrow passage, and was conscious instantly of the smell and sound of pigeons. Coo-coo, coo-coo, coo-coo! He looked up. No pigeons were visible, but on the half landing the bathroom door stood open revealing a small string of washing: long black stockings and several white garments. Hers, thought Joe delightedly, swiftly; but he masked his eyes before she had time to blush. She did blush though, for that neglected door, and her tone was suddenly shrewish as, with a toss of her head, she declared:

"It's in *here* if you want to know. The back room!"

He went after her, entering "the back room," a small blowsy much-lived-in apartment, full of old bits of horse-hair furniture, penny magazines, presents from Whitley Bay and bags of pigeon meal. Two blue chequer homers sat solemnly on the mantelpiece. Beside the hot fire, rocking herself gently in a squeaky chair, reading *Home Chat*, sat an indolent, untidy woman, with big eyes and a lot of hair piled up on the top of her head.

"Here, ma, it's somebody about the room." And flinging herself haughtily upon the broken-springed sofa, Jenny picked up a battered magazine and took, most conspicuously, no further interest in the matter.

Mrs. Sunley went on with her rocking comfortably. Only the crack of doom would have stopped Ada Sunley making herself comfortable. She was always making herself comfortable: taking off a shoe, or easing her stays, or having a little baking soda to break the wind, or a cup of tea, or a little sit down, or a look at a paper till the kettle boiled. Ada was a fat, friendly, dreamy slattern. Occasionally she nagged her husband, but mostly she was easy-going. She had been in service in her "young days," a "good family," she always insisted. She was romantic, she liked to look at the new moon; and superstitious, she never wore green, walked under a ladder or spilled salt without throwing it over her left shoulder; she adored a good novelette, especially the kind where the dark quiet one "got him" in the end. She wanted to be rich, she was always going in for competitions, limericks chiefly, and hoping to win a lot of money. But Ada's limericks were hopeless. She often had remarkable ideas, Ma's brain waves, they were called, amongst the family: to repaper a room or cover the sofa in a nice pink plush, or re-enamel the bath, or retire to the country, or start a hotel, or a ribbon shop, or even to write "a story"—she was sure she had the *gift*. But none of Ada's ideas ever came to fruit. Ada never got far from her rocker. Alf, her husband, frequently said to her mildly: "My Gawd, Ada, you're barmy!"

"Oh," she said now. "I thought it was the club-man." Pause. "So you're looking for a room?"

"Yes, mam."

"We only take one young man." When she met people for the first time, Ada always tried to put on a faint air, but it soon slipped off. "Our last gentleman left a week ago. Should you require part board as well?"

"Yes, mam, if it wouldn't trouble you."

"You should have to sit down with the family. We're six in family here. Me, my husband, Jenny there, who's out all day at Slattery's, Phyllis, Clarice and Sally, my youngest." She paused, considered him more shrewdly: "Who are you, by the bye? And where are you from?"

Joe's eyes fell humbly, but a wave of panic swept him. He had come in for a bit of a lark really, a kind of try-on just for fun, but now he knew he must get in, he simply *must*. She was a plum, that Jenny, she really was a plum, she had him simply gasping. But what the hell was he going to say? Strings of sympathetic lies flashed through his head and were instantly rejected. Where was his luggage, his money to pay in advance? Hell! He sweated. He despaired. Suddenly the inspiration came, nothing better surely than the truth, ah, that was it—he glowed inside—the truth, not the whole truth, of course, but something like the truth. He flung up his head and faced her. He said with conscious honesty:

"I could tell a pack of lies to you, mam, but I'd rather tell you the truth. I've run away from home."

"Well I never!"

The magazine was lowered, and this time the rocking did stop: Mrs. Sunley and Jenny both stared at him with a new interest. Romance in the best tradition had flown into the frowsy room.

Joe said:

" I had a terrible time, I couldn't bear it no longer. My mother died, my father used to leather me till I could hardly stand. We had a strike an' all at wor pit. I diddent . . . I diddent have enough to eat." Manly emotion glistened in Joe's eyes as he went on . . . oh, it was glorious . . . glorious . . . he had them eating out of his hand!

" So your mother died ? " Ada breathed.

Joe nodded dumbly—the last convention was fulfilled.

Ada let her big balmy eyes travel over his brushed and combed handsomeness with a rising sympathy. He's had a hard enough time, poor young man, she reflected, and that good-looking too, with his bright brown eyes and curly hair. But curly hair don't pay the rent, no indeed it don't, with Sally's music to think of. . . . Ada started to rock again. For all her sluttish indolence Ada Sunley was no fool. She took herself in hand.

" Look here," she declared in a matter-of-fact tone, " you can't come to us on pity. You've got to have a shop, a regular shop. Now, my Alf said to-day they was taking on at Millington-Yarrow's, the foundry in Yarrow, you understand, Platt Lane way. Try there! If you're lucky, come back. If you're unlucky, do the other thing."

" Yes, mam."

Joe held his chastened probity till he was out of the house, then in his exultation he bounded across the street.

" Here, you with the face! " He grabbed a passing message boy by the collar. " Tell us the road to Millington's Foundry or I'll break your blasted neck! "

He almost ran to Yarrow, and it was a long, long way. He presented himself at the Foundry. He lied nobly, obscenely, and showed his sweating muscle to the foreman. His luck held, they were in urgent need of hands, he was taken on, as puddler's assistant, at twenty-five shillings a week. After the pit it was riches. And there was Jenny, Jenny, Jenny . . .

He came back to Scottswood Road in easy stages, holding himself in, telling himself he must be careful, do nothing in a hurry, work it up slow. But triumph rose gloating through the thin veneer of caution as he came into the back room once more.

The whole family sat there, had just finished tea. Ada lounged at the top of the table and next to her sat Jenny. Then came the three younger girls: Phyllis, cast in the image of her mother, blonde, languid, and thirteen years of age, Clarice, dark, leggy and eleven and a half, with a beautiful scarlet ribbon, removed from a chocolate box of Jenny's, in her hair, and finally Sally, a queer thing of ten, with Jenny's big mouth, hostile black eyes and a self-possessed stare. At the end of the table was Alfred, husband of Ada, father of the four girls and head of the house, an insignificant pasty-faced man with drooping shoulders and a sparse ginger moustache. He had also a crick in his neck, no collar and watery eyes. Alf was a house-painter, a house-painter who swallowed a fair amount of white lead in the process of slabbing it upon Tynecastle house fronts. The lead gave him his pallid face, sundry pains in his "stummick" and that faint blue line which could be made out along the edge of Alf's gums. The crick in his neck, however, came not from painting but from pigeons. Alf was a fancier, his passion was pigeons, blue and red chequers, homers, lovely prize homers. And flighting his homers, watching them fly the empyrean blue, had gradually brought Alf's neck to this singular obliquity.

Joe surveyed the company, exclaimed joyously:

"They've taken me on. I start to-morrow. Twenty-five bob a week."

Jenny had obviously forgotten him; but Ada looked pleased in her indolent way.

"Didn't I tell you, now? You'll pay me fifteen a week, that'll leave you ten clear, in the meantime that's to say. You'll soon have a rise. Puddlers earn good money." She yawned delicately behind her hand, then sketchily cleared a space upon the littered table. "Sit in and have a pick. Clarry, fetch a cup and saucer from the scull'ry and run round to Mrs. Gresley's, there's a dear, for three penn'orth corned ham, see you watch her weight too. Might as well have something tasty for a start. Alf, this is Mr. Joe Gowlan, our new gentleman."

Alf stopped his slow mastication of a final tea-soaked crust to give Joe a laconic yet impressive nod. Clarry slammed in with a newly washed cup and saucer, inky tea was poured, the corned ham appeared with half a loaf and Alf solemnly pushed across the mustard.

Joe sat next to Jenny on the horse-hair sofa. It intoxicated him to be beside her, to think how marvellously he had managed it. She was wonderful, never before had desire stricken him so deeply, so suddenly. He set himself to please, to captivate them—not Jenny, of course, oh, dear no, Joe knew a thing or two better than that! He smiled, his open good-hearted smile; he talked, made easy converse, invented little anecdotes connected with his past; he flattered Ada, joked with the children; he even told a story, a splendidly proper funny story he had once heard at a minstrel entertainment given by the Band of Hope—not that he had really belonged to the Band of Hope—he had joined the night before the concert, dissevered himself abruptly from the pious movement on the following morning. The story went well: for all except Sally who received it scornfully and Jenny whose haughtiness remained unmoved. Ada shook with laughter, her hands on her fat sides, shedding hairpins all over the place:

"An' Bones found the blue-bottle in his sarsparilla . . . well, I say, Mr. Gowlan . . ."

"Ah, call me Joe, Mrs. Sunley. Treat me like one of the family, mam."

He was getting them, he'd get them all soon enough, the thrill of it went to his head like wine. This was the way, he could do it, he could take hold of life, squeeze the fat out of it. He'd get on, have what he wanted, anything, everything, just wait and see.

Later, Alf invited Joe to see him feed his pigeons. They went out to the yard, where the pearly doves preened themselves, ducked their heads in and out of Alf's home-made dovecote, delicately pecked the grain. Removed from the presence of his wife, where he sat mute and mild as milk, Alf revealed himself a little hero of a man with views beyond his pigeons upon beer, patriotism and Spearmint's prospects in the Derby. He was affable to Joe, proffered a friendly fag. But Joe chafed, burned to be back with Jenny. When the cigarette was smoked, he excused himself, drifted back into the house.

Jenny was alone in the back room. She still sat upon the sofa, deep in the same magazine.

" Excuse me," Joe murmured. " I was wondering if you would show me my room."

She did not even lower the magazine which she held with her little finger elegantly crooked.

" One of the kids will show you."

He did not move.

" Don't you go out for a stroll at night . . . on your half-day . . . like this ? "

No answer.

" You serve in a shop, don't you ? " he tried once more, patiently. He had a vague remembrance of Slattery's—a big plate-glassed drapery stores in Grainger Street.

She condescended to look at him.

" What if I do ? " she said flatly. " It's none of your business. And when it comes to that I don't *serve*. That's a low common word and I hate it. I'm *at* Slattery's. I'm in the millinery and extremely refined work it is too. I hate anything that's common and low. I hate men who work dirty more than anything." And the magazine went up again with a jerk. Joe rubbed his jaw reflectively, taking her all in, neat ankles, slender hips, trim little bosom. So you don't like men who work dirty, he thought with a secret grin; well, by gum, you're going to like a dirty worker in me.

VIII

For Martha the disgrace was terrible; never in all her life had she dreamed of such a thing, no, never. It was horrible. As she went about her work in the kitchen, testing the potatoes with a fork, lifting the pot lid to see that the stew was right, she tried not to think about it. But it was no use, she had to think. In vain she fought it, battled it away, the thought that she, Martha Redpath that was, should have come to this. They had always been decent folk her folks, the Redpaths, decent chapel folk, decent Methodist folk, decent collier folk, she could go back a full four generations with pride and find never a blemish on the stock. They had all worked underground decently and conducted themselves decently above. But now ? Now she was not a Redpath, she was a Fenwick, the wife of Robert Fenwick. And Robert Fenwick was in gaol.

A spasm of bitterness went over her face. In gaol. The scene burned her, as it had done a hundred times, the whole burning scene: Robert standing in the dock with Leeming beside him, Leeming of all men; James Ramage on the bench, coarse and red-faced and bullying, not mincing his words, saying exactly what he thought. She had gone to the court. She *would* go, it was her place to go. She had been there, she had seen and heard everything. Three weeks without the option. She could have screamed when Ramage sentenced him. She could have died; but her pride kept her up, helped her to put on a stony face. Her pride had helped her through those frightful days, helped her even this afternoon when, returning with her messages from the town, the wife of Slogger Leeming had waylaid her at Alma corner and remarked with loud-voiced sympathy that their men would be out on Saturday. *Their* men and *out*!

With a look at the clock—the first thing Sammy had got out of pawn for her—she pulled the tin bath before the fire and began to fill it with hot water from the wash-house. She used an iron pot as dipper and the journeys to and fro with the heavy weight taxed her severely. Lately she had not been well, indeed, she knew she was not well and just now she felt weak and shaky. She had a pain too. For a minute she had to stop to ease the catch in her side. Worry, she knew, had done it, she was a strong woman; she felt she would be better if only the child within her showed signs of life. But there was no movement, nothing but a dragging heaviness, a weight.

The clock struck five, and shortly after the tramp of feet echoed along the Terrace, the slow tramp of tired men. Nine hours from bank to bank and the Terraces to climb at the end of it. But it was good honest work, bred in their bones, and in her bones too. Her sons were young and strong. It was their work. She desired no other.

The door opened upon her thought and the three came in, Hughie first, then David, and finally Sammy with a sawn balk of timber tucked under his arm, for her kindling. Dear Sammy. Always thoughtful of her. A rush of warmth came round the brooding coldness of her heart, she wanted suddenly to have Sammy in her arms and to weep.

They were searching her face; the house had been oppressive these last days; and Martha had been oppressive too, hard on them and difficult. She knew that and she knew that they were searching her face. Though she had been to blame it hurt her.

" How, mother," Sammy smiled, his teeth showing white against the black coal dust that sweat had caked on him.

She loved the way he called her mother, not that " mam " in common usage here; but she merely nodded towards the bath that was ready and turned back to set the table.

With their mother in the room the three lads took off their boots, jackets, their pit drawers and singlets, all sodden with water, sweat and pit dirt. Together, naked to the buff, they stood scouring themselves in the tiny steaming bath. There was never much room and it was always friendly. But there was not much joking to-night. Sam in a tentative way nudged Davey and grinned:

" Ower the bed a bit, ye elephant." And again remarked: " Whey, mon, have ye swallowed the soap ? " But there was nothing genuine in the way of fun. The heaviness in the house, in Martha's face, precluded it. They dressed with no horse-play, sat in to their dinner almost in silence.

It was a beautiful dinner, huge helpings of savoury stew with onions and floury potatoes. Martha's dinners were always beautiful, she knew the value of a good dinner to a man. Now, thank God, that the wicked strike was stopped she could let them have their food. She sat watching them eat, replenishing their plates. Though she did not feel like eating herself, she drank some tea. Yet even the tea didn't help her much. A stray pain started in her back, tugged at her breasts, and slipped out of her again before she recognised the nature of the pain.

Her sons had finished dinner. David was the first to rise, going to the corner where his books were kept, seating himself on a low stool by the cheek of the fire with a pencil in his hand and jotter upon his knee. Latin, Martha thought glumly, he's doing Latin now, and the thought, striking across her bitter mood, irked her strangely. It was part of Robert's doing, this education, this wanting the boy to go to college, to sit for the scholarship next year, to get above himself. Robert had started him with Mr. Carmichael at the old Bethel Street night classes. And she, coming of a long line of pitmen, a proudly class-conscious woman, despised book learning in her own kind, and felt that no good would come of it.

Hughie got up next, went into the wash-house, returned with a hammer and last, his old football boots and twelve new leather studs. At the back of the kitchen, away from everyone, he squatted down, bent his dark head, still shiny from the bath, and began, in his own way, both taciturn and absorbed, to hammer in the studs. Last Saturday he had kept back sixpence of his pay from her, never saying a word, simply keeping it back. She might have guessed why. Football! Not just the love of the sport, though he loved it with all his heart. No, no. Hughie's interest, she knew, lay deeper. Hughie wanted to be a star, a footballer in the big league, an athlete who drew six pounds a week for his supreme cleverness at the game. That was at once the secret, the ambition of Hughie's soul. That kept him from cigarettes, from touching even one glass of beer which he might have had on Sundays; that kept him from talking to the girls—Hughie never so much as looked at a girl, she knew, though plenty of them looked at Hughie; that set him running miles at night, training he called it; tired or not he would go out, she might rest assured, the minute he had finished his boots.

Martha's frown deepened. She approved with all her heart Hughie's spartan life, nothing could be better. But to what cause? To leave the pit! He, too, striving with all his soul to leave the pit. She had no faith in his glittering illusion and no fear that he might achieve it. Yet it worried her, this queer intensity of Hughie's, oh yes, it harassed her.

Instinctively her eyes turned to Sammy, who still sat at the table, restlessly making patterns on the oilcloth with the back of his fork. He was conscious of her gaze for, after a moment, he laid down the fork and sheepishly got up. He hung about with his hands in his pockets, then went to the tiny square of mirror above the sink. He took the comb that lay always on the back of the enamel soap rack, wetted it, and carefully parted his hair. Then he took a clean collar, she had starched and ironed it only that afternoon, which hung on the rail by the fire. He put on the collar, arranged his tie freshly, smartened himself up. Then, whistling self-consciously, he whipped up his cap and moved jauntily to the door.

Martha's hand, lying upon her knee, clenched so tightly the knuckles showed like bone.

" Sammy! "

Sam, half out the door, turned as if he had been shot.

" Where are ye going, Sammy? "

" I'm goin' out, mother."

She would not let his smile soften her.

" I know ye're goin' out. But where are ye goin' out to? "

" I'm goin' down the street."

" Are ye goin' down Quay Street? "

He looked at her, his plain honest face flushed and dogged now.

" Yes, I am goin' down Quay Street, mother, if ye want to know."

Her instinct was true, then: he was going to see Annie Macer. She hated the Macers, distrusted them, the improvident father, that wild Pug Macer, the son. They were in the same category as the Leemings—not quite respectable. They were not even colliers, they were " fisher-foak," part of that separate community which lived an uncertain life—" waste and wantry " Martha called it, faring on the fat of the land one month, boat and nets mortgaged the next. She had nothing against Annie's character, some held she was a decent lass. But she was not the lass for her Sammy. She came from the wrong stock, she hawked fish in the open street, she had even gone to Yarmouth, one bad year, to retrieve the Macers' fortunes, as a herring gutter. Sammy, her own dear son, whom she hoped one day to see the finest hewer in the Neptune, married on a herring gutter. Never. *Never!* She drew a long, deep breath.

" I don't want ye to go out to-night, Sammy."

" But you know, mother, I promised. Pug Macer and me was goin' out. And Annie's comin' too."

" Never mind that, Sammy." Her voice turned harsh, strident. " I don't want ye to go."

He faced her; and in his loving, dog-like eyes she saw an unexpected firmness.

" Annie's expecting me, mother. I'm sorry, but I'm going."

He went out and very quietly closed the door.

Martha sat perfectly rigid: for the first time in his life Sammy had disobeyed her. She felt as if he had struck her on the face. Conscious of the covert glances of David and Hughie, she tried to take command of herself. She rose, cleared the table, washed the dishes with hands that trembled.

David said:

" Shall I dry for you, mother ? "

She shook her head, dried the dishes herself, sat down with some mending. With some difficulty she threaded her needle. She took up an old pit singlet of Sammy's, so patched and darned scarcely any of the original flannel remained. The sight of the old pit singlet tore at her heart. She had been too harsh with Sammy, she felt suddenly that she had not taken him the right way, that she, not Sam, had been to blame. The thought pierced her. Sam would do anything for her, anything, if only she treated him properly.

With clouded eyes, she made to take up the singlet when all at once the pain in her back came on again. The pain was bad this time, transfixing her, and in the instant she knew it for what it was. Dismayed, she waited. The pain went, returned. Without a word she got up and went out of the back door of the kitchen. She walked with difficulty up the back. She went into the closet. Yes, it was that.

She came out, stood for a moment surrounded by the quiet darkness of the night, supporting herself against the low dividing fence with one hand, holding her swollen body with the other. It had come upon her then, while her husband was in prison, the last indignity. And before her grown sons. Inscrutable as the darkness which lay about her, she thought rapidly. She would not have Dr. Scott, nor Mrs. Reedy, the midwife, either. Robert had flung away their savings madly in the strike. She was in debt, she could not, she would not tolerate further expense. Within a minute her mind was made up.

She returned to the house.

" David! Run round to Mrs. Brace. Tell her to look in to me now."

Startled, he looked at her questioningly. She was never a great one for

David, who had always been his father's boy, but now the expression in his eyes moved her. She said kindly:

" Never worry, Davey. I'm just not well." As he scurried out she went over to the kist where she kept such linen as she had, unlocked it. Then, awkwardly, lifting one foot up to the other, she climbed the ladder to the lads' room above.

Mrs. Brace, the neighbour, came in presently from next door. She was a kindly woman, short of breath and very stout: indeed, she looked, poor soul, as though she were going to have a baby herself. But it was not so. Hannah Brace was *ruptured*, as she phrased it, she had a big umbilical hernia, the result of repeated pregnancies, and, though her husband Harry faithfully promised her the article every Christmas, as yet no truss to restrain it: every night when she went to bed she solemnly pushed back the bulging mass, every morning when she got up the thing bulged out again. She had become almost attached to her rupture, it formed a topic of conversation, she spoke about it to her intimates as people do about the weather. She went up the ladder very cautiously too, and disappeared into the room above.

David and Hughie sat in the kitchen. Hughie had given over his cobbling, and now pretended to interest himself with a paper. David also pretended to read. But from time to time the two looked at each other, confronted by the mystery secretly unfolding in the room above, and in the eyes of each there was a strange shame. To think of it; and their own mother!

No sound came from the bedroom but the heavy thump of feet as Mrs. Brace moved about. Once she called down for a kettle of hot water. Davey handed it to her.

At ten o'clock Sam came back rather pale about the gills, his jaw set to meet a most tremendous row. They told him. He flushed, as he did so easily, and remorse flooded him. Sam never could bear ill will. He lifted his eyes to the ceiling.

" My poor mother," he said. It was the most any of them dared to say.

At twenty minutes to eleven Mrs. Brace came down carrying a small newspaper package. She looked saddened and put out; she washed her red hands at the sink, took a drink of cold water; then she addressed herself to Sammy—the eldest:

" A little lass," she said, " a bonny thing, but dead. Ay, still-born. I'd have done as well as Mrs. Reedy, don't you fret. But I niver had no chance. I'll come in te-morrow an' lay the littlin out. Take yer mother up a cup of cocoa now. She's fair to middling; an' I've my man's bait to see to for the fore shift." She lifted the package carefully, smiled gently at David who saw that red was coming through the newspaper, then she waddled out.

Sam made the cocoa and took it up. He remained about ten minutes.

When he came down, his face was pale as clay, and the sweat had broken on his brow. He had come from his courting to look on death. David hoped that Sam might speak, say that their mother was comfortable. But all Sam said was:

" Get into bed, here, lads. We'll sleep three thegither in the kitchen for a bit."

Next morning, which was Tuesday, Mrs. Brace came in to see to Martha and, as she had promised, she laid out the still-born child. David returned from the pit earlier than the others; that night he had been lucky and ridden to bank two cage-loads ahead of the main shift. He entered the kitchen in the half-darkness. And there, upon the dresser, lay the body of the child.

He went over and looked at it with a queer catch of fear and awe. It was very small, its hands no bigger than the petals of a water lily. The tiny fingers had no nails. The palm of his own hand would have covered its face; the pinched, marble-white features, were perfect; the tiny blue lips parted as in wonderment that life was not. Mrs. Brace, with the real professional touch, had stuffed the mouth and nostrils with cotton-wool. Looking over his shoulder now, not without pride, she explained:

" It looks mortal pretty. But she couldna bear it upstairs wi' her, your mother, Davey."

David hardly heard her. A stubborn resentment surged within him as he gazed at the dead-born infant. Why should it be so? Why shouldn't his mother have had food, care, attention, all that her condition demanded. Why was this child not living, smiling, sucking at the breast? It hurt him, stirred him to a fierce indignation. As on that occasion when the Wepts had given him food, a chord vibrated deeply, painfully within his being; and again he swore with all the inarticulate passion of his young soul to do something . . . something . . . he didn't know what or how . . . but he would do it . . . strike some destroying stroke against the pitiful inhumanities of life.

Sam and Hughie came in together. They looked at the baby. Still in their pit clothes they ate the fried bacon Mrs. Brace had prepared. It was not the usual good meal, the potatoes were lumpy, there was insufficient water for the bath, the kitchen was upset, everything untidy, they missed their mother's hand.

Later, when Sammy came down from upstairs he looked at his brothers furtively. He said awkwardly:

" She won't have no funeral. I've talked an' talked, but she won't have it. She says since the lock-out we can't face the expense."

" But, Sammy, we must," David cried. " Ask Mrs. Brace . . ."

Mrs. Brace was called to reason with Martha. It was useless, Martha was inexorable, an iron bitterness had seized her over this child she had not wanted and which now had no want of her. No funeral was exacted by law. She would not have it, none of the trappings or panoply of death.

Hughie, always clever with his hands, made a neat enough coffin from plain pit boards. They put clean white paper inside and laid the body in the rude shell. Then Hughie nailed on the lid.

Late on Thursday night Sam took the box under his arm and set out alone. He forbade Hughie and David to accompany him. It was dark and windy. They did not know where he had gone until he came back. Then he told them. He had borrowed five shillings from Pug Macer, Annie's eldest brother, and given it to Geddes, the cemetery keeper. Geddes had let him bury the child privately in a corner of the graveyard. David often thought of that shallow grave; he never knew where it was; but he did know it was not near the pauper graves; this much Sammy told him.

Friday passed and Saturday came: the day of Robert's release. Martha had been confined on Monday night. By Saturday afternoon she was up, waiting . . . waiting for him, for Robert.

He arrived at eight o'clock, to find her in the kitchen alone. He entered so quietly she did not know he was there until the sound of his cough made her spin round as she stood, still bent over the fire. They stared at each other, he quietly, without rancour, she with that terrible bitterness burning like dark fire in her eyes. Neither spoke. He flung his cap on the sofa, sat down at the table like a weary man. Immediately she went to the oven, drew out his plate of cooked dinner kept hot for him there. She placed it before him in that same terrible silence.

He began to eat, casting quick glances at her figure from time to time, glances that became charged with a strange apology. At length he said:

" What's like the matter, my lass ? "

She quivered with anger.

" Don't call me your lass."

He understood then what had happened; a kind of wonder stirred in him.

" What was it ? " he asked.

She knew he had always wanted a daughter. And to cut him more she told him that his daughter was dead.

" So that was the way of it," he sighed; and then: " Did ye have a bad time, lass ? "

It was too much. She did not deign to answer at once; but with embittered servitude she removed his empty plate and placed his tea before him; then she said:

" I'm used to bad times like, since ever I knew you."

Though he had come home for peace, her savage attitude provoked his tired blood.

" I canna help the way things hev gone," he said with a sudden bitterness to match her own. " I hope ye understand they gaoled me for nowt."

" I do not understand," she answered, hand on her hip, facing him.

" They had their knife in me ower the strike, don't ye see! "

" I'm not surprised," she retorted, panting with anger.

It was then that his nerves broke. What, under heaven, had he done? He had brought the men out, because in his very marrow he feared for them in Scupper Flats, and in the end they had scoffed at him and spat upon him and let him go to gaol for nothing. Fury seethed in him, against her and against his fate. He lifted his hand and struck her on the face.

She did not flinch, she received the blow gratefully. Her nostrils dilated.

" Thanks," she said. " That was good of ye. 'Twas all I needed."

He sank back into his chair, paler than she. Then he began to cough, his deep booming cough. He was torn by this paroxysm. When it had passed he sat bowed, defeated; then he rose, threw off his clothes, got into the kitchen bed.

Next day, Sunday, though he awakened at seven, he stopped in bed all forenoon. She was up early and went to chapel. She forced herself to go, enduring the looks, slights and sympathy of the Bethel Street congregation, partly to show him up, partly to establish her own respectability. Dinner was a misery, especially for the lads. They hated it when open anger came between their father and mother. It paralysed the house, lay upon them like a degradation.

After dinner Robert walked down to the pit. He expected to find himself sacked. But he was not sacked. Dimly he realised that his friendship with Heddon, the miners' agent, and with Harry Nugent of the Federation had helped him here. Fear of real trouble with the Union had saved his job for him at the Neptune.

He came straight home, sat reading by the fire, went silently to bed. Next morning the caller woke him, at two o'clock he was in the pit working the early fore shift.

All day long she prepared for his return in that same storm of unappeased bitterness. She would show him, make him pay . . . she kept looking at the clock, waiting for the hours to pass.

At the end of the shift he returned, dead beat and soaked to the skin. She prepared to wound him with her silent anger, but somehow the sight of him killed all the rankling in her heart.

" What's like the matter? " she asked instinctively.

He leaned against the table, stifling his cough, gasping for breath.

" They've couped the cavils," he said, meaning that the draw for positions in the Paradise had been overruled. " They've black-listed me, gi'en me the worst place in the whole district. A scabby three-foot roof. I've lay on my stomach in water, hewin', all the shift."

A throb of compassion beat within her. And with that beat of anguish something she had thought dead came painfully alive. She reached out her hands.

" Let me help ye, my lad. Let me help ye with your claes."

She helped him strip the filthy sodden clothes. She helped him to the bath. She knew she still loved him.

IX

David, five hundred feet underground and two miles from the main shaft, reckoned it was nearly bait time. He was in the Paradise, the Mixen-section of Paradise, the lowest level of the Neptune pit with Globe Coal two hundred feet above, and Five Quarter a hundred higher still. He had no watch, but the number of journeys he had made with his tubs from the flat to the landing gave him the clue. He stood beside Dick, his galloway, in the landing—where the full tubs which he, the horse putter, drove up, were hitched to the mechanical haulage and pulled outbye on the Paradise haulage road. He was waiting for Tally Brown to switch the empties. Though he hated the Paradise, David always liked the landing. It was cool, after a hot sweaty run, and he could stand upright without fear of banging his head.

While David waited he reflected on his own good fortune. He could barely believe it, that this should be his last Saturday in the Neptune. Not only his last Saturday; but his last day! No, he could not fully realise his luck.

He had always hated the pit. Some of the lads liked it, took to the work like a duck to water. But not he. Never! Perhaps his imagination was too vivid, he couldn't lose the sense of being shut up, buried in these dark little warrens, deep down underground. He always remembered, too, in the Five Quarter Seam, that he was under the sea. Mr. Carmichael, the junior master at Bethel Street Council School, who had helped him over the scholarship, had told him the name of that queer sensation of feeling shut down. Deep underground; deep under the sea. While above the sun shone, the wind blew fresh, the waves broke white and lovely.

He always set himself stubbornly against that feeling. He'd be hanged if he'd give way to a thing like that. Yet, he was glad, glad to be leaving the Neptune, the more so as he had always had the odd notion that once a boy went down the pit, the pit claimed him, refused to let him go. Old pit-men said that, joking. In the darkness David laughed to himself, it was a joke, that, right enough.

Here Tally switched the empty tubs. David coupled them in a train of four, sprang on to the bar, clicked his tongue to Dick and set off down the pitch-black incline. Bang, bang went the tubs, jerking and crashing behind him on the badly laid track as he gathered speed. David prided himself on driving fast, of all the horse putters in the Paradise he could drive the fastest; and he was used to the banging of the tubs, he did not mind the din. What he did mind was the bother when a tub ran off; it nearly killed him, the raxing and straining to lift it back upon the line.

Down he went, down, down, smashing along at a glorious pace, balancing, guiding, knowing when to duck his head and when to throw his weight against the curve, It was reckless, terribly reckless, his father often checked him for driving so fast. But David loved the thrill of it. He drew up with a magnificent jolt at the putters' flat.

Here, as he had anticipated, Ned Softley and Tom Reedy, the two hand putters who pushed the tubs from the coal face to the flat, were squatted in the refuge hole eating their bait.

" Come on, ye old beggor, and have yer snap," Tom called out with his mouth full of bread and cheese, and he moved up the refuge hole to make room.

David liked Tom—a big, good-natured lad who had taken Joe's place in the flat. He had often wondered where Joe had got to, what he was doing; and he wondered, too, why he missed Joe so little—Joe, after all, had been his mate. Perhaps it was because Tom Reedy had made so good a substitute: as genial as Joe, more willing to help with a run-off tub, less ready in the matter of lewd profanity. But though David was fond of Tom's company he shook his head negatively:

" I'm going inbye, Tom."

David really wanted to eat his bait with his father; whenever he got the chance he took his bait-poke and went in; he wasn't going to miss it this last day.

The slant to the coal face was so low he had to bend himself double. The tunnel was like a rabbit run for size, so inky black his naked light, smoking a little, seemed hardly to carry a foot, and so wet, his feet made squelching noises as he plugged along. Once he hit his head against the hard scabby whinstone roof and swore gently.

When he reached the face his father and Slogger had not knocked off, but were still hewing coal to fill the empty tubs that Tom and Ned would shortly bring in. Stark naked except for boots and pit drawers, they were working bord and pillar. The place was awful, David knew, the work frightfully hard. He sat down on a dry bit, watching, waiting till they should finish. Robert, twisted sideways under the jud, was nicking the coal ready to bring it down. His breath came in short gasps, sweat ran out of every pore of his body, he looked done. There was no room to turn, the roof was so low it seemed to flatten him. Yet he worked tenaciously, with experience and wonderful skill. With him worked the Slogger. His enormous hairy torso and bull neck made him a titan beside Robert. He never spoke a word, kept chewing tobacco furiously, chewing and spitting and hewing. Yet David, with a quick pulse of gratitude, saw that he was saving his father, taking the heavy end of the stick, doing all the hardest bits himself. The sweat rained off Slogger's bashed-in face, he bore no resemblance to the Pitboy Wonder.

At last they knocked off, wiped themselves with their singlets, slipped them on, came over and sat down.

" How, Davey ? " said Robert when he saw his son.

" How again, dad ? "

Harry Grace and Bob Ogle emerged from another heading and joined them. Hughie, his brother, followed silently. They all began to eat their bait.

To Davey, after a hard morning's driving, the bread and cold bacon his mother had put up for him was delicious. He saw, however, that his father barely ate, merely drinking enormous draughts of cold tea from his bottle. And he had pie, too, in his poke. Since Robert and Martha had been reconciled she had made him the most appetising pokes. But Robert gave half of the pie to Slogger; he said he was not hungry.

" It ud take any mon's appetite away," remarked Harry Brace with a nod towards Robert's heading. " It's a bitch of a place for sure."

" There's no bloddy head room," agreed Slogger, chewing pie with the noisy relish of a man whose missus usually gave him cut bread and dripping. " But this is bloddy good pie."

" It's the wet," commented Ogle. " We hev it an' all. Man, the roof fair bleeds water."

There was a silence, broken only by the snoring of air through the wind-bore cast of the pump. The sound echoed in the darkness, mingled with the suck and gurgle of water through the lower snore-holes. Though they barely heard that sound, subconsciously each man approved it, aware, deep down within himself, that it meant the proper functioning of the pump.

Harry Brace turned to Robert.

" It's not as wet as in the Scupper, though."

" No! " said Robert quietly, " we're well out o' that sheugh."

Slogger said:

" If the wet irks ye, Harry, lad, ye better ask the missus for a clout."

Everybody laughed. Carried away by his success, Slogger gaily nudged David in the ribs.

" You're a clivor young fella, Davey. Can ye do onything about my wet backside ? "

" What about kicking it ? " Davey suggested dryly.

There was a louder laugh than ever. Slogger grinned: in the dim light of that dark place he looked like some gay gigantic devil bent on a rich Satanic jest.

" Good lad! Good lad! That would warm it reet enough." He approved Davey, taking his measure with one white eye. " Ye *are* a clivor fella after all. Is't true what I hear, that yer goin' te the Baddeley College to teach all the professors in Tynecassel ? "

David said:

" I hope they'll teach me, Slogger."

" But for why in all the world are ye going ? " expostulated Slogger with a wink at Robert. " Don't ye want to grow up a proper collier like me wi' an elegant figger an' face ? An' a canny bit o' money tucked away in the Fiddler's bank."

This time Robert did not see the joke.

" He's going because I want him to get out of *this*," he said sternly; and the burning stress he laid upon that word silenced them all. " He's taken his chance. He's worked hard, has got his scholarship, he goes to Tynecastle Monday."

There was a pause, then Hughie, the silent one, suddenly declared:

" I wish I could get the length of Tynecassel. I'd fair love to see the United regular." The longing in Hughie's voice made Slogger laugh again.

" Don't ye worry, lad." He slapped Hughie on the back. " Ye'll be playin' for the United yerself one of they days. I've seen ye, I know what ye can do. Mon, I heard the Tynecassel spotter wor coming down to watch ye at the next Sleescale match."

Hughie coloured under his dirt. He knew Slogger was pulling his leg. But he didn't care. He'd get there one day, for all their jokes. He'd show them, and show them soon, he would!

All at once Brace lifted his head, cocked one ear towards the slant.

" Hey! " he exclaimed, " what's like the matter wi' the pump ? "

Slogger stopped chewing, every one sat perfectly still, listening into the darkness. The snoring of the pump had stopped. For a full minute none of them spoke. David felt a queer cold pricking run down his spine.

" Dammit," Slogger said slowly with a sort of obtuse wonder. " Will ye lissen to that! The pump has let up on us."

Ogle, who was not long working in the Paradise, got to his feet and felt for the feeder. Hastily, he called out:

" The level's rising. There's more water here. A heap more water." He paused, fumbling about with his arm in the water of the feeder; then, with sudden anxiety: " I'll better fetch the deputy."

" Wait! " Robert stopped him with a sudden sharp command; then in a reasoning tone he added: " Don't be runnin' outbye like a bairn, mon. Let Dinning bide where he is. Hover a bit! Hover a bit! There's never any trouble with a bucket pump. And there's nowt serious the matter wi' this pump. It's only some sludge choked up the clack. I'll see to it myself."

He got up in a quiet, unhurried style and went down the slant. The others waited, not speaking. In five minutes there came the slow suck of the cleared valve, the throaty gurgle of the restarted pump. Another three minutes and the healthy snoring was restored. The tension binding the men relaxed. A great sense of pride in his father's knowledge broke over David.

" I'll be damned . . ." Ogle sighed.

Slogger derided him.

" Don't ye know there's niver need to worry wi' Robert Fenwick in the sett. Come on and fill some tubs. You'll addle nowt by sittin' here all day." He rose, tugged off his singlet; Brace, Hughie and Ogle went back to their heading; David started towards his tubs, passing Robert as he came down the dip.

" You made short work o' that, Robert," Slogger said. " Ogle nearly had us roofed! " and he laughed extravagantly.

But Robert did not laugh. He pulled off his singlet with a curiously remote expression on his drawn face. Then he threw it down without looking. The singlet fell in a puddle of water.

They restarted. Swinging their picks, cutting, bringing down the coal. The sweat broke out on them again. The pit dirt clogged their skin. Five hundred feet down, two miles from shaft bottom. The moisture seeped slowly from the roof, it dropped incessantly like unseen rain in a pitch-dark night. And over and above it all there rose the measured stertor of the pump.

X

At the end of that shift David led his galloway to the stables and saw him comfortable.

This was the worst bit of all, he had known it would be the worst of all, but it was worse even than he had thought. With firm strokes David caressed the pony's neck. Dick turned his long head, seemed to look at David with those soft blind eyes, then nuzzled towards the pocket of his jacket. Often David saved a bit of bread from his bait, or maybe a biscuit. But to-day there was something special; he pulled out a lump of cheese—Dick went simply mad about cheese—and slowly fed the pony, breaking off little pieces, holding them flat on his palm, spinning out the pleasure for Dick and for himself. The wet velvety feel of the galloway's muzzle on his hand brought a lump to his throat. He slowly rubbed his wet hand on the lapel of his jacket, took a last look at Dick and went rapidly away.

He walked outbye down the main road, passing the place where a fall of roof had killed three men the year before: Harrower, and the two brothers Neil and Allen Preston, he had been there when they dug them out, all mangled, flattened, their chests caved in and bloody, their mouths pressed full of dirt. David would never orget that fall. He always walked slower under the place with a stubborn determination to show that he was not afraid.

Along the road he was joined by Tom Reedy and his brother Jack, Softley, Ogle, young Cha Leeming, son of the Slogger, by Dan Teasdale and some others. They reached the shaft bottom where a big crowd stood waiting to ride the bank, jammed together yet patient. The cage was single and could take only twelve persons at a time. Besides the Paradise the cage was serving Globe and Five Quarter Coal, the levels above. David found himself squeezed next to Wept, away from the larking of Tom Reedy and Softley. Wept fixed him with his dark, intense gaze.

" Ye're going to college, then, to Tynecassel ? "

David nodded. Again it seemed to him too strange to be real. Perhaps he was a little worn by the last six months, the strain of working by night, of studying with Mr. Carmichael, whirling to Tynecastle to sit the scholarship, learning joyfully of the result. The silent struggle between his mother and his father had worried him too: Robert doggedly intent that he should get the scholarship and leave the pit, Martha equally determined he should remain. When the news had come of his success, she had said nothing, not one word. She had not even prepared his clothes for his departure, she would have no hand in it, she would not.

" Ye must mind Tynecassel, lad," Wept said. " Ye're takin' your journey into the wilderness where they meet with darkness in the daytime and grope in the noonday as in the night. Here! " He slipped his hand into his inside pocket and pulled out a thin folded finger-marked booklet much soiled by coal dust. " You'll find counsel in this! It's been good company to me many a bait time in this very pit."

David took the tract, colouring. He did not want it; at the same time he did not want to hurt Wept's feelings. Awkwardly he turned the pages—the light was bad, he could barely see, but he could think of nothing else to do. Suddenly his lamp flickered and a phrase leaped up to him: *No servant can serve two masters, ye cannot serve God and mammon.*

Wept watched him with intent eyes. Over his shoulder Tom Reedy whispered slyly:

" Has he gi'en ye the winner of the three o'clock ? "

Around him the men were beginning to sway. The cage crashed down. From the back someone shouted:

" All in, lads! All in."

There was a rush, the usual squash for places. David jammed in with the rest. The cage lifted, swishing up the guides, up, up as though plucked by a gigantic hand. Daylight came flooding down to meet it. There came a clang, the bar lifted, the men crushed out into the sweet daylight as though welded in a solid mass.

David clattered down the steps with the men, crossed the pit yard, took his place in the pay line outside the offices. It was a bright June day. The hard outline of the headgear, stocks and spinning pulleys, even the smoking upcast stack, was softened by the languid beauty of the day. A wonderful day to be leaving the pit.

The line moved slowly forward. David saw his father come out of the cage, he had been the last to ride the bank, and take his place right at the end of the line. Then he observed the dogcart from the Law drive through the yard gates. The occurrence of the dogcart was quite normal: every pay-Saturday Richard Barras drove down to the offices while the men stood lined up for their envelopes. It was a sort of ritual.

The dogcart took a neat sweep, its yellow spokes flashing in the sun, and brought up opposite the offices. Richard Barras descended, holding himself erect, and disappeared through the main door of the offices. Bartley was already at the horse's head. Arthur Barras, who had been wedged between the two, remained seated in the dogcart.

From a distance, as he moved slowly forward, David studied Arthur; wondered about him idly. Without in the least knowing why, he felt a strange sympathy for Arthur; an extremely odd sensation, peculiar, paradoxical almost, as if he were sorry for Arthur. It was ridiculous considering their respective situations. Yet the small boy, undersized for his age, perched all by himself upon the seat of the dogcart with his soft fair hair ruffled by the breeze, looked so very much alone. He invoked protection. And he was so serious, his gravity, his serious preoccupation lay upon him like a sadness. When he discovered that he was pitying Arthur Barras David almost laughed aloud.

His turn at the window came. He went forward, received his pay envelope thrust through the opening by Pettit, the cashier. Then he lounged over to the yard gates to await his father. As he reached the gate post and leaned his back against it, Annie Macer passed down Cowpen Street. At the sight of him she smiled and stopped. She did not speak; Annie seldom spoke until she was spoken to; no, she stopped and smiled out of friendship; but she waited until he should speak to her.

" All by yourself, Annie ? " he said companionably. He liked Annie Macer; he really did like her; he could understand perfectly why Sam should be so gone on her. She was so simple, fresh, homely. She had no pride. She was herself. Transparently there was no nonsense about Annie. For some absurd reason he associated Annie with a little silvery fresh herring. Yet Annie was not little, nor had she the least resemblance to a herring. She was a big-boned strapping girl of his own age, with generous hips and a fine firm bosom; she wore a blue serge skirt and coarse hand-knitted stockings. Annie knitted these stockings herself; she had never read a book in her life; but she had knitted a great many pairs of stockings.

" It's my last day this, Annie," he declared, making conversation to detain her. " I'm done with the Neptune for good . . . water, muck, ponies, tubs and all."

She smiled tolerantly.

"I'm not sorry," he added. "No, you may bet your life I'm not sorry."

She nodded her head understandingly. There fell a silence. She looked up and down the street. Then with her friendly smile she nodded again and went off.

Pleased, he followed her with his eyes. It struck him that she had not spoken a single word. Yet he had enjoyed every minute of her company. Good for Annie Macer!

Turning again he looked towards his father: he was still a long way from the window. What a time Pettit was taking to-day. He leaned back, kicking his heels against the post.

Suddenly he became aware that he, in his turn, was being observed: Barras, escorted by Armstrong, had returned to the dogcart, they stood together, the owner and the viewer, staring directly at him. He stared back at them, dourly, determined not to be put down by them; after all, he was leaving the pit, wasn't he?—he didn't give tuppence now. For a minute they continued talking, then Armstrong laughed respectfully, raised his hand and beckoned him over. He had half a mind not to go, yet he did go, taking care, however, to go slowly.

"Mr. Armstrong tells me that you have won a scholarship at the Baddeley."

David saw that Barras was in high good humour; yet felt the keen scrutiny of his small cold eyes.

"I'm very pleased," Barras went on, "to hear of your success. What are you after—at the Baddeley?"

"I want to take my B.A."

"H'm—your B.A.? Why don't you go in for mining engineering?"

David answered defiantly, something in Barras provoked his defiance: "I've no interest in the work."

His defiance slid off Barras like water off cold stone.

"Really . . . no interest?"

"No! I don't like it underground."

"You don't like it," Barras echoed aloofly. "You want to take up teaching."

David saw that Armstrong had told him.

"No, no. I'll not stop at teaching." He regretted the remark instantly. That hot defiant pride had betrayed him into revealing himself. He felt the incongruity of it, standing there in his pit clothes with Arthur there in the dogcart looking and listening; he felt like some sickly hero of an autobiography—Log Cabin to White House; but he was stubborn enough not to withdraw. If Barras asked, he'd tell him outright what he meant to do.

But Barras seemed to have no curiosity whatever, no consciousness of antagonism. He simply went on, as though he had not heard David, went on to moralise:

" Education is a fine thing. I never stand in anyone's way. When you finish at the Baddeley you might let me know. I'm on the Board! I might get you into one of the County schools. We always have a place for junior teachers."

He seemed to recede from David behind the strong lenses of his glasses. Remotely, thus, he slipped his hand into his trousers pocket, pulled out a large white palmful of silver. In his unhurried style he picked out a half-crown, weighed it mentally; then he put it back, selecting instead a two-shilling piece.

" Here's a florin," he said calmly, rather majestically, making it a gift and a dismissal.

David was so dumbfounded he took the coin. He stood with it in his hand while Barras mounted, took his seat in the dogcart. He was dimly conscious of Arthur's friendly smile upon him. Then the dogcart moved off.

A wild impulse to laugh came over David. He recollected the text in the tract Wept had given him. " Ye cannot serve God and mammon." Inwardly he repeated: " Ye cannot serve God and mammon. Ye cannot serve God . . ." It was funny, oh, it was funny!

He turned abruptly and went towards the yard gates where Robert now stood, in his turn, waiting for him. David saw that his father had been a spectator of the whole scene. He saw that his father was furious. Robert was pale with fury, he kept his eyes down, not looking at David.

They went out of the yard together, side by side, walking up Cowpen Street. Not a word passed between them. A little way up they were joined by Swee Messer. Immediately Robert began to talk to Swee in an ordinary friendly way. Swee was a good-looking blond-haired lad, always light-hearted and gay, a filler, not in the Paradise but in Globe Coal, higher up. Swee's real name was Oswey Messuer, his father was the barber in Lamb Street, a naturalised Austrian who had been settled twenty years in Sleescale. They were popular, father and son, each in his own sphere, the son gaily filling tubs in the pit, the father meekly lathering chins in the parlour of his shop.

Robert went on talking to Swee as though nothing had happened to disturb him. As Swee branched off along Freehold Street he said:

" Tell your dad I'll be down four o'clock as usual."

But the moment Swee was gone Robert's face relapsed into its former bitterness. His features seemed to contract, to tighten upon the bone. In silence he tramped along with David until they reached half-way up Cowpen Street. Then he paused. Opposite was Middlerig, the back yard of the old cow-stalls, a filthy place, an eyesore to the town, rank with rotting straw, ordure and an enormous dung-heap. He faced David.

" What did he gie ye, son ? " he asked quietly.

" He gave me two shillings, dad." And David exposed the florin which he still kept, from shame, gripped tightly, secretly in his palm.

Robert took the coin, looked at it, silently, then flung it from him with a savage force.

" There," he said, as though the word hurt him. " *There!* "

The florin pitched right into the centre of the dung-heap.

XI

The night, the great night of the Millington Social arrived. Millington's, situated at the dead end of a lane off Platt Street, employed about two hundred men and, though small, was not without impressiveness, especially if viewed on a dull March afternoon. From the chimneys of the furnaces, in which the iron was melted, tongues of red flame and dense clouds of smoke belched upwards. The drab sky, illuminated by the white-hot stream of molten metal flowing from the cupolas to the ladles, seemed to burn with a brassy glare. Pungent fumes rising from the foundry floor as the liquid iron poured into the moulds assailed the nostrils. The ears were stung by the heavy thud of hammers, the ringing of the fettlers' chisels as they dressed the iron castings, the whirring of driving belts and gear wheels, the piercing scream of the lathes and the milling machines, the burr of the saws as they gnawed into metal. And through the haze emerging from the open doors the eye picked up the dim figures of men, stripped to the waist because of the tremendous heat.

The chief product of the foundry was colliery equipment—iron tubs, haulage gear, roofing bars and heavy forged shackle-bolts, but competition was keen in this market, and Millington's kept going more through their conservative connection with old-established firms than through enterprise. Millington's was itself an old-established firm. Millington's had tradition. And part of that tradition was the Social Club.

Millington's Social Club, founded in the 'seventies by the Grand Old Man—Wesley Millington, catered in the most benevolent manner for the Workman and the Workman's Family. The Club had four sections: Literary, Rambling, Photography—Dark Room included—and Athletic. But the scintillating event in the Social Club's calendar was the Dance, known from time immemorial as the Social, and held, invariably, in the Oddfellows' Hall.

To-night, Friday, March 23rd, was the actual night of gaiety and gladness; yet Joe went home from his work at the foundry in a crush of sombre meditation. Naturally Joe was going to the Social, he was already a prime favourite in the Club, a rising member in the boxing section, likely candidate for the novices' billiards handicap. Joe had done pretty well in these last eight months, filled out substantially, put more muscle on his shoulders and, in his own phrase, made a deuce of a lot of pals. He was a grand mixer, Joe, a hearty slapper on the back, with a resonant: " How *do*, ole man! " a ready laugh—a fine manly laugh—a firm handshake and he was, oh, such a lovely teller of a smutty story. Everybody at the works, from Porterfield, the foreman, to Mr. Stanley Millington himself, everyone who really mattered, seemed to take to Joe; at least everyone but Jenny.

Jenny! Joe thought of her as he tramped over the High Level Bridge, reviewing the situation with a moody eye. She was going to the Social with him, certainly she was. But what did that mean, when all was said and done? Nothing, plain nothing at all! How far had he got with Jenny in these eight months? Not so very far, by gum, no, not so very far. He had taken her out plenty—Jenny loved to go out—spent money on her, yes, spent his good money like water. But what had he received in return? A few kisses, a few short kisses, surrendered unwillingly, a few pushed-away embraces which only whetted his appetite for more.

He let out a long, gloomy breath: if Jenny thought she'd make a mug out of him she was mistaken, he'd tell her a few plain truths, chuck the whole thing and be done with her. But no, he'd said that before. He'd said that a dozen times before. And he hadn't chucked her. He wanted her, even more than on that first day . . . and even then he had wanted her badly enough. He cursed right out loud.

She puzzled him: treating him sometimes with a haughty arrogance, sometimes with coquettish intimacy. She was always pleasantest to him when he was all dressed up in his new blue serge suit and the derby hat she had made him buy. But if by chance she met him in his dirty dungarees she sailed past him with a distant air, almost froze him with her look. It was the same when they went out: if he took her to a good seat at the Empire, she purred, smiled up into his face, let him hold her hand; yet, if he suggested a stroll after dark round the Town Moor, she would accompany him quite pettishly, her head well in the air, her answers short and snappy, keeping herself a full yard from his side. When he asked her to McGuigan's coffee-stall for sausage and mash she would sniff and say: " That's the sort of place my father goes to." But an invitation to Leonard's High Class Tea Rooms in the High Street found her beaming, snuggling to his side. She wanted to be above her family, better than they; she corrected her father, her mother and her sisters, Sally especially. She was always correcting him, too, pulling him up, disdainfully telling him how to raise his hat, carry his cane, walk on the outside of the pavement, and crook his little finger when he drank his tea. She was terribly genteel, crammed with etiquette culled from the columns of the women's penny journals. From the same columns she got her fashion hints, " shapes " for the dresses she made herself, advice on how to keep her hands white, how " the white of an egg mixed with the rinsing water " would bring out the glossy lustre of her hair.

Mind you, he did not mind this striving towards refined gentility, in fact he liked it, little things like her Jockey Club scent or her lace camisole—pink ribbon threaded, seen through her blouse—excited him, made him feel that she was *different* from the street tarts he had possessed occasionally, during these tantalising months of hope deferred.

The very thought of what he had endured goaded his desire intolerably. As he went up the front steps of 117A Scottswood Road he told himself that he would bring matters to a head to-night or know the reason why.

When he went into the back room he saw from the clock that he was late. Already Jenny had gone upstairs to dress. Mrs. Sunley was lying down in the parlour with a sick headache. Phyllis and Clarry had gone into the street to play. It was left to Sally to give him his tea.

" Where's your dad ? " Joe asked suddenly when he had wolfed his two kippers and the best part of a new loaf, and swilled down three big cups of tea.

" Gone to Birmingham. The secretary couldn't go, so dad went instead. He's taken all the club homers and ours too. For to-morrow."

Joe lifted his fork and picked his teeth reflectively. So Alf had a free trip to Birmingham for the Saturday Pigeon Flight. Lucky dog!

Studying Joe critically, Sally now loosed upon him a shaft from her precocious wit.

" Don't swallow that fork," she warned him gravely. " It'll rattle when you do the polka."

He scowled at her. He was only too well aware that Sally loathed him, however much he tried he could not win her round. He had the uncomfortable feeling, under her dark eyes, that Sally saw through him; sometimes her shrill derisive laugh cutting into his manly conversation would take him completely aback, rend his composure from him, make him blush horribly.

His scowl gratified her; her eyes sparkled. Though she was only eleven, her sense of drollery was acute. Gaily she went on with the game of taking him off.

" You ought to be a good dancer, too, you've such big feet. Can you reverse, Miss Sunley ? Yes indeed, Joe, I mean Mr. Gowlan, excuse the liberty. Shall we try ? Please do, Mr. Gowlan, dear. Isn't the music too lovelee ? Ouch! ye beggor, ye tramped on me corn."

She was really very funny, screwing up her comic little face, rolling her big black eyes, mimicking Jenny's fastidious accent to perfection.

" Shall I stand you an ice, my deah ? Or would you prefer tripe ? Beautiful tripe. Straight from the cow. You can have all the curly bits." She jerked her head upwards. " She's curling her hair upstairs. Miss

Sunley. Jenny, the lady toff what sleeps with the clothes-peg on her nose. Been at it for an hour. Come straight from in the millineree, not serving mind you, that's what the slaveys do, that's comming! Made me heat the irons, she did, caught me a cuff on the ear for the good of the house. There's temper for you, Joseph, take a stitch in time before you leap! "

" Ah, be quiet will you . . . you cheeky little brat." He rose from the table, made for the door.

She pretended to blush, remarking mincingly:

" Don't be so formal, Mr. Gowlan, dear. Just call me plain Maggie. With such lovelee eyes ain't it a shame you smoke. Oh, don't think of leaving me so soon," deliberately she got in his way, " just let me sing you a song before you go, Mr. Gowlan. One tiny little song." Folding her hands in coy imitation of Jenny standing at the piano she began, very falsetto:

" *See the little pansy faces,*
Growing in the garden there . . ."

She stopped when the door banged behind him, burst into a peal of delighted laughter, then took a flying header on to the sofa. She lay curled up on the edge whanging the springs with her own delight.

Upstairs Joe shaved, scrubbed himself, robed carefully in the best blue serge, knotted a new green tie, neatly laced his shiny brown boots. Even so he was ready before Jenny; he waited impatiently in the hall. Yet when she did come down she took his breath away, knocked the puff right out of him: dressed in a pink frock, white satin shoes, a white crochet shawl—known in the vogue of the moment as a *fascinator*—over her hair. Her grey eyes had a cool lustre in her clear, petalled face. She was delicately sucking a scented cachou.

" By gum, Jenny, you look a treat! "

She accepted his homage as a matter of course, slipped her everyday cloth coat over her finery, took the front door key with a womanly air and put it in her coat pocket. Then she caught sight of his brown boots. Her lip drooped.

" I wish, Joe," she said peevishly, " that you had got yourself a pair of pumps. I told you to a week ago."

" Ah, all the fellows wear these at the Social, I asked them."

" Don't be a fool! As if I didn't know! You'll make me look ridiculous with these brown boots. Have you got the cab ? "

" Cab! " His jaw fell; did she think he was Carnegie ? he said sulkily: " We're going by tram."

Her eyes frosted with temper.

" I see! So that's what you think of me! I'm not good enough to have a cab."

From the landing above Ada called out:

" Don't be late, you two. I've taken a Daisy powder and I'm going to bed."

" Don't you worry, ma," Jenny answered in a mortal huff. " We certainly shan't be late."

They caught a red tram which was, unfortunately, very full. The tram's fullness made Jenny more sulky, she stared the conductor out of countenance when he asked Joe for something smaller. During the whole journey she did not speak. But at last they reached Yarrow, got out of the crowded red tram. They approached the Oddfellows' Hall in the chill silence of her offended dignity. When they entered the hall the Social had already begun.

Actually, it was not a bad Social, an intimate informal affair rather like the annual gathering of a large and happy middle-class family. At one end of the hall were tables set out with the supper: cakes, sandwiches, biscuits, green jellies, lots of small hard oranges that looked full of pips and were, bright red bottles of kola and two huge brass urns for tea and coffee. At the other end on a very high platform, screened by two aspidistras and a palm, was the orchestra, a grand orchestra, it had a full bass drum, used without stint, and Frank McGarvie at the piano. No one could put in more wonderful " twiddley-bits " than Frank. And the time? Impossible to put a foot wrong with Frank McGarvie's time, it was so wonderful, as though bunged out with a hammer—*La* de dee, *La* de dee, *La* de dee—the floor of the Oddfellows' Hall went up on the la and down, reverberating, on that final dee.

Every one was matey, there was no side, no nonsense of pencil and programme. Two foolscap sheets—beautifully written out by Frank McGarvie's sister—were pasted on opposite walls indicating the number and order of the dances! *Valse . . . Nights of Gladness, 2 Valetta . . . In a Gondola with You*, and so on. Much companionable crowding took place round the lists, giggling, craning of necks, linking of arms, commingling of perfume, perspiration and exclamations: " Hey, Bella, hinny, can ye do the military two-step? ": in which fashion partners were achieved. Or a young husky, having scanned the list, might take a gallant slide across the slippy powdered floor, his impetus carrying him straight on to the bosom of his beloved. " It's lancers, lass, diddent ye know? Come on an' dance it wi' us."

Jenny took a look at the assembly. She saw the poor refreshments, the pasted programmes on the steamy walls, the cheap and gaudy dresses, bright red, blue and green, the ridiculous dress suit of old Mike McKenna, the honoured master of ceremonies; she saw that gloves and slippers were considered by many to be non-essential; she saw the coterie of fat elderly puddlers' wives seated in a corner, conversing amicably while their offspring skipped and hopped and slid upon the floor before them. Jenny saw all this in one long look. Then she turned up her pretty nose.

" This," she sniffed to Joe, " gives me the pip."

" What ? " he gaped.

She snapped at him then,

" It's not *nice*, it's not classy, it's *low*."

" But aren't you going to dance ? "

She tossed her head indifferently.

" Oh, we might as well, I suppose, take the benefit of the floor. The tickets are paid for, aren't they ? "

So they danced, but she held herself well away from him, and well apart from all the hand-clapping and stamping and screeches of merriment round about.

" Who's that ? " said she disdainfully as they two-stepped past the door.

Joe followed her eyes. *That* was an inoffensive looking fellow, a middle-aged man, with a round head, a compact figure and slightly bandy legs.

" Jack Lynch," Joe said. " He's a blacksmith in the shop. Seems to have a notion of you."

" Him! " Jenny said, smirking stiffly at her own wit. " I've seen better in a cage."

She lapsed into her monosyllabic mood, lifting her eyebrows, keeping her head well up in the air, condescending. She wanted it to be seen that she was, in her own phrase, above all this.

Yet Jenny was a little premature. Gradually, as the evening wore on, people began to drop in: not the workpeople, the plain members of the Club who had crowded to the Social at the start, but the honorary members, a few draughtsmen from the drawing office, Mr. Irving, the accountant, and his wife, Morgan, the cashier, and actually old Mr. Clegg, the works manager. Jenny unbent slightly; she even smiled at Joe:

" It seems to be improving."

No sooner had she spoken than the doors swung open and Stanley Millington arrived, Mr. Stanley himself, *our* Mr. Stanley. It was a great moment. He entered genially, crisp and well-groomed in a very smart dinner suit, bringing his fiancée with him.

This time Jenny really sat up, fixing her shrewd noticing stare upon the two smart young people as they smiled and shook hands with several of the older members of the Club.

" That's Laura Todd with him," she whispered breathlessly. " You know, her father's the mining engineer in the Groat Market, I see her about plenty I can tell you. They got engaged last August, it was in the *Courier*."

Joe stared at her eager face. Jenny's burning interest in the " smart " society of Tynecastle, her delight in being posted to the last detail, left him quite nonplussed. But she now unbent completely towards him.

" Why aren't we dancing, Joe ? " she murmured, and rose to twirl languorously in his arms near Millington and Miss Todd.

" That frock of hers . . . a model . . . straight out of Bonar's," she whispered confidentially in Joe's ear as they swept past. Bonar's was, of course, the last word in Tynecastle. " And that lace . . ." she lifted her eyes expressively . . . " well . . ."

The gaiety increased, the drum thundered, Frank McGarvie put in more twiddley-bits than ever, the pace got fast and furious. Every one was so glad that young Mr. Stanley had found " time to come." And to bring Miss Laura with him, too! Stanley Millington was " well thought of " in Yarrow. His father had died some years before while Stanley was seventeen and still at school at St. Bede's. Stanley had therefore come hot foot to the works—athletic, upstanding, very fresh complexioned, with the small beginnings of a moustache—to learn the business under old Henry Clegg. Now, at twenty-five, Stanley was in command, enthusiastic and indefatigable, always extremely eager to do what he called the correct thing. Every one agreed that Stanley had the right spirit, it was the advantage of having been " at a good school."

Founded fifty years before by a group of rich northern nonconformist merchants, St. Bede's, in the short span of its existence, had achieved the true public school tradition. Prefects, fags, tuck shop, *esprit de corps*, inspiring school song, St. Bede's has them all and more, as though Dr. Fuller, the first head master, had gone round all the ancient schools of England with a butterfly net, capturing skilfully from each the choicest of its customs. Sport bulks largely at St. Bede's. Colours are awarded freely. They are pretty colours: purple, scarlet and gold. Stanley, passionately devoted to his old school, was naturally devoted to its colours. Usually he wore something on his person—tie, cuff links, braces or suspenders, emblazoned in the famous purple, scarlet and gold—a kind of testimony to the true sportsmanship for which St. Bede's has always stood.

In a manner of speaking, Mr. Stanley's sportsmanship was the reason of his coming to the Social. He wanted to be decent, to do the decent, the correct thing. And so he was here, extremely agreeable, shaking horny hands, interspersing his waltzes with Laura with several dances with the heavier wives of the old employees.

As the evening wore on, Jenny's bright smile, which had developed upon the entry of our Mr. Stanley and Laura Todd, became a trifle fixed; her laughter, which always seemed to ripple out, as she wheeled past either the one, or the other, or both, a trifle forced. Jenny was burning to be " noticed " by Miss Todd, dying simply for our Mr. Stanley to ask her to dance. But, no, nothing happened, it really was too bad. Instead Jack Lynch kept staring at her, following her about, trying to get the chance to ask her for a dance.

Jack was not a bad lad, the trouble was that Jack was drunk. Everybody knew that Jack was fond of a bead and to-night, nipping in and out of the Hall to the adjacent Duke of Cumberland, Jack had strung a good few beads on his alcoholic rosary. In the ordinary way Jack would have stood by the Hall door, nodding happily to the music and at the end gone home unsteadily upon his bandy legs to bed. But to-night Jack's bad angel hovered near.

The last dance before supper Jack straightened his tie, and swaggered over to Jenny.

" Come awa', hinny," he said in his broad Tyneside. " You an' me'll show them."

Jenny tossed her head and looked pointedly across the room. Joe, sitting beside her, said:

" Away you go, Jack. Miss Sunley's dancing with me."

Jack swayed on his feet:

" But aw want her to dawnce wi' me." He reached out his arm with rough gallantry. There was not an ounce of harm in Jack but he staggered, so that his big paw fell accidentally on Jenny's shoulder.

Jenny screamed dramatically. And Joe, rising in a sudden heat, planted a right hook dexterously on the point of Jack's chin. Jack measured his length on the floor. Hubbub broke.

" I say, what's all this ? " Mr. Stanley, thrusting his way forward, came though the crowd to where Joe stood gallantly with his chest stuck out and his arm round the pale-faced, frightened Jenny. " What's happened ? What's the trouble ? "

The manly Joe, with his heart in his boots, replied virtuously:

" He was drunk, Mr. Millington, rotten drunk. A fellow's got to draw the line somewhere." Joe had been out on a beautiful blind with Lynch the Saturday before, they had both been chucked out of the Empire Bar, but he forgot, oh, he rose above that now. " He was drunk and interfered with my friend, Mr. Stanley. I only protected her."

Stanley took in the pair of them—the clean-limbed young fellow . . . beauty in distress; then, with a frown, the figure of the fallen drunkard.

" Drunk," he exclaimed. " That's too bad, really too bad. I can't have any of that here! My people are decent people and I want them to enjoy themselves decently. Carry him out, will you. Attend to it, Mr. Clegg, please. And let him come and see me at the office to-morrow. He can have his ticket."

Jack Lynch, the obscenity, was carried out. Next day he was sacked. Stanley turned again to Joe and Jenny; smiled in answer to Joe's grin and Jenny's melting winsomeness.

" *That's* all right," he nodded reassuringly. " You're Joe Gowlan, aren't you ? I know you perfectly. I know all you chaps, make a point of it. Introduce me to your girl, Joe. How do you do, Miss Sunley. You must dance with me if you will, Miss Sunley, take that little unpleasantness away if we can. And you, Joe, let me introduce you to *my* girl. Perhaps you'll dance with her, eh ? "

So Jenny floated away ecstatically in the arms of Mr. Stanley, holding herself very, very properly, elbow fashionably straight, conscious that every eye in the room was fixed upon her. And Joe pranced heavily with Miss Todd, whose eyes seemed to find amusement in him and a certain interest.

" That was a lovely punch," she said with the little humorous twist to her lips that was her mannerism.

He admitted the punch to be a superior punch, feeling virtuous and painfully ill at ease.

" I like a chap," she casually commented, " to be able to take care of himself." She smiled again. " But don't look as if you'd suddenly joined the Good Templars."

Stanley, Miss Todd, Jenny and Joe took supper together. Jenny was in heaven. She smiled, showed her pretty teeth, cast her dark lashes down entrancingly; she ate jelly with her fork; left a little of everything upon her plate. She was a little shaken when Laura Todd, lifting an orange, bit into the skin off-handedly with her white teeth. She was even more shaken when Laura nonchalantly borrowed Stanley's handkerchief. But it was rapture, rapture, all of it, every moment. And to crown all, when it was over, and the Social breaking up, Joe, in atonement for that earlier sin of omission, magnificently commandeered a cab.

The last compliments were exchanged; good-byes called, much waving of hands. In a flutter of petticoats and excitement Jenny stepped into the greenish mildewed vehicle which smelt of mice, funerals, weddings and damp livery stables. The little woolly balls of her fascinator dangled deliriously. She sank back in the cushions.

" Oh, Joe," she gushed. " It's been perfectly lovely. I didn't know you knew Mr. Millington so well. Why didn't you tell me? I'd no idea. He's very nice. She is too, of course. Not good-looking, mind you, a bit of a one to go, I should say. Real style, though. That dress she had on cost pounds and pounds let me tell you, the last word, and I should know. Did you notice when she bit that orange, though? and the hanky? . . . I could have dropped. My! I wouldn't have done a thing like that. Not at all ladylike. Do you hear me, Joe, listen! "

He assured her tenderly that he heard. Alone with her in the dark cab, the longing he had for her rose suddenly to fever heat. His whole body flamed, swelled with that longing. All the evening he had held her in his arms, felt her thinly covered body against his. For months she had staved him off. Now he had her, here, alone. Burning, he shifted his position, carefully edged nearer to her, as she lay back in the corner of the cab, and slipped his arm round her waist. She was still talking nineteen to the dozen, excited, lifted out of herself, gay.

" Some day I'll have a dress like hers, Miss Todd's I mean. Satin it was and real lace edging. She knows what's what I'll be bound. She's got the look of a real fast one, too, you can always tell."

Gently, very gently he drew her close to him, murmured, making his voice caressing:

" I'm not wanting to talk about her, Jenny. I didn't notice her at all. It's you I noticed. I'm noticin' you now! "

She giggled, well pleased.

" You're far, far better lookin' than her. And your dress looked a heap prettier an' all."

" Two and four the material cost, Joe . . . I got the pattern out of Weldon's."

" By gum, you're a wonder, Jenny . . ." He continued skilfully to flatter her. And the more he flattered, the more he fondled her. He could feel she was excited, strung up, letting him do little things he had never been allowed to do before. Elation swelled in him. Thirsting for her, he moved ever so cautiously.

Suddenly she called out sharply:

" Don't, Joe! Don't! You got to behave."

" Ah, what's your worry, my dear," he soothed her.

" No, Joe, no! It's wrong. It isn't right."

" It isn't wrong, Jenny," he whispered piously. " Don't we *love* each other ? "

Tactically it was perfect. Whatever his status in the billiards handicap, Joe certainly was no novice in the seducer's gentle art. Flustered, feeling him close to her:

" But, no, Joe . . . well, not *here*, Joe."

" Ah, Jenny . . ."

She struggled.

" Look, Joe, we're nearly there. See, Plummer Street. We're nearly home. Let me go, Joe. Let me go."

Sullenly he lifted his hot face from her neck, saw that she was right. Burning with disappointment, he almost gave way to loud profanity. But he got out, helped her to alight, flung a shilling to the scarecrow of a jarvie, followed her up the steps. The curve of her figure from behind, her simple act of taking the key and sliding it into the keyhole maddened him with desire. Then he remembered that Alf, her father, was away for the night.

In the kitchen, lit only by the firelight, she faced him: for all her offended maidenhood she seemed reluctant to go to bed. The excitement, the unusualness of it all worked in her, and her triumph at the Social still buzzed in her head. She postured a little coyly.

" Will I light the gas and make you some cocoa, Joe ? "

With an effort he mastered his sullenness, his frantic desire to seize her. Plaintively he said:

" You don't give a fella a chance, Jenny. Come on and sit on the sofa a bit. I haven't had a word with you all night."

Half-awakened, half-afraid, she stood undecided; it was so dull to say good night and go to bed; and Joe really looked awful handsome to-night; taking that cab, too, he had *behaved* handsome. She giggled again:

" Well . . . it won't hurt us to *talk*." She moved to the sofa.

On the sofa he took her close in his arms: it was easier now that he had done it before; she tried only half-heartedly to snatch herself away. He felt the excitement, the unusualness of the whole evening vibrating through her body.

" Don't, Joe, don't. We got to behave." She kept on repeating it, not knowing what she said.

" Ah, Jenny, you must. You know I'm mad about you. You *know* we love each other."

Fascinated, terrified in one breath, resisting, yielding, lost in fear, pain and something unknown:

" But, Joe . . . You're hurting me, Joe."

He knew he had her now, knew with a wild delicious knowledge that this, at last, was Jenny.

The fire was going out. The grate empty. Now that it was long over and her period of snivelling done, she whispered:

" Hold me tight, Joe . . . tighter, Joe dear."

God! Could you beat it, and him lying there uncomfortable as the devil, with some of her hair getting in his mouth. As she snuggled up to him, offering her pale, tear-stained, pretty face—now shorn of all silly affectation—for his kiss she was for once simple and beautiful like one of her father's little pearly doves. Yet now he almost, yes, he almost could have kicked her. There was, of course, the extenuating circumstance: this was, as he had said, Joe's first real love.

XII

SATURDAY night had its routine at the Law. After cold supper Hilda played to her father upon the organ. And to-night, the last Saturday of November 1909, at eight o'clock, Hilda was playing the first movement of Handel's *Water Music* while Barras sat in his chair supporting his forehead in his hand, listening. Hilda did not like playing to her father. But Hilda played. It was part of Barras's routine that Hilda should play.

Richard Barras held closely to his routine. This did not stamp Barras as a creature of habit. In stature he was above habit. And routine was not his master but the echo rather, the constantly resounding echo of his principle. To comprehend Richard Barras it is necessary to begin by admitting this principle. He *was* a man of principle and not, be it understood, of hypocritical principle. He was sincere.

He was, too, a moral man. He despised those weaknesses into which humanity is so requently and unhappily betrayed. He was incapable, for example, of thinking of any woman but his wife. Though Harriet was an invalid she was in effect his wife. His wife. He despised the grosser appetites of men; rich food and wines, overeating, overdrinking, oversleeping, luxury, sensuality, all the excesses of bodily indulgence were abhorrent to him. He ate plainly and usually drank water. He did not smoke. Though his suit was always well made and of good material, he had few clothes and no vanity for dress.

He had his pride, of course, the natural pride of a liberal, enlightened man. He knew himself as a man of position and substance; he was a mine owner, the owner of the Neptune, whose family had worked the Neptune pits for just one hundred years. He took a real satisfaction in the family succession, beginning with Peter Barras who in 1805 had originally sunk No. 1 shaft into the Snook, known now as the Old Neptune, leaving a tidy little pit to his son William who in his turn had sunk shafts Nos. 2 and 3. As for Peter William, Richard's own father, he had bored No. 4, a shrewd and well-judged stroke from which Richard was now benefiting hugely. The foundation of the family name and fortune by these shrewd, hard-headed men gratified Richard deeply. He prided himself on inheriting, on developing the qualities of his forebears, on his own shrewdness and hard-headedness, his ability to drive a hard bargain.

Socially, he was not openly aspiring. When, in conversation, the name of some county notable cropped up Barras had a way of calmly interjecting: " And what's he worth ? " inferring with a mild amusement that his neighbour's financial position was contemptible. Thus while he enjoyed the deference of his banker and his lawyer he was not a snob—he despised the pettiness of the word. Though Harriet Wandless was of a county family he had not married Harriet for the distinction of her pedigree. He had married Harriet to make Harriet his wife.

The suggestion of a passion arises here. Yet Barras was a man of no apparent passions. The strength of his personality was terrific; but it was a static, a glacial strength. He had no violence, no towering passions, no gusts of fiery emotion. What was alien to him he rejected; what was not alien he possessed. The evidence of Harriet, taken in camera, is, positively, the clue. But Harriet, on the mornings which succeeded these regular nocturnal idylls, merely ate a large breakfast soulfully—with the placid satisfaction of a cow that has been successfully milked. Such visible biological evidence as Harriet's modesty afforded was both positive and negative. But the examination of Harriet's stomach contents would undoubtedly have revealed cud.

Richard himself gave a few clues. He was a secret man. This secrecy was definitely a quality. Not the ordinary banal secrecy of concealment, but a subtler secrecy, a secrecy which sternly resented prying and froze all familiarity with a look. He seemed icily to say, I am myself and will be myself but that is no concern of any one but myself. And to continue, I dominate myself but I will be dominated by no one but myself. The static glacier again.

It must not be assumed, however, that Richard's qualities were cast entirely in this out-size arctic mould. Barras had some very individual characteristics. His love of organ music, of Handel, of the *Messiah* in particular. His devotion to art, to sound established art as manifested in the expensive pictures upon his walls. His loyalty to the domestic unities. His inveterate neatness and precision. And finally his acquisitiveness.

Here, at last, lies the hidden intention of Richard's soul, the very core of the man himself. He loved his possessions passionately, his pit, his house, his pictures, his property, everything that was *his*. This accounted for his abomination of waste, of which the pale reflection was Aunt Carrie's acquired inability " to throw anything out." Aunt Carrie often protested this openly and Barras was always pleased. Barras himself never threw anything out. Papers, documents, receipts, records of transactions, everything—all neatly docketed and locked away in Barras's desk. It was almost a religion, this docketing and locking away. It had a spiritual quality. It was most exemplary. It rang in harmony with his love of Handel. It had, like Handel, impressive breadth and depth and a kind of impenetrable religiosity, but it had its basis in simple avarice. For, beyond everything, the secret and consuming passion of Barras's soul was his love of money. Though he masked it cleverly, deceiving even himself, he adored money. He hugged it to him and nourished it, the glowing scene of his wealth, his own substance.

Meanwhile Hilda had finished with Handel. At least she had finished with *Water Music*. And in the normal way she would have restored her music to the long piano stool and gone straight upstairs. But to-night Hilda seemed determined to propitiate. Staring straight at the keyboard she said:

" Would you like *Largo*, father ? "

It was his favourite piece, the piece which impressed him beyond all others, the piece which made Hilda wish to scream.

She played it slowly and with sonorous rhythm.

There was a silence. Without removing his hand from his forehead he said:

" Thank you, Hilda."

She got off the stool, stood on the other side of the table. Though her face wore the familiar forbidding look, she was trembling inside. She said:

" Father! "

" Well, Hilda! " His voice appeared reasonable.

She took a long breath. For weeks she had been nerving herself to take that breath. She said:

" I'm nearly twenty, now, father. It's nearly three years since I came home from school. All that time I've been at home doing nothing. I'm tired of doing nothing. I want to do something for a change. I want you to let me go away and do something."

He uncovered his eyes and measured her curiously. He repeated:

" Do something ? "

" Yes, do something," she said violently. " Let me train for something. Get some position."

" Some position ? " The same remote tone of wonder. " What position ? "

" Any position. To be your secretary. To be a nurse. Or let me go in for medicine. I'd like that best of all."

He studied her again, still pleasantly ironic.

" And what," he said, " is to happen when you marry ? "

" I'll never get married," she burst out. " I'd hate to get married. I'm far too ugly ever to get married."

Coldness crept into his face but his tone did not change. He said:

" You have been reading the papers, Hilda."

His penetration brought the blood to her sallow face. It was true. She had read the morning paper. The day before there had been a raid by suffragists on Downing Street, during a Cabinet meeting, and violent scenes when some women attempted to rush the House of Commons. It had brought Hilda's brooding to a head.

" An attempt was made to rush," he quoted musingly, " to rush . . . the House of Commons." He made it sound the last insanity.

She bit her lip fiercely. She said:

" Father, let me go away and study medicine. I want to be a doctor."

He said:

" No, Hilda."

" Let me go, father," she said.

He said:

" No, Hilda."

" *Let me.*" An almost frantic intercession in her voice.

He said nothing.

A silence fell. Her face had gone chalky white now. He contemplated the ceiling with an air of absent interest. For about a minute they remained like this, then, quite undramatically, she turned and went out of the room.

He did not seem to notice that Hilda had gone. Hilda had broken an inviolable convention. He sealed his mind against Hilda.

He sat for about half an hour, then he rose and carefully turned out the gas and went up to his study. He always went to his study after Hilda had played to him on Sunday nights. The study was a spacious and comfortable room, thickly carpeted, with a massive desk, dark red curtains screening the windows, and several photographs of the Colliery hung upon the walls. Barras sat down at his desk, pulled out his ring of keys, selected one with meticulous care and unlocked the top middle drawer. From the top middle drawer he took out three ordinary red-backed account books and with a familiar touch began to examine them. The first was a list of his investments, written carefully in his own neat handwriting. He considered it detachedly, a pleased yet non-committal smile touching his lips. He lifted a pen, without dipping it in the ink and ran the point delicately down the row of figures. Suddenly he paused, reflected seriously, deciding to sell that block of 1st Preference United Collieries. They had touched their peak recently; his confidential information regarding their current profits was of an adverse nature; yes, he would sell. He smiled again faintly, recognising his own shrewd instinct, his money sense. He never made a mistake, and why need he? Every security in this little book was virtually gilt-edged, guaranteed, impregnable. Again he made a rapid calculation. The total pleased him.

Then he turned to the second book. This second book gave the list of his house property in Sleescale and the district. Most of the Terraces belonged to Barras—it was a sore point with him that Ramage, the butcher, had half of Balaclava Row—and in Tynecastle he had several sound blocks of " weeklies." These tenements, which lay down by the river, and yielded their rents to a weekly collector, were immensely profitable. Richard never regretted these tenements, his own idea, though Bannerman, his lawyer, handled the actual business with a quiet discretion. He made a note to speak to Bannerman on a point of costs.

And finally, with a sense of relaxation, a fondling touch, he drew the third book towards him. There was the list of his pictures with the prices he had paid for each. He considered it tolerantly. It amused him to consider that he had spent twenty thousand pounds, a fortune, virtually on pictures. Well, it was a sound investment too—they were on his walls, appreciating in value, growing rare and old like the Titians and Rembrandts . . . but he would buy no more. No, he had paid his homage to art. It was enough.

He looked at his watch. His lips made a little clicking sound that it should be so late. Carefully, he put his books away, relocked the top middle drawer and went up to his bedroom.

He took out his watch again and wound up his watch. He took a drink of water from the carafe beside his bed. Then he began to undress, The quiet movements of his powerful figure had a set inevitability. The movements were regular and systematic. The movements admitted no other movements. Each movement had a deliberate self-interest. The white strong hands spoke a dumb alphabet of their own. This way . . . like this . . . the best way to do it is this way . . . the best way for me . . . there may be other ways . . . but this way is the best way for me . . . for me. In the half light of the bedroom the symbolism of the hands was strangely menacing.

At last Barras was ready. He circled on his dark purple dressing-gown. He stood for a moment smoothing his jaw with his fingers. Then he went steadily along the corridor.

Hilda, sitting in the darkness of her own room, heard the heavy tread of her father as he entered her mother's room next door. Her body contracted, she held herself quite rigid. Her face wore a tormented look. Desperately she tried to shut her ears but she could not shut her ears. She could never shut her ears. The tread advanced. Subdued voices. A heavy deliberate creak. Hilda's whole body shuddered. In an agony of loathing she waited. The sounds began.

XIII

Joe lounged in the living-room at Scottswood Road paying not the slightest heed to Alf Sunley who sat by the table reading aloud the selections of Captain Sanglar for Gosforth Park Races. This afternoon Joe and Alf were going to the races, though Joe, from the sullen expression in his face and his contemptuous indifference to the Captain's information, did not appear to exult unduly at the prospect. Replete with dinner, he lay back in his chair with his feet on the window-sill, indulging himself in surly meditation.

" Taking form for courses I confidently nap Lord Kell's Nesfield for the Eldon Plate, making that well-tried filly my three-star selection for the day . . ."

As Alf's voice droned on Joe's eyes roved glumly round the room. God, what a sickening place! What a hole! And to think, to think actually that he had put up with it for over three years! Nearly four, in fact! Was he going to stick it much longer ? He couldn't believe it, the way time had slipped in, and left him still here, like a stranded whale. Where, curse it, was his ambition ? Was he going to waste himself here *all* his life ?

Soberly reviewed, the position impressed him as being not altogether lively. At Millington's in these four years he had got on well enough. Yes, well enough . . . but well enough was not good enough, not nearly good enough for Joe Gowlan. He was puddling now, earning his regular three pounds a week; and that, at twenty-two, was something. He was popular—a faint complacent gleam broke through his present gloom—wonderfully popular. He was one of the lads! Mr. Millington appeared to take an interest in him, too, always stopped and spoke as he came through the works, but nothing definite ever seemed to come of it. Nothing, dammit, thought Joe, glooming.

What had he done for himself? He had three suits instead of one, three pairs of brown boots and a lot of fancy ties; he had a few quid in his pocket; he had improved his physique, even boxed at St. James's Hall; he knew his way around the town; he knew some tricks. But what else? Nothing, dammit, nothing, thought Joe, again, glooming worse. He was still a workman living in lodgings, with no money to brag about, and he was still . . . still mixed up with Jenny.

Joe moved restlessly. Jenny represented the peak, the crisis, the goading thorn of his present discontent. Jenny was in love with him, clinging to him, mucking him up. Could anything be bloodier? At first, naturally, his vanity had been tickled, it had been a bit of all right having Jenny running after him, hanging on his elbow as, with his chest well out, and his derby well back, he brown-booted jauntily down the street.

But now he wasn't so jaunty, by a half of a long chop. He was fed up with Jenny. Well, no, perhaps he wouldn't put it so strong as that—she was still soft, still desirable in his arms, and their love-making, the fierce consummation of his desire, snatched secretly here in this room, in his own room, outside after dark, in doorways, round by the back of Elswick stables, in all sorts of queer and unexpected places, *that*, he had to admit, was still sweet. But it was . . . oh, it was too easy now. There was no difficulty, no resistance in Jenny; there was even a faint eagerness about her sometimes, and sometimes a sense of neglect when he left her alone too long. Oh, hell! He might just as well have been *married* to Jenny.

And he didn't want to be married to Jenny, nor to any other Jenny. Not to be tied up for life, not him. He was too wise a bird for that sort of snare. He wanted to get on, make his way, pile up some money. He wanted to scrape some of the gilt, the real gilt off the gingerbread.

He frowned. She was too much in his life, changing it too much, she really was upsetting him. This very afternoon, for instance, hearing that he was going to Gosforth with her father and leaving her at home she had dissolved in sudden scalding tears, had been pacified only at the cost of promising to take her with them. She was upstairs, dressing, now.

Oh, blast! Joe took a sudden fierce kick at the stool in front of him, making Alf stop reading and look up in mild surprise.

"You're not lissenin', Joe," Alf remonstrated. "What's the good of me wastin' my breath if you don't lissen."

Joe answered disagreeably:

"That fellow don't know nowt. He gets his tips straight from the horses' mouths. An' the horses is all liars. I'm goin' to get my information from Dick Jobey on the course. He's a pal o' mine and a man as knows what he's talkin' about."

Alf gave a short expressive laugh.

"What's like the matter with you, Joe? I'd stopped readin' about the horses ten minutes ago. I was readin' about the new aeroplane this fella

Bleeryoh has got, you know, him that flew the Channel last year."

Joe grunted:

" Aw'll have a fleet o' bloody aeroplanes myself one o' these days. You watch."

Alf squinted over the edge of the paper.

" I'll watch," he agreed with enormous sarcasm.

The door opened and Jenny came in. Joe looked up grumpily:

" You're ready at last."

" I'm ready," she admitted brightly; all traces of her recent weeping had vanished and, as was often the case after a bout of tearful petulance, she was brisk, blithe as a lark. " Like my new hat ? " she asked, tilting her head for him archly. " Pretty nice, mister ? "

Through all his moodiness he had to grant that she did look nice. The new hat, which she wore so dashingly, set off her pale prettiness. Her figure was extraordinarily attractive, she had the most beautifully modelled legs and hips. Physically the loss of her virginity had improved her. She was riper, more assured, less anæmic; she had more *go* in her; she was near her point of perfection.

" Come on, then," she laughed. " Come on you too, dad. Don't keep me waiting or we'll be late."

" Keep *you* waiting! " Joe expostulated.

And Alf, nodding his head commiseratingly, sighed.

" Women! "

The three set out for Gosforth Park by tram, Jenny sitting between the two men, very straight and happy, while the tram bumped and bounded along North Road.

" I want to make some money," she remarked confidentially to Joe, patting her handbag.

" You're not the only one," Joe answered rudely.

They went into the two-shilling ring which was pleasantly full, just enough people to interest Jenny, not enough to crowd her. She was delighted; the white railings against the bright green of the course, the colours of the jockeys, the sleek lovely horses, the shouts of the bookies under their big blue and gold umbrellas, the movement, animation and excitement of the ring, the fashionable dresses, the celebrities seen not too distantly in the paddock.

" Look, Joe, look," she cried, clutching his arm. " There's Lord Kell! Isn't he a gentleman! "

Lord Kell, doyen of British sport, millionaire landowner of the North, florid, sidewhiskered and genial, stood chatting to a little scrap of a man, Lew Lester, his jockey.

Joe grunted enviously:

" If he thinks Nesfield's goin' to win he's up a gum tree." Then he barged off to find Dick Jobey.

He had a lot of trouble in finding Dick, for Dick was in the ten-shilling enclosure; but by getting hold of the tick-tacker, Joe managed to summon Dick to the railings.

" Sorry to bother you, Mr. Jobey," Joe began with ingratiating friendliness. " I was just wondering if you had anything. I'm not botherin' about myself. I never do have much on. But I've got my young lady and her dad along with us . . . my lass, you see . . . she'd just dance with delight if she took a couple of shillings off the ring."

Dick Jobey tapped the toe of his neat black shoe against the railings, very pleasant and non-committal. The convention that bookmakers are full-bodied and purple-faced, talking with one corner of the mouth whilst a large cigar occupies the other, receives the lie from Dick Jobey of Tynecastle. Dick was a bookmaker, a bookmaker in quite a large way, with an office in Bigg Market and a branch in Yarrow across the road from the Catholic Church. But Dick smoked the mildest of cigarettes, drank only mineral water. A nice, quiet, affable, plainly dressed, medium-sized man who never swore, never bellowed the odds, and was never seen on any race-course but the local Gosforth Park. It was rumoured, indeed, amongst his many friends, that Dick went to Gosforth once a year to pick buttercups.

" Have you anything, then, Mr. Jobey, that I can tell the lass ? "

Dick Jobey inspected Joe. He liked the tone of Joe's remark; he had seen Joe box at St. James's Hall; he felt, altogether, that Joe was a " likely lad." And as Dick had a weakness for likely lads, he allowed Joe to cultivate him, to run odd commissions for him. Altogether Joe had been assiduous in worming his way into Dick Jobey's favour. Dick spoke at last.

" I wouldn't let her do anything till the last race, Joe."

" No, Mr. Jobey."

" But she might have a little on, then. Not much, you know, just half a crown for fun."

" Yes, Mr. Jobey."

" Of course you never can tell."

" No, Mr. Jobey." An excited pause. " Is it Nesfield you fancy ? "

Dick shook his head.

" She hasn't an earthly, that one. Let your young lady have a half a crown on Pink Bud. Just half a crown, mind you. And just for fun."

Dick Jobey smiled, nodded and quietly strolled away. Thrilling with triumph, Joe elbowed his way back to Alf and Jenny.

" Oh, Joe," Jenny protested, " wherever have you been ? There's the first race over and I've never even betted yet."

In a right good humour he assured her that she could bet now to her heart's content. Blandly he listened while she and Alf discussed their fancies. Jenny was all for picking out the pretty names, the nicest colours, or a horse belonging to someone particularly notable. Joe beamed approval. With continued blandness he accepted her money, placed her bets. She lost, lost again, and once again.

" Now isn't that too bad ? " Jenny exclaimed, completely dashed at the end of the fourth race. She had wanted so much to win. Jenny was not mean, she was generous to a fault, and quite careless of her few half-crowns; but it would have been simply lovely to win.

Alf, who had been following Captain Sanglar doggedly with nothing to show for it but an odds-on place, reassured her.

" We'll get it all back on Nesfield, lass. She's the three-star nap of the day."

Gloating inside, Joe heard him plump for Nesfield.

Jenny studied her programme doubtfully.

" I'm not so sure about your old Captain," she said. " What do you think, Joe ? "

" You never can tell," Joe suggested artlessly. " That's Lord Kell's filly, isn't it ? "

" So it is." Jenny brightened. " I forgot about that. Yes, I think I better have Nesfield."

" What about Pink Bud ? " Joe ventured rather vaguely.

" Never heard of it," Alf said promptly.

And Jenny:

" Oh no, Joe . . . Lord Kell's horse for me."

" Well! " said Joe, moving off. " Have it your own way. But I think I'll do Pink Bud."

He took all the money he had with him, four pounds in all, and boldly slammed it on Pink Bud. He got fives about the animal, saw the price shorten rapidly to three. Then they were off. He stood at the rails, holding on tight, watching the massed horses swing round the bend. Faster, faster; he sweated, hardly dared to breathe. Panting, he watched them enter the straight, approach the post. Then he let out a wild yell. Pink Bud was home by a good two lengths.

The minute the numbers were up he collected his winnings, stuffed the four five-pound notes tight into his inside pocket, slipped the four sovereigns in his vest, buttoned up his coat, cocked his hat and swaggered back to Jenny.

" Oh, Joe," Jenny nearly wept, " why didn't I . . ."

" Yes, why didn't you ? " he bubbled over. " You should have taken my tip. I've won a packet. And don't say I didn't warn you. I told you I was going to do it. I'd a notion about Pink Bud all the time." He could have hugged himself with the delight of having got ahead of them. The sight of her pale, woebegone face made him laugh. He said patronisingly: " Don't make a song about it, Jenny. I'll take you out with me to-night. We'll paint the old town red."

Skilfully, they gave Alf the slip on the way out. They had done it before; and this time it was easy. Alf, plodding along with his head down, was far too busy cursing Captain Sanglar to see that they were dodging him.

They got to Tynecastle shortly after six, strolled up Newgate Street into Haymarket. All Joe's earlier despondency had vanished, swept away by a sort of boisterous magnanimity. He condescended towards Jenny with a large, forgiving geniality; he even let her take his arm.

Suddenly, as they turned the corner of Northumberland Street, Joe stiffened, gasped:

" By gum, it can't be him! " Then he let out a whoop. " Davey! Hey, Davey Fenwick, man! "

David stopped, turned; a slow recognition spread over his face.

" Why, Joe . . . it's not you! "

" Ay, it's me right enough," Joe crowed, falling upon David with manly exuberance. " It's me and none other. There's only one Joe Gowlan in Tynecassel."

They all laughed. Joe, with a princely wave of his hand, making the necessary introduction.

" This is Miss Sunley, Davey. Little friend of mine. An this is Davey, Jenny, a regular pal of Joe's in the good old days."

David looked at Jenny. He looked right into her clear, wide eyes. Then, under her smile, he smiled too. Admiration dawned upon his face. Very politely they shook hands.

" Jenny and me was just going to have a bit of snap," Joe remarked, irresistibly taking charge of the situation. " But now we'll all have a bit of snap. Fancy a bit of snap, Davey ? "

" You bet," David agreed enthusiastically. " We're quite near Nun Street. Let's pop into Lockhart's."

Joe nearly collapsed.

" Lockhart's," he repeated to Jenny. " Did ye hear him say Lockhart's ? "

" What's wrong ? " inquired David blankly. " It's a jolly good spot. I often go there for a cup of cocoa in the evening."

" Cocoa," moaned Joe weakly, pretending to support himself against an adjacent lamp-post. " Does he take us for a couple of true blue Rechabites ? "

" Now, behave, Joe, do," Jenny entreated him, exchanging a demure glance with David.

Joe galvanised himself dramatically. He went up to David with great effect.

" Look here, my lad. You're not in the pit now. You're with Mr. Joe Gowlan. An' he's standing' treat. So shut yer gob an' come on."

Saying no more, Joe thrust his thumb in his arm-hole and led the way down Northumberland Street to the Percy Grill. David and Jenny followed. They entered, sat down at a table. Joe's exhibitionism was superb. This was one of the things he really enjoyed: showing off his ease, address, aplomb, showing off himself. In the Percy Grill he was at home: this last year he had frequently been here with Jenny. A small place it was, common and showy, with a good deal of gilt and a good many red lamp shades, a kind of annexe to the adjoining pub known as the Percy Vaults. There was one waiter with a napkin stuffed into his waistcoat, who came fawning upon them in answer to Joe's sophisticated call.

" What'll you have ? " Joe demanded. " Mine's a whisky. An' yours, Jenny ? A port, eh ? An' yours, Davey ? Be careful now, lad, an' don't say cocoa."

David smiled, remarked that in this instance he would prefer beer.

When the drinks were brought, Joe ordered a lavish meal: chops, sausages and chip potatoes. Then he lolled back in his seat, inspecting David critically, finding him lankier, maturer, curiously improved. With a burst of curiosity he asked:

" What are ye doin' with yerself now, Davey ? Ye're changed a lot, man."

David had certainly changed. He was nearly twenty-one now but his pale face and smooth dark hair made him a little older. His brow was good, his chin as stubborn as before. He was inclined to leanness about the jaw, he had a taut and rather finely drawn look, but his shy smile was a delight. He smiled now.

" There's nothing much to tell, Joe."

" Ah, come on now," said Joe patronisingly.

" Well . . ." said David. . . .

These last three years had not been easy for him, they had left their mark, knocked the immaturity out of his face for good. He had come up to Baddeley on his scholarship of sixty pounds a year, taking lodgings at Westgate Hill opposite the Big Lamp. The money was ridiculously inadequate, his allowance from home sometimes did not come—Robert had once been laid up for two months on end—and David had frequently been up against it. On one occasion he had carried a man's bag from Central Station to earn a sixpence for his supper.

It was nothing really, his enthusiasm carried him through it with a rush. The enthusiasm came from the discovery of his own ignorance. The first month at Baddeley had demonstrated him as a raw pit lad who had stumbled by good luck, hard elementary coaching and a little natural-born sense into a scholarship. At that David had set himself to get hold of something. He began to read: not the stereotyped reading prescribed by the classes, not just his Gibbon, Macaulay, Horace. He read everything he could lay his hands on from Marx to Maupassant, Goethe to Goncourt. He read unwisely perhaps but he read well. He read entranced, bewildered sometimes, but stubborn always. He joined the Fabian Society, squeezed sixpence for a gallery seat at the symphony concerts, came to know Beethoven there and Bach, wandered to the Tynecastle Municipal Gallery to discover the beauty of Whistler, Degas and the solitary glowing Manet there.

It was not easy, it was in fact a little pathetic, this troubled, solitary seeking. He was too poor, shabby and proud to make many friends. He wanted friends, but they must come to him.

Then he began to teach, going out to the poorer districts—Saltley, Witton, Hebburn—as a pupil teacher in the elementary schools. He should, of course, by reason of his ideals, have loved it; instead he hated it—the pale, undernourished and often sickly children from the slum areas distracted his attention, distressed him horribly. He wanted to give them boots, clothes and food—not thump the multiplication table into their bemused little heads. He wanted to cart them away to the Wansbeck and set them playing there in the sunshine, instead of rowing them for failing to learn ten lines of incomprehensible " poetry," about Lycidas dying ere his prime. His heart bled at times for these wretched kids. He knew immediately and irrevocably that he was no use at a black-board, would never be any good; that this teaching was only a means to an end, that he must get out of it presently, into another, more active, more combative sphere. He must take his B.A. next year, quickly, then move on.

David stopped suddenly: his rare smile broke out again.

" O Lord! Have I been talking all this time? You asked for the sad, sad story . . . that's my only excuse! "

But Jenny refused to let him make light of it; she was terribly impressed.

" My," she remarked, animated yet bashful. " I'd no idea I was going to meet anybody so important." The port had brought a faint flush to her cheeks; she sparkled upon him.

David looked at her wryly.

" Important! that's a rich piece of sarcasm, Miss Jenny."

But Miss Jenny did not mean it for sarcasm. She had never met a student, a real student of Baddeley College before. Students of the Baddeley belonged mostly to a social world on which Jenny had as yet merely gazed with envy. Besides, she thought David, though rather shabby beside Joe's smooth opulence, quite a good-looking young man—interesting was the word! And finally she felt that Joe had treated her abominably lately—it would be " nice " to play off David against him and make him thoroughly jealous. She murmured:

" It frightens me to death to think of all these books you study. And that B.A. too. My! "

" It'll probably land me in some nice unventilated school, teaching underfed little kids."

" But don't you want to? " She was incredulous. " A teacher! That's a lovely thing to be! "

He shook his head in smiling apology and was about to argue with her when the arrival of the chops, sausages and chips created a diversion. Joe divided them thoughtfully. He divided them extremely thoughtfully. At first Joe had heard David with an envious, slightly mocking grin, with a guffaw all ready, perfectly ready to take David down a peg. Then he had seen David look at Jenny. That was when it came to Joe, the marvellous, the wholly marvellous idea. He lifted his head, handed David his plate solicitously.

"That's all right for you, Davey, boy?"

"Fine, thanks, Joe." David smiled: he hadn't seen a plateful like that in weeks.

Joe nodded, graciously passed Jenny the mustard and ordered her another port.

"What was that you were saying, Davey?" he inquired kindly. "About getting on beyond the teaching like?"

David shook his head deprecatingly.

"You wouldn't be interested, Joe, not a bit."

"But we are—aren't we, Jenny?" Real enthusiasm in Joe's voice. "Go on an' tell us more, man."

David gazed from one to the other: encouraged by Joe's grave attention, by Jenny's bright eyes. He plunged into it.

"It's just like this, then. Don't think I'm drunk, or a prig, or a candidate for the City Asylum. When I've got my B.A. I may have to take up teaching for a bit. That'll only be for bread and butter. I'm not educating myself to teach. I'm not cut out for teaching—too impatient, I suppose. I'm educating myself to fight. What I honestly want to do is different, and it's hard, terribly hard to explain. But it just amounts to this. I want to do something for my own kind, for the men who work in the pits. You know, Joe, what the work is. Take the Neptune, we've both been in it, you know what it's done to my father. You know what the conditions are . . . and the pay. I want to help to change things, to make them better."

Joe thought, he's mad, quite bleeding well barmy. But he said, very suavely:

"Go on, Davey, that's the stuff to give them."

David, glowing to his subject, exclaimed:

"No, Joe, you probably think I'm talking through my hat. But you might get a better idea of what I mean if you take a look at the history of the miners—yes, the history of the miners in Northumberland only sixty or seventy years ago. They worked under something like the feudal system. They were treated as barbarians . . . outcasts. They had no education. Learning was checked amongst them. The conditions were terrible, improper ventilation, accidents through the owners refusing to take precautions against firedamp. Women and children of six years of age allowed to go down the pit . . . children of six, mind you. Boys kept eighteen hours a day underground. The men bonded, so they couldn't stir a foot without being chucked out their houses or chucked into prison. Tommy shops everywhere—kept usually by a relative of the viewer—with the pitman compelled to buy his provisions there and his wages confiscated on pay day to settle the balance. . ."

All at once he broke off and laughed awkwardly towards Jenny.

" This can't possibly interest you! I'm an idiot to bother you with it."

" No, indeed," she declared admiringly. " I think it's most awfully clever of you to know all that."

" Go on, Davey," urged the genial Joe, signalling another port for Jenny. " Tell us more."

But this time David shook his head definitely.

" I'll keep it all for the Fabian Society debate. That's when the windbags really get going. But perhaps you do see what I mean. Conditions have improved since those terrible days I'm talking about, we've marched a certain distance. But we haven't marched far enough. There still *are* appalling hardships in some of the pits, rotten pay, and too many accidents. People don't seem to realise. I heard a man in the tram the other day. He was reading the paper. His friend asked him what was the news. He answered: ' Nothing. Nothing, at all. Just another of these pit accidents.' . . . I looked over his shoulder and saw that fifteen men had been killed in an explosion at Nottingham."

There was a short pause. Jenny's eyes dimmed sympathetically. Jenny had swallowed three large ports and all her emotions were beautifully responsive; she vibrated, equipoised, ready to laugh with the joy of life or weep for the sadness of death. She had come to like port quite a lot, had Jenny. A ladylike drink she considered it, a *wine*, too, which classed it as a beverage infinitely refined. Joe, naturally, had introduced her to it.

Joe broke the silence:

" You'll go far, Davey," he said solemnly. " You're streets ahead of me. You'll be in Parliament while I'm puddlin' steel."

" Don't be an ass," David said shortly.

But Jenny had heard; her attention towards David increased. She began, really, to devote herself to him. Her demure glances now became more demure, more significant. She sparkled. She knew all the time, of course, that she was playing David against Joe. It was extremely fascinating to have two strings to her bow.

They talked of lighter things; they talked of what Joe had done; talked and laughed until ten o'clock, all very merry and friendly. Then with a start David became aware of the time.

" Heavens above! " he exclaimed. " And I'm supposed to be working! "

" Don't go yet," Jenny protested. " The evening's young."

" I don't want to, but I must, I really must. I've got a History Class exam. on Monday."

"Well," Joe declared roundly, " we'll see you on Tuesday, Davey lad, like we've arranged. And ye'll not get away from us so easy next time."

The party broke up, Jenny retired to " tidy up," Joe paid the bill with a flourish of five-pound notes.

Outside, while they waited on Jenny, Joe suddenly stopped masticating his toothpick:

" She's a nice lass that, Davey."

" She is indeed. I admire your taste."

" My taste! " Joe laughed quite heartily. " You've got it all wrong, lad. We're just friends. There's not a thing between Jenny and me."

" Really ? " David sounded interested all at once.

" Ay, really! " Joe laughed again at the very idea. " I'd no idea you were getting hold of the wrong end of the stick."

Jenny joined them and they walked three abreast to the corner of Collingwood Street, where David branched off along Westgate Road.

" Don't forget now," Joe said. " Tuesday night for sure." The final handshake was cordial; Jenny's fingers conveyed just the politest sensation of a squeeze.

David walked home on air to his scrubby room; propped up Mignet's *Histoire de la Révolution Française*, and lit his pipe.

Simply grand, he thought, meeting Joe so unexpectedly; odd, too, that they should not have met before. But Tynecastle was a big place with, as Joe had said, only one Joe Gowlan in it.

David seemed to be thinking quite a lot about Joe. But the face which danced through the pages of Mignet was not Joe's face. It was the smiling face of Jenny.

XIV

David called at 117A Scottswood Road on the following Tuesday. It was unfortunate, considering how much he had looked forward to the evening, that Joe should be detained at Millington's working overtime. But there it was and couldn't be helped: poor Joe had to work his overtime. David, nevertheless, enjoyed himself hugely. Though his opportunities had been so few, his nature was really sociable, he came prepared to enjoy himself and he did. The Sunleys, pre-informed by Jenny, were inclined at first to treat him with suspicion. They expected superiority. But soon the atmosphere thawed, supper appeared on the table, and hilarity filled the air. Mrs. Sunley, shedding her lethargy for once, had made a rarebit—and, as Sally remarked, Ma's rarebits were a treat. Alf, with the help of two tea-spoons and the pepper pot, had demonstrated his own especial method of dovecote construction. A fortune it would have made him, if he'd only patented it. Jenny, looking delicious in a fresh print frock, had poured the tea herself—Ma being too flushed and flustered from her exertions in the kitchen.

David couldn't keep his eyes off Jenny. Against the slipshod background of her home she bloomed for him. During his years in Tynecastle he had hardly spoken to a woman; at Sleescale, of course, he had been far from the stage of " walking out "—as it was traditionally known in the Terraces. Jenny was the first . . . absolutely the first to lay the spell of sex upon him.

A warm air wafted in through the half-open window of the back room; and though it bore the exhalation of ten thousand chimney pots it held for David the scent of spring. He watched, waited for Jenny's smile: the soft crinkling of her lip was the most delicious thing he had ever seen. It was like the unfolding of a flower. When she passed him his cup and their fingers touched a divine softness flowed into him.

Jenny, conscious of the effect she was producing, was flattered. And when Jenny felt flattered she was at her very best. Yet actually she was not greatly attracted to David, when their fingers met she knew no answering thrill. Jenny was in love with Joe.

Jenny had begun by despising Joe, his bad manners, his roughness, the fact, as she expressed it, that " he worked dirty." Strange as it may seem, these were the very qualities which had subdued her. Jenny was made to be bullied, deep down in her being lay an unconscious recognition of the brutality which had mastered her. Meanwhile, however, Jenny was very pleased with this new conquest: it would " learn " Joe, when he heard of it, not to treat her so casually.

Supper over, Alf suggested music. They went into the parlour. Outside was the subdued evening hum of the street, inside it was pleasantly cool and airy. While Sally played her accompaniments, Jenny sang *Juanita* and *Sweet Marie, come to me*. Though her voice was thin and rather forced Jenny was very effective by the piano. When she finished *Sweet Marie* she offered to sing *Passing By*, but Alf, loudly supported by Clarry and Phyllis, had begun to clamour for Sally.

" Sally's the top of the bill," he remarked confidentially to David. " If we can get her started you'll see some fun. She's a great little comedienne. Her and me go to the Empire regularly every week."

" Come on, Sally," Clarry begged. " Do Jack Pleasants."

Phyllis urged:

" Yes, Sally, please. And Florrie Forde."

But Sally, perched apathetically on the piano stool, refused. Picking out melancholy bass notes with one finger:

" I'm not in the mood. He," jerking her head towards David, " he wants to hear Jenny, not me."

Aside, Jenny gave a superior little laugh:

" She only wants to be coaxed."

Sally flared instantly:

" All right, then, Miss Sweet Marie Sunley, I'll do it without the coaxing." She straightened herself upon the stool.

At fifteen, Sally was still small and tubby, but she had something, a queer something that gripped and fascinated. Now her short figure became electric. She frowned, then into her plain little face there flowed an irresistible mockery. She struck a frightful discord.

" By special request," she mimicked, " the *other* Miss Sunley will sing *Molly o' Morgan.*" And she let herself go.

It was good, terribly good. The song was nothing, just a popular number of the day, but Sally made it something. She did not sing the song; she parodied it: she burlesqued it; she went falsetto; she suddenly went soulful: she wept almost, for the tragedy of Molly's forsaken lovers.

" *Molly o' Morgan with her barrel organ,*
The Irish Ey-talian girl."

Forgetting what Jenny would have called her manners, she concluded with a disgraceful impersonation of the monkey which might reasonably have been expected to accompany Miss o' Morgan's organ.

Everyone but Jenny was convulsed. But Sally, without giving them time to recover, dashed into *I was standing at the corner of the street.* She ceased to be the monkey. She became Jack Pleasants; she became a dull bumpkin, sluggish as a turnip, supporting the wall of the village pub. You saw the straw in her hair as she sang:

" *A fellow dressed in uniform came up to me and cried,*
How did you get into the army ? I replied:
I . . . was standing at . . . the corner . . . of the street."

Vociferously Alf clapped his appreciation. Sally smiled at him wickedly from the corner of her eye; she winked, restoring her sex, and sang *Yip I addy I ay.* She developed a bosom, a rich deep voice and wonderful hips. It was Florrie Forde. Florrie, to the life.

" *Sing of joy, sing of bliss, it was* never *like this*
Yip I addy I ay."

She ended suddenly. She slid from the stool, swung round, and faced them, smiling.

" Rotten," she exclaimed, screwing up her nose. " Not worth a slab of toffee. Let me get out before the ripe tomatoes come." And she skipped out of the room.

Later, Jenny apologised to David for Sally's oddity.

" You must excuse her, she's often terribly queer. And temper. My!

I'm afraid," lowering her voice. "It's very stupid, but I'm afraid she's rather inclined to be jealous of me."

"Surely not," David smiled. "She's just a kid."

"She's getting on for sixteen," Jenny contradicted primly. "And she really does hate to see anyone paying me attention. I can tell you it makes things pretty difficult for me. As if I could help it."

Assuredly Jenny could not help it: Heavens! that was like blaming a rose for its perfume, a lily for its purity.

David went home that night more convinced than ever that she was adorable.

He began to call regularly, to drop in of an evening. Occasionally he encountered Joe; more often he did not. Joe, with an air of tremendous preoccupation, was working overtime feverishly and seldom in evidence at No. 117A. Then David asked Jenny to go out with him: they began to take excursions together, curious excursions for Jenny, walks on the Aston Hills, a ramble to Liddle, a picnic, actually to Esmond Dene. Secretly, Jenny was contemptuous of all this junketing. She was accustomed to Joe's lordly escort, to the Percy Grill, the Bioscope, Carrick's—"going places" meant, for Jenny, crowds, entertainment, a few glasses of port, money spent upon her. David had no money to spend upon her. She did not for a moment doubt that he would have taken her to all her favourite resorts had his purse permitted. David was a *nice* young man, she liked him, though occasionally she thought him very odd. On the afternoon they went to Esmond Dene he quite bewildered her.

She was not very keen to visit Esmond, she thought it a common place, a place where it cost nothing to get in, and the very lowest people sprawled upon the grass and ate out of paper bags. Some of the commonest girls from the shop went there with their fellows on Sundays. But David appeared so much to wish her to go that she agreed.

He began by taking her the long way round so that he might show her the swallows' nests. Quite eagerly he asked:

"Have you ever seen the nests, Jenny?"

She shook her head.

"I've only been here once, and I was a kid then, about five."

He seemed astounded.

"But it's the loveliest spot, Jenny! I take a walk here every week. It's got moods, this place, just like the human soul, sometimes dark and melancholy, sometimes sunny, full of sunshine. Look! Just look at these nests, under the eaves of the lodge."

She looked very carefully; but she could see only some daubs of mud plastered against the wall. Baffled, feeling rather angrily that she was missing something, she accompanied him past the banqueting hall, down the rhododendron walk to the waterfall. They stood together on the little arched stone bridge.

"See these chestnuts, Jenny," he exclaimed happily. "Don't they open out the sky? And the moss there on these stones. And the mill there, look, isn't it wonderful? It's exactly like one of the early Corots!"

She saw an old ruin of a house, with a red tiled roof and a wooden mill-wheel, covered with ivy and all sorts of queer colours. But it was a queer kind of tumbled-down place, and in any case it was no good now, it wasn't working. She felt angrier than ever. They had tramped quite a long way, her feet were swollen, hurting her in her new tight shoes which she had thought such a bargain, four and eleven reduced from nine shillings, at the sales. She had seen nothing but grass, trees, flowers and sky, heard nothing but the sound of water and birds, eaten nothing but some damp egg sandwiches and two Canary bananas—they were not even the big waxy Jamaica kind which she preferred. She was confused, puzzled, all "upside down"; cross with David, herself, Joe, life, her shoes—was she really getting a corn?—cross with everything. She wanted a cup of tea, a glass of port, something! Standing there, on that lovely arched stone bridge, she compressed her rather pale lips, then opened them to say something extremely disagreeable. But at that moment she caught sight of David's face.

His face was so happy, so rapt, suffused with such ardour, intensity and love that it took her all of a heap. She giggled suddenly. She giggled and giggled; it was so funny she could not stop. She had a perfect paroxysm of almost hysterical enjoyment.

David laughed too, out of sheer sympathy.

"What's the matter, Jenny?" he kept asking. "Do tell me what's the joke!"

"I don't know," she gasped, going into a fresh spasm of mirth. "That's just it. I don't know . . . I don't know what I'm laughing at."

At last she dried her streaming eyes on her small lace-edged hanky—an extra nice hanky, a lady had left it in the toilet at Slattery's.

"Oh dear," she sighed. "That was a scream, wasn't it?" This was a favourite phrase of Jenny's: all events of unusual significance, when they lay beyond Jenny's comprehension, were classed sympathetically as *screams*.

She felt quite restored, however, rather fond of him now; she allowed him to take her arm and be very close to her as they climbed the steep hill of the Dene towards the tram. But she cut the afternoon shorter than it might have been, pleaded tiredness, refused to let him see her to her home.

She went along Scottswood Road in a restless, excitable mood, nursing the idea which had come to her as she sat beside David in the tram. The street teemed with life. It was Saturday, about six o'clock; people were starting to stroll about, to enjoy themselves; it was a time that Jenny loved, the time when she most commonly set out with Joe.

She let herself into the house quietly and, by a stroke of luck which made her heart leap, she met Joe in the passage coming out.

" Hello, Joe," she said brightly, forgetting that for a week she had cut him dead.

" Hello! " he said, not looking at her.

" I've had such a scream of an afternoon, Joe," she went on gaily, coquettishly. " You'd have died, honestly you'd have died. I've seen every kind of swallow but a real one."

He darted a quick suspicious glance at her as she stood in the dim passage blocking his way. She saw the look and came a little closer, making herself seductive, asking him with her face, her eyes, her body.

" Couldn't you and I go out to-night, Joe ? " she murmured seductively. " Honest, I've had a sickening afternoon. I've missed you a lot lately. I want to go out with you. I want to. Here I am ready, all dressed up . . ."

" Ah, what——"

She pressed against him, began to smooth his coat lapel, to slip her white finger into his buttonhole, with a childish yet suggestive appeal.

" I'm just dying to have a fling. Let's go to the Percy Grill, Joe, and have a rare old time. You know, Joe . . . you know what . . ."

He shook his head rudely.

" No," he said in a surly voice. " I'm busy, I'm worried, I've got things on my mind." He brushed past her, banged through the door and was gone.

She lay back against the wall of the passage, her mouth a little open, her eyes upon the street door. She had asked him, lowered herself to ask him. She had held herself wide open, wide open, longing for him, and he had chucked a surly refusal in her face. Humiliation rushed over her; never, in all her life, had she been so wounded, so humiliated. Pale with temper, she bit her lips fiercely. She lay there for a moment mad, simply, with fury. Then she gathered herself, flung her head in the air, went into the back room as if nothing had happened.

Tossing her hat and gloves upon the sofa, she began to make herself a cup of tea. Ada, reclining in the rocker, lowered her magazine and watched her with displeasure.

" Where you been ? " Ada asked laconically, very coldly.

" Out."

" H'umph . . . out with that young Fenwick fella, eh ? "

" Certainly," Jenny agreed with a calm tranquillity. " Out with David Fenwick. And a most lovely afternoon I've had. Simply perfect. Such wonderful flowers and birds we've seen. He's a nice fellow, oh, he really is *nice*."

Ada's indolent bosom heaved ominously.

" So he's nice, is he ? "

" Yes, indeed." Jenny paused in her unruffled measuring of the tea to nod graciously. " He's the nicest and best fellow I've ever met. I'm quite carried away by him." And very airily she began to hum.

Ada could stand it no longer.

" Don't hum at me," she quivered with indignation. " I won't have it. And let me tell you this, madam, I think you're behaving shocking. You're not treating Joe right. For four years now he's run after you, taken you out and all, as good as your intended. And the minute this other young man comes along you turn Joe down and go cohorting all over the place with *him*. . . . It's not fair on Joe."

Jenny paused and sipped her tea with ladylike restraint.

" I think nothing of Joe Gowlan, ma. I could have Joe just by the raising of my little finger. But I haven't raised it. Not just yet."

" So that's it, my lady! Joe isn't good enough for you now . . . not grand enough now this school teacher has come on the carpet. You're a fine customer, right enough. I should think so. Let me tell you, my lady, that I didn't go about it that way with your dad. I treated him proper and human. And if you don't treat Joe the same you'll lose him as sure as your name's Jenny Sunley."

" A lot I care, ma." Jenny smiled pityingly. " Even if I never did set eyes on Joe Gowlan again."

Mrs. Sunley exploded.

" You might not then. Joe's upset. Joe's terrible upset. He's just been in here talking to me now. There was tears in his eyes, poor fella, when he was speaking to me about you. He don't know what to do. And he's got trouble on him, too, trouble at the foundry. You're treating him shameful, but mark my words, no man'll put up with that kind of thing for long. So just look out. You're a bad heartless girl. I've had a good mind to tell your dad." Ada delivered the final threat and sealed off the conversation by raising her magazine with a jerk. She had said her say, done her duty, and Jenny could like it or lump it!

Jenny's smile was still superior as she finished her tea. Still condescending and even more superior as she picked up her hat and gloves, swept from the room and mounted the stairs.

In her own bedroom, however, something went wrong with Jenny's smile. She stood alone, in the middle of the cold worn linoleum like a wretched, forsaken, spoiled child. She let her hat and gloves slip from her. Then with a great gulp she flung herself upon the bed. She lay flat upon the bed as though embracing it. Her skirt, caught above one knee, exposed a tender patch of white skin above her black stocking. Her abandon was unutterable. She sobbed and sobbed as if her heart would break.

Joe, strutting down Bigg Market to see Dick Jobey, with whom he had private and important business, was telling himself gleefully:

" It's working, lad! By gum, it's working."

XV

Ten days later, early in the forenoon, Joe presented himself at the foundry offices and asked to see Mr. Stanley.

" Well, Joe, what is it ? " Stanley Millington asked, looking up from his desk, set in the centre of the old-fashioned high-windowed room, full of papers, books and blue prints, with maroon walls covered by photographs of employee groups, officials of the firm, outings of the Social Club and big castings dangling precariously from cranes.

Joe said respectfully:

" I've just worked my week's notice, Mr. Millington. I didn't want to go without saying good-bye."

Our Mr. Stanley sat up in his chair.

" Heavens, man, you don't mean to say you're leaving us. Why, that's too bad. You're one of the bright lights of the shop. And the Social Club too. What's the trouble ? Anything I can put right ? "

Joe shook his head with a kind of manly melancholy.

" No, Mr. Stanley, sir, it's just private trouble. Nothing to do with the shop. I like it there fine. It's . . . it's just a matter between my lass and me."

" Good God, Joe! " Mr. Stanley burned. " You don't mean . . ." Our Mr. Stanley remembered Jenny; our Mr. Stanley had recently married Laura; our Mr. Stanley was straight, so to speak, from the nuptial bed and his mood was dramatically propitious: " You don't mean to say she's chucked you."

Joe nodded dumbly.

" I'll have to get out. I can't stick the place any longer. I'll have to get right away."

Millington averted his eyes. Bad luck on the man, oh, rotten bad luck. Taking it like a sportsman, too! To give Joe time he tactfully took out his pipe, slowly filled it from the tobacco jar on the desk bearing the St. Bede's colours, straightened his St. Bede's tie and said:

" I'm sorry, Joe." Chivalry towards woman permitted him to say no more: he could not indict Jenny. But he went on: " I'm doubly sorry to lose you, Joe. As a matter of fact I've had you at the back of my mind for some time. I've been watching you. I wanted to make an opening for you, give you a lift."

Dammit to hell, thought Joe grimly, why didn't you do it then ? Smiling gratefully, he said:

" That was good of you, Mr. Stanley."

" Yes! " Puffing thoughtfully. " I like your style, Joe. You're the type of man I like to work with—open and decent. Education counts very little these days. It's the man himself who matters. I wanted to give you your chance." Long pause. " However, I won't attempt to dissuade you now. There's no good offering a man stones when he wants bread. In your circumstance I should probably do exactly the same thing. Go away and try to forget." He paused again, pipe in hand, realising with a sudden fullness of heart how happy was his position with Laura, how *different* from poor old Joe's. " But remember what I've said, Joe. I really mean it. If and when you want to come back there'll be a job waiting on you here. A *decent* job. You understand, Joe ? "

" Yes, Mr. Stanley," Joe managed manfully.

Millington got up, took the pipe from his mouth and held out his hand, encouraging Joe to face his present destiny.

" Good-bye, Joe. I know we'll meet again."

They shook hands. Joe turned and went out. He hurried down Platt Street, caught a tram, urged it mentally to speed. He hurried along Scottswood Road, entered No. 117A quietly, slipped softly upstairs and packed his bag. He packed everything. When he came to the framed photograph of herself which Jenny had given him he contemplated it for a minute, grinned slightly, detached the photograph and packed the frame. It was a good frame, anyway, a silver frame.

With the bulging bag in his big fist he came downstairs, plumped the bag in the hall and entered the back room. Ada, as usual, was in the rocker, her untidy curves overflowing while she took what she called her forenoon go-easy.

" Good-bye, Mrs. Sunley."

" What! " Ada almost jumped out of the chair.

" I'm sacked," Joe announced succinctly. " I've lost my job, Jenny's finished with me, I can't stand it any longer, I'm off."

" But, Joe . . ." Ada gasped. " You're not serious ? "

" I'm dead serious." Joe was not doleful now: this would have been dangerous, invoking protests from Ada that he should remain. He was firm, determined, controlled. He was going, a man who had been outraged, whose mind now was inexorably made up. And as such the impressionable Ada accepted him.

" I knew it," she wailed. " I knew it the way Jenny was going on. I told her. I told her you wouldn't stand it. She's treated you shocking."

" Worse than shocking," Joe amended grimly.

" And to think you've lost your job on top of it, oh, Joe, I'm sorry. It's wicked. What on earth are you going to do ? "

" I'll find a job," Joe said resolutely. " But it'll be far enough from Tynecastle."

" But, Joe . . . won't you . . ."

" No! " bawled Joe suddenly. " I won't. I won't do anything. I've suffered enough. I've been done down by my best friend. I'll stand no more of it."

David, of course, was Joe's trump card. But for David, Joe would never have slipped out of the affair like this. Impossible. In every way impossible. He would have been questioned, pursued, spied on at every turn. Even as he spoke this thought flashed across Joe's mind; and a great surge of elation at his own cleverness came over him. Yes, he was clever; he was an artist; it was marvellous to be standing here pulling the wool over her eyes, laughing up his sleeve at every one of them.

" Mind you, I bear no ill feeling, Mrs. Sunley," he declared finally. " Tell Jenny I forgive her. And say good-bye to the others for me. I can't face them. I'm too upset."

Ada didn't want to let him go. She, indeed, was the one who seemed upset. But what could she do with this injured man ? Joe left the house as he had entered it: in the best tradition and without a stain on his character.

That evening Jenny returned late. It was Slattery's Summer Sale and this being Friday, the last full day of that hateful period, the establishment did not close until nearly eight o'clock. Jenny came in at quarter past.

Ada was alone in the house: with remarkable energy she had arranged it so, sending Clarry and Phyllis " out," Alf and Sally to the first house of the Empire.

" I want to speak to you, Jenny."

Something unusual vibrated in her mother's voice, but Jenny was too tired to bother. She was dead tired, indisposed too, which made it worse, she'd had a killing day.

" That Slattery's," she declared wearily, flinging herself on a chair. " I'm sick of it. Ten blessed hours I've been on my feet. They're all hot and swollen. I'll have varicose veins if I go on much longer. I used to think it was a toney job. What a hope! It's worse than ever, the class of women we're getting now is fierce."

" Joe," remarked Mrs. Sunley acidly, " has left."

" Left ? " Jenny echoed, bewildered.

" Left this morning! Left for good."

Jenny understood. Her pale face went absolutely blanched. She stopped caressing her swollen stockinged feet and sat up. Her grey eyes stared, not at her mother, but at nothing. She looked frightened. Then she recovered herself.

" Give me my tea, mother," she said in an odd tone. " Don't say another word. Just give me my tea and shut up."

Ada drew a deep breath and all the pent-up scolding died upon her tongue. She knew something of her Jenny—not everything, but enough to know that Jenny must at this moment be obeyed. She " shut up " and gave Jenny her tea.

Very slowly Jenny ate her tea, it was really dinner, some cottage pie kept hot in the oven. She still sat very erect, still stared straight in front of her. She was thinking.

When she had finished she turned to her mother.

" Now, listen, ma," she said, " and listen hard. I know you're all ready to begin on me. I know every word that's ready to come off your tongue. I've treated Joe rotten and all the rest of it. I know, I tell you. I know it all. So don't say it. Then you'll have nothing to regret. See! And now I'm going to bed."

She left her dumbfounded mother and walked wearily upstairs. She felt incredibly tired. If only she had a port, a couple of ports to buck her up. Suddenly she felt she would give anything for one cheering glass of port. Upstairs she threw off her things, some on to a chair, some on to the floor, anywhere, anyhow. She got into bed. Thank God Clarry, who shared the room, was not there to bother her.

In the cool darkness of her room she lay flat upon her back, still thinking . . . thinking. There was no hysteria this time, no floods of tears, no wild beating at the pillow. She was perfectly calm; but for all her calmness she was frightened.

She faced the fact that Joe had thrown her over, a frightful blow, a blow almost mortally damaging to her pride, a blow which had struck her psychologically at the worst possible time. She was sick of Slattery's, sick of the long hours of standing, stretching, snipping, sick of being politely patronising to the common women customers. Only to-day her six years at Slattery's had risen up to confront her; she had told herself firmly she must get out of it. She was sick of her home, too; sick of the crowded, littered, blowsy place. She wanted a house of her own, her own things; she wanted to meet people, give little tea parties, have proper " society." But suppose she never had her wish? Suppose it was a case of Slattery's and Scottswood Road all her life—there lay the vital cause of Jenny's sudden alarm. In Joe she had lost one opportunity. Would she lose the other?

She put in a great deal of cold hard thinking before she fell asleep. But she woke next morning feeling refreshed. Saturday was her half-day and when she came home at one o'clock she ate her lunch quickly and hurried upstairs to change. She spent a great deal of time upon her dressing: choosing her smartest frock, a pearl grey with pale pink trimmings, doing her hair in a new style, carefully smoothing her complexion with Vinolia cold cream. The result satisfied her. She went down to the parlour to wait for David.

She expected him at half-past two, but he came a good ten minutes before his time, thrilling with eagerness to see her. One glance reassured Jenny: he was head over ears in love with her. She let him in herself and he stood stock still in the passage, consuming her with his ardent eyes.

" Jenny," he whispered. " You're too good to be true."

As she led the way into the parlour she laughed, pleased: David, she was forced to admit, had a way of saying things far beyond Joe's capacity. But he had brought her the stupidest little present: not chocolates or candy or even perfume; nothing useful: but a bunch of wallflowers, hardly a bunch even, a small sort of posy which couldn't have cost more than twopence at one of the market barrows. But never mind, never mind about that now. She smiled:

" I'm that pleased to see you, David, really I am, and such lovely flowers."

" They're nothing much, but they're sweet, Jenny, and so are you. Their petals have a kind of mist on them . . . it's like the lovely mist on your eyes."

She did not know what to say; this style of conversation left her completely at a loss; she supposed it came from all the books he'd read in these last three years—" poems and that like." Ordinarily she would have bustled away with the wallflowers, making the correct ladylike remark: " I really do love arranging flowers." But this afternoon she did not wish to bustle away from him. She wanted to keep near him. Still holding the flowers she sat down primly on the couch. He sat beside her, smiling at the stern propriety of their attitudes.

" We look like we were having our photograph taken."

" What ? " She gazed at him blankly, making him laugh outright.

" You know, Jenny," he said, " I've never met anyone more . . . oh, more completely innocent than you. Like Francesca . . . Hither all dewy from her cloister fetched . . . a man called Stephen Phillips wrote that."

Her eyes were downcast. Her grey dress, pale soft face and still hands clasping the flowers did give her a queer nun-like quality. She remained very quiet after he had spoken, wondering what on earth he meant. Innocent ? Was he—could he be kidding her ? No, surely not, he was too far gone on her for that. She said at length:

" You're not to make fun of me. I haven't been feeling too well this day or two."

" Oh, Jenny." His concern was instant. " What's been wrong ? "

She sighed, began to pick at the stem of one of his flowers.

" They've all been down on me here, all of them . . . Then there's been trouble with Joe . . . he's gone away."

" Joe gone ? "

She nodded.

" But why ? In the name of goodness why ? "

She was silent a moment, then, still plucking pathetically at the flower:

" He was jealous . . . He wouldn't stay because . . . oh, well, if you must know, because I like you better than him."

" But, Jenny," he protested, confused. " Joe said . . . do you mean . . . do you really mean that after all Joe was fond of you ? "

" Don't let's talk about it," she answered with a little shiver. " I won't talk about it. They've been on about it all the time. They blame me because I couldn't stand Joe . . ." She lifted her eyes to his suddenly. " I can't help myself, can I, David ? "

At the subtle implication in her words his heart beat loudly, with a quick and exquisite elation. She preferred him. She had called him David. Gazing into her eyes as on that first evening when they met, he lost himself, knowing only that he loved her, wanting her with all his soul. There was no one in the world but Jenny. There would never be anyone but Jenny. The thought, simply of her name, Jenny, was enchantment: a lark singing, a bud opening, beauty and sweetness, melody and perfume in one. With all the ardour of his young and hungry soul he desired her. He bent towards her, and she did not draw away.

"Jenny," he murmured above the beating of his heart. "Do you mean that you like me?"

"Yes, David."

"Jenny," he whispered. "I knew right from the start it would be like this. You do love me, Jenny?"

She gave a little nervous nod.

He took her in his arms. Nothing in all his life transcended the rapture of that kiss. He kissed her lightly, almost reverently. There was a tragic youthfulness, a complete betrayal of his inexperience in the tender awkwardness of that embrace. It was the queerest kiss she had ever known. Some curious quality in the kiss helped a tear tremulously down her cheek, another, and another.

"Jenny . . . you're crying. Don't you love me? Oh, my dear, tell me what's wrong."

"I do love you, David. I do," she whispered. "I haven't got anybody but you. I want you to go on loving me. I want you to take me out of here. I hate it here. I hate it. They've been beastly to me. And I'm sick of working in the millinery. I'll not put up with it another minute. I want to be with you, right away. I want us to be married and happy and, oh, everything, David."

The emotion in her voice moved him beyond the edge of ecstasy.

"I'll take you away, Jenny. As soon as ever I can. Whenever I take my degree and get a post."

She burst into tears.

"Oh, David, but that's another whole year. And you'll be in Durham, at the University, away from me. You'll forget me. I couldn't wait as long as that. I'm sick of it here, I tell you. Couldn't you get a post now?" She wept bitterly; she did not know why.

It distressed him terribly to see her crying: he saw that she was overwrought and highly strung: but every sob she gave seemed to pierce him like a wound.

He soothed her, stroking her brow as her head lay upon his shoulder.

"It's not so very long, Jenny. And don't worry, oh, my dear, don't worry. Why, I daresay I could get a post now if it came to the bit. I'm quite qualified to teach, you see. I've got the B.Litt already, you can take that in two years at the Baddeley. It's not worth anything, nothing like the B.A., but I daresay if it came to a push I could get a job on the strength of it."

"Could you, David?" Her streaming eyes implored him. "Oh, do try, David! How would you set about it?"

"Well." Still stroking her brow he humoured her. Only the madness of his love made him go on. "I might write to a man at home who's got some influence. A man named Barras. He might get me in somewhere in the county. But you see . . ."

"I do see, David," she gulped. "I see exactly what you mean. You must take your B.A. But why not take it *afterwards*? Oh, think, David, you and me together in a nice little house somewhere. You working in the evenings with all your great big important books on the table and me sitting there beside you. It's not so very hard to teach during the day. Then you can study, oh, ever so hard at night. Why, David, it would be wonderful. Wonderful!"

The picture, painted so romantically by Jenny, stirred him to a smiling tenderness. He looked at her protectively.

"But you see, Jenny, we must be practical . . ."

She smiled through her tears.

"David, David . . . don't say another word. I'm so happy, I don't want you to spoil it." She jumped up, laughing. "Now, listen! We'll go for a beautiful walk. Let's go to Esmond Dene, it's so lovely there, I do love it so, what with the trees and that *beautiful* old mill. And we'll talk it all over, every bit of it. After all it wouldn't do any harm just to write to this gentleman, Mr. Barras . . ." She broke off, fascinating him with her lovely eyes, all liquid and melting with her suppressed tears. She kissed him quickly, then ran off to get ready.

He stood smiling; uplifted, enraptured, perhaps a little perplexed. But nothing mattered beside the fact that Jenny loved him. She loved him. And he loved her. He thrilled with tenderness, an ardent hope for the future. Jenny would wait, of course she would wait . . . he was only twenty-two . . . he *must* take his B.A., she would come to see that later.

While he remained there, waiting for Jenny, the door flew open and Sally came into the room. She stopped short when she saw him.

"I didn't know you were here," she said, frowning. "I only came to get some music."

Her frown was like a cloud sailing into the clear sky of his happiness. She had always been very odd with him, abrupt, caustic, perversely disagreeable. She seemed to have a grudge against him, an instinct for flicking him on the raw. Suddenly he wanted to be on good terms with Sally now that he was so happy, now that he was marrying her sister. And on an impulse he said:

"Why do you look at me that way, Sally? Is it because you dislike me?"

She faced him steadily: she wore an old blue drill costume, relic of her last year's school days; her hair was very untidy.

" I don't dislike you," she said, with none of her usual precocious flippancy.

He saw that she was speaking the truth. He smiled.

" But you're . . . you're always so sour to me."

She answered with uncommon gravity:

" You know where to get sugar if you want it." And lowering her eyes suddenly she turned and went out of the room.

As Sally went through the door Jenny came swimming in.

" What's the little cat been saying to you ? " Not waiting for his reply she took his arm with a proprietary air, gave it a gentle squeeze. " Come along now, dear. I'm dying for us to have our lovely, lovely talk."

She was bright now, yes, bright as a bird was Jenny. And why not ? Hadn't she every reason to be pleased, with a fiancé, not just a " boy " but a real fiancé, qualified to be a teacher. Oh! Marvellous to have a fiancé who was a teacher. She'd get out of Slattery's right away, and out of Scottswood Road as well. She'd show them, show Joe too, she'd have a church wedding to spite them all, with a notice in the paper, she'd always set her mind on a church wedding, now what would she wear, something simple but nice . . . oh, yes, nice . . . nice . . . nice.

When David returned from his walk he wrote to Barras, " just to please " Jenny. A week later he had an answer, offering him a post as junior master at the New Bethel Street Council School in Sleescale. He showed it to Jenny, torn between reason and the rapture of his love for her, thinking of his parents, his career, wondering what she would say. She flung her arms round his neck.

" Oh, David, darling," she sobbed. " Isn't that marvellous, too marvellous for words. Aren't you glad I made you write ? Isn't it really *wonderful* ? "

Pressed against her, his eyes shut, his lips on hers holding her, oh, so tight, he felt with surging intoxication that she was right: it was really quite wonderful.

XVI

THAT morning, even before the telegram arrived for his father, Arthur was conscious of a singular elation. He awoke into it, was aware from the moment he opened his eyes upon the square of blue sky through his open window that life was very precious—full of sunshine and strength and hope. Naturally he did not always wake this way. Some mornings there was no sunshine, nothing awaited him but heaviness, a kind of immobile darkness, and the dismal sense of his own deficiencies.

Why was he so happy? That, like his moods of misery, remained inexplicable. Perhaps a premonition of the morning telegram, or of seeing Hetty in the afternoon. More likely the joyful recognition of his own improvement for, lying in bed with his hands clasped behind his head and the long span of his eighteen-year body luxuriously stretched, his first real thought had been: " I didn't eat the strawberries."

Of course, the strawberries, though he was very fond of them, were nothing in themselves; they were a symbol, they stood for his own strength. Half-smiling, he recapitulated. The table last night, Aunt Caroline, head on one side as usual, purring, portioning the luscious bowl of home-grown strawberries—a rare luxury on Barras's austere table. And the cream too, he nearly forgot the big silver jug of yellow cream—nothing he liked better than strawberries and cream. " Now, Arthur," he heard Aunt Caroline say, preparing to delve generously for him. Then, himself, quickly: " No thank you, Aunt Carrie. I shan't have any strawberries to-night." " But, Arthur . . ." Surprise, even consternation in Aunt Carrie's voice; his father's aloof eye fixed momentarily upon him. Aunt Carrie again: " Aren't you well, Arthur, my dear? " Himself, laughing: " Perfectly well, Aunt Carrie, I just don't feel like strawberries to-night." He had sat, with watering teeth, watching them eat the strawberries.

That was the way to do it, a little thing, perhaps, but the book said bigger things would follow. Yes, he was satisfied this morning. " I do wish Arthur would show more character." His mother's petulant remark, overheard as he passed along the corridor outside her room, and fixed through all these months in the very centre of his mind, receded now, answered by his conduct towards the strawberries!

He jumped out of bed—it was wrong, really, to lie dreaming in bed—went through his exercises vigorously before the open window, dashed into the bathroom and took a cold bath: really cold, mind you, not a trickle, even, from the hot tap to temper the icy plunge. He came back to his room, glowing, dressed in his working suit with his eyes fixed religiously upon the placard which hung on the wall opposite his bed. The placard said in large heavily inked letters: *I will!* Beneath this was another: " *Look every man straight between the eyes!* "

Arthur finished lacing his boots, his heavy boots, for he would be going inbye to-day, and was ready. He went to a drawer, unlocked it and picked out a small red book; *The Cure of Self-consciousness*, one of a series of such books entitled *The Will and the Way*—and sat down seriously upon the edge of his bed to read. He always read one chapter before breakfast when, as the book declared, the mind was most receptive; and he preferred his bedroom because of its privacy—these little red books were a secret, guarded jealously.

Outside the edge of his concentration he heard the movements of the house: the slow pad, pad of Aunt Carrie in his mother's room, Grace's laugh and scurry towards the bathroom, the sullen thud of Hilda overhead as she grudgingly got out of bed to face the day. His father had been up an hour ago; early rising was part of his father's routine, inevitable somehow, never questioned, expected.

Arthur paused momentarily in his reading: *The human will is capable of controlling not only the destiny of one man but the destinies of many men. That faculty of mind which determines either to do or forbear to do, that faculty whereby we determine, among two courses, which we shall embrace or pursue can affect not only our own lives but the lives of many others.*

How true that was! If only for that single reason one must cultivate the will—not for the effects upon oneself but for these wide and far-flung consequences upon others. He wanted to be strong, to have control, resolution, mastery over himself. He knew his own defects, his natural shyness and awkwardness, his proneness to burrow in his own reserve, but beyond everything his incorrigible tendency to dream.

Like all gentle and sensitive natures, he was tempted to escape from the harsh reality of life through the gateway of his imagination. How wonderful were these dreams! How often he saw himself performing some terrific act of heroism at the Neptune . . . or perhaps it was a little child he saved from drowning or from an express train, walking away quietly without giving his name, only to be discovered afterwards and carried shoulder high by a delirious crowd . . . or it was a hulking brute he knocked out for bullying a woman . . . or he stood upon a platform, spellbinding an enormous audience with his oratory . . . or again, at some select dinner table, partnered by Hetty Todd, he fascinated her and the company at large by the ease and brilliance of his address . . . oh, there was no limit to the dazzling wonder of those dreams. But he realised their danger, he had put them behind him, he would be strong now, magnificently strong. He was nearly nineteen; in a year would finish his course in mining engineering. Life had . . . oh yes, life really had begun, and it was necessary to bring courage to bear upon it. Courage and determination. I will, Arthur said firmly, closing the book and staring zealously at the placard. He shut his eyes tight and repeated the phrase several times into himself, burning the words, as it were, into his soul. I will, I will, I will . . . Then he went down to breakfast.

His father, who preferred to breakfast half an hour before the others, had almost finished; he was drinking a last cup of coffee, reflectively, with the paper on his knee. He nodded silently in answer to Arthur's good morning. There was nothing peremptory in that nod, none of the freezing curtness which sometimes cut Arthur to the bone. The nod this morning held an indulgent tranquillity: it fell upon Arthur like a caress, it reinforced, admitted his devotion, acknowledged him as an individual.

He smiled with happiness, began intently to chip the top from his egg, warmly conscious of his father's continued gaze.

" I think, Arthur," Barras said, suddenly, as though he had decided to speak, " I think we may have interesting news to-day."

" Yes, father ? "

" We have the prospect of a contract."

" Yes, father ? " Arthur looked up, blushing. That " we " simply was magnificent, including him, making him one with his father, enrolling him already as a partner in the mine.

" A first-rate contract, I may add, with P. W. & Company."

" Yes, father."

" You're pleased ? " Barras inquired with amiable satire.

" Oh yes, father."

Barras nodded again.

" It's our coking coal they want. I had begun to think we should never get started on that seam again. But if they meet our price we shall start work there next week. Start to strip the Dyke in Scupper Flats."

" When shall you know, father ? "

" This morning," Barras answered; and as though Arthur's direct question had made him suddenly resent his previous unbending, he raised his paper and from behind it said authoritatively: " Be ready at nine sharp, please. I don't wish to be kept waiting."

Arthur returned to his egg industriously, gratified at the information he had received. But suddenly a thought disturbed him. He remembered something . . . something most disturbing. Scupper Flats! He lifted his eyes quickly towards the screened figure of his father. He wanted to ask . . . he most terribly wanted to ask a question. Should he, could he, or had be better not ? While he vacillated, Aunt Carrie came in with Grace and Hilda. Aunt Carrie wore her usual look of pleasantness which she put on every morning, regularly, naturally, just as she put in her false teeth.

" Your mother's had a splendid night." Brightly she apostrophised Arthur. Though the information was for Richard, Carrie knew better than address him outright: all Aunt Carrie's methods were indirect, protective of her own and the general peace.

Arthur passed her the toast without hearing a word. His mind was focused entirely upon his own disturbing thought . . . Scupper Flats. He did not feel half so happy now, he began to feel worried and upset. He kept his eyes upon his plate. And under his brooding the splendour of the morning slowly waned. He could have cried out with vexation: why should it always be, this sudden turn of his being from ecstatic lightness to heaviness and dismay ?

He gazed across at Grace in a sort of envy, watching her as she dealt with the marmalade cheerfully and happily. Grace was always the same: at sixteen she had the same sweetness, the same happy unconsciousness that he remembered so vividly in those days when they used both to tumble off Boxer's back. Why, only yesterday he had seen her come up the Avenue with Dan Teasdale, munching a big red apple, with a sort of cheerful comradeship. She, who was going next month to a finishing school at Harrogate, went chewing apples through the town in broad daylight, and with Dan Teasdale, the baker's son! He, no doubt, had given her the apple, for he was munching its neighbour. If Aunt Carrie had seen her there would have been a row and no mistake.

Here Grace caught his eyes upon her before he could remove them, smiled at him and silently articulated a single word. At least she shaped her lips to the word, just breathed it across the table towards him. But he knew what it was. Grace, still smiling at him cheerfully, was saying " Hetty! " Whenever Grace caught him in a mood of introspection she deduced that he was dreaming of Hetty Todd.

He shook his head vaguely—an action which seemed to cause her the most intense amusement. Her eyes glistened with fun, she simply bubbled with some inward joy. But as her mouth was full of toast and marmalade, the result was calamitous. Grace spluttered suddenly, coughed, choked and got very red in the face.

" Oh dear," she gasped at last. " Something went the wrong way."

Hilda frowned at her:

" Drink some coffee quickly, then. And don't be such a little jay."

Grace obediently drank her coffee. Hilda watched her; sitting erect and severe, the frown still lingering, making her dark face harsh.

" I don't think," she said firmly, " that you will ever learn to behave."

The remark was like a rap across the knuckles. That at least was how Arthur would have felt it. And yet, he knew that Hilda loved Grace. Curious! Yes, it struck him always as intensely curious this love of Hilda for Grace. It was violent somehow, yet disciplined; like a caress united to a blow; watchful; both dormant and possessive; made up of sudden anger and tenderness quickly subdued. Hilda wanted Grace to be with her; Hilda would give everything to be loved by Grace. Yet Hilda, he felt, openly scorned the least demonstration of affection which might attract Grace to her, which might evoke Grace's love.

With a quick impatience he turned from the thought—that was another fault he must correct, the wandering tendency of his too inquisitive mind. Hadn't he enough to occupy him since that conversation with his father ? He finished his coffee, rolled his napkin in the bone ring and sat waiting for his father to rise. On the way to the pit he would ask . . . or perhaps mightn't it be better on the way home ?

At last Barras finished with the paper. He did not let it drop beside him; he folded it neatly with his white, beautifully kept hands; his fingers smoothed, preserved the paper; then he passed it to Aunt Carrie without a word.

Hilda always took the paper the moment Barras went out, and

Barras knew that Hilda took it. But he chose rather loftily to ignore that obtrusive fact.

He went out of the room followed by Arthur and in five minutes both were in the dogcart spanking towards the pit. Arthur nerved himself to speak. The words were on his tongue a dozen times and in a dozen different ways. " By the bye, father," he would say: or simply " Father, do you think . . ." or perhaps " It has suddenly struck me, father . . ." would be a more propitious opening. All the permutations and combinations ranged themselves for his choice: he saw himself speaking, heard the words he spoke. But he said nothing. It was agony. Then, to his infinite relief, Barras calmly cut right into the heart of his distress.

" We had a little trouble some years ago over the Scupper Flats. Do you remember ? "

" Yes, father, I remember." Arthur stole a quick glance at his father, who sat upright and composed beside him.

" A wretched business! I didn't want it. Who does want trouble ? But that trouble was thrust upon me. It cost me dearly." He disposed of the matter, slid it back quietly into the archives of the past, moralising: " Life is a hard business, sometimes, Arthur. It is necessary to preserve one's position in the face of circumstance." Then in a moment he said: " But this time we shall have no trouble."

" You think not, father ? "

" I'm sure of it. The men had a lesson last time they won't be in a hurry to repeat." His tone was considered, reasonable; he balanced the argument dispassionately. " No doubt the Scupper will turn out a wet section, but for that matter Mixen and the whole of Paradise is wet. They're used to these conditions. Quite used to them."

As his father spoke, saying so little yet conveying so much, a tremendous wave of comfort flowed over Arthur, obliterating all the nebulous anxieties and fears which had tormented him for the last hour. They became effaced, like puny sand castles washed straight and clean by some vigorous advancing tide. Gratitude overwhelmed him. He loved his father for this serenity, for this calm, unruffled strength. He sat silent, conscious of his father's presence near to him. He was untroubled now. The brightness of the morning was restored.

They bowled down Cowpen Street at a fine pace, entered the pit yard, went straight into the office. Armstrong was there, obviously waiting, for he stood at the window idly tapping the pane with his thumb. He spun round as Barras entered.

" A wire for you, Mr. Barras." And, in a moment, showing that he knew the telegram's significance, " I thought maybe I'd better wait."

Barras took up the orange slip from the desk and opened it without hurry.

" Yes," he said calmly. " It's all right. They've agreed to our price."

" Then we start in the Flats on Monday ? " Armstrong said.

Barras nodded.

Armstrong stroked his lips with the back of his hand, an odd self-conscious gesture. For no apparent reason he had a sheepish look. Suddenly the telephone rang. Almost with relief, Armstrong walked over to the desk and lifted the receiver to his ear.

" Hello, hello." He listened for a moment, then glanced across at Barras. " It's Mr. Todd of Tynecastle. He's been on twice this morning already."

Barras took the instrument from Armstrong.

" Yes, yes, this is Richard Barras . . . yes, Todd, I'm glad to say it's settled."

He broke off, listening, then in an altered tone he said:

" Don't be absurd, Todd. Yes, of course. What? I said *of course*! "

Another pause while the familiar impatient furrow gathered on Barras's forehead.

" I tell you *yes*." A rasp entered his voice. " What nonsense, man! I should think so. Not over the 'phone. What? I don't see the slightest need. Yes, I shall be in Tynecastle this afternoon. Where? At your house? What's that? Indigestion? Dear, dear . . ." The sarcastic emphasis in Barras's voice grew more pronounced and his eyes, searching the office irritably, found Arthur's suddenly and remained there, communicating, derisive. ". . . Your liver again? What a pity! Something disagreed with you. Well, since you're seedy I suppose I'd better call on you. But I refuse to take you seriously. Yes, I absolutely refuse. Listen, I'll bring Arthur with me. Tell Hetty to expect him."

He rang off abruptly, stood for a few seconds, the contemptuous smile still touching his lips, then he remarked to Arthur:

" We might as well look up Todd this afternoon. He seems to have been a trifle indiscreet again . . . in his diet. I never heard him sound so dismal." He gave the brittle smile that served him for a laugh and turned to go. Armstrong, with an obsequious echo of Barras's amusement, threw open the office door. The two men went into the pit yard together.

Arthur remained in the office with mixed and rather curious thoughts. He knew, of course, that Todd's indiscretion was drink, not violent spasms of intoxication, but a quiet, melancholy and diligent application to the bottle which from time to time laid him up with jaundice. Though these bouts were not serious and had come to be accepted generally as inevitable and innocuous, Arthur never learned of them without pain. He liked Adam Todd, pitied him as a pathetic and defeated figure. He sensed that Todd, in his own youth, had known the burning ardours, the fears and hopes which afflict the sensitive soul. It was impossible to conceive that Todd, a small morose seedy man, stained with nicotine and soaked with alcohol, had once been eager and responsive to the promise of life, that his torpid eye had ever brightened or been stirred.

But it was so. In his young days, when he served his apprenticeship along with Richard Barras in the Tyecastle Main, Todd had been a lively blade, full of enthusiasm for the career he had mapped out. Then the years had rolled over him. He lost his wife in child-birth. A case, the important North Hetton case, in which he was retained as the expert witness by the Briggs-Hetton Company went against him. His reputation suffered, his interest flagged, he distrusted his own decisions, his practice started to decline. His children began to grow away from him: now Laura, his favourite, had married; Alan seemed more set on the pursuit of " a good time " than the reanimation of the firm; Hetty was intent on enjoyment and her own affairs. Gradually Todd had withdrawn into himself, had stopped going out except to the County Club where, from eight until eleven on most nights, he could be found in his customary chair, drinking silently, smoking, listening, throwing out an occasional word, wearing the fixed and slightly apathetic air of a man who has finally accepted disillusionment.

As he went about his work that morning Arthur somehow couldn't get the thought of old Todd out of his head. And when, at three o'clock in the afternoon, he accompanied his father to Tynecastle and walked up College Row towards Todd's house he had a strange and unaccountable sense of expectation, as though some chord vibrated between his own eager personality and the snuffy personality of Adam Todd. He could not understand the feeling, it was baffling and new.

Barras rang the bell and almost at once the door opened. Todd himself let them in—that was typical of him, he never stood on ceremony—wearing an old dun dressing-gown and down-at-heel slippers.

" Well," Barras said, glancing sideways at Todd. " You're not in bed."

" No, no, I'm all right." Todd pushed up the gold-rimmed glasses that always lay at the end of his veinous nose; the glasses immediately slipped down again. " It's just a chill. I'll be right as rain in a couple of days."

" Quite," Barras agreed suavely. That Todd should always attribute his bilious attacks to chill really amused Barras, though he did not show it. He had the bland air of condescending to his old friend, even of humouring him. He had, too, an air of immense prosperity and success standing above the seedy little man in the stained dressing-gown within that narrow and rather dingy hall, where the maroon wall-paper, the heavy umbrella stand and presentation fumed oak barometer gave out a resigned, a patient sadness.

" I wanted to talk to you, you know, Richard." Todd addressed the remark to his slippers and he did so with a certain hesitation.

" So I gathered."

" You didn't mind my ringing you this morning ? "

" My dear Todd, why should I ? " Richard's condescension grew more expansive; and Todd's hesitation correspondingly increased.

" I felt I had to speak to you." It was almost an apology.

" Quite so."

" Well," Todd paused, " we'd better go in the back room. I've a spot of fire there. I find it chilly, my blood's thin I suppose." He paused again, preoccupied, worried, and let his eyes drift round to Arthur; he smiled his indefinite smile. " Perhaps you'd like to go up to Hetty, Arthur. Laura looked over from Yarrow this afternoon. They're upstairs in the drawing-room now."

Arthur coloured instantly. The conversation had excited him. Todd had something unusual to discuss with his father, he had hoped to be included, maturely, in their conversation. But now he saw himself discarded, sent ignominiously to join the women-folk. He felt utterly humiliated; he attempted to cover it by pretending not to care.

" Yes, I'll go up," he said glibly, forcing a smile.

Todd nodded:

" You know your way, my boy."

Barras turned his glance of critical indulgence upon Arthur.

" I shan't be long," he said off-handedly, " we must catch the five-ten home." Then he followed Todd into the back room.

Arthur remained standing in the hall, his cheek still twitching from that attempted smile. He felt horribly slighted. It was always the same: one word, the mere inflection of a voice, would do it, he was so easily offended, so quickly abashed. A kind of torment at his own wretched temperament took hold of him, mixed up with a provoked, indignant curiosity as to what Todd's business might be with his father. Was it money Todd wished to borrow, or what ? Why was Todd so anxious, his father so contemptuous and masterful ? A smarting wave of exasperation surged over Arthur when suddenly he raised his head and saw Hetty coming down the stairs.

" Arthur! " cried Hetty, hurrying down. " I thought I heard you. Why on earth didn't you sing out ? "

She came to him and held out her hand. Immediately, with an almost magical abruptness, his mood altered. He looked down at her in welcome, forgetting his father and Todd in an overmastering desire to impress her. All at once he wanted to shine before Hetty, and more, he felt himself capable of doing so. Not that it was his nature to be like this; the whole thing was the reaction of that preceding rebuff.

" Hello, Hetty," he said briskly. Then, observing that she was dressed for the street, " I say, are you going out ? "

She smiled without a trace of shyness—Hetty was never shy.

" I said I'd walk down with Laura. She's just going." Pausing, she made a pert little face. " I've been doing the heavy with the rich married sister all the afternoon. But I'll dash back and give you tea the minute I get rid of her."

" Come and have tea with me at Dilley's," he suggested on an impulse.

She clapped her hands at the unexpected invitation.

" Lovely, Arthur, lovely! "

He studied her, thinking how pretty she looked since she had put her hair up. Now, at eighteen, Hetty was more than ever a pretty little thing. Though Hetty's features were not pretty, though Hetty ought not to have been pretty, she was pretty. She was small-boned with thin wrists and small hands. She had large greenish eyes and an insignificant nose and a palish skin. But her hair was soft and blonde and she wore it attractively fluffed out from her smooth white narrow forehead. Her eyes always had a moist lustre and occasionally her pupils were wide and black, and those big black pupils against the soft blonde hair were extremely attractive. That was Hetty's secret. She was not beautiful. But she was attractive, composed and vivacious, and provocative and appealing, rather like a nice sleek little cat. Now she smiled most appealingly at Arthur and said in a kind of artless baby talk she sometimes used:

" Nice Arthur to take Hetty to Dilley's. Hetty likes to go to Dilley's."

" You mean you like going with me? " he inquired with that same factitious confidence.

" Mmm! " she agreed. " Arthur and Hetty have nice time at Dilley's. Much nicer than here." Unconsciously she stressed the last word. Hetty did not care much for the background of her home. It was an old house, 15 College Row, with an out-of-date atmosphere which particularly annoyed her and made her keep on trying to force her father into moving to a smarter residence.

" It's those old coffee éclairs you're keen on," he persisted, striving for more balm to ease his wounded pride. " And not me? "

She screwed up her nose at him—very artless and sweet.

" Will Arthur really buy Hetty nice coffee éclair? Hetty adores coffee éclairs."

A warning cough made them both swing round. Laura stood in the hall beside them, pulling on her gloves with too obvious preoccupation. Immediately the kittenish expression faded from Hetty's face. Quite sharply she declared:

" What a start to give anyone, Laura! You ought to let people hear you coming."

" I did cough," Laura said drily. " And I was just going to sneeze."

" Clever! " said Hetty, darting a sharp glance at her sister.

Laura continued to pull on her gloves, gazing from one to the other quizzically. She was beautifully but quietly dressed in a dark navy costume. Arthur had not seen much of Laura since her marriage to Stanley Millington. For some obscure reason he was never quite comfortable with Laura. Hetty he understood, she was sweet, oh, transparently guileless! But Laura left him always at a loss. Her restraint in particular, that curious emotional flatness, the sense of some carefully hidden quality, a watchfulness almost, behind her pale, humorous face, disturbed him strangely.

" Come along, then," Hetty exclaimed pettishly; Laura's placidity, her well-turned-out air seemed to annoy her further. " Don't let's stand here all day. Arthur's taking me to Dilley's."

A slight smile came to Laura's lips; she did not speak. As they went through the door into the street Arthur turned the conversation hastily.

" How is Stanley ? " he asked.

" He's very well," Laura answered pleasantly. " I think he's golfing this afternoon."

They continued to talk of trivialities until they reached the corner of Grainger Street, where Laura said good-bye good-naturedly and left them to keep an appointment with Bonar, her tailor.

" She's mad about clothes," Hetty explained with a sharp laugh the minute Laura had gone. She let her fingers come to rest lightly on Arthur's arm as they walked towards Dilley's. " If she wasn't so extravagant she might be a little more decent to me."

" How do you mean, Hetty ? "

" Well, she only gives me five pounds a month for *my* dress allowance, and pocket money and everything."

He gazed at her in astonishment.

" Does Laura really allow you that, Hetty ? Why, that's pretty generous of her."

" I'm glad you think so." Hetty looked piqued, almost sorry she had spoken. " She can jolly well afford it, anyhow. She made a good match, didn't she ? "

There was a pause.

" I can never quite fathom Laura," Arthur said, puzzled.

" I'm not surprised." Hetty gave her ingenuous laugh again. " I could tell you a few things about her, not that I would though, not for anything in the world." She dismissed the subject with a virtuous little shiver. " I'm glad I'm not like her, anyway. So don't let's talk of it."

Here they entered Dilley's and Hetty, responding to the warm note of gaiety which met them, switched her mood to one of composed vivacity. It was half-past four and the place was crowded: Dilley's was considered smart for tea in Tynecastle. The Resort of the Élite!—this was the proud boast used in the advertisement columns of the *Courier*. An orchestra was playing behind some palms, a pleasant chatter of voices met them as they went into the Mikado room, done after Sullivan in the Japanese taste. They sat down at a bamboo table and Arthur ordered tea.

" Rather nice, here." He leaned across towards Hetty, who was nodding brightly to her friends in the crowded room. There was, in fact, a regular clientèle for afternoon tea at Dilley's, mainly the younger generation of Tynecastle, sons and daughters of the well-to-do doctors, lawyers and merchants of the city, a perfect aristocracy of provincial snobbism and style. Hetty was quite a figure in this smartish little clique. Hetty was really popular. Though old man Todd was only a mining engineer in a not very flourishing way of business Hetty went out a great deal. She was young, sure of herself and in the swim. She was known to have a head on her shoulders. The wise ones who had prophesied a good match for pretty little Hetty, always smiled knowingly when she was seen about with Arthur Barras.

She sipped her tea nonchalantly.

" Alan's over there." Gaily, with a wave of recognition, she indicated her brother. " With Dick Purves and some of the Nomad Rugger crowd. We ought to go across."

Arthur looked over dutifully to where her brother Alan, who ought to have been at the office, lounged with half a dozen young fellows at a table in the centre of the room, the smoke from their cigarettes rising with heroic languor.

" Don't let's bother about them, Hetty," he murmured. " It's nicer by ourselves."

Hetty, sitting up with a sparkle in her eye, aware of admiring glances directed towards her, toyed absently with her cake fork.

" That Purves boy," she remarked. " He's too absurdly good-looking."

" He's just an ass." Arthur glared across at a vapidly handsome youth with crinkly hair parted in the middle.

" Oh no, Arthur, he's quite a nice boy, really. He dances beautifully."

" He's a conceited fop." Jealously taking Hetty's hand under the table he whispered: " You like me better than him, don't you, Hetty ? "

" Of course, you silly boy." Hetty laughed lightly and let her eyes come back to Arthur. " He's only a stupid little bank clerk. He'll never be anything worth while."

" *I* will, Hetty," Arthur declared fervently.

" Well, *naturally*, Arthur."

" Wait till I go in with father . . . just wait . . . you'll see." He paused, excited suddenly by the prospect of the future, eager to impress her with his own ardour. " We landed a new contract to-day, Hetty. With P. W. & Co. A whacking good one. You just wait and see."

She widened her eyes at him ingenuously.

" Going to make lots and lots more money ? "

He nodded seriously.

" But it isn't just that, Hetty. It's . . . oh, everything. Being in with father, pulling my weight at the Neptune, the way all we Barrases have done, thinking of settling down too, having someone to work for. Honestly, Hetty, it thrills me when I think about it."

Quite carried away, he gazed at her, his face alight with eagerness.

" It *is* rather nice, isn't it, Arthur ? " she agreed, studying him with a sympathetic smile. She really was quite drawn to him at this moment.

He looked his best with a faint colour in his cheeks and this ardour in his eyes. Of course, he was not really good-looking, she had regretfully to admit it, his fair eyelashes, pale complexion and thin jaw gave him too sensitive an air. He couldn't for an instant be compared to Dick Purves, who was the *most* handsome boy. But he was, on the whole, rather a dear, with the Neptune pit and pots of money simply waiting on him. She let him hold her hand under the table again.

" I'm enjoying myself tremendously, this afternoon," he said impulsively. " I don't know why."

" Don't you ? "

" Well, yes, I do."

They both laughed. Her laugh, whereby she showed her small even teeth, enthralled him.

" Are you enjoying it too, Hetty ? "

" Yes, of course."

The feel of her fragile hand beneath the table set his heart thumping with its silent promise. A kind of intoxication mounted to his head, a glorious sense of hope—in himself, in Hetty, in the future. He reached the crisis of his boldness. Nerving himself, he said with a rush:

" Listen, Hetty, I've been meaning to ask you for a long time, why can't we be engaged ? "

She laughed again, not in the least disconcerted, pressing his hand lightly.

" You're such a dear, Arthur."

His colour came and went. He blurted out:

" You know how I feel about you, Hetty. I think I've always felt that way. Remember how we played at the Law when we were kids. You're the nicest girl I know. Father'll be giving me a partnership soon . . ." His own incoherence brought him up short.

Hetty considered swiftly. She had been proposed to before, callow offers made usually in the semi-darkness when " sitting out " at dances. But this was different, this was the real thing. And yet her shrewdness warned her not to hurry. She saw quite sharply how ridiculous her premature engagement to Arthur might be, the subject of gossip, malicious innuendo. Besides, she wanted to have her fling before she settled down.

" You're a dear, Arthur," she breathed, with downcast lashes. " A perfect dear. And you know how fond I am of you. But I do think we're both a little young for anything, well, official. We've got our understanding, of course. Everything's all right between us."

" You do like me then, Hetty ? " he whispered.

" Oh, Arthur, you *know* I do."

An immense elation possessed him. At the facile intensity of his emotion tears came into his eyes. He felt unbelievably happy. He felt mature and manly, capable of anything, he could have thanked her on his knees for loving him.

A few minutes passed.

" Well," she said with a sigh, " I suppose I must get back and see how old man Todd is getting on."

He looked at his watch.

" Twenty to five. I promised to meet father at the five-ten train."

" I'll walk with you to the station."

He smiled at her tenderly. Already her devotion to himself, as to her invalid father, entranced him. He beckoned to the waitress with a lordly confidence and paid the bill. They rose to go.

On the way out they stopped for a moment at Alan's table. Alan was a good sort, a big heavy smiling fellow, inclined perhaps to be lazy and a little wild. But there was no real harm in him. He played football for the Northern Nomads, was in the Territorials and knew a few barmaids by their Christian names. Now amidst a certain amount of chaff and laughter he began to jolly Arthur for taking Hetty out to tea. Usually Arthur was painfully shy under banter, but this afternoon he scored off Alan right and left. His spirits bounded higher. He felt strong, happy, confident. He knew that little things would never worry him again, his flushing, his fits of lassitude and depression, his complex of inferiority, his jealousy. Purves, for instance, " glad-eyeing " Hetty, trying " to get off with her," was no more than a silly little bank clerk, completely negligible. With a final repartee that set the table in a roar he lit a cigarette and gallantly escorted Hetty to the street.

They walked to the Central, Arthur bathed in a warm, unusual glow of self-approval, like an actor who has given a brilliant performance in a leading part. Yes, he had done well. He understood that Hetty wanted him to be like this: not stammering and sheepish but full of confidence, assured.

They entered the station and walked up the platform together, a little early, for the train was not in and Barras had not yet arrived. Suddenly Hetty stopped.

" By the way, Arthur," she exclaimed, " I've just been wondering. Why did your father come to see mine to-day ? "

He drew up, facing her, completely taken aback by the unexpectedness of her remark.

" It's rather odd," she smiled, " now I come to think of it. Dad can't bear seeing any one when he's seedy and yet he got on the telephone to Sleescale three times this morning. Why was it, Arthur ? "

" I don't know," he hesitated, still staring at her. " As a matter of fact I was wondering why myself." He paused. " I'll ask father."

She laughed and pressed his arm.

" Of course not, silly. Don't look so serious, what in all the world does it matter ? "

XVII

AT half-past four that afternoon David emerged from Bethel Street School and crossed the hard concrete playground towards the street. The school, already known as New Bethel Street to distinguish it from the old shut-down school, was a building of shiny, purplish bricks erected on a high piece of waste land at the top of Bethel Street. The opening of New Bethel Street six months ago had caused a general shuffle round amongst the county educational staff and a vacancy for one new junior teacher. It was this appointment that David had received.

New Bethel Street School was not pretty. It was semi-detached severely into halves. Upon one half, in grey stone inset, was carved the word BOYS; upon the other, in equally huge letters, GIRLS. For each sex, separated by a menacing spiked fence, there was a vaulted entrance. A great many white tiles had got into the construction of the school and a smell of disinfectant somehow managed to permeate the corridors. Taken altogether the school succeeded in resembling a large public convenience.

David's dark figure moved rapidly under the lowering and wind-swept sky and seemed to indicate that he was eager to leave the school. It was a cold night and as he had no coat he turned up the collar of his jacket and fairly spurted down the windy street. Suddenly he recognised and was inclined to smile at his own eagerness. He was still unused to the idea of himself as a married man and a master at New Bethel Street. He must, as Strother said, begin to cultivate decorum.

He had been married six months and was settled with Jenny in a small house behind the Dunes. A most tremendous business it had been finding the house—the *right* house, as Jenny put it. Naturally the Terraces were impossible: Jenny wouldn't have looked at a miners' row "for love nor money"; and David felt it wise in the meantime to be at the other end of the town from his parents. Their reaction to his marriage had made things difficult.

High and low they had searched. Rooms furnished or unfurnished Jenny would not have. But at last they had pitched on a small plaster-fronted detached house in Lamb Lane, the straggling continuation of Lamb Street. The house belonged to Wept's wife, who had one or two "bits" of property in her own name in Sleescale, and who let them have the house for ten shillings a week because it had stood unlet for the previous two quarters and now showed signs of damp. Even so, the rent was more than David could afford on a salary of £70 a year. Still he had not wished to disappoint Jenny, who had from the first taken quite a fancy to the house, since it did not stand vulgarly in a row and had actually a patch of front garden. Jenny insisted that the garden would afford them a most refined seclusion and hinted romantically at the wonders she would work in the way of cultivating it.

Nor had he cared to stint her over the house's furnishing: Jenny was so bright and intrepid, so set on having " the exact thing " that she would tirelessly ransack a dozen shops rather than confess defeat—how, in the face of such enthusiasm, could he freeze her warm housewifely spirit! Yet he had eventually been obliged to take a stand and in the end they had compromised. Three rooms of the house were furnished on credit: kitchen, parlour, bedroom—the last with a noble suite of stained walnut, the pride of Jenny's heart. For the rest she had taken it out in chintzes, muslin curtains and a superb selection of lace doyleys.

David was happy . . . very happy in this house behind the Dunes—these last six months had been far and away the happiest of his life. And before that there had been the honeymoon. Never, never would David forget the joy of that week . . . those seven blessed days at Cullercoats. Naturally he had thought a honeymoon out of the question. But Jenny, tenacious as ever where romantic tradition was involved, had fiercely insisted; and Jenny, revealing unsuspected treasure, had produced fifteen pounds, her six years' money from the Slattery savings fund, and handed it firmly to him. She had, moreover, in the face of all his protests, argued him into buying himself a new ready-made suit out of the money to replace the shabby grey he wore. Her way of putting it involved no humiliation. Jenny, at least, was never mean; where money was concerned Jenny never thought twice. He had bought the suit; they had spent the honeymoon on Jenny's money. He would never in all his life forget Jenny for that.

The wedding ceremony had been a failure—though he had been prepared for worse—a chilly affair in the Plummer Street church with Jenny unnatural and stiff, a pretentious breakfast at Scottswood Road, a horrible rigidity between the opposing factions of Sunleys and Fenwicks. But the week at Cullercoats had blown it all away. Jenny had been wonderful to him, revealing an ardour—startling yet beautiful. He had expected her to be timid; the depth of her passion had overwhelmed him. She loved him . . . she loved him . . . she really loved him.

He had discovered, of course, that she had been unfortunate, there was no escape from the stark physiology of this fact. Sobbing in his arms that first bitter-sweet night she had told him the whole story; though he had not wished to hear and had begged her, unhappily, to stop. But she would, she must *explain*, it had happened, she wept, when she was just, oh, just a girl, a well-to-do commercial traveller, in the millinery line, of course, a perfect brute, a *beast* of a man, had taken advantage of her. He was drunk and forty, she not yet sixteen. He was bald, too, she remembered, with a little mole on his chin, and his name, oh, his name was Harris. She had not been untrue to herself; she had struggled, fought, but her resistance had been useless; terrified, she had been afraid to tell her mother. It had happened only once and never, never, *never* again with any one in all the world.

Tears filled David's eyes as he held her in his arms, compassion added to his love, his ardour leavened by a sublime pity. Poor Jenny, poor, darling little Jenny!

After the honeymoon they had come direct to Sleescale where his work at New Bethel Street had immediately begun. Here, alas, the run of his good luck was checked.

He was not happy at the school. He had always recognised that teaching would never be his trade, he was too impulsive, too eager for results. He wanted to reform the world. And now, in charge of Standard IIIA, a class full of little boys and girls of nine, inky, untidy, apathetic, he was conscious of the irony of this beginning. He chafed at the creaking system, controlled by bell and whistle and cane, loathed equally the *Grand March* as thumped on the piano by Miss Mimms, his opposite number in IIIB, and her acidulous " now children " heard through the thin partition fifty times a day. As in his period of pupil-teaching, he wanted to change the whole curriculum, cut the idiotic non-essentials on which visiting inspectors set such store, ignore the Battle of Hastings, the latitude of Cape Town, the sing-song recitation of capitals and dates, substitute Hans Andersen for the prim Crown Reader, awaken the children, fan their flickering interest, stimulate the mind rather than the memory. Of course all his attempts, his suggestions towards this end had met with the chilliest reception. Every hour of every day he felt that he did not belong to this environment. In the Staff Room it was the same, he felt himself alien, treated distantly by his colleagues, frozen by the virgin Mimms. Nor could he disguise from himself the fact that Strother, the head master, disliked him. Strother was a square, official man, an M.A. of Durham with a ponderous manner and a fussy, pedantic mind. He wore black suits, had a heavy black moustache, was something of a martinet. He had been second master at the old school, knew all about David, his family and origin; despised him for having worked in the pit; for not having taken the B.A.; felt that he had been foisted upon him; went out of his way to be difficult, contemptuous and severe. If only Mr. Carmichael had been head, everything would have been different; but Carmichael, though applying for the post, had not even reached the short leet. He had no influence. In disgust he had accepted a village school at Wallington. He had written a long letter to David asking David to visit him soon, to come for a week-end occasionally. The letter was full of the pessimism of a discouraged man.

But David was not discouraged: he was young enthusiastic, determined to make his way. And as he swung round the corner of Lamb Street, braced by the keen wind, he swore to himself that he would get on, out of New Bethel Street, away from Strother's paltriness, into something finer. The chance would come. And, by heaven, he would take it.

Half-way down Lamb Street he saw a figure advancing on the same side of the road: it was Ramage, James Ramage, the butcher, vice-chairman of the school board, mayor in prospect for the town. David prepared to nod civilly. He did nod. But Ramage passed without the slightest recognition; his lowering gaze dwelt blankly upon David as though he looked through him.

David coloured, set his jaw hard. There, he thought, is an enemy of mine. Coming at the end of a trying day this last snub cut him pretty deeply. But as he let himself into his house he tried to banish it, calling out cheerily to Jenny as soon he came inside the door.

She appeared in a fetching pink silk blouse which he had never seen before, her hair newly shampooed and smartly arranged.

" Why, Jenny, you look like the queen."

She held him off, posing nicely, coquettishly:

" Now, don't crush my new blouse, Mister Man." Lately she had taken to calling him Mister Man: it jarred abominably, he must tell her to stop. Not now, of course . . . she might stop of her own accord. With his arm round her trim hips he steered her to the kitchen where, through the open door, he saw a comforting fire. But she protested:

" No, not there, David. I won't have us in the kitchen."

" But, Jenny . . . I'm used to kitchens . . . and it's so lovely and warm there."

" No, I won't have it, bad Mister Man. You know what we said. No falling off. We got to use the front room. It's terribly common to sit in the kitchen."

She led the way to the parlour where a green fire smoked unpromisingly.

" Now you sit there till I fetch the tea."

" But hang it all, Jenny . . ."

She settled him with a pretty little gesture, bustled out. In five minutes she brought in tea: a tray first, then a tall nickel-plated cake stand—a recent purchase, such a bargain, bought on the near prospect of people calling—and finally two little Japanese paper serviettes.

" Now you be quiet, Mister Man." Again she stilled his bewildered protest almost before he uttered it. She poured him a cup of not very hot tea, politely handed him a serviette, placed the cake stand at his elbow. She was like a small girl playing with a doll's tea-set. He could stand it no longer.

" My heavens, Jenny," in humorous exasperation, " what in the name of thunder does this mean? I'm hungry. I want a good high tea, a kipper or eggs, or a couple of Wept's prepare to meet thy God's."

" Now, David, don't swear. You know I wasn't brought up to it. And don't be impatient. Just wait and see. A cup in your hand is very nice once in a while. And I'll be having visitors soon enough. I want to try things out. Have some of that seed-cake. I bought it in Murchison's."

He swallowed hard, choking down his resentment with an effort.

In silence he made the best of " a cup in his hand," Murchison's damp seed-cake, stringy shop bread streaked with bought jam. For a split second he couldn't help thinking of the tea his mother used to set before him when he was working, earning a wage not half what he earned now: a home-baked crusty loaf to hack at will, a big pot of butter, cheese and home-made blaeberry jam—bought jam, like bought pastry, was never in Martha's home. But the very disloyalty of that swift vision brought him swiftly back to Jenny. He smiled tenderly at her.

" In your own inimitable words, Jenny, you're a scream."

" Oh, I am, am I ? You're coming round, I see, Mister Man. Well, what's been happening at the school to-day ? "

" Nothing much, Jenny, darling."

" It's always nothing much! "

" Well, Jenny . . ."

" Well, what ? "

" Oh, nothing, dear."

He filled his pipe slowly. How could he tell her the dull tale of his struggle and rebuffs. Some might like that, but not Jenny. She expected some glittering story of success, of how the head master had commended him, of a dazzling stroke which would bring him quick promotion. He didn't want to upset her. And he couldn't lie to her.

A short silence followed, then, lightly, she switched to another perilous topic.

"Tell me, then. Have you made up your mind about Arthur Barras?"

" Well . . . I'm not eager to take him on."

" But it's such a chance," she protested. " To think that you were asked by Mr. Barras himself."

He answered shortly:

" I think I've had too much to do with Barras. I don't like him. I'm sorry in a way I ever wrote to him. It's hateful to feel that I'm indebted to him for my job."

" You're so stupid, David. He's got such influence. I think it's splendid he should have an interest in you, asking you to tutor his son."

" I don't take it as an interest. He's a man I've no time for, Jenny. It's merely an attempt to make his benevolence convincing."

" And who should he want to convince ? "

Quite sharply he answered:

" Himself! "

Pause. She had no idea what he meant. The fact was that Barras, meeting David in Cowpen Street on the previous Saturday, had stopped him with an air of patronage, questioned him with an aloof interest and finally asked him to come to the Law three nights a week to brush up Arthur's mathematics. Arthur was weak in maths. and would need tuition before he could sit the final examination for his certificate.

Jenny tossed her head.

" I don't think," she informed him, " that you know what you're talking about." She looked for a minute as if she might add something. But she said no more, and in a huff gathered together the tea things, carried them out of the room.

Silence in the little room with the new wood fire and the new wood furniture. Then David got up, laid his books out upon the table, stirred up the fire with the poker. He made an effort. Deliberately he closed his mind to the Barras affair and sat down to work.

He was behind the schedule he had mapped out for himself and it worried him. Somehow he did not find the opportunities for study he had expected. Teaching was hard, much harder than he had imagined. He was often tired when he came home; he was tired to-night; and distractions had a way of cropping up. He gritted his teeth, propped his head up with both hands, fastened his attention firmly upon Jusserand. He must, he simply must work for this confounded B.A.: it was the only way to get on: to lift up Jenny and himself.

For half an hour he worked splendidly, undisturbed. Then Jenny slipped in and perched herself upon the arm of his chair. She was repentant for her petulance, kittenish, coy.

" David, dear," she slipped her arm round his shoulder. " I'm sorry I was cross, really I am. I've had such a dull day, p'raps that's why I've been looking forward to to-night ever and ever so much."

He half smiled, pressed his cheek against her round young breast, his eyes still firmly upon the book.

" You weren't cross and it is dull for you."

She stroked the back of his head, coaxing.

" It has really been dull, David. I've hardly spoken to a soul but old Mr. Murchison in the stores and the woman where I priced some silk, oh, and one or two people who came to the door. I . . . I was thinking we might go out to-night to cheer ourselves up."

" But I've got to work, Jenny. You know that as well as I do." Eyes still fastened upon the book.

" Oh . . . you haven't always got to bury yourself in these stupid old books, David. You can take to-night off . . . you can work some other time."

" No, honestly, Jenny, it's important."

" Oh, you could, David, you could if you wanted to."

Astounded, perplexed, he lifted his eyes at last and studied her for a moment.

" But where on earth can you want to go to ? It's cold and wet outside. Home's the best place."

She had it all ready, arranged, carefully planned. She brought it out with a rush.

" We could take the train to Tynecastle; the six-ten. There's a popular concert in the Eldon Hall, something really nice. I looked up the paper and some of the Whitley Bay entertainers are to be there; that's what they do in the winter, you know. There's Colin Loveday, for instance, he's got such a lovely tenor. The tickets only cost one and three, so the money's nothing. Oh, do let's go, David, we'll have a lovely time. I've been so down, I do want a bit of a fling. Don't be an old stick-in-the-mud."

There was a short silence. He did not wish to be an old stick-in-the-mud. He was tired, obsessed by the necessity for study; it was, as he had said, a wet, inhospitable night outside; the concert did not attract him. Suddenly an idea, a grand idea, struck him. His eyes lit up:

"Listen, Jenny! How about this! I'll take to-night off, like you suggest. I'll run up and fetch down Sam and Hughie. We'll bank up the fire, make a hot-pot supper and play rummy. Talk about your entertainers . . . they're not in the hunt with Sam. Our Sammy's the best you ever heard, he'll keep you in stitches all the time." It honestly was, he felt, a great idea: he had been worried over his estrangement from his family, he wanted to be one with his brothers again, this was a marvellous opportunity to break the ice. But as his face brightened, Jenny's fell.

"No," she said coldly, "I wouldn't like that at all. Your family hasn't treated me right, David. I'll not have them make a back door of my house."

Another silence. He compressed his lips firmly. He felt that she was unreasonable and unjust, it was not fair to ask him to go into Tynecastle on a night like this. He would not go. Suddenly he saw tears rise smarting to her eyes. That did it. He could not bully her into tears.

He sighed, rose up, closed the book.

"Right, Jenny. Let's go to the concert then if you feel you'd like it."

She gave a little trill of delight, clapped her hands, kissed him excitedly.

"You are nice, David darling, really you are! Now you wait a minute, I'll run up and put on my hat. I won't be long, we've plenty of time to catch the train."

While she was upstairs he went into the kitchen and cut himself a wedge of bread and cheese. He ate this slowly, staring into the fire: Jenny, he reflected with a wry smile, had probably made up her mind to drag him to the concert days ago.

He had just finished eating when a knock came to the back door. Surprised, he opened it.

"Why, Sammy," he exclaimed delightedly. "You old dog."

Sammy, with the hardy grin irremovably fixed on his pale healthy face, rolled into the kitchen.

"Me and Annie was just passin'," he announced, not—despite the grin—without a certain shyness. "I jest thought I'd look ye up."

"That's great, Sammy. But, man . . . where's Annie?"

Sam jerked his head towards the outer darkness. The etiquette was perfect. Annie was waiting outside. Annie knew her place. Annie was not sure of her welcome. David saw it all: the obscure figure of Annie Macer strolling quietly, contentedly, outside the house waiting until she be judged worthy to enter. He cried instantly:

" Tell her to come in at once, you big idiot. Go on! Fetch her in this minute."

Sammy's grin broadened.

Then Jenny, all dressed to go out, walked into the room. Sammy, on his way to the door, hesitated, not quite sure, gazing at Jenny, who advanced on him with her best company manners.

" This is a great pleasure," Jenny remarked, smiling ever so politely. " And such a stranger too. What a shame you've caught David and me just going out."

" But Sammy's dropped in to see us, Jenny," David broke in. " And he's brought Annie. She's outside."

Jenny's eyebrows went up; she paused for just the appropriate time; smiled sweetly at Sam.

" Isn't that a pity! Too bad, really it is, that you should have caught us on the way to the concert. We've promised to meet some friends in Tynecastle and really we couldn't disappoint them. You must look in another time."

Sammy clung tenaciously to his grin.

" Ah, that's all right. Annie and me never have much to do. We can come any old time."

" You're not to go, Sammy," burst out David. " Fetch Annie in. And both of you stop and have a cup of tea."

Jenny threw a pained look towards the clock.

" Not at all, lad." Sammy was already on his way to the door. " Aw wouldna stop you an' the missus from goin' out for anything. Annie an' me'll just take a stroll up the Avenue. Good night to ye both."

Right to the end Sammy's grin persisted; but beneath it, David saw that Sammy was bitterly hurt. Out Sammy would go to Annie and mutter:

" Come on, lass, we're not good enough for the likes o' them. Since our Davey's turned schoolmaster he fancies himself too much, I'm thinking."

David winced, torn between his desire to run after Sammy and his promise to take Jenny to the concert. But Sammy was already gone.

Jenny and David caught the six-ten for Tynecastle, a slow, crowded train which stopped at every station. They went to the Eldon Hall. The tickets cost two shillings each, the cheaper seats being filled when they reached the hall. They sat through three hours of steamy performance.

Jenny adored it, clapping with the rest for encores, but to David it was ghastly. He tried not to be superior; tried hard to like it; but the entire concert party defeated him. Oh! They're first rate, Jenny kept breathing enthusiastically. But they were not first rate. They were fourth rate: the left-overs from holiday pierrot troupes, the comedian relying mainly upon his mother-in-law and Colin Loveday upon a fruity vibrato and a hand laid soulfully upon his heart. David thought of Sally's little performance in the parlour of Scottswood Road, so vastly superior to this; he thought of his books lying unopened; he thought of Sammy and Annie Macer strolling arm in arm down the Avenue.

When the performance was over Jenny nestled up to him as they came out of the hall.

" It's an hour till the last train, David ; we must take that, it's such a quick one . . . first stop Sleescale. Let's run round to the Percy Grill for something. Joe always used to take me there. Only a port or that, we can't wait at the station."

At the Percy they each had a port. Jenny was delighted to be back, recognised familiar faces, chaffed the napkin-stuffed waiter whom, recalling a joke of the red-nosed comedian, she called Chawles.

" A scream, wasn't he ? " she added, giggling.

The port made things a little different for David, outlines less incisive, colours rosier, atmosphere a trifle hazy. He smiled across at Jenny.

" You're a reckless imp," he said, " and what an influence on a poor man! I see I shall have to take to coaching young Barras after all."

" That's the way to look at it, darling." She approved warmly, instantly. She enticed him with her eyes, pressed her knee against his under the table. And with a gay daring she ordered Chawles to bring her another port.

After that they had to run quickly for the train. Quickly, quickly, they caught it in a whirl, flung themselves into an empty smoker.

" Oh dear! Oh dear! " Jenny giggled, panting. " That was a scream, David darling, wasn't it now ? " She paused, recovered her breath, saw that they were alone, remembered with a queer catch deep down in her that the train did not stop until Sleescale . . . another half-hour at least. She liked queer places, always had, even with Joe. Suddenly she snuggled up close to him: " You've been so good to me, David, I can't thank you enough. Pull down the blinds, David . . . it's cosier that way."

He looked at her doubtfully, closely, as she lay in his arms; her eyes were shut—under the lids they seemed full; her pale lips were moist and a little apart as if vaguely smiling; her breath held the generous fume of port; her body was soft and very warm.

" Go on," she murmured. " Pull down the blinds. *All* the blinds."

" No, Jenny . . . wait, Jenny . . ."

The train jolted a little; shook up and down as it took some point on the track. He rose and pulled down all the blinds.

" That's wonderful, David."

Afterwards she lay against him; she fell asleep; she snored gently. He stared straight in front of him, a curious look upon his set face. The carriage reeked of stale pipes, port and engine smoke; someone had thrown orange peel upon the floor. Outside it was black as pitch. The wind howled, battered the heavy rain against the carriage window. The train thundered on.

XVIII

At the beginning of April, when David had been coaching Arthur Barras at the Law for close on three months, he received a message from his father. Harry Kinch, a small boy from the Terraces, brother of that little Alice who had died of pneumonia nearly seven years before, brought the note to David at New Bethel Street school one morning. *Dear David will you come up the Wansbeck—trouting Saturday yours Dad.* It was clumsily written in copying-ink pencil on the inside of an old envelope.

David was deeply touched. His father still wished to go fishing with him as in those days when he had taken him, a little boy, up the Wansbeck stream! The thought made him happy. For ten days Robert had been out the pit with a flare-up of tubercular pleurisy—he passed it off lightly as " inflammation "—but he was up now and about. Saturday would be his last free day; he wished David to spend it with him. The invitation came like a peace offering straight from his father's heart.

Standing at his desk in the humming class-room, David's thoughts flashed swiftly back over these past months. He had gone to the Law against his own inclination, perhaps because of Jenny's importunities, certainly because they needed the extra money. But it had upset his father greatly. And, indeed, he felt it strangely unreal himself, that he should now be on familiar terms with the Barrases, who had always figured in his mind as apart from him and his life. He reflected. Aunt Carrie, for instance, so curious and worried about him at the start, inclined to look at him as she did at people who came into the house with muddy boots or at Ramage's bill when she thought he had overcharged her for the sirloin. Her near-sighted eyes had worn that worried distrustfulness for quite a while.

But the look had faded from Aunt Carrie's eyes in time. She had " taken " to David in the end and would send up hot milk and biscuits to the old schoolroom about nine o'clock when Arthur and David were due to finish their work.

Then Hilda, strangely enough, had started to drop in with the hot milk and the biscuits. She had begun by treating him—not like the person who came in with dirty boots—but like the actual dirt upon the boots. He took no notice, he was quick enough to see it as the symptom of Hilda's conflict. Hilda interested him. She was twenty-four; her forbidding manner and dark unattractiveness ingrained more deeply now. Hilda, he thought, is not like most unattractive women. They will go on deluding themselves, dressing up, making the best of themselves, reflecting before the mirror, this blue *does* suit me, or my profile is really quite good, or isn't my hair charming with this middle parting ? deluding themselves until they die. But Hilda from the start had resolutely made up her mind that she was ugly, and with that forbidding manner, she resolutely made the worst of her ugliness. Apart from this, he saw that Hilda lived in conflict: perhaps her father's strength fought against her mother's weakness within her. Hilda always struck David as the unwilling union of these two elements, as if she had been conceived unwillingly, fought with herself in embryo and came into the world finally in a state of threshing discord. Hilda was not happy. She revealed herself gradually, not knowing that she revealed herself. She was missing Grace, who was now at school in Harrogate, acutely. Though her remarks usually took this form: " They'll never teach her anything, she's a perfect little jay! " or, as when reading a letter: " She can't even spell yet! "—David saw that Hilda adored Grace. She was a queer sort of feminist, she was militant within herself. On March 12th the papers were full of a campaign of destruction organised by suffragists in the West End of London. Windows had been smashed in all the principal streets and many hundreds arrested, including Mrs. Pankhurst. Hilda glowed. She started a magnificent argument that night, quite taken out of herself. She wanted to be part of the movement, she said, to do something, go into the active whirl of life, work madly to relieve the crushing oppressions on her sex. Her eyes flashed as she instanced the Armenian women and the white-slave traffic. She was disdainful, magnificent. Men ? Of course she detested men! Hated and detested them. She launched into arguments, she knew her Doll's House by heart. It was another symptom of her conflict, her ugliness, her psychosis.

Though she never openly revealed the fact, it was evident that Hilda's aversion to men was rooted in her father. He was MAN, the phallic symbol, her father. His calm suppression of all her wishes inverted her more fiercely, magnified and deepened her repressions. She wanted to get away from the Law and out of Sleescale, she wanted to work for her living—anything and anywhere so long as she was amongst her own sex. She wanted to *do* something. But all her frantic desires beat themselves out against her father's calm detachment. He laughed at her, made her feel a fool with one inattentive word. She swore she would get away, that she would fight. Yet she remained, and the fight took place only within herself. Hilda waited . . . waited for what ?

From Hilda, David got one view of Barras. The other, of course, came from Arthur. At the Law David never came in contact with Barras, he remained a remote and unapproachable figure. But Arthur talked a great deal about his father, he was never happier than when talking about him. After the quadratic equations were disposed of Arthur would begin . . . anything would serve to set him going. But while Hilda's disclosure wore the taint of hatred, Arthur's rang out like an ecstasy.

David grew very fond of Arthur—yet through his fondness lingered that same sense of pity which had come to him in the pit yard when he first saw Arthur upon the high seat of the dogcart. Arthur was so earnest, so pathetically earnest. And yet so weak! He would waver even upon the kind of pencil he must use—an H or an HB. A quick decision comforted him like a kindness. He took everything to heart, he was inordinately sensitive. Often David tried gently to move Arthur from his shyness with a joke. It was no use, Arthur had not the faintest sense of humour.

As for Arthur's mother, David came to know her too. One evening Aunt Carrie brought the hot milk into the schoolroom with an air of conferring a favour even greater than usual.

She said with dignity:

" Mrs. Barras, my sister, would like to see you."

Lying back upon her pillows, Harriet wanted to know about Arthur, just his " opinion," of course, about Arthur. He was a great anxiety to her, Arthur, her son, and a great responsibility. Oh, a great responsibility, she said, asking him if he would mind handing her the bottle of Cologne from the little side table. Just there, if he please, by his elbow. Cologne soothed her headaches when Caroline was too busy to brush her hair. Yes, she went on, it would be such a disappointment to Arthur's father if Arthur did not turn out well. Perhaps he might try, in his own way, since Caroline had spoken so highly of him, to influence Arthur's character for good to prepare him for life. And, without taking breath, she asked him if he believed in thought healing. She had felt lately that she might try thought healing for herself, the difficulty being that in thought healing the bed should, strictly speaking, face to the north and it was awkward in this room from the position of the window and the gas stove. She could not, naturally, dispense with her gas stove. Impossible! Now, she continued, since he knew mathematics did he honestly believe that thought healing would be equally effective if the bed faced north-west which could be managed with a little difficulty by moving the chest of drawers against the other wall.

Jenny was delighted that David had made such a good impression at the Law, delighted that he had become " so friendly with the Barrases." Jenny's desire for society was such that it pleased her even to take it by proxy. When he came back at night she would urge David to tell her all that had happened: now did she really say that, and did they hand the biscuits round or just leave the barrel on the tray? That Hilda might have an interest in David did not worry her in the least. She had no jealousy, she was " dead sure " of David, and in any case that Hilda was the dowdiest thing.

Jenny's reactions to the Law amused David, often he invented the most elaborate incidents to tease her. But Jenny was not so easily taken in. Jenny, in her own words, had a head on her shoulders. Jenny was Jenny.

David, all this time, was becoming acquainted with Jenny. It often struck him as strange that he should only now be getting to know his own wife, but it was not so strange when he reflected that he certainly had not known her before her marriage. Then Jenny had been the projection of his love, a flower, a sweetness, the very breath of spring.

Now he began to know the real Jenny, the Jenny who wanted " society," clothes, amusement, who liked " going about " and was fond of a glass of port, who was passionate yet easily shocked, who smilingly put up with big discomforts and cried over the little ones, who suddenly demanded love and sympathy and " petting," who had a habit of flat contradiction with no argument to support it, who combined logic and wild unreason in the same sweet breath.

He still loved Jenny, he would never stop loving her, he knew. But they started now to have frequent and violent quarrels. Jenny was stubborn and he was stubborn. And there were certain things in which Jenny must not have her way. He would not have her drinking port. On the night when she had ordered herself a port in the Percy Grill he had felt that Jenny was too fond of port. He would not let her have port in the house. They fought over that port: " You're a killjoy right enough . . . you ought to join the Salvation Army . . . I hate you, I *hate* you . . ." Then would come a burst of tears, a big reconciliation and love. " Oh, I do love you, David, I do, I *do* . . ."

They fought over David's examination as well. She wanted him to take his B.A., of course. She was mad that he should take it, she would like to spite that Mrs. Strother and a few of them. But she simply would not give him time to study. There was always something for them to do at nights, or if they were alone it was a case, very pathetically, of: " Take me on your knee, David darling, it seems ages since I had the littlest bit of petting." Or perhaps she had given herself a tiny cut with the potato knife—lost such a lot of blood and when do you think we'll have a maid, David ?—and must have no one but him to bind it up. The B.A. receded at such moments. David had already put it back six months and it looked now, with this extra coaching at the Law, as though another six months would be added to the other. In desperation he took to cycling the fifteen miles to Wallington, the village where Carmichael now lived. In the school house he got peace and judicious advice: what best to go on with and what to leave alone. The disillusioned Carmichael was kind to him, really decent. Often he stayed the whole week-end with Carmichael.

And they fought finally, Jenny and he, about their families. It worried David terribly, the estrangement his marriage had brought about between his own family and himself. There was of course a certain coming and going between Inkerman Terrace and the house in Lamb Lane. But it was not what David wanted. Jenny was stiff, Martha cold, Robert silent, Sammy and Hugh uncomfortable. It was queer that when David saw Jenny, in all her patronising gentility, with his own family he could have beaten her and the moment they went out he felt himself loving her again. His marriage had been a shock, he realised, to Martha and Robert. Martha naturally received the blow with an air of bitter justification: Jenny wasn't nearly good enough, she had always known harm would come of David's coming out the pit, and now this silly early marriage clearly proved her right.

Robert's attitude was different. He retired into his silence. To Jenny he was always kind, he went out of his way to be kind, but though he tried so hard to be encouraging there was a sadness about it all. He had been ambitious for David, he had built so much on all that he would do, he had in a sense put his whole life into David's future. And David at twenty-one had married a silly shop-girl—that, in his secret heart, was how Robert viewed it.

David felt his father's sadness. It hurt him horribly. He lay awake at nights thinking about it. His father resented his marriage. His father resented his having applied to Barras for a job. His father resented his coaching of Arthur Barras at the Law. Yet his father had written and asked him to go fishing up the Wansbeck.

With a start David came back to himself. Rather guiltily he silenced his noisy class. Quickly, he wrote a short reply to his father's note for Harry to take back. Then he flung himself into the work of the day.

All that week he looked forward to Saturday. He had always been, in the local phrase, " a great one for the fishing," though his opportunities to fish had lately been so few. Spring was again in the air; he knew the Wansbeck valley would be lovely now; he suddenly longed to go there with all his soul.

Saturday came, a good fishing day, warm, with blinks of sun amongst the clouds and a soft westerly wind. He rose early, gave Jenny her morning cup of tea, prepared some jam sandwiches; then he had a look at the little greenheart rod his father had given him on his tenth birthday—how well he remembered going to Marriot's in West Street to buy it. He tried the rod, it was still whippy and useful as ever. He put on his boots, whistling softly. Jenny was still in bed when he left the house.

He climbed the Terraces, along Inkerman—it gave him a queer feeling, this soft spring morning—into his own home. Sammy and Hughie were both working their shift, but his mother stood at the table tying up Robert's picnic lunch with thin twine and greased paper. Martha saved twine and greased paper as though they were both fine gold. At the sight of him, though she nodded, her lips drew down ominously, he saw she had not forgiven him yet.

" Ye don't look well," she said, penetrating him with her bleak eyes.

" I feel perfectly well, mother." It was not true; off and on he had been feeling seedy these last few months.

" Ye have a face white as a clout."

He answered shortly:

" I can't help my face. I tell you I feel all right."

" I'm thinkin' ye felt better when ye stopped in this house and worked decently in the pit."

He felt his temper rise in him. But he said:

" Where's my dad ? "

" Gone out to get some grubs. He'll be back presently. Are ye in such a hurry ye can't sit down for a second and speak a word to your own mother ? "

He sat down, watching her as she carefully tied the last tight bow—there were no knots in the string, for Martha wanted it back. She had aged little: her big solid body was still active, her movements sure, her deep-set eyes shrewd and masterful as ever in her gaunt healthy vigorous face. She turned:

" Where's your lunch ? "

" In my pocket."

" Show me."

He pretended not to hear.

She held out her hand; repeated:

" Show me."

" I will *not* show you, mother. My lunch is in my pocket. It's my lunch. I'm going to eat it. So that's an end of it."

She still kept out her hand, grimly, her expression unrelaxed. She said:

" So ye want to disobey me to my face now . . . like ye've done behind my back."

" Oh, hang it, mother, I don't want to disobey you. It's just . . ." Angrily he lugged the paper bag out his pocket.

She received it coldly and as coldly opened it, exposing the three jammy hunks of stale bread he had prepared himself. Her face did not change, she expressed no disdain, she simply laid the bag aside. She said:

" It'll go in my bread pudding." And in return she handed him her own solid package, not commending it, remarking simply: " There's more than enough for the two of you there."

There was injustice in her attitude but there was justice too. And it was the justice which struck him like a blow. He said hotly:

" Mother, I do wish you'd give Jenny a chance. You've always had a down on her. It's not fair. You don't try to get things straight between you. You haven't been to see her half a dozen times in these last three months."

" Does she *want* me to come and see her, David ? "

" You don't give her a chance to want you, mother. You ought to be nicer to her. She's lonely in this place. You ought to cheer her up."

Grimmer than ever, Martha sneered:

" So she needs to be cheered up, then ? " She paused. Cold anger filled her, stifled her. She showed nothing outwardly but from the depth of her anger she fell unconsciously into the broad dialect of her youth. " An' she's lonely, is she ? What cause hev she to be lonely wi' her mon and her house te tend te. Aw'm not lonely. Aw niver hev time te be lonely. But she's aalways gaddin' aboot the place, meykin' up te foaks above hersel'. She'll niver meyk friends that wey, not the reet kind ov friends. An' if aw were ye aw'd tell her not te order so mony bottles ov port at Murchison's."

" Mother! " David jumped up, red flaming into his pale face. " How dare you say a thing like that . . ."

As they faced each other, he burning . . . she pale, cold . . . Robert came in through the open door. He took in the situation at a glance.

" Well," he said mildly. " I'm all ready, Davey. Come on the now, ye'll be seein' your mother when ye come back."

A long sigh came from the very bottom of David's breast. He lowered his eyes to cover up the hurt in them.

" All right, dad."

They went out together.

On the way down Cowpen Street Robert talked more than usual. He made quite a bit of conversation about the fishing; he had got some beautiful grubs out the bone-works on the Spit, he said, and a few nice brandlings from Middlerig. The wind was in the right quarter too, they ought to do well. And he had arranged for them to get a lift in Teasdale's van. The ordinary van man was ill and Dan Teasdale, off duty from the pit, was doing the Saturday delivery to help his father out. He would take them as far as Avory's Farm . . . a couple of miles from Morpeth. Decent of him it was . . . a decent chap Dan Teasdale.

David listened, tried to listen, but he saw through Robert's flow of conversation. He stood a little apart outside Teasdale's shop while Dan and Robert talked. What hurt was not that his mother should have said these things; it was the tiny germ of truth behind her words which rankled and gnawed at him and would not let him alone.

When the van was ready Dan Teasdale clambered up, Robert followed, putting his foot first upon the brass hub, getting up slowly, with an effort, then David—there was not much room. They drove off.

Immediately they had cleared the outskirts of the town Dan began to talk in his friendly style: he would take them straight to Avory's, he said, do his deliveries on the way back. He wished he was going with them, he went on cheerily; he was fond of the fishing, but never got much chance. Altogether he was fond of the country, and loved the country life; really he had always wanted to be a farmer, to use his limbs in the open air, not down the mucky old pit. But you know how things went . . . here Dan laughed, rather ashamed of having revealed himself.

They drove on, striking away from the flat drab land with its grim pit chimneys and head stocks, into a countryside that was like a new world clothed with new green leaves and new green grass. It was as if God had just made that bit of world and dropped it down the night before and men had not yet found and dirtied it. There were the most beautiful fields of yellow dandelions, thousands of dandelions, and without a doubt they did look fine.

Even David cheered up under the influence of these fields and fields of lovely dandelions. He roused himself:

" Fine! " he said to Dan.

Dan nodded and said:

" Fine. They make the milk good." Silence for a minute, then Dan looked furtively at David. Then he said: " How do you like it, going to the Law ? "

David said:

" Not so bad, Dan. Not so bad."

For no earthly reason that David could determine a sort of shame imposed itself on Dan's fresh-coloured face. He gave a short laugh, fixing his candid blue eyes on David.

" You know them all, eh ? You're bound to know them all by now. You've met Grace, haven't you ? "

When Dan came to Grace's name something like reverence fell on him; he swallowed as though he were taking a sacrament. David did not notice. He shook his head.

" I haven't seen Grace. She's away at present, isn't she ? In Harrogate ? "

" Yes," Dan agreed, contemplating the jogging ears of the horse. " She's in Harrogate."

Pause; heavy pause; then Dan Teasdale sighed:

" She's an awful nice girl is Grace! "

He sighed again, an honest sigh and quite a heavy one too, a sigh which epitomised the longing, the impossible longing which had lain hidden in his heart for nearly eight years.

By this time they were approaching Avory's Farm, and at the head of the road Dan stopped the van. Robert and David got down. They thanked Dan again, set off across the fields to the Wansbeck.

They reached the stream: there was plenty of water and a good colour. Not looking at his son, Robert said:

" I'll go beyond the bridge, Davey; you start here . . . this is the best place. Fish up to me and we'll have our snap when we meet." He nodded and strode off along the bank.

David put up his rod, slowly; not caring much, he threaded the line; then he chose his flies: greenwell, march brown and blue spider. As he tried the cast a faint thrill went through him: it was like old times again. Rod in hand, he came over to the water edge, balanced on a hot dry boulder. A trout rose almost silently in mid stream. That faint sucking plop went straight to the marrow of David's bones. It affected him like the sound of a cork leaving a bottle might affect a toper who has not seen wine for years. He began to fish.

He fished up stream, covering all the water he could, the likely places. The sun came out from behind the clouds, steeped him in a warm brightness. The sound of running water sank into his ears, the soft eternal sound of running water.

He caught five fish, the biggest a pound at least, but when he rejoined his father by the bridge, he found that Robert had beaten him. A dozen trout lay in a row upon the grass and Robert lay on his elbow smoking, beside them. He had given over an hour ago when he had made his dozen.

It was three o'clock, and David was hungry. They ate their snap together: cold bacon sandwiches, hard-boiled eggs, a thick cut of veal pie and one of Martha's raspberry jam sponges; there was even a bottle of milk which Robert had put to cool in a shallow channel of the stream.

Robert, unlike most people with chronic phthisis, had, as a rule, a poor appetite and to-day, although the food was tempting, he took very little. He was soon back at his pipe.

David noticed. He studied his father a while, concerned, thinking that his figure seemed sparer . . . a little shrunken. People went to Switzerland and Florida and Arizona with consumption. They went to beautiful expensive sanatoria; got tapped all over by expensive doctors, spat in expensive rubber-capped flasks. Robert went down the pit, got tapped by nobody, and spat in *Tit-Bits*. All the old feeling came over David. He said:

" You've eaten nothing, dad. You don't half take care of yourself."

" I'm fine," Robert said quite sincerely. He had the optimism of his disease. Consumptives usually think they will recover but it was not only that with Robert, he had had the thing so long; the cough, the sweats, the sputum, everything, it all was part of him, he did not regard it with hostility. Indeed he never thought of it except to think that he would get better of it. Now he smiled at David and tapped his chest with the stem of his pipe. " Don't you fret. This . . . this'll never kill me."

David lit his pipe now. They both lay smoking, looking at the sky and the white clouds that raced each other across the sky. The air smelled of grass and primroses and tobacco smoke and the brandlings still left in Robert's worm-bag. It was a good smell. Fields and meadows and trees all round about them, not a house in sight. Lambing time was on, they could hear the thin bleating of it everywhere, restful and quiet. Everything seemed quiet, the only moving things were the white clouds and the little white lambs that skipped about and butted under the bellies of their mothers, who stood chewing, waiting, their black hind legs planted wide apart. The little white lambs butted hard, and tugged and butted again but they did not stay long. They were away, skipping again, getting ready to butt harder, harder.

Robert wondered if David were happy . . . he wondered that very much. Happy on the surface, perhaps, not really happy underneath. But he couldn't ask David, he couldn't set his teeth like Martha and tear into the heart of David's relations with Jenny. He felt the spring in the air and he thought: a primrose, a bird singing and it's done; the only birds, he thought again, that ought to be allowed to sing in the spring are the cuckoos. If only David had just taken her, she looked the kind for that, he would not be lying here now with that strained look on him. But no, he was too young to know, it all had to be dressed up in a wedding. And now he was hacking away in the elementary school, coaching young Barras for money, the B.A. and all the glorious plans they used to talk about laid aside, perhaps forgotten. He hoped to God that David would pull himself out of it soon, go ahead and make a name for himself, do something real; he had it in him to do something big. Oh, he hoped to God he would. At that Robert left it alone, for he had other things upon his mind.

Suddenly David roused himself.

" You're very quiet, dad. There's something bothering you."

" Oh, I don't know, Davey. It's pretty good up here! " He paused. " Better than down the Scupper Flats."

Understanding broke on David; he said slowly:

" So that's where you're cutting now ? "

" It is. We're in the Scupper Flats at last. We started to strip the Dyke three months since."

" You did."

" We did."

" Is it wet ? "

" It is! " Robert puffed quietly. " Near up to the ear holes in my stall. It's that put me badly last week."

The placidity in his father's voice made David suddenly sad. He said:

" You fought pretty hard to keep out Scupper Flats, dad."

" Maybe I did. We got beat though, diddent we ? We'd 'a gone back in the Scupper right away if Barras hadn't lost his contract. Well, he's gotten another contract now, so here we are again, right where we begun. Life's just like a wheel, man, round it comes if you wait long enough."

A short silence came; then Robert went on:

" Mind ye, as I said afore, I don't mind the wet. All my time I've worked in wet places and worse and worse places as my time had gone on. It's the water in the waste that bothers me. You see, Davey, it's like this." He paused and placed his hand edgeways upon the ground. " Here's the Dyke, the Universal Dyke, that's the barrier, a down throw fault that runs due north and south. On the one side of the Dyke you've got all the old workings, the waste of all the old Neptune sinkings that run down from the Snook. All the low levels of the waste are full of water, they're bound to be, bung full of water. Well, man, on the other side of the Dyke, the west side, is Scupper Flats where we're working now. And what are we doing ? We're stripping coal off the Dyke, we're weakening the barrier."

He began to smoke again.

David said:

" I've always heard that the Dyke would stop anything, it's a natural barrier in itself."

" Maybe," Robert said, " but I just can't help thinking what would happen if we stripped too near the old waterlogged workings. Their natural barrier might look pretty thin then."

Robert spoke reasonably, almost musingly; he seemed to have lost his old bitterness completely.

" But, dad, they know what they're doing, they're bound to know if they're near the old workings, they're bound to have the plans."

Robert shook his head:

" They have no plans of the Old Neptune workings."

" They must have plans. You ought to go to the inspector, you ought to go to Jennings."

" What's the use ? " Robert said quietly. " He can't do nothing. He can't enforce a law that doesn't exist. There's no law about mines abandoned afore 1872, and these old Neptune workings was abandoned long afore that. They wasn't made to keep a record of the plans then. So the plans have just got lost. That water might be right on the other side of the Dyke for all they know or it might be half a mile away." He yawned suddenly as though tired of the subject, then he smiled at David. He added: " I hope it's the half mile."

" But, dad . . ." David paused, worried by his father's attitude. Robert seemed weary, enveloped by a sort of fatalism.

Robert saw the expression and smiled again. He said:

" No, I'm not makin' a song about it this time, Davey. They'd none of them believe me, none of the lads, 'twas only the chance of a half-penny raise what brought them out the last time. I'm not bothering . . . not bothering my head." He broke off, looked at the sky. " I think I'll come here next Sunday. You better come too. It's the right time of year for the Wansbeck." He coughed, his soft yet booming cough.

David said quickly:

" You ought to get out oftener with that cough of yours."

Robert smiled:

"I'm going to retire here one of these days." He tapped his chest with his pipe. "But that's nothing, that cough. It and me are old friends now. It'll never kill me."

David looked at his father with a silent anxiety. His nerves, all on edge these days, resented the intolerable situation: Robert's cough, his cheerfulness, his apathy under the hardships of Scupper Flats. And suppose there really was danger in the Flats? David's heart contracted. With a sudden determination he thought: I must speak to Barras about Scupper Flats. I'll speak to him this week.

XIX

Meanwhile Joe was having a splendid time; he described it frequently to himself as "a high old time," or "this is the life." He liked Shiphead, a friendly sort of town with good pubs, two handy billiard saloons, a dance hall and a regular Saturday night boxing show. He liked the change, his lodgings, his office—a single room across from the Fountain Hotel, complete with telephone, two chairs, a desk for his feet, a safe, a racing calendar and walls pasted with cut-outs of everybody from Jack Johnson to Vesta Victoria. He liked his new light brown suit, his new watch-chain worn between the two top pockets of his waistcoat. He liked his finger-nails—cultivated with a pen-knife while his hat sat on the back of his head and his feet rested on the top of his desk—he liked the way he was getting off with the nice little pusher who glittered in the pay box of the new picture palace. And above all he liked his work. The work was a pinch, nothing to do but collect the slips and the money, 'phone the slips through to Dick Jobey in Tynecastle and hold the money till Saturday night when Dick came over himself to collect it. Dick had thought him the right man for the job, the right man to open this new branch in Shiphead, a likely lad, a good mixer, open and hearty, able to get in with the boys, steer clear of the police, run things smart and lively. Dick hadn't wanted a figgering-machine, no, by gum! not no kind of a clerk to sit mopey in the office till business came. Dick wanted a smart lad, a likely, honest lad with a head on his shoulders . . .

And had Dick been wrong? Joe smiled genially towards the lady in the tights who seemed in the act of "la savatting" the White-eyed Kaffir on the opposite wall. A smart lad, with a head on his shoulders . . . Had Joe a head on his shoulders? Joe could have laughed, split himself, it was too easy, too, too easy, it was money for jam. It was all the front you put on; doing the other fellow before he did you. He shifted the toothpick, slid his hand into his inside pocket, pulled out a thin, mottle-covered book. The book pleased Joe. The book said between the red ruled lines two hundred and two pounds ten shillings and sixpence to the credit of Mr. Joe Gowlan, 7 Brown Street, Shiphead. The book proved that Joe was a considerable success.

The 'phone rang, Joe lifted the receiver.

" Hello! Yes, Mr. Carr, yes. Certainly. The two-thirty. Ten shillings Slider, any to come Blackbird in the four o'clock. You're on, Mr. Carr."

Carr, the chemist in Bank Street that was, Joe ruminated; funny the people what bet you never think would bet. Carr looked as though he thought of nothing but jalap and titties, went to chapel every Sunday with his wife and had ten bob on regular twice a week. Won, too. Won a packet often. You could pretty well tell the ones what won, they were cautious and up to the game, never showed it when they won. And the losers, you could tell them just the same. Take Tracy, now, that young Tracy who had come to Shiphead last month, there was a born loser for you, if you like. With mug written all over his silly dial. From the minute young Tracy had made up to him in Markey's Billiard-room over a game of pin-pool and put a quid on Sally Sloper, finished last in a field of fourteen, he had taken young Tracy's number. Young Tracy was anybody's meat, thin, sloppy, fade-away chin, woodbine and laugh. And for all the woodbine young Tracy had money to play the horses, a matter of twenty quid straight he'd had on in the month and lost it all, lost every blinking time. Young Tracy had stopped being anybody's meat, he was Joe's meat now, and don't you make no mistake, thought Joe.

'Phone again.

" Hello! Hello! " Whatever Joe's private simplicities he was magnificent upon the 'phone. He had improved. He was sonorous, breezy, classy—as the occasion demanded. He did not murder King's English now, except to register extreme affability. He lolled back, grinning, not business this time, just the little lady from the pay box of the Picturedrome giving him a tinkle before her boss came down:

" Hello, Minnie, uh-huh, who did you think it was—Ching-lung-soo? Ha! Ha! Oh, you're barmy, Minnie! What! For the three o'clock . . . or any race? Hellup, Minnie, what d'ye think I am . . . Dr. Barnardo's Homes? Expect me to give away state secrets for nowt—I mean nothing. Not on your sweet little Pearl White life, Minnie! I told you before . . . *What!* . . ." His mouth open, gloating suddenly, Joe listened. " Well, that's different, Minnie, didn't I always say I would, Minnie? It was you that got up in the air about it. Why, yes, Minnie . . . if you've changed your mind I think I can put you on a cert." Swelling with elation, Joe kept his tone calm, persuasive, flattering. " You leave it to me, Minnie. Why yes, a cert . . . I always said you had it in you, Minnie. I'll do something for you if you do something for me, that's our motto, eh, Minnie? But listen, if you think you can slip it across me you're . . . oh, all right, Minnie. I was only thinking. Eleven o'clock then, outside the Drome, you bet your garters I'll be there. I'll bring your winnings! "

Joe rang off exultantly. He'd always said, hadn't he, that that was the way to do it . . . like in the school book, make the mountain come to Mahommey. His chest swelled. He wanted to get up and dance, do a cake-walk up and down the office. But no, he was beyond that now, a man of the world, cool, up to a thing or two. He composed himself, rested his toothpick in his waistcoat pocket, expertly lit a cigarette and got down to work.

First he took out all the morning's slips. He considered each slip expertly, scrutinised and weighed it before he passed it. In the end he had two heaps: one large heap of likely bets and another consisting of three slips, all of which, barring three separate and individual miracles, he knew for certain losers. Tracy, for instance, had three pounds—the biggest plunge he'd ever had—on Hydrangea, an old tubed pace-maker of a horse that wasn't even trying. Joe smiled slightly for the witless Tracy, as he did a mental calculation—no head for figgers, eh?—tore Tracy's slip into tiny fragments. Fulbrook and Sweet Orb were on the other slips—he tore these up also. Still smiling he looked at the clock: half-past one, no more coming in. Genially, he picked up the 'phone, chaffed the operator a bit, got through to Tynecastle, a few miles down the wire.

" Hello, that Dick Jobey! This is Joe, Dick. Not a bad day. Ha! Ha! That's right, Dick. Are you ready, right, Dick, off we go " . . . Joe began to read out the undestroyed slips. He read them out smartly, clearly, rather sonorously. He finished. " Yes, that's all, Dick. What? Am I sure? You bet I am, Dick. Ever know me make a mistake? Yes, that *is* the lot, Dick. Yes. So-long. See you Saturday."

Joe smacked down the receiver heartily, rose, winked at the lady in tights, cocked his hat, locked the office and went out. He crossed the bustling street to the Fountain, went through the bar, nodding here, there, everywhere. They all knew him . . . him . . . Joe Gowlan . . . commission agent . . . Big Joe Gowlan . . .

He had a beefsteak, a large thick juicy beefsteak, cooked red, the way he liked it with onions, chips and a pint of three X. He enjoyed every bit of the beef, every drop of the bitter. A rare capacity for enjoyment had Joe. Then he had a lump of Stilton and a roll. Good, that Stilton was . . . by God, it was good . . . what had he known about Stilton a couple of years ago? . . . he was going up, up, up in the world . . . him . . . Joe Gowlan.

The afternoon was more or less his own. He had a chat with Preston, Jack Preston the landlord of the Fountain . . . nice fella Jack was. Then he strolled down to Markey's and played a couple of games of snooker. Tracy was not there, funny Tracy not being there, but never mind, Tracy's three quid was safe and sound in Joe's inside pocket.

After the snooker Joe rolled over to Young Curley's gymnasium. Joe was a regular patron of Young Curley—a fella couldn't do nothing if he wasn't fit! Couldn't enjoy himself neither! Now *could* he? A little of everything in its right place, thought Joe blandly, remembering eleven o'clock and Minnie.

In the gym Joe stripped his beefy twelve stone, did a turn on the bars, shadow boxed, then sparred three rounds easy with Curley himself. He sweated beautifully, then got into the bath, soaked long and hot. After that a needle shower and a hard rub down. Curley didn't rub him hard enough.

" Harder, man, harder," Joe urged, " what d'ye think I pay you for? " He was the boss, wasn't he? and he had to take it out of Curley somehow. Curley had caught him too loud a wallop on the ear that last third round. Pink and glowing, Joe slid off the table like a big smooth seal. He padded to his cubicle, dressed carefully, threw Curley half a crown and sauntered out.

Five o'clock—just right for the office. On the way back to the Square he bought a late special, inspected the stop-press with a confident untroubled eye. As he had expected, Hydrangea nowhere, Fulbrook fourth in a field of six, Sweet Orb also ran. Joe gave no sign, only the mugs did that, perhaps there was a shade more swagger in his walk as he crossed the street and let himself into the office.

At his desk Joe went through the day's accounts, picked up the telephone and rang Tynecastle.

" Hello! Dick Jobey there? Hello . . . what? . . . Mr. Jobey left early . . . oh, all right, I'll ring again in the morning."

So Dick had left early; well, no wonder, thought Joe pleasantly, Dick couldn't have had none too good a day. He rose, whistling, straightening his tie. Then the door opened and Dick Jobey walked into the room.

" Why, he-*lo*, Dick, this is great. . . . I didn't expect you here . . ."

" Shut up, Gowlan. And sit down." Quiet and unsmiling, Dick Jobey indicated the chair.

Joe's jaw dropped:

" But, Dick, ole man . . ." Then Joe went a sickly green. Behind Dick Jobey, young Tracy came in, and behind Tracy an extremely large red-faced man with shoulders like the side of a house and a hard unpleasant eye. The large man shut the door and leant carefully against it. Young Tracy, looking a little less like a mug, put a woodbine in his mouth and gazed without pity upon Joe.

" Gowlan," Jobey said, " you're a dirty rotten rigger."

" What! " Joe gathered himself together, made an agonised effort to carry off a bluff. " Half a chance, Dick. What are you talking about? I've just rung you up at Tynecastle a minute ago trying to get you to tell you I'd forgotten to put through Hydrangea. *His* bet . . ." He indicated Tracy and went on with growing indignation. " Honest to God, Dick, I did forget and I rang you up the minute I remembered."

" Shut up, Gowlan. It isn't only to-day you've cribbed me. For a month Tracy has been punting with you. He's lost thirty-five pounds and I haven't had a penny of it."

" What! " roared Joe. " He says that, does he, the dirty liar. Don't you believe him, Dick. It's a blasted lie. My word's as good as his . . ."

" Shut up, Gowlan," Jobey said for the third time, almost wearily. " Tracy's with me. He works a month on all my branches like he's done with you. What kind of a leg do you take me for ? D'you think I don't check up on everything ? Everything, you fool! I know you've been cribbing me. You've had a good job, and a good chance. But now you're out, see, out on your neck, you low-down dirty rigger! "

All up, thought Joe. Rage burst over him. He blustered.

" Look out who you're calling a rigger. I could have you up for that . . . I . . ." He choked, for two pins he'd have taken a crack at Jobey, but there were three of them, curse it, three of them. And besides, he didn't care, he was well in over the business, yes, he was quids in. Then he went absolutely cold. Jobey, turning aside with a gesture of distaste, remarked:

" Go through him, Jim."

Jim removed himself from the door, came forward hard eye and all as if he meant to go through the wall. Oh, God! thought Joe, he's going to scrounge my dough. A sudden fury burst over him. I'll be damned, he flamed, I'll be damned if I let them. He set himself in a crouch and took a vicious crack at Jim's jaw. The blow landed but the jaw was cast iron. Jim lowered his bullet head and rushed in.

For three minutes the office rocked under the riot of the scrap. But it was no use, Joe was giving away two stone, at the end of it he took the floor with a terrific bump. He lay prone, Jim sitting on his chest. No use . . . no use at all . . . I'm giving him two stone . . . he had to let Jim go through him: five-pound notes and the mottled bank-book were placed upon the desk.

As Dick Jobey delicately pocketed the notes and lifted the bank-book Joe picked himself off the floor and began to blubber.

" For Gord's sake, Mr. Jobey, sir. It's my own money, my own savings . . ."

Jobey looked at his watch, quickly took up the 'phone, called the manager of the bank. Blubbering, Joe listened dazedly.

" I'm sorry to trouble you after hours but this is most important. Mr. Gowlan wants to cash a cheque most urgently. It's Jobey of Tynecastle speaking, yes, Mr. Dick Jobey . . . would you as a special favour to me oblige Mr. Gowlan. Thank you, yes, right away, I'm extremely obliged to you."

" I won't go," shrieked Joe. " I'll be damned if I go."

" I give you one minute to make up your mind," Jobey said sadly. " If you don't go I'll call up the police."

Joe went. The silent procession of four marched to the bank, and as silently marched back to the office.

" Hand it over," Jobey said.

" For the love of Gord," Joe howled, " some of it's my own money."

" Hand it over," Jobey said. Jim stood there, ready.

O Christ, thought Joe, he'll only bounce me again. He handed it over, all of it, in twenties, fives and sovereigns, all of his lovely money, his lovely two hundred pounds, all that he had . . .

" For Gord's sake, Mr. Jobey," he implored abjectly.

On his way to the door Dick Jobey paused. A look of contempt came into his face. He picked a single sovereign from the money in his pocket, flung it at Joe.

" Here," he said. " Buy yourself a hat." And with Tracy and Jim he went out.

For ten minutes Joe sat rocking himself in a passion of misery, tears running down his cheeks. Then he rose and picked up the sovereign. A perfect fury possessed him. He kicked at a chair, kicked and kicked at it. He began to wreck the office. He wrecked the office thoroughly, viciously. It was all second-hand cheap furniture and very little of it. What there was he battered to matchwood. He spat upon the floor. He cursed Jobey, cursed and cursed him. He took a blue pencil and wrote big on the wall, *Jobey is a dirty bastard.* He wrote further fierce, unutterable obscenities. Then he sat down on the window-sill and counted his money. With the pound and some change in his pocket he had exactly thirty shillings. Thirty shillings. Thirty pieces of silver!

He banged out of the ruined office, went straight to the Fountain. He put ten shillings in his waistcoat pocket. With the rest he got drunk. He sat drinking, until half-past ten, all by himself. At half-past ten he was broodingly, rampantly drunk. He rose and swayed over to the Picturedrome.

At eleven Minnie came out, blasé, yellow-haired, narrow-chested, sporting her gold-crowned tooth and all. There was no doubt about it, Minnie was a tart.

Joe took Minnie in, swaying gently, looking her up and down.

" Come on, Minnie," he said thickly. " I've got your winnings here. Ten bob. Nothing to what I'll get you to-morrow."

" Oh," said Minnie in a disillusioned voice. " You all want the same thing."

" Come on," said Joe.

Minnie came on. Joe didn't buy himself a hat that night. But because of that night he bought several later on.

XX

The trees of the Avenue stood silent in the teeming rain, their smoke-grimed branches dripping water, vague dismal shapes, like mourning women, lining the Avenue in the dank twilight, weeping. But David, walking quickly up the wet pathway, paid no attention to the weeping trees. His head was bent, his expression concentrated and fixed. Under the stress of some positive emotion, he entered the grounds of the Law, rang the bell and waited. In a moment the door was opened, not by Ann, the maid, but by Hilda Barras, and at the sight of him she flushed unexpectedly.

"You're early!" she exclaimed, controlling herself immediately. "Much too early. Arthur's with father in the study."

He entered the hall and took off his wet coat.

"I came early because I wanted to see your father."

"Father?" For all her assumption of irony she observed his face intently. "You sound serious."

"Do I?"

"Yes, quite painfully serious."

He felt the sarcasm in her voice but he did not answer. Somehow he liked Hilda, her uncompromising rudeness was at least sincere. A pause followed. Though clearly she was curious to know what was in his mind she did not press him further. Indifferently she remarked:

"They're in the study then, as I said."

"May I go up?"

She shrugged her shoulders without answering. He was conscious of her dark eyes upon his, then she spun upon her heel and was gone. He stood for a moment collecting himself before ascending the stairs. Then he knocked and went into the study.

The room was brightly lit and warm; a good fire blazed on the hearth. Barras was seated at the desk, while Arthur stood beside the fireplace, in front of him. As David entered Arthur smiled in his usual friendly manner, but Barras's welcome was much less cordial. He swung round his padded leather chair and stared at David with a blank inquiry.

"Well?" he said abruptly, "what is it?"

David looked from one to the other. He compressed his lips firmly.

"I wanted to have a word with you," he said to Barras.

Richard Barras lay back in his chair. He was, actually, in an excellent humour. By the afternoon post he had received a letter from the Lord Mayor of Tynecastle asking him to accept the convenership of the organisation committee in connection with the building of the new wing for the City Royal Hospital. Barras was already on the Bench, three years president of the local education committee, and now this. He was pleased, sniffing the prospect of a knighthood like a well-fed mastiff the chances of a meaty bone. In his own exquisitely precise handwriting—

no such machine as a typewriter existed at the Law—he was framing a suitable acceptance. As he sat there he embodied an almost sensual satisfaction that life should be so gratifying an affair.

" What is it you have to say ? " he exclaimed; and observing David's glance towards Arthur he added impatiently: " Go on, man. If it's about Arthur he'd better hear it."

David took a quick determined breath. Under the almost judicial force of Barras's personality what he was going to say suddenly seemed presumptuous and absurd. But he had resolved to speak to Barras; nothing would shake him.

" It's about the new workings in the Paradise," he rushed on before Barras could interpose. " I daresay I've no right to talk, I'm out of the Neptune now, but my father's there and my two brothers. You know my father, Mr. Barras, he's been thirty years in the pit, he's not an alarmist. But ever since you got the new contract and started stripping off the barrier he's been worried to death you'll have an inrush."

Silence in the room. Barras continued to measure David with a coldly inquiring eye.

" If your father doesn't like the Paradise he can leave it. He had this same insane notion seven years ago. He's always been a trouble maker."

David felt his blood rise; but he made himself speak calmly.

" It isn't just my father. Quite a number of the men don't like it. They say you're travelling too near the old waste, the workings of Old Neptune which must be chock full of water."

" They know what to do then," Barras said icily. " They can get out."

" But they can't. They've got their living to think of. Almost every one of them has a wife and children to support."

Barras's features hardened imperceptibly.

" Let them go to that Heddon fellow then. That's what he's there for, isn't it ? They pay him to exploit their grievances. The matter has nothing to do with you."

A sudden tension gathered in the air and Arthur gazed from David to his father with growing uneasiness. Arthur hated trouble, anything approaching a scene caused him acute distress. David kept his eyes on Barras. He had turned pale but his expression remained determined and controlled.

" All I'm asking is that you should give a fair hearing to what these men have got to say."

Barras laughed shortly.

" Indeed," he answered cuttingly. " So you expect me to sit here and let my workmen teach me my business."

" You'll do nothing ? "

" Emphatically, no! "

David clenched his teeth, restrained the turmoil of indignation within him. In a low voice he said:

" Very well, Mr. Barras. If you will take up my meaning wrongly, I can't say any more. No doubt it was quite out of place for me to say anything at all." He stood for a moment as though hoping Barras might speak, then he turned and quietly left the room.

Arthur did not immediately follow. The silence lengthened; then diffidently, with his eyes on the floor, Arthur said:

" I don't think he meant any harm, father. He's a good chap, David Fenwick."

Barras did not answer.

Arthur flushed. Although he had taken a great many cold baths and knew his series of little red books almost by heart he still flushed abominably. But he continued with a sort of desperation:

" You don't think he has any justification then ? It sticks in my mind —what he said. As a matter of fact a queer thing happened in the Paradise to-day, father. The Scupper pump was overcome in the afternoon shift."

" Well ? "

" There was quite an accumulation of water in Swelly."

" Indeed! " Barras picked up his pen and inspected the nib.

Arthur paused: the information seemed to mean nothing to his father. He still sat enthroned, judicial and half abstracted. Lamely, Arthur went on:

" It appeared to me there was quite a come of water in Scupper Flats. In fact it looked as if a block of undercut coal was forced off the Dyke as if there was pressure behind it. I thought you might like to know, father."

" Like to know," Barras repeated almost as though he recollected himself. " Oh yes! " Then his sardonic pleasantry: " I am obliged to you, of course, Arthur. I have no doubt you have anticipated Armstrong by a good sixteen hours, it's very gratifying."

Arthur looked downcast and hurt, his eyes travelled over the pattern of the carpet.

" If only we had the plans of the Old Neptune workings, father. We should know then for certain. It's the most maddening thing to me, father, that they didn't keep plans in those old days, father."

The motionless quality of justice had never left Barras's figure. He could not sneer. His voice held merely a cold rebuke:

" You are a little late with your condemnation, Arthur. If you had been born eighty years ago, I have no doubt you would have completely revolutionised the industry."

There was another silence. Barras gazed at the half-finished letter on the desk before him. He picked it up and seemed to study it with a certain stern admiration for its phrasing. He thought out a fresh turn to the final sentence, lifted his pen. Then he rediscovered Arthur still standing by the door. He studied Arthur deliberately, as he had studied the letter, and gradually the severity went out of his face. He looked as near amusement as he could ever get. He said:

" Your interest in the Neptune is very satisfactory, Arthur. And I'm glad to see you have ideas on its management. In a few years' time I have no doubt you will be running the mine—and me! " Had Barras been capable of real laughter he must certainly have laughed now: " In the meantime I suggest you confine yourself to the elementary things and leave the complicated business alone. Go and find that Fenwick fellow and get some trigonometry into your foolish head."

When Arthur had gone, apologetic and vaguely ashamed, Barras returned to his letter of acceptance. Where had he got to again ? What was that phrase again ? Oh yes, he remembered. In his precise, resolute handwriting he continued: " For myself . . ."

XXI

THE months passed quickly, summer to autumn, autumn to winter, and David's recollection of his interview with Barras became less painful. Yet often, when he thought of it, he winced. He had been a fool, a presumptuous fool. Work still proceeded in Scupper Flats, the contract would be completed by the New Year. His visits to the Law had ceased. Arthur had taken his certificate with honours; and at the same time Dan Teasdale had obtained his ticket.

And now he had flung himself, with a kind of fury, into his own work. His final B.A. examination came on December 14th and he had made up his mind to take the thing then, to take it if it killed him. Putting off and putting off had sickened him, he shut his ears to Jenny's wheedlings, got down to the last of his correspondence classes, and spent every second week-end with Carmichael at Wallington. He felt he would be all right, it was just a question of making sure.

Jenny became the poor neglected little wife—Jenny was always little when she required sympathy, she shrank from sheer pathos. She complained that she had no " callers," no friends, she looked around for companionship, she even cultivated Mrs. Wept, who was of course already a " caller " in so far as she called for the rent. It went well until Mrs. Wept took Jenny to the meeting. Jenny returned from the meeting much amused. David could not get out of her what had happened except that the whole thing had been very unrefined.

As a last resource Jenny turned back upon her own family, imagining that it would, perhaps, be nice to have one of them through to stay. But who ? Not ma, this time, ma was getting so fat and heavy she just sat and sat, so much dead weight in the house. Phyllis and Clarry couldn't come, they were both working in Slattery's now and couldn't get away. Dad couldn't either, and when he could it was always pigeons; turn into a pigeon himself would dad one of these days!

Sally remained. Sally was not at Slattery's. Sally had begun very brightly by being in the Tynecastle Telephone Exchange and all might still have been right with Sally had Sally stayed on at the telephone exchange. It was clean and classy work being in the Tynecastle Exchange, with all the advantages. Unfortunately dad had never got it out of his silly head that Sally had talent for the stage. Always taking her to music-halls, encouraging her to mimic the variety stars, sending her to tap-dancing, generally playing the fool. And as if this were not enough, he had actually persuaded Sally to enter for a Saturday night go-as-you-please at the Empire. They were low, these go-as-you-please competitions, all the rag-tag went in for them.

It was very sad, but Sally had won this go-as-you-please. Not only had she won the first prize but she had so knocked the low Saturday night gallery crowd that the management had given her an engagement for the whole of the following week. At the end of that week Sally had got the offer of a six weeks' tour on the Payne-Gould northern circuit.

Why, oh, why, asked Jenny sadly, had Sally been fool enough to take that offer? For Sally had taken the offer, chucked the classy exchange with all the advantages and done her six weeks' circuit. That, of course, was the end of Sally, the finish, absolutely.

Sally had been out of a job four months now. No more circuit, no more offers, no more anything. As for the telephone exchange they wouldn't even look at Sally again. Pity! But then the Exchange was classy and would never have you back if once you did the dirty on it. Yes, sighed Jenny, she's done for herself now I'm afraid, poor Sally!

Still it would be nice to have Sally through to stay, nice, and a kindness to the unfortunate girl. Perhaps Jenny had a complacent sense of patronage behind her sisterly benevolence. She always wanted to *show* people did Jenny.

Sally arrived in Sleescale towards the third week in November and was greeted with rapture by her sister. Jenny was delighted, hugging her dearest Sally, full of "well I nevers" and "isn't this just like old times," full of little confidences and ripples of laughter and showings to the newly furnished spare bedroom and running upstairs with hot water and clean towels and gay tryings on of Sally's hat. Oh, my dear, isn't it *just*! David was pleased: he had not seen Jenny so happy or excited for a long time.

But the rapture went out of it comically soon, the running upstairs soon became a bore, the ripples of laughter wore themselves out and all the beautiful novelty of dearest Sally faded and was finished. "She's changed, David," Jenny announced sadly towards the end of the first week, " she's not the same girl at all, mind you I never did think much of . . ."

David did not find Sally changed except that she might be quieter and improved. Perhaps Jenny's effusiveness made her subdued. Perhaps the thought that she was finished sobered Sally down. She had lost her pertness. There was a new thoughtfulness behind her eyes. She made herself useful running errands and about the house. She did not ask to be amused and all Jenny's arrangements and display merely served to shut her up. Once or twice in the kitchen, seated on the plain deal table swinging her legs before the big fire she condescended, as Jenny put it, to come out of herself. Then she chattered away sixteen to the dozen, telling them in a frank and merry way of her experiences on the Payne-Gould tour, of the landladies, the managers, the " moth-eaten " dressing-rooms, of her own greenness and nervousness and mistakes. She had no pretentiousness. She could take off people beautifully but now she took off herself even better. Her best story was terribly against herself, of how she got the bird in Shiphead—Jenny simply loved to hear that story!—but Sally told it joyfully, without a trace of bitterness. She had a carelessness about herself. She never did up, never bothered about the kind of soap she used, always washed her face in cold water, she had very few clothes and, unlike Jenny who was always altering and stitching and pressing, keeping her clothes in the most beautiful condition, she took no care of them whatever. She had one brown tweed costume and wore it nearly all the time; as Jenny remarked, that thing was never off her back. But Sally's method was to buy a suit, wear it out, then buy another one. She had no good clothes, Sunday hats, or *adorable* fancy underwear. She wore plain serge knickers and flat shoes. Her figure was short and rather tubby. She was very plain.

David enjoyed Sally quite a lot though Jenny's increasing petulance began to worry him again. One evening, however, it was the first of December, when he came in from school Jenny met him with a return of her old animation.

" Guess who's in Sleescale ? " she demanded, smiling all over her face.

Sally, setting the table for David's tea, said sadly:

" Buffalo Bill."

" Be quiet," Jenny said. " Just because you don't happen to like him, Miss Impudence! But really though, David, you never would guess, honestly you'd never. It's Joe! "

" Joe! " David repeated, " Joe Gowlan ? "

" Mm-huh! " Jenny nodded brightly. " And, *my*, doesn't he look well. You could have knocked me down with a feather when I met him in Church Street. Of course *I* wasn't going to recognise him, not me, I wasn't too pleased with Joe Gowlan the last time I saw him, but he came up and spoke to me nice as nice. He's improved wonderful."

Sally looked at her sister.

" Is it cold meat for David's tea ? " she said.

" No, no," said Jenny absently, " just a plain tea to-night, we'll keep the meat for supper. I've asked Joe to drop in, I knew you would want to see him, David."

" Why, yes, of course."

" Not that I'm *all that* anxious myself, mind you. But I did think I'd like to let Mr. Joe Gowlan see he's not the only one that has got on. Believe me, with my blue china and the doyleys and cold meat and heated-up peas I'll show Mr. Joe a thing or two. Pity it wasn't the cod we had yesterday, I could have used the new ivorine fish slice. Never mind, though, I'll borrow Mrs. Wept's carvers, we'll have a pretty nice display I can tell you."

" Why don't you hire a butler when you're about it ? " Sally said mildly.

Jenny coloured. The pleasantness left her face. She turned on Sally. She said:

" You're an ungrateful little hussy, you are, to stand there and talk to me like that. I think I've done pretty well by *you* when it comes to the bit. The idea of you standing there criticising me because I ask a gentleman to supper in my own house. The idea! And after all that I've done for you. You go home, my lady, if you don't like it."

" I'll go home, if you want me to," Sally said. And she went to get David's tea.

Joe dropped in about seven o'clock. He wore his light brown suit, his watch-chain, that really impressive derby, and an air of affable simplicity. He was not loud, nor boisterous, nor full of brag, he was nothing that David might have feared. Joe had really been forced to come home and, though Joe could never look that way, Joe was quite a bit under the weather. In plain truth, Joe was still out of a job. He was turning over in his mind the idea of going back to Millington's; after all hadn't Stanley Millington promised to give him a lift up, hadn't he now, the big sod ? Yes, he would go to Millington's all right. But not yet, not just yet. There was something else, something on Joe's mind that Joe didn't enjoy. Joe was worried about himself, worried about something. God, what a fool a fella could be, but maybe it wasn't something, maybe it was nothing after all.

The general effect of this bodily and spiritual uncertainty was to throw an air of subdued virtue about Joe, to establish him as a man who had at last returned to see his aged father and was modestly reticent about his obvious success in life. And he was so pleased to see David, so deeply touched to see his " ole pal " again! It was quite affecting.

Towards Jenny, Joe was very humble, apologetic and subdued. He praised her china, her doyleys, her frock, her food. He ate, for one prosperously acquainted with a richer diet than cold beef and peas, a considerable supper. He was struck, oh, immensely struck by the improvement in Jenny's social setting.

" By gum," he kept repeating, " I must say this goes one better than Scottswood Road! " His manners were quite elevated. He no longer foraged with his knife for errant peas. He " helped " the ladies. He was handsomer than ever and his tone was almost reverent.

It was honey to Jenny, her formal " company " manner slowly slid from her, she became pleasantly arch, condescending, chatty in a lady-like way.

Not that Joe talked much to Jenny. No, no! It was clear that Joe had little time for " wimmen " now—his interest in Jenny was merely friendly and polite. As for Sally, he never looked at her at all. Joe was all for David, full of questions, interest, admiration. It was great that David was sitting his B.A. in a fortnight, those week-ends of study with Carmichael were certainly a brain wave of the first degree. Always the lad to have brain waves, eh, Davey ole man ? Joe and David talked long after supper and Jenny kept slipping in and out, humming pleasantly and graciously inquiring from time to time how they were getting on. Sally was washing the dishes, with a certain restrained vehemence, in the scullery.

" It's been fine seeing you again," David said at last as Joe rose to go.

" No more nor seeing you, ole man," Joe said. " Believe me it's the whole cheese. I'll be here a week or two, I expect, we got to see more of each other. Walk down the road with me now. Ah, come on. It's early yet. By the bye," Joe paused, twiddling his watch-chain, a candid amusement in his eye. " I almost forgot, Davey, I cleaned myself out over the old dad this afternoon, gave him a packet, a regular packet, everything I'd got, felt sort of generous like seeing him again I suppose. You couldn't lend us a couple of quid or so—just till I hear from the bank ? Just an ole couple of pounds."

" A couple of pounds . . . Joe ? " David stared at Joe, taken aback.

" Oh, never mind, then." Joe's smile departed, he looked hurt, offended; " palship " and decency outraged suffused his shiny face. " Never mind if you don't want to . . . it's nothing to me . . . I'll get it easy somewhere else."

" Well, Joe . . ." Joe's wounded expression cut David, he felt mean, horrible. He had about ten pounds tucked away in the chest of drawers in the bedroom, money saved for his examination expenses, and it was money that had taken some saving. He said suddenly: " Of course I'll lend you it, Joe. Hold on . . ." He dashed upstairs and took three pounds and came back and offered them to Joe.

" Right, Davey." Joe's belief in humanity was mercifully restored. He beamed. " I knew you'd oblige an ole pal. Just till the end of the week, you understand."

As they went up the street together Joe cocked his hat a trifle. His good night to David rang like a benediction.

David turned down Cowpen Street. He had meant to go up to see his father to-night, but it was getting towards ten o'clock now. Joe had kept him longer than he expected, and Martha had a way of frowning upon him when he slipped in late as if the very lateness of his visit were a slight on her. He walked along Freehold Street, meaning to cut through Bethel Street, when suddenly he saw his brother Hughie coming through the darkness, running swiftly down the crown of the road in his shorts and singlet. David called:

" Hughie! Hughie! " He had to call quickly, Hughie was going so fast.

Hughie stopped and crossed over. Although he had run three miles his breath came easily, he was in perfect condition. When he saw that it was David he gave a whoop and promptly fell upon his neck.

" Davey, you son of a gun! "

David disentangled himself.

" For heaven's sake, Hughie."

But Hughie for once was irrepressible.

" It's happened, Davey. It's happened at last. Did you know ? I had the letter this afternoon. I got it when I came out the pit. They've asked me, Davey. Oh, help, isn't it great! "

" Asked you what, Hughie ? " asked David, bewildered. He had never seen Hughie like this, never, why . . . if he didn't know Hughie, he'd have sworn Hughie was drunk.

The silent Hughie was drunk, intoxicated with delight.

" Asked me to play for Tynecastle! Could you believe it, man! They were watching the match last Saturday and I never knew a thing about it . . . and I scored three goals . . . I did the hat trick, Davey . . . and now they've asked me to play a trial with the reserves at St. James's Park on Saturday week. Oh, heavens, isn't it great. If I do all right I'm signed, Davey . . . signed for the United, Davey, *the United*! " Hughie's voice cracked amongst delirious heights.

David understood: it was here at last, Hughie's hoped for, longed for, impossible dream. Not for nothing had Hughie martyred himself, bound himself to monkish ways, steeled himself against those glamorous glances, that so often sought out his in Lamb Street on Saturday nights. Suddenly David felt glad, a rush of genuine happiness came over him, he held out his hand in congratulation.

" I'm delighted, Hughie." How comically inadequate words were to express the real joy he felt.

Hughie went on.

" They've had their eye on me for months. Did I tell you that before ? I can't think what I'm saying. But you may be sure of one thing. I'll play the game of my life on Saturday week. Oh, Davey, man, isn't it wonderful! " That last ecstasy seemed to bring Hughie to himself. He coloured and stole a look at David. He said: " I'm fair sloppy to-night.

It's excitement." He paused. " You'll come to the match though, Davey ? "

" I'll be there, Hughie. I'll come and shout my head off."

Hughie smiled: his old diffident smile.

" Sammy's coming too. He says if I don't score six he'll wring my neck! " He balanced on his heels for a minute in his familiar style, then he said: " I'd better not catch cold. I'm not taking any chances now, lad. Good night, Davey."

" Good night, Hughie."

Hughie went off, running, disappearing into the darkness of the night.

David returned home, with a sense of warmth about his heart. He let himself into the house. Sally was alone, sitting crouched up in a chair by the fire with her legs tucked in and her lips drawn down. She looked very small and silent. After Hughie's elation it struck David that she was sad.

" Where's Jenny ? " he asked.

" Gone to bed! "

" Oh! " He paused, disappointed. Right away he had wanted to let Jenny know about Hughie. Then, smiling again, he began to tell Sally.

Crouched there, she studied him, watching him steadily with her face masked by the shadow of her hand.

" Isn't that grand ? " he concluded. " You know, not so much what he's got . . . but because he was so set on getting it."

She sighed. She was silent. Then she said:

" Yes, it's pretty nice getting what you want."

He looked at her.

" What's the matter ? "

" Nothing."

" You don't look like it was nothing. You look upset."

" Well," she said slowly, " I've been rather stupid. Just before you came in I had a row with Jenny."

He looked away quickly.

" I'm sorry about that."

" Don't be sorry. It's not the first and I'm afraid it's been coming for a long, long time. I shouldn't have told you. I should have been noble and just smiled myself away to-morrow all polite and self-sacrificing."

" Are you going to-morrow ? "

" Yes, I'm going. It's time I was getting back to Alfred. He doesn't get his place in the house and he smells of pigeons but I'm rather struck on old Alfred for all that."

He said:

" I wish I understood what the trouble was."

She said:

" I'm glad you don't."

He stared at her doubtfully.

" I don't like you going this way. Please don't go."

" I must go," she said. " I didn't bring a change of lingerie." She gave a short laugh and then burst straight into tears.

He simply didn't know what to make of her.

She stopped crying at once. She said:

" Don't pay any attention. I've been slightly unstuck ever since I came to bits on the prima donna act. I don't want any sympathy. It's better to be a has been than a never was. I'm quite cheerful and I think I'll go to bed."

" But I am sorry, Sally."

" Shut up," she said. " It's high time you stopped being sorry for other people and started being sorry for yourself."

" What on earth have I got to be sorry about ? "

" Nothing." She got up. " It's too late to be soulful. I'll tell you in the morning." Abruptly, she said good night and went to bed.

Next morning he did not see her. She had risen early and left by the seven o'clock train.

All that day David worried about Sally: when he returned from school he spoke to Jenny.

Jenny gave her little complacent laugh.

" She's jealous, my dear, absolutely jealous."

He drew back disgusted.

" Oh no," he said, " I'm convinced it isn't that."

She nodded indulgently.

" She always had her eye on you, even in the Scottswood Road days. She hated to see you spoony on me. And she hates it even worse now! " She paused, smiling up at him. " You still *are* spoony on me, aren't you, David ? "

He looked at her queerly, with a queer hardness in his eyes. He said:

" Yes, I do love you, Jenny. I know you're chock full of faults—just as I am myself. Sometimes you say and do things that I loathe. Sometimes I simply can't stand you. But I can't help myself. I love you."

She did not attempt to understand him but took the general drift of his remarks as complimentary.

" Funny bones," she said archly. And went back to her novel.

He was not accustomed to analyse his feeling for Jenny. He simply accepted it. But two days later, on the following Friday, an incident occurred which disturbed him strangely.

As a rule he did not leave the school until four o'clock. But on this particular day Strother came along at three o'clock to " take his class." It was Strother's habit to take a class once a week, on this day and at this hour, to determine the progress of the class and to make forcible and pointed comment in the presence of the master of that class. Lately, however, Strother had been kinder to David since he had been working so strenuously for the B.A.; he said curtly, yet pleasantly enough, that

David might go.

David went. He went first of all to Hans Messuer's for a hair cut. While Hans, a fat meek smiling man with a moustache turned up like the Kaiser's, was cutting his hair David talked to Swee who had just come out the Neptune and was shaving himself in the back shop. He had a cheerful and unedifying conversation with Swee. Swee was always cheerful and could be very unedifying. He could shave and talk and be cheerful and unedifying all at the same time without cutting himself. The talk with Swee did David good but it took only half an hour. He reached home at half-past three instead of quarter-past four. Then as he came up the lane behind the Dunes he met Joe Gowlan coming out of his house.

David stopped. He stopped absolutely dead. He had not seen Joe since he loaned him the money; it gave him the most singular sensation to see Joe walking out the house as though actually it were Joe's house. He felt the sensation like an acute embarrassment especially as Joe seemed acutely embarrassed too.

" I thought I'd left my stick the other night," Joe explained, looking everywhere but at David.

" You didn't have a stick, Joe."

Joe laughed, glancing up and down the lane. Perhaps he thought the stick might be there.

" I did have a stick . . . a cane . . . I always carry it, but I'm blowed if I haven't lost it somewhere."

Just that; then Joe nodding, smiling, hurrying; hurrying to get away.

David went up the path and into his house thoughtfully.

" Jenny," he said, " what did Joe want here ? "

" Joe! " She darted a look at him; got very red in the face.

" I've just met him . . . coming out of this house."

She stood in the middle of the floor in that lost, taken aback way, then her temper flared.

" I can't help it if you did meet him. I'm not his keeper. He only looked in for a minute. What are you staring at me like that for ? "

" Nothing," he said, turning away. Why had Jenny said nothing about the stick ?

" Nothing *what* ? " she insisted violently.

He looked out of the window. Why had Joe called at an hour when he was likely to be at the school ? Why on earth ? Suddenly an explanation struck him: the unusual time of Joe's call, Joe's nervousness, his hurry to get away, everything. Joe had borrowed three pounds from him, and Joe was still unable to pay it back!

His face lightened, he swung round to Jenny.

" Joe did call for his stick . . . didn't he ? "

" *Yes*," she cried, quite hysterically, and came right into his arms. " Of course he did. What in the world did you think he came for ? '

He soothed her, patting her lovely soft hair.

" I'm sorry, Jenny, darling. It did give me the oddest feeling, though, to see him walking out of my house as if he owned it."

" Oh, David," she wept, " how can you say such things ? "

What had he said ? He smiled, his lips touched her white slender neck. She pleaded:

" You're not angry with me, David ? "

Why under heaven should he be angry with her ?

" Heavens, no, my dear."

Reassured, she lifted her limpid swimming eyes. She kissed him. She was sweet to him all that evening, most terribly sweet. She got up actually next morning, which was Saturday, to give him his morning tea. When she saw him off on his bicycle that same afternoon to spend the week-end working with Carmichael she clung to him and would hardly let him go.

But she did let him go after one last big hug, as she called it. Then she went into the house, humming lightly, pleased that David loved her, pleased with herself, pleased with the nice long free week-end before her.

Of course she wouldn't let Joe come to supper to-night, she wouldn't dream of such a thing, the cheek, indeed! of Joe for even suggesting it. To talk about old times he had said, well, could you believe it. She hadn't even bothered to tell David about Joe's impertinence, it was not the kind of thing a lady cared to mention.

That afternoon she took a pleasant stroll down the town. Outside Murchison's she paused, debating, as it were, and deciding well, yes, it was a useful thing to have in the house. She went in and elegantly ordered a bottle of port, invalid port, to be sent down, this afternoon, for sure now, Mr. Murchison. David didn't like it, she knew. but David had lately been most unreasonable and he was away in any case and would never know. What was the old saying again, what the eye didn't see the heart didn't grieve for. Good, wasn't it ? Smiling a little Jenny went home, changed her dress, scented herself behind her ears, like it said in *Home Chat*, and made herself nice, Jenny did, even if it was only to be nice for herself.

At seven o'clock Joe came to the door. Jenny answered his ring.

" Well, I declare," she exclaimed, shocked. " After all I said."

" Ah, come on now, Jenny," Joe said ingratiatingly, " don't be hard on a fella."

" The very idea," said Jenny. " I've a good mind not to let you in."

But she did let him in. And she did not let him out till it was very late. She was flushed and disarranged and rather sheepish. She giggled. The port, the invalid port was finished.

XXII

On the next day, Sunday the 7th of December, Jack Reedy, eldest of the Reedy brothers, and his marrow, Cha Leeming, worked their shift in the Scupper Flats, an extra shift because they were doubling to complete the P. W. contract. Robert was in the same shift though much further up the Flats at the head of the slant. His heading was bad. The heading of Reedy and Leeming was good, about one mile and a half from the pit-bottom. At five o'clock the shift stopped work and came out of the pit. Reedy and Cha Leeming, before they came out, left a fine jud of unworked coal on the face of their heading. About five or six tubs of coal would be in this jud when it was brought down, good coal and easy to get when they came in next morning.

Well satisfied, Jack Reedy and Cha stopped at the Salutation for a drink on the way home. Jack had a bit of money. For all it was Sunday night they had several drinks and then several more. Jack got merry and Cha was half-seas over. Arm in arm together they rolled up the Terraces, singing. They went to bed. Next morning both slept in. But neither appreciated the point of this sleeping in till later.

At half-past three of the morning of Monday Dinning, the deputy in charge of the district, entered the Paradise section and made his examination of the workings. He did this before admitting the morning shift. Stick in hand, head bent, Dinning plodded diligently through the Mixen and Scupper Flats. Everything seemed satisfactory so Dinning returned to his kist in the Scupper ropeway and wrote out his statutory report.

The shift then came in, one hundred and five persons, made up of eighty-seven men and eighteen boys. Two of the shift, Bob Ogle and Tally Brown, made up to Dinning in the ropeway.

"Jack and Cha slep' in," Bob Ogle said.

"To hell!" Dinning said.

"Can Tally and me hev that heading?" Bob said. "It's a bitch of a one we hev."

"To hell," Dinning said. "Take it, then!"

Ogle and Brown went up the ropeway with a bunch of men, amongst whom were Robert, Hughie, Slogger Leeming, Harry Brace, Swee Messer, Tom Reedy, Ned Softley and Jesus Wept. Tom Reedy's young brother Pat, a boy of fifteen, whose first week it was inbye proper, followed on behind.

Robert was in good spirits. He felt well and hopeful. He had slept soundly, his cough had not been so troublesome; in the last few months, with a strong sense of relief, he had come to the conclusion that his fears of flooding had been unfounded. As he walked up through the blackness of the slant, which was low and narrow, four foot high, six hundred feet below the surface and two miles from the main shaft, he found himself beside little Pat Reedy, youngest of the Reedy tribe.

"Eh, Pat," he joked, encouraging him. "It's a fine place ye've come for your holidays." He clapped Pat on the back and went down through the dip known as the Swelly and up to his far heading with Slogger. The heading was drier than it had been for weeks.

Ogle and Brown were already in their heading further back. They found the jud left by Jack and Cha. They started work, drilled two yard shot holes into the face of the jud and another of the same depth to the right of the projection. At quarter to five Dinning, the deputy, came along. He charged and fired the shots. Eight tubs of coal came down.

Dinning saw that the shots had fired well and the line of the coal face straightened.

"To hell, lads," he said, nodding his satisfaction, "that's all reet." He went back up the Scupper ropeway to his kist.

But ten minutes later Tom Reedy, the putter, came after him. Tom said, in a great hurry:

"Ogle says will you come inbye. There's water comin' through the shot holes, he says."

Dinning appeared to reflect.

"To hell, he says."

Tom Reedy and Dinning went back to the heading. Dinning took a look at the face, a real good look. He found a thin trickle of water coming through the middle of it between the two shots he had fired. There appeared to be no pressure behind it. He smelled the water. The water had a bad smell, a smell of styfe which meant black damp about, he knew it was not virgin coal water. He did not like the look of it at all.

"To hell, lads," Dinning said, dismayed. "Ye've holed. Ye better try and get rid of some o't."

Ogle, Brown and Tom Reedy began to tub the water, to try and get rid of it by letting it through the pack walls on the low side of the drawing road. At that moment Geordie Dinning, who was Dinning's son, and a hand putter with Tom Reedy in Scupper Flats, came by.

"Here, Geordie, lad," Dinning cried. Though Dinning said to hell without offence and without knowing he said it, strangely enough he never said it before his son.

Dinning took his son Geordie back to the kist with him. While he was hurrying to his kist he thought about the branch telephone but the telephone was some way off and it was still so early he was afraid Hudspeth might not yet have come to bank. Besides, Dinning was not very good at thinking. At the kist he got out his stub of copying-ink pencil and wrote two notes. He wrote laboriously, wetting the pencil occasionally on his tongue. In the first note this is what Dinning wrote:

Mr. Wm. Hudspeth, Under-Viewer, Dear Sir,

The water has holed into Scupper No. 6 *Branch and is over the boots in the slope and more is coming and there is more going to the haulage than the pumps can manage. You might come inbye and see it and I will be at the kist in Paradise ropeway if not there in Mixen number two Bench. P.S. There is very great danger of flooding out. Yours H. Dinning.*

In the second note this is what Dinning wrote:

The water has broken through Scupper No. 6 Branch. Frank will you warn the other men in the Paradise in case. Yrs. H. Dinning.

Dinning turned to his son. He was a slow man, a slow thinker and speaker. But now he spoke quicker than usual. He said:

" Run, Geordie, to Frank Logan, the fireman, and gie him this note. Then go outbye and up to the under-viewer's house with this. Run now, Geordie, man, run."

Geordie went off with the two notes. He went quickly. When he came to the junction he looked for the onsetter but the onsetter was not there. Then Geordie heard a faint thump and the air commenced to reverse. Geordie knew that meant trouble in the Scupper Flats. He knew he wanted to get outbye but he knew also what his father had told him to do and between the two he lost his head and began to walk up the middle of the Paradise roadway.

As young Geordie Dinning walked up the middle of the Paradise roadway suddenly out of the darkness came a train of four loaded tubs running loose. The tubs had broken amain from further up. Geordie shouted. Geordie jumped half a second too late. The train of tubs smashed down on him, took him twenty yards with a rush, flung him, went over him, and left his mangled body on the roadway. The train of tubs roared on.

After his son had gone Dinning stood for some moments satisfied that he had done what he ought to do. Then he heard a loud bang, it was the thump his son had heard, only being nearer he heard it as a bang. Suddenly petrified, Dinning stood with his mouth open. He had expected trouble but nothing so sudden or terrible as this. He knew it was an inrush. Instinctively he turned into the Flats, but after going ten yards he saw the water rushing towards him. The water came roof high in a great swell of sound. In the water were the bodies of Ogle, Brown and ten other men. The gas in front of the rushing water extinguished his lamp. For two seconds while he stood in the sounding darkness waiting for the water Dinning thought: To hell, I'm awful glad I sent Geordie out of the pit! But Geordie was already dead. Then the water took Dinning too. He fought, struggled, tried to swim. No use. Dinning's drowned body made fourteen drowned bodies in the flooded Scupper ropeway.

Frank Logan, the Paradise fireman, did not get Dinning's note. The note lay in the darkness covered with some blood, clenched in the completely severed hand of Geordie Dinning. But Frank heard the slight thump too and in a minute he felt the water coming knee-deep down the incline. He knew now without receiving the note that the water had holed. Fifteen men were working near him. Two of these men he ordered to go quick by the return airway to tell other men in the lower workings of the Paradise. The other thirteen he encouraged to push on to the pit-shaft one mile outbye. He himself remained. He knew that the Scupper workings were the deepest in the Paradise. He knew they would be flooded first. In the face of that he went back and down to warn the eighteen men in these workings. These men were drowned before he set out. And Frank Logan was never again seen alive.

The thirteen men pushing outbye, the men Frank Logan, the fireman, had sent outbye, reached the Atlas Drift. Here they hesitated and held a rapid conference. The Atlas connected the Paradise with the Globe Coal, which was the seam above. They decided the higher seam was less likely to hold water, that it would be safer to reach the pitshaft along Globe Coal. They went up the Drift into Globe Coal. Here they came upon some bricklayers who had been working in the main haulage road and knew nothing at all about the holing until the air reversed. The bricklayers were talking together, talking for a minute then listening for a minute, worried, not knowing whether to go outbye or remain. But now they decided to go outbye; they joined the thirteen men who had come up the Atlas Drift and proceeded all together along the main haulage road of Globe Coal towards the pit-shaft.

Three minutes later the inrush of water came down the main Paradise haulage, swept up the Atlas Drift and along the main road of Globe Coal. The men heard the water and started to run. The road was good with plenty of headroom and a hard-beaten floor and the men, all of whom were young, were able to run very fast. Some had never run faster in their lives.

But the water ran faster still. The speed of the water was terrific, it chased them with animal ferocity, surged upon them with the velocity, the inevitability of a tidal wave. One minute there was no water in Globe Coal and the next it had wiped them out.

The water swept on, reached the pit-shaft and began to spout down the shaft in tremendous volume. The meeting of the waters now took place. The water cascading from Globe Coal joined the water in Paradise pit-bottom. There was a backlash of water which swirled upon all the men who had managed to make pit-bottom and drowned them swiftly. The water then foamed round the stables and inundated the stalls.

The only four ponies still alive were in the stalls—Nigger, Kitty, Warrior and Ginger—all whinnying with terror. Warrior lashed out with heels at the water and went amuck in his stall; he almost broke his neck before he was drowned, but the others just stood whinnying, whinnying until the water rose above them. By this time the water had risen in the two main shafts, sealing both Globe and Paradise and preventing all access to the workings from the surface.

The suddenness of the calamity was unbelievable and deadly. Not more than fifteen minutes had elapsed from the instant of inrush and already eighty-nine were dead from drowning, violence or black damp suffocation.

But Robert and his mates were still alive. They were far inbye at the top of the slant and the inrush went away from them.

Robert heard the thump when it happened and fifty seconds later he felt the reversal of the air. He knew. Into himself he said: My God, that's it. Beside him in the heading Slogger Leeming got up slowly from his knees.

" Did ye hear that, Robert, mon ? " Slogger said, dazedly. Instinctively he turned to Robert for his opinion.

Robert said rapidly:

" Keep everybody here till I come back. *Everybody*." He ducked out of the heading and made his way down the slant and into the Scupper ropeway. He ran along the Scupper ropeway, his ears deafened by the sound of water pouring into the ropeway. He splashed on, getting deeper and deeper over his boots, his knees, his waist. He knew he must be near the Swelly, the depression that ran north and south across the Scupper ropeway. Suddenly he lost his footing and went right out of his depth into the Swelly. The water lifted him until his head hit the whinstone roof. He clawed the roof with his hands, kicked out his legs in the water, worked himself out the way he had come. He got into his depth, waded back, stood in the shallow water, shivering with cold. He knew exactly what had happened. The inrush had roofed in the Swelly: for fifty yards a barrier of water blocked the ropeway. All the escape roads were filled to the roof where they crossed the Swelly.

The cold of the water made Robert cough. He stood coughing for a minute, then he swung round and retook his way up the slant, bumping into little Pat Reedy half-way up. Pat was very frightened.

" What's like the matter, mester ? " he asked.

" It's nowt, Pat, mon," Robert answered. " You come along wi' me."

Robert and Pat reached the top of the slant where they found the remaining men collected round Slogger. There were ten altogether and amongst them were Hughie, Harry Brace, Tom Reedy, Ned Softley, Swee Messer and Jesus Wept. They were all waiting for Robert. Although they could not guess the fact, they were the sole survivors in the Neptune pit.

" How, then, Robert ? " Slogger called out as Robert came up. He looked intently at Robert.

" How, again, Slogger ? " Robert paused, making everything he said sound ordinary and perfectly all right. He wrung the water out his jacket.

" They're holed down there and let a drop water in the Swelly. But we're high enough here not to bother about that. We must find another road outbye."

Silence. They all knew enough to make them silent. But Tom Reedy asked:

" Can we not get through the Swelly, then ? "

Slogger let out at him savagely.

" Shut up yer gob, you silly runt, until yer asked to open it."

Robert went on as though nothing had happened.

" So what we'll do is this, lads. We'll travel the return airways into Globe and win outbye through the Globe."

Keeping Pat Reedy next and very close to him Robert led the way into the return airways. All the party followed but Tom Reedy. Tom was a splendid swimmer. He knew he was a splendid swimmer both under water and above and he knew that he could swim the Swelly. Once through the Swelly it would be easy to get outbye, then he would bring help and show the Slogger whether he was a silly runt or not. Tom lagged behind till the others had gone. He ran down the slant, slipped off his boots, took a deep breath and slid into the Swelly. He swam the Swelly in one deep breath. But what Tom didn't bargain for was the mile and a half of water beyond the Swelly. On the other side the main inrush caught him. Tom got outbye right enough. Five minutes later his body swirled gently into the sump at the bottom of the flooded shaft.

Robert crawled on, leading his party through the airway. He knew they must be near the Globe by now. Suddenly his lamp went out as if extinguished by a soft breath and at the same moment Pat Reedy choked and lay quietly down beside him. Not water this time. Black damp.

" Get back," Robert said. " Get back everybody."

The party went back, forty yards back, where they revived Pat Reedy. Robert, watching Pat Reedy come round, thought very hard. There must be men, he thought, in the dead end of the Globe. At length he said:

" Who is coming to try into the Globe with me again ? "

Nobody answered; they all knew black damp, and this whiff of it had made them know it better. It was not so easy to think of penetrating Globe in these circumstances. Hughie said:

" Don't go, dad, there's styfe in there."

Jesus Wept had said nothing up till now. But now Jesus Wept said: " I'll go." He understood that Robert wanted to bring out any men in the Globe who might be overcome with black damp and still alive. He was not brave, but it was his religion to go with Robert.

Robert and Wept crawled back along the airway into the Globe. They took off their jackets and wrapped them round their heads, though this was simply a tradition against black damp and did little good. They also went flat on their stomachs. Wept was very frightened. from time to time gave little nervous convulsive jerks, but he kept on, praying into himself.

The black damp or styfe was gas full of carbon monoxide driven from the old waste workings by the water and it seemed to lift and die. It had lifted slightly when Robert and Wept got into the Globe. Although they felt sick and sleepy they were able to go on. But it had been heavy before: they found four men overcome by the gas. The men were sitting in a little group as though gazing at each other, perfectly natural and at ease. They looked extremely well: the gas had given a nice pink colour to their faces and hands which were hardly dirty, since the shift had just come in. They looked healthy. They looked cheerful. They were all dead.

Robert and Wept dragged out the men; that was why they had come into the Globe; they dragged them out, but nothing the party could do revived the four dead men. At the sight of these four dead men Pat Reedy, who had never looked upon death before, burst into tears.

" Oh, help," he blubbered. " Oh, help. What in the name ov wonder am I doin' here ? And where's my brother Tom ? "

Wept said:

" Don't cry, lad, the Lord will look after us all." There was something terribly impressive in the way Jesus Wept said those words.

Silence. Robert stood thinking. His face was worried. If there's gas in the Globe, he thought, there's water too. The waste black damp could only have reached that upper seam with a full head of water behind it. The men were trapped by the water first, then overcome by the gas. Yes, he concluded, the Globe is sealed too, there's no escape that way. Then Robert remembered the telephone in the far end of Scupper Flats.

" We can't get into the Globe, lads," he said. " There's gas and water there both. We'll win back to the Scupper and telephone the surface."

At the mention of the telephone every face brightened.

" By Christ, Robert," said the Slogger admiringly.

The very thought of telephoning took all the sting out of the return journey through the airway, they did not think of it as going back nor remember that they were trapped. They thought of the telephone.

But when Robert came into Scupper Flats again he looked more worried than ever, he looked really worried. He saw that the water level in the Flats was up and rising fast. This meant only one thing: the inrush had washed away the timbering; the unsupported roof beyond the Swelly had fallen, thereby blocking the outlet of the water down the main roadway; and now the water was turning back upon them. With every escape road blocked they had perhaps fifteen minutes in which to get out of the dead end of Scupper Flats.

" Wait here," Robert said. He went on to the telephone himself, spun the little handle violently, then lifted the receiver. He was very pale. Now . . . he thought.

" Hello, hello." His voice, the voice of a man not yet dead rose out of the dark tomb, fled in despairing hope over waterlogged wires to the surface two miles away.

The answer came instantly.

" Hello, hello! "

Robert nearly fainted. It was Barras, from his office, insistently repeating:

" Hello, hello, hello, hello . . ."

Robert answered, speaking feverishly:

" Fenwick on Scupper Flats telephone. The water has holed beyond the Swelly and roofed. There's been a fall beyond. A party of nine cut off here beside me. What are we to do ? "

The answer came immediately, very hard and clear.

" Travel the airways to Globe Coal."

" We've tried the airways."

" What! "

" The Globe's chock full of black damp and water."

Silence. Thirty seconds of agonised silence which seemed like thirty years. Then Robert heard the slam of a door as though, still sitting at his desk, Barras had kicked the door shut. It really was very odd hearing the slam of that office door from far away up there upon the surface.

" Listen to me, Fenwick! " Barras spoke rapidly now, yet every word struck incisively and hard. " You must make for Old Scupperhole shaft. You can't come this way, both shafts are water sealed. You must travel the old workings to Old Scupperhole shaft! "

" Old Scupperhole shaft! " What in the name of God was he talking about . . .

" Go right up the slant," Barras went on with that same inflexible precision. " Break through the frame dam at the top east side, above the dyke. That takes you into the upper level of the Old Neptune waste. Don't be afraid of water, that's all in the bottom levels. Go along the road, it's all main road, don't take the branches nor the right dip, keep bearing due east for fifteen hundred yards until you strike the old Scupperhole shaft . . ."

Christ! thought Robert, he knows these old workings, he knows them, he knows them. The sweat broke upon Robert's brow. Oh, sweet Christ, he's known them all along . . .

" Do you hear me ? " asked Barras faintly, distantly. " The rescue party will meet you there. Do you hear me ? "

" Yes," shouted Robert. Then a water blast tore out the wires and left the instrument dead in his hand. He let it fall, it swung dangling . . . Christ! he thought again, weak with a terrible emotion.

" Quick, dad," Hughie cried, approaching, frantically. " Quick, quick, dad. The water's coming up on us."

Robert turned, splashed over to the others. Christ! he thought again. He shouted:

" We're going into the waste, lads. We can't do no more."

He led the way at the double up the slant, a dead end no one ever thought of trying. Yes, there was the old frame dam, not so much a dam as simple stopping, a row of three-inch planks set on edge eighteen inches apart with clay between. Slogger kicked a way through in two minutes. The party entered the waste of the Old Neptune workings.

The waste was cold and full of a curious smell. It was not styfe, though there was black damp about, but the smell of disuse. The waste had not been worked for eighty years.

Led by Robert they pressed forward with rising hope . . . it was dry here, they were leaving the water. Oh, thank God, they were leaving all that water. Six of them had lamps still lit, and Harry Brace had three pit candles in his pocket. They could see the way. There was no difficulty. There was only one road, the main road, the road that struck due east.

For about a quarter of a mile they followed the abandoned road. Then they checked. In front of them the roof had fallen.

" Never mind, lads," shouted Slogger. " It's nowt but rubble. Us'll soon be through." He threw off his jacket and tightened his leather belt. He led the attack on the fall.

They had no tools, all their tools, bait pokes and waterbottles lay submerged half a mile away. They worked with their bare hands, scraping, scraping, tearing out the loose stones. They worked in pairs: and Slogger worked double shift. How long they worked nobody knew, they worked so hard they did not think of time, nor of their bleeding hands, but they worked actually seven hours straight and went through fifteen yards of fallen rubble. Slogger crawled through first:

" Hurrah! " he yelled, pulling Pat Reedy after him. They all came through, all talking at once, laughing, triumphant. Famous it was to be through that fallen rubble. They laughed like children.

But fifty yards further on they stopped laughing. Another fall, and this time no rubble. Stone, hard solid whinstone, impenetrable to anything but a diamond drill. And they had their bare hands. Only one road. And the one road blocked. Solid whinstone, thick and hard as the face of a cliff. Their bare and bleeding hands. A silence. A long, cold silence.

" Well, lads," Robert said with studied cheerfulness, " here we are and not that far off the Scupperhole either. They're comin' in for us now. They're sure to reach us sooner or later. We've nowt to do but crook our houghs and jowl. And keep our spirits up."

They all sat down. Harry Brace, crouched next the fallen roof, picked up a heavy lump of whinstone and began to jowl, beating out a sort of tattoo on the rock face so that the rescuers might hear. Occasionally he raised his voice and let out a long high call. Deep in the abandoned waste, quarter of a mile inbye from the old Scupperhole shaft, they waited. Jowling and calling, they waited there.

XXIII

A LITTLE before six that morning Richard Barras was wakened by a light knocking on his door. The knocking had been going on for some time. He called out:

" Who is it ? "

Aunt Carrie's voice, diffident and frightened, came through the door:

" I don't wish to disturb you, Richard, but the underviewer is here from the pit. He *will* see you." Aunt Carrie shrank from the word which Hudspeth had flatly used . . . let Hudspeth himself say that terrifying word to Richard.

Richard dressed and came downstairs; it was in any case near his usual time for rising.

" Good morning, Hudspeth." He saw that Hudspeth was only half clothed and extremely agitated; he saw that Hudspeth had been running. And Hudspeth burst out immediately:

" There's water in both main shafts, Mr. Barras, covering all levels. We can't drop the cage below Five Quarter Seam."

There was a terrible pause.

" I see." It came out just like that, reflex, with automatic composure.

" The whole of the foreshift has gone into Globe Coal and Paradise." Hudspeth's usually stolid voice shook. " We can't get near them, not one of them has come outbye."

Barras carefully inspected Hudspeth:

" How many in the shift ? " he asked, with that mechanical precision.

" A round hundred men and boys, I don't know, something like that, I'm not five minutes out my bed, one of the lamp-men fetched me, I sent him running to Mr. Armstrong and came on up here as fast as I could."

Richard hesitated no longer. Six minutes later they were in the pit yard. Jimmy, the lamp-man, stood with the banksman, the assistant banksman and Cousins, the timekeeper, in a silent, intimidated group. As Barras arrived the banksman said:

" Mr. Armstrong has just come, sir. He went up in the winding room."

Barras said to Hudspeth:

" Fetch him."

Hudspeth ran up the steps to the winding room. Meanwhile Barras went into the office where the round clock fixed on to the wall above the fireplace indicated six-fifteen. As Barras entered the empty office the underground telephone rang. He picked up the receiver instantly. In his hard impersonal voice he said:

" Hello, hello, hello . . ."

Robert Fenwick's voice answered from Scupper Flats. It was the call from the entombed party, and when the conversation had terminated and the instrument lay dead in his hand Barras blindly replaced the receiver. Then he inflated his chest, took command of himself. A moment later Armstrong and Hudspeth came into the office.

" Now tell me, Mr. Armstrong," Barras began instantly in a voice of authority, " tell me everything you know."

Armstrong, labouring under some strain, told him. All the time Armstrong was speaking, which was about two minutes, Armstrong kept thinking, the end of this is the end of my job. The skin under one of his eyes began to twitch, he put up his hand to hide it.

" I see," Barras said; then, abruptly: " Ring Mr. Jennings."

Armstrong answered hurriedly:

" I sent Saul Pickings for him, Mr. Barras, that's the first thing I did; he'll be here any minute now."

" That was well done," said Barras in a pleased manner. His command was perfect, under that beautiful command Armstrong and Hudspeth were recovering themselves. Armstrong especially. Barras continued: " Get on the telephone, Mr. Armstrong. Instantly. Ring the Rigger and Headstock Co., Tynecastle, ring Messrs. T. & R. Henderson of Seaton, ring Amalgamated Collieries, and the Horton Iron Co.—ask especially for Mr. Probert senr. here—give them all my compliments, inform them of our situation, ask for every assistance, *every* assistance if you please. We shall want headgear, all pumping and electrical equipment they can give us. Ask Tynecastle especially for steam winding gear. Ask Amalgamated Collieries for any rescue men they can spare. At once if you please, Mr. Armstrong."

Armstrong ran to the telephone in his office. Barras turned to Hudspeth:

" Take ten men and go to the Old Scupper shaft. Make an inspection. As quick and complete as you can. Find out all you can about the condition of the shaft. Then hurry back to me."

As Hudspeth went out, Mr. Jennings arrived. The mines inspector was a blunt, compact, red-faced man with a cheerfully determined manner. It was well known that Jennings would stand no nonsense, he was unassertive yet strong, rather too hail-fellow-well-met perhaps, yet everybody liked and respected him. Just now he had a large boil on the back of his neck.

" Ouch," he said as he clumped down in a chair. " This hurts me like hell. What's up ? "

Barras told him.

Jennings forgot about his boil. All of a sudden he looked perfectly aghast.

" No," he said, in a tone of absolute dismay.

There was a silence. Barras said formally:

" Will you inspect the bank ? "

Although he had just sat down Jennings got up. He said:

" Yes, I'll have a look up top."

Barras led the way. Jennings and Barras inspected the bank. The pumps were completely overcome, the water had risen another six feet in both shafts. Jennings questioned the winding-engineman. Jennings and Barras returned to the office. Jennings said:

" You'll need extra pumps on these shafts, Mr. Barras. You'll need them soon. But there's that much head of water I question if they'll do much good . . ."

Barras listened with determined patience. He let Jennings talk himself out. He made no comment whatsoever. But when Jennings had finished he declared, in his clear, judicial voice, as though Jennings had not spoken at all:

" It will take days to dewater these main shafts. We must go in from Scupperhole in the hope of travelling a roadway. That much is positive. Hudspeth will be back immediately from Old Scupperhole shaft. The instant it is possible we must go in."

Jennings looked a little put down. He felt the impact of a personality stronger than his own, it subordinated and depressed him. His boil was paining him too. Yet Barras's definition of the position was crystal clear, his scheme for the rescue the only logical course. A grudging admiration showed in Jennings' blunt face.

" That's about it," he said, and then: " But how'll you manage without plans ? "

" We *must* manage," retorted Barras with sudden intensity.

" Well, well," Jennings conciliated, " we can but try." He sighed. " But if only we'd had these plans we wouldn't be in this bloody mess now. God, what idiots they were in those days! " He winced from the pain in his neck. " Oh, damn this carbuncle I've got on me. I'm taking yeast for it. But I don't think it's doing a hate of good."

As Jennings fumbled painfully with the dressing on his boil Hudspeth returned. Hudspeth said:

" I've had a good look, Mr. Barras, sir. The shaft at Old Scupperhole isn't that bad. There's rubbish in the shaft, not that much though. But there's black damp there too, a bad bit of black damp. We lowered a man on a crab rope and he came out pretty sick. I fancy we could clear the shaft of stowing and black damp in twenty-four hours."

Barras said:

" Thank you, Mr. Hudspeth. We'll go over to Scupperhole shaft now." There was no question: Barras was in charge. There was something sublime in his calm and resolute command, he dominated without effort, he subdued panic, he was absolute.

As the four men came out of the office young Dr. Lewis, who was now Dr. Scott's partner, came hurrying across the pit yard. He said:

" I've just heard . . . on my way back from a confinement case. . . . Can I do anything ? " He paused expectantly, seeing himself doing dramatic heroism down the mine. He was pink-cheeked and eager, his ideals and enthusiasms simply bubbled within him; in Sleescale he was always referred to as *young* Dr. Lewis. Jennings looked as if he would like to kick young Dr. Lewis's young backside. He turned away.

Barras said kindly:

" Thank you very much, Dr. Lewis. We may need you. Go in the office and Saul Pickings will make you a hot cup of cocoa. We may need you later."

Young Dr. Lewis bustled away happily. Barras, Jennings, Armstrong and Hudspeth went on to Old Scupperhole shaft. It was only now beginning to get light. It was very cold. A few thin snow-flakes began to fall, trembling gently out of the unseen sky. A party of twenty-five men went with them, moving in silence across the troubled ground, until the snow enwrapped and curtained them. This was the first rescue party.

And now the news began to travel through the town. Doors in the Terraces flew open and men and women rushed through the open doors. They ran down Cowpen Street. As they ran, more ran with them. They ran as if they could not help themselves, as if the pit had suddenly become a magnet drawing them, drawing them irrespective of their own volition. They ran because they had to run. They ran in silence.

Martha heard the news from Mrs. Brace. Her first thought was less of anguish than of gratitude: Thank God my Sammy isn't down. Clutching her breast, she wakened Sammy, then threw on her coat and ran with Sammy to the pit. Old Hans Messuer was running too. Hans had been shaving an early customer when he heard, and running, he still held the lather brush in his left hand. David heard as he cycled into the town. He tore straight to the pit. The Slogger's wife heard in bed, and Cha, the Slogger's son, heard at the side-door of the Salutation. Susan Wept heard as she said her morning prayer. Mrs. Reedy, the midwife, heard at her case with young Dr. Lewis. Jack Reedy, her eldest son, heard on his way to pick up a stiffener at the pub. Joining Cha Leeming, Jack ran towards the pit. Ned Softley's mother heard on her way to the public wash-house. Old Tom Ogle heard in the closet. Buttoning his trousers, Tom Ogle ran.

In no time at all five hundred men and women stood packed on the outskirts of the pit yard and there were more outside. They stood in silence, the women mostly in shawls, the men without overcoats, all very black against the white snow. They stood like some vast chorus, massed in silence under the snow-dark sky. They were not the actors in the drama but they were of it none the less. In silence they stood, in mortal silence, under that immortal snow-dark silent sky.

It was nine o'clock and snowing hard when Barras, Jennings and Armstrong recrossed the Snook and came into the pit yard. Armstrong looked at the crowd. Armstrong said:

" Will I have the yard gates shut ? "

" No! " said Barras, inspecting the people with his remote, myopic eyes. " Have a fire lighted in the yard. A large fire. Light it in the middle of the yard. It is cold for them standing there."

They lit the fire. Charley Gowlan, Jake Wicks and the banksmen brought lots of timbering to feed the fire. Just as the fire was going well the first party of volunteers rolled in from the Seaton collieries. They went immediately to the Scupperhole. Then the riggers came from Tynecastle bringing three truckloads of their gear. Armstrong stood by the telephone. Barras and Jennings went back to the Scupperhole. The black damp made it impossible to descend the shaft but soon they would clear the black damp. Already they had started to fit headgear, winding engine and a fan.

At eleven o'clock Arthur Barras arrived. Arthur had been spending the week-end with the Todds at Tynecastle, he had just arrived by the ten forty-five train. He dashed into the office with nervous haste.

" Father! " he exclaimed, " this is terrible."

Barras turned slowly.

" It is heart-breaking."

" What can I do ? I'll do anything. What a thing to happen, father."

Barras looked at his son with heavy eyes. He made a gesture with his hand. He said:

" It is the will of God, Arthur."

Arthur stared back at his father with anguish in his face.

" The will of God," he repeated in a strange voice. " What does that mean ? "

At that moment Armstrong rushed in.

" They're pulling out two pumps at the Amalgamated. They'll be on their way over presently. A new turbine pump is coming from Horton's, Mr. Probert says no trouble is too great."

" Thank you, Mr. Armstrong," Barras said mechanically.

There was a strained silence until old Saul Pickings limped in with three large cups of hot cocoa. He was over seventy was Saul, and though he had a wooden leg he could get along very fast; he limped about doing surface jobs and was good at cocoa. Arthur and Armstrong each took a cup; Barras refused. But Arthur and Armstrong pressed Barras to drink the cocoa, saying that it would do him good, Armstrong adding that it was impossible to work on an empty stomach. But Barras still refused; he seemed a little exalted.

Saul Pickings said:

" Young Dr. Lewis wants to know if you still want him. If he's to wait I'll take him in this cup of cocoa." Young Dr. Lewis had already had four cups of cocoa, his heroism was slightly diluted now. And he had been obliged to ask, politely, for the lavatory.

Barras looked at Armstrong.

" It would be a good thing if the doctors of the town could manage for one of their number always to be on duty here for the next few days. Let them take turns."

" That's a splendid idea, Mr. Barras," Armstrong exclaimed. He hurried out to use the telephone again.

" Father," Arthur said in a kind of desperation, " how did this happen ? I've got to know."

" Not now," Barras answered. " Not now."

Arthur turned away and pressed his brow against the cold, feathered window-pane. For the moment his father's tone had silenced him.

Then Firemaster Ebenezer Camhow puffed in. He had changed into his uniform, which carried a pleasant amount of bright red braid and eight important brass buttons kept beautifully shined by Mrs. Camhow. The firemaster was short, round and bald-headed, he was like an orb. He was fond of uniforms, had started early with a pill-box cap in the boys' brigade, was now both firemaster and bandmaster of Sleescale. He played four musical instruments, including the triangle, and won prizes regularly for his sweet peas at the county show. In the last five years he had extinguished one small fire at a disused brewery.

" I'm at your service, Mr. Barras," he declared. " I've got my men outside. Outside in the yard. They're there in a row. Every one has a first-aid certificate. You've only got to command me, sir."

Barras thanked the firemaster, Saul Pickings gave the firemaster the cup of cocoa that was left over, then the firemaster went out. As he went into the yard the firemaster looked so official and important that two reporters who had just arrived from Tynecastle took his portrait, which appeared next morning in the *Tynecastle Argus*. The firemaster cut it out.

Offers of assistance kept pouring in, telegrams, telephone calls, Mr. Probert of the Horton Iron Co. came over in person, three further relays of rescue men came in from Amalgamated Collieries.

Before twelve o'clock Barras and Arthur went out to inspect the erection work at Old Scupperhole shaft. The shaft lay in the wretched piece of waste land known as the Snook, all hummocks and subsidences, covered with snow and swept by a bitter wind. Troubled land was what they called it. In spite of the fire in the pit yard nearly everybody had left the yard and stood gathered on the Snook. They stood well back from the riggers who were raising headgear, working fast and hard. As Barras and Arthur approached the crowd parted silently, but one group of men did not give way. It was then that Arthur saw David.

David stood at the head of the group of men which did not give way. Jack Reedy, Cha Leeming and old Tom Ogle were also in the group. David waited until Barras came up to him. His skin seemed drawn upon his cheek-bones with cold and the hidden tension of his mind. His eyes met the eyes of Barras. Under that accusation Barras dropped his gaze. Then David spoke.

" These men want to know something ? "

" Well ? "

" They want to know that everything will be done to rescue the men underground."

" It is being done." A pause. Barras raised his eyes. " Is that all ? "

" Yes," David said slowly. " For the meantime."

It was here that old Tom Ogle thrust himself violently forward.

" What's all this talking ? " he shouted at Barras. He was a little out his mind. He had already tried spectacularly to jump down the Scupperhole shaft. " Why don't ye save them ? All this rigging does nothing. My son's down there, my son Bob Ogle. Why don't you send inbye and fetch him out ? "

" We're doing what we can, my man," Barras said, very dignified and calm.

" I'm not yer man," Tom Ogle snarled and raising his fist he hit Barras full in the face.

Arthur shivered. Charley Gowlan and some others pulled Tom Ogle away, struggling, shouting. Barras stood upright. He had not defended himself, he had received the blow in a kind of spiritual exaltation as though, deep down in the centre of his being, the blow satisfied him. He proceeded calmly to the shaft, ordered another fire to be lit, remained supervising the work of erection.

He remained at the pit all that day. He remained until Old Scupperhole shaft had been fitted with headgear, steam winding engine and fan, until the shaft was cleared of black damp. He remained until relays of men were started in to remove the stowing which marked the road into the waste. He remained until both main shafts of No. 17 had been fitted with new pumps, the one sending out two hundred and fifty gallons per minute from main winding, the other, a turbine, four hundred and fifty gallons per minute in the upcast. Then, alone, he walked back to the Law.

He did not feel tired nor particularly hungry, he swung between the torpor of his body and that curious exaltation of his mind. He was impersonal; what he was doing was illusory. He was like a man sentenced to death who receives the verdict calmly. He did not quite understand. His belief in his own innocence remained unassailable.

Aunt Carrie had seen to it that oxtail soup was ready for him—Aunt Carrie knew that when Richard had a " hard day," he liked oxtail soup better than anything. He ate the soup, a wing of chicken and a slice of his favourite blue cheddar cheese. But he ate very sparingly and he drank only water. Of Aunt Carrie, who hung in a fluttering servitude in the background, he took no notice whatever; he did not see Aunt Carrie.

At the table Hilda sat opposite, she kept her eyes fixed upon him with a sort of desperate intensity. At last, as though she could bear it no longer, she said:

" Let me help, father. Let me do something. I beg of you to let me do something." In the face of this emergency Hilda's lack of opportunity maddened her.

He raised his heavy eyes to hers, observing her for the first time. He answered:

" What is there to do? Everything is being done. There is nothing for a woman to do."

He left her then. He climbed the stairs, went in to his wife. To her, as to Arthur, he said:

" It is the will of God." Then, inscrutable and stern, he lay down fully dressed upon his bed.

But in four hours he was back at the pit and immediately proceeded to Old Scupperhole shaft. He knew that the real chance of penetrating to the Paradise lay through the Scupperhole. He went down the shaft.

They were working in relays down the Scupperhole, working so fast they were clearing the stowing from the main road at the rate of six feet an hour. There was more stowing than they had thought. But the relays launched themselves in waves, they battered into the stowing, there was something frantic and abandoned in their assault. It was more than human this progress through the stowing, one relay slipped in as another staggered out.

" This road runs due west," Jennings said to Barras. " It ought to take us pretty near the mark."

" Yes," said Barras.

" We ought to be near the end of the stowing," Jennings said.

" Yes," said Barras.

In twenty-four hours the relays had cleared one hundred and forty-four feet of stowing from the old main road. They broke through into clear road, into an open section of the old waste. A loud cheer rang out, a cheer which ascended the shaft and thrilled into the ears of those who waited on the surface.

But there was no second cheer. Immediately beyond the stowing the main road ran into a dip or trough which was full of water and impassable.

Dirty, covered with coal dust, wearing no collar and tie, an old silk muffler round his swollen neck, Jennings stared at Barras.

" Oh, my good God," he said hopelessly, " if only we'd had a plan we'd have known this before."

Barras remained unmoved.

" A plan would not have removed the trough. We expect difficulties. We must blast a new road above the trough." There was something so sternly inflexible in the words that even Jennings was impressed.

" My God," he said, exhausted almost to the edge of tears, " that's the spirit. Come on then and we'll blast your blasted roof."

They began to blast the roof, to blast down the iron-hard whinstone into the water so that the trough might be filled and a road established above water level. A compressor was erected to supply the drills; the finest diamond drill bores were used. The work was killing. It proceeded in darkness, dust, sweat and the fume of high explosive. It proceeded in a sort of insane frenzy. Only Barras remained calm. Calm and impenetrable. He was there. He was the motive, the directing force. For a full eighteen further hours' he did not leave the Scupperhole.

Fresh back from six hours rest, Jennings pleaded with him:

"Take some sleep, for God's sake, Mr. Barras, you're fair killing yourself."

Mr. Probert, Armstrong and several of the senior officials from the Department all pleaded with him: he had done so much, it would take at least five days to blast above the trough, let him spare himself until then. Even Arthur pleaded with him:

"Take some sleep . . . please . . . father . . . please . . ."

But Barras snatched only an odd half-hour in his office chair; he did not go home again until the evening of the fourth day. Once more he walked home. It was still bitter cold and the snow still lay upon the ground, freshly fallen snow. How white was the snow! He walked thoughtfully up Cowpen Street . . . yet he did not think. Since the accident he had refused to think, subconsciously his mind had detached itself, developed this powerful attack upon the pit, fixed itself inflexibly upon the work of rescue. His icy detachment persisted and sustained him. Strong currents were working deep beneath the crust of outer coldness. He did not feel these currents. But the currents were working there.

About him the streets were deserted, every door closed, not a single child at play. Many of the shops were shuttered. A still agony lay upon the Terraces, the stillness of despair. From opposite ends of Alma Terrace two women approached. They were friends. They passed each other with averted faces. Not a word. Silence: even their footsteps silenced by the snow. Within the houses the same silence. In the houses of the entombed men the breakfast things were laid out upon the table in preparation for their return. It was the tradition. Even at night the blinds remained undrawn. In No. 23 Inkerman Martha was making a fresh pot pie: Robert and Hughie both liked a fresh pot pie. Sammy and David sat in silence, not watching her. They had both come back from Scupperhole shaft; they had both been helping there; David had not been near the school for four full days. He had forgotten about school, forgotten about his examination, forgotten about Jenny. He sat in silence, his head buried in his hands thinking of his father, thinking his own bitter thoughts.

After the heat and clamour of the Scupperhole this cold seemed to strike at Barras. As he went on, a great sigh broke from his chest. He was not conscious of that sigh. He was conscious of nothing. He entered the Law. An enormous correspondence awaited him, letters of praise, sympathy, condolence, a telegram from Stapleton, the member for

Sleescale, another from Lord Kell, owner of the Neptune royalties, another from the Lord Mayor, Tynecastle—*Your heroic endeavours on behalf of the entombed men evokes our highest admiration we pray God success attend your further efforts.* And yet another, a Royal Message, pregnant with gracious condolence. He studied them carefully. Curious! He studied a letter from the wife of a rubber-tubing manufacturer in Leeds offering to supply *free*—underlined—five hundred yards or *more*—underlined—of her husband's quarter-inch tubing so that hot soup might be conveyed to the buried miners. Curious! He did not smile.

He returned to the pit early next morning. They had lowered the water level in the main shaft sufficient to allow divers to descend. The divers had to contend with a maximum head of eighteen feet of water in the levels. In spite of this they fought their way along Globe and Paradise levels as far as the fall. They made an arduous, exhaustive search. No one knew better than Barras how useless this search would be. All that the divers found was seventy-two drowned bodies.

The divers came back. They reported the absence of any living soul. They reported that at least another month would be required to dewater the levels completely. Then they started to bring out the bodies: the drowned men, roped together, dangling out of the mine into the brightness of the day they did not see.

Everything now concentrated on the approach by Scupperhole: it was fully realised that men unaccounted for might be imprisoned in the waste. Though it was now ten days since the date of the disaster these men might still be alive. In a fresh frenzy of endeavour, efforts above the trough were redoubled. The men spurted, strained every nerve. Six days after blasting was begun the last charge was fired, they broke through and regained the old main roadway beyond the trough. Exhausted but jubilant the rescuers pressed forward. They were met, sixty paces due west, by a complete fall of whinstone roof. They drew up hopelessly.

" Oh, my God," Jennings moaned. " There might be a half mile of this. We'll never reach them, never. This is the end at last." Utterly spent, he leaned against the whinstone rock and buried his face in his arm.

" We must go on," Barras said with sudden loudness, " we must go on."

XXIV

HARRY BRACE was the first to die. Harry's heart was weak, he was not a young man, and his immersion in the Flats had been severe, he died from sheer exhaustion. No one knew how or when he died until Ned

Softley knocked his hand against Harry's death-cold face and cried out that Harry was gone. Actually that was towards the end of the third night, though, of course, it was always night with them now, for the lamps had burned out and all the pit candles were used except one that Robert had kept and was saving for emergency. The darkness was not so bad, it clothed them, linked them in comradeship, hid them and was kind.

There were nine of them altogether: Robert, Hughie, Slogger, Pat Reedy, Jesus Wept, Swee Messer, Ned Softley, Harry Brace and two other men named Bennett and Seth Calder. The first day they had spent jowling, chiefly in jowling . . . ta-ta . . . ta-ta . . . ta-ta-ta-ta-tap . . . on and on . . . ta-ta . . . ta-ta . . . ta-ta-ta-ta-tap . . . like a hard tattoo beat out upon a tribal drum. Jowling was good; it signified their position in this unfathomable darkness; dozens of men had been rescued by jowling their rescuers towards them. Ta-ta . . . ta-ta . . . ta-ta-ta-ta-tap . . . they took turns upon the stone. But towards the second day Slogger shouted suddenly:

"Stop! For Christ's sake, stop, I can't stand that bloody hammering any longer."

Ned Softley, whose turn it was, stopped at once. In fact everybody seemed glad when the jowling stopped. It stopped for about an hour, then they all agreed, and Slogger did too, that the jowling must go on. They must be very near them now, the men coming in through the Scupperhole. Oh, they must be hellofa near now, Swee Messer said. So Ned resumed: . . . ta-ta . . . ta-ta . . . ta-ta-ta-ta-tap.

It was shortly after this that Wept held his first service. Jesus Wept had been upon his knees a great deal, praying by himself, away from the others, praying with a passionate intensity like Jesus Himself in the Garden of Gethsemane. Wept was a silent earnest little man, he did not impose himself upon others except through the silent medium of his tracts and sandwich boards. At Whitley Bay or the Sleescale football matches Wept would be silent amongst the noisy crowds, just standing silent, or walking slow and silent, advertising the tears of Jesus, back and front. He was the quietest publicity man Jesus ever had and not by any means the worst. So it wasn't Wept's nature to force the others to a service. But oddly enough, Robert, who never went to chapel, suggested they ought to have a service.

Though Wept had not mentioned the service he had wanted the service. He had wanted it badly and he took it gladly, gladly. He began with a prayer. It was a very good prayer with nothing about rending of garments or the scarlet woman in it. It was full of good faith and bad grammar and it ended quietly—" . . . so get us out of here, dear God, for Jesus' sake, Amen." Then Wept gave a short address. He took the text simply: John viii. 12, *I am the light of the world: he that followeth me shall not walk in darkness, but shall have the light of life.*

He simply talked to them, he spoke quite ordinarily.
Then they sang the hymn: *Come, Great Deliverer, Come.*

> " *I've wandered far away o'er mountains cold,*
> *I've wandered far away from home.*
> *Oh, take me now and bring me to thy fold.*
> *Come, Great Deliverer, come!* "

An echoing silence fell. None of them seemed to want to break that silence. They all sat very still, Slogger in particular sat gritting his teeth, but Slogger was the one who gave way.

" O God," Slogger groaned, " oh, my God Christ so help me God." And Slogger began to cry. A hard case was Slogger, but with streaks of softness in him. He sat now with his head in his hands, shaking with dry sobs, and his racking grief was horrible to hear. They were all a little unstrung by this time, each found it difficult to keep his manhood on an empty belly. They had no food and no water but a tiny puddle that bled down slowly from the roof above. It was strange to have come away from that terrific flood of water and to have so little now, just enough for each, a mouthful of brackish coaly fluid.

Wept went over to Slogger and began to comfort him. A great joy was in Wept that he should have saved the Slogger and for a little while the joy was in Slogger too.

Then some of them felt hungry. Pat Reedy, being the youngest, felt the want of food the most. Robert had three cough sweets in his pocket. He slipped one to Pat and then another. How long was it between each sweet ? . . . five minutes or five days ? God alone knew! After the second Pat whispered:

" That was good, that was, mester."

Robert smiled. He made to give Pat the third sweet, but the curious understanding that it was the last held him back. I'll keep it for him, he thought.

This same desire to keep something in reserve made Robert withhold the last pit candle, though at first the darkness was not kind but difficult, terribly difficult to bear after the yellow glow of the candle set like a tiny camp fire in their midst.

The darkness made time much harder to compute. Only Robert amongst them had a watch and it had stopped when he went into the water of the Swelly. Hughie especially was worrying about time. Hughie was always a silent one, but now more so than ever; since they had come upon the fall of rock Hughie had hardly said one word. He sat beside his father, his brow knitted, brooding. His whole body was tense with this secret brooding. At last he said in a low voice:

" Dad! How long have we been in ? "

Robert said:

"I cannot tell ye, Hughie."

"But, dad, how long do ye think?"

"Two days, maybe, or maybe three."

"What day is this, then, dad?"

"I don't know, man, Hughie . . . it's Wednesday likely."

"Wednesday . . ." Hughie sighed, settled back stiffly against the wall. If it was only Wednesday that wasn't quite so bad, that left three whole days to go, three days until the match. He must get out of this pit by Saturday, he must, he must . . . in a sudden torment of anxiety Hughie picked up the stone and began to jowl . . . ta-ta . . . ta-ta . . . ta-ta-ta-ta-tap!

When Hughie stopped jowling there was a long silence. It was then that Ned Softley put his hand out to move himself and touched Harry Brace's face. At first he thought Harry was asleep; he tried again gingerly and his fingers went right into Harry's cold, dead, open mouth.

Robert lit the candle. Yes, Harry Brace was gone. Poor Harry, he'd never given his missus the truss for her rupture he'd always promised her. Robert and Slogger lifted Harry. He lifted very heavy. Or were they just weak? They carried him down the roadway about thirty yards. They placed him upon his back, Robert crossed Harry's hands on his pit singlet and shut Harry's eyes. Wept was asleep, sleeping for the first time in three days, snoring deeply. Robert did not waken him. He recited the Lord's Prayer over Harry, then Slogger and he came back.

"We'll burn another inch of candle, lads," Robert said. "Just to keep our spirits up."

Pat Reedy was crying quietly again; he had met with death for the second time and still he did not like it much.

"Hover a bit, man," Robert said. He put his arm round Pat's shaking shoulders. "It's time I was giving you something to do. Will you have a turn jowling?"

Pat shook his head.

"I want to write to my mam," he said, letting himself go altogether.

"Very well," Robert said gravely. "You shall write to your mam. I have a pencil. Who has some paper?"

Ned Softley had a notebook for checking tubs. He passed it to Robert. Robert tore out a narrow double sheet, slapped it on the back of the notebook, passed it over with the pencil to Pat.

Pat took the paper and the notebook and the pencil with a gulp of gratitude. He cheered up. He began straightway and wrote in big round letters: *My dear mam* . . . Then he stopped, head on one side, reading what he had written. *My dear mam* . . . he stopped again. *My dear mam* . . . he read it again and stopped. Then he began to cry in earnest. He cried bitterly. He was only fifteen.

When the candle had burned down its inch he was a little easier. Robert took back the notebook and the pencil and the narrow double sheet of paper and slipped them in his pocket. He put out the candle. He placed his left arm round Pat Reedy as though protecting him. In that position Pat Reedy fell asleep.

Robert drowsed off himself. Time passed. He awoke into the silent, the unceasing darkness and had a long bout of coughing, his silent, intimate, familiar cough. His wet clothes had dried on him and that was not good for him. I'll have another attack for sure when we get out, he thought. Then with a vague coldness about his heart he thought, if we get out. More time passed. Surely they must be near them now, the men coming in, oh, surely they must be near them now!

" Dad," Hughie again. " What day is it, dad ? "

" I cannot say, Hughie, lad." Robert tried to speak calmly, reasonably.

" But, dad . . . what day is it ? "

" I cannot say, Hughie, lad." Robert again tried to to speak calmly, reasonably, but his voice remained flat and weary.

" But, dad . . . what day is it ? It's the match, dad . . . the United, dad . . . the United . . . I've got to be out by Saturday. I've got to . . . I've got to, dad." Hysteria shrilled into the silent Hughie's voice. He rocked himself to and fro in the darkness. He must be out by Saturday, he must, he must be out by Saturday! It was then Sunday evening.

Slogger woke up. Everybody seemed to be sleeping a bit now; there must be traces of black damp in the air, or was it simply weakness ? Slogger said:

" Oh, my God, what a dream I was having. If my poor old missus only knew. Oh, my God, if only I had a pint of beer. I'm not hungry no more, it's just the beer I want. O God, what am I sayin', diddent I promise to give up the drink if Ye got us out of here, O God, get us out of here, God, for God's sake." His voice rose to a shout.

Ned Softley shouted too. Several of the others joined in. " Get us out! Get us out! " Even Wept was losing himself now. He called out suddenly in a high voice:

" How long, O Lord, until Thou deliverest us ? " It was like the roaring of caged beasts.

Bennett died next and Seth Calder six hours after him. They were marrows who had worked with each other for nearly fourteen years. For fourteen years they had worked, got drunk, played pot-stour bowls together. But it didn't seem in the least appropriate to them that they should die together. Bennett was the quieter of the two, Seth Calder, when he felt himself sinking, kept moaning:

" I don't want to die. I'm a young man yet. I've got a young wife. I don't want to die." But for all that he did die.

Everyone was too weak now to move the bodies of Bennett and Seth Calder, and besides Robert had only two matches left in his pocket with his stump of candle. He gave the last cough sweet to Pat Reedy. Surely to God it wouldn't be long now before they broke through from the Scupperhole. Surely to God! Oh, let them come in quick, dear God, or it won't be no use!

They just lay there now, too weak to move themselves. They were too weak even to move up to the place they used. They just lay. Lying there Robert had an idea. He called out each name three times. If no answer came back after the third time he knew it was finished.

Ned Softley stopped answering next. He must have died as quietly as Harry Brace. Ned always had the name for being weak-witted, but he died well. He never said a whimper. Then Swee Messer went, a lewd fellow was Swee, but he'd finished with his funny stories now for good.

It was after Swee died that Wept went mad. Like the rest of them he had been quiet for a long time. But now he got up on his feet. He stood there in the darkness, they could feel his madness as he stood there in the darkness. He said:

" I see them! I see the seven angels which stood before God! I hear their trumpets. It is revealed to me."

At first they tried to take no notice, but Wept went on:

" I hear them sound their trumpets. The first angel sounds and then follows hail mingled with blood."

Slogger said:

" Oh, for God's sake, man, shut up."

Wept continued louder:

" Then the second angel sounds and as it were a great mountain burning with fire is cast into the sea and the third part of the sea becomes blood. Not water, my brethren, but blood. It is not water that has brought us here, but blood."

Slogger sat up. He said:

" Wept, for the love of God, I can't stand no more of that."

Wept went on in that rapt voice:

" The third angel sounds and the star Wormwood falls. Wormwood and gall, my brethren, is our lot upon earth, we are crushed by the greed of man. And the fourth angel sounds and the fifth and another star falls into the bottomless pit and there arises a smoke out of the pit. We are in the pit, my brethren, and the air is darkened by reason of the smoke in the pit and the seal of God is upon our foreheads, and punishment will come upon those in high places who brought us here. I see it, my brethren. To me is given the gift of prophecy. I am a prophet in the Paradise pit."

Then Robert knew that Wept was mad. He said:

" Sit down, man, do." He coaxed Wept. " Sit down, now, do. It cannot be long till they reach us now. Sit down and wait quiet like. It isn't long now."

Wept went on:

" And the sixth angel sounds and a voice from the four horns of the golden altar which is before God and the four angels loosed which are prepared to slay the third part of men by smoke and by brimstone and the rest of men which are not killed by these plagues yet repent not of the works of their hands, nor repent they of their murders nor of their sorceries, nor of their fornications, nor of their thefts."

Wept's voice rose gradually to a shout that echoed, reverberating, and seemed to rock the very roof.

Slogger groaned:

" I cannot stand no more of this." He crawled forward to Wept, feeling with his hands.

Wept went on in a terrible voice:

" And now the seventh angel sounds . . ."

But before the seventh angel sounded, Slogger caught Wept by the ankle and pulled the feet from him. Wept collapsed, moaning.

" But the seventh angel sounds. I see it. I see the millennium brought by the madness and the greed of man. Money, money, money . . . we are crushed and killed for it. I will prophesy. . . . From high places they fall . . . not water, but blood . . . the blood of the Lamb . . . come mother pass the hymn-books and we'll sing love is poke my hand mother hold me tight for it is no sin come great Deliverer come. . . ."

His voice trailed off, he lay groaning for a few minutes, then he was silent. He had exhausted himself with prophesy. He cried a little. For a minute Jesus Wept wept. Then Jesus Wept died.

Time passed. Robert gave Pat Reedy a drink. Pat was only half conscious, he retched back the coaly water over Robert's cupped hands.

" O God, let them come quick," Slogger said in a kind of delirium, " or it won't be no use them comin' at all." He crawled over to the fall and began to jowl. But he was too weak to jowl now, the stone fell from his slack fingers.

Time passed. Slogger put his hand to his throat and croaked:

" God, Robert, mon, I'd give anything for a pint." Then he fell over on his side and did not move again.

Pat Reedy died next. He lay relaxed in Robert's arms with his head resting upon Robert's flat chest like an infant upon his mother's breast. He rambled a little towards the end. At the last he said:

" Come on, mam, an' make us truly thankful."

After that Robert called every one in turn. Then he said:

" It's only you and me, Hughie, lad."

Hughie said mechanically:

" What day is it, dad ? " He said it again, then he said: " I wish I had a drink, dad, but I cannot be bothered."

Robert crawled over and got Hughie a drink.

Hughie thanked him.

" It's all over now, dad," he said. He was still thinking about the match. " They'll never give me another chance now."

Robert said:

" No, Hughie."

Hughie said:

" I would have liked to have played, dad."

Robert said:

" I know, Hughie."

Robert had given up hope. He had listened and listened and heard never a sound of the men coming in. They must have met something, water, or a terrible fall of roof. He was beyond hope and beyond bitterness.

Gently he put Pat Reedy's body down and put his arm round Hughie's shoulder. He had never devoted himself enough to Hughie, perhaps. Hughie was too like himself, too silent and contained. He had not loved Hughie enough.

He tried to talk to Hughie but it was difficult, the words came out of his mouth all wrong. He coughed and the cough tasted salt and ran out of his mouth like the wrong words.

Time passed. A last faint sigh passed over Hughie's body. Hughie died thinking about the match he would never play, he died really of a broken heart.

Time passed. Robert kissed Hughie on the brow, tried to fold Hughie's dead hands like he had done Harry's hands. He was too weak almost to do it. He was too weak even to cough. He said the Lord's Prayer silently. The words of the Lord's Prayer right, though the cough did not come right.

Robert's thoughts wandered: he felt it strange that he should be the last to die, that he who was consumptive should last out so many healthy men. Well, he had always said his cough would never kill him . . . it would not kill him now. He lost the sense of time and place, was back on the Wansbeck fishing with David, his little boy David . . . showing David how to cast . . . watching David land his first small speckled trout . . . eh, Davey boy, isn't it a beauty!

Time passed. Robert stirred, opened his eyes. He lit the last small piece of candle. He thought, a pity not to use it. Since he had the choice he felt he would rather not die in the dark.

The candle cast a yellow glow upon the silent spectral forms of the dead around him. He knew that he too would soon be dead. He had no fear, no anything . . . but he did think at last that he would like to write to David . . . he had always loved David.

He fumbled for the notebook and the pencil and the sheet of paper. He set himself to think painfully, then he wrote:

Dear David, you will get this when they find me. We have done our best, but it is no use. We holed in the Flats. I managed to telephone surface and Barras directed us to the Scupperhole, but this fall stopped us, a very bad fall.

Hughie has just gone. He died without pain. Tell your mother we had service. I hope you will get on Davey and make something out of life. Yours dad.

He thought for a moment without knowing that he thought, then he added on the back:

P.S. Barras must have had plans of this waste his instructions were correct.

He folded the paper, put it under his singlet next to his emaciated chest. He sat huddled with his back against the fallen roof, as if thinking. Formless swathes of darkness floated into his brain. He coughed, his intimate kindly cough, the cough that was he. Then his body slid down slowly and sprawled out. He lay upon his back with his arms outstretched as though pleading. His dead eyes were open. He lay there amongst his dead comrades. The candle guttered feebly and went out.

END OF BOOK ONE

BOOK II

I

THE final session of the formal Inquiry, held under Section 83 of the Coal Mines Act, into the causes and circumstances of the Neptune disaster, was drawing to a close. The Town Hall in Lamb Street was crammed to suffocation, crowds waited outside, a sense of tension filtered with the afternoon sunshine through the high leaded windows into the steamy atmosphere of the court. Upon the bench sat the Commissioner, the Rt. Hon. Henry Drummond, K.C., supported by the Technical Assessor, the Deputy Chief Inspector of Mines. In the body of the hall were the Divisional Inspector and Mr. Jennings, the local Inspector, both representing the Mines Department; Mr. Lynton Roscoe, K.C., instructed by Mr. John Bannerman, solicitor, Tynecastle, acting for Richard Barras of the Neptune Colliery; Harry Nugent, M.P., and Jim Dudgeon on behalf of the Miners' Federation of Great Britain; Tom Heddon on behalf of the Sleescale Miners' Lodge; Mr. William Snagg, solicitor, Tynecastle, representing the dependants of the deceased; and Colonel Gascoigne, watching the case on behalf of Lord Kell, owner of Royalties. Occupying the front seats were Barras, Arthur, Armstrong, Hudspeth and the officials of the Neptune. Three rows of witnesses came next with David, Jack Reedy, Harry Ogle and some men from the Terraces placed immediately behind Nugent. Then followed the relatives of the dead men, mostly women, rigged out in cheap black, a few bare-headed and in shawls, all faintly bewildered, uncomprehending and over-awed. The rest of the hall was packed with miners and townspeople, not an inch of space remained.

Following the customary official practice, a certain period of time had been allowed to elapse between the calamity and the subsequent investigation. But now, for six full days, since July 27th, 1914, the court had been in session, the hall humming with voices, fifty-four witnesses called and recalled, fifteen thousand questions asked and answered, words flying to and fro, angry, persuasive, bitter, hundreds of thousands of words. There was Heddon, with his hot violence, losing the thread of his argument, being sharply called to order; Jim Dudgeon, genial and ungrammatical, supporting Nugent's calm logic; Colonel Gascoigne with his technicalities of bench-marks, ordinance datum and geological formation; Lynton Roscoe, practised in the art of oratory, master of gesture and smoothly turned periods.

But it was all drawing to a close now, quickly drawing to a close. Lynton Roscoe, K.C., was at this moment on his feet, a portly, imposing figure, heavy jowled, with long upper lip and a florid port-wine colouring. Since two o'clock he had been re-examining witnesses and now, with a full dramatic gesture, he turned to the Commissioner. A silence.

The Commissioner: Have you an application to make, Mr. Roscoe?

Lynton Roscoe: It is the question of Mr. Richard Barras, sir. I think it would bring matters to a fitting conclusion if for the last time I recalled him.

The Commissioner: By all means then, Mr. Roscoe.

Richard Barras was called. He left his seat immediately and entered the witness-box, where he stood upright, his reserve gone, a faint flush on his high cheek-bones, his head inclined forward as though eager to answer every question with the utmost candour. Arthur, stooping in his seat, kept his eyes upon the floor, shielding his face so that it remained invisible.

Lynton Roscoe: Mr. Richard Barras, I am sorry to trouble you again, sir, but there are certain points which I wish to emphasise. I think you have told us that you are the owner of the Neptune Colliery, a mining engineer of some thirty-five years' standing?

Barras: That is so.

Lynton Roscoe: Inevitably, your experience in mining engineering has been wide?

Barras: Yes, I think I may say that.

Lynton Roscoe: Once again, Mr. Barras (slowly), had you any idea when you started to strip the Dyke that you were in any way near the water-logged workings of the Old Neptune pit?

Barras: I had no idea.

Lynton Roscoe: I take it, Mr. Barras, in plain language that there are only two ways of getting to know your whereabouts underground. The one is by boring and the other is by resort to records, in short a plan?

Barras: Quite.

Lynton Roscoe (persuasively): But a bore, after all, will only tell you what is in its own track. And you may have very large faults. In fact boring will often teach little or nothing?

Barras: Not in a case such as this.

Lynton Roscoe: Precisely. And as for the other method. Had you any record, or plan, or tracing of these Old Neptune workings?

Barras: No.

Lynton Roscoe: Such a plan, if it ever existed, must in these early days of mining, when records were not treated with the respect due to them, have been mislaid or destroyed. It was never in your possession?

Barras: Never.

Lynton Roscoe: You had, then, no knowledge of the impending peril. (Dramatically) And in the light of logic and reason, you were as much a victim of the disaster as those unhappy men who perished. (Turning to the Commissioner) That, sir, is the point I thought fit to re-emphasise. I have no wish to trouble Mr. Barras further.

The Commissioner: Thank you, Mr. Barras, I am much obliged.

Barras stepped out of the box, head well up, as if inviting the inspection of every eye. So admirable was his bearing that an involuntary murmur of applause came from the sides of the court. There was genuine sympathy for Richard. His conduct during the Inquiry had been commented on most favourably and, coming on top of his efforts during the rescue operations, had raised him almost to popularity.

As Barras sat down beside Arthur, Harry Nugent, M.P., rose quietly. Nugent was a quiet man with an air of purpose and stability and an eye that was luminous and direct. He was tall, rather emaciated, with a bony cadaverous face and a fine brow across which a few thin strands of hair were streaked. Unprepossessing at first sight, there was a warmth, a quiet sincerity about Nugent which wore down the prejudice created by his appearance. For the last five years he had represented the Tyneside borough of Edgely, he was recognised as a rising force in the Labour Movement and some of his adherents spoke of him as the future leader of the Party. He faced the Commissioner, stooping slightly as he spoke.

Harry Nugent: Since my friend has recalled his principal witness, Mr. Chairman, have I your permission to put David Fenwick in the box again?

The Commissioner: If you feel that any useful purpose will be served.

The name of David Fenwick was called. David got up and moved quickly to the front, his expression controlled and serious. For these last six days he had been in and out of the witness-box, questioned and cross-questioned, threatened, flattered, ridiculed and cajoled, but all the time holding grimly to his point. He took the Book and was sworn.

Harry Nugent: Once again, Mr. Fenwick, about your father, Robert Fenwick, who lost his life in the disaster. . . .

David: Yes.

Harry Nugent: Do you reaffirm that while working in Scupper Flats he expressed alarm about the possibility of an inrush?

David: Yes, he spoke of it several times.

Harry Nugent: To you?

David: Yes, to me.

Harry Nugent: Now, please, Mr. Fenwick, did you attach any importance to what your father said?

David: Yes, I did, I was worried. In fact, as I've told you, I went so far as to speak to Mr. Barras himself.

Harry Nugent: You actually took this matter to Mr. Barras himself?

David: Yes.

Harry Nugent: And what was his attitude?

David: He refused to listen to me.

Lynton Roscoe (rising) : Sir, I protest. Mr. Nugent, not only in connection with this witness but with other witnesses, has laboured this matter beyond all bounds. I find it quite impossible to leave it where it is.

The Commissioner: Mr. Roscoe, you will have full opportunity to cross-examine this witness again if you so desire. (Turning to Nugent) But I suggest, Mr. Nugent, that we have nothing more to learn from this witness.

Harry Nugent: I have no more to say, Mr. Chairman. I have merely drawn your attention again to the possibility that the disaster might have been avoided.

Nugent sat down. But Lynton Roscoe sprang to his feet again and with a pompous gesture stopped David as he made to leave the box.

Lynton Roscoe: One moment, sir. Where did this alleged conversation take place?

David: On the Wansbeck stream. We were fishing.

Lynton Roscoe (incredulously): Do you really ask us to believe that your father, although in mortal fear of death, went calmly to amuse himself by fishing? (Sardonic pause.) Mr. Fenwick, let us be frank. Was your father an educated man?

David: He was an intelligent man.

Lynton Roscoe: Come, come, sir, confine yourself to my questions. Was he educated, I ask you?

David: Not in the restricted sense of the word.

Lynton Roscoe: I take it, sir, despite your unwillingness to admit the fact, that he was *not* educated. He had, for instance, no knowledge of the science of mining engineering? Answer me, yes, or no.

David: No.

Lynton Roscoe: Have you such knowledge?

David: No.

Lynton Roscoe (sarcastically): You follow the teaching profession, I understand?

David (hotly): What has my teaching got to do with the Neptune disaster?

Lynton Roscoe: That is exactly the question I propose to ask you, sir. You are a junior teacher in a County Council School without even, I believe, the qualification of the B.A. degree. You have admitted your complete ignorance of the science of mining engineering. And yet——

David: I——

Lynton Roscoe: One moment, sir. (Thumping the table.) Had you or had you not any authority from the men to act in this matter?

David: No.

Lynton Roscoe: Then how did you expect Mr. Barras to do other than ignore your presumptuous interference?

David: Was it presumptuous to try to save the lives of these hundred men?

Lynton Roscoe: Don't be insolent, sir.

David: Insolence doesn't belong exclusively to you.

The Commissioner (interposing): I think, Mr. Lynton Roscoe, as I remarked before, we have already exhausted the usefulness of this witness.

Lynton Roscoe (throwing out his hand): But, sir——

The Commissioner: I think it may close this matter if I state, without prejudice, that I impute no motives to Mr. Richard Barras other than the very highest.

Lynton Roscoe (smiling and bowing): I respectfully thank you, sir.

The Commissioner: Do you wish to address me further, Mr. Lynton Roscoe?

Mr. Lynton Roscoe: If you please, sir, merely to affirm the facts shortly. We may congratulate ourselves that the issue arising out of the disaster is so clear. The absence of any plan, drawing or sketch which demonstrated the Old Neptune workings is beyond doubt. These old workings, as I have shown, were abandoned in 1808 at a time long before there was any legislative provision requiring the filing of plans or the lodging of information regarding the abandonment of a pit, and when, as you may imagine, the keeping of records, indeed the conduct of mining in general, was primitive in the extreme. We are, by your leave, sir, not responsible for that! The evidence is that Mr. Richard Barras was a trusted employer and that he controlled the operations in Scupper Flats in the best and highest tradition of the industry. He did not know of the impending peril.

I cannot believe that Mr. Nugent, in the course of his cross-examination of the witness Fenwick, really implied that certain of the men who had lost their lives in the disaster had previously expressed their apprehension at water flowing into Scupper Flats.

I ask you, sir, having considered Fenwick's evidence, on the matter of his father's communications to him, to say that there is not one fragment of foundation for such a monstrous suggestion. At best it is a casual conversation; we have the sworn evidence of every responsible official of the colliery that not one of the workmen or local inhabitants expressed any fears or misgiving to them.

The witness Fenwick has insisted, with an acrimony which we deplore, upon his interview with Mr. Richard Barras on the night of the 13th April previous. But, sir, what importance could the manager of any colliery attach to such an irrelevant and impertinent approach as that made by Fenwick on the night in question? Had some responsible and competent person, say Mr. Armstrong, Mr. Hudspeth or some other official raised this query the case would have been altogether different. But an outsider, speaking in such uninformed and ambiguous terms of danger and water and wetness in the pit? The Neptune, sir, was essentially a wet pit and the amount of water flowing therein conveyed no possible indication of the approaching inrush.

In a word, sir, we have fully established that the management had no knowledge of the fact that they were in immediate proximity to old waterlogged workings. There was no plan, owing to a defect in the legislation previous to 1872. That, sir, is the crux of the situation. And there, with your permission, I leave it with you.

The Commissioner: Thank you, Mr. Roscoe, for your admirable and lucid summary of the case. I am not sure, Mr. Nugent, whether you wished to address me.

Harry Nugent rose slowly to his feet.

Harry Nugent: Mr. Chairman, I have little more to say at present. Later, I intend to raise the whole question of the legislation affecting wet mines in the House of Commons. This is not the first inrush of water that has taken place. We have had similar cases, lack of opportunity to see necessary plans and a large loss of life. I must repeat how serious this question is. If we are going to get safety in mines it is high time something was done about it. We are all familiar with cases where colliery owners are careless, I might even say worse than careless, underground when they get near a boundary, particularly if it presents prospects of desirable coal. It is an irregularity inseparable from the system of private ownership. Even in our good years in the mines of this country we averaged killing four men every day, 365 days of the year. Think of it, sir, a man killed every six hours, a man injured every three minutes. We have been accused of acrimony in this case. I want you to understand that I concern myself less with this local issue than with the general issue of safety in mines. We are forced to use these accidents to agitate for better conditions and more favourable legislation, for it is only when these accidents happen that we get a little sympathy. The so-called progress in the coal industry, instead of resulting in the diminution of the death and accident rates, has resulted in their increase. And we honestly believe that so long as the economic system of private ownership exists this waste of human life will continue. That, sir, is all I have to say at present.

The Commissioner (briefly): Then I have now to declare this Inquiry closed. I should like, however, to express my indebtedness to all who have taken part in the investigation. I wish also to convey my sympathy to the bereaved families, particularly towards those of the ten men whose bodies have not yet been recovered from the pit. In conclusion, I want to congratulate Mr. Richard Barras on his heroic efforts on behalf of the entombed men and to place immediately on record that, from the evidence heard before me, he leaves this court without a stain on his character.

A murmur, a great sigh of relaxed tension filled the court. As the Commissioner rose, there was a clatter of chairs, a rapid hum of talk. The double doors at the back were thrown open, the court began to empty quickly. When Barras and Arthur reached the steps outside, Colonel Gascoigne and a number of others pressed forward in congratulation. Actually a faint cheer was raised. More people crowded round, eager to shake hands. Bareheaded, slightly flushed, holding himself erect, Barras stood on the topmost step with Arthur, still deadly pale, behind him. He seemed in no hurry to move from the glare of publicity. He looked about him, an eager, vindicated expression on his face, readily accepting any hand held out to him. Something emotional in his attitude flowed towards the waiting men. Another cheer went up and another, louder than before. Deeply gratified, Barras began to move slowly down the steps, still hatless, accompanied by Gascoigne, Lynton Roscoe, Bannerman, Armstrong, Jennings and, last of all, by Arthur. The crowd parted deferentially before this imposing group. Barras led the way across the pavement, head well up, his eye eagerly picking out known faces, acknowledging salutations, dropping a grave word here and there, feeling the popular sentiment veering towards him, a man leaving the court without a stain on his character, unsmirched by the mud flung at him, those last words ringing in his ears: " Your truly heroic efforts on behalf of the entombed men." The party's progress towards the Law became something of a triumph.

Inside the hall David remained motionless in his seat, hearing the cheers, the heavy movement of feet outside, staring at the blank sweating walls, the flies buzzing on the dirty window panes. Deliberately he held himself in check. No use to give way, no use at all.

A touch on the shoulder made him turn slowly. Harry Nugent stood beside him in the deserted hall. Nugent said kindly:

" Well, it's all over."

" Yes."

Studying David's impassive face, Nugent sat down beside him.

" You didn't expect anything else, did you ? "

" Well, yes." David seemed to reflect seriously. " Yes, I expected justice. I know he was to blame. He ought to have been punished. Instead of that they compliment him, cheer him, let him go."

" You mustn't take it too hard."

" I'm not thinking about myself. Why should I ? Nothing has happened to me. It's the others."

A faint smile came upon Nugent's lips. It was a very friendly smile. Throughout the Inquiry he had seen a lot of David, and he was strongly drawn to him.

" We haven't done so badly," he meditated. " Now we'll be able to force the Mines Department to act over this question of abandoned waterlogged mines. We've been waiting on the chance for years. That's the main issue. Can you see it that way ? "

David raised his head, stubbornly fighting the emptiness within him, the ache of defeat.

" Yes, I see that," he muttered.

The look in David's eyes moved Nugent suddenly from his serenity. He slipped his arm round David's shoulders.

" I know how you feel, lad, but don't fret. You did well. Your evidence helped us more than you believe."

" I did nothing. I wanted to, but I didn't. All my life I've been talking about doing something. . . ."

" And so you will. Give yourself a chance. I'm going to keep in touch with you. I'll see what can be done. And in the meantime keep your pecker up." He rose, glancing towards the door where Heddon stood in conversation with Jim Dudgeon, awaiting him. " Listen, David. Be at the station at six to-night. I'll have another word with you then."

He nodded encouragingly and walked over to Heddon and Dudgeon. The three moved off towards the temporary lodge office in Cowpen Street.

A moment later David rose and reached for his hat. He walked out of the hall and down Freehold Street. He was completely fagged. With typical intensity he had concentrated everything on the Inquiry, for six days he had not been near the school. And the result was this. He hunched his shoulders doggedly, taking hold of himself again. This was no time for the luxury of going to pieces, for petty spite and hysteria.

Along Freehold Street he went, across the road, and into Lamb Street. But there, opposite the Scut, a man called after him. It was Ramage. The butcher wore a dirty blue linen coat with an enormous blue and white apron belted round his middle. He had just come up from his slaughter-house where he had been down at the killing, the backs of his hands were mottled with dried blood. The warm afternoon set a haze of red about him.

" Hey, Fenwick, here a minute! "

David stopped but did not speak. Ramage eased his thick neck away from his collar, then stuffed both thumbs in his leather belt, and lay back, studying David.

" So y've finished your day's work at the Town Hall ? " he declared with heavy sarcasm. " No wonder y'look proud of yourself. God Almighty, y've been a credit to Sleescale this past week. Standin' up to argue with Lynton like y' were bloody lawyer." His sneer grew. He was evidently posted in the last details of the Inquiry. " But if I were in your shoes I wouldn't look so set up about it. Maybe y'll find this business has cost more'n ye bargained for."

David waited, facing Ramage. He knew that something was coming. There was a pause, then Ramage abandoned his sarcasm, his brows drew down in that bullying way.

" What the hell d'y' think y've been up to, leaving the school without permission, these last six days ? D'y think ye own the bloody place . . ."

" I went to the Inquiry because I had to."

" Y' didn't have to. Y' went out of downright spite. Y' went to sling muck at one of the leadin' men in the town, a public man like myself, a man who got ye the job what ye never deserved. Y've turned round and bit the hand that fed ye. But, by God, y're goin' to regret it."

" I'm the best judge of that," David said curtly and he made to go.

" Wait a minute," Ramage bawled, " I've not done with ye. I've always thought ye were a trouble maker like your father afore ye. Y're nothing but a rank rotten socialist. We've no use for your kind teachin' in our schools. Y're goin' to be chucked out."

A pause. David considered Ramage.

" You can't put me out."

" Oh, can't I ? Can't I though ? " Triumph blared into Ramage's snarl. " Y' might like to know we called a meetin' of the School Board last night to consider y're conduct an' agreed unanimous to demand your resignation."

" What ! "

" No whats about it. Ye'll get your notice from Strother in the morning. He wants a man what's gotten a B.A. t'is name; not a half-baked pitman like yourself." For a full minute Ramage indulged himself in the delicious satisfaction of watching David's face, then, with a sardonic grin fixed on his meaty lips, he swung round and barged his way into his shop.

David walked along Lamb Street, head down, eyes on the pavement. He let himself into his house, went into the kitchen and began automatically to make himself some tea. Jenny was in Tynecastle at her mother's, he had sent her there this last week to spare her the worry of the Inquiry. He sat down at the table, stirring his cup, round and round, not even tasting the tea. So they were trying to sack him. He knew at once that Ramage meant every word he had spoken. He could fight, of course, appeal to the Northern Teachers' Association. But what would be the use ? His face hardened. No, let them do what they liked. He would talk to Nugent at six, he wanted to be out of this blind alley of teaching, he wanted to do something. O God, he did want to justify himself, to *do* something at last.

At quarter to six he left the house and set out for the station. But he had not gone more than half-way when he heard a commotion at the head of the street and, looking up, he saw two news-boys tearing down the hill with their billheads wildly fluttering. He stopped and bought a paper, all the rumours and latent fears which the Inquiry had overlaid flashing into the foreground of his mind. And there across the front page sprawled the headline: *British Ultimatum Expires Midnight.*

II

TOWARDS one o'clock on the second Saturday of September, 1914, Arthur came home from the Neptune to the Law. Normal conditions prevailed at the pit again, work had recommenced, the whole tragic business of the disaster appeared buried and forgotten. But Arthur's face expressed no satisfaction. He walked up the Avenue like a tired man. He entered the grounds of the Law and, as he had expected and dreaded, the new car had arrived. Bartley, who had been to Tynecastle for a month's tuition, had brought the new car down himself and it was drawn up in the drive in front of the Law, a landaulet, all smooth maroon enamel and shiny brass. Barras stood beside the new car and as Arthur passed he called out:

" Look, Arthur, here she is at last! "

Arthur stopped. He was in his pit suit. He stared heavily at the car and he said at length:

" So I see."

" I have so much to do I must have a car," Barras explained. " It was quite ridiculous not to have seen that before. Bartley tells me she runs magnificently. We'll run in to Tynecastle this evening and try her out."

Arthur appeared to be thinking. He said:

" I'm sorry . . . I can't come."

Barras laughed. The laugh, like the car, was new. He said:

" Nonsense. We're spending the evening with the Todds. I've arranged for us all to have dinner at the Central."

Arthur stopped staring at the car and stared at his father instead. Barras's face was not flushed but it gave the impression of being flushed: the eyes and the lips were fuller than they had been, the small eyes behind the strong lenses in particular had a protruding look. He seemed restless and vaguely excited, perhaps the arrival of the new car had excited him.

" I didn't know you were in the habit of giving dinners at the Central," Arthur said.

" I'm not," Barras answered with a sudden irritation. " But this is an occasion. Alan is going to the front with his battalion. We are all proud of him. Besides I haven't seen Todd for some time now. I want to look him up."

Arthur thought for another minute, then he asked:

" You haven't seen Todd since we had the disaster at the pit? "

" No, I haven't," Barras replied shortly.

There was a pause.

" It always struck me as odd, father, that you didn't ask Todd to come over and support you at the Inquiry."

Barras turned sharply.

" Support! What do you mean, support? The findings were pretty satisfactory, weren't they ? "

" Satisfactory ? "

" That's what I said," Barras snapped. He took out his handkerchief and flicked a fine spot of dust from the radiator. " Are you coming to Tynecastle or not ? "

With his eyes on the ground Arthur said:

" Yes, I'll come, father."

There was a silence, then the gong sounded. Arthur followed his father in to lunch, Barras walking a little faster than usual. To Arthur it seemed almost as though he were hurrying; lately his father's walk had briskened to a point where it simulated haste.

" A remarkably fine car," Barras informed the table, looking down towards Aunt Carrie. " You must come for a spin one of these days, Caroline."

Aunt Caroline coloured with pleasure but before she could answer Barras had picked up the paper, a special edition which Bartley had brought down from Tynecastle. Rapidly scanning the centre page he said with sudden satisfaction:

" Aha! Here is some news for you. And good news, too." His pupils dilated slightly. " A serious repulse for the Germans on the Marne. Heavy losses. Enfiladed by our machine-gun fire. Enormous losses. Estimated at four thousand killed and wounded."

It struck Arthur that his father seized upon these losses, upon the slaughter of these four thousand men with a queer unconscious avidity. A faint shiver passed over him.

" Why, yes," he said in an unnatural tone, " it is enormous. Four thousand men. That's about forty times the number we lost in the Neptune."

Dead silence. Barras lowered his paper. He fixed his protruding eyes upon Arthur. Then in a high voice he said:

" You have an odd sense of values, to mention our misfortune at the pit in the same breath as this. If you don't give over brooding about what is done with and forgotten you'll become morbid. You must take yourself in hand. Don't you realise we are facing a national emergency ? " He frowned and resumed his paper.

There was another silence. Arthur choked down the rest of his lunch and immediately went upstairs. He sat down on the edge of his bed and stared moodily out of the window. What was happening to him ? It was true enough, no doubt, what his father said. He was becoming morbid, horribly morbid, but he could not help it. One hundred and five men had been killed in the Neptune pit. He could not forget them. These men lived with him, ate with him, walked with him, worked with him. They peopled his dreams. He could not forget them. All this carnage, as his father named it, this horrible carnage, this slaughter of thousands of men by shells, bullets, bombs and shrapnel seemed merely to intensify and swell his morbid introspection. The war was nothing by itself. It was the echo, the profound reverberation of the Neptune disaster. It was at once a new horror and the same horror. The war victims were the pit victims. The war was the Neptune disaster magnified to gigantic size, a deepening of the first flood, a spreading of the morass in which was sunk the beautiful ideal of the preciousness of human life.

Arthur moved uneasily. Lately his own thoughts terrified him. He felt his mind a delicate flask in which terrific thoughts were agitated and convulsed like chemicals which might coalesce and suddenly explode. He felt himself unable to withstand the action and reaction of these chemically active thoughts.

What terrified him most of all was his attitude towards his father. He loved his father, he had always loved and admired his father. And yet he found himself repeatedly at his father's elbow, watching, criticising, observing carefully and adding one observation to another like a detective spying upon God. He wanted with all his soul to abandon this unholy espionage. But he could not: the change in his father made it impossible. He knew his father to be changed. He knew it. And he was afraid.

He sat on his bed thinking for a long time. Then he lay back and closed his eyes. He felt tired suddenly as though he must have sleep. It was late afternoon when he awoke. As he recollected himself he sighed and got up and began to dress.

At six o'clock he went downstairs and found his father waiting for him in the hall. As Arthur approached Barras looked at his watch significantly, lately he had acquired a perfect mannerism with his watch, flicking it open and frowning at the dial like a man pressed for time. Indeed time seemed to have acquired a new significance for Barras now, as though every moment must be utilised.

" I was afraid you were going to be late." And without waiting for an answer he led the way to the car.

When Arthur got into the car with his father and they glided off in the direction of Tynecastle he felt less despondent. It was, after all, rather pleasant to be going out like this. He hadn't seen Hetty for ages, his spirits rose at the thought of seeing her. The car behaved beautifully too, he was not insensible to the gracious springing, the smooth flow of movement. He glanced sideways at his father. Barras was seated upright with a pleased expression on his face, an intent expression, like a child with a new toy.

They drove into Tynecastle. The streets were crowded, reflecting a certain movement and unrest which seemed to gratify Barras. At the Central Hotel the head porter opened the door of the car with a kind of flourish head porters reserve for expensive cars. Barras nodded to the hotel porter. The porter saluted Barras.

They went into the lounge, which was crowded and rather restless like the streets. Many of the men were in uniform. Barras let his eye rest upon the men in uniform with approval.

Then Hetty signalled them gaily from a corner of the lounge, a good corner by the fireplace, and Alan her brother stood up as Barras and Arthur came over. The first thing Barras said was:

" Where is your father ? "

Alan smiled. He looked very well in his second lieutenant's uniform and very light-hearted because he was already a few drinks to the good.

" Father's got the old complaint. A touch of the jaundice. Sent his regrets."

Barras looked put out, his face fell.

A distinct silence followed; but Barras quickly recovered himself. He smiled vaguely at Hetty. In a moment the four of them went in to dinner.

In the restaurant Barras picked up his napkin and let his eyes go round the room, which was filled with people and gaiety. Most of the gayest people were in khaki. He said:

" This is very pleasant. I've had a certain amount of strain lately. I'm glad to have some recreation for a change."

" You're glad it's all settled," Alan said, looking at Barras rather knowingly.

Barras said shortly:

" Yes."

" They're just a lot of twisters," Alan went on. " They'd twist *you* if they got the chance. I know that Heddon, he's a swine. He's paid to be a swine, but he is a natural-born swine as well! "

" Alan! " Hetty protested, with her little pout.

" I know, Hetty, I *know*," Alan said airily. " I've had to do with men. You've got to get them down or else they'll get you down. It's self-preservation."

Covertly, Arthur looked at his father. Something of the old frozen expression was back on Barras's face. He seemed trying to adapt himself to a new outlook. With a definite attempt to turn the conversation he said:

" You leave on Monday, Alan ? "

" That's right."

" And glad to get into it, I suppose ? "

" Certainly," Alan agreed loudly. " It's a regular lark."

The wine waiter came over. Barras took the red-covered list and meditated over it. Yet he was not so much debating with the wine list as debating with himself. But at length he took a decision.

" I think we ought to have a little celebration. After all this is an occasion." He ordered champagne and the waiter bowed himself away.

Hetty looked pleased. She had always been slightly in awe of Barras, his formality and aloof dignity had somehow intimidated her. But to-night he was surprising, with his sudden exciting hospitality. She smiled at him, the sweetest, respectful smile.

" This is nice," she murmured. She fingered her beads with one hand and the stem of her full wine-glass with the other. She turned to Arthur: " Don't you think Alan suits his uniform beautifully ? "

Arthur forced a smile:

" Alan would look well in anything."

" Oh no, but seriously, Arthur, don't you think the uniform sets him off ? "

Arthur said with stiff lips:

" Yes."

" It's the very devil answering salutes," Alan remarked complacently. " Wait till you get into the Women's Emergency Corps, Hetty, you'll know all about it."

Hetty took another tiny sip of her champagne. She reflected, her pretty head atilt.

" You'd look simply gorgeous in uniform yourself, Arthur."

Arthur went absolutely cold inside. He said:

" I don't see myself in uniform, somehow."

" You're slim you see, Arthur, you've really got a good figure for a Sam Browne. And your colouring, too. You'd be marvellous in khaki."

They all looked at Arthur. Alan said:

" It's a fact, Arthur. You'd have knocked 'em good and proper. You ought to have been coming out with me."

For no reason that he could determine, Arthur felt himself trembling. His nerves were overstrung, he saw the whole evening as abnormal and abominable. Why was his father here, sitting in this crowded hotel drinking champagne, sanctioning Alan Todd's patriotic bluster, so restless and unlike himself ?

" D'you hear, Arthur ? " Alan said. " You and I ought to be in the show together."

Arthur compelled himself to speak. He struggled to speak lightly.

" I expect the show will get on without me, Alan. I'm not very keen on it to tell you the truth."

" Oh, Arthur! " Hetty said, disappointed. Because she regarded Arthur as her own property she liked him always to show up well, to shine, as she phrased it. And this last remark of Arthur's was not a very shining one. She screwed up her vivacious little face, fascinating and disapproving. " That's a ridiculous way to talk, Arthur. Why, anyone that didn't know you would imagine you were scared."

" Nonsense, Hetty," Barras said indulgently. " Arthur just hasn't had time to think it out. One of these days you may see him making a dash for the nearest recruiting office."

" Oh, I know! " Hetty said, warmly casting down those ingenuous eyes, a little sorry for having spoken.

Arthur said nothing. He sat with his eyes on his plate. He refused champagne. He refused dessert. He let the others talk on without him.

An orchestra struck up at the far end of the room where there was a clear space of floor waxed and ready for dancing. The orchestra played " God save the King " very loudly, and everyone stood up with a loud clatter of chairs and there was loud and prolonged cheering at the end, then the orchestra began not so loudly to play dance music. They always had dancing at the Central on Saturday nights.

Hetty smiled across at Arthur: they were both good dancers, they loved dancing together. Hetty had often been told what a charming couple she and Arthur made when dancing together. She waited for him to ask her to dance. But he sat there with his eyes glumly fixed on his plate, and he did not ask Hetty.

His moodiness became quite obvious at last and Alan, always ready to oblige, leaned across to Hetty.

" Care to take the old war-horse for a walk, Hetty ? "

Hetty smiled with more than her usual vivacity. Alan was a bad dancer, a heavy dancer, he did not like dancing, and it was not the least pleasure for Hetty to dance with him. But Hetty pretended that she was pleased; she got up, and she and Alan danced together.

While they were dancing Barras said:

" She is a nice little thing, Hetty. So modest and yet so full of spirits." He spoke pleasantly, more restfully; since his dinner and the champagne he seemed more quiescent.

Arthur did not answer; out of the corner of his eye he watched Hetty and Alan dancing and he tried hard to overcome his incomprehensible mood.

When Hetty and Alan came back he did, for politeness' sake, ask her to dance. He asked her stiffly, still chilled and hurt inside. It was wonderful dancing with Hetty, she was soft in his arms and the perfume that was herself seemed to flow into him with every movement of her body, yet because it was so wonderful he swore perversely he would dance this one dance and no more.

Afterwards Hetty sat beating time to the music with her neat slippered foot, until at last she could bear it no longer. With that fetching expression of vivacious distress:

" Is nobody going to dance to-night ? "

Arthur said quickly:

" I'm tired."

There was a silence. Suddenly Barras said:

" If I were any use to you, Hetty, I'm at your disposal. But I'm afraid I don't know any of these new steps."

She stared at him doubtfully, rather taken aback.

" But it's quite easy," she said. " You simply walk."

He had the new smile, the vague, rather pleased, smile upon his face.

" Well, if you are not afraid, by all means let us try." He rose and offered her his arm.

Arthur sat perfectly rigid. With a set face he stared at the figures of his father and Hetty moving slowly in each other's arms at the end of the room. His father had always treated Hetty with a patronising aloofness and Hetty had always been timid and deferential to his father. And now they were dancing together. He distinctly saw Hetty smile, her uplifted flirtatious smile, the smile of a woman who is flattered by the attention she is receiving.

Then he heard Alan speak to him, asking him to go out, and mechanically he rose and went out with Alan. Now Alan was certainly not sober. He glowed. In the lavatory he faced Arthur, wavering slightly on his feet.

" Your old man's loosened up a treat to-night, Arthur; I wouldn't have believed it; given the old war-horse a marvellous send off."

He turned on both taps so that they ran at full strength into the basin, then he swung round to Arthur again. He said with great confidence:

" Y'know, Arthur, my old man was pretty sick at your old man for not asking him over to back him up at the Inquiry. Never said much, but I know, the old war-horse knows, Arthur."

Arthur stared at Alan uneasily.

" No need to worry, you know, Arthur." Alan waved a hand with wise and friendly confidence. " Not the slightest need to worry, Arthur. All between friends you know, all between the best of old friends."

Arthur continued to stare at Alan. He was speechless. A great confusion of doubt and uncertainty and fear rushed over him.

" What are you trying to say ? " he asked at length.

Suddenly the lavatory basin overflowed and all the water came gushing over the floor, flowing, flowing over the floor.

Arthur's eyes turned to the flooding water dazedly. The water in the Neptune pit had flooded like that, flooded through those tortuous and secret channels of the mine, drowning the men in horror and darkness.

His whole body was shaken by a spasm. He thought passionately: I mean to discover the truth. If it kills me I will discover the truth.

III

In the car on the way home Arthur waited until they were clear of the traffic of Tynecastle, then as they hummed along the straight stretch of silent road between Kenton and Sleescale he said quickly:

" There's something I want to ask you, father."

Barras was silent for a moment; he sat in his corner supported by the soft upholstery, his features masked by the interior dimness of the car.

" Well," he said, unwillingly. " What is it you want ? "

Barras's tone was completely discouraging but Arthur was beyond discouragement now.

" It's about the disaster."

Barras made a movement of displeasure, almost of repugnance. Arthur felt rather than saw the gesture. There was a silence, then he heard his father say:

" Why must you keep on with that subject ? It's extremely distasteful to me. I've had a pleasant evening. I enjoyed dancing with Hetty, I'd no idea I should master these steps so well. I don't want to be bothered with something which is completely settled and forgotten."

Arthur answered in a burning voice.

" I haven't forgotten it, father. I can't forget it."

Barras sat quite still for a moment.

" Arthur, I wish to God you would give this over." He spoke with a certain restraint as though forcing this restraint upon a rising impatience; the result was the injection of a gloomy kindness into his words. " Don't think I haven't seen it coming. I have. Now listen to me and try to be reasonable. You're on my side of the affair, aren't you ? My interests are your interests. You're nearly twenty-two now. You'll be my partner in the Neptune very shortly. Whenever this war is over I intend to see to it. When every living soul has forgotten about the disaster don't you think it's madness for you to keep harping on it ? "

Arthur felt sick. In reminding him of his interest in the Neptune it was as if his father had offered him a bribe. His voice trembled.

" I don't look on it as madness. I want to know the truth."

Barras lost his self-control.

" The truth," he exclaimed. " Haven't we had an Inquiry ? Eleven days of it, with everything investigated and settled. You know I was exonerated. There's the truth for you. What more do you want ? "

" The Inquiry was an official inquiry. It's very easy to suppress facts at that kind of Inquiry."

" What facts ? " Barras burst out. " Have you gone out of your mind ? "

Arthur stared straight in front of him through the glass partition at the stiff outlines of Bartley's back.

" Didn't you know all the time that you were taking a risk, father ? "

" We've got to take risks," Barras answered angrily. " Every one of us. In mining it's a case of risks and risks and more risks, day in and day out. You can't get away from them."

But Arthur was not to be turned aside.

" Didn't Adam Todd warn you before you started stripping coal from the Dyke ? " he asked stonily. " You remember that day you went to see him. Didn't he tell you there was a danger? And yet you went on in spite of him."

" You're talking nonsense," Barras almost shouted. " It's my place to make the decisions. The Neptune is my pit and I've got to run it my own way. Nobody has the right to interfere. I run it the best way I can."

" The best way for whom? "

Barras struggled violently for self-control.

" Do you think the Neptune is a Benevolent Institute? I want to show a profit, don't I? "

" That's it, father," Arthur said tonelessly. " You wanted to make a profit, an enormous profit. If you had pumped the water out of the Old Neptune workings before you started to strip that coal there would have been no danger. But the expense of dewatering the old workings would have swallowed up your profit. The expense, the thought of spending all that money in pumping out waste water was too much for you. So you decided to take the chance, the risk, to ignore the waste water and send all these men into danger."

" That's enough," Barras said harshly. " I won't have you talk to me like that." The lights of a passing vehicle momentarily illuminated his face, which was congested, the forehead flushed, the eyes indignant and inflamed. Then all was darkness in the car again. Arthur clung tremblingly to the seat of the car, his lips pale, his whole being rent by an incredible dismay.

Once again he felt that strange unrest behind his father's words, the sense of hurry, of evasion; it impressed him dully as an act of flight. He remained silent while the car swung into the drive of the Law and drew up before the front porch. He followed Barras into the house and in the high, bright vestibule they faced each other. There was a singular expression on Barras's face as he stood with one hand upon the carved banister preparatory to ascending the stairs.

" You've had a great deal to say lately, a very great deal. But don't you think it would fit you better if you tried to do something for a change? "

" I don't understand you, father."

Over his shoulder, Barras said:

" Hasn't it occurred to you that you might be fighting for your country? " Then he turned and heavily went upstairs.

Arthur stood with his head thrown back watching the retreating figure of his father. His pale, upturned face was contorted. He felt finally that his love for his father was dead, he felt that out of the ashes there was arising something sinister and terrible.

IV

EARLIER on that same Saturday night Sammy walked down the Avenue with Annie Macer. Every Saturday night for years Sammy and Annie had taken this walk. It was part of the courtship of Sammy and Annie Macer.

About seven o'clock every Saturday night Sammy and Annie met at the corner of Quay Street. Usually Annie was there first, strolling up and down in her thick woollen stockings and well-brushed shoes, strolling quietly up and down, waiting, waiting for Sammy. Sammy always was the late one. Sammy would arrive about ten past seven, dressed in his good blue suit, very newly shaved about the chin and very shiny about his nobby forehead.

" I'm late, Annie," Sammy would remark, smiling. He never expressed regret for being late, never dreamed of it; Annie, indeed, would have felt it very out of place if Sammy had said that he was sorry he had kept her waiting.

They set out for their walk " up the Avenue." Not arm in arm, there was nothing like that in the courtship of Sam and Annie, no holding of hands, or squeezing, or kissing, none of the more exuberant manifestations of affection. Sam and Annie were steadies. Sam respected Annie. In the darkest part of the Avenue Sam might quietly and sensibly encircle Annie's waist as they strolled along. No more than that. Sammy and Annie just walked out.

Annie knew that Sammy's mother " objected " to her. But she knew that Sammy loved her. That was enough. After they had walked up the Avenue they would come back to the town, Sammy nodding to acquaintances " How do, Ned," " How again, Tom," back along Lamb Street and into Mrs. Wept's pie-shop where the bell went *ping* and the loose glass pane in the door rattled every time they went in. Standing in Mrs. Wept's dark little pie-shop they would each eat a hot pie with gravy and share a big bottle of lemonade. Annie preferred ginger ale but Sam's favourite drink was the lemonade and this meant, of course, that Annie always insisted on lemonade. Sometimes Sammy had two pies, if he was flush after a good week's hewing, for Mrs. Wept's pies were the last word. But Annie refused, Annie knew a woman's place, Annie never had more than one. She would suck the gravy from her fingers while Sam made inroads upon the second pie. Then they would have a chat, maybe, with Mrs. Wept and stroll back to Quay Corner where they stood for a while watching the brisk Saturday night movement in the street before they said good night. And as he walked up the Terraces Sammy would think what a grand evening it had been and what a fine girl Annie was and how lucky he was to be walking her out.

But to-night as Sam and Annie came down the Avenue it was plain that something had gone wrong between them. Annie's expression was subdued while Sammy, with a harassed look, seemed to struggle to explain himself.

" I'm sorry, Annie," kicking moodily at a stone which lay in his way. " I didn't think you'd take it that sore, lass."

In a low voice Annie said:

" It's all right, Sammy, I'm not minding that much. It's quite all right." Whatever Sammy did was always all right with Annie; but her face, seen palely in that dark avenue of trees, was troubled.

Sammy took a kick at another stone.

" I couldn't stand the pit no longer, honest I couldn't, Annie. Goin' down every day thinkin' on dad and Hughie lyin' inbye there, it's more nor I could stand. The pit'll never be the same to me, Annie, never, it won't, till dad and Hughie gets brought out."

" I see that, Sammy," Annie agreed.

" Mind you, I'm not exactly wantin' to go," Sammy worried on. " I don't hold with all this ruddy buglin' and flag flappin'. I'm just makin' it the excuse. I've just got to get out that pit. Anything's better'n the pit now, anything."

" That's right, Sammy," Annie reassured him. " I see what you mean."

Annie saw perfectly that Sammy, a fine hewer who liked, and was needed in, his job, would never be going to the war but for the disaster in the Neptune. But the sadness in Annie's acquiescence set Sammy more at cross-purposes than ever.

" Ah, Annie," he exclaimed with sudden feeling. " I wish't this thing had never happened on us in the Neptune. As I was bringin' out my tools at the end of the shift the day, that's just what I kept thinkin'. There's our Davey, now. I'm proper put down ower what it's done to him. I'm worrit, lass, at how he's took it." He went on with sudden heat: " It wasna fair the way they sacked him out the school. Ramage done it, mind ye, he's always had his knife in wor lot. But God, it was shameful, Annie."

" He'll get work some other place, Sammy."

But Sammy shook his head.

" He's done wi' the schoolmasterin', lass. He's got in wi' Harry Nugent someways. Harry took a heap of notice of Davey when he was up, something'll come out of that, I'm thinkin'." He sighed. " But there's a proper change come ower him, lass."

Annie made no reply: she was thinking of the change which had come over Sammy too.

They walked along the Avenue without speaking. It was now almost dark, but as they passed the Law, the moon sailed out from a bank of cloud, and threw a cold hard light upon the house which sat there square and squat, with a self-complacency almost malignant. Beside the big white gate, under one of the tall beeches which flanked it, two figures stood together—the one a young fellow in uniform, the other a bareheaded girl.

Sammy turned to Annie as they reached the end of the Avenue.

" Did you see that ? " he said. " Dán Teasdale and Grace Barras."

" Ay, I saw them, Sammy."

" I'm thinkin' it wouldn't do for Barras to see them there."

" No, Sammy."

" Barras! " Sammy jerked his head aside and spat. " He's come out of the sheugh all right. But I'll not work for him no more, no, not if he came and begged us."

Silence continued between Annie and Sammy as they walked towards Mrs. Wept's shop. Annie was bearing up, but the thought that Sammy was going to the war paralysed her; anyone but Annie would have refused to go to the shop. Yet Annie felt that Sammy wanted to go, so Annie went and struggled gamely with her pie. To-night Sammy had only one pie and he left half a tumbler of his lemonade.

As they stood at the corner of Quay Street Sammy said, with an effort at his old smile:

" Don't take on, Annie, lass. The pit hasn't done that much for me after all. Maybe the war'll do a bit more."

" Maybe," Annie said: and with a sudden catch in her breath: " I'll see you to-morrow, Sammy. I'll see you for sure before you go."

Sammy nodded his head, still holding his smile, then he exclaimed: " Give us a kiss, lass, to show you're not angry wi' us."

Annie kissed Sammy, then she turned away for fear Sammy should see the tears that were in her eyes. Holding her head down she walked rapidly towards her home.

Sammy climbed the Terraces slowly. He was a fool, he knew he was a fool to be leaving Annie and his good job for a war that did not interest him. And yet he couldn't help himself. The disaster had done something to him—ay, just like it had to David. Where he was going didn't matter; all that mattered was that he was getting out of the pit.

When he reached Inkerman his mother was sitting up for him as usual in her own hard, straight-backed chair by the window and the minute he came in she rose to get him some hot cocoa.

She gave him his cocoa, and, standing by the grate where she had just put the steaming kettle, she watched him, her hands folded beneath her breast, elbows rather gaunt, eyes sombre and loving.

" Will I cut you a piece of cake, son ? "

He had sat down rather wearily at the table with his cap pushed back on his head and now he raised his eyes and looked at her.

She had altered. Though she did not fight within herself against the disaster but received it sombrely with the calm fatality of a woman who has always known and accepted the danger of the pit, the calamity at the Neptune had left its mark on Martha too. The lines on her face were deeper and her cheeks more fallen in, one grey strand made a curious streak on the black of her tight-drawn hair, there was a little pattern of furrows graven upon her brow. But she still held herself erect without effort. Her vitality seemed inexhaustible.

Sammy hated to have to tell his mother; but there was no other way: and as he was without subtlety he spoke directly.

" Mother," he said, " I've joined up."

She went an ashen grey. Her face and her lips turned as grey as the grey strand of her hair; and her hand flew instinctively to her throat. A sudden wildness came into her eyes.

" You don't mean "—she stopped, but at last she brought herself to say it—" the army ? "

He nodded moodily:

" The Fifth Fusiliers. I fetched my tools outbye this afternoon. The draft leaves for camp on Monday."

" On Monday," she stammered, in that same tone of wild and incredulous dismay.

Still looking at him she sat down upon a chair. She sat down very carefully, her hand still pressed to her throat. She seemed shrunken, crushed into that chair by what he had told her; but still she refused to believe it. In a low voice she said:

" They'll not take you. They want the miners back here at home. They can't possibly take a good man like you."

He avoided her beseeching eyes.

" They have taken me."

The words extinguished her. There was a long silence, then almost in a whisper she asked:

" What way did you have to do a thing like that, Sammy ? Oh, what way did you have to do it ? "

He answered doggedly:

" I cannot help it, mother, I cannot go on any longer wi' the pit."

V

It was about five o'clock on the following Tuesday evening and though still light the streets were quiet as David walked along Lamb Lane and entered his house. In the narrow hall he stopped, his first glance towards the little electro-plated tray upon which Jenny, with her deathless sense of etiquette, always placed his mail. One letter lay upon the tray. He picked it up and his dark face brightened.

He went into the kitchen, where he sat down by the small fire and began to take off his boots, unlacing them with one hand and staring at the letter in the other.

Jenny brought him his slippers. That was unusual, but lately Jenny had been most unusual, worried and almost timid, looking after him in small ways, as though subdued by his sombre uncommunicativeness.

He thanked Jenny with a look. He could smell the sweet odour of port on her breath but he refrained from speaking, he had spoken so often and he was tired of words. She took very little, she explained, just a glass when she felt low. The disgrace—her own word—of his dismissal from New Bethel Street had naturally predisposed her to lowness.

He opened the letter and read it slowly and carefully, then he rested it on his knee and gazed into the fire. His face was fixed and unimpassioned and mature. In those six months since the disaster he seemed to have grown older by a good ten years.

Jenny moved about the kitchen pretending to be busy but glancing at him furtively from time to time, as if curious to know what was in the letter. She felt that deep currents were working secretly within David's mind; she did not fully understand; a look, almost of fear, was in her eyes.

" Is it anything important ? " she asked at length. She could not help asking, the words slipped out.

" It's from Nugent," he answered.

She stared at him blankly, then her features sharpened with temper. She distrusted this sudden and spontaneous friendship with Harry Nugent which had sprung from the disaster at the Neptune; it struck her almost as an alliance; she felt excluded and was jealous.

" I thought it was about a job, I'm about sick of you going idle."

He roused himself and looked at her.

" In a way it is about a job, Jenny. It's the answer to a letter I wrote Harry Nugent last week. He's joining the ambulance corps, going out to France as a stretcher-bearer, and I've decided that the only thing to do is to go with him."

Jenny gasped—her reaction was unbelievably intense. She turned quite green, a ghastly colour, her whole body wilted. She looked cowed. He thought for a moment she was going to be sick, she had lately had some queer bouts of sickness, and he jumped up and went over to her.

" Don't worry, Jenny," he said. " There isn't the slightest reason to worry."

" But why must you go ? " she quavered in that odd frightened voice. " Why have you got to let this Nugent drag you in ? You don't believe in it, there isn't any need for you to go."

He was moved by her concern; lately he had resigned himself to the conviction that Jenny's love for him was not what it had been. And he hardly knew how to answer her. It was true that he had no patriotism. The political machinery which had produced the war was linked in his mind with the economic machinery which had produced the disaster in the Neptune. Behind each he saw that insatiable lust for power, for possessions; the quenchless self-interest of man. But although he had no patriotism he felt he could not keep out of the war. This was exactly Nugent's feeling too. It was awful to be in the war but it was more awful not to be in the war. He need not go to the war to kill. He could go to the war to save. To stand aside palely while humanity lay locked in the anguished struggle was to proclain himself a fraud for ever. It was like standing upon the pit-bank of the Neptune watching the cage descend filled with men upon whose foreheads was the predestined seal of the disaster, standing aside and saying, you are in the cage, my brothers, but I will not enter with you because the terror and the danger which await you should never have arisen.

He put out his hand and stroked her cheek.

" It's difficult to explain, Jenny. You know what I've told you . . . since the disaster . . . since I got the sack from the school . . . I'm chucking the B.A., teaching, everything. I'm going to make a complete break and join the Federation. Well, while this war is on there's not much chance to do what I want to do at home. It's a case of marking time. Besides, Sammy has gone and Harry Nugent is going. It's the only thing."

" Oh no, David," she whimpered. " You can't go."

" I'll be all right," he said soothingly. " There's no need to worry about that."

" No, you can't, you can't leave me now, you can't desert me at a time like this." She created the picture of herself forsaken, not only by him, but by everyone she had trusted.

" But, Jenny——"

" You can't leave me now." She was quite beside herself, her words came all in a rush. " You're my husband, you can't desert me. Don't you see I'm going . . . that we're going to have a baby."

There was a complete silence. Her news staggered him, not for an instant had he suspected it. Then she began to cry, letting her head droop while the tears simply ran out of her eyes, to cry as she always cried when she had offended him. He could not bear to see her cry like this; he flung his arm round her.

" Don't cry, Jenny, for God's sake don't cry. I'm glad, I'm terribly glad; you know I've always wanted this to happen. You took me by surprise there for a minute. That was all. Don't cry, Jenny, please, don't cry like that, as if it was your fault."

She sniffed and sobbed on his chest, snuggling up to him. The colour came back into her face, she looked relieved now that she had told him. She said:

" You won't leave me now, will you, David, not until our baby's born at any rate?"

There was something almost pitiful in Jenny's eagerness to share the baby with him; but he did not see it.

" Of course not, Jenny."

" Promise ? "

" I promise."

He sat down and took her on his knee. She still kept her head against his chest as though afraid to let him read her eyes.

" The idea," he said gently, " crying like that. Surely you knew I'd be pleased. Why on earth didn't you tell me before ? "

" I thought you might be angry. You had that much to worry you and you're different lately. I don't mind telling you you've frightened me."

He said mildly:

" I don't want to frighten you, Jenny."

" You won't go then, will you, David ? You won't leave me till it's all over ? "

He took her chin gently in his fingers and raised her tear-stained face to his. Looking into her eyes he said:

" I'll not think about the army until you're all right, Jenny." He paused, holding her glance firmly in his. She looked vaguely frightened again, ready to shrink, to start, to weep. Then he said: " But will you promise to give over drinking that confounded port, Jenny ? "

There was no quarrel. A sudden final relief swept over her and she burst into tears.

" Oh yes, David, I promise," she wailed. " I really do promise, I swear to you I'll be good. You're the best husband in the world, David, and I'm a silly, stupid, wicked thing. But oh, David . . ."

He held her closely, soothing her, his tenderness strengthened and renewed. Amongst all the troubled darkness of his mind he felt a shaft of light strike hopefully. He had a vision of new life rising out of death, Jenny's son and his; and in his blindness he was happy.

Suddenly there came a ring at the bell. Jenny raised her head, flushed now and relieved, her mood altered with almost childish facility.

" Who can it be ? " she queried interestedly. They were not used to front-door callers at such an hour. But before she could surmise the bell rang again. She rose smartly and hurried to answer it.

She was back in a minute, quite excited and impressed.

" It's Mr. Arthur Barras," she announced. " I showed him in the parlour. Can you think of it, David, young Mr. Barras himself? He's asked to see you."

The fixed look returned to David's face, his eyes hardened.

" What does he want ? "

" He didn't say. I didn't think to ask him, naturally. But imagine him calling at our house. Oh, goodness, if I'd only known I'd have had a fire going in the front room."

There was a silence. The social occasion did not seem to strike David as important. He rose from his chair and went slowly to the door.

Arthur was walking up and down in the parlour in a state of acute nervous tension and as David entered he started quite visibly. He looked at David for an instant with wide, rather staring eyes and then came hurriedly forward.

" I'm sorry if I'm disturbing you," he said, " but I simply had to come." With a sudden gesture, he sank into a chair and covered his eyes with his hand. " I know how you feel. I don't blame you a bit. I wouldn't have blamed you if you had refused to see me. But I had to come, I'm in such a state I had to see you. I've always liked you and looked up to you, David. I feel that you're the only one who can help me."

David sat down quietly at the table opposite Arthur. The contrast between them was singularly pathetic: the one rent by a painful agitation, the other firmly controlled with strength and forbearance in his face.

" What do you want ? " David asked.

Arthur uncovered his eyes abruptly and fixed them on David with a desperate intentness.

" The truth, that's what I want. I can't rest, I can't sleep, I can't be still until I get it. I want to know if my father is to blame for the disaster. I must know, I must. You've got to help me."

David averted his gaze, struck by that strange recurrent pity which Arthur seemed always destined to evoke in him.

" What can I do ? " he asked in a low voice. " I said all I had to say at the Inquiry. They wouldn't listen to me."

" They can reopen the Inquiry."

" What would be the use ? "

An exclamation broke from Arthur, a sound lost in bitterness, between a laugh and a sob.

" Justice," Arthur exclaimed wildly. " Ordinary decency and justice. Think of these men killed, cut off suddenly, dying horribly. Think of the suffering among their wives and children. O God! it won't bear thinking of. If my father is to blame it's too brutal and horrible to think it should all be glossed over and forgotten."

David got up and went to the window. He wanted to give Arthur the chance to collect himself. Presently he said:

" I felt exactly that way too at first. Worse, perhaps . . . hatred . . . a terrible hatred. But I've tried to get over it. It's not easy. It's human nature to have these violent reactions. When a man throws a bomb at you, your first reaction is to pick it up and throw it back. I talked all this out with Nugent when he was here. I wish you'd met Nugent, Arthur, he's the sanest man I know. But throwing back the bomb isn't a bit of good. It's far better to ignore the man who threw the bomb and concentrate on the organisation which made it. It's no good looking for individual punishment over this Neptune disaster when the whole economic system behind the disaster is to blame. Do you see what I mean, Arthur? It's no good lopping off a branch when the disease is at the very roots of the tree."

"Does that mean you are going to do nothing?" Arthur asked desperately. The words seemed to stick in his throat. "Nothing? Absolutely nothing?"

David shook his head, his features rigid and saddened.

"I'm going to try to do something," he said slowly. "Once we get rid of the war. I can't tell you, I can't say. But, believe me, I am going to try."

A long silence fell. Arthur passed his hand across his eyes with that nervous, bewildered gesture. Perspiration was beaded on his brow. He stood up to go.

"So you won't help me?" he said in a suppressed voice.

David held out his hand.

"Give it up, Arthur," he said in a sincere and affectionate tone. "Don't let it become an obsession with you. You'll hurt yourself most of all. Forget about it."

Arthur flushed violently, his thin boyish face looked faltering and afraid.

"I can't," he said in that same tormented voice, "I can't forget about it."

He left the room and went into the tiny hall. David opened the front door. Outside it was raining. Without looking at David, Arthur said good-bye, and plunged into the wet darkness. David stood for a moment upon the doorstep of his house listening to the rapid footsteps dying down the lane. Then all that he heard was the slow patter of the rain.

VI

ARTHUR did not reach the Law until after seven. In the tumult and disorder of his mind he wished to be alone, he hoped that supper would be over. But supper was not over. Everyone was seated at table as he went in.

Barras was jubilant, he had been to Tynecastle and brought home the news of another victory. It was the battle of Loos, fought on September 26th, and the British forces on the Western front had won a glorious victory at the cost of only 15,000 men. The *Tynecastle Argus* computed the enemy losses at 19,000 killed and wounded, 7,000 prisoners and 125 guns captured. The *Northern Star* went a little better with 21,000 enemy killed and wounded and 3,000 prisoners.

Barras glowed with an excited satisfaction. As he ate his cutlets he read the *communiqué* aloud from the *Northern Star* in a firm official voice. Barras had never taken an evening paper before, *The Times* had always satisfied him, but now he was never without an evening *Argus* or *Star*, or both. With the paper in his hand he jumped up from the table, and went over to the opposite wall where a big-scale map hung all pricked out with the flags of the allied armies. Consulting the paper carefully Barras moved half a dozen of the tiny Union Jacks. He moved the tiny Union Jacks forward.

Watching his father covertly Arthur was seized by a terrifying thought. Barras, the flag-mover, was the genetic impulse behind the war. In his jubilation over the gain of a few hundred yards of torn-up trenches he was guilty, in essence, of the deaths of those thousands of men.

When he had moved the flags Barras studied the map intently. He was heart and soul in the war now, he had lost himself in the war, he was a patriot, he lived in a whirl of forgetfulness. He was on six committees already, and had been nominated for the Northern Refugee Council. The telephone rang all day long. The car tore up and down the road to Tynecastle. Coal was coming out Five Quarter and Globe Seams and selling magnificently at forty shillings a ton pit-head price.

Barras came back to the table. As he sat down he stole a look at Hilda and Grace and Arthur as though to discover whether they had observed his generalship with the flags, then in obvious satisfaction he resumed his paper. His odd preoccupation and detachment were gone; the arteries of his temples stood out a little and showed the beat of his pulse. His air was vaguely restless, almost feverish; he was like a patient who insists on being about in defiance of his doctor's orders, a patient whose metabolism is accentuated and every function accelerated. As he read the paper he drummed incessantly with his fingers upon the table. The drumming sound was not unlike the sound of quick jowling in the pit.

For a few minutes everything was silence but for that quick jowling of Barras's fingers; then it happened, the incredible thing. Barras read a small item in the news twice over. Then he raised his head.

" Lord Kell has most kindly offered his London house as a temporary hospital for the wounded. The work of conversion will be completed in a month. They are asking already for volunteer nurses. Lord Kell has expressed the wish that all V.A.D. nurses should be if possible from the North." Barras paused. He looked at Hilda and at Grace with that bland intentness. " How would you like to go ? "

Arthur sat rooted in his chair. His father, the rock of family unity, the immovable rock upon which all Hilda's pleading had previously broken in vain. Arthur went very pale. His eyes darted towards Hilda almost in apprehension.

Hilda had coloured deeply, violently. She seemed unable to believe her ears. She said:

" Do you mean that, father ? "

Blandly intent, Barras said:

" Do I usually mean what I say, Hilda ? "

The wave of colour receded from Hilda's face as swiftly as it had come. She looked at Grace, large-eyed and eager beside her. Her voice trembled with joy.

" I think we should both like to go, father."

" Very well! " Barras briskly resumed his paper. It was settled.

A quick glance between Hilda and Grace. Hilda said:

" When may we expect to go, father ? "

From behind the paper:

" Shortly, I should imagine. Probably next week. I am seeing Councillor Leach at Tynecastle to-morrow. I shall speak to him and make the necessary arrangements." A pause, then significantly: " I shall feel happy that at least you, Hilda, and Grace are doing your country's work."

Arthur felt the perspiration break out on his palms. He wanted to rise and walk out of the room but he was unable to rise. His eyes remained fixed upon his plate. The sense of sickness which agitation always brought came upon him now.

Hilda and Grace went out, he could hear them flying upstairs to discuss the miracle. Aunt Carrie was already upstairs attending to his mother. Once again he made the effort to rise, but his legs refused to move. He sat paralysed, bound by the current of animosity which flowed towards him from behind the paper. He waited.

As he had expected, his father lowered the paper. His father said:

" I am very pleased at the eagerness of your sisters to serve their country."

Arthur winced. A whole ocean of emotion boiled and surged within him. Once it had been love. Now it was fear, suspicion, hatred. How had the change occurred ? He knew and yet he did not know, he was tired from the tension of the day, his brain felt thick and stupid. He answered heavily:

" Hilda and Grace only want to get away from here."

The mottled flush spread over Barras's forehead. In rather a high tone he said:

" Indeed! And why should they ? "

Arthur replied listlessly; he seemed not to care now what he said:

" They can't stand it here any longer. Hilda has always hated it here but now Grace hates it too. Ever since the disaster. I heard them talking the other day. They said how much you had changed. Hilda said you were living in a fever."

Barras seemed to allow the words to slip over him. It was a faculty he had lately developed of shutting out any issue which might be likely to disturb him, the supreme faculty of judicial inhibition; to Arthur it seemed like Pilate when he washed his hands. He paused, then said in a measured voice:

"Your attitude is worrying me, Arthur. You are very different."

"It's you who are different."

"It isn't only I who am worried. I saw Hetty to-night at the Centra Organisation offices. She is extremely worried and unhappy about you."

"I can't help Hetty," Arthur said with that same listless bitterness.

Barras's dignity increased.

"Alan has been mentioned in dispatches. They have just had the news. Hetty told me to-day. He is recommended for the M.C."

"I can't help Alan either," Arthur answered.

The duskiness on Barras's brow spread behind his ears and into the loose tissue of his neck. The vessels in his temples thickened and throbbed. He said loudly:

"Have you no wish to fight for your country?"

"I don't want to fight for anything," Arthur answered in a stifled tone. "I don't want to kill anybody. There's been enough killing already. We started off pretty well in the Neptune. That's sickened me against killing." His voice rose suddenly, shrill, hysterical. "Do you understand? If that hadn't happened I might have run out like the rest of them with a gun, run out looking nice and pretty in my uniform, run out looking for a man to kill. But it has happened. I saw these men killed and I'm not satisfied. I've had time to think, you see. I've had time to think. I've had time to think. . . ." He broke off, his breath coming quickly. He dared not look at his father, but he felt his father looking at him.

There was a long, a heavy silence. Then Barras performed the usual gesture, a measured movement towards his left-hand waistcoat pocket, an impressive inspection of his watch. Arthur heard the click as the watch was shut and the significance of the action bore down upon him as pathological and alarming. His father had an appointment in Tynecastle, another committee meeting, another and yet another, his father whose habit it had been never to go out, who used to sit listening to Handel in the quiet of his own home, his father, who had sent all these men down the Neptune to die.

"I hope you understand," Barras said, rising from the table, "that you are not indispensable to me at the Neptune. Turn that over in your mind. It may help you to do your duty." Then he went out and shut the door. In two minutes Arthur heard the purr of the car as it slid away down the drive.

Arthur's lip trembled, his whole body trembled again as a rush of stubborn weakness flooded him.

"He won't." he shouted suddenly to the empty room. "He won't!"

VII

Towards the end of September, abruptly and extremely early in the morning, Joe Gowlan had quitted Sleescale. Though he said neither why nor where Joe had his own good reasons for going. He returned, by a discreet route, to Yarrow and set out for Platt Lane.

Trudging along the Lane on that damp autumn morning he became aware of an unusual activity at Millington's. Above the high paling he saw a long corrugated shed in course of erection and a lorry, backed into the yard, discharging heavy equipment. Cautiously, he applied his eye to a knot hole in the fence. Holy Gee, there was a do on right enough! Two new lathes going into the machine-shop, a drilling machine, new moulds and trays, men hauling and heaving, Porterfield the foreman shouting merry hell, Irving tearing out of the drawing office with a bunch of papers in his fist. With a thoughtful air Joe straightened up and stepped into the offices.

He had to cool his heels interminably in the Inquiry Room before gaining admittance to Millington's office but neither the delay nor the reluctant eye of Fuller the head clerk damped him. He went in firmly.

" It's Joe Gowlan, Mr. Stanley." He smiled—deferential yet confident. " Maybe you don't remember me. You promised you might have an opening for me when I came back."

Stanley, who sat in his shirt-sleeves before a littered table, raised his head and glanced at Joe. Stanley was plumper about the face and his waist line had increased, he was a trifle paler, too, his hair beginning to recede from his forehead, he had a flabby and irritable look. He frowned now; he recollected Joe at once, yet he was rather puzzled; remembrance associated Joe with dungarees and a certain amount of grime. He said perplexedly:

" Why, yes, Gowlan, of course. But are you after a job now ? "

" Well, yes, sir." Joe's smile though still deferential was quite irresistible and despite himself Stanley smiled slightly in sympathy. " I've been doing pretty well, mind you, but I wanted a change and I've always felt I'd like to come back to you."

" I see," Stanley declared drily. " Unfortunately we don't want puddlers here now. And what about the army ? A stout young fellow like you ought to be at the front."

Joe's brightness dissolved into an expression of disconsolate regret. He had anticipated this difficulty and he had no intention ever of being at the front. Without hesitation he answered:

" They've rejected me twice, sir. It's no use. It's my knee, a cartilage or something, must have jiggered up when I was boxing."

Stanley had no reason to believe that Joe was lying. There was a pause, then he inquired:

" What have you been doing with yourself since you were here ? "

Without blinking an eyelash Joe said modestly:

" I've been on construction work in Sheffield. I was foreman of the job. I had thirty-odd men under me. But I've never right settled down since I left Millington's. I've always felt you might give me an opening here like you promised."

Another pause. Millington picked up a ruler and began to twiddle it fretfully. He was in a perfect jam of work and schedules and contracts. Suddenly an idea struck him. He welcomed it. Like most dull men in a position of responsibility he flattered himself upon what he called his ability to make quick decisions. He felt himself making a quick decision now. He looked up abruptly, rather patronising, very much on his dignity.

" We've rather changed things here. Did you know that ? "

" No, Mr. Stanley."

Millington inspected the ruler with a kind of fagged triumph.

" We're making munitions," he announced impressively. " Hand grenades, shrapnel, eighteen-pounder shells." Fagged or not, there was good reason for Stanley's air of triumph. For Millington's was on the map at last. During those last years trade had languished painfully, old markets waning and new difficult to find. A good many hands had been sacked and the social club had turned slightly less social than before. For all Stanley's hearty efforts it looked as though Millington's might finally have to close down.

But immediately upon the outbreak of war old Mr. Clegg had wheezed his way to Stanley. Old Clegg was very asthmatic now, very old, done up and worried but, on this occasion, quite heaven inspired.

" It's all up with us short of one thing," Clegg put it with brutal bluntness. " There's a war on now and we might as well try to sell our tubs and shackle-bolts in Greenland. But they'll need munitions, tons and tons of them, more than all the arsenals in kingdom come can give them. We've got to chance it, Mr. Stanley, and turn over quick. If we don't we'll shut down in six months. For the love of God talk it over with me, Mr. Stanley ? "

They talked it over, old Clegg wheezing and puffing his project into Stanley's startled ears. Their present plant with some additions would be adequate. They had the foundry, the machine-shop, four furnaces, and one cupola, nothing, of course, which lent itself to the manufacture of the larger implements of war, but they could concentrate on the small material, shrapnel, shrapnel bullets, hand grenades, and small shells. That's the stuff, Clegg observed with emotion, the stuff to show the profit and win the war.

That final argument, firing Stanley's patriotism, had tipped the scale. He had adopted Clegg's idea, realised all his resources, put in six new melting-pots and another cupola. Millington's had begun to make munitions and, for the first time in five years, to make, simply to coin money, as though they minted sovereigns instead of shrapnel. It was ridiculously easy, the simplicity of the process took Stanley's breath away. A Government department met his advance with a feverish acceptance, asking for half a million Mills bombs and offering £3,500 per ten thousand. Shrapnel was demanded urgently, insistently, one, two, three hundred tons a week. Already Stanley had a sheaf of contracts in hand; he was fitting eighteen-pounder shell moulds and heavy lathes; and the filling factories were clamouring, shrieking for material faster than he could turn it out.

This was the situation which caused Stanley to fix his eyes importantly on Joe. He made a brisk, decisive movement.

" It looks as though you'd turned up at the right moment, Gowlan. I'm short-handed, chiefly through enlistment, for I never stop a man who wants to go. Hughes, the foundry foreman, has just gone and I need somebody in his place. Mr. Clegg isn't fit to deal with that himself. He's been seedy lately; in fact I'm doing part of his work myself. But in the shop I need a foreman, I can't be three places at once, and I've half a mind to try you out there. Six pounds a week and a month's trial. What do you say to it ? "

Joe's eye glistened, the offer was far better than he had expected; he could scarcely conceal his eagerness.

" I say, yes, Mr. Stanley," he blurted out. "Just give me the chance to show you what I can do."

The enthusiasm behind Joe's words seemed to gratify Millington.

" Come along, then." He rose. " I'll turn you over to Clegg."

They found Clegg in the melting-shed superintending the installation of new moulds. He looked a sick man, stooping over a stick, his grey moustache clotted with rheum. He had no recollection of Joe, but at Stanley's request he led him into the foundry. From his previous experience one glance assured Joe of his own competence to deal with the work. There were six pots in all and the process was extremely simple: pig and lead mixed with twelve per cent. antimony for hardening, fired underneath, then into the moulds. While old Clegg rambled on Joe made pretence of attentive listening, but all the time his alert eye was darting round, taking in the forty-odd men who worked in the red glare, feeding the pots, serving the moulds, breaking up, tubbing away the cast grenades that looked like small unripe pineapples. A walk over, he kept thinking to himself, I know it backwards already.

" It's a matter of handling the men," Mr. Stanley observed. He had followed them into the shop. " To keep the output up."

With quiet efficiency Joe said:

" You can trust me, Mr. Stanley. I'll get down to it all right."

Mr. Stanley nodded and walked off with Clegg.

There and then Joe set himself, in his own phrase, to get down to it. From the start he let it be seen that he was the boss. Though he had never before held a position of authority he felt himself eminently adapted to the part; he had no diffidence, no qualms, he was breezy and expansive. He threw himself into the work, was here, there, everywhere, superintending the mixing, the firing, the moulds, with a ready word of praise and a healthy line of blasphemy.

At the end of the first month the shop output indicated a distinct rise and Millington was pleased. He congratulated himself upon his own decision and called Joe to his office to compliment him personally and confirm his appointment. Joe certainly spared no pains in making himself useful. Millington never came into the shop but Joe hung on to his sleeve, pointing out something that was being done, advancing a suggestion, coming forward with a new idea, all bustle and efficiency. In Joe's own phrase, he soaped Stanley a treat and Stanley, who was temperamentally inclined to become bothered and confused by a sudden rush of work, began to think of Joe as a real stout fellow.

Joe spent his evenings quietly. For a moment he had entertained the thought of taking up his lodgings again with the Sunleys. But only for a moment. There were many reasons why Joe did not wish to return to Scottswood Road to be mixed up with his old associations again. He had an idea that at last he was on a good thing: Millington's was humming, money dancing in, the air full of excitement and change. On the recommendation of Sim Porterfield, the machine-shop foreman, he took a room at 4 Beech Road, Yarrow, with Mrs. Calder, a decent elderly woman, a member of Penuel, very dried and sinewy, who from her age, respectability and the shine on her linoleum, could not possibly tamper with Joe's virtue and so upset his prospects.

As the months went on Joe concentrated more and more on the main chance. And the more he concentrated the more his eye drifted in the direction of the machine-shop and Sim Porterfield. Sim was a short silent sallow-faced man with a small black beard, a pious acrimonious wife and a passion for the game of quoits. His taciturnity gave him the reputation of " a thinker," he was a member of the Yarrow Fabian Society, he plodded again and again with ponderous lack of understanding through the works of Karl Marx. He was not popular with the men nor with Stanley who half suspected Sim of being " a socialist." Yet he was a kindly man, it was he who had engaged Joe on that memorable afternoon seven years before and given him his first chance at Millington's.

Natural, then, that Joe should pal up with Sim, endure his heavy comradeship, forgo the lighter pleasures of Saturday afternoon to accompany him to the quoit ground and heave metal rings into squashy clay. More natural still that Joe should spend a lot of time studying Sim, genially figuring things out as to how Sim might be undermined. The trouble was Sim's steadiness. He never drank more than a pint, had no time for women and never pinched so much as a one-inch nut from the shop. Joe began to think he would never manage to get Sim in wrong, until one evening, leaving the works in the gathering dusk a stranger furtively thrust some pamphlets into his hand before vanishing down Platt Lane. Joe glanced indifferently at the sticky handbills under the nearest street lamp: *Comrades! Workers of the World! Down with War! Don't let the war-mongers put a gun in your hands and send you to kill a German worker. How do they treat you when you strike for a living wage? They can't fight this war without you. Stop it now! The German worker doesn't want to fight any more than you. Don't let them send you out for cannon fodder. Munition workers, down tools! British armaments are being sold to Germany by the capitalists. Down with Capitalism! Down with War!* . . .

Joe recognised the literature and was about to throw it into the gutter when all at once a thought struck him. He folded the sheets tenderly and placed them in his pocket-book. Smiling slightly, he walked off towards his lodgings.

On the following day he was extra affable, slipped in and out of the machine-shop, lunched with the shirt-sleeved Sim in the corner of the canteen, then, suddenly serious, advanced upon the office and demanded to see Millington. He was closeted with Stanley quite a time.

At six o'clock that evening, when the hooter blared, and the men, struggling into their jackets, milled out of the machine-shop, Stanley and Clegg and Joe stood by the door. Millington's face was ablaze with indignation. As Sim came past he thrust out an arm and stopped him.

" Porterfield, you've been spreading sedition in my works."

" What? " Sim said stupidly. Everybody turned to stare.

" Don't deny it." Outrage quivered in Stanley's voice. " I know all about it. You and your damned Marx. I ought to have suspected you before."

" I've done nowt, sir," gasped Sim.

" You're a barefaced liar," shouted Stanley. " You've been seen distributing pamphlets! And what's that in your inside pocket? " He plucked a sheaf of papers out of Sim's open jacket. " Look, is that *nowt*? Seditious poison! And in *my* works! You're sacked on the spot. Call and get your money from Mr. Dobbie and don't show your pro-German face near Millington's again."

" But, listen, Mr. Millington . . ." cried Sim wildly.

No use. Stanley's back was turned, he was stalking off with Joe and Clegg. Sim stared stupidly at one of the pamphlets on the floor, picked it up, like a man in a dream, to read. Five minutes later as he stumbled out of the works a crowd of men were awaiting him at the gates. An angry shout went up. Somebody yelled: " Here's the bloody pro-German! Here's the bastard, lads. We'll give him hell! "

They closed in on Sim.

" Let us be," he panted, his ridiculous little beard cocked defiantly. " I tell you I ain't done nowt." By way of answer a steel bolt caught him on the ear. He struck out with his fists blindly. But a heavy kick caught him in the groin. He sank to his knees in a red haze of pain. " Pro-German! Dirty swine! " fading into the red dark haze. A last violent stab of pain as an iron-bound boot bashed against his ribs. Then blackness.

Three weeks later Joe called to see Sim who lay in bed, his right leg in splints, his ribs in plaster, a dazed expression imprinted on his face. " Christ Almighty, Sim," Joe almost blubbered, " I wouldn't have believed it. I'm all to bits over it. And to think they've gone and given me your job as well. O Christ, Sim, why did you do it ? "

Before he went Joe thoughtfully left a clipping from the *Yarrow News*: *British Workers' Lesson to a Skunk.* At the end of which was the line: " Mr. Joseph Gowlan now occupies the post of combined superintendent of the foundry and machine-shop at the Millington Munitions Works." Sim read it woodenly through his narrow spectacles, then woodenly picked up the book beside his bed. But he did not really understand Marx.

After this Joe's stock was high with Millington and his prestige at the works immense. Then came that memorable Monday morning when Stanley arrived late, rather put out by a telephone message that Clegg was laid up and would not be in to business. Joe was already in the office, ostensibly for the purpose of going over his check sheets with Stanley.

Stanley, however, seemed rushed, in one of his moods of irritability under pressure when he gave the impression of supporting enormous enterprises entirely upon his own shoulders. He fussed in with his overcoat flapping and his scarf undone and as he hung up the scarf and pulled off his gloves he called through to Fuller to send in Dobbie, the Cashier. Then, feeling in the side pocket of his overcoat he paused, and made a gesture of impatience.

" Damn it all," turning to Joe, " I've forgotten my counterfoils." He ran his hand through his hair. " Take the car like a good chap and run up to Hilltop for them. Ask Laura, Mrs. Millington I mean, or ask one of the maids for the long envelope I left in the breakfast-room—on the table, I think, or perhaps it was in the hall. Go on, quick, now, before Dodds gets away."

Joe hastened to comply. He went out of the office and into the yard where Millington's car stood drawn up with the engine still running. He explained the matter to Dodds and in a minute they were on their way to Hilltop.

The morning was cold and fine with a crisp exhilaration in the air. Joe sat beside Dodds in the front seat and the wind of the car's passage whipped a fine colour into his cheek. He had a swelling sensation of his own fitness, of his rising importance in the world. When the car reached Hilltop, about two miles from the works, and ran into the semi-circular drive of Millington's house, a large modern villa with an outlook towards the golf-course, he jumped out, ran up the front steps and pressed the bell.

A neat maid let him in. He smiled in a brotherly fashion to the maid—Joe never neglected anybody.

" I'm from the works," he announced, " to see Mrs. Millington."

The maid showed him into the lounge where he stood up by a fine coal fire and waited carefully. Though the chairs were deep and looked easy to sit in, Joe felt that it would be safer for him to stand. He liked the lounge, it was comfortable and different, there was a single picture on one of the walls and no more. But it was, reflected Joe, a classy bit of work. And he had enough knowledge to understand that the furniture was antique.

Then Laura entered. She descended the stairs slowly looking cool and trim in a dove-grey dress with white cuffs and collar. With an air of complete detachment, she gave him a rapid, impersonal glance and said:

" Yes ? "

In spite of his assurance Joe felt intimidated. He stammered:

" I came for some papers. Mr. Millington left them on the breakfast table."

" Oh yes." She stood half-looking at him with a kind of curiosity and he blushed to the roots of his hair, not knowing what to do, conscious that he was being scrutinised, weighed up and judged. Although he cursed his unusual embarrassment, it stood him in good stead, for suddenly she smiled faintly, the smile of a bored woman responding to a momentary whim.

" Haven't I seen you before somewhere ? " she asked.

" I had the pleasure of dancing with you once, Mrs. Millington," he gabbled. " At the social."

" Yes." She nodded. " I do remember now."

He gave a deferential laugh; he was recovering himself.

" I haven't forgotten, at any rate, Mrs. Millington. That was something I couldn't forget."

She continued considering him with a certain interest. He really looked extraordinarily handsome standing there in his neat blue suit with that fine colour in his cheeks, his strong white teeth showing in a smile, his curly hair and dark brown eyes.

" Stanley spoke about you the other day," she said reflectively. " You're doing well." A pause. " You're the one the young lady jilted." She smiled her cool faintly amused smile. " Or was it the other way round ? "

He looked down hurriedly, feeling that she saw through him and was making fun of him.

" It's finished with, anyhow," he blurted out.

She did not answer for a minute.

" Well, I'll get you the papers." She moved towards the door but on the way out she paused in her impersonal way. " Would you like a drink ? "

" I don't usually touch it," he answered. " Not in the morning. I want to get on, you see."

As if she had not heard she took the decanter which stood on the top of the walnut cocktail cabinet and mixed him a whisky and soda. Then she went out of the room.

He was sipping the whisky and soda when she returned. She handed him the papers, remarking:

" So you want to get on ? "

" Well, naturally, Mrs. Millington," he answered with eager deference.

There was a silence while she stared in a bored fashion into the fire. He watched her dumbly. She was not beautiful. She had a very pale face with faint blue shadows under her eyes and the whites of her eyes were not clear. She had ordinary black hair. Her figure was not remarkable. It was quite a good figure but it was not remarkable. Her ankles were not slim and her hips were inclined to be full. But she was extremely smart, not smart in the ordinary sense, but impeccably smart. Her dress was in remarkable taste, her hair and hands beautifully kept. In that same dumb admiration Joe grasped that Laura was a fastidious woman, he could not help thinking how wonderful her underwear must be.

But he had finished his whisky now and could make no further pretext for delay. He put his glass down upon the mantelpiece and said:

" Well, I must get back to the works."

She did not speak. She looked up from the fire and once again she smiled her cool, faintly ironic smile, held out a cool, firm hand. He shook hands, terribly deferential and polite—his own hands were well kept too—and the next minute he was out of the house.

He took his seat in the car with his head in a whirl. He did not know, he could not be sure, but he had the wild, impossible notion that he had made some sort of impression on Laura Millington. The idea was crazy, perhaps, but he felt it nevertheless and a tremendous exultation surged inside his chest. He was perfectly aware that he was extremely attractive to women; he could not walk down the street without being conscious of admiring glances flung towards him. Laura had said nothing, done nothing, her behaviour was altogether restrained and cold; yet Joe knew women; and he had seen something too firmly controlled, a flicker under the bored indifference in Laura's eye. Joe, who had not one moral scruple in his whole composition, gloated inwardly. If only it were true ? He had always wanted a *lady* to take a fancy to him. Often in Grainger Street, strolling as one of the common crowd, he would observe some car draw up and a smartly dressed, disdainful woman pass quickly across the pavement into an expensive shop leaving a peculiar exasperating perfume and the insufferable sense of her inaccessibility. In the past that had always goaded Joe, made him ram his hands in his pockets and, powerfully aware of his own virility, swear to have a woman like that, a lady, some day. By God, he would! Tarts were all right, but a real lady was different. And at the thought he would drift along with the herd again, shouldering his way forward, lip thrust out, pausing perhaps outside a window where gossamer lingerie was displayed. That was what they wore and his imagination, rejecting the cotton crudities available to him, soared towards a future time when he could command the full subtleties of his desire.

All this recurred to Joe as he drove back to the works; he could hardly sit still for sheer excitement. He kept looking at himself in the driving mirror and admiring himself, running his hand over the glossy, natural wave in his hair. At the office he handed over the papers to Stanley and went into the melting-shop in a perfect glow.

But as the days passed and nothing, absolutely nothing, happened, Joe's complacency began to shrink. He waited for some sign, some vague indication of Laura's interest. But for all the interest Laura evinced he might never have existed. He began to think he had been mistaken; then he was convinced he had been mistaken. He became surly and ill-tempered, took his spite out on the men in the melting-shop, and ended up with a wild night spent in the company of a blatant and unknown young female whose dirty toe-nails eventually disgusted him.

Three months passed and then, one frosty afternoon in late November, while Joe happened to be in consultation with Stanley over some defective moulds, Laura dropped into the office. She had her own car outside and had called to drive Stanley into Tynecastle. She entered quietly, a soft silver fox fur enhancing the pale oval of her face, and Joe's heart took one enormous bound.

Stanley glanced up from his papers with a slight irritation. During that autumn Stanley's tendency to irritation had increased; in the steam-heated office he looked pale, wilted and moist. " Sheer overwork," he would protest in a voice of grievance. " Think of it, I haven't had Clegg inside the office in six weeks." Actually, having given birth to the idea of conversion to munitions—as though the process of delivery had been too much for his enfeebled constitution—old Mr. Clegg had taken to his bed and the doctor had reported that his lying-in would be prolonged. There was, in fact, a possibility that he would not get up again. This worried Stanley. Lately, Millington had run a little to seed and he was liable to impulsive bemoanings of his waist band, his lack of condition and his inability to get his regular bi-weekly golf. His tone on these occasions was the tone of a man who has just lost his collar stud and indicts the entire household.

" I'll be ready in a minute, Laura," he grunted. " You know Gowlan, don't you? Joe Gowlan. Only man besides myself who works in this place."

Joe hardly dared to raise his eyes. He blundered out some formal remark and, as soon as he could, gathered up his papers and left the office.

Stanley yawned and threw down his pen.

" I'm tired, Laura," he said, " damned tired. Too many gin and Its last night and not enough sleep. I've been like a washed-out rag all day. God! when I think how fit I used to be. I'm missing my golf I tell you. I must start my cold showers in the morning again. I'd like to have time to get really fit. I'm sick of this driving on. Money pouring in, but what the dickens of good is it ? Clegg's still laid up, you know. I can't put up with it much longer. I shall have to pension him off and get a new man, a new works manager."

" Of course you must," she agreed.

He stifled another yawn, his expression peevish.

" So damned difficult, getting a good man. They're all booked up or at the front, lucky devils. I must advertise though. I'll do it Monday."

Laura smoothed her soft fur with her pale flexible fingers as though enjoying the feel of its voluptuous silkiness.

" Why don't you give this man Gowlan a trial ? " she remarked idly.

Stanley stared at her in amazement.

" Gowlan! " he exclaimed with a short laugh. " Joe Gowlan, my works manager! That shows how little you savvy about business, my dear. Gowlan was a workman himself not so long ago. Why, the thing's ridiculous."

" Yes, I suppose it is," she remarked indifferently. " I don't understand." She turned towards the door. But he did not follow.

" Clegg's job is a damned responsible post. It means looking after the whole show when I'm not here. It's idiotic to think Gowlan could handle it." He rubbed his chin indecisively. " And yet I don't know. He *is* a damned capable fellow. He's helped me no end of ways these last three months. He's popular with the men and smart, yes, straight as a die, too. Think how he put me up to that swine Porterfield. Hang it all, Laura, I don't know but what there might be some sense in the idea after all."

She looked at her tiny wrist watch, worn on the outside of her glove.

" Oh, never mind your idea, Stanley, it really is time we were going."

" No, but listen, Laura. I honestly believe this solves my difficulty. There's a war on, you know and that's when men do get promotion. I believe I might do worse than try Gowlan in the job."

" You must do exactly as you think best."

" Good Lord, Laura, as if I ever did anything else. But, honestly, I'm rather keen on this now. How would it do to ask him up to supper some night and see how he strikes us ? "

" Just as you wish. But we must go now or we'll be late."

Stanley stood for a moment with his brow corrugated in thought, then suddenly he clapped on his bowler and reached for his coat. He followed Laura down the corridor and on the way across the yard he shouted to the machine-shop for Joe.

Joe advanced slowly and Stanley, straightening himself inside the coat, remarked offhandedly:

" By the way, Joe, I nearly forgot. I want you to come up and have supper with us some night. How about to-morrow ? That suit you all right ? "

Joe stood incapable of speech.

" Yes," he stammered at last, " that would suit me perfectly."

" It's settled then," Stanley declared. " Half-past seven in case I forget."

Joe nodded. He was conscious of Laura's dark eyes inspecting him non-committally over Stanley's shoulder. Then they both turned and walked off.

He gazed after them with a violently beating heart. He wanted to whoop for joy. At last! At last! He had been right after all. In a sweat of triumph he returned to his work.

That night when he went home he could not be still. He had to tell someone, it was impossible to contain this delicious exultation within himself. A strange desire seized him, a temptation, and he could not resist it. He took a tram across the bridge to Tynecastle and carried his gloating along to Scottswood Road.

He strolled in upon the Sunleys with a casual air while they sat at supper, Alfred, Ada, Clarry and Phyllis—Sally was not there, she was with a concert party which had just left for France—and their welcome caused him to feel even more magnificent.

" Well, I declare," Ada kept repeating. " It's a regular treat to see you again."

He accepted his old chair by the fire and let her send out for some cold ham and give him a second supper—he called it a snack—and while he ate her sandwiches he informed them all of his success at Millington's. Reaching for the mustard he added carelessly: " As a matter of fact, I'm having supper with Stanley and Mrs. Millington at Hilltop to-morrow night."

Their astounded admiration gave him a glorious thrill. Joe was a natural boaster, particularly when the audience was receptive, and now he boasted to his heart's content. He expatiated on the beauty and nobility of his calling. Somebody, he announced through a large mouthful of ham, had got to make the bullets, bombs and shells for the boys at the front. There was a future in munitions, too. He had heard only the other day that they were going to put up a line of sheds at Wirtley on the waste ground at the top of Yarrow Hill, filling sheds, and quite near the foundry too. Mr. Stanley had said they would soon be employing hundreds of girls there, filling the shells with T.N.T. Mr. Stanley had got the news from London straight. Joe looked at Clarry and Phyllis in a friendly way. He said:

" Why don't you two get in on that? They'll be paying you three times what you get at Slattery's and the work's a pinch."

Ada looked interested. She said:

" Is that a fact, Joe? "

Joe said largely:

" Certainly it's a fact. What do you take me for? I know, don't I? I know! "

Ada pondered flabbily in the rocker. House painting in Tynecastle in these early days of the war was inclined to be slack; there was not as much money coming into the house as Ada would have liked, certainly Clarry's and Phyllis's money was very small. She said:

" I wish you'd let me know if you hear anything further, Joe."

Ada had always had a weakness, a soft maternal tenderness towards Joe. To-night she thought he looked wonderful handsome—quite the gentleman, sort of dashing and alive. Ada sighed; she had always wanted to have Joe her son-in-law; it was pitiful the chance Jenny had thrown away now that things had turned out so well for Joe.

When Clarry and Phyllis had gone out and Alf was busy with his pigeons in the back, Ada looked across at Joe and breathed very sadly and confidentially:

" You haven't heard about Jenny? "

" No," Joe said. And taking out his case he busied himself in lighting a cigarette.

Ada sighed.

" She's expecting next month, yes, I've got to go through and see to her myself. At the beginning of December."

The smoke from his cigarette got into Joe's throat. He coughed and choked and got quite red in the face. After a pause he said:

" You mean there's going to be an addition? "

Ada nodded mournfully.

" It's just about the limit, poor Jenny, and he will have it he's going in the army. And after that Gawd knows what'll happen. He's got the chuck from the teaching. Can you beat it? I always said she threw herself away that time, Joe. And now to think she's been and went and let herself get caught."

Joe's cough convulsed him again.

" Well, well. These things do happen, I suppose."

After that Ada became more confidential with Joe. They had a pleasant intimate talk in the half darkness of the room. At the end of it when Joe had to go Ada was greatly consoled, she felt that Joe's visit had done her a power of good.

Joe walked back to Beech Road, Yarrow, with a curious expression on his face. Thank God he'd got out of Sleescale when he did! He was unusually agreeable to his withered landlady that night, spoke to her kindly and seemed generally to congratulate her that she was old and ugly and daughterless.

The next day came and Joe could think of nothing but his engagement in the evening. When he had finished work he slipped into Grigg's the barber's at the foot of Beech Road and had a shave, very close, and a hair-trim. Then he went home to his lodgings and took a bath. He sat on the edge of the bath quite naked, whistling softly and doing his nails. To-night he was determined to be at his best.

When he had bathed he padded into his bed-sitting-room, dressed extra carefully in his very best suit, a light grey with a faint pin stripe, a pattern copied from a suit he had once seen a heavy swell wearing in a musical comedy at the Empire. He had ambitions for a dinner suit, terrible tearing ambitions for a dinner suit, but he knew that the time for the dinner suit was not yet. Still, even in the ordinary grey he looked splendid, chin tenderly smooth, hair brilliantined, eye bright and vital, his thin watch-chain girded high on his waistcoat, a paste-pearl stud in his tie. He smiled at his scintillating reflection in the mirror, tried a bow and a few positions of careless elegance; then his smile became a grin and he thought to himself: " You're in amongst it at last, my boy, just you watch yourself and there's nothing can stop you."

He became grave again and as he walked up the road to Hilltop he rehearsed the right note, deferential yet manly; his expression as he went up the steps, ready to conquer, was masterly.

The same neat maid, Bessie, showed him into the lounge where Laura stood alone with her bare arm resting on the mantelpiece and one slipper extended to the fire. She was dressed very plainly in black and she made a marvellously effective picture with the firelight warming her pale face and glinting on her beautiful polished nails. Joe suddenly had a thrilling admiration for her. She's great, he thought to himself, by gum she's *it*; and, gripped by a most familiar tenseness of his middle, yet with a touching humility on his face, he advanced and greeted her.

Then an awkward pause occurred. He rubbed his hands, smoothed his hair, straightened his tie and smiled.

" It's been cold to-day, terrible cold for the time of year. Seems to be freezing outside to-night."

She extended her other slipper to the fire, then she said:

" Is it? "

He felt snubbed; she thrilled and overawed him; he had never known anyone like her in his life. He persevered:

" It certainly is good of you to ask me up to-night. It's a real honour, I assure you. When Mr. Stanley gave me the invitation you could have knocked me down with a feather."

Laura looked at him with that unsmiling smile, taking in his flashy chain, fake pearl, his deadly emanation of hair-oil. Then, as though wishing him free of such atrocities, she looked away. She said to the fire:

" Stanley will be down in a moment."

Damped, he could not make her out. He would have given everything he had to know absolutely and completely the nature of her real self and how he stood with her.

But he did not know and he was half afraid of her. To begin with she was undoubtedly a lady. Not " ladylike " in Jenny's silly sense—he could have laughed when he remembered Jenny's shallow gentility, the crooking of the little finger, the bowing, the " so good of you " and " after you please " nonsense. No, Laura was not like that, Laura had real class. She did not have to try; in Joe's memorable phrase, she was already *it*.

She had a curious indifference, too, which pleased and fascinated him. He felt that she would never insist; if she did not agree she would simply let the matter drop and keep her own opinion with that queer unsmiling smile. It was as though Laura had a secret, mocking self. He suspected that she was extremely unconventional within herself, that she probably disagreed utterly with the set ideas of life. Yet she was not unconventional outwardly; she was extremely fastidious in her person and her taste in dress was quietly perfect. Nevertheless he could not help the feeling that she was contemptuous of convention; he had a crazy half-formed intuition that she despised everybody—including herself.

His thoughts were interrupted by Stanley's entry: Stanley came in breezily, shook hands with Joe and clapped him on the back, too obviously trying to put him at his ease.

" Glad to see you in my house, Gowlan. We don't stand on ceremony here, so make yourself at home." He planted his feet apart in the middle of the hearthrug, exposing his back to the heat of the fire, and exclaimed: " What about it though, Laura? What about the rum ration for the troops? "

Laura went over to the walnut cabinet where a shaker stood with glasses and some ice. They each had a dry martini; then Joe and Millington had a second; and Millington, who drank his quickly, had a third.

" I get outside too many of these, Gowlan," he remarked, smacking his lips. " Don't get enough exercise, either. I want to get thoroughly fit one of these days, get my old form back, exercises, aha! Harden myself up like I used to be at St. Bede's." He flexed his biceps and felt it with a frown.

To cheer himself up Stanley had another drink and they went in to supper.

" It's very curious," Stanley lamented, spreading his napkin and addressing himself to his cold chicken, " how soon you can get out of condition. Business is all very well, making money and chaining yourself to an office, but hang it all health is the best wealth. Shakespeare or somebody said that, didn't they? "

" Emerson, wasn't it ? " suggested Laura, with her eyes on Joe.

Joe did not answer. His library at his lodgings consisted of a torn paper-backed edition of *Saucy Stories from the French*, and Mrs. Calder's Bible, planted encouragingly in front of the glass case of waxed fruit, out of which Joe, on Sunday afternoons when feeling especially pious, would read what he termed the dirty bits.

" I wish I could have joined the army," Stanley meditated complainingly. He had the dull man's habit of worrying a subject to death. " That's the place to get you really into shape."

A short silence. Stanley crumbled his roll in a momentary discontent. Interspersed with his breeziness he was much given to these bouts of grumbling, the peevish regret of a man who sees himself approaching baldness and middle age. But Stanley had always been liable to impulsive dissatisfactions with his present lot in life. Six months ago he had longed to make money and re-establish the position of the firm; yet now that he had done it his sense of unfulfilment still persisted.

Stanley continued to monopolise the conversation. Laura spoke very little and Joe, though his assurance was increasing, made only an occasional and careful observation, agreeing with some remark which Stanley had made. Occasionally, while Stanley discoursed upon bridge or golf, once especially when he was detailing at some length the manner in which he had played a particular hole, Joe's eyes encountered Laura's across the table and the deliberate blankness of her gaze gave him a secret chagrin. He wondered what her feelings were for Stanley. She had been married to him for seven years now. She had no children. She was always extremely nice to Stanley, listening to everything he said, or was she listening? Had she no feelings at all under that cold indifference ? Was she merely icy ? Or what in the name of heaven was it ? Stanley, he knew, had been crazy about her at the start, their honeymoon had lasted for six weeks or longer but now Stanley was not quite so crazy. He was a little less of the dashing Don Juan. Often, in Joe's phrase, he looked all washed out.

After the sweet, Laura left them, Joe blundering in an access of politeness to the door to open it for her. Then Stanley selected a cigar, lit up, and pushed across the box to Joe magnanimously.

" Help yourself, Gowlan," he said. " You'll find these all right."

Joe took a cigar with a look of humility and gratitude. Secretly he was irked by Millington's condescending air. Just wait a bit, he thought into himself, and I'll show him something. But in the meantime he was all deference. He lit his cigar without removing the band.

A longish silence followed while Stanley, with his legs stretched under the table and his stomach at ease, pulled at his cigar and stared at Joe.

" You know, Gowlan," he announced at length, " I like you."

Joe smiled modestly and wondered what the hell was coming.

" I'm a liberal man," Stanley went on expansively—he had drunk half a bottle of Sauterne on top of the cocktails and was inclined to be expansive. " And it doesn't matter a tinker's damn to me what a man is so long as he's decent. He can be a duke's son or a dustman's son, I don't care, it's all the same to me so long as he's straight. Do you get me ? "

" Why, yes, I get you, Mr. Stanley."

" Well, look here, Joe," Millington continued, " I'll go a bit further since you understand what I'm after. I've been watching you pretty closely this last month or two and I've been pretty pleased with what I've seen." He broke off, switching the cigar round his mouth, inspecting Joe. Then he said slowly: " Clegg's *finito*, that's point number one. Point number two, I've got an idea, Gowlan, that I'm going to try you out as my new works manager."

Joe nearly swooned.

" Manager! " he whispered feebly.

Millington smiled.

" I'm offering you Clegg's job now. It's up to you to see if you can hold it."

Joe's emotion was so great the room swam before him. He had scented something in the wind but nothing, oh, nothing like this. He went white as mutton fat and dropped his cigar on to his plate.

" Why, Mr. Stanley," he gasped. He didn't have to act this time, he was natural and convincing. " Why, Mr. Stanley . . ."

" That's all right, Joe. Just take it easy. I'm sorry if I caught you unexpected. But there's a war on, see. That's when the unexpected happens. You'll soon pick up the ropes. I've an idea you'll not let me down."

A wave of exhilaration swept over Joe. Clegg's job . . . him! . . . works manager at Millington's!

" You see, I trust you, Joe," Millington explained cordially. " And I'm prepared to back my judgment. That's why I'm offering you the job."

At that moment the telephone rang in the lounge and before Joe could speak again Laura entered.

" It's for you, Stanley," she declared. " Major Jenkins wants you."

Stanley excused himself and went out to the telephone.

There was a silence. Joe could feel Laura there, he could feel her standing by the doorway, opposite him, near him, looking at him. A terrific elation throbbed in him, he felt strong, intoxicated, gloriously alive. He lifted his eyes and faced her. But she avoided his gaze and said quite curtly:

" There's coffee in the lounge before you go! "

He did not answer. He could not speak. As they stood there, in this fashion, the sound of Stanley's voice at the telephone came into the room.

VIII

THE time of Jenny's confinement drew near and Jenny's behaviour was in every way exemplary. Since that Tuesday afternoon when she had told David, Jenny had been " a changed woman." She had her little querulous moments of course—who in her condition would not ?—and what she called her " fancies," the sudden desire at awkward moments for strange and exotic forms of nourishment—more simply denoted as " something tasty." A craving for ginger snaps for instance, since she had " gone off " bread, or a pickled onion, or soft herring roes on toast. Ada, her mother, had always had her fancies and Jenny felt herself fully within her rights in having her fancies too.

She was making a fetching outfit for the little baby girl—she was sure it would be a girl, she did want a little girlie so, to dress up nicely, boys were horrid!—and she sat night after night on the opposite side of the fire from David in the most domestic manner stitching and crocheting and fashioning the garments from the directions given in *Mab's Home Notes* and the *Chickabiddy's Journal.* Dreamily she planned the future of the little one. She was to be an actress, a great actress, or better still a great singer, a prima donna in Grand Opera. Her mother's talent would unfold in her and she would have triumph upon triumph at Covent Garden with great men and bouquets scattered at her feet, while Jenny from a box would gaze tenderly and understandingly upon the success which might have been hers too, if only she had been given her chance. There were temptations here though, great temptations, and at that Jenny's brow would crease. The scene became changed suddenly and she saw a nun, an Anglican nun, pale and spiritual with a hidden sorrow in her heart and the stage and the world cast behind her, passing through the cloister of a great convent and entering the dim chapel. Service began, the organ sounded, and the nun's voice pealed out in all its lovely purity. Tears came to Jenny's eyes and her sad romantic fancy took even more tragic flights. There would be no little girl after all, no prima donna, no nun. She herself was going to die, she felt it in her heart, it was absurd to imagine she would ever have the strength to have a baby, and she had always had the premonition of dying young. She remembered that Lily Blades, a girl in the Millinery at Slattery's who was something wonderful at fortunes, had once seen a terrible illness in her tea-cup. She saw herself dying in David's arms while with riven and anguished countenance he implored her not to leave him. A great bowl of white roses stood by the bedside and the doctor, though a hard man, stood in the background in an agony of distress.

Real tears flowed down Jenny's cheeks and David, looking up suddedly, exclaimed:

" Good Lord, Jenny! What on earth's the matter ? "

" It's nothing, David," she sighed with a pale, angelic smile. " I'm really quite happy. Quite, quite happy."

After this she decided she must have a cat because it was domestic and human and cheerful about the house. She asked everyone she knew to get her a kitten; everyone, simply everyone must search high and low to get her a kitten, and when Harry, the butcher's boy, brought her a little tabby she was delighted. Later when Murchison's van man brought her another kitten and Mrs. Wept on the following day sent round yet another, she was less ecstatic. It was impossible to return the two kittens in the face of her wide-spread appeal, and they were not very clean about the house. She had in the end to drown them, it hurt her terribly, the little helpless darlings, yet what could a girl do? However, she took a lot of trouble in thinking out a name for the survivor. She called it *Pretty*.

Then she began to take up her music again. She sat at the piano through the day practising and trying out her voice and she learned two lullabies. She wanted to be more accomplished. At this stage her attitude expressed a secret remorse: she was not good enough for David, she should have been better in every way, more talented, more intellectual. She wanted to be able to talk to David, to have discussions, real discussions upon the subjects which interested him, all about things that mattered, social and economic and political problems. With this in mind she dipped into his books once or twice to elevate her intellectual plane and bring grist to the mills of philosophical discussion. But the books were not very encouraging and in the end she was obliged to give them up.

Still, if she could not be clever she could be good. Ah, yes, she could be good. She purchased a little volume entitled *Sunny Half-hours in the Happy Home* and she read it devotedly. She read it like a child learning a lesson, her lips moving slightly over the words, the book resting in her lap on top of the crochet work. After one particularly sunny half-hour she fastened her swimming eyes on David and exclaimed emotionally:

" I'm just a silly little thing, David. But I'm not bad really. It says here we all make mistakes but we can lift ourselves up again. I'm not bad, am I, David, I'm not really bad ? "

He assured her patiently that she was not bad.

She looked at him for a moment, then said with a sudden gush:

" Oh, David, you're the best man that ever was. Really you are, David, the best in all the world."

Never before had Jenny seemed to him so much a child. She was a child. It was simply ridiculous that she should be having a baby. He was gentle with her. Often at nights when they lay in bed together and she would start, troubled and frightened in her sleep, and cling to him, he could feel her swollen body and the infant moving within her. Tenderness came over him and he soothed her through these midnight whimperings.

He had asked Jenny if she would like Martha, his own mother, to look after the house and nurse her while she was lying-in and Jenny, with her new submissiveness, had agreed. But when Martha came down to make arrangements that one interview proved the reconciliation to be impossible. Martha met David on his way home. Her colour was high. "I can't do it," she declared in a contained voice. "It's no use at all. The less I have to do with her the better. I cannot stand her and she cannot stand me. So that must just be the end of it." She walked off before he could reply.

So it was arranged for Ada Sunley to come through from Tynecastle. Ada arrived on the 2nd of December, a wet and windy day, stepping heavily out of the train with a small yellow suit-case made secure with cord. David met her at the station, carried the suit-case to Lamb Lane. Ada's mood was very offhand, she did not seem particularly pleased to come, at least she did not seem pleased with David. She was reserved and rather cold towards him and inclined to be cross at the household's limitations; she was not an hour in the house before she sent him out to buy a bedpan. Her preparations, her fussings and bustlings were tremendous. Shorn of the comfort of her own slatternly back room, prised from the indolent ease of her favourite rocker, she assumed an unnatural activity, the terrible waddling activity of the fat woman. She was assiduous towards Jenny, assiduous and pitying. "Come away, my poor lamb," she seemed to say. "At least you have your mother beside you."

Ada's tongue was particularly active. She gave Jenny all the news. Sally had finished up unexpectedly on her winter pantomime tour, the show had suddenly come to grief, it wasn't any good, and Sally was out of work again and looking for an engagement. Sally never seemed to be doing anything else but looking for an engagement, Ada added ruefully. There was some talk of concerts being organised for the wounded soldiers and Sally might be asked to take part in those, but it would be voluntary work without a penny piece of pay. Ada deplored equally Sally's inability to earn a decent settled wage and the stupid ambition which drove her to continue with the whole hopeless business of the stage. She wished to heaven that Sally had never chucked the Telephone Exchange.

By a gradual process of approach Ada arrived at the topic of Joe. They were in the kitchen together, Jenny and Ada, on the day following Ada's arrival and Ada was making Jenny a cup of tea. With a very casual air Ada remarked:

"By the bye, you didn't know that Joe had been to see us?"

Jenny, who was reclining upon the sofa, stiffened suddenly and her pale languorous face sealed up like an oyster. There was a silence, then she said in a frozen voice:

"I don't know anything about Joe Gowlan and I don't care either. I despise him."

Ada carefully adjusted the cosy on the tea-pot.

" He did come though, Jenny, dropped in as nice as you please, and dropped in once or twice since, he has. You needn't run him down because you missed him, Jenny. That was your mistake, my lady. He's a nice fellow, if it's the last word I say. He's going to get Phyllis and Clarry into the munitions when it goes up at Wirtley. He's back again at Millington's and doing wonderful."

" I tell you I don't want to hear about Joe Gowlan," Jenny exclaimed in a tense voice. " If you want to know, I loathe and detest the very sound of his name."

But Ada, seating herself at the table and placing her plump hands on the cosy as though to warm them, went on, maddeningly:

" You can't think how wonderful he's got on. He's the head of the department, works clean and everything, dresses a perfect treat. Why, Jenny, the last time he come in he told us he was going up to supper at the Millingtons' house. Up to their house on Hilltop, Jenny, can you beat that? I'm telling you, my lady, you made a big mistake when you let Joe slip through your fingers. He's the man I'd have liked to see my son-in-law."

Jenny's face was very white, she clenched her fists tight, her voice turned shrill.

" I won't have you speak that way, mother. I won't have you mention Joe in the same breath as David. Joe's an absolute rotter and David's the best man that ever lived."

She stared at Ada challengingly. But this time Jenny could not dominate her mother. Her condition made her weak physically; and spiritually she was in a state of curious compromise. Ada had an excellent chance to make Jenny " lie down to her for once " and Ada took that chance.

" Huh! " she declared with a toss of her head. " What a way to talk. You would never think you had played about with him to hear you."

Jenny's eyes fell. She shivered slightly and was silent.

At that moment the door opened and David entered. He had just returned from the Harbour Board offices where he had been given temporary clerical work. Ada turned towards him with a little condescending smile. But before she could speak Jenny, upon the sofa, gave a dolorous cry and clapped her hand to her side.

" Oh dear," she whispered. " I've got a pain."

Ada hesitated, contemplating her daughter between resentment and doubt.

" You can't," she said at last. " It's a week before your time."

" Oh yes, I can," Jenny answered in a breathless voice. " I know I can. See, here it is again."

" Well I never," Ada declared. " I believe it is." Sympathy rushed over her. " My poor lamb! " She knelt down and put her hand on

Jenny's stomach. "Yes indeed it is, well, well, did you ever?" And then to David as though the whole situation were completely altered, and he, in some mysterious manner, to blame: "Go on. Fetch the doctor. Don't stand there looking at her."

With a quick look at Jenny David went for Dr. Scott, whom he found taking his evening surgery. Scott was an elderly red-faced bony man, very offhand and laconic, with a disconcerting habit of hawking and spitting in the middle of a conversation. He was in every way extremely unprofessional. He always wore riding-breeches and a long check jacket with enormous pockets stuffed full of everything: pipe, pills, half a bandage, some blue raisins, two empty thermometer cases, a pocket lance never sterilised, and a gum elastic catheter which whipped across the room whenever he pulled out his musty handkerchief. But in spite of his oddity, untidiness and complete lack of asepsis he was an excellent doctor.

Yet he seemed to attach little urgency to Jenny's first pain. He hawked, spat and nodded:

"I'll look round in an hour." Then he called out through the open door into his waiting-room: "Next, please."

David was upset because Scott did not come at once. He returned home to find that Jenny and Ada had both gone upstairs. He waited restlessly for Scott's arrival.

Yet when the doctor appeared at seven o'clock, though Jenny's pains were much worse, he assured David that he could do nothing in the meantime. David understood that a first confinement was always a protracted business and he asked the doctor if Jenny would have to suffer long. Staring into the kitchen fire a minute before spitting into it Scott replied:

"I don't think she'll be that long, mind ye. I'll look back before twelve!"

It was hard to wait until twelve. Jenny's pains became rapid and severe. She seemed to have no strength and no spirit to endure the pains. She was by turns peevish, anguished, hysterical, exhausted. The bedroom on which she had expended such care and thought, with the befrilled cot in one corner and the new muslin curtains on the windows, and the pretty lace doyleys set upon the dressing-table became littered and disordered. It was bad enough when Ada upset the kettle, but the climax came with a faint mewing which set Jenny screaming and revealed the fact that "Pretty" was below the bed.

Then Jenny gave up. Though Ada told her she must walk about, she lay across her bed sprawling, holding her stomach, weeping on a huddle of twisted bed-clothes. She forgot all about the *Chickabiddy's Journal* and *Sunny Half-hours in the Happy Home*. She got completely out of hand, lying on her back across that disordered bed with her legs apart, her night-dress drawn up, her hair tumbled about her pale thin face, her brow streaming with sweat. From time to time she closed her eyes and screamed. " Oh dear God," she screamed, " ah, ah, ah, there it is again, oh my God my back, ah, ah, ah, oh mother give me a drink that water there it's worse quick dear God, mother." It was not quite so romantic as Jenny had imagined.

Scott came at twelve sharp and went straight upstairs. The door slammed upon Scott, Ada and the screeching Jenny. There was more screeching, the heavy tramp of Scott's boots, then silence.

Chloroform, thank God, David thought. He sat hunched up in a chair in the kitchen before the nearly out fire. He had suffered every pain with Jenny and now the chloroform silence brought him an almost agonised relief. Human suffering always affected him profoundly and Jenny's suffering seemed the epitome of all inevitable human pain. He thought of her with tenderness. He forgot all the quarrels and disputes and bickerings that had occurred between them. He forgot her pettiness, her petulance and her vanities. He began to consider the child and once again the child appeared to him as a symbol—a new life rising from amongst the dead. He had a vision of the battlefields where the dead lay in attitudes stranger even than they had lain within the pit. Soon he would be there, in France, on these battlefields. Nugent had written to him from the front where he was serving as a stretcher bearer in an ambulance unit attached to the Northumberland Fusiliers. By joining up at the same headquarters at Tynecastle, he also would get out with the Fusiliers and he hoped his unit would be near to Nugent's.

A moaning came from the room overhead and then a singing, Jenny's voice singing. He heard it quite plainly, a verse from one of her old sentimental songs, but the words came curiously ribald and slurred. That was another effect of the chloroform. It made people sing as though they were drunk.

Then again there was silence, a very long silence broken by the sudden coming of another voice, a thin new voice, not Jenny's or Ada's or Scott's voice, but an altogether new voice which cried and piped like a little flute. The sound of that thin voice emerging from the pain and the shouting and the dark succeeding silence struck into David's heart. Again the symbol: out of the chaos the new dawn. He sat perfectly still, his hands clasped together, his head uplifted, a strange presentiment in his eyes.

Half an hour later Scott clumped down the stairs and entered the kitchen. His face wore that tired and distasteful look which confinements often bring to the faces of over-worked and disillusioned doctors. He fumbled in his pocket for a blue raisin. Scott always declared that he carried about these blue raisins to give to children; they were a marvellous cure for worms, he said. But Scott really liked the blue raisins himself and that was why he carried them about.

He found a blue raisin and began to chew it. He said in a non-committal way:

" Well, the little article's arrived."

David did not speak. He swallowed; nodded his head.

" A boy," Scott said with a sort of automatic response, trying to infuse enthusiasm into his words, but failing.

" Is Jenny all right? "

" Oh, your wife's quite comfortable, perfectly comfortable." Scott paused and threw a very queer look at David. " The baby's inclined to be delicate though. He'll need a bit of attention one way and another."

He threw another queerly suspicious look at David, but he said no more. He was a coarse old man with a low-class country and colliery practice. But he was not coarse now. He looked merely fatigued with life which, at a moment such as this, seemed to him terrible and incomprehensible. Stretching his arms above his head he yawned. He nodded to David and he spat into the fire that had gone out. Then he went out himself.

David stood in the centre of the empty kitchen for a few moments before going upstairs. He knocked at the bedroom door and entered. He wanted to be beside Jenny and the child. But Jenny was overcome, completely overcome, not yet fully recovered from the anæsthetic and inclined to be hysterical as well. Ada, too, was bustling and cross, fussing him out of the room at once. He had to leave it at that and return downstairs. He made his bed on the parlour sofa. The house was completely silent before he slept.

But next morning he saw the baby. While he sat at his breakfast of cocoa and bread Ada brought the baby down quite proudly as though she had done it all herself. The baby was freshly washed and powdered and dressed up in a lace-trimmed Carricoat, from the Chickabiddy's set. which draped its tiny body most importantly. But for all its important trimmings the baby was very ugly and puny. It had black hair and blinking eyes and a flat pushed-in watery little nose and was pale and sickly and small. The baby was so ugly and small that David's heart melted into fresh tenderness. He put down the cup of cocoa and took the baby on his knee. The feel of the baby upon his knee was absurd and wonderful. The baby's eyes blinked timidly towards his. There was an apology in the timid blinking of the baby's eyes.

" There, now, there! " Ada took up the baby again and dandled it up and down. " Your father's clumsy with the pet! "

She had the stupid convention that no man was capable of holding a baby without serious consequences to the baby. Strangely enough the baby had been good as gold on David's knee. But now it began to cry and was still crying when Ada carried it from the room.

David went out to his clerking thinking about the baby and when he returned at the end of his day's work he was still thinking about the baby. He had begun to be fond of the small, ugly baby.

It was perfectly clear that the baby was delicate. Jenny admitted it herself and in course of time adopted a neatly descriptive phrase which she used in the presence of visitors. Looking compassionately towards the baby she would remark all in one breath: " Poor little mite, he's not very robust, the doctor says! "

Powders were prescribed by Dr. Scott for the baby with an ointment to rub in and Jenny, after a few initial protests, fed the baby herself. The doctor insisted on that, too.

Already the memory of her confinement—considered at the time to be excruciating and unforgettable—had become dimmed and Jenny was brightening up, recovering from her disappointment that the baby was not a girl. She wanted to call the baby David. She implored David very prettily to let her call the baby after him.

" He's yours, David," she remarked with a naïve logic. She faced him with her clear, beautiful eyes and smiled. " It's only right he should have your name."

But David wanted the baby to have the name of Robert: his dead father and his living son both Robert. And Jenny, after countering with several other names, notably Hector, Archibald and Victor, which she thought superior in point of sound and importance, very meekly gave in. She wanted to please David in every possible way. So the baby became Robert.

Three weeks passed. Ada went back to Tynecastle. Jenny was able to leave her room and recline languidly upon the sofa downstairs. Yet she found the duty of nursing Robert a tax on her in many ways. As her strength returned and her life approached the normal the resolutions formed by her romantic imagination gradually seemed less attractive. Robert, from being a dear little mite, had now become a dear little nuisance. She was pleased to let David give Robert his medicine and to bath Robert when she felt tired. And yet in a way Jenny was queerly resentful of David's interest in the child.

" You do love me best, don't you, David ? " she exclaimed one evening. " You don't love him better than you love me ? "

" Of course not, Jenny." He laughed at her as he knelt with rolled-up shirt-sleeves beside the tin bath where Robert lay in the soapy water.

She did not reply. And, still watching them, the look of discontent deepened upon her face.

Indeed, as the New Year approached Jenny became increasingly discontented and restless. Everything seemed wrong, nothing right. She wanted David to go to the front and yet she did not want him to go. She was proud one minute and afraid the next. To distract her mind she took to reading a great many paper-backed novelettes, *Sunny Half-hours in the Happy Home* having been mislaid. She had forgotten about her music now, never touched the piano and never sang her lullabies. She studied her reflection in the glass for long periods on end to reassure herself that her looks and her figure had not suffered. Once again she felt she had no friends. She was out of things, life was passing over her. She was missing everything. It was very trying and upsetting for Jenny, she might as well be dead. The weather was wet, too, and though she was able to get about now it was useless to go out in the rain. Besides, Robert had to be fed every four hours and that naturally interfered with any decent outing she might make up her mind to take.

But on New Year's Eve the rain ceased and the sun came out and Jenny felt that she could stand it no longer. She really must have a little jaunt. She must, she must. It was years, hundreds of years since she had had a little jaunt. She would go and see her mother at Tynecastle. Her face brightened at the decision, she rushed upstairs, dressed herself nicely and came down. It was four o'clock. She fed Robert, put him in his cot and scribbled a hurried note for David saying she would be back at eight.

David was quite glad when he returned and found Jenny's note, pleased to think that Jenny was having an outing and pleased in some singular way to have Robert to himself.

Robert was asleep in his cot in the corner beside the kitchen range. David took off his boots and walked about in his socks in order not to make a noise. He got his tea and enjoyed his tea in Robert's company. Then he took a book and sat down to read beside the cot. The book was Nietzsche's *Beyond Good and Evil* and David was interested in Nietzsche. But David looked more frequently at Robert than at Nietzsche.

At half-past seven Robert woke up and got ready to be fed. He lay perfectly quietly on his back, looking up at the much-befrilled ceiling of his cot. What a queer view of the world he must have, thought David.

For a good half-hour Robert kept on contentedly taking his queer view of the world, meanwhile staving off his appetite with his thumb. But in the end the thumb was not satisfactory and after a few preliminary whimperings Robert began to cry. David lifted Robert out of his cot and soothed him. That was successful for a little while, then Robert began to cry again.

Anxiously David looked at the clock. Half-past eight: Jenny must have missed her train and the next did not arrive till ten! It struck David how utterly dependent Robert was upon Jenny.

He did the best he could. He saw that Robert was uncomfortable and wet, and though he had not much experience with napkins he took Robert's napkin off. Robert seemed pleased and by way of gratitude when David lifted him aloft again he clutched hard at David's hair.

David laughed and Robert laughed too. He seemed hungry, but otherwise much relieved. David put Robert down on the hearthrug and Robert sprawled and kicked before the fire. He seemed altogether a healthier baby these last few weeks, he was fatter, his rash had gone and he did not snuffle so much. But now he was extremely hungry, he cried a good deal again as it came towards ten o'clock.

With a rising indignation at Jenny's lateness David got down on his hands and knees and began to talk to Robert, to try to soothe and reassure him. At that moment the door swung open and Jenny came in. She was in tremendous spirits. She had been to the pictures with Clarry and had her glass of port. She stood in the doorway with one hand on her hip and a broad smile on her red lips, then all at once she began to laugh; she was convulsed with laughter at the picture made by David and Robert on the hearthrug.

David drew his lips together.

"Don't laugh like that," he said sharply.

" I can't help it," she giggled. " It's something . . . something just come in my head."

" What do you mean ? "

" Oh, nothing," she said hurriedly. " Just a kind of joke."

There was a short pause. He got to his feet and lifted the child.

" Robert's hungry," he said, still angry and indignant. " Can't you see he wants his feed ? "

She came forward rather unsteadily.

" Here, then," she said, " I'm the one that can see to that, amn't I ? "

She took Robert from him and sat down with a bump on the sofa. Perhaps two glasses of port gave a certain generosity to her movements. David watched her grimly. She ripped open her blouse. Her big full breasts protruded like udders, veined and white and fat, the milk was already dripping from them. As Robert nestled to one breast and sucked the milk spurted from the other. Flushed and happy Jenny smiled, rocking sensuously back and forward on the sofa, careless of the dripping milk.

But David turned away. He felt suddenly revolted. He made a pretence of stirring up the fire, then he faced her again.

" Remember! " he said in a low, serious tone, " I expect you to look after Robert when I'm away! "

" I will, David," she gushed. " Oh, you know I will."

He left for Tynecastle the following day and from there he was drafted straight away to camp at Catterick. Three months later, on the 5th of April, he went with the field ambulance unit attached to the fifth battalion of the Northumberland Fusiliers to France.

IX

On that second Sunday of September, 1915, Hetty's car drew up briskly on the gravel drive of the Law. As he stood at the dining-room window with his hands in his pockets Arthur watched Hetty get out, very smart in her khaki, and advance towards the front door.

Arthur had known that Hetty was coming to the Law to-day. Impossible not to know of Hetty's coming. Aunt Carrie had mentioned it, his mother had mentioned it, and at lunch, on Saturday, Barras had looked down the table and remarked with unusual significance:

" Hetty will be here for tea to-morrow. She has asked the day off specially."

Arthur had not answered. Did they take him for a fool? It was too obvious; that " specially " had a grim humour all its own.

During these last eight months Hetty had been frequently at the Law. Hetty, as one of the first to join the Women's Emergency Corps, had now secured a commission in the W.V.R., executive headquarters, Tynecastle. She was often useful to Barras in his activities, dashing between Tynecastle and Sleescale in her two-seater runabout, bringing official papers for his signature. But on this Sunday Arthur was fully aware that Hetty's duties would not be official. Hetty was having a day off to be sweetly unofficial. He saw it plainly and for all his bitterness he could have laughed.

She came into the room. And at the sight of him there, by the window, she smiled brightly and extended her hands with a little twitter of pleasure.

" You've been looking out for me," she said. " How nice of you, Arthur."

She was extremely bright; but he had anticipated that. He did not smile back. He said flatly:

" Yes, I expected you."

His tone might perhaps have warned her, but she was not dismayed.

" Where are the others ? " she asked lightly.

" They've all disappeared," he said. " They're all conveniently out of the way so that we can be alone."

She laughed reprovingly:

" You sound as if you didn't want us to be alone. But I know you don't mean to be unkind. I know you better than you do yourself. Come on, now, what shall we do ? Shall we go for a walk ? "

He coloured slightly and looked away from her. But in a moment he said:

" All right, then, Hetty, let's go for a walk."

He got his hat and coat and they set out on the walk they usually took together, though they had not taken it for some months now, the walk through Sluice Dene. The autumn day was calm, the dene was full of russet colour, the bracken crackled under their feet. They walked in silence. When they reached the end of the dene they sat down on the high root of an oak tree which a subsidence had unearthed. It was their usual seat. Below, the town lay subdued in the Sunday quiet and the sea stretched out beyond, shimmering away into the distance and merging with the sky. The headstocks of the Neptune rose up black and high against the clear background of sea and sky. Arthur stared at the headstocks, the gallows headstocks of the Neptune pit.

And presently, having tucked her skirt round her trim legs with seductive modesty, Hetty followed his gaze.

" Arthur," she exclaimed. " Why do you look at the pit like that ? "

" I don't know," he said bitterly. " Business is good. Coal selling at fifty shillings a ton."

" It isn't that," she said with an impulse of curiosity. " I do wish you'd tell me, Arthur. You've been so queer lately, so unlike yourself. Do tell me, dear, and perhaps I can help you."

He turned to Hetty, a warmth penetrating through his bitterness. He had an impulse to tell her, unburden himself of the awful weight that pressed upon him and crushed his very soul. He said in a low voice:

" I can't forget the disaster at the Neptune."

She was staggered, but she concealed it. She said as she might have humoured a troubled child:

" In what way, Arthur dear ? "

" I believe the disaster could have been prevented."

She stared at his melancholy face, exasperated, feeling that she must get to the bottom of this irritating enigma.

" Something is really worrying you, Arthur dear. If you could only tell me ? "

He looked at her. He said slowly:

" I believe the lives of all these men were thrown away, Hetty." He broke off. What was the use ? She would never understand.

Yet she had a vague glimpse of the morbid obsession that burned in his mind. She took his hand. She humoured him. She said gently:

" Even if it were so, Arthur, don't you think the best way is to forget about it ? It's so long ago now. And only a hundred men. What's that compared with the thousands and thousands of brave fellows who have been killed in the war ? That's what you've got to remember now, Arthur dear. There's a war on now. A world war, and that's a very different affair from the tiny little disaster in the pit."

" It is not different," he said, pressing his hand against his brow. " It's the same thing exactly. I can't see it any other way. I can't separate them in my mind. The men at the front are being killed just like the men in the pit, needlessly, horribly. The disaster and the war mean exactly the same thing to me. They've become united in one great mass murder."

Hetty took the situation in hand. She abandoned the tortuous labyrinths into which he was leading her and took the short cut home. She was, in a way, quite fond of Arthur. She was practical, prided herself on being practical. And she meant to be kind.

" I'm so glad you've told me, Arthur," she said briskly. " You've been worrying yourself sick and all about nothing. I've seen you were queer lately, but I hadn't the least idea. I thought, well, I didn't know what to think."

He stared at her glumly.

" What *did* you think ? "

" Well," she hesitated, " I thought maybe you were, well, that you didn't *want* to go to the war."

" I don't," he said.

" But I meant, Arthur dear, I meant *afraid* to go."

" Perhaps I am afraid," he said dully. " I may be a coward for all I know."

" Nonsense! " she said decisively and patted his hand. " You've got yourself into a perfect state of nerves. The very bravest of people get like that. Why, Alan told me before he went over the top and got his M.C. he was in a complete blue funk. Now you listen to me, my dear. You've been thinking and worrying far too much. You want a little action for a change. It's high time I was taking you in hand."

Her look became inquiring. She smiled, very sweet and sure of herself, aware of her sex, her attraction, her poise.

" Now listen to me, you dear silly boy. Do you remember, Arthur, that week-end at Tynecastle when you wanted us to be engaged and I said we were both too young ? "

" Yes," he said slowly. " I remember that day. I shan't forget it in a hurry."

She raised her dark-pupilled eyes towards him intimately, and began to stroke his hand. " Well . . . it would be different if you were in the army, Arthur dear."

He stiffened. It had come at last, what he dreaded, come under the odious pretence of tenderness. But she did not notice the sudden aversion that held him rigid and speechless. She was carried away by her own feeling, which was not love but the sense of immolating herself. She came nearer to him and murmured:

" You know I'm fond of you, Arthur. Ever since we were little. Why don't we get engaged and stop all these stupid misunderstandings. You're worrying your father, worrying everybody, including poor little me. You'd be so much happier in the army, I'm sure of it. We'd both be happier, we'd have a wonderful time."

He still said nothing, but as she lifted her face, a little flushed now, with her smooth blonde hair fluffed appealingly about her cheeks, he answered stiffly:

" I've no doubt it would be wonderful. Unfortunately I've made up my mind not to join the army."

" Oh no, Arthur," she cried. " You can't really mean that."

" I do mean it."

Her first reaction was dismay. She said hurriedly:

" But, listen, Arthur. Please do listen. It isn't going to be a matter of choice. It's not going to be so easy as you think. They'll be bringing in conscription soon. I know. I heard it at headquarters. Everybody between eighteen and forty-one who's not exempt. And I don't think you'd be exempt. Your father, he'd have to say if you were entitled to a badge."

" Let my father do what he likes," he answered in a low and bitter voice, " I can see you've been talking about me, all right."

" Oh, please," she begged. " For my sake. Please, please."

" I can't," he said in a tone of dead finality.

Her face went a vivid red with shame. The shame was partly for him but chiefly for herself. She snatched her hand away from him. To give herself time she pretended to arrange her hair, her back towards him, then she said in quite a different voice:

" I hope you understand that this is pretty horrible for me, to be virtually engaged to a man who refuses to do the one decent thing that's asked of him."

" I'm sorry, Hetty," he said in a low voice, " but, don't you see——"

" Be quiet," she cut in furiously, " I've never been so insulted in my life. Never. It's . . . it's impossible. Don't think I'm so much gone on you as all that. I only did it for your father. He's a real man, not a feeble attempt like you. It can't go on, of course. I can't have anything more to do with you."

" Very well," he said, almost inaudibly.

The satisfaction of hurting him was now almost as great as had been her previous satisfaction of surrender. She bit her lip fiercely.

" There's only one conclusion I can come to, only one conclusion anybody can come to. You're afraid, that's what you are." She paused and threw the word at him. " You're a coward, a miserable coward."

He went very pale. She waited for him to speak but he did not and with a gesture of suppressed contempt she got up.

He got up too. They walked back to the Law in complete silence. He opened the front door for her, but once inside the house he went straight up to his room, leaving her in the hall. She stood with her head in the air, her eyes swimming with temper and self-pity, then abruptly she turned and went into the dining-room.

Barras was there. He was alone, studying the beflagged map upon the wall, and he turned at the sight of her, rubbing his hands together, rather effusive in his welcome.

" Well, Hetty," he exclaimed. " Anything to report ? "

All the way home Hetty had borne up well. But that bland kindness in Barras's face quite broke her down. She burst into tears.

"Oh dear, oh dear," she sobbed. "I'm so horribly upset."

Barras came over. He looked down at her and on an impulse slipped an arm round her thin, enticing shoulders.

"Why, my poor little Hetty, what's the matter?" he inquired protectively.

Overcome, she could not tell him, but she clung to him as to a refuge in a storm. He held her in his arm, soothing her. She had a queer feeling that he was taking care of her, saving her from Arthur, and a sense of his vitality and strength stole upon her. She closed her eyes and gave herself up to this strange new sense of his protection.

X

For six months following his appointment as works manager Joe found plenty to occupy him. He arrived early at Platt Lane and left late; he was always on the spot when he was wanted; he created the impression of boundless energy and enthusiasm. At the start he went cautiously. With natural astuteness he saw that Fuller the chief clerk, Irving head of the drawing room and Dobbie the cashier had not taken kindly to his promotion. They were elderly men prepared to resent the authority of a young man of twenty-seven who had risen so rapidly from nothing. Dobbie in particular, a dried-up, angular adding machine, with pince-nez balanced on a beak of a nose and a high peakless collar like a parson's, was sour as vinegar. But Joe was careful. He knew that his time would come. And in the meantime he continued to ingratiate himself with Millington.

Nothing was too much trouble for Joe. He had a way of relieving Stanley of small unpleasant duties which in course of time produced an extension of his own. In March he suggested the Saturday morning conference between Millington and himself at which all the important business of the week came to be discussed. At the end of the same month he pressed for six additional melting-pots and advanced the idea that women be engaged upon the extra traying work. He put Vic Oliver in charge of the machine-shop, and old Sam Doubleday in the foundry; and both Oliver and Doubleday were in his pocket. In April Mr. Clegg died and Joe sent an enormous wreath to his funeral.

Gradually Joe came to stand very near Millington and to know the intricacies of the business. The profits the works were making staggered Joe. The Mills bombs alone, for which the Government paid Stanley 7*s*. 6*d*. the piece, cost on an average about 9*d*. And they were turning them out by the tens of thousands. God Almighty, thought Joe; and the itching in his hands was terrible. His salary, now seven-fifty per annum, became as nothing. He redoubled his efforts. Stanley and he became intimate; often lunched together in the office on sandwiches and beer; went out occasionally to Stanley's club—the County, and to the lounge of the Central Hotel. It actually came about that Joe accompanied Millington to the first meeting of the Local Munitions Committee. This all happened adroitly and smoothly. When Stanley was away the responsibility seemed to descend upon Joe's broad shoulders perfectly naturally and rightly. " See Mr. Gowlan about it " became a recognised phrase of Stanley's when he wanted to escape the tedium of an irritating interview. In this way Joe began to make important contacts, even to do a certain amount of the buying: scrap, lead, and particularly antimony. The price of antimony went as high as £25 per long ton. And over the price of antimony Joe first fell in with Mawson.

Jim Mawson was a large man with a double chin and a small, comprehensive, carefully hooded eye. His beginnings were even more obscure than Joe's, which caused Joe to regard him favourably from the outset. He described himself broadly as a merchant and contractor. The nucleus of his business was centred in a large depot on Malmo wharf where his original sign, now almost obliterated, read as follows: *Jim Mawson, Iron and Metals, Old Rope, Canvas, Hair and Tallow, Rubber Waste, Rabbit Skins, Rags, Bones, &c., Wholesale and General Contractor and Merchant.* But Mawson's activities went further than that; he was in the new Wirtley " hutting " contract; he was active on the Tynecastle Exchange; he was one of the men who were taking advantage of the war; known as a warm man, he was growing richer every day. One especial side-line of Mawson's particularly tickled Joe, when he came to hear of it, and struck him as typical of Mawson's cleverness. Already the paper shortage had hit Tynecastle, and Jim Mawson, well aware of the situation, had engaged a squad of girls—young shawlies from the Malmo slums—who went out regularly at five every morning and cleared the paper out of half the garbage bins in the city. They collected paper and cardboard—cardboard was the best—and each of the drabs got two and six a week, which was more, Jim said, than they deserved. As for Jim, the price he got was stupendous. But it was the idea that appealed to Joe: what " a knock out " to make " a packet " out of garbage!

Joe really felt himself blood brother to Jim Mawson; he was not obliged to disguise his motives in Mawson's company; and he had an idea that Mawson was drawn to him in much the same way. After their preliminary talk on the subject of antimony Mawson invited Joe to his house in Peters Place, a large untidy mansion—a mortgage which Mawson had foreclosed upon and moved into—full of ponderous yellow furniture, slovenly stair-carpet and dirt. There Joe met Mrs. Mawson, who was frizzy-haired and elderly and shrewd, and took pride in the fact that she had once owned a pawnshop. Joe exerted himself with Ma Mawson, he greeted her with jovial deference, bending over her beringed, shop-soiled hand as though he could have licked it. Supper consisted of a ferocious beef-steak and onions served out of the pan, and several bottles of stout, and after supper Mawson slipped Joe a quiet tip on the Exchange. Speaking out of the corner of his mouth, sitting placid and laconic in a big leather armchair, Mawson said: "Hm. Might buy yourself a few Franks' Ordinary. They wassent worth a damn afore the war. They make the mouldiest biscuits outa chokey. Y'wouldn't give them to a dog. But they're goin' great in the trenches. They're coming out with a fifteen per cent. divvy. Better get in afore the dividend gets out."

Buying on margin Joe cleared three hundred pounds on Mawson's tip and, rejoicing, he visioned the future in Mawson's co-operation. This was only the beginning, too. The war was going on for a long time yet and it was going to be the making of him. It was the most wonderful war he had ever seen; he hoped it would go on for ever.

Only one flaw marred the splendour of Joe's prospects—Laura. Whenever Joe thought of Laura, and that was often, his brow registered a puzzled and frustrated frown. He could not, simply could not fathom her. He was convinced that in some subtle way he owed his present position to Laura; indeed he owed her more than his position. Unconsciously he found himself taking hints from Laura, puzzling things out and modelling himself to her standard, wondering how she would like this . . . or that. He was still ignorant, but he did not do badly. The brilliantine was stopped, that strongly scented hair dressing which had made one eyebrow of Laura's faintly lift; the brown boots were worn only with the brown suit; the ties became less florid; the watch-chain now stretched between the bottom pockets of his waistcoat; the bunch of near-gold seals and the imitation pearl had been flung, one dark evening, into the Tyne. And in matters of more intimate detail this unseen influence of Laura prevailed. For instance, after one look at the bathroom at Hilltop with its bath-salts, crystals, toilet ammonia, loofah and spray, Joe had gone straight to the chemist's and resolutely bought himself a tooth-brush.

But the trouble was that Laura remained so wickedly inaccessible. They met frequently, but always in Stanley's company. He wanted to be alone with her, he would have given largely to charity to be alone with her, but he was afraid to make the first move. He was not completely sure; he was terrified of making a horrible mistake, of losing his wonderful position and his more wonderful prospects. He did not dare.

At nights he sat in his room thinking about her, wanting her, conjuring up her image, wondering what she was doing at that especial moment: taking a bath, doing her hair, pulling on her long silk stockings. Once the situation so fevered him, he jumped up and rushed out to the nearest telephone box. With a bumping heart he rang her number; but it was Stanley's voice which answered from the other end; and in a cold panic Joe dropped back the receiver and slunk back to his room.

It was maddening. He felt towards Laura as towards the first sexual experience of his life: she represented something strange and new, something he wanted to find out. But he could not find out. She remained, thus far, an enigma. He tried terribly hard to probe into her character and occasionally vague glimmerings of understanding came to him. He suspected, to begin with, that Laura was tired to death of Stanley's gush, of his bouts of moody grumbling, and of his patriotism, which had lately become intense. She was bored to tears with his public-school spirit, high ideals and the special brand of baby talk which Stanley preserved for their moments of endearment. "How is my little kittikins?" he had once heard Stanley murmur and he could have sworn that Laura stiffened. Yet Laura was loyal to Stanley—that, Joe repeated, was the curse of it.

Joe had a great deal of vanity. He saw himself as a fine handsome dashing fellow. But did Laura see him that way?

Laura was interested in him. She seemed to recognise his possibilities, to take a sort of mocking interest in him. She had no illusions regarding his morality. Her unsmiling smile met all his protestations of good faith and high ideals; yet when, skilfully, he approached her on the opposite tack the result was quite disastrous. On one occasion at tea he had made a slightly vulgar joke. Stanley had laughed boisterously, but Laura had turned blank, completely blank and frigid. Joe had blushed as he had never blushed before, the shame of it had nearly killed him. She was a queer one, Laura. She was not a type. She was herself.

The question of war-work illuminated Laura's queerness pretty well. All the ladies in Yarrow were crazy about war-work, there was a rash of uniforms and a perfect epidemic of corps, committees and guilds. Hetty, Laura's sister in Tynecastle, was never out of her khaki. But Laura would have none of it. She went only to the canteen at the new munition sheds at Wirtley because, as she put it ironically to Joe, she liked to see the beasts fed. She served coffee and sandwiches to the munition workers there, but no more than that. Laura kept to herself, and Joe, to his infinite exasperation, could not get near her.

June came and this state of affairs still went on. Then, on the 16th of the month, Stanley gave Joe the second staggering surprise of his life. It was a quarter-past twelve and Millington, who had been out all the forenoon, put his head round the door of Joe's office and said:

"I want to see you, Gowlan. Come into my office."

The serious quality in Stanley's tone startled Joe. With a slightly guilty air he got up and walked into the private office where Stanley flung himself into a chair and began restlessly to shuffle some papers on his desk. Stanley had been very restless lately. He was a curious fellow. As far as could be made out he was extremely ordinary; spiritually he was full of clichés; he had the ordinary cut and dried ideas and he liked to do the ordinary things. He was fond of bridge and golf; he liked a good detective story or yarns which dealt with buried treasure; he believed that one Britisher was better than any five foreigners; in peace time he never missed the Motor Show; he was a bore, too; he told the same stories over and over again; he would talk for hours on how, in his last year at St. Bede's, the first fifteen had beaten Giggleswick. But through all this ran a curious strain of discontent, a buried complex of escape. He would arrive at the office, on a Monday morning, with a listless droop to his mouth, and his manner seemed to say, oh lord, must I still go on with this!

His business was flourishing and, at the beginning, that had sent the mercury soaring to the sky. He wanted to make money; and it had been *ripping* watching profits flow in at the rate of a round £1,000 a week. But now "money wasn't everything." His discontent grew when the Ministry of Munitions came into existence. Then Millington's became part of the official scheme; they were sub-contracted to the new Hutton filling sheds at Wirtley; the pioneer work was finished; everything was set, ordered and official; there was altogether less for Stanley to do; a sort of lull set in; and, though he had grumblingly demanded ease, he did not like it when it came.

He began to feel troubled. Bands in particular began to trouble Stanley. Whenever a band went down the street blaring *Tipperary* or *Good-byee*, a faint flush would come to Stanley's cheek, his eyes would kindle, his back straighten. But when the band was gone and the music stilled and the tramp of marching men an echo merely in his heart, Stanley would sigh and let his figure slump.

The notices worried him too. Yarrow had responded well to the call for men and a great many windows of the Yarrow houses bore the notice: *A MAN has gone from this house to fight for King and Country.* The MAN was in out-size letters and Millington had always prided himself on being an out-size man.

As for the posters, that stern look on Kitchener's face and the finger, which pointed at him and would not let him alone, oh, when passing those posters Stanley fumed and fretted and flushed, and clenched his pipe between his teeth, and wondered how long he would be able to endure it.

It was not the pointing finger, however, but the Old St. Bedean's Dinner which had brought Stanley to a head. The dinner had taken place at Dilley's Rooms in Tynecastle upon the previous evening. And now Millington looked across his desk at Joe and announced gravely:

"Joe, there's a great adventure taking place in France, and I'm missing it!"

Joe did not understand, his main feeling was relief that Stanley had not uncovered his antimony deals.

" I think you ought to know," Stanley went on, his voice rising, a little hysterical, " I've made up my mind to join the army."

An electric silence. The shock was so great that Joe became completely unnerved. He paled and blurted out:

" But you can't. What about here ? "

" We'll talk about that later," Stanley said, pushing it away from him and speaking rapidly. " You can take it from me, I'm going. Last night convinced me. The dinner last night. My God, how I ever got through it I can't imagine. Would you believe it—everyone but myself in uniform. All my pals in uniform and me there in civilians. I felt an absolute outsider. They all looked at me, you know—how's the profiteer? —that sort of thing. Hampson, who was in my form, a regular decent fellow, cut me absolutely dead. He's a major in the Public Schools Battalion now. And there was Robbins, a little worm who wasn't even in the second eleven, he's a captain now with a couple of wound stripes. I tell you I can't stand it, Gowlan. I've *got* to get into it."

Joe took a trembling breath, trying to collect his scattered wits. He could not yet believe it, the thing was too good to be true.

" You're doing work of national importance. They'll never let you go."

" They'll have to let me go," Stanley barked. " This place runs itself now. The contracts are automatic. Dobbie handles the accounts, and there's you—you know it all backwards, Joe."

Joe lowered his eyes quickly.

" Well," he muttered, " that's true enough."

Stanley jumped up and began to march up and down the office.

" I'm not a spiritually-minded chap, I suppose, but I will say I've felt uplifted since I decided to answer the call. The spirit of St. George for England lives still, you know. It isn't dead, you know, it isn't really. We're fighting for the right. What decent fellow could sit down under it, these air raids and submarine attacks, and innocent women raped, and shelling hospitals and babies even—O God, even to read it in the papers makes a man's blood boil."

" I know how you feel," Joe said with his eyes on the floor. " It's the devil. If I didn't have this old knee of mine . . ." The knee, it may be remembered, was a complaint which Joe had discovered by visiting an obscure surgery in Commercial Road and planking down seven and six for a certificate, and it made Joe limp horribly whenever the air was military.

But Stanley, marching up and down, was solely occupied with Stanley.

" I'm qualified for a commission, you know. I was three years in the corps at St. Bede's. I'll take a few weeks to make my arrangements, then I'll get into uniform with the Public Schools Battalion."

Another silence.

" I see," Joe said slowly; he cleared his throat. " Mrs. Millington won't like this."

" No, naturally, she doesn't want me to go." Stanley laughed and clapped Joe on the back. " Cheer up, there's a good fellow. It's decent of you to be upset, but the bally old war won't last long once I get into it." He broke off, glanced at his watch. " Now look here, I've got to run down and meet Major Hampson for lunch. If I'm not back by three you might look over to Rutley's and see them about these last grenades. Old John Rutley made the appointment, but you can tell him all there is to it."

" All right," Joe said sadly. " I'll go."

So Joe went over to Rutley's and met old John in a tiresome and involved discussion upon blow-hole castings while Stanley tore down excitedly to have lunch with Hampson. At five o'clock when Stanley, several drinks to the good, lay back in a club chair convulsed by one of Hampson's stories about a certain mademoiselle in a certain estaminet, Joe was shaking hands in a firm but deferential fashion with Rutley himself, while the old man thought, with grim approval, there's a young fellow who knows what he's about.

That night Joe went posting round to Mawson's with the news. Mawson was silent for a long time, sitting upright in his chair, clasping his stomach with both hands, his high bald forehead creased, his small eyes fixed thoughtfully on Joe.

" Well," he reflected. " This is goin' to be helpful."

In spite of himself Joe grinned.

" You and me's goin' to do well out of this, Joe," Mawson said unemotionally, then raising his voice he bawled: " Mother, fetch me and Joe a bottle of Scotch."

They finished the bottle between them, but towards midnight when Joe walked home the thrilling intoxication in his blood was not due to whisky. He was drunk with the sense of his opportunity, the chance of power, money, everything. He was in it at last, as Jim had said, absolutely set right up to the ear-holes in it, in with the big men, he only had to watch himself to be big himself, *bloody* big. O Christ, wasn't it great! A great place, Tynecastle, wonderful air, wonderful streets, wonderful buildings—there was an idea now, property, he'd have property, a hell of a lot, some day. What a wonderful night it was. Look at the moon shining on that white place over there. What was it? Public lavatory, eh? Never mind—wonderful public lavatory! At the corner of Grainger Street a tart spoke to him.

" You little bitch," said Joe kindly, " get out! " He strode on, laughing, wide awake, exultant. Better than that, he thought, much better than that. He gloated upon Laura, her fastidiousness, her aloof charms. To hell with tarts. Women like Laura were different, see, *different*. His idyllic fancy took him far with Laura that night, especially when he reached his lodgings and went to bed.

But next morning he was at Platt Lane upon the tick of nine, fresh as a daisy and more deferentially alert towards Stanley than ever. There were an astonishing number of things to be gone into. Joe was thoroughness itself: nothing escaped him.

" Good lord, Joe," Stanley exclaimed, yawning, after they had been hard at it for a couple of hours. " You're a regular tartar. I'd no idea you'd got such an eye for detail."

He patted Joe on the shoulder gaily. " I appreciate it immensely. But in the meantime I'm going out to have a spot with Hampson. See you later."

There was a queer look on Joe's face as he watched Stanley's figure disappear briskly through the office door.

The days passed, the final arrangements were completed, and at last the afternoon of Stanley's departure for Aldershot arrived. He had arranged to drive over to Carnton Junction and join the express direct, instead of taking a slow local from Yarrow. As a special sign of his regard he had asked Joe to come with Laura to the station to see him off.

It was a wet afternoon. Joe arrived too early at Hilltop, he had to wait ten minutes in the lounge before Laura came in. She wore a plain blue costume and a dark soft fur which gave her pale skin that queer luminous quality which always excited him. He jumped up from his chair, but she walked slowly to the window as though she did not notice him. There was a silence. He watched her.

" I'm sorry he's going," he said at last.

She turned and considered him with that secret look which always puzzled him. He felt that she was sad, perhaps angry too; she didn't want Stanley to go; no, she didn't want him to go.

Here Stanley entered breezily, as if a row of medals were already on his chest. He rubbed his hands cheerfully.

" Filthy day, isn't it? Well, the wetter the day the better the deed, eh, Joe? Ha! Ha! Now what about the rum ration for the troops, Laura? "

Laura rang the bell and Bessie brought in a tray of sandwiches and tea. Stanley was dreadfully hearty. He chaffed Bessie out of her long face, mixed himself a whisky and soda, and walked up and down the room munching sandwiches and talking.

" Good sandwiches, these, Laura. Don't suppose I'll be getting this kind of stomach-fodder in a week or two. You'll need to send me some parcels, Laura. A fellow was saying last night that they absoblooming-utely look forward to getting parcels. Varies the jolly old bully beef and plum and apple." Stanley laughed. He could now say plum and apple without a blush. He could laugh, really laugh at the Bairnsfather cartoons. He crowed: " Hampson, old dodger that he is——" another laugh, " was telling me of a scheme they have for making Irish stew in a ration tin. Some of the batmen are wonderful. Wonder what my luck will be. Did you see the *Bystander* this week? Good it was, oh, *damned* good!" Then he began to be patriotic again. Swinging up and down the room he talked glowingly of what the Major had told him—counter-attacks, gas-masks, pill boxes. Very lights, the musketry handbook, number nines and British pluck.

While Stanley talked Laura sat by the window, her almost sad profile outlined by the dripping laurel bush beyond. She was listening loyally to Stanley's patriotism. Suddenly Stanley slapped down his tumbler.

" Well, we better get along now. Mustn't miss the old joy waggon." He glanced out of the window. " Better put your mac on, old girl, looks like more rain."

" I don't think I'll mind," Laura answered. She stood up, arresting all Stanley's fussing by the perfect immobility of her manner. " Have you everything in the car? "

" You bet," Stanley said, leading the way to the door.

They got into the car, not the office car, but Stanley's own, an open sports model now two years old, which stood with the hood up in front of the porch. Stanley jabbed at the starter with his thumb, threw in the gear and they drove off.

The road ran uphill through the outskirts of Hillbrow, left the last isolated villa behind and stretched out across open country towards the moor. Stanley drove in a kind of exhilaration, using his cut-out on all the corners.

" Goes like an aeroplane, doesn't she? " he threw out high-spiritedly. " Almost wish I'd joined the Flying Corps."

" Look out you don't skid," Joe said, " the roads are pretty greasy."

Stanley laughed again. Joe, alone in the back seat, kept his eyes on Laura's calm profile in front. Her composure was both baffling and fascinating: Stanley driving like a mug, and she not turning a hair. She didn't want to come to a sticky end yet, did she? He didn't, at any rate not yet, by God, no!

They flashed past the old St. Bede's Church, which stood grey and gauntly weatherbeaten, surrounded by a few flat, lichened tombstones, isolated and open on the edge of the moor.

" Wonderful old building," Stanley said, jerking his head. " Ever been in, Joe? "

" No."

" Got some wonderful oak pews. Some time you ought to have a look at them."

They began to slip downhill, through Cadder village and a few outlying farms. Twenty minutes later they reached Carnton Junction. The express was late and after seeing to his baggage Stanley began to walk slowly up and down the platform with Laura. Joe, pretending to make affable conversation with the porter, watched them jealously from the corner of his eye. Damn it, he thought, oh, *damn* it all, I believe she's in love with him after all.

A sharp whistle and the thunder of the approaching train.

" Here she is, sir," the porter said. " Only four minutes behind her time."

Stanley came hurrying over.

" Well, Joe, here we are at last. Yes, porter, a first smoker, facing the engine if you can. You'll write to me, old man. I can leave everything to you. Yes, yes, that's all right, splendid, splendid. I know you'll do everything." He shook hands with Joe—Joe's grip was manly and prolonged—kissed Laura good-bye, then jumped into his compartment. Stanley was to the core a sentimentalist and now that the moment of departure had come he was deeply affected. He hung out of the window, feeling himself every inch a man going to the front, facing his wife and his friend. Quick tears glistened in his eyes but he smiled them away.

" Take care of Laura, Joe."

" You bet, Mr. Stanley."

" Don't forget to write."

" No fear! "

There came a pause; the train did not move. The pause lengthened awkwardly.

" It looks like more rain," Stanley said, filling in the gap. Another hollow pause. The train started forward. Stanley shouted:

" Well, we're off! Good-bye, Laura. Good-bye, old man."

The train shuddered and stopped. Stanley frowned, looking up the line.

" Must be taking in water. We'll be a few minutes yet."

Immediately the train started again, pulled away smoothly and began to gather speed.

" Well! Good-bye, good-bye."

This time Stanley was away. Joe and Laura stood on the platform until the last carriage was out of sight, Joe waving heartily, Laura not waving at all. She was paler than usual and there was a suspicious moisture in her eyes. Joe saw this. They turned to the car in silence.

When they came out from cover of the station and reached the car it was raining again. Laura went towards the back seat but, with an air of solicitude, Joe put out his hand:

" You'll get all the rain in there, Mrs. Millington. It's coming on heavy."

She hesitated, then without speaking she got into the front seat. He nodded, as though she had done a most reasonable and sensible thing, then climbed in and took the wheel.

He drove slowly, partly because of the rain blurring the windscreen, but chiefly because he wanted to prolong the journey. Though his attitude was respectful, openly deferential, he was bursting with the knowledge of his position: Stanley tearing off to God knows where, every minute getting farther and farther away, Laura in the car with him, here, now. Cautiously, he glanced at her. She sat at the extreme end of the seat, staring straight in front of her; he could feel that every fibre of her was resentful, defensively alert. He thought how careful he must be, no gentle pressure of his knee against hers, a different technique, weeks perhaps or months of strategy, he must be slow, cautious as hell. He had the queer feeling that she almost hated him.

Suddenly he said, in a voice of mild regret:

" I don't think you like me much, Mrs. Millington."

Silence; he kept his eyes on the road.

" I haven't thought about it a great deal," she answered rather scornfully.

" Oh, I know." A deprecating laugh. " I didn't mean anything. I only thought, you'd helped me at the start a bit, at the works you know, and lately you'd . . . oh, I don't know . . ."

" Would you mind driving a little faster," she said. " I've got to be at the canteen by six."

" Why, certainly, Mrs. Millington." He pressed his foot down on the accelerator, increasing the car's speed, causing the rain to shoot round the windscreen. " I was only hoping you'd let me do anything for you I can. Mr. Stanley's gone. A great chap Stanley." He sighed. " He's certainly given me my chance. I'd do anything for him, anything."

As he spoke the rain began to fall in torrents. They were on the open moor now, and the wind was high. The car, sheltered only by its thin hood, quite unprotected by side screens, caught the full force of the driving rain.

" I say," Joe cried, " you're getting drenched."

Laura turned up the collar of her costume.

" I'm all right."

" But you're not. Look, you're getting soaked, absolutely soaked. We'll stop a minute. We must take shelter. It's a perfect cloudburst."

It actually was a deluge and Laura, without her mackintosh, began to get extremely wet. It was obvious that in a few minutes she must be drenched to her skin. Still, she did not speak. Joe, however, sighting the old church upon their left, suddenly swerved the car towards it and drew up with a jerk.

" Quick," he urged. " In here. This is awful, simply awful." He took her arm, impelling her from the car by the very unexpectedness of his action, running with her up the short path into the dripping portico of the old church. The door was open. " In here," Joe cried. " If you don't you'll catch your death of cold. This is awful, awful." They went in.

It was a small place, warm after the biting wind and rather dark, impregnated with a faint scent of candle grease and incense. The altar was dimly visible and upon it a large brass crucifix and, remaining from the previous Sunday's service, two globular brass vases holding white flowers. The atmosphere was quiet and still, belonging to another world, different. The drumming of the rain upon the leaded roof intensified the warm silence.

Gazing about him curiously, Joe walked up the aisle, subconsciously noting the heavy carved pews to which Stanley had referred.

" Damn funny old place, but it's dry anyway." Then, his voice solicitous, " We won't have to wait long till it goes off. I'll get you back in time for the canteen."

He turned and saw, suddenly, that she was shivering, standing against one of the benches with her hands pressed together.

" Oh dear," he said in that beautiful tone of self-reproach. " I've let you in for it. Your jacket's soaking. Let me help you off with it."

" No," she said, " I'm all right." She kept her eyes averted, biting her lip fiercely. He sensed vaguely some struggle within her, deep, unknown.

" But you must, Mrs. Millington," he said with that same regretful, reassuring kindness, and he put his hand on the lapel of her jacket.

" No, no," she stammered. " I'm all right, I tell you. I don't like it here. We ought never to have come. The rain . . ." She broke off, struggled quickly out of the jacket herself. She was breathing quickly, he saw the rise and fall of her breasts under the white silk blouse which, dampened in places, adhered to her skin. Her composure seemed gone, torn from her by the dim secrecy of the place, the drumming rain, the silence. Her eyes fluttered about in frightened glances. He stared at her dumbly, uncomprehendingly. She shivered again. Then all at once he understood. A suffocating heat flushed over him. He took a step forward.

" Laura," he gasped. " Laura."

" No, no," she panted. " I want to go, I want . . ." As she spoke his arms went round her. They clasped each other wildly, their lips seeking each other's. She gave a moan. Even before her mouth opened to his he knew that she was mad about him, had been fighting it all these months. A wild intoxication mounted in him. Linked together they moved to the foremost pew, cushioned and wide as any bed. Their hands moved together, her lips were moist with desire. The rain drummed upon the roof and the darkness of the church reddened and enclosed them. When it came, her cry of physical exaltation rose before the altar. The figure on the cross looked down on them.

XI

When the Derby Scheme came into force the situation between Arthur and his father had become intolerable, it was a state of unconcealed hostility. Arthur's name was on the National Register, yet although he received his papers under the new Scheme he did not attest. His failure to attest produced no immediate comment. At the Law, by coming in late for all his meals, he avoided Barras as far as he was able, while at the Neptune he spent most of his time underground, arriving early and getting inbye with Hudspeth before Barras reached the pit. But in spite of his precautions it was impossible to escape the inevitable encounters, full of animosity and strain and conflict. When he entered the office, dirty and tired at the end of the day, Barras pretended to ignore him in great flurry of business, conveying to Arthur the unmistakable sense of how little he was needed at the pit. And then, lifting his head from a mass of papers, Barras would appear suddenly to discover Arthur and frown as though to say: " Oh, you're there, *still* there ? " And when Arthur turned away in silence Barras would follow him with his eyes, fuming, drumming his fingers rapidly upon the desk, wearing that flushed look of injury and high displeasure.

Arthur saw that his father hated having him about the pit. Towards the beginning of January he was forced to complain about the quality of the new timber props in Five Quarter Seam. Barras flared instantly.

" Mind your own business, and leave me to mind mine. When I want your advice I'll ask for it."

Arthur made no reply. He knew that the props were inferior, some of them quite perished at the base. He was appalled at the quality of the material his father was using. With mounting prices and feverish production money flowed into the Neptune. Yet, despite the lesson of the disaster, nothing was being spent to ensure better and safer conditions in the pit.

That same evening the Tynecastle *Argus* announced in double headlines that the Military Service Act had become law.

When he read the news Barras could not conceal his satisfaction.

" That'll shake the shirkers up a bit," he announced from the head of the table. " It's high time we had a comb out. There are too many of them tucked away in their funk holes." He gave a short triumphant laugh. " This'll give them something to think about."

It was supper, one of the rare occasions when Arthur was present; and although Barras addressed his remarks to Aunt Carrie the sting in them was for Arthur.

" It's quite scandalous, Caroline," he went on loudly, " the number of able-bodied young men who ought to be fighting for their country. They've got out of it so far by digging themselves into jobs where they're not wanted. They've refused to take the hint, don't you see, to join the army. Well, upon my soul, it's high time they were kicked into it."

"Yes, Richard," Aunt Carrie murmured, with a trembling glance towards Arthur, who kept his eyes fixed upon his plate.

"I knew it was coming of course," Barras continued in the same tone. "And I've no doubt I shall have a hand in the working of it. Between ourselves I've been approached to sit on the local Tribunal."

"The Tribunal, Richard?" Aunt Carrie faltered.

"Yes, indeed," Richard declared, studiously avoiding Arthur's eye. "And I shan't stand any nonsense, I assure you. This is serious at last and the sooner everyone realises it the better. I was discussing it with Hetty only the other day. She feels pretty strongly that it's high time the slackers were wakened up. And weeded out."

Arthur raised his eyes slowly and looked at his father. Barras was dressed in a new grey suit and he wore a flower in his buttonhole. Lately he had ordered himself a number of new suits, much smarter than his usual style—Arthur suspected him of having changed his tailor in Tynecastle—and he had taken to wearing a buttonhole regularly, a pink carnation usually, picked from the new plants in the conservatory. His appearance was exaggeratedly spruce, his eye bright, he had an intent, oddly excited air.

"You wait and see, Caroline," he laughed, with immense satisfaction, "what a rush to the colours when the tribunals get busy!"

There was a silence while Aunt Carrie, in an access of distress, fluttered her glance from one to the other. Then Barras looked at his watch: the usual gesture. "Well," he remarked in a conscious tone, "I must get along now, Caroline. Don't let anyone trouble to stay up for me. I shall be late I expect. I'm taking Hetty to the King's. Must carry on in spite of the war. It's 'The Maid of the Mountains,' very good I'm told, the full London Company. Hetty is tremendously keen to see it." He rose, fingering the flower in his buttonhole. Then, ignoring Arthur, but with a brisk nod to Caroline, he strode out of the room.

Arthur remained seated at the table, perfectly still and silent. He was well aware that Hetty and his father went about together a great deal: the new suits, the buttonhole, the spurious veneer of youth were all indicative of that fact. It had begun in an attitude of reparation—Arthur had treated Hetty shamefully, and the obligation of "making it up to Hetty" had devolved upon Barras. Yet Arthur suspected that the relationship had progressed beyond the bounds of mere amendment. He did not know. He sighed heavily at his own thoughts. That sigh made Aunt Carrie stir uneasily.

"You've eaten scarcely anything to-night, Arthur," she murmured. "Why don't you have some of this trifle?"

"I'm not hungry, Aunt Carrie."

"But it's so good, my dear," she remonstrated in her troubled voice.

He shook his head silently, seeing her through his pain. He had a sudden impulse to unburden himself to her, to pour out the whole affliction that lay upon his mind. But he restrained himself, he saw clearly that it would be purposeless. Aunt Carrie was kind, she loved him in her own way, yet her timidity, her awe of his father, rendered her incapable of helping him.

He got up from the table and went out of the dining-room. In the hall he stood with head bent, undecided. At a moment such as this his gentle nature thirsted for sympathy. If only Hetty had been here . . . a lump came into his throat . . . he felt lost and helpless. Turning, he went slowly upstairs. And then, as he passed his mother's room, he stopped suddenly. With a spontaneous gesture he put his hand upon the door knob and entered the room.

" How are you to-night, mother ? " he asked.

She looked round sharply, propped up on her pillows, her pale fat face both querulous and questioning.

" I have a headache," she answered. " And you gave me such a start opening the door so sharp."

" I'm sorry, mother." He sat down quietly on the edge of the bed.

" Oh *no*, Arthur," she protested. " Not there, my dear, I can't bear anyone sitting on my bed, not with this headache, it worries me so."

He stood up again, flushing slightly.

" I'm sorry, mother," he said once more. He made himself see her point of view, refusing to let himself be hurt. She was his mother. Out of subliminal depths a memory of early tenderness affected him, a vague sensation of her bending over him, her lace gown open and drooping upon him, enclosing and protecting him. Now he yielded to that childish recollection and, craving her loving kindness, he exclaimed in a broken voice:

" Mother, will you let me talk something over with you ? "

She considered him querulously.

" I have such a headache."

" It won't take long. Oh, I do want your advice."

" No, no, Arthur," she protested, closing her eyes as though his eagerness startled her. " Really, I can't. Some other time perhaps. My head does ache so frightfully."

He drew back, silenced, his whole expression altered by the rebuff.

" What is it, do you think, Arthur," she went on with closed eyes, " that keeps on giving me these headaches ? I've been wondering if it's the gun-fire in France, the vibrations, you know, travelling through the air. Of course I can't hear the firing, that I do fully understand, but it has occurred to me that the vibrations might set up something. Naturally that wouldn't explain my backache and that has been quite bad lately, too. Tell me, Arthur, do you think the gun-fire has any influence ? "

" I don't know, mother," he answered heavily and paused, collecting himself. " I should hardly think it could affect your back."

" Mind you, I'm not complaining too much about my back. The liniment Dr. Lewis has given me helps it tremendously. Aconite, belladonna and chloroform. I read the prescription, three deadly poisons. Isn't it strange that poison should be so beneficial externally? But what was I saying? Oh yes, the vibrations. I was reading in the paper only the other day that they were responsible for the heavy rain we've been having lately. That seems to prove my point. It shows that they are, well, about. And Dr. Lewis tells me there is a distinct condition known as gun headache. Of course the root cause of the whole thing is nerve exhaustion. That's always been my trouble, Arthur dear, sheer nerve exhaustion."

" Yes, mother," he agreed in a low voice.

There was another slight pause, then she began to talk again. For half an hour she talked of her own condition, then raising her hand suddenly to her head she begged him to leave the room as he was tiring her. He obeyed in silence. Fifteen minutes later as he came back along the corridor he heard the loud sound of her snoring.

The sense of being isolated in his own trouble grew upon Arthur as the days passed, the sense of being cut off from the other people, almost of being outcast. Instinctively he began to curtail the sphere of his activities. He went out only to his work, and even there he caught strange glances directed towards him—from Armstrong and Hudspeth, from certain of the men. In the streets on his way to and from the Neptune abuse was frequently shouted after him. His differences with his father were common knowledge and were attributed to his refusal to join up. Barras had not hesitated to define his views openly; his firm and patriotic attitude was applauded on all sides; he was considered to be doing a fine thing in refusing to allow his natural feeling to interfere with his sense of what was due in this great national emergency. It paralysed Arthur to realise that the whole town was watching the conflict between his father and himself.

During February things steadily got worse, then in the middle of March the Sleescale Tribunal came into action. The Tribunal was made up of five members, James Ramage, Bates the draper, old Murchison, the Rev. Enoch Low of New Bethel Street Chapel and Richard Barras, who, by a unanimous vote, was elected Chairman. Besides these five there was the Military Representative, Captain Douglas from Tynecastle Barracks, a standing Counsel on behalf of the Army authorities. Rutter, the clerk to the Sleescale Town Council, acted as clerk to the Tribunal.

With a strained and painful interest Arthur watched the early activities of the Tribunal. He was not long in doubt of its severity; case after case was refused exemption. Douglas was a hardened autocrat, he had a way of browbeating applicants, then looking up and declaring summarily: " I want that man "; Ramage and his father were both swollen with unbridled patriotism; the others were of little account.

The line taken was extreme. The Tribunal argued that since the applicant had to prove an objection to combatant service it was only from combatant service they could exempt him. Combatant service became the vital issue; and the alternative to service was prison.

As the days passed Arthur's indignation rose passionately against the arbitrary methods of the Tribunal. With a pale suppressed face he observed his father return from the administration of justice. Barras's mood was invariably elated, and for Arthur's benefit he often described to Caroline the choicer incidents of the session. On the last day of March Barras came home in exactly this fashion, late for tea, but in an even greater flow of spirits than usual. Ostentatiously disregarding Arthur he sat down and helped himself largely to hot buttered toast. Then he led off with the case which had most engaged him that afternoon: a young divinity student claiming exemption on religious grounds.

" Do you know what Ramage's first question was ? " he remarked with his mouth full of soft toast. " He asked him if he ever took a bath." He paused in his mastication to laugh triumphantly. " But Douglas went one better than that. Douglas gave me a side look, then he barked at him: ' Do you know that a man who refuses military duty is liable to be shot ? ' That got him all right. You should have seen him crumple up. He agreed to join up. He'll be in France in three months." He laughed again.

Arthur could stand it no longer. He jumped up from the table, pale to the lips.

" You think it's amusing, don't you ? You like to feel you've shoved a gun into his hands against his will. You're glad you've forced him to go out and shoot, kill, murder somebody in France. Kill or be killed. What a lovely motto. You ought to have it made into a banner and hung above your seat at the Tribunal. It suits you. I tell you it suits you. But I've got some respect for human life if you haven't. You won't frighten me into killing. You won't, you won't." Panting, Arthur broke off. With a hopeless gesture he swung round and made for the door, but as he did so Barras stopped him.

" Wait a minute," he said. " You and I have got to have a talk."

Arthur turned; he heard Aunt Carrie catch her breath.

There was a pause.

" Very well," Arthur said in a suppressed voice. He came back and sat down again.

Barras helped himself to more toast and ate steadily with his eyes in front of him. Aunt Carrie had turned a sickly grey. She endured the silence for a few moments in a palpitating agony; then she could bear it no longer. She excused herself in a trembling voice, rose hurriedly and went out of the room.

Barras finished his tea, wiped his mouth with a restless movement, then fixed Arthur with that full, injected eye.

" It's just this," he said in a contained tone. " For the last time, are you going to join the army ? "

Arthur returned his father's look; his face was very pale but quite determined. He answered:

" No."

A pause.

" I'd like to make it quite clear that I don't need you at the Neptune."

" Very well."

" Doesn't that help you to change your mind ? "

" No."

Renewed pause.

" In that case," Barras said, " you might as well know that your case will come up before the Tribunal on Tuesday of next week."

A sickening sense of apprehension rushed over Arthur. His eyes fell. In his secret heart he had not expected his father to go as far as this. Though he had no official position at the Neptune he had imagined himself outside the scope of the present Act.

" It's about time you realised that being my son isn't going to protect you," Barras went on heavily. " You're a young, fit man. You have no excuse. My views are well known. I'm not going to have you hide behind my back any longer."

" You imagine you can force me into the army that way," Arthur said in a shaking voice.

" I do. And it's the best thing that could happen to you."

" You're quite mistaken." Arthur felt himself trembling violently inside. " You think I'm afraid to go before the Tribunal ? "

Barras gave his short laugh.

" Exactly! "

" Then you're wrong. I'll go. I'll go."

The blood rose to Barras's brow.

" In that case you'll be dealt with like any ordinary shirker. I've talked it over with Captain Douglas. There'll be no preferential treatment. My mind is made up. You'll have to go to the army just the same."

There was a silence.

" What are you trying to do to me ? " Arthur asked in a low tone.

" I'm trying to make you do your duty." Barras rose abruptly. He stood for a moment by the sideboard, erect, with his chest thrown out. " Get into Tynecastle to-morrow and join up. For your own sake. Join up before you're made to. That's my last word." And he walked out of the room.

Arthur remained seated at the table. He still felt himself trembling and he leaned his elbow upon the table, supporting his head upon his hand.

Aunt Carrie, stealing back into the room ten minutes later, found him in this attitude. She came forward and slipped her arm round his bowed shoulders.

"Oh, Arthur," she whispered, "it'll never do to go against your father. You must be reasonable. Oh, for your own sake you must."

He did not answer but continued to stare palely in front of him.

"You see, Arthur dear," Aunt Carrie went on appealingly, "there's some things you can't stand out against. No one understands that better than me. You've just got to give in whether you like it or not. I'm so fond of you, Arthur. I can't see you ruin your whole life. You must do what your father wants, Arthur."

"I won't," he said, as though to himself.

"Oh no, Arthur," she pleaded, "don't go on like that. Please, please. I'm afraid something awful will happen. And think of the disgrace, the terrible disgrace. Oh, promise me you'll do what your father wants."

"No," he whispered, "I must go through with it in my own way." Rising, he gave her the pitiful semblance of a smile and went up to his own room.

Next morning he received his summons to appear before the Tribunal. Barras, who was present when the post came in, observed him with a sidelong scrutiny as he opened the thin buff envelope. But if he expected Arthur to speak he was disappointed. Arthur put the letter in his pocket and walked out of the room. He was aware that his father had calculated upon his submission. And he was equally determined that he would not submit. His nature was not strong but now a form of exaltation gave him strength.

The intervening days went by and the morning of Tuesday arrived. The time of Arthur's summons was ten o'clock and the place Old Bethel Street School. The Tribunal had been set up in the hall of the old school where there was ample accommodation for the court and a gallery at the back to accommodate the public. At the top of the hall was a raised platform with a table at which the five members sat. Rutter the clerk occupied one end of the table and Captain Douglas, Military Representative, the other. A large Union Jack hung upon the wall behind, and beneath it was a disused blackboard, a few left-over chalks, and a ledge bearing a chipped water-bottle covered by a tumbler.

Arthur reached Old Bethel Street School at exactly five minutes to ten. Roddam, the sergeant on duty, informed him that his case was first on the list, and with a brusque sign led him through the swing door into the court.

As Arthur entered the court an excited hum went up. He lifted his head and saw that the gallery was packed with people; he made out men from the pit, Harry Ogle, Joe Kinch, Jake Wicks the new checkweigher, and a score of others. There were a great many women, too, women from the Terraces and the town, Hannah Brace, Mrs. Reedy, old

Susan Calder, Mrs. Wept. The reporters' bench was full. Two cameramen stood together against a window. Arthur dropped his eyes quickly, painfully aware of the sensation his case was creating. His nervousness, already extreme, became intensified. He sat down in the chair assigned to him in the middle of the hall and began in an agitated manner to fumble with his handkerchief. His sensitive nature shrank at all times from the glare of publicity. And now he was in the centre of the glare. He shivered slightly. It was the intensity of his weakness which had brought him here, which held him fast in the determination to go on. But he had no hardihood. He was acutely aware of his position, of the mass hostility of the crowd, and he suffered abominably. He felt like a common criminal.

Here, another buzz of sound broke out in the gallery and was immediately subdued. The members of the Tribunal filed in from a side door accompanied by Rutter and Captain Douglas, a stocky figure with a reddish, pock-marked face. Roddam, from behind Arthur, said "Stand!" and Arthur stood. Then he raised his head and his eyes, as though magnetised, fell upon his father now in the act of seating himself in the high official chair. Arthur stared at his father as at a judge. He could not withdraw his eyes, he existed in a web of unreality, a hypnotised suspense.

Barras leaned across the table to Captain Douglas. They had a lengthy conference, then Douglas nodded his head with an approving look, squared his shoulders and rapped sharply with his knuckles on the table.

The last whispers of conversation in the gallery and body of the hall died out and a tense silence succeeded. Douglas let his gun-metal eyes travel slowly round, embracing the audience, the press reporters and Arthur in one firm and comprehensive glance, then he faced his colleagues at the table. He spoke loudly so that everyone could hear.

" This is a particularly painful case," he said, " in so far as it concerns the son of our esteemed chairman who has already done such yeoman service on this Tribunal here. The facts are clear. This young man, Arthur Barras, holds a redundant position at the Neptune pit and is eligible for combatant service. I need not repeat what you already know. But before we open the case I must affirm my personal admiration for Mr. Barras senior, who with wholehearted courage and patriotism has not shirked his duty in the face of his own natural feelings. I think I am right in saying that we all respect and honour him for what he has done." Here a burst of applause broke out in the court. No effort was made to restrain it and when it had ended Douglas continued: "Speaking in my capacity as representative of the military authorities I should like to advance the statement that we on our side are prepared to come halfway over this unhappy and distressing case. The applicant has only to accept his liability for combatant service and he will receive every consideration in the matter of regimental draft and training."

He looked across the court at Arthur with his hard inquiring stare. Arthur moistened his dry lips. He saw that an answer was expected of him. Gathering himself, he said:

" I refuse combatant service."

" But come now, you can't be serious ? "

" I am serious."

There was an imperceptible pause, a further heightening of the tension. Douglas exchanged a quick glance with Barras as though expressing his inability to do more and James Ramage, thrusting his head forward pugnaciously, demanded:

" Why do you refuse to fight ? " The examination had begun.

Arthur turned his eyes upon the thick-necked butcher whose low brow and small deep-set eyes seemed to commingle the attributes of bull and pig. He answered in an almost inaudible voice:

" I don't want to kill anyone."

" Speak up," shouted Ramage. " You couldn't hear that below a bowl."

Huskily, Arthur repeated: " I don't want to kill anyone."

" But why ? " Ramage persisted. He had killed a great many live things in his time. He could not understand this puzzling mentality.

" It's against my conscience."

A pause. Then Ramage said coarsely:

" Ah, too much conscience is bad for anybody."

The Rev. Enoch Low hurriedly interposed. He was a tall thin cadaverous man with pinched nostrils and a poor stipend. James Ramage, the main adherent of his church, paid half that stipend and the Rev. Low could always be depended on to support Ramage and cover up his little pleasantries.

" Come now," he addressed Arthur. " You're a Christian, aren't you ? There's nothing in the Christian religion which prevents lawful killing in the service of your country."

" There's no such thing as lawful killing."

The Rev. Low cocked his bony head.

" What do you mean ? "

Arthur answered rapidly:

" I haven't got any religion very much, not religion in your sense. But you talk about Christianity, the religion of Christ. Well, I can't imagine Jesus Christ taking a bayonet in His hands and sticking it into the stomach of a German soldier or an English soldier either for that matter. I can't imagine Jesus Christ sitting behind an English machine gun or a German machine gun mowing down dozens of perfectly guiltless men."

The Rev. Low coloured with horror. He looked unutterably shocked.

" That's blasphemy," he muttered, turning to Ramage.

But Murchison would not allow the argument to lapse. The snuffy little grocer wanted to show his knowledge of Holy Writ. Bending forward, rather slyly, as though weighing a bare half pound of ham:

" Don't you know that Jesus Christ said an eye for an eye and a tooth for a tooth ? "

The Rev. Low looked more uncomfortable still.

" No," cried Arthur, " He never said that."

" He did, I tell you," Murchison bellowed, " it's in the Book." He lay back, victorious, in his chair.

Bates the draper now interposed. He had one stock question, a question he never failed to put, and now he felt the time was ripe for it. Caressing his long drooping moustache he asked:

" If a German attacked your mother what would you do ? "

Arthur made a hopeless gesture; he did not answer.

With another tug at his moustache Bates repeated:

" If a German attacked your mother what would you do ? "

Arthur bit his trembling underlip.

" How can I explain what's in my mind by answering a question like that! Perhaps they're asking it in Germany, too. Don't you see ? About our soldiers."

" Would you rather kill the German or let the German kill your mother ? " Bates persisted ponderously.

Arthur gave it up. He did not answer and Bates, with an air of childish triumph, looked round at his colleagues.

There was a silence. Everyone at the table now seemed to wait on Barras. And Barras seemed to wait upon himself. He cleared his throat abruptly. His eye was bright and there was a slight flush on his high cheek-bones. He stared fixedly over the top of Arthur's head.

" Do you refuse to admit the necessity of this great national emergency, this tremendous world conflict which demands sacrifices from us all ? "

As his father spoke Arthur felt himself trembling again and a sense of his own weakness bound him pitifully. He longed for calmness and courage, for the power to express himself with resolution and eloquence. But instead his lips quivered, he could only stammer:

" I can't admit the necessity for herding men together to slaughter one another nor the necessity for starving women and children all over Europe. Especially when no one really knows what it is all for."

Barras's flush deepened:

" This war is being fought to end war."

" That's what has always been said," Arthur exclaimed with a rising inflexion in his voice. " It'll be said in the same way to make people kill one another when the next war comes along."

Ramage moved restlessly. He picked up the pen in front of him and began to stab it into the table. He was used to a more forceful method in the Tribunal and this digression exasperated him.

" Stop the shilly-shally," he threw out an irritable aside, " and let's get on with the job."

Barras, who in the past had always affected to despise Ramage, gave no sign of resenting the interruption. His expression remained statuesque. He began to drum with his fingers on the table.

" What is your real reason for refusing to join the army ? "

" I've told you," Arthur answered with a quick intake of his breath.

" Good God ! " Ramage interjected again. " What is he talking about ? What's he talking round corners for ? Let him speak plain or keep his mouth shut."

" Explain yourself," the Rev. Low said to Arthur with a sort of patronising pity.

" I can't say any more than I have said," Arthur replied in a suppressed voice. " I object to the unjust and unnecessary sacrifice of human life. I'll be no party to it either in the war or out of it." As he said these last words, Arthur kept his eyes fixed upon his father's face.

" Good God," Ramage groaned again. " What a bloody awful state of mind to be in."

But here an interruption occurred. In the gallery a woman stood up, small, very matter of fact and composed. It was Mrs. Wept, and in a clear voice she called out: " He's quite right and all the lot of you are wrong. Thou shalt not kill. Remember that and the war'll end tomorrow."

Immediately there was an uproar, a storm of protest. Several voices shouted:

" Shame! "

" Shut up! "

" Put her out! "

Mrs. Wept was surrounded, pushed towards the door and bundled violently from the court.

When order was restored, Captain Douglas rapped loudly on the table.

" Another interruption like that and I'll order the court to be cleared."

He turned to his colleagues. A moment arose in every case when it became necessary to concentrate the digressive forces of the committee and bring the situation rapidly to a head. And here matters had clearly gone too far. Douglas had listened to Arthur with ill-concealed contempt. He was a dominating type, severe and illiterate, promoted after years of non-commissioned service, with a hard face, a tough hide and the proved mentality of the barrack square. He addressed Arthur curtly.

" Let's take this another way if you don't mind. You say you object to serve. But have you considered the alternative ? "

Arthur went very pale, conscious of the dark current of animosity flowing from Douglas to himself.

" That won't alter my attitude."

" Quite so! But for all that you don't want to be locked up for two or three years."

Dead silence in court. Arthur felt the fascinated attention of the crowd upon him. He thought, I am not really here, in this horrible position. He said at last in a laboured voice:

" I don't want to be locked up any more than most soldiers want to go to the trenches." Douglas's eye hardened. In a louder voice he declared:

" They go because they think it is their duty."

" I may think it my duty to go to prison."

A faint sigh went up from the crowd in the gallery. Douglas glanced upwards angrily; then he slewed round towards Barras. He shrugged his shoulders and at the same time flung his papers on the desk with a final gesture as if to say: " I'm sorry, but this is hopeless."

Barras sat up very stiff and rigid in his chair. He passed his hand carefully across his brow. He appeared to listen to the low discussion which now went on amongst his colleagues round about him. Then he said formally:

" I see you are all of the same opinion as myself." And he held up his hand for silence.

A minute's interval occurred, then, in that same dead silence, still staring over Arthur's head, Barras pronounced the verdict.

" The Tribunal have carefully considered your case," he declared, using the precise, the habitual formula. " And they find that they cannot grant you any exemption."

There was an immediate outburst of applause, loud prolonged cheers, which Rutter, the clerk, did not order to be suppressed. From the gallery a woman called out:

" Well done, Mr. Barras. Well done, sir." Captain Douglas leaned across the table and offered his hand. The other members of the Tribunal did likewise. Barras shook hands with them all, his air impressive yet vaguely remote, his glance directed towards the gallery from where the applause and the woman's voice had come.

Arthur remained standing in the centre of the court, his features drawn and colourless, his head drooping. He seemed waiting for something to happen. He had an agonised sense of anti-climax. He raised his head as though endeavouring to catch his father's eye. A shiver went over him. Then he turned and walked out of the court.

That evening it was late when Barras returned. In the hall he encountered Arthur. He paused and in that curious manner, half mortified and half bewildered, he suddenly said:

" You can appeal if you wish. You know you can appeal."

Arthur looked steadily at his father. He felt himself calm now.

" You've driven me into this," Arthur said. " I shan't appeal. I shall go through with it."

There was a pause.

" Very well," Barras said, almost plaintively. " It's on your own head." He turned and went into the dining-room.

As Arthur went upstairs he was dimly conscious of the sound of Aunt Carrie weeping.

That night there was great excitement in the town. Barras's action had caused a tremendous sensation. Patriotism rose to fever heat and a crowd of people marched down Freehold Street, waving flags and singing *Tipperary*. They broke the windows of Mrs. Wept's house, then marched on Hans Messuer's shop. For some time now old Hans had been suspect as an alien and in this access of patriotic zeal the suspicion was confirmed. His shop was wrecked, plate-glass window smashed, bottles broken, curtains slit, the red and blue striped pole—pride of old Messuer's heart—snapped into bits. Hans, risen from his bed in a panic, was assaulted, and left senseless on the floor.

Two days later Arthur was arrested and taken to Tynecastle Barracks. It happened with perfect quietness and order. He was in the machine now, everything moved smoothly and independent of his own volition. At the Barracks he refused to accept uniform. He was immediately court-martialled, sentenced to two years' hard labour and ordered to be removed to Benton Prison.

As he came out of this second court he wondered how it had all happened. And he had a queer memory of his father's face: flushed, confused, vaguely bewildered.

XII

THE Black Maria stopped with a jerk outside Benton Prison and there was the sound of bolts being withdrawn. Arthur sat up in his dark little stall, still trying dazedly to realise that he was here, inside this prison van.

The van jerked forward again and jerked to a stop. Then the door of the van was unlocked and thrown open, letting in a sudden rush of cool night air. From beyond the door a warder's voice cried:

" Out."

Arthur and four others rose from their narrow partitioned stalls and got out. It had been a long cramped journey from Tynecastle to Benton but now they were at the end of that journey and in the courtyard of the prison. The night was heavy and overcast and it was raining heavily, puddles of water lay in the depressions of the asphalt. Arthur looked about him hurriedly: high grey walls with a sharp castellated coping, row upon row of iron-barred clefts, warders in glistening oilskins, silence and a shapeless darkness relieved only by a weak blur of yellow from the light above the archway. The five prisoners stood in the streaming rain, then one of the warders shouted a command and they were marched through another door into a small whitewashed room, the brightness of which was dazzling to the eyes after that outer darkness. An officer sat at a table in this bare bright room with a number of papers and a register in front of him. He was an elderly man with a bald, shiny head.

The warder of the prison van went up to the officer and spoke to him. While they talked Arthur looked at the four prisoners who had accompanied him in the van. The first two were small scrubby men with black ties and long quakerish faces so oddly alike it was obvious that they were brothers. The third man had a weak despondent chin and gold-rimmed pince-nez, he looked like a down-at-heel clerk and, in common with the two brothers, seemed harmless and ill at ease. The fourth man was big and unshaven and dirty, he was the only one who did not appear surprised or distressed to find himself here.

The officer at the table stopped speaking to the warder of the van. He picked up his pen and called out:

" Line up there, will you ? " He was the reception clerk of the prison. He began perfunctorily to read out the particulars of each man's sentence and to enter it in the register with the name and occupation and religion and the amount of money each had come in with.

The dirty man was first and he had no money at all, not one red farthing. He was convicted of assault with violence, had no occupation and was due to serve three years' hard labour. His name was Hicks. Arthur's turn came next. Arthur had four pounds six shillings and tenpence halfpenny exactly. When the officer finished counting Arthur's money he said sarcastically, addressing the neat pile of silver upon the notes:

" This Cuthbert is well-off."

The two brothers and the down-at-heel clerk followed. They were all three of them conscientious objectors and the officer made a peevish remark under his breath, deploring the necessity for dealing with such swine.

When he had finished the entries he rose and unlocked an inner door. He jerked a silent command with his thumb and they filed into a long room with small cells on either side. The officer said:

" Strip."

They stripped. The quaker brothers were upset at being obliged to undress before the others. They shed their clothes slowly and timidly and before arriving actually at the buff they stood for a moment in their drawers shivering self-consciously. Hicks must have thought them funny. Stripped stark naked Hicks revealed an enormous unclean hairy body covered in parts with reddish pustules. Standing with his legs planted well apart he grinned and made a ribald gesture towards the quakers.

" Come on, girls," he said. " We's all goin' shrimpin'."

" Shut up, you," the officer said.

" Yes, sir." said Hicks obsequiously. He walked over and stepped on to the scales.

They were all weighed and measured. When that was over Hicks, who clearly knew the ropes, led the way across the concrete floor to the bath. The bath was half full of dirty tepid water with a slight scum on the surface and the bath itself was dirty.

Arthur looked at Hicks who was already splashing his pustular body in the dirty bath. He turned to the officer and asked in a low voice:

" Do I have to go into the bath ? "

The officer was gifted with a sense of humour. He said:

" Yes, dear." Then he added: "No talking." Arthur got into the bath.

After the dirty bath they were given their prison clothes. Arthur received a yellow flannel vest and pants, a pair of socks, and a very small khaki uniform stamped all over with black broad arrows. The trousers barely reached below his knees. As his eyes rested on the tight short tunic he thought dully, khaki at last.

An inner door opened and the doctor came in. The doctor was a round, reddish-faced man with a number of small gold fillings in his front teeth. He entered briskly with his stethoscope already dangling from his ears and he used it rapidly. He took one swift blank look at each man, stood away from him, perfectly machine-like and impersonal. He ordered Arthur to say ninety-nine, gave him a few swift taps, and asked him if he had ever had venereal disease. Then he passed on. Arthur did not blame the doctor for being quick. He thought, if I were the doctor here I should probably be quick too. Arthur forced himself to be fair. He had sworn to himself to be calm. It was the only way, a quiet acceptance of the inevitable. He had thought it out carefully on the previous night. He saw that otherwise he might easily go mad.

After the medical examination the bald officer went out with the doctor, leaving them in charge of a new warder who had silently come in and who now silently surveyed them. This warder was short and burly with a squat head and a forbidding way of holding himself. He had a short upper lip, very thin lips, and his broad deformed head seemed always to protrude, as in an attitude of watching. His name was Warder Collins.

When he had finished his silent scrutiny Warder Collins in a leisurely fashion gave them each a number and a cell number. Arthur's number was 115 and his cell number 273. Then Warder Collins unlocked a heavy iron gate. He said:

" Step out now. March lively."

They stepped out, and under the dispassionate eye of Warder Collins they marched in line into the main body of the prison.

The prison was built like a well, an enormous deep resounding well with cells all round, galleries of cells reaching in tiers to a great height. Every gallery was heavily barred so that the front of the combined galleries presented the appearance of an enormous cage. The air was cold and in spite of the smell of disinfectant had a cold earthy prison smell. The smell made Arthur shudder.

Warder Collins showed Arthur to Cell 273. It was in the third gallery. Arthur went into Cell 273. The cell was six feet by thirteen feet and extremely high. The walls were of brick painted a yellowish brown on the lower half and whitewashed on the upper. High up on one wall was a very small heavily barred window which was scarcely a window at all. Very little light came through even on bright sunny days. An armoured electric globe, operated from outside, gave a dim glow to the cell. The floor of the cell was of cement and on the cement floor stood an enamel jug and a utensil. The stench of hundreds of these utensils made the prison smell.

The bed was a board six feet long by two and a half feet broad with a blanket but no mattress. Above the bed was a ledge with an enamel mug, a plate and spoon and a tin knife. A slate and pencil were hung up above the ledge and propped up invitingly under the slate stood a small Bible.

Arthur turned from his inspection to find Warder Collins standing by the door, as if waiting for Arthur's opinion of the cell. His lip was a little drawn back and his head thrust forward. When he saw that Arthur had nothing to say he swung round without a word and padded silently away.

As the door clanged, a heavy door with a small barred peep-hole, Arthur sat down on the edge of the board that was his bed. He was in prison. This was a prison cell and he was in the prison cell. He was not Arthur Barras now. He was number 115.

In spite of his resolution a cold dismay broke over him: it was worse, far worse than he had expected. Outside it was easy to talk glibly of prison when you had no idea what prison was like, but inside it was not so easy. Prison was a horrible place. He gazed round the small, dim shut-in cell. No, it was not going to be so easy after all.

At seven o'clock supper was served. This was an extra supper, a special supper for the newcomers consisting of a bowl of watery porridge. Though it nauseated him, Arthur forced himself to eat the porridge. He ate standing and when he had finished he sat down again on the edge of his bed. He knew it was fatal to think. Yet he had nothing else to do. He could not see to read the Bible and there was nothing in particular he wished to write upon the slate.

He thought, why am I here? He was here because he refused to kill, because he refused to go out and plunge a bayonet into the body of another man in a desolate stretch of mud in France. It was not because he had committed murder that he was here but because he had refused to commit murder.

It was queer, it was quite amusing, but the more he thought of it the less amusing it became. Soon the sweating of his palms, the physical evidence of his neurosis, began. The sweat poured out of his palms until he thought it would never cease.

All at once, as he sat there, a sudden sound, a sort of howling, made him start. It came from the bottom of the prison well, the lowest gallery of all, from the solitary confinement cells, a brute noise, perfectly inhuman and uncontrolled. Arthur jumped up. His nerves quivered in sympathy, like the strings of a violin, to that horrible howling. He listened tensely. The howling rose to an unbearable crescendo. Then it stopped suddenly. It was shut off with an almost violent abruptness. The succeeding silence hummed with conjectures as to how the howling had been stopped.

Arthur began to pace up and down his cell. He paced quickly and gradually increased his pace. He kept waiting for the howling to begin again but it did not. He was almost running up and down the concrete floor of his cell when suddenly a bell clanged and the lights went out.

He stood stock still in the centre of his cell, then slowly he took off his arrow-stamped khaki in the darkness and lay down on the board bed. He could not sleep. He argued with himself that he could not expect to sleep, that he would in time get used to the hardness of his board. But meanwhile a great kaleidoscope of bitter thought whirled and flashed within his brain, like an enormous wheel whirling and swelling until it filled the cell. Faces and scenes whirled within the whirling wheel. His father, Hetty, Ramage, the Tribunal, the Neptune, the dead men in the Neptune, men stretched upon the battlefields with dead protesting eyes, all mingled and whirling, faster, faster, whirling in the bitter wheel. He clung with sweating hands to the edge of his board supporting himself against this chaos, while the night passed.

At half-past five in the morning when it was still dark the prison bell rang. Arthur got up. He washed, dressed, folded his blanket and cleaned up the cell. He had barely finished when the key turned in the lock. The sound of the key turning in the lock of his cell was peculiar, a rasping squeak like two raw metals forced across each other unwillingly. It was a sound which grated into the marrow of the bones. Warder Collins threw some mail bags into the cell. He said:

"Stitch these." Then he slammed the door shut.

Arthur picked up the mail bags, coarse pieces of whitey-brown sacking. He did not know how to stitch them. He laid the bags down again. He sat staring at the shaped canvas bags until seven when the key sounded and his breakfast was handed in. The breakfast consisted of watery porridge and a chunk of brown bread.

After breakfast Warder Collins thrust his squat head round the door. He took a good look at the unsewn mail bags, then he looked at Arthur in a curious fashion. But he made no comment. He merely said, rather softly:

" Step out for exercise."

Exercise took place in the prison yard. The yard was a square of greasy asphalt with enormous high walls and a raised platform at one end. On the platform a warder stood watching the circle of men as they shuffled round. He watched the men's lips to see that they did not talk. From time to time he shouted: " No talking "; the old lags were such experts they could talk to one another without moving their lips.

In the middle of the yard was a lavatory, a circular band of metal supported on low pillars. As the men circled the yard they held up their hands to the warder asking permission to go to the lavatory. When they went to the lavatory their heads were seen above the metal band and their legs below. It was considered a great treat to be allowed to sit a long time in the lavatory, a privilege which the warder allowed only to his favourites.

Arthur shuffled round with the others. In the pale light of the early morning the circle of shuffling men was incomprehensible to reason, it became grotesque, like a circus of the insane. The faces of the men were debased, brooding, sullen, hopeless. Their bodies had the prison stench, their arms hung inhumanly.

Two places in front of him he made out Hicks who leered at him in recognition across his shoulder.

" D'y like a fag, sissy ? " asked Hicks, making the words come back from the corner of his mouth.

" No talking," shouted Warder Hall from his platform. " You, No. 514, no talking, there! "

Round and round, circling, circling, like the wheel in Arthur's brain, circling round the obscene focus of the lavatory. Warder Hall was the ring master, his voice cracked like a whip.

" No talking. No talking." The crazy merry-go-round of exercise.

At nine they went into the shop, a long bare workroom where the mail bags were stitched. Arthur was given more mail bags. Warder Beeby, the shop inspector, gave Arthur the mail bags, and observing his rawness, as he handed out the canvas he bent over and explained:

" See here, stupid, you rope them like this." He pushed the big needle through two folds of the thick canvas, indicating, good-naturedly, the manner in which the stitches should be made. And he added, with not unfriendly irony: "If you rope a nice lot of mail bags you get cocoa at night. See, stupid ? A nice hot bowl of oko! "

The kindness in Warder Beeby's voice put a new heart into Arthur. He began to rope the mail bags. About a hundred men were roping mail bags. The man next to Arthur was old and grey-whiskered and he roped skilfully and quickly, making sure of his cocoa. Every time he threw down a mail bag he scratched himself under his armpit and threw a furtive look at Arthur. But he did not talk. If he talked he would lose his cocoa.

At twelve o'clock the bell rang again. They stopped work in the shop and filed back to the cells for dinner. The key sounded in Arthur's cell. Dinner was skilly and bread and rancid margarine. After dinner Warder Collins slid back the peep-hole. His eye, seen through the peep-hole, seemed sinister and large. He said:

" You don't come here to do nothing. Get on with these mail bags."

Arthur got on with the mail bags. His hands were sore from pushing the heavy needle through the canvas and a blister had risen on his thumb. He worked in a reflex manner. He did not know what he was doing or why he was doing it; already his actions had become automatic, on and on, roping the mail bags. Once again the key sounded. Warder Collins came in with the supper, watery porridge and a chunk of bread. When he entered the cell he looked at the mail bags, then he looked at Arthur and his short upper lip drew back from his teeth. There was no doubt about it, for some reason Warder Collins had a down on Arthur. But he was in no hurry, he had a great many months in which to work and from long experience he knew how much more pleasure he got out of it by taking time. He merely said, reflectively:

" Haven't you done no more nor that? We can't have no scrimshankin' here."

" I'm not used to it," Arthur answered. Unconsciously he made his tone propitiating as if he realised the importance of being on the right side of Warder Collins. He raised his eyes, tired with close work, and it seemed as if Warder Collins had become enlarged. His head especially, his broad deformed head was fantastically enlarged and menacing. Arthur had to shade his eyes to look at Warder Collins.

" You better bloody well hurry up and get used to it." Though he spoke ever so gently, Warder Collins brought his deformed head a little nearer. " Don't think you've dodged out of the army to have a cushy job here. Get on with the bags till you hear the bell."

Arthur got on with the bags until he heard the bell. He heard the bell at eight o'clock. The clanging of the bell filled the deep well of the prison with a great volume of sound, and Arthur knew that he had all night before him in which to be alone.

He sat on the edge of his board staring at the broad black arrows stamped on his khaki trousers and he started to trace the pattern of the arrows with his forefinger. Why did he have arrows stamped upon him? He was covered with arrows; his entire body, enwrapped in a daze, in a blind stupor, was pierced by flights and flights of broad black arrows. He had a queer sense of having ceased to exist, a sense of spiritual annihilation. These arrows had killed him.

At nine o'clock the lights went out and after sitting stupidly for a minute in the darkness he fell back, dressed as he was, upon the board as though he had been stunned. He slept.

But he did not sleep long. Soon after midnight he was awakened by the howling which had disturbed him on the night before. But this time the howling went on and on, as if forgotten. It was wild and altogether lost. Arthur sprang up from the bed in the darkness. His sleep had re-created him. He was alive again, horribly and painfully alive, and he could not stand the howling nor the darkness nor the solitude. He lifted up his voice and shouted.

" Stop it, stop it, for God's sake stop it," and he began to pound the door of his cell with his closed fists. He shouted and pounded in a frenzy and in a minute he heard others shouting and pounding too. From the dark catacombs of the gallery rose a great sound of shouting and pounding. But no one took any notice and the great sound of shouting and pounding fell away gradually into the darkness and the silence.

Arthur stood for a moment with his cheek pressed against the cold shut grating of the door, his chest heaving, his arms outstretched. Then he tore himself away and began to pace the floor of his cell. There was no space in which to move yet he had to keep moving, it was impossible for him to be still. His hands remained clenched and he seemed to have no power to unclench his body. From time to time he flung himself upon the board but it was no use, the torment of his nerves would not let him alone. Only the pacing relieved him. He had to go on pacing.

He was still pacing when the key sounded. The sound of the key opened another day. He jumped at the sound, then he stood in the centre of his cell facing Warder Collins. He panted:

" I couldn't sleep for that howling. I couldn't sleep for it."

" What a shame," sneered Warder Collins.

" I couldn't sleep. I couldn't sleep. What is that howling ? "

" No talking! "

" What is that howling ? What is it ? "

" No talking I tell you. It's a bloke gone mad if you want to know, he's under observation for mental. Shut up. No talking! " And Warder Collins went out.

Arthur pressed his brow into his hands, striving with all his force to control himself. His head drooped, his legs seemed incapable of supporting his body. He felt mortally ill. He could not eat the skilly which warder Collins had left for him in the usual earthenware bowl. The smell of the skilly sickened him to death. He sat down on the board bed. He could not eat the skilly.

Suddenly the key sounded. Warder Collins came in and looked at Arthur and drew back his lip. He said:

" Why don't you eat your breakfast ? "

Arthur looked at him dully.

" I can't."

" Stand up when I address you."

Arthur stood up.

" Eat your breakfast! "

" I can't."

Collins's lip came back, very thin and blue.

" Not good enough for you, eh? Not fancy enough for Cuthbert? Eat your breakfast, Cuthbert."

Arthur repeated dully:

" I can't."

Warder Collins stroked his chin softly. It was beginning to get good.

" Do you know what'll happen to you? " he said. " You'll be fed forcible if you don't look out. You'll have a tube forced down your gullet and your soup run into your stomach, see. I've done it before and I'll do it again."

" I'm sorry," Arthur said with his eyes on the ground. " If I eat it I know I'll be sick."

" Pick up the bowl," Collins ordered.

Arthur stooped and picked up the bowl. Warder Collins watched him do it. From the start Collins had taken a violent dislike to Arthur as being well-bred, educated and a gentleman. There was the other reason too. Collins explained the other reason slowly:

" I been lookin' at you, Cuthbert. I don't like Cuthberts. I sort of picked on you the minnet you came in. I got a son in the trenches, see. That explains a lot, see. It explains why you be goin' to eat that breakfast. Eat your breakfast, Cuthbert."

Arthur began to eat the skilly. He swallowed half of the watery mess, then in a laboured voice he said:

" I can't." And as he said it his inside revolted. He vomited over Warder Collins's boots.

Warder Collins went livid. He thought Arthur had tried to vomit back the skilly over his boots. He forgot the technique of his sadism. Without any hesitation he hit Arthur a violent blow in the face.

Arthur turned bone white. He stared at Warder Collins with tormented eyes.

" You can't do that," he said, breathing painfully. " I'll report you for striking me."

" You will? " Warder Collins drew back his sneering lip as far as it would go. " Report that at the same time then." He swung his fist hard and knocked Arthur down.

Arthur struck the concrete floor of the cell and lay still. He moaned weakly and at that sound Warder Collins, thinking of his son in the trenches, smiled grimly. He wiped his soiled boots on Arthur's tunic, then, with his thin lip still drawn back, he walked out of the cell. The key sounded.

XIII

On the day that Arthur lay senseless in the puddle of skilly on the cement floor of his cell, Joe sat very sensibly before some oysters in the Central Hotel, Tynecastle. Amongst other things, Joe had recently discovered oysters. They were amazing, oysters were, amazing in every way, especially amazing in the number a man could eat. Joe could manage a dozen and a half quite easily when he was in the mood, and he was usually in the mood. And, by God, they were good—with a dash of tabasco and a squeeze of lemon. The big fat ones were the best.

Even though certain food-stuffs, meat for instance and chicken, were rather more restricted, the people who knew their way about could always get oysters in season at the Central. For that matter Joe could get pretty well anything at the Central. He dropped in so often he was a known man there now, they all ran after him, and the head waiter, old Sue—his name was really Suchard but Joe had the hail-fellow-well-met habit of abbreviation—ran faster than any. " Why don't you buy yourself some Crocker and Dicksons ? " Joe had blandly suggested to old Sue some months before. " Ah, don't look so frightened, I know you don't speculate—a family man and all that, eh, Sue ?—but this is *different*, you ought to buy yourself a hundred just for fun." A week later Sue had been waiting for Joe at the entrance to the Grill Room, fawning with gratitude, almost genuflecting, showing him to the best table in the room. " Ah, that's all right, Sue, don't bother to say it. H'much d'you knock out of it ? Sixty pounds. Keep you in cigars for a bit, eh, Sue ? Ha, ha! That's right, just you look after me, y'understand, and I'll look after you."

Money!—thought Joe, pronging the last oyster and letting it slide skilfully down his gullet—it certainly delivered the goods. While the waiter removed the pearly litter and brought his steak he surveyed the Grill Room genially. The Grill Room of the Central was a perfect health resort these days; even on Sundays it was bung full, the place where all the successful men gathered, the business men who were up to the elbow in the pie. Joe knew most of them, Bingham and Howard, both on the Munitions Council, Snagg the lawyer, Ingram, of Ingram Toogood the brewers, Wainwright the big noise on the Tynecastle Exchange, and Pennington, whose speciality was synthetic jam. Joe had deliberately set out to make contacts; the people with money, anyone who might be useful to him. Personal liking meant nothing, he cultivated only those who could advance him; but he was so hearty in his manner, such an excellent mixer that he passed, everywhere, as the best of good fellows.

Two men at the window caught his eye. He nodded and they waved to him in recognition. Joe smiled with a secret gratification. A clever pair, Bostock and Stokes—yes, they'd both cut their eye teeth all right.

Bostock was boots, just in a small way of business before the war began, with a little hand-me-down factory in East Town. But in these last eighteen months Bostock had reached himself a handful of army contracts. It wasn't the contracts, of course, though they were good enough. It was the boots. There wasn't an inch of leather in Bostock's boots. Not one bleeding inch. Bostock had let it out to Joe the other night at the County when Bostock was just the littlest bit screwed. It was some kind of bark Bostock put in his boots and the bark was guaranteed not to last. But what was the odds, Bostock had tearfully confided, the boots lasted out most of the poor devils that wore them. Pity! " O Gord, Sho, washn't it a pity ? " Bostock had blubbered suddenly into his cham in a passion of patriotic grief.

Stokes's line was tailoring. In the last few months he had bought all the property over his shop and could now refer casually to " his factory." He was the biggest patriot in the whole Crockerstown district; he was always talking of " the national necessity," he made all his women work unpaid overtime, cribbed down their dinner hour, drove them often till 8 p.m. on Sundays. Even so, most of his work was " given out " to the surrounding tenements. He paid 7*d.* per pair of breeches, and 1*s.* 6*d.* the complete uniform. Khaki shirts he gave out at 2*s.* a dozen less 2¾*d.* a reel for the cotton. Soldiers' trousers he farmed out to be finished at 1¼*d.* a pair, body belts at 8*d.* a dozen, needles and cotton provided by the women. And the *profit* ?—Joe moistened his lips, hungrily. Take these body belts for instance: Joe knew for a fact that they were being bought from Stokes by somebody " higher up " at 18*s.* a dozen. And the total cost to Stokes was 2*s.* 10*d.*! God, it was marvellous. True enough, some socialist swine had worked it out that Stokes paid on an average 1*d.* an hour to his tenement out-workers and had raised the question of sweated labour in the Council. Bah! thought Joe. Sweated labour be damned! These women fought to get the work, didn't they ? There were plenty of them too—just take a look at the draggled mob that made up the margarine queues, for instance! And besides, wasn't there a war on ?

Joe's experience was that there was nothing like a war for helping a man to throw his weight about. At least Joe put it down to the war. At Millington's he had thrown his weight about to some tune, they were all scared of him now, Morgan, Irvine, even that old stickler Dobbie. Joe smiled. He lay back in his chair and carefully peeled the band off a light Havana cigar. Stokes and Bostock might smoke their cigars with the band on, the blinking profiteers, but he knew one better than that. Joe's smile became dreamy. But suddenly he sat up, alert and welcoming, at the sight of Jim Mawson appoaching. He had been expecting Mawson, who always took his Sunday dinner at home, to drop in about two.

Jim edged along quietly through the crowded room and sat down at Joe's table. His heavy, hooded eyes lifted towards Joe who nodded silently in return: the greeting of two men who knew their way about. A pause while Mawson surveyed the restaurant with boredom.

" Whisky, Jim ? " asked Joe at length.

Jim shook his head and yawned. Another pause. " How's things upbye ? "

" Not so dusty." Joe pulled a slip from his waistcoat pocket in leisurely fashion. " Output last week was 200 tons shrapnel, 10,000 Mills grenades, 1,000 whizz bangs, you know, stick bombs, and 1,500 eighteen-pounders."

" Christ," said Jim, reaching without emotion for a toothpick out of the little glass dish, " you'll finish the bloody war all by your bloody little self, Joe, if you're not careful."

Joe grinned cautiously. " Don't you fret, Jim. Some of these shells wouldn't finish a coco-nut. God, I never saw so many blow-hole castings as we got last week. It's that last pig you delivered, Jim. Shocking. Half of them come out like Gruyère cheeses. Duds. We had to clay up the holes and slash on two coats of paint."

" Ah," Jim sighed. " Won't carry true, eh ? "

" Not on your bloody life, Jim, they'll about go round corners if they clear the muzzle."

" Pity," agreed Jim, working overtime with the toothpick. Then, " How much can you take this week ? " he asked.

Cocking his head Joe affected to consider: " You better send me 150 tons."

Mawson nodded.

" And look here, Jim," went on Joe, " invoice it as 350 this week. I'm sick of piking at an extra hundred."

Jim's enigmatic eye inquired, is it safe ?

" We don't want to go too quick," he said at last, thoughtfully. " There's Dobbie."

" Ah, what about him! If the invoice comes in he doesn't know what the hell we're using in the foundry. So long as his bloody figures add up right he thinks he's got the whole issue taped." Perhaps Joe spoke a little violently: his early tentative efforts to corrupt Dobbie, the angular, pince-nez-ed, finicking cashier, had proved singularly unsuccessful. Fortunately Dobbie, if interfering, was easy to hoodwink. His whole being was bound up in the scrupulosity of his returns. But he knew nothing of the practical side. For months past Joe had been conducting these amusing little deals with Mawson. To-day, for instance, he had ordered 150 tons of scrap iron, but the invoice which he would initial as correct would be for 350 tons. Dobbie would pay for 350 tons and Mawson and Joe would split even on 200 tons at £7 a ton. A trifling matter of £1,400 profit. Only a side issue perhaps, in the combined activities of Jim and Joe. But for all that enough to make them mildly grateful for the boon of war.

Business satisfactorily concluded, Mawson lay back in his chair holding his stomach tenderly. A silence.

" Here's them two —— comin' over," he declared at length.

Stokes and Bostock had risen and now came over and stood by their table. Both were flushed by food and drink, happy yet important. Stokes offered his cigar case to Joe and Mawson. As Joe put away his half-smoked Havana and bent selectively over the gold-bound crocodile case, Stokes said with quite an unnecessary wink:

" You don't have to smell them, they cost me half-a-dollar apiece."

" It's no bloody joke, these prices," Bostock said with great solemnity. He had only had four brandies. He swayed slightly but he was superbly grave. " Do you know that one bloody egg costs fivepence ? "

" You can afford it," Joe said.

" I don't eat eggs myself," Bostock said. " Bilious things eggs, and besides I'm too busy. I'm buying myself a bloody big house in Kenton, and the wife wants it and the daughter. Ah, wimen, wimen. But what I mean is, how in hell is the war going on if an egg costs fivepence ? "

Cutting his cigar, Mawson said:

" You can insure that risk. I've done it myself. Fifteen per cent. against the war ending this year. It's worth it."

Bostock argued very soberly:

" I'm talking about eggs, Jim."

Stokes winked at Joe. He said:

" Why does a hen cross the road ? "

Bostock looked at Stokes. He said very solemnly:

" B—s."

" B—s yourself," Stokes answered, steadying himself lovingly against Bostock's shoulder.

Instinctively Joe and Mawson exchanged a quick glance of contempt: Stokes and Bostock could not carry their money, they were braggers, they would not last the pace, one of these days they would go up in a puff of smoke. Joe's self-esteem was immensely flattered by this silent interchange of understanding between Mawson and himself. He began almost to despise Stokes and Bostock, he was above them now, above them both. He caressed his cigar opulently between his lips and let out a cool derisive puff.

" Wha' y' doin' this afternoon, Jim ? " Stokes benignantly inquired of Mawson.

Mawson looked inquiringly at Joe.

" The County, I suppose."

" Tha' suits us," said Bostock. " Le's all go roun' th' Club."

Joe and Mawson rose and they strolled in a bunch to the door of the Grill. A woman commissionaire revolved the door obsequiously to these four triumphant males, magnificently fed and clothed, masters of the universe. They made an impressive group on the steps of the Central

Grill, Joe a little behind, adjusting his blue silk scarf.

Mawson turned, intimately:

" Come on, Joe, we may as well. We'll have a four at pool."

Joe inspected his neat platinum wrist watch with an air of regret.

" Sorry, Jim, I've got business."

Bostock neighed with laughter, wagging a fat forefinger:

" It's a skirt, it's a lady called Brown."

Joe shook his head.

" Business," he said suavely.

" 'S war work," Stokes suggested with a ribald leer. " 'S war work wish a wack."

They inspected him with envy.

" Cheerio, then," Bostock said. " Na poo, toodeloo, good-bye-ee."

Mawson, Bostock and Stokes went off to the Club. Joe watched them go, then he stepped on to the pavement and crossed briskly to where his car stood parked. He started the engine and set out for Wirtley: he had promised to pick up Laura at the canteen. Driving thoughtfully through the quiet Sunday streets, his head filled with Mawson's scheme, by money, business, shells, steel, and his belly with rich food and drink, he found himself comfortably aware of the afternoon before him. He smiled: a glossy self-satisfied smile. She was all right, Laura, he owed a bit to her. She'd shown him so many things, from how to tie his new dress tie to where to find the little self-contained flat which he had now occupied for six months. She'd improved him. Well, it pleased her, didn't it, to do things for him, like getting him put up for the County and, by an equally discreet approach, invited to the Howards', the Penningtons', even to Mrs. John Rutley's house. She was completely gone on him. His smile deepened. He understood Laura perfectly now. He had always flattered himself that he *knew* women: the frightened ones, the cold ones—these were the commonest—the " pretenders "; but never before had he met a type like Laura. No wonder she hadn't been able to hold out against him, or rather against herself.

As he slid into the square below Wirtley Munition Works—for obvious reasons they always met here—Laura turned the corner, walking smartly. Her punctuality pleased him. He lifted his hat and, not getting out of the car, held the door open for her. She got in and, without a word, he drove off towards his flat.

For some minutes they did not speak, the silence of complete familiarity. He liked having her beside him; she was a damned well-turned-out woman; these navy costumes always suited her. His feeling for her now was that of a husband still quite fond of his wife. Naturally there was not so much excitement now, the very consciousness of her attachment to him took the edge off his appetite.

" Where did you lunch ? " she asked at length.

" The Central." He answered casually. " What about you ? "

" I had a bacon sandwich at the canteen."

He laughed graciously: he knew her interest did not lie in food.

" Aren't you fed up with that place yet? " he said. " Standing serving swill to the canaries? "

" No." She deliberated. " I like to think I still have some decent instincts in me."

He laughed again, dropped the subject, and they began to talk of ordinary things until they reached the far end of Northern Road where, in a quiet crescent behind the main thoroughfare, Joe's flat was situated. It was actually the lower half of a subdivided house, with high-ceilinged rooms, fireplaces and mouldings in the Adams style and a discreet sense of space accentuated by open gardens fore and aft. Laura had furnished it for him in decided taste—Laura had a flair for that sort of thing. It was easily run. A woman came in the forenoons to do for him, and as it lay a full five miles from Yarrow it was, from the point of their intimacy, absolutely safe. To those who saw Laura come and go she passed, in the nicest possible way, as Joe's sister.

Joe opened the door with his latch-key and went in with Laura. He switched on the electric heater in the living-room and, sitting down, began to take off his shoes. Laura poured herself a glass of milk and stood drinking it with her eyes upon his back.

" Have a whisky and soda," she suggested.

" No, I don't feel like it." He picked up the Sunday paper which lay on the table and opened it at the financial column.

She studied him for a moment in silence, finishing her milk. For a few minutes she pottered about the room, straightening things up, as if waiting for him to speak, then she went unobtrusively into the bedroom next door. He heard her moving about, taking off her things and, lowering his paper, he grinned faintly. They went to bed every Sunday afternoon, quietly and decently, as people go to church, but lately since his own desire was less acute it had amused him to " kid Laura on a bit." Now he waited a full half-hour, pretending to read, before, with an obvious yawn, he went into the bedroom.

She lay upon her back in his bed in a plain white nightdress of beautiful material and cut, her hair charmingly arranged, her clothes neatly folded upon a chair, a faint perfume of her, like an evocation, in the room. He had to admit that she had class. A week ago he had taken a little flutter with a munitionette from the Wirtley Works—gone home with her to her room in fact—oh, a nice enough girl, no doubt, her ginger colouring had appealed to him after Laura's bushy darkness, but somehow her flashy nightdress, the poor sheets upon the bed had disgusted him. Yes, there was no question but that Laura had educated him: clearly the best way to learn manners was to sleep with a well-bred woman.

He undressed slowly, aware that Laura was watching him, taking a long time to arrange his keys, gold cigarette case and loose silver upon the chest of drawers. He even stood in his underwear, deliberately counting his money before he came over and sat upon the edge of the bed.

" Were you working out how much you'd give me ? " she inquired in her controlled voice.

He broke into a roar of laughter, glad in a way to get rid of his simmering amusement in one explosive burst.

" As a matter of fact, Joe," she went on in that same ironic manner, " I've just been thinking that I'm the one who's done most of the giving. Cigarette case, watch, cuff links, all these little presents, the use of the car too. You even wangled this furniture out of me. Oh, I know you're always *going* to give me the cheque and I don't give a hang whether you do. I hope to God I'm not petty. It's just that I wonder often whether you realise what I've done for you one way and another."

He felt his biceps in high good humour.

" Well," he said, " you did it because you wanted to."

" So that's the way you look at it ? " She paused. " When I think how it began. That morning you came up about the counterfoils. A silly weak moment. And now this."

" Ah," he grinned sheepishly, " it'd have been the same in any case. You know you're mad about me."

" What a pretty way to put it. You know, Joe, I honestly believe you don't care for me at all. You've simply used me, used me for all you were worth, used me to get on . . ."

" And haven't I been some use to you ? "

A silence.

" You're an adept," she said slowly, " at making me hate myself."

" Ah, don't say that now, Laura," he protested. And, throwing off his singlet, he slipped into bed beside her. She gave a sigh that was almost a moan, as at her own weakness, her own desire, then turned upon her side, yielding herself to him.

They slept for about an hour afterwards, Joe rather restlessly. It always irked him that she clung to him after his own desire was satisfied. In their early days together it had gratified his vanity to demonstrate his own virility to her, to contrast his own fine body with Stanley's obvious flabbiness. But now he was tired of that: he had no intention of depleting his physical resources for her. When she opened her eyes and looked at him he sustained her gaze across the pillow with a slightly mocking stare.

" Don't you love me any more, Joe ? " she asked.

" You know I do."

She sighed: her eyes fell.

" Oh dear," she said.

" What's the matter ? "

" Nothing. You can be hateful when you choose. Sometimes you make me feel horrible." A pause. " I am horrible, I daresay, but I can't help it."

He continued to look at her, conscious of that inward chuckle which had affected him all day. He had reached the subtlety of deriving a curious satisfaction from the play of emotion upon her face; he watched especially in their moments of climax, obtaining a sense of his importance as the mitigator of this inner turmoil. Yes, he was " the boss," as he put it, right enough. He was still fond of her, of course, but it was good for her to feel her dependence on him once in a while. Now, since he saw she was in the mood for tenderness, he affected a playful briskness.

" I think we ought to have our tea," he said. " I'm parched."

He had begun to grin, when suddenly the telephone rang. Still grinning, he leaned across her and picked up the receiver.

" Hello," he said. " Yes, this is Mr. Gowlan. Yes, Morgan. . . . Yes. . . . I don't know, no I haven't the least idea. . . . What! " Joe's voice altered slightly. There was a longish pause. " Is that so. . . . Good God, you don't say so . . . came to the office did it. . . . Yes, Morgan. . . . Yes, of course. . . . I'll be over shortly. Yes, I'll be over myself."

Joe hung up the receiver, came back slowly to his own side of the bed. A silence followed.

" What was it ? " Laura asked.

" Well——" Joe cleared his throat. " You see . . ."

" Well, what ? "

He hesitated, picking at the edging of the sheet.

" A wire's just come to the office."

Laura raised herself in the bed. All at once she said:

" Is it Stanley ? "

" It's nothing," Joe said hurriedly. " He's absolutely all right. It's only shell-shock."

" Shell-shock," Laura said. Her lips went quite pale.

" That's all," he answered. " Not a thing more."

Laura pressed her hand against her brow.

" O God," she said in an extinguished voice. " I knew something like this would happen, I knew it. I knew it."

" But it's nothing," he repeated. " Don't upset yourself. He isn't scratched. He only got buried by a shell and they've sent him home to get over it. He's not even wounded. I tell you, it's nothing." He tried to take her hand but she snatched it away.

" Leave me." She burst into tears. " Leave me alone . . ."

" But he isn't even wounded . . ."

She turned from him violently, jumped out of bed, and, sobbing, pulled off her nightdress. Naked, her white body bent, she fumbled at the chair, began to huddle on her clothes.

"But, Laura," he said, protestingly. He had never seen her cry before.

" Be quiet," she cried, " anything you say can only make it worse. You've done something to me. You've made me hate myself. And now Stanley . . . O God . . ."

Flinging on her jacket, she snatched up her hat and ran, bareheaded and sobbing, from the room.

He remained upon his elbow for a minute, then with a shrug of his bare shoulders he reached out towards the bedside table, yawned, and lit himself a cigarette.

XIV

It was the spring of 1916, nearly fourteen months since Hilda and Grace had come to nurse in London, and Hilda was happier than she had ever been. The disturbing changes in her father, all the painful echoes of the Neptune disaster, the whole grim business of Arthur's imprisonment, as related in Aunt Carrie's woeful letters, affected her very little. When Grace came to her, weeping: " Oh, Hilda, we must do something about Arthur. We can't stay here and let this happen," Hilda snapped: " What can we do? Nothing. Except keep out of it." Whenever Grace attempted to broach the subject Hilda cut her short in this brusque fashion.

Lord Kell's house was in Belgrave Square, a large mansion which had been stripped—except for the beautiful cut-glass chandeliers, a few pictures and some tapestry panels—and converted into an adequate hospital, for which purpose it was admirably suited. Six of the rooms were enormous, each as big as an average ballroom, with high ceilings and polished oak floors, and these became the wards. The big conservatory at the back was transformed to an operating theatre; and it was here that Hilda had her happiest moments.

Hilda had got on wonderfully at Belgrave Square; in six months she had at her finger ends as much as the average nurse acquires in a three years' training. Already Miss Gibbs, the matron, had her eye upon Hilda as something quite out of the ordinary. Miss Gibbs had commended Hilda and moved Hilda to the theatre. In the theatre Hilda's qualities seemed exactly right. Dark, self-contained and precise, Hilda functioned in that theatre with forbidding and unerring accuracy. Hilda's spare-time studying had been extensive but it was her instinct, her temperament which made her so pluperfect. You looked at Hilda and saw that it was impossible for her to blunder. Mr. Ness looked at Hilda several times during her first week in the theatre, his quick darting glance, when Hilda had anticipated something which he required. Ness was the honorary, a short blunt gingery man who sweated offensively while he worked, but a wonder at abdominal surgery. Later, he suggested quietly to Miss Gibbs that Hilda might shortly be useful as his theatre sister.

When Hilda was told of Ness's interest in her work she showed no elation—the signal honour, as Miss Gibbs euphoniously named it, left Hilda quite unmoved. She had a little thrill of inward satisfaction, quickly suppressed, but she was not overcome. Success had firmed Hilda's predetermination and set her ambition higher than before. When she stood by Ness watching him make his incisions, sutures and anastomoses, she did not fix her mind upon the time when as theatre sister she would intimately assist him in this work. No, she watched Ness operate and fixed her mind upon the day when she herself would operate. That was Hilda's ambition, she had always wanted to be a doctor—a surgeon. Always. She was a little late in beginning, perhaps, but she was still young, only twenty-five. And since her miraculous emancipation from the Law Hilda had sworn to herself that nothing would stop her in achieving her goal. In the meantime Hilda was happy—she had an end in view, she had her work, and she had Grace.

Grace had not achieved Hilda's crashing success, indeed Grace was not a success at all. Untidy, unpunctual, inaccurate—poor Grace had none of the qualities essential to success. While Hilda rose like a rocket to the giddy heights of the operating theatre, Grace remained scrubbing floors and basins in the basement. Grace didn't mind. Grace was perfectly contented: so contented that she had twice been before Miss Gibbs for giving tea to patients' wives in the ward kitchen and once for smuggling Gold Flake in to a sergeant disciplined for swearing at the ward sister. Grace, as Miss Gibbs did not hesitate to say, was incompetent, hopelessly incompetent—Grace would never be *anything*, Miss Gibbs said, unless she mended her ways.

But these ways were Grace; and nobody but Miss Gibbs and Hilda seemed to want Grace to mend them. Grace was a great favourite with the other nurses. At the nurses' home, a house in Sloane Street, quarter of a mile away, there was always someone in Grace's untidy little cubby hole begging or giving a cigarette, or a *Bystander*, or a gramophone record, or one of the make-believe chocolates that the war had produced. Or asking Grace out to tea, or to the pictures, or to meet a brother home on leave.

Hilda hated this. No one came to Hilda's austerely tidy room and Hilda did not want anyone to come: no one except Grace. Yes, Hilda wanted Grace, wanted Grace all to herself and with all her heart. She froze the friendly visiting, nipped Grace's friendships in the bud.

"Why," she scornfully remarked one morning towards the end of March, "must you go out with that Montgomerie creature?"

"Old Monty's not a bad sort, Hilda," Grace answered apologetically, "we only went to the Kardomah."

" The woman's impossible! " said Hilda jealously. " You must come out with me on your next half-holiday. I'll arrange it."

Hilda arranged most things for Grace, continued, in her possessive love, to dictate to Grace. And Grace—artless, simple and sweet-natured as ever—submitted cheerfully.

But Grace would not submit to Hilda about the letters. Grace did not argue, she did not contradict. On this point she simply refused to submit to Hilda. And these letters worried Hilda to death. Every week and sometimes twice a week the letters came from France, with the field postmark and the same handwriting, a man's handwriting. Hilda saw that Grace was in close correspondence with someone at the front and at last Hilda could bear it no longer. One April evening, as she walked through the darkened streets to the home with Grace, Hilda said:

" You had another letter, to-day, another letter from France? "

Staring hard at the pavement in front of her Grace said:

" Yes."

Because she was upset, Hilda's manner became colder and more forbidding.

" Who is it writes to you? "

At first Grace did not answer. She flushed quickly in the darkness. But she did answer—there was never evasion or artifice about Grace.

" It's Dan Teasdale."

" Dan Teasdale." Hilda's voice was both shocked and scornful. " You mean Teasdale, Teasdale the baker's son? "

Grace said very simply:

" Yes."

" Good heavens! " Hilda burst out. " You don't mean to say—well, in all my life I never heard anything so sickeningly idiotic——"

" Why is it idiotic? "

" Why? " Hilda sneered. " Why, indeed? Don't you think it rather cheap to work up a romance with a baker's lout? "

Grace was very pale now, and her voice extremely quiet.

" You can say unkind things, Hilda," she said. " Dan Teasdale has nothing to be ashamed of. He writes me the nicest letters I've ever had in my life. I don't think there's anything cheap about that."

" You don't," Hilda said scathingly. " Well, I do. And I won't have you behaving like an infatuated school-girl. Too many silly women have thrown themselves away already. Their war heroes!—oh, it's disgusting, *disgusting*. You've got to stop these letters."

Grace shook her head.

" I'm sorry, Hilda."

" You've got to, I tell you."

Grace shook her head again.

" I won't," she said. Tears stood in Grace's eyes but there was a queer finality in her voice which knocked the rage right out of Hilda and really frightened her.

Hilda said no more that evening: but she took up an attitude and tried to coerce Grace by that attitude. She froze Grace, spoke to her cuttingly, generally ignored her with a sort of scornful contempt. This lasted for a fortnight and the letters still came.

Then in a secret panic Hilda suddenly changed. She unbent completely, apologised to Grace, petted and wheedled Grace and took Grace out to the Kardomah, a café greatly favoured by the nurses, for the nicest tea that money and Hilda's influence with the proprietress could procure. For a whole week Hilda spoiled Grace and Grace received the spoiling as submissively as she had received the scolding. Then Hilda tried once again to persuade Grace to give up writing to Dan. No use, no use at all, Grace would not give up writing to Dan.

Hilda watched the letters, these abominable interminable letters, she went down early every morning to inspect the letter rack, in a kind of hatred. And then, one morning in June she noticed with a start that the postmark of the letter just arrived was Loughborough.

She stopped Grace after breakfast. In a controlled voice she asked:

" Is he wounded ? "

" Yes." Grace kept her eyes averted.

" Seriously ? "

" No."

" In hospital ? "

" Yes! "

A secret relief flooded Hilda, deep down within herself she was overwhelmed by relief—Loughborough was a long way off, a very long way off. Since the wound was not serious Dan would soon be back in France. But her lip curled. She sneered:

" He really ought to have been brought here, of course. That's how it happens in the best penny-farthing romances."

Grace turned away quickly. Yet before she could go Hilda went on:

" So lovely for him to come out of the anæsthetic and find you by his bedside ready to fling your arms round his neck."

The quivering in Hilda's voice showed how much it hurt Hilda to say that—it hurt her horribly. Yet she had to say it. She was inflamed with jealousy.

Grace did not answer Hilda. She went into the ward carrying Dan's letter in the pocket of her apron. She read it several times while she was on duty.

Dan had been in the big push at the Somme, had been wounded in the left forearm and wrist. He would be well almost immediately, he wrote, his arm did not hurt him in the slightest, it was just that he could not use his hand.

Dan's letters became irregular about the end of July, but on the evening of the very last day of the month as Grace walked down Sloane Street, she saw someone in uniform standing with his arm in a sling exactly opposite the home. She was alone and walking rather slowly for she was tired, saddened by the thought of Arthur, of all the changes at home in Sleescale. For once everything seemed wrong. Miss Gibbs had given her another lecture for untidiness, and she was upset at not hearing from Dan—it was amazing how much she had come to depend on these letters of Dan's. At the sight of that figure in uniform she stopped, not very sure. And then all at once she was sure. Her heart leaped within her breast. It was Dan. He crossed the street and saluted her.

"Dan! I thought . . . yes, I thought it was you." The pleasure she felt at seeing him shone in her face; she did not feel tired now but, forgetting all about being tired and sad, she held out her hand.

Not speaking, he shook hands shyly. His shyness of her amounted almost to a disease, he seemed afraid almost to look at her. Grace had never seen anyone afraid of her before, it was so ridiculous she wanted to laugh and cry at once. Quickly, before she should do anything so stupid as that, she said:

"Have you been waiting, Dan? Didn't you go into the home?"

"No," he said, "I didn't want to be worrying you. I thought I might see you for a minute as you went in."

"A minute!" She smiled again; suddenly she looked at his wounded arm.

"How is your arm?"

"They've had some trouble with the wrist . . . the tendons," he said. "I'm sent up here for orthopædic treatment at the Langham clinic. Electricity and one of these new exercise machines. Six weeks' treatment before I can go back."

"Six weeks!"

Her gasp of pleasure almost reassured him. He said awkwardly:

"I was wondering if you, that's to say if you wouldn't mind . . . if you hadn't anything better to do . . ."

"No," she said with a little rush, "I wouldn't mind. And I've got *nothing* better to do." She paused, gazing at him with bright eyes. Her hair stuck out comically from her nurse's cap; there was a distinct smut on her cheek. "I've got two hours off to-morrow. Shall we have tea?"

He laughed, his eyes still on the ground:

"That's what I wanted to ask you."

"I know, I know, it's awful, I've invited myself," she ran on, "but oh, Dan, it's too marvellous for words. There's hundreds of things we can do in six weeks." She broke off. "There isn't any other girl you've been writing to you want to take around?"

He lifted his eyes in such concern that now it was her turn to laugh. She laughed happily. It was splendid seeing Dan again. Dan had always been the most marvellous companion, from those very early days when he had given her a drive on the van up the Avenue and made her pick a most beautiful cream bun out of the basket. The same Dan who had made whistles for her out of willow shoots, and shown her the golden wren's nest in Sluice Dene and brought her harvest plaits from Avory's farm. And for all his second-lieutenant's uniform and his arm in a sling Dan wasn't a bit changed from these good old days. He ought, she knew, to have come back from the front very curt and commanding, completely reorganised inside and out. But Dan, like herself, would never be reorganised: he was the same shy, humble Dan. Grace did not dream that she was in love with Dan but she did know that she had not been so happy since she left the Law. She held out her hand.

" To-morrow at three, Dan. Wait for me outside. And don't come too near or you'll get Mary Jane the sack." She ran up the steps before he could reply.

They met next day at three and they went to the new Harris's in Oxford Street for tea. They talked and talked. Dan, when he got over his shyness, was the most interesting talker—that, at least, was what Grace thought—and he on his side wanted her to talk, was eager to listen to what she said, which struck Grace as unusual and pleasant. Encouraged, she poured out to him all her worries about Arthur and her father. He heard her in silence, sympathetically.

" Things haven't been right at home since the disaster, Dan," she concluded, her eyes earnest and sad. " I can't think of it as the same place. Somehow I can't think that I'll ever go back."

He nodded his head.

" I understand, Grace."

She gazed at him earnestly: " You won't go back to the Neptune, will you, Dan? Oh, I'd hate to think of you going back to that awful pit."

" Well," he answered, " I think I've had enough. You see, I've had time to think it over. I never liked it, I daresay, but—oh, what's the use of saying it again? It's been said so many times before, you know, the disaster and everything." He paused. " If I get through the war I want to go farming."

" Yes, Dan," she said.

They went on talking. They talked so long that the waitress came twice to demand haughtily if they required anything further.

Afterwards they took a walk through the Park; they went round the Serpentine, then back by Hyde Park Corner. Five o'clock came before they realised it. Outside the Nurses' Home Grace paused. She said:

" If I haven't been a complete nuisance, Dan, perhaps we can go out again? "

Grace and Dan began to go out regularly. They went to the oddest places and they enjoyed themselves—oh, how they enjoyed themselves!

They walked on the Chelsea Embankment, took the steamboat to Putney and the bus to Richmond, they found out queer little tea shops, they had macaroni and minestrone in Soho—it was all banal and beautiful, it had happened a million times before and yet it had never happened to Grace and Dan.

But one evening as they came back from a walk in Kensington Gardens they ran directly into Hilda, outside the Home. Hilda knew all about Grace's expeditions with Dan and Hilda though burning to speak had kept herself cuttingly aloof. But now Hilda stopped. She smiled freezingly at Dan and said:

" Good evening."

It was like a blow in the face; Dan answered:

" Good evening, Miss Barras."

There was a pause, then Hilda said:

" You seem to be making the most of the war, Mr. Teasdale."

Grace exclaimed hotly:

" Dan got himself wounded if that's what you mean."

" No," Hilda said in that same insufferable patronising tone. " I didn't quite mean that."

Dan coloured. He looked straight into Hilda's eyes. An uncomfortable silence fell, then Hilda spoke again.

" It'll be such a relief when it's over. Then we can all get back to where we belong."

Her meaning was unmistakable. Dan looked very unhappy. He said good night quickly, shook hands without looking at Grace and walked off down the street.

Inside the Home, Hilda turned contemptuously to Grace:

" Do you remember when we played happy families, Grace? Master Bun the Baker's son ? " And with her lips fixed in that cold and bitter smile she began leisurely to climb the stairs.

But Grace ran after her and caught her fiercely by the arm:

" If you dare to speak like that to me again," she panted, " or to Dan either, I'll never have anything more to do with you as long as I live."

The eyes of Grace and Hilda met in a long and burning look. It was Hilda's eyes that fell.

The next outing which Dan and Grace had arranged was on the Thursday of Dan's last week and it was to be their last. Dan's wrist was well now, he had left off the sling and he was due to rejoin his battalion on the following Monday.

They went to Kew Gardens. Dan had been eager to see the Gardens; he had a passion for gardens, and they had saved up Kew for their final jaunt. But it did not look like being brilliantly successful. To begin with the day was dull and threatening and Hilda had upset them both. Dan was silent and Grace was sad. Grace was very sad.There was not the slightest doubt about it now, Grace knew that she loved Dan, and the thought that Dan was going back to France without knowing that she loved him nearly broke Grace's heart. Dan couldn't care for her, naturally. He looked upon her as a friend. Who on earth could love her ? She was silly and careless and untidy and not even pretty. An intolerable ache rose up in Grace's throat as she walked silently beside the silent Dan.

They went to look at the water-fowl on the little lake just above the bluebell wood. They were beautiful ducks and Dan said they were beautiful ducks. He added gloomily:

" If ever I get the chance I'd like to raise ducks like these."

Grace said:

" Yes, Dan," which was as much as Grace felt like saying.

They stood together, two rather forlorn figures by the water's edge, watching the gaily plumaged birds. Suddenly the rain came on, a heavy shower.

" Oh dear," Grace said.

" We'll have to run," said Dan. " It's going to pour." They dashed for shelter; they dashed for shelter to the orchid house. At an ordinary time there would have been a world of fun in that dash for shelter but there was no fun in it now. No fun at all.

Grace had her blue uniform coat but Dan had none and his tunic got wet through. When they reached the orchid house and had got their breath again Grace turned to Dan. Her brow creased in concern.

" Your tunic's soaked, Dan." She looked round: they were quite alone. " You can't possibly keep it on. Let me dry it for you on the pipes."

Dan opened his mouth to refuse, then closed it again. Without a word he slipped off his tunic and handed it to Grace. He had always done what Grace told him and he did so now. Then, as Grace took the tunic an old gardener came up the other side of the orchid house. He had seen them run for shelter. He nodded to Dan and smiled at Grace.

" Come round here and dry it, nurse. There's better pipes over here."

Grace thanked the gardener and followed him round to a little recess where there was a coil of warm pipes. She shook Dan's tunic and laid it inside out on the warm pipes. Then she looked at herself in the little square of mirror which the gardener kept above the pipes. The wind had blown about her hair, she was untidier than ever; heavens, she thought wretchedly, I'm a fright; no wonder Dan hates the sight of me.

She waited until Dan's tunic dried, half listening, out of politeness, to the gardener, who was old and garrulous and who kept coming and going and talking—chiefly about the difficulty in getting fuel for heating. When the tunic was dry she took it back to Dan. He was staring out at the rain. He turned dismally:

" It's going to be a wet week-end."

She said:

" Yes, it looks like it."

Then, stretching out her arms, she held out the tunic, meaning to help him into it. He looked at her quite wildly as with open arms, all disconsolate and windblown, she stood before him. He looked and looked and all at once something like a groan broke from him.

" I love you, Grace, I love you," he cried and they were in each other's arms.

The tunic lay on the ground. Her heart beat madly, madly with happiness.

" Oh, Dan," she whispered.

" I must tell you, Grace, I must, I must, I can't help it . . ." he kept on repeating his excuses to her.

Her heart still beat madly, madly with happiness; her eyes were swimming with tears; but strength and calmness were in her now.

" Do you really love me, Dan ? "

" Oh, Grace . . ."

She looked up at him.

" When do you go back, Dan ? "

A pause.

" Monday."

" What day is to-day, Dan ? "

" Why, it's Thursday, Grace."

She considered him tranquilly.

" Let's get married on Saturday, Dan," she said.

Dan went perfectly white. He gazed down at her and his whole soul was in his eyes.

" Grace," he whispered.

" Dan! "

The old gardener, playing at Peeping Tom behind the orchids, forgot all about the coal shortage and nearly had a heart attack.

They were married on Saturday. Grace fought Miss Gibbs for a week-end off. That was their honeymoon. They spent it at Brighton. As Dan had predicted, it was a wet week-end, a very wet week-end, it rained all the time, but the rain made no difference to Grace and Dan.

XV

Late that August afternoon the cage rose slowly from the Paradise and Barras, accompanied by Armstrong and Hudspeth, stepped out into the pit yard. Barras wore his pit clothes: dark Norfolk jacket and breeches, round leather skullcap, a stout stick in his hand; and he stood for a moment outside the offices talking to Armstrong and Hudspeth, conscious of the glances of the banksmen, rather like an actor taking an important curtain.

" I think," he said, as though deliberating, " you'd better give it to the papers. The *Argus*, anyway. They'll be glad to know."

" Certainly, Mr. Barras," said Armstrong. " I'll ring them to-morrow for sure."

" Let them have full particulars of the estimated cost of the new roadway."

" Very good, sir."

" Oh, and by the bye, Armstrong, you might let them know that my main reasons for this step are patriotic. Once we are into the Paradise again we shall double our output."

Barras nodded and turned away towards the yard gates; then, aware of the simple dignity conferred by his underground suit, he walked through the town towards the Law. Every few yards he was obliged to raise his hand, acknowledging nods, greetings, respectful salutes. He was now incredibly popular. His patriotic activities were enormous. Strangely, Arthur's imprisonment had intensified these activities. At first Barras had faced this staggering result of his persuasive methods with a catch of dismay. But readjustment came swiftly. His imagination, choked by the hurrying succession of his own affairs, admitted no disturbing images of his son, existing and suffering in prison. He took his stand, openly admitting the fact of Arthur's imprisonment, going out of his way to refer to it publicly with a kind of upright regret.

Everyone agreed that Barras had behaved magnificently. The case was widely reported—the *Argus* giving it in a double column under the caption " Spartan Father," the *Sunday Echo* featuring a special article, " Hats off to a Patriot "; it had created a tremendous sensation, not only in Sleescale, but in Tynecastle itself. Barras moved in a perfect blaze of glory which was far from being distasteful to him. Upon several occasions when dining at the Central with Hetty he observed himself being pointed out, and he could not repress a thrill of gratification. He went about a great deal now, basked in the general approval. He had arrived at that state of mind when the whole procedure of his existence was deliberately extroverted. In the beginning the reaction had been defensive; but now it was deliberate. He had no private moments of reflection, quiet introspection or self-examination. No time, no time! His figure, breathless and a little flushed, seemed to throw the words backwards across his shoulders, hurrying, hurrying away. He was engrossed by the external, increasingly absorbed by his public performance, diverted only by the limelight, by noise, cheers and crowds.

His activities upon the Tribunal were redoubled. It became almost an impossibility for even the most genuine cases to secure exemption when Barras took his seat upon that arbitrary bench. Drumming impatiently upon the table, he would appear to listen to incoherent arguments and agitated protestations with an affectation of impartiality. Yet he was not attentive to the logic of the case; his decision was already taken. No exemption.

As time went on and the inveteracy of his decisions began to pall he briskened his methods and, speeding the cases one upon the other, began to pride himself on the numbers he could dispose of in each session. Upon the evenings of such successful days he would return home with a warm satisfaction and the sense of having earned the approbation of his fellow men.

Yet, as he walked up Cowpen Street, at this moment an even deeper satisfaction was imprinted on his face. The arrangement he had concluded at the Neptune to-day gave him a glowing sense of self-approval. For months past he had deplored the enforced closure of the Paradise, but he could not bring himself to face the heavy expense of driving a new roadway through the flood-undermined whinstone. Now, however, by judicious representations in the proper quarter he could offset the cost of the necessary roadway against subsequent deliveries to the Government of Paradise coal. The road was paid for before it was begun. Nothing need interfere with the fascinating accumulation of his wartime profits. Pit-head prices had risen a further ten shillings a ton and at the Neptune he was making money faster than he could ever have believed. Deep in the very centre of his being the secret knowledge of his own substance enraptured Barras, sustained him like a drug.

He was not a miser, but had simply an awareness of his money. He would spend money—indeed it gratified him, almost childishly, to reflect that in this respect five pounds meant as little to him as fivepence. And his present excitement demanded a kind of petty cash expenditure, that life with such potentialities laid open should not pass him by uneventfully. He had developed a new acquisitiveness. Already he had carried out striking changes at the Law. New furniture and carpets, a new gramophone, the car, a number of luxurious easy chairs, a special water softener, the old American organ removed and an electric pianola substituted. It was significant that he bought no more pictures. This belonged to his earlier phase of more constrained acquisitiveness and though the sense of his art " treasures " still brought him comfort—as instanced by his frequent complacent remark, " I have a fortune locked up in my pictures! "—he did not augment his collection during these war years. His indulgence was more showy, spontaneous and erratic. He would buy upon a whim; he developed a craze for " picking up a bargain "; he became a constant frequenter of the Tynecastle Arcade, where junk and curio shops abounded, and he never returned from such expeditions without triumphantly bringing home some purchase.

The presents he made to Hetty were expressive of the same momentum. Not the simplicities of his previous paternal devotion, not sweets, perfumes or a beribboned box of handkerchiefs, but presents upon a different psychological scale.

Here he smiled consciously. Almost insensibly he had come to regard Hetty as the normal relaxation to his strenuous endeavours. Hetty had always pleased him. Even in those early days when as a little girl of twelve she would skip astride his knee, to demand a clear gum—one of the pastilles he carried in his waistcoat pocket—he had experienced a curious reaction to Hetty. Her soapy, well-washed scent had filled his nostrils and he had reflected that Hetty would make a sweet little wife for Arthur. But now, in the face of Arthur's contemptible behaviour, this was wholly changed. The change had begun on that Sunday when Hetty, bursting into tears, had allowed Barras to comfort her in the dining-room of the Law. From that moment Barras began " to make up " for Arthur's deficiencies. Ostensibly the motive was sympathy: Hetty had to be compensated, taken out of herself and, when the final catastrophe of Arthur's imprisonment occurred, made to forget. All this attuned with Barras's mood, and now with this new restlessness urging him forward, the process was intensified. He smartened himself visibly, changed his tailor, wore silk ties and socks, acquired the habit of dropping in to Stirrocks near Grainger Street for a face massage, and a vibro-electric treatment for his hair. Gradually he began to take Hetty about with a certain conscious gallantry. To-night she was accompanying him to the King's Theatre to see the new revue Zig Zag.

A sense of anticipation tingled in Barras as he walked up the drive of the Law and let himself into his house. He went straight upstairs and took a bath, lying full length in the steaming water, conscious of his own virility. Then he dressed carefully and came down to pick himself a button-hole.

In the conservatory he found Aunt Carrie, who had just finished a half-hour's rubbing of Harriet's back, and was now on her way to cut come asparagus in the kitchen garden. Aunt Carrie had made the kitchen garden her especial care during these war years, even extending her activities to poultry and ducks, so that while meatless days and restricted meals became the general rule, while many stood in queues for hours on end to purchase a few pounds of potatoes, or a scrap of meat or an ounce or two of margarine, there was always an abundance of excellent food on dear Richard's table.

As Richard entered, Aunt Carrie raised her eyes. She murmured:

" You've had a hard day, Richard."

He studied her with unusual indulgence.

" I've decided to cut the new roadway into Paradise, Caroline."

" Oh, Richard," she fluttered at the favour of his confidence, " that's good, isn't it ? "

" We shall be able to bring out those ten men," he said gravely. " That pleases me, Caroline."

" Yes, Richard."

" There must be a public funeral. I'll arrange it. A token of respect."

Aunt Carrie inclined her head. A pause. She moved towards the door.

" I was going to cut some asparagus for your dinner. The first of the season." And she waited eagerly: Richard had always praised her for the excellence of her asparagus.

He nodded.

" By the bye, leave out some sandwiches to-night, Caroline. I may be late coming back. I'm taking Hetty to the theatre."

Aunt Carrie coloured and her heart sank from her faded tussore blouse right into her old cracked gardening boots. She answered in a tremulous voice:

" Yes, Richard." Then she went out to the garden.

But she cut her asparagus with an uneasy mind. Coming on top of Arthur's misfortune—it was like Aunt Carrie to soften his prison sentence to this ambiguity—the situation between Hetty and Richard distressed her frightfully. Richard, of course, was beyond reproach. But Aunt Carrie was not so sure about Hetty now; she viewed with misgiving these recent presents; at times Aunt Carrie almost hated Hetty.

All that evening Aunt Carrie worried and worried and would not go to bed until Richard should return.

It was, in fact, nearly eleven when Barras came back to the Law. And Hetty came with him. He had suggested that they take the cool drive together, after the heat of the theatre. Bartley would drive her home later.

They entered the drawing-room in good spirits.

" I can't stay, you know," Hetty declared brightly. She took the cigarette he offered her and perched on the arm of a chair, her legs crossed, one neat ankle swinging.

" You'll have a sandwich ? " he suggested with a sheepish smile. And he went into the dining-room to find the tray Aunt Carrie had prepared.

There was no doubt about it, he was reluctant to let her go. He did not ask himself why. He had always held himself a moral man, mechanically content to satisfy his physical needs at the legitimate fount of love upstairs. But since the disaster he was different. The state of tension in which he lived had accelerated his functions, infused a fever through his blood. He was experiencing the Indian summer of his ductless glands. Sometimes the sense of his own physical well-being was extraordinary. It is true that one or twice he had experienced a sharp attack of giddiness, almost of vertigo, which had made him reel and clutch at the nearest article of furniture to save himself from falling. But this, he knew, was nothing, nothing whatever; he had never felt better in his life.

He went back into the drawing-room.

" Here you are, my dear."

She accepted a chicken sandwich in silence.

" You're very quiet all of a sudden," he observed, after several side glances towards her small, appealing profile.

" Am I ? " she answered, averting her eyes.

The fixed admiration in his face made her suddenly uneasy. It was impossible not to realise the change in him. For some weeks past, indeed, his manner, attentions and repeated presents had suggested the possibility of a climax approaching, and this did not suit Hetty at all. She did not like it. She wanted to keep on receiving the advantages without giving anything in exchange. To begin with, Hetty was, in her own phrase, a good girl. Actually she had no morality; she was pure by design, saved from sin by the marketable value of her virginity. Her fixed idea was to make a good match, a marriage which would give her money and position, and to this end she knew perfectly how important it was to maintain her maiden state. This was easy, for though her effect was aphrodisiac, in herself she had no sexual impulses—Laura, her sister, had received the double supply. At the outset Barras's attentions had flattered and soothed her. Arthur's imprisonment had fallen as a dreadful blow upon her vanity, removing Arthur at one stroke from her pleasant plannings for the future. She could never marry him now, never, never. It was natural for her to accept Barras's sympathy; the mere fact of being seen with him in public helped tremendously to " save her face "; they were united against a weakling who had wretchedly let them down.

The drawing-room was lit by several of the new shaded lamps, which cast soft pools of light upon the carpet and left the ceiling mysterious and dark.

" How pretty! " she exclaimed, arising and moving towards the shades and fingering their fringes. Then she turned brightly.

" Why don't you smoke a cigar ? "

She had the idea that he would be safer if engaged with a cigar.

" I don't want a cigar," he replied ponderously, his eyes dwelling on her face.

She laughed lightly, as if he had made a joke, and remarked:

" I'll have another cigarette then."

When he had lit her cigarette she moved over to the gramophone and set Violet Lorraine to sing: *If you were the only girl in the world.*

" I'm having tea with Dick Purves and his sister at Dilley's to-morrow," she remarked inconsequently.

His face altered. He had now reached the stage of jealousy; he detested this young Purves. Flight-Lieutenant Dick Purves, the comparatively undistinguished companion of Hetty's childhood, was now the hero of the hour. During the last air raid upon the North-East counties he had flown solo above a wind-driven Zeppelin and released the bomb out of the high darkness which had brought down the dirigible in flames. Tynecastle had gone mad about Dick Purves; it was rumoured he was to have the V.C., and in the meantime he had only to show himself in a restaurant to be greeted by wild demonstrations of hero-worship.

All this recurred to Barras and he said quite sulkily:

" You seem to do a good deal of running after this Purves fellow."

" Oh no," she protested. " You know I don't. It's just that he's so much in demand just now. You know what I mean. Everyone'll be looking at our table and envying us. It makes the party quite exciting."

He moved impatiently, seeing the vapidly handsome youth with his baby blue eyes, the flaxen hair parted in the middle and plastered smooth as wax upon his head, the conceited smile playing about his lips as he smoked his cigarette and continually looked round in search of admiration. He smothered his irritation with difficulty. He had returned to the settee, flushed and breathing rather thickly. And in a moment he said:

" Come and sit here, Hetty."

" I like moving about," she replied airily, " after sitting in the theatre."

" But I want you to sit beside me."

A pause. She saw that it was impossible to refuse without seriously offending him, and unwillingly she came over and sat down on the far corner of the settee.

" You're bullying me to-night," she said.

" Am I ? "

She nodded her head archly, at least, she tried to be arch again, but it was not very successful. She was too conscious of his presence beside her, his congested face, thick-set shoulders, even the fleshy creases of his waistcoat.

" You like the bracelet I gave you ? " he asked at length, fingering the thin platinum strip on her wrist.

" Oh yes," she said quickly. " You spoil me, really you do."

" I'm a pretty rich man," he said. " I can give you a number of things." He was extremely clumsy and inexperienced: his emotion mastered him, almost choked him.

" You've always been kind to me," she said, casting down her eyes.

He reached up to take her hand, but just then the gramophone stopped, and with the sense of being saved she jumped up and went to the machine.

" I'll play the other side," she remarked, and started the record.

He watched her heavily from under his brows with that fixed and vaguely ogling smile. His breathing was more difficult than ever, his under lip protruded.

" It's pretty, that," she went on, " terribly smart and catchy."

She snapped her fingers to the time, resolved not to be led back to the settee again, moving about to the rhythm of the music. But as she passed him, he stretched out suddenly, caught her thin wrist and drew her on to his knees.

It happened so spontaneously, both of them were taken by surprise. She did not know whether or not to scream. She did not struggle. She simply stared at him.

And then, while they remained in this attitude, the door opened behind them suddenly, and Aunt Carrie entered the room. The unusual noise so late at night had caused her to come down, but at the spectacle upon the settee she paused as though turned suddenly to stone. Her eyes dilated with horror. She went absolutely grey. It was the most awful moment of her life. For one dreadful instant she felt she was going to faint, but with a supreme effort she recovered herself, and swinging round she almost fell out of the room. Then, like a haunted spirit, she fled and went stumbling upstairs.

Neither Barras nor Hetty had observed the incident. Barras was blind to all but Hetty, her nearness, her perfume, the pressure of her thin hip bones upon his thighs.

" Hetty," he said thickly, " you know that I'm fond of you."

His words brought her out of that queer, trance-like state.

" Don't," she said, " please don't hold me like that."

He relaxed his hold and put his palm upon her knee.

" Oh no," she cried, resisting vigorously. " You mustn't do that. I don't like it."

" But Hetty——" he panted.

" No, no," she cut him short. " I'm not that kind of girl, not that kind of girl at all."

She hated him suddenly for putting her in this position, for spoiling everything, ending his protection and his presents by this horrible anti-climax. She hated his heavy, congested face, the lines under his eyes, his fleshy nose. She thought, with sudden contrast, of Purves' clear-cut, youthful features, and she cried:

" Let me go, will you. Let me go, or I'll scream."

He answered by pressing her to him and burying his mouth into her neck. She did not scream, but she tore herself free, like a little cat, and banged her hand against his cheek. Then she jumped up, adjusting her dress and her hair, and spat out the words:

" You're a horrid, beastly old man. You're worse than your wretched son. I hate you. Don't you know I'm a good girl. I'm a good girl, I tell you, a good girl. You ought to be ashamed of yourself. I'll never look at you again as long as I live."

He rose up excitedly, trying to speak, but before he had time she dashed out of the room and left him there. He stood for a moment, with his hand outstretched, as if still trying to detain her. His heart was hammering in his side, his brain dazed, his ears buzzing. He had a crushed sense of prostration, of his age, which had defeated his attempt to ravish her. He remained upon his feet, swaying slightly in the empty, softly lighted room, almost overcome by an attack of vertigo. He thought for a second that he was going to have a stroke. Then he raised his hand to his bursting head and sank down limply upon the settee.

XVI

MEANWHILE, seated in the darkness of her own room Aunt Carrie heard the sound of the car setting out for Tynecastle with Hetty. She saw the two soft beams of the headlights slide terrifyingly round the room and in the darkness and the silence which succeeded she trembled wretchedly. What Aunt Carrie had seen in the drawing-room tore at the very roots of her most sacred belief. To think that Richard—*Richard!* Aunt Carrie's trembling increased; she shook in all her limbs with a simply pitiful agitation and the two huge tears which had formed in her eyes were shaken from her eyes by the palsied shaking of her inclined head. Oh dear, oh *dear*, thought Aunt Carrie in a paroxysm of grief.

Aunt Carrie's belief was Richard. For fifteen years she had served Richard with hand and foot and soul. She had served Richard at a distance but that had not prevented her from adoring Richard and locking her adoration jealously in the centre of her being. No other man existed for Aunt Carrie. True, she had at one time entertained an affection for the memory of the late Prince Albert whom she rightly regarded as a good man, but it was a pale moon beside the sun of her adoration for Richard. Aunt Carrie existed for that sun, basked in it, warmed her whole cramped life at it. And now after fifteen years of sunshine, after fifteen years of putting out his slippers, arranging his meals, sorting his laundry, cutting his asparagus, filling his hot-water bottle, religiously keeping the moth out of his woollen underwear, knitting his socks, stockings and scarves—after fifteen years of slavish heavenly servitude Aunt Carrie had seen Richard fondling Hetty Todd upon his knee. In an access of pity and pain Aunt Carrie buried her shaking head in her shaking hands and sobbed bitterly.

Suddenly, while she sat weeping and overcome, she heard Harriet's stick. Whenever Harriet wanted attention she lifted the walking-stick which lay beside her bed and thumped on the wall for Aunt Carrie to come in. It was the recognised procedure and Aunt Carrie knew at this moment that Harriet was thumping for her medicine. But she had not the heart to go in. She could not move for the thought of Richard, this new Richard, this poor Richard, both terrifying and terrible.

Aunt Carrie did not understand that the new Richard was an exfoliation of the old Richard; she did not dream that these new propensities which shocked her were sprouting from the old propensities. She fancied Richard, poor Richard, the victim of some strange calamity. She had no knowledge of what the calamity might be. She simply saw a god turned clown, an archangel become a satyr, and her heart was broken. She cried and cried. Richard with Hetty Todd upon his knee. She cried and cried and could not bear it.

Then with a start she was once again aware of Harriet's knocking. Harriet had been knocking for a full five minutes now and though dimly conscious of that knocking Aunt Carrie had not moved to answer the summons. She could not go in to Harriet with blind and swollen eyes and trembling hands and this insufferable choking in her breast revealing the obvious fact that something was seriously wrong. And yet she must go. Harriet must have her medicine. If Harriet did not have her medicine she would go on knocking louder and louder and bring the house down and there might be some fresh and terrible development which would finish Aunt Carrie for good and all.

Mastering her sobbing as best she could Aunt Carrie wiped her blind and swollen eyes and went fumbling along the corridor to Harriet's room. It was dark in the corridor for it was a dark night and Aunt Carrie in her agitation had not switched on the electric light at the head of the stairs. Harriet's room was dark too, a dim darkness which the green glow of the bedside lamp did little to dispel. Because of her headaches Harriet was averse to a glare and now Aunt Carrie was tremblingly glad of that fact because the dim darkness hid her tear-stained face. She did not offer to switch on the light.

Upon Aunt Carrie's entry Harriet quivered upon the bed where her pale, cow-like outlines were obscurely visible. She was trembling with temper and she bared her false teeth at Aunt Carrie with a click.

" Why didn't you come, Caroline ? " she cried. " I've been knocking for a good half-hour."

Aunt Carrie stifled a big sob. Controlling her voice the best way she could she said:

" I'm sorry, Harriet dear, I can't think what came over me. Shall I—shall I give you your medicine now ? "

But Harriet was not going to let it go so easily as that. She lay there on her back in the bed in the dim darkness of the room surrounded by her bottles and her flat moon face was pale with passion and self-pity.

" It's becoming a disgrace," she said, " the way I'm neglected. I'm lying here with a splitting headache. I'm dying for my medicine and not a soul looks near me! "

Sad and shamefaced, her head bent, blinking her timid swollen eyes, Aunt Carrie gulped:

" I'm sure I beg your pardon, Harriet. Shall I give you your medicine now ? "

" I should think so."

" Yes, Harriet." And hiding her face Aunt Carrie moved blindly to the little table, thinking, oh, dear goodness, let me give Harriet her medicine and get out of this room quickly before I break down completely.

" Your valerian, Harriet ? " she asked.

" No," Harriet said peevishly. " I want my old bromide to-night, the old aromatic bromide that Dr. Lewis gave me. I think that does best with me after all. On the shelf there at the corner."

" Yes, Harriet." Aunt Carrie turned obediently to the shelf and began to grope and fumble amongst the bottles. There were so many bottles too. " Where did you say, Harriet ? "

" There," Harriet snapped. " You're a perfect fool to-night. There under your hand. I put it there myself the last time I was up. I remember perfectly."

" This one ? " Aunt Carrie knew she would break down again. Oh, dear goodness, she thought again, let me get out of here before I give way completely. " This one, Harriet ? "

" No! The one next to it, that green bottle there. What on earth is the matter with you ? Yes, that one, that's right."

Aunt Carrie lifted the bottle dazedly and went to the little table. Her hand shook so much she could hardly pick up the measuring glass.

" How much do you take, Harriet ? "

" Two tablespoonfuls! Don't you know that much ? Can't you even read ? "

But Aunt Carrie could not read, Aunt Carrie was blind and dumb and desolate. Her movements were automatic, her mind far away in a grotesque and horrible land where Richard held Hetty Todd upon his knee. She could only do as she was told and then all that she wanted was to get back into her own room and give way to the floods of tears which welled within her. She fumbled out two tablespoonfuls of the medicine she thought Harriet had indicated. Dimly, through the dim darkness of the room, and the confusion of Harriet's nagging, and the terrible desolation of her own heart, she thought the medicine had a queer smell. But it must be the saltness of her shed and unshed tears which made her think the medicine smelled queer, and Harriet was asking for the medicine and for her to hurry and not to be a fool.

She advanced to the bed, drooping, her head averted, her hand outstretched. Harriet sat up and snatched the medicine glass crossly.

" You've been very stupid and slow to-night, Caroline," she said sharply. " Just when you saw I was dying for my medicine."

Closing her eyes tight in the way she had, Harriet swallowed the medicine at one ill-tempered gulp. She swallowed the medicine at one ill-tempered gulp and for one second remained sitting upright with her eyes tight closed and the medicine glass in her hand. Then she opened her eyes and screamed.

" It's not the medicine." She screamed and the glass fell out of her hand

Aunt Carrie's tears were frozen with horror. For half a second she stood petrified, then she rushed to the switch and turned on the full illumination of the room. She dived for the bottle. A shrill cry came from her like a frightened rabbit. The bottle said liniment. She had given Harriet a poisonous liniment. She screamed, louder than Harriet.

Harriet was clutching her stomach and writhing on the bed. For the first time since she took to her bed Harriet knew real pain. She was in agony. Her face was a greenish white and her lips all puffed and burned by the liniment.

" Water," she gasped feebly, clutching with both hands now, clutching at her fat white stomach. " It's burning on fire."

Swooning with horror Aunt Carrie fled to the water bottle on the wash-basin and tore back with a tumbler of water. But the water would not go down. Harriet could not drink the water; it ran out of her puffed useless mouth all over the nice clean bed-clothes.

Harriet did not seem to realise that the water was wetting her in all the wrong places.

" Water," she still gasped feebly. " It's burning on fire." But however much she tried, she could not drink the water to put out the fire.

A glimmer of reason now pierced Aunt Carrie's panic and, clattering the tumbler upon the commode, she bolted out of the room to fetch a doctor. Along the corridor she raced and down the stairs, her long bunioned feet performing a miracle of speed, and in the back vestibule she brushed into Ann who was on her way upstairs to bed.

Aunt Carrie clutched at Ann.

" The doctor," she moaned. " Telephone for the doctor, any of them, to come at once, quick, quick, the doctor."

Ann took one look at Aunt Carrie. She was a sensible woman, habitually taciturn, and realising that something dreadful and serious had occurred she did not stop to ask any questions. She went instantly to the telephone and very capably rang up Dr. Lewis who promised to come immediately. Ann thought for a moment, then, in case there should be some unavoidable delay, she rang up Dr. Proctor, her own doctor, and asked him to come as well.

Meanwhile Aunt Carrie had darted to the pantry in search of whiting. She had the belief that whiting was an antidote of value. And, returning with the packet of whiting in her hand, she suddenly observed Richard emerge from the drawing-room. He came slowly, disturbed from his own meditation by the unusual flurry, and supporting himself against the lintel of the door he said heavily:

" What is the matter ? "

" It's Harriet," she gasped, holding the whiting so tightly in her agitation that a thin white stream poured out of the corner of the packet.

" Harriet ? " he repeated dully.

She could not wait, she could not endure it; she turned with another cry, and fled upstairs. He followed slowly.

Harriet was still stretched upon her bed under the bright glare, lying amongst her rows and rows of bottles. She had stopped moaning now. She lay sideways and twisted up and her puffed-up mouth was fallen open. A gummy mucus had formed on her blackened lips.

Occasionally Harriet's legs gave a little twitch and with that twitch Harriet's breath came back to her in one quick snore. Sick with terror at that quick infrequent snore, Aunt Carrie mixed the whiting in a frenzy of haste and endeavoured to get some of it past Harriet's swollen lips. She was still trying to do this when Richard entered the room. He stood staring at Harriet, quite stunned.

" Why, Harriet," he said in a thickened voice.

Harriet answered by puking back some of Aunt Carrie's whiting.

Richard came forward in a kind of stupor.

" Harriet," he mumbled again in a besotted sort of way.

He was interrupted by the abrupt entry of Dr. Lewis who walked in cheerfully with his black gladstone bag. But when Dr. Lewis saw Harriet his cheerfulness dropped from him. His manner altered completely and in a subdued tone he asked Aunt Carrie to 'phone for Dr. Scott to come immediately. Aunt Carrie ran to do this at once. Richard retreated to the alcove by the window where, like some strange figure of destiny, he stood silent, watching.

Dr. Scott came with great dispatch and Dr. Proctor, who had walked up from Sleescale, arrived at exactly the same time. The three doctors put their heads together over Harriet. They did a great many things to Harriet. They injected Harriet with little syringes and lifted Harriet's unresistant eyelids and pumped at Harriet's stomach. They pumped and pumped at Harriet's stomach and got the most extraordinary amount out of Harriet's stomach. They all saw what a good dinner Harriet had eaten—it was incredible the quantity of asparagus she had put away. But Harriet did not see. Harriet, being dead, would not see any more.

At last, after a final attempt at resuscitation, the doctors were obliged to give it up and, wiping his forehead, Dr. Lewis advanced towards Richard who still stood rigidly in the window alcove.

" I'm sorry, Mr. Barras, sir." He looked genuinely distressed. " I am afraid we can do no more."

Barras did not speak. Dr. Lewis, looking at him, saw the hard pounding of his temporal arteries, the dusky suffusion of his brow, and mingling with his sympathy came the instinctive thought that Barras's blood pressure must be high. " We have done everything possible," he added.

" Yes," Richard said in a strange voice.

Another wave of sympathy rushed over Dr. Lewis. He gazed at Barras with sorrow in his eyes. He did not know of course that he was, to all intents, looking at Harriet's murderer.

XVII

Even Hilda was distressed. For weeks after Grace and she had returned to hospital from attending their mother's funeral at Sleescale she remained taciturn and brooding. Now she admitted the abnormal atmosphere at the Law. Because she was worried she snapped at the patients, was rude to Ness, went through her work with a tireless efficiency. And towards Grace she was again possessive, jealously affectionate.

It was the end of their half-day off and they were walking slowly along Regent Street, making for Oxford Circus to take a bus for Knightsbridge. Hilda, concluding a bitter diatribe on the humiliating complications of family life, glanced towards Grace sarcastically:

" You're always on about wanting to straighten things out. Now's your chance to go back home and try it."

" Well," Grace said quietly, " I wouldn't be much use now."

" How do you mean ? "

Here their bus swung into the kerb.

Grace waited until they had taken their seats. Then, the minute they sat down she broke the news that she was going to have a baby.

Hilda flushed horribly. She looked as if she were going to be ill. She remained absolutely still while the woman conductor came and took their fares; then in a low, wounded voice she said:

" As if it wasn't bad enough getting married. As if we hadn't had enough trouble lately. You're a fool, Grace, a ghastly little fool."

" I don't think I'm a fool," Grace answered.

" Well, I do," Hilda jerked out, very pale now and bitter. " War babies aren't amusing."

" I never said they were, Hilda, only mine might be."

" Just a silly little fool," Hilda hissed, staring hard in front of her. " Losing your head with that Teasdale and now this. You'll have to leave the hospital. It's sickening. I'll have nothing to do with it. I've kept out of the family complications up till now and I'll keep out of this. Oh, it's so silly, it's so beastly ordinary, it's what silly ordinary beastly little nurses are doing all over the country. Having war babies to war heroes! O God, it's . . . it's disgusting. I'll have nothing to do with it, nothing; you can go away and have your beastly infant by yourself."

Grace said nothing. Grace had a simple way of saying nothing when to say nothing was the best answer in the world. She and Hilda had never really come together again since her marriage with Dan. And now this! That Grace, whom she had petted and protected, dear little Grace, who had slept in her arms, should be having a baby, a war baby, shocked and nauseated Hilda and made her swear that she would keep herself clear of the whole disgusting affair. Tears stood in Hilda's eyes as she rose stiffly at Harrod's and marched out of the bus.

So Grace had to make her own arrangements. Next morning she went to see Miss Gibbs. Traditionally, Miss Gibbs should have been kind, but, like Hilda, Miss Gibbs was not kind. Miss Gibbs said, with a glint of teeth and temper:

" I'm sick and tired of this sort of thing, Nurse Barras. What do you think we have you here for—to nurse the wounded or propagate the race ? We've taken the trouble to train you and educate you to a certain usefulness. This is how you repay us! I'm afraid I'm not very satisfied with you, Nurse Barras. You are not the success your sister has been. *She* doesn't turn round and say she'll have a baby. She stops in the theatre doing her job. This last month you've been three times reprimanded for carelessness and talking in the corridors. And now you come with this story. Things are very difficult. I am not pleased. That will do."

Grace felt almost as if she were not married at all, Hilda and Miss Gibbs had made it sound so indecent. But Grace was not easily cast down. Grace was simple and artless and careless, the most unassertive person in the world, but she had a quiet way of keeping up her heart even although, as Miss Gibbs said, things were difficult.

In her individual way Grace went ahead with her plans. Since her mother's funeral her dread of returning to the Law had increased. She wrote to Aunt Carrie and Aunt Carrie's reply, full of suppressed fears and pious premonitions, and ending with a fluttering postscript, twice underlined, made Grace feel that she could not go home.

She thought a little over Aunt Carrie's letter, then she decided what she would do. Somehow it was easy for Grace to make a decision; matters which would have worried Hilda for a fortnight never worried Grace at all, she hardly seemed to consider them but just made up her mind. Grace had the capacity of making molehills out of mountains. It was because she never thought about herself.

On the first Saturday of January when she had a whole day off from the hospital, Grace took the train into Sussex. She had an idea that she would like Sussex, that it would be warm and sunny there, different from the inhospitable bleakness of the North. She did not know a great deal about Sussex but one of the nurses had once spent a holiday at Winrush, near Parnham Junction, and she gave Grace the name of the woman, Mrs. Case, with whom she had stayed.

The train bowled Grace down into Sussex and bowled her out on the platform of Parnham Junction. It was rather uninspiring, the junction, a few corrugated sheds, empty cattle pens and stacks of dented milk cans. But Grace was not put down.

She spied a signpost on which was written the word Winrush, and as the distance marked down was only a mile she set out to walk to Winrush.

The day was windy and fresh and green. There was a most beautiful smell of moist earth in the wind mixed up with the salty smell of the sea.

It struck her with a kind of pain that, when the world could be so lovely a place as this, the war should go on, mutilating the face of nature, wrecking beauty, destroying men. Her young brow clouded as she walked along. But it cleared slightly when she came to Winrush. Grace felt that Winrush was wonderful the minute she walked into it. Winrush was a very small village, just one little street with the country at one end and the sea at the other. In the middle of that one little street was one little shop which bore a very home-made, very hand-painted notice: *Mrs. Case—Grocery, Drapery, Chemistry.* There was not much sign of chemistry, except for a packet of seidlitz powders in the window, but Grace liked that little shop very much and she looked in the window a long time making out all the things she had known in her youth. There was a sweet called Slim Jim, rather thin and rationed-looking to be sure, and another called Gob Stoppers, big beautiful red and white balls, which were built only to deceive, because you thought there was a nut inside and there wasn't. Altogether Grace entertained herself a good deal at the window, then she took an impulsive breath and walked into the shop. She went into the shop so impulsively she stumbled and nearly fell, for it was dark in the shop and there was a step which she had not seen. As Grace fetched up with a bump against a barrel of nice seed potatoes, from behind the counter a voice said:

" Oh, my dear . . . that wicked old step."

Clinging to the barrel Grace looked at the person who had called her my dear. She decided that it must be Mrs. Case. She said:

" I'm quite all right. I'm always clumsy. I hope I haven't damaged the barrel."

Mrs. Case said, with a little nod of approval at her own repartee:

" Oh, my dear, I hope you haven't damaged yourself."

Grace smiled; anyone would have smiled at Mrs. Case for Mrs. Case was such an oddity, a small old woman with bright beady eyes and a hump back. Mrs. Case's hump oughtn't to have been romantic—it was her spine which was deformed since she had suffered from Pott's disease when a child—but somehow it was romantic; indeed her head was so sunk into her body and her eyes so bright and beady that Mrs. Case actually gave the comical impression of sitting upon her own shoulders like an old hen sitting upon eggs. A brown hen, of course, for Mrs. Case's skin was all a warm wrinkled russet except under her nose where it was darker. The dark spot under Mrs. Case's nose advanced the suggestion that Mrs. Case took snuff. And Mrs. Case did.

" I came in to see you about rooms," Grace went on politely. " Nurse Montgomerie, a friend of mine, recommended me to come."

" Oh yes." Mrs. Case rubbed her hands together reflectively. " I remember her, she was a sparky one. Did you want the rooms for next summer ? "

" Oh no. It would be the spring," Grace said quickly; then she added: " You see, it's rather different with me. You see, I'm going to have a baby."

" I see," Mrs. Case said after a longish time.

" You see, that makes it rather different."

" Yes, my dear, I see. That do make it rather different. Oh, I do see that."

Here Grace burst out laughing; there had been such a lot of seeing between Mrs. Case and herself and it was such a dark little shop. In a minute Mrs. Case laughed too but not altogether heartily. Then she said:

" You do seem fond of a joke, I will say. Have you any objection to my asking if you got your husband in the war or anywhere, my dear ? "

Grace had no objection. Grace told Mrs. Case about Dan. Grace more or less explained herself and Mrs. Case looked friendly again and slightly relieved. She said:

" I did know to be sure, my dear, I can tell a face when I see one. But people have got to be careful what with these Germans and the price of butter. Perhaps you'd like me to show you the rooms, my dear."

The rooms were splendid; at least, that was what Grace thought. There were two of them, connecting, and on the second floor. The floors were uneven and the ceilings given to unexpected bulges; you had to duck your head pretty sharp as you went over to the bed, and the sitting-room was unquestionably not a room to stand in, but they were very clean, these rooms, with fresh darned muslin curtains, a handsome picture of Queen Victoria's coronation, a case of birds' eggs collected by Mrs. Case's nephew, an enlargement of Mrs. Case's husband who had worked on the railway and died of a floating kidney, and a lovely view of the garden. It was a long garden with an orchard of cherry trees and Grace saw them as they would be in spring, all trembling upon the edge of blossom. There were cows in the field beyond and a line of elms. Grace stood at the window and one tiny tear came into her eye—it was all so beautiful, it hurt her a little and made her think of Dan.

She turned to Mrs. Case:

" I'd like to take the rooms if you would let me have them."

Pleased, Mrs. Case nodded.

" You come down, my dear, and have a cup of tea and we'll talk it over."

They went downstairs, Grace and Mrs. Case—Mrs. Case holding to the banister because she had a limp—and they had several cups of tea and talked it over. Mrs. Case was *free* from now onwards and Mrs. Case was never grasping.

" If I said fifteen shillings a week," remarked Mrs. Case, her head to one side like an inquiring bird, " considering the circumstances, my dear, would that be asking too much ? "

" No indeed," said Grace, and the matter was settled without a word of argument.

They continued to talk in growing understanding. Mrs. Case was a mine of useful information. There was a telephone in the village, at old Mr. Purcell's farm, and he would surely oblige them with the use of it. And Fittlehampton was only three miles away and there were numbers of estimable doctors in Fittlehampton. It was a long, long conversation between Grace and Mrs. Case, and though in the end it involved confidences as to how the late Mr. Case's kidney had floated him to glory, it was extremely warm and satisfactory.

Later, as she caught the four-ten from Parnham Junction, Grace felt extraordinarily happy and uplifted. Grace was not clever. Hilda and Miss Gibbs might contend that Grace was careless and stupid and easy-going. Hilda and Miss Gibbs would have recommended Grace to a competent maternity hospital replete with water-beds and douche cans; they would have thought her mad had they seen her setting out for Parnham Junction and pressing her slightly snub nose against the pane of Mrs. Case's shop window.

When she returned to the Home Grace felt so happy she wanted to make it up with Hilda. Glowing, she went to Hilda's room. Standing on the threshold, her cheeks brightened by the fresh night air, her eyes full of confidence and hope, she said:

" I've fixed up, Hilda. I've found the most lovely spot in Sussex."

" Really! " Hilda said coldly. She burned to know where Grace had been and what she had arranged but she was too hurt and proud to show it.

Gradually the glow died out of Grace's face.

" Shall I tell you about it ? " she asked doubtfully.

" Some other time," Hilda said, picking up a magazine and beginning to turn the pages.

Grace turned and went out of the room. The instant the door closed Hilda jumped up to follow her. But Hilda did not follow her—it was against Hilda's nature to follow anyone. She remained frowning, motionless, with a look of pain upon her pale face, then she flung the magazine violently into the corner of the room. That same night there was an air raid over London and when there was a raid Grace usually came to Hilda's room and crept into bed beside her. But to-night, though Hilda waited and longed for Grace to come, Grace did not come.

Time drew on. Whenever she had her half-day Grace went round buying little things that might be useful to her or which, perhaps, might not. She had a great deal of enjoyment that way, especially in the cheap department stores. Dan wrote twice a week. He hoped he could get leave in time for the great event. He would beg, borrow or steal leave, he would desert and swim the Channel—it all depended, of course, even the swimming of the Channel, on whether there was going to be an offensive.

Dan's letters were more of a comfort to Grace than ever. She still hoped that Hilda would be friends again. But on her very last day at the hospital when she climbed up to Hilda's room to say good-bye, Hilda was in the theatre. Grace had to go and leave it at that. She felt sad leaving it that way.

XVIII

On the sixteenth of April, 1917, Stanley Millington returned to Tynecastle. All those intervening weeks Laura had been down at Sawbridge in Warwickshire where Stanley was in the special hospital for functional war neuroses. Joe had heard nothing until he learned indirectly at the office of the telegram to Hilltop announcing their return. Actually, he had not had a line from Laura since that evening when she had rushed from the flat in tears. But the fact that he had received no invitation to be present did not deter Joe from attending at the station. Oh dear, no. Joe had a splendid combination of brazen nerve and rhinoceros hide which enabled him to carry off the most delicate situation. Besides, he knew they would expect him—why not ? He was quite ready to overlook that last scene Laura had made and genuinely prepared to demonstrate his warm admiration for Stanley's heroism and his delight in Stanley's recovery. He drove to the station to meet Stanley full of welcome and sympathy and the manly affection of one good fellow for another.

But when the train got in, one look at Stanley took the beam out of Joe's smile.

" Hello, Stanley," he said, with guarded enthusiasm.

Stanley allowed himself to be shaken hands with.

" I got buried by a shell," he said.

Joe darted a glance at Laura's set face. The platform was very crowded, people pushing past them, porters struggling with luggage, and Stanley standing stiffly there seemed to be in everybody's way. Avoiding Joe's eyes, Laura took Stanley's arm and led him to the barrier. On the way to the barrier Stanley confided in Joe again.

" I got buried by a shell."

They got into the car. All the way from Central Station to Hilltop Joe sat in the car looking sideways at Stanley, yet trying not to look sideways and saying to himself, Good God, could you ever believe it!

He hoped Stanley wouldn't say it again.

But Stanley said it again. For the third time Stanley said:

" I got buried by a shell! "

Looking sideways, yet trying not to look sideways, Joe said:

" That's right, Stanley, you got buried by a shell."

Stanley said nothing. He sat on the edge of the back seat as though cut out of wood. His eyes were away in front of him. His face was quite blank, all his plump body seemed to have melted away from him. He held on to the side of the car with both hands. Mr. Stanley, our Mr. Stanley, held on.

" We're nearly there now," Joe said encouragingly. He had thought that Stanley was all right, absolutely unscratched and good as new. But this was Stanley, this was Stanley here. Joe had to keep telling himself to believe it. This . . . here . . . this. He took a furtive glance towards Laura. She sat with that expressionless look, supporting Stanley with her arm.

The car drew up at Hilltop and Joe jumped out. He was terribly solicitous and helpful.

" This way, now. Watch the step. Careful now."

Mr. Stanley was careful. Holding on, he got out of the car and stood himself on the pavement. He was extremely careful. He kept his head very still as if he wanted to be careful of his head. He looked like a man with a bad stiff neck until you saw that all his body was stiff. The movements of his body were effected by a series of little impulses. The movements were not quite co-ordinated. They were like the movements of a very nearly perfect mechanical man.

Joe said:

" Will I give you a hand ? "

Stanley did not answer—he had a way of not answering—but in a minute he said:

" The legs work pretty well but it's the head. I've been in hospital. I got buried by a shell! "

While Laura remained at the gate giving the chauffeur instructions about the luggage, Joe led Stanley into the house. Bessie, the parlour-maid, stood on the doorstep, waiting to let them in. Bessie's eyes dropped out of her head at the sight of Mr. Stanley. Joe exclaimed very heartily:

" Here's Mr. Stanley back then, Bessie."

Taking no notice of Bessie at all, Stanley walked straight into the lounge and sat down on the edge of a chair. The house did not belong to him and he did not belong to the house. He fingered his waistcoat buttons, then he looked at Bessie. This time he must have noticed Bessie for he explained himself to her.

Without any warning whatever Bessie burst into tears.

Joe took off Mr. Stanley's cap.

" There! " he said kindly. " He'll feel better when he's had his lunch, eh, Bessie." He smiled at Bessie, she was a nice girl Bessie was, he had always treated Bessie nice.

Bessie went out to see about the lunch. Joe could hear her weeping in the kitchen, weeping and telling the cook.

Stanley looked round the lounge. To look round the lounge he did not turn his head, he turned his body very slowly and carefully upon the edge of the chair. As he did so Laura came in.

" It's fine to see you back, Stan," Joe said, rubbing his hands together heartily. " Isn't it, Mrs. Millington ? "

" Yes." Laura went over to Stanley. From her face the strain was almost unsupportable.

" Would you like to come upstairs now ? " she said.

But Stanley answered, no. He hadn't much interest in Laura. In fact he seemed in some queer way to resent Laura's interest in him. He kept looking round the lounge. His eyes were curious, and there was a curious undercurrent in his eyes. They seemed darker, his eyes, with a film of darkness, and below the film the undercurrent played. When the undercurrent played near the surface Stanley's face came nearest to emotion. It was difficult to make out the emotion for it came to the surface so suddenly and darted so suddenly away. But it was a horrible emotion. It was fear, no particular fear, simply fear. Stanley was not afraid of anything. He was just afraid. He finished looking round the lounge. He remarked:

" We had a good journey."

" Fine, fine! "

" Except for the noise."

" The noise, Stanley ? "

" The wheels. In the tunnels."

What the hell, thought Joe.

" I got——"

" That's right," Joe said quickly. The gong sounded softly. " Come on and have your lunch. He'll feel better when he's had his lunch, won't he, Mrs. Millington ? Nothing like a spot of lunch for pulling a man together."

" I've got to lie down after lunch," Stanley said. " That's one of the things the doctors told me. They made me promise before I came away."

They went in to lunch. Laura paused pointedly in the doorway of the dining-room.

" Haven't you got to be at the works ? " she asked in a flat voice, not looking at Joe.

" Not a bit of it," said Joe heartily. " Things are going grand there."

" I think perhaps Stanley would rather you left him now ? "

A flutter of irritation came over Stanley.

" No, no. Let Joe stop on."

A short silence; Joe smiled genially; Laura moved reluctantly away. They sat down to lunch.

When he had finished his soup, to show he had not forgotten his instructions, Stanley remarked again to Joe:

" I've got to lie down after lunch, that's one of the things they told me. And when I get up I've got to do my knitting."

Joe's mouth fell open—it's not funny, he thought, O God, no, it's not funny. In an awed voice he said:

"Your knitting?"

Laura made a movement of pain, as though to interpose. But Mr. Stanley went on, explaining himself; he seemed happiest when explaining himself:

"My knitting helps the head. In the hospital I learned to do my knitting after I got buried by the shell."

Joe removed his eyes hurriedly from Stanley's face. Knitting, he thought . . . knitting. He thought back. He kind of remembered Stanley, and Mr. Stanley's remarks in this same room a year before. The topping fellow who wanted a smack at the Fritzes, don't you know, for St. George and England, the full-blooded Briton who wished he'd joined the Flying Corps . . . great adventure, what? Very lights, Public Schools Battalion, number nines . . . *our* Mr. Stanley, who thought war simply *marvellous*. Christ, thought Joe, I wonder what he thinks about it now; and all of a sudden Joe wanted to laugh.

But at that moment Stanley very nearly began to cry.

"I can't," he whimpered, "I can't."

Laura intervened in a low voice, bending forward:

"What's wrong, dear?"

Stanley's face twitched under its frozen mask.

"I can't close the mustard-pot." He was trying to close the mustard-pot and he could not do it. He was beginning to shake all over because he could not close the mustard-pot.

Joe jumped up.

"Here," he said, "let me do it for you." He shifted the spoon so that the lid of the mustard-pot could close and while he was about it he took his napkin and wiped the gravy off Stanley's chin. Then he sat down.

All at once Laura seemed to give way. She rose abruptly. In a shaking voice she excused herself.

"I must see to something." With her head averted she went out.

Silence for a few minutes while Joe turned things over carefully in his mind. At length he said:

"You know it's great to see you back, Stan, old man. We're making a lot of money at the works these days. Last month was marvellous."

Stanley said, yes.

"That Dobbie fellow we have in the office isn't worth a damn though, Stanley. Seein' you're back now we ought to get rid of him."

Stanley said, yes.

"In fact I was thinkin' myself I could give him his notice at the end of this month. Does that seem to be all right with you, Stanley?"

Stanley said, yes. Then Stanley got up from the table very stiff and sudden, although Joe had not nearly finished his dessert. He said:

" I've got to go to bed."

" Certainly, Stan, old man," Joe agreed blandly. " You'll do whatever you like." In an access of helpfulness Joe jumped up and took Stanley's arm. Laura was waiting at the foot of the stairs, a small damp handkerchief clenched tightly in her hand. She made to take Stanley's arm but Joe was not to be dispossessed. And Stanley himself appeared to lean on Joe, to depend upon him. He said peevishly:

" Leave me, Laura." Joe helped him upstairs to his room and helped him to undress.

Stanley stripped sheer skin and bone. Stripped, Stanley was less like a mechanical man, and more like a mechanical corpse. He seemed ready for his bed but before he got into bed he went through a quiet little ritual. He got down and looked under the bed then he got up and looked under the pillows. He looked inside the two cupboards and behind the curtains of both windows. Then he climbed into bed. He lay flat upon his back with his hands and legs stretched out straight. His dead, wide-open eyes stared towards the ceiling. Joe tiptoed from the room.

In the lounge at the foot of the stairs Laura was waiting on Joe with red and swollen eyes. She faced him determinedly, biting her lower lip that way he knew so well.

" I've just one thing to say." She spoke with difficulty, her breast rising and falling quickly. " And that's to ask you to keep away from this house."

" Now, don't, Laura," he remonstrated mildly. " You're in a spot of trouble with Stan and you want all the help you can get."

" You call it help! "

" Why not ? " he reasoned soothingly. " There's nobody more upset than me, nobody in all the world, but we've got to discuss things." He shook his head sensibly. " Stanley's finished as far as the front is concerned. I'm thinking about the works . . ."

" You would," she said bitterly.

" I mean," he threw out his hand with the air of a man who has been wronged. " Oh, damn it all, Laura, give us some credit. I want to help you both. I want to get Stanley down to the works, interest him in things again, give him all the hand I can."

" If I didn't know you I'd think you meant it."

" But I do mean it. After all, we've got to help one another over this. Honest to God, Laura, I'll do what I can."

There was a silence, her swollen eyes remained fixed upon his face; her breath came quicker, agonised.

" I don't believe you'll do anything," she choked. " And I hate you for what you've done . . . almost as much as I hate myself." She spun round and walked rapidly out of the lounge.

He remained where he was, caressing his chin gently with his hand; then he smiled into himself and left the house. He came back next morning, though, bustling in about eleven to keep his promise to take Stanley to the works. Laura had gone out but Stanley was up and dressed, seated upon the edge of a chair in the lounge playing the gramophone to himself. The gramophone was all right, of course, but the music, the music Stanley was playing, set Joe's teeth on edge. Joe protested:

"Why don't you play something lively, Stanley? Something out of the Bing Boys, what?"

"I like this," Stanley said, putting the same record on again. "It's the only one I like. I've been playing it all morning."

Puzzled, Joe endured the record once more. The combination of the record and Stanley listening to the record was horrible. Then Joe walked over and looked at it. *Marche Funèbre*, Chopin. Joe swung round.

"Holy smoke, Stanley, what d'you want with this stuff? Come on now, brace up, I've got the car at the door and we're all set. We're going down to the works."

They drove quietly to the works and went straight into the melting-shop. Joe had arranged it beforehand. All the Union Jacks were hung and a big banner, which Joe had raked out of an old locker, stretched across the shop—WELCOME. When Stanley walked into the shop with Joe everybody stopped work and gave him a rousing cheer. A great many women were in the shop now, Joe found them much cheaper and quicker than the older men, and these women cheered wildly. Stanley faced the cheering women, the women in the overalls, the women who were making shrapnel bullets for the shells. He looked as if he did not quite know what to do before all these women, he seemed more than ever to belong to nowhere. In an undertone Joe suggested:

"Say something, Stanley, say anything you like." And he held up his hand for silence.

Mr. Stanley faced the women. He said:

"I got buried by a shell. I've been in hospital."

There was another cheer and under cover of the cheer Joe prompted swiftly:

"Say you're glad the output is going up and you hope they'll keep on working like they're doing."

Mr. Stanley repeated in a high voice:

"I'm glad the output is going up and I hope you'll keep on working like you're doing."

Another cheer, a loud long cheer. Then Joe took the matter in hand. He raised his hand again for silence. He thrust his hat well back on his head, put his thumb in his arm-hole and beamed on them. He said:

"You're all delighted to see Mr. Stanley and so am I. Mr. Stanley isn't going to talk about what he's done so I'll do a little of the talking instead. I'm not going to say much because you've got work to do for your country, work that must be done, and you can't knock off to listen to anybody; but I'm going to say this: I'm going to say to his face here that we're proud of Mr. Stanley. I'm proud to be associated with him in business and I know you're proud to work for him. We've been making plans, Mr. Stanley and me, and he says he hopes you'll all continue to do your bit here just the same as he's done his bit in France. You've got to work, you understand, work like hell to keep the output up. Now that's all, but before you go back to work I want us all to sing the National Anthem and then lift the roof off with a cheer for Mr. Stanley."

A silence fell, then—very affectingly, because of the women's voices—they sang *God Save the King.* It was extremely moving, there were tears in Joe's eyes.

When they had asked God to save their king they cheered Mr. Stanley, they cheered Joe, they cheered mostly everybody. Then in a mood of almost religious fervour they went back to the shrapnel, the Mills bombs and the eighteen-pounder shells.

Joe and Stanley started along the corridor towards the office. But they did not get very far. Half-way down the passage there stood an enormous shell. Joe had not made that shell although Joe would greatly have liked to make such a shell as that. The shell was a present to Joe from John Rutley, old Rutley of Yarrow, who sat with him on the Munitions Committee. Rutley's had an enormous plant and turned out enormous shells and Joe was extremely proud of that beautiful seventeen-inch shell which indicated many things, not the least being that John Rutley was, so to speak, a friend of Joe's. The shell had been mounted by Joe upon a fine polished wood base and now it stood, shining and gigantic, pointing its snout heavenwards in a kind of silent ecstasy.

It was the shell which stopped Stanley. He stared at the big shining shell with those frozen eyes.

Joe clapped the snout of the shell affectionately.

" She's a beauty, eh? I call her Katie! "

Mr. Stanley did not speak but the dark light played and played beneath the film upon his eyes.

" I wish we were making the big stuff," Joe remarked. " There's a hell of a lot of money in big stuff too. Oh well, come on in the office now. I've got Morgan and Dobbie there and we're going to talk to them."

But Mr. Stanley did not come on, he could not get past the shell. He stared and stared at the shell. It was a shell like this which had blown him up. His soul shrank and shuddered before that shell.

" Come on, man," Joe said impatiently. " Don't you know they're waiting on you? "

" I want to go home." His voice sounded very odd and he began to drag himself backwards stiffly from the shell.

Christ, thought Joe, he's at it again. He took Stanley's arm to help him past the shell. But Stanley could not get past the shell. The skin of his forehead twitched, and in his eyes the buried agony of fear came leaping, leaping underneath the film. He gasped:

" Let me go. I want to go home."

" You're all right, Stanley," Joe said. " Take it easy, now, you're all right. It won't bite you, it isn't even filled. Be sensible, Stanley, man."

But Stanley could not be sensible. All Stanley's splendid sense had got blown out of Stanley by a shell like this in France. Stanley's whole face was twitching now, a rapid twitching, and the fear behind his eyes was horrible to see.

" I've got to go home." Hardly able to say it now. Under the dead cold face worked an unbelievable agony and excitement.

Joe gave a groan of resignation.

" All right, then, you'll go home, Stanley. Don't make a song about it." Joe didn't want a scene at the works, good God, no, not when everything had gone off so well. Still holding Stanley's arm Joe walked Stanley very nicely down the shop. Joe's smile indicated that everything was perfectly in order. Mr. Stanley was not quite fit yet, just out of hospital you see, oh yes, just that!

The car drove off to Hilltop with Stanley sitting upright on the back seat, and Joe, with a last friendly, reassuring smile, returned to his own office. He shut himself in his office and lit a cigar. He smoked the cigar thoughtfully. It was a good cigar, but Joe did not think about the cigar. He thought about Stanley.

There was no doubt about it, Stanley was washed out. The minute he had clapped eyes on Stanley at the station he had seen it; this shell-shock was a bigger thing than he had ever imagined. Stanley was going to be months and months before he got back to normal. If he ever did get back. In the meantime Joe would have to take Millington's in hand more than ever. And that was hardly fair on Joe unless Joe got a little more out of Millington's than he had been getting. Hardly fair. Joe carefully inspected the glowing end of his cigar, calculating shrewdly. About two thousand a year he was pulling down at the moment, all in, as Jim Mawson would have put it. But that was nothing, nothing at all. There was the future to think about. And God, what a chance this was to consolidate his future, to get in big, oh, bigger than ever. Joe sighed ever so gently. There would have to be some sort of readjustment . . . that was the word . . . in Millington's. Yes, that was it, that was the exact idea.

Moistening his lips Joe reached for the telephone. He rang up Jim Mawson. Never before had he been so glad to know Mawson, to feel sure of his co-operation. A clever fellow Jim, who knew exactly how to set about a thing and steer just the right side of trouble.

" Hello, Jim, that you, ole man ? " Joe took pains to put the case justly to Mawson. And sympathetically, too. " It would break your heart to see the poor fellow, Jim. He's perfectly sensible and all that, as sane as you and me, but it's his nerves. Shell-shock, you understand.

Yes, certainly, shell-shock, that's right, Jim, you've got me."

A pause while Mawson's voice came back over the wire. Then Joe said:

" To-morrow night at your house then, Jim. Certainly, I know there's no hurry. Certainly I know Snagg, I met him at Bostock's, didn't he handle that contract case? Yes, certainly, oh, what the *hell*, Jim, what do you think I am . . . now *listen*, oh, all right, not on the 'phone . . . certainly . . . how's the wife? . . . that's grand, Jim, that certainly is grand, all right, ole man, so long for the meantime."

Joe hung up the receiver; but only for a minute. His big hand reached out again, he rang Laura at Hilltop, his voice quiet, sympathetic, reasonable:

" I must talk to you, Laura, honestly I must. Ah, what's the use going on that way, Laura. Surely I know how you feel about it, I don't blame you, but we're only human, aren't we, and we've got to make the best of it. Yes, yes, call me anything you like, I daresay I deserve it, but for God's sake let's get things straight. I've got to see you, there's no getting away from it. What! All right, all right, Laura, I can't force you to meet me, if you won't come, you won't . . . but I'll be at the flat all evening in case you should change your mind. . . ." He continued talking for a couple of minutes more before he realised that she had hung up at the other end. Then he smirked, replaced the receiver and fell joyously upon his work.

That night he went without his usual dinner at the County and got home by six o'clock. Whistling, he built up the fire, helped himself to whisky and a cold mutton pie, then washed and brushed himself, slipped on his new checked dressing-gown and sat down to read the paper and wait.

From time to time his eyes strayed towards the clock. Occasionally the sound of a car in the crescent outside made him straighten expectantly in his chair. As the hands of the clock moved round, a frown began to mar the smooth handsomeness of his brow, but at nine o'clock the sharp ring of the door bell sent him eagerly to his feet.

Laura entered with a kind of nervous violence. She wore a raincoat and an old brown hat that fitted closely on her head. There were splashes on her shoes; he had the feeling that she had walked all the way from Hilltop. She was very pale.

" I came, you see," she declared with bitter hostility, her hands thrust in her raincoat pockets, her whole figure braced. " Now what have you got to say? "

He did not attempt even to approach her. He kept his eyes on the floor.

" I'm glad you came, Laura."

" Well? " she queried in that same suppressed voice. "You'd better say it quickly. I can't wait long."

" Sit down," he said in a brotherly voice. " We can't talk like this. You're tired, you look absolutely all in." Tactfully he turned away and began to stir the fire into a fresh blaze. She watched him with a cold irony, then with a sigh of fatigue she let herself sink into a chair. She said bitterly:

" I haven't had a minute's peace since I left this wretched room."

" I know." He sat back in his own chair, chastened, staring into the fire. " But we couldn't foresee this, Laura, how could we ? "

" Every time I look at him," a sob rose in her throat. " Every minute of the day. He can't bear me now. You've seen that, haven't you ? He seems to hate to have me near him. He's got to go to Bournemouth, to a rest home there. He actually asked me not to come with him. It serves me right, it serves me right. O God, how I loathe and detest myself."

He made a mutter of sympathy.

" Don't," she cried. " I loathe and detest you too."

" Stanley doesn't need to know anything about us," he reasoned. " Not one single thing."

" I should hope not." She turned on him with savage irony. " You don't propose to tell him, do you ? "

" Oh no," he answered in a queer voice. He got up and went to the sideboard where he mixed a stiff whisky and soda. " Not if you stand in with me, Laura. Here, you better try this. You look absolutely done."

She accepted the tumbler mechanically, still staring at him.

" How do you mean, stand in with you ? "

" Well, we got to be friends, Laura." He took a sip at his own drink, meditating sombrely. " Friends all round, that's my motto, I've always been a friendly sort of chap. You see it would be pretty awkward if there was a burst up. It wouldn't do Stanley any good, or any of us for that matter. Stanley needs me in the business now, I've all sorts of ideas for expanding, amalgamating. Why, only the other day I was talking to Jim Mawson of Tynecastle. You know Mawson—one of the best business men in Tynecastle. Well, if Mawson and Stanley and myself got together, you've no idea how we could reorganise the foundry. We'd make a perfect gold mine out the place."

" I see," she whispered, " I see what you want. You're sick of me in any case. And now you want to use me, use all that's happened between us——"

" For God's sake, Laura, have a heart. This is absolutely on the level! We'll have a company, there's pots of money in it for all of us."

" Money! You think of nothing but money. You're contemptible."

" I'm only human, Laura. We're all only human. That's why I fell in love with you."

" Don't! " she said fiercely.

A silence came; she drank her whisky. It restored her. Joe at least was practical in what he did. She took a look at him, hating him. For all these weeks she had hated him, visualizing his loudness, his vulgarity, his insatiable egoism, his physical grossness. And yet he wasn't really gross, she had to admit it despite herself. He was handsome, extraordinarily handsome. His figure was beautifully muscled, he had the most winning brown eyes. And she had taught him so much, how to dress, to groom himself: in a sense she had created him.

" Are you still angry with me, Laura ? " he asked humbly.

" I'm not even thinking about you." A pause. Rudely, she held out her empty glass. " Here, get me another of these. I think I deserve it."

He hurried to obey. He sighed.

" I've thought about you a lot these last weeks. I've missed you."

She gave a short laugh, swallowing her drink as though it was bitter.

" You're lying. You've got off with someone else while I was away. While I've been nursing a man who loathes me, a man who's been blown up and dried up, you've been sleeping with some other woman. Come on, now, own up, speak the truth."

" I am speaking the truth," he lied earnestly.

" I don't believe you," she said; but for all that her heart gave a sudden throb. She added: " In any case it doesn't matter. I'm myself again, thank God. I don't care if you have a hundred women. I'm going to devote myself to Stanley now."

" I know, Laura," he said. " Just let's be friends." He reached over to take her empty glass but instead he took her hand.

" How dare you, how *dare* you." She snatched her hand away. Her eyes filled with tears, she began all at once to cry.

" Just friends, Laura," he pleaded. " Just the best of pals."

" How can you make me so unhappy. Haven't I been through enough? I'm going . . . going." She rose quite blindly and at the same moment his arms were round her, gently restraining, holding her with confident strength.

" You can't go like this, Laura."

" Leave me, leave me, for God's sake leave me." She tried to break away from him, weeping hysterically.

" Please, Laura, please."

As she struggled she felt herself trembling. She felt the trembling of her body against his.

" Oh, how can you, Joe," she cried. " How could you be so beastly to me."

" Laura! " He kissed her.

" No, Joe, no," she whispered weakly. But his lips again prevented her from speaking. Everything dissolved and fell away from her except the sense of his nearness. Reaction flooded her too. All those awful weeks at Sawbridge, her loneliness, Stanley's peevishness—the deadly monotone of the machine man, whose sex lay buried in that shell-hole, somewhere in France. She closed her eyes. A shiver went over her. Joe didn't really love her, he was merely using her, would throw her over. But it was no use for her to try. She felt him carrying her to the bedroom.

When she got back to Hilltop it was nearly ten o'clock and Mrs. John Rutley sat waiting in the lounge.

"Oh, my dear," said Mrs. John, rising and taking both Laura's hands in warm sympathy. "They told me you'd gone out to get some air but I simply had to wait. I'm so sorry about Stanley, my dear. I had to run down. You look so upset. And no wonder, as I was saying to John, you were always such a little pair of love-birds. But don't you worry, my dear, you'll soon get him right."

Laura stared at the older woman. Her face broke into a distorted smile.

XIX

TOWARDS the middle of November 1917 Martha heard about Annie Macer. It was Hannah Brace who told Martha that sharp winter morning and Hannah Brace was distressed that such a misfortune should have come on a decent girl like Annie. She stood on the pavement of the Terraces, her blowsy hair gathered under a man's peaked cap, her nose blue with cold, her figure sagging, the door-mat she had come out to shake dangling from her hand.

"You could have knocked me down with a feather," she said, "when I saw Annie was that way!"

The dismay in Hannah's good-natured face was not reflected in Martha's. Her expression revealed nothing as, without waiting for the gossip which Hannah so obviously desired, she went into her own house and closed the door. But for all that a great rush of triumphant vindication overwhelmed her. She sat down at the able and rested her chin on her big knuckled fist and thought about what Hannah had just told her. A stern smile came upon her lips. She had always said, hadn't she, that Annie was no good, and now it was proved that Annie was no good. She was right, she, Martha Fenwick was right.

Sammy was responsible, of course. Sammy had been out a great deal during his last leave; he had even, to her serious displeasure, stayed away from home an entire week-end. And this was the result. Yes, Sammy was responsible; but that was nothing. By Martha's reasoning the man was never to blame. Martha was glad, yes, she admitted it to herself savagely, glad that things had turned out this way. Sammy would not respect Annie now. Never! Martha knew there was nothing a man hated worse than to get a girl in trouble. Besides Sammy was away, far out of the way in France. And when he came home she, Martha, would manage Sammy. She would manage Sammy away from Annie Macer. She knew how she'd do it, she knew exactly.

The first step, naturally, was to see that Hannah Brace was right. At eleven o'clock that same forenoon Martha put on her coat and walked slowly down Cowpen Street listening for the sound of Annie's bell. At present the Macers were having a struggle; Pug had drifted into the army and old Macer, landlocked by mines and handicapped by increasing rheumatism, had to make the best of it by hand-lining off shore for whiting. Annie helped him with the hand-lining, digging the lugs when the tide was out, putting her shoulder to the boat in the early morning, baiting the snecked steel hooks, setting with her father out beyond the harbour while the dawn broke gently over the grey water. Then, in the forenoon, when the town had wakened, Annie hawked the catch with a creel on her back and a little brass bell in her hand through the streets of Sleescale.

This forenoon Martha heard Annie's bell at the foot of Cowpen Street. It was always an irritation to Martha, that bell of Annie's, but to-day when Martha saw Annie she forgot all about the bell. One eagle glance from Martha's eye deduced the fact that Hannah Brace was right. Annie was that way.

Along the street Martha went, slow and formidable, until she came abreast of Annie, who had laid down her creel on the pavement to serve Mrs. Dale of the Middlerig Dairy. Martha stood watching Annie while Annie took the clean gutted fish in her clean chapped hands and put them on the plate Mrs. Dale gave her. Martha had to admit that Annie was clean. Her weather-blown face was hard scrubbed, her blue apron newly washed and stiff from fresh ironing, her arms, bare to the elbow, pink and firm, her eyes clear as though they had been polished by the wind. This grudging admission of Annie's cleanness made Martha more bitter. With her lips drawn in she stood waiting until Annie had finished with Mrs. Dale.

Annie straightened herself from the creel at last. She noticed Martha and her face lightened slowly, imperceptibly. Annie's expression never changed quickly; it had a quiet, almost stolid repose, but now it did undoubtedly brighten. She thought Martha wanted her fish and that was an honour which Martha had never bestowed on Annie before. Annie smiled diffidently.

" I have nice whiting, Mrs. Fenwick," she said. A pause while Annie reflected she might have been too forward. So she added: " They're bigger than usual, anyway."

Martha did not say anything, she continued to look at Annie.

Annie did not understand yet. With an easy movement of her fine body, she lifted the creel by its black leather strap and showed the catch to Martha.

" Dad and me got these at four this morning," she said. " They take best with a mist on the water. I'll put a couple on your step as I go past, there's no need for you to carry them up." It was a long speech for Annie, an extremely long speech; it was extremely long because Annie was extremely anxious to please.

Martha said nothing but, as Annie raised her eyes from the freshly caught fish, Martha gave Annie one insolent ice-bound look: the look knew everything, said everything, was significant of everything. Annie understood. Then Martha said:

"I don't want your fish nor anything else you're like to have." Then she waited, tall, erect, formidable, waiting for Annie to answer her back. But Annie did not speak. Her eyes fell towards her creel, as if humiliated.

A cruel wave of triumph swept over Martha. She still waited until, seeing that Annie would not speak, she turned, with her head high in the air, and walked away.

Annie lifted her eyes and stood looking after Martha's retreating figure. There was a nobility about Annie at that moment. Her open, weather-burnished face expressed neither shame nor confusion nor anger, but a kind of sorrow was mirrored there. She remained for a moment as though steeped in some profound regret, then she shouldered her basket and went up the street. Her bell rang out quiet and clear.

After that Martha went out of her way to humiliate Annie. She did not hesitate to "give Annie her character" in the Terraces. It was a strange reaction. Martha was never one for idle talk: as for scandal, she scorned and despised the mention of the word; but now she took a bitter pleasure in speading the news of Annie's trouble.

She made it her duty to encounter Annie as often as she could and she never passed without giving Annie that withering look. Nothing was said; but there was always that look. She discovered a favourite walk of Annie's, a walk Annie took by herself in the evening, which was the only time she had a moment to herself, a walk which led along the shore and up the steep hill beyond the Snook. Martha, who never went beyond the Terraces of the town, began to take this walk too. Sometimes Annie was on the cliff first, staring out across the sea, and sometimes Martha was there first; but whatever the way of it Martha always gave Annie that silent look. Often Annie seemed to wish to speak to Martha, but Martha's look froze all speech. For years she had suffered because of Annie; now Annie could suffer because of her!

Not that Martha gave a hint of the situation to Sammy; in her letters to Sammy Martha never said a word. She was too wise for that. She sent him more parcels than ever, most wonderful parcels she sent to Sammy; she made Sammy feel her worth. She had Sammy's allowance every week on Sammy's ring paper and that allowance enabled Martha to do what she wanted. She could never have got along without Sammy's allowance.

The days passed and the weeks passed. Little enough was happening in Sleescale. At the Neptune they were well advanced with the new road into the Paradise. Jenny was still living in Tynecastle with her people and Martha never heard from her. Harry Ogle, son of old Tom Ogle, had been elected to the Town Council. Hans Messuer had been removed from the cottage hospital to an internment camp. Mrs. Wept opened her pie shop on two days of the week. Jack Reedy had returned from the front with bad gas-poisoning. Letters from David arrived quite regularly, once a month. Life still went on.

And Annie Macer still went on hawking the fish which she and her father hand-lined in the early morning when the pale mist lay on the water. Everyone said it was a disgrace that Annie should go on hawking fish, but Annie could not very well do anything else. Annie's brother, Pug, was not the kind to send allowances and hawking that fish was the livelihood of Annie and her dad. So Annie went on with it in spite of the disgrace.

But one day Annie did not go on with it. The day was the 22nd March and on that day Annie did not appear with her basket and her little bell. Martha looked for Annie in vain. And Martha thought with a savage thought, Is this her time, is she come to it at last ?

It was not Annie's time. In the evening Martha took the walk along the shore, past the Snook and up the cliff beyond. She took the walk partly from her newly formed habit and partly to see if Annie would be there. Annie was not there. And Martha stood erect and vigorous, looking down the path, thinking her savage thought that it was Annie's time, that Annie had come to the bearing of her bastard at last.

But it was not Annie's time. As Martha stood there she stiffened slightly, for at the foot of the cliff path she saw Annie, and Annie was coming up the path.

Annie came up the path slowly and Martha waited with her look ready, waited until Annie should come up. To-night Annie took a long time. She climbed slowly, slowly as though labouring under a great burden. But at last she got to the top. Then Martha threw her look at Annie.

But Annie took no notice of the look. She paused before Martha, unusually pale and breathless from her climb and she stooped slightly as if tired, as though still she laboured under a great burden. She gazed at Martha, then she gazed out to the sea, as she always had done, gazing towards the place where Sammy might be. Then, as though she spoke the simplest fact:

" Sammy and me got married in August."

Martha drew back as if she had been stung. Then she straightened herself.

" It's a lie," she said.

Still looking towards the place where Sammy might be, Annie said again, sadly, almost wearily:

"We were married, Sammy and me, his last leave in August."

"It's not true," Martha said. "It can't be true." With a triumphant rush, "I'm getting Sammy's allowance."

Still looking towards the place where Sammy might be, Annie said:

"We wanted you to get the allowance, Sammy and me. We didn't want it stopped on you."

Martha was harsh and pale with anger. Her masterful pride throbbed in her. Between her clenched teeth she said:

"I don't believe it. I'll *never* believe it."

Slowly Annie withdrew her eyes from the place where Sammy might be. Her eyes were dry. A great shadow lay upon her face, she looked more than ever as though she laboured under a heavy burden. She handed Martha the telegram in her hand.

Martha took the telegram. The telegram was to Mrs. Annie Fenwick. The telegram said: *Regret to inform you your husband Corporal Samuel Fenwick killed in action March 19th.*

XX

On the 24th of April, 1918, Arthur's sentence expired and at nine o'clock of that day, dressed in his own clothes, he passed through the prison gates. He came out of the grey stone archway with his head down and walked cautiously away. It was a grey, dank morning, but to Arthur the sense of light and space was unbelievable. He could scarcely understand, his eyes blinked apprehensively. Why was there no cell, no wall to stop him? He walked faster, suddenly aware that the walls lay behind him now. He wanted to get away.

But soon he had to give over walking quickly; he wasn't fit for that. He was like a man just out of hospital, very weak and easily tired, with a stoop and a sickly pallor ingrained into him. His hair was cropped close, too, right down to the bone—Warder Collins had seen to that a couple of days before, it was Collins' last little joke—so that he looked as if he had been through an operation on his brain, a serious operation on his brain in that large hospital he had left behind.

It was this operation on his brain, no doubt, which made him glance nervously at everybody he met to see if they were looking at him. Were people looking at him? Were they looking? Were they?

He walked for about a mile until he came to the outskirts of Benton, then he went into a workman's coffee-house: *Good pull up for lorries* was on the sign outside. He sat down, keeping his hat on to cover his shaven head, and his eyes on the table, and he ordered coffee and two poached eggs. He did not look at the man who served him, but he saw the man's boots and dirty apron and yellow nicotined fingers. The man asked to be paid whenever he brought the coffee and poached eggs.

Bowed over the table with his hat on, Arthur drank the coffee and ate the poached eggs. The strong knife and fork felt clumsy in his hands after the tin cutlery of the prison, and his clothes sat loosely and awkwardly upon him. He had shrunk a little in the place back there. But he thought, I'm out. I'm out, he thought. Oh, thank God, I'm out.

The coffee and eggs made him feel better and he was able to look at the man on the way to the door and ask him for a packet of cigarettes.

The man had red hair and an expression of vulgar inquisitiveness.

" Twenty ? "

Arthur nodded abruptly and put a shilling on the counter.

The red-haired man put on a confidential air.

" Been in long ? " he asked.

Then Arthur knew that the man knew he had been in prison—probably most of the convicts stopped at this place on their release—and a wave of colour rushed into his sallow face. Without answering he walked out of the shop.

The first cigarette was not very good, it made him slightly giddy but it made him feel less conspicuous in the street. A little boy going to school saw him open the packet and ran after him asking for the cigarette card. Arthur fumbled eagerly for the card with his calloused and insensitive fingers and held it out. It helped him in some mysterious way to be spoken to by this little boy, to feel for an instant the warm contact of his hand. He felt himself suddenly more human.

At Benton terminus he took the tram to Tynecastle and in the tram he sat thinking with his eyes on the floor. When he had been in prison he could think of nothing but the outside. Now he was outside he could think of nothing but the prison. The good-bye of the governor, of the prison chaplain, rang in his ears: " I hope this has made a man of you." The doctor's inspection: " Pull up your shirt, let your trousers down." Hicks's final pleasantry over the shoulder at exercise: " Little bit of skirt to-night, Cuthbert ? " Yes, he remembered. He remembered particularly the last satire of Warder Collins. Something had made him offer his hand to Collins when the warder had made the key sound for the last time. But Warder Collins had said:

" Not on your bloody life, Cuthbert," and expectorated neatly into Arthur's hand. As he thought about it Arthur instinctively wiped his palm against his trouser leg.

The tram blundered into Tynecastle, through crowded familiar streets, and finally stopped outside Central Station. Arthur got out of the tram and entered the station. He meant to buy a ticket for Sleescale, but when he got to the booking-office he hesitated. He could not bring himself to do it. He went up to a porter.

" When is the next train for Sleescale ? "

" Eleven fifty-five."

Arthur looked at the big clock above the bookstall. He had five minutes in which to take his ticket and catch the train. No, no, he couldn't decide so quickly, he didn't want to go home yet. He had been informed, at the time, of his mother's death and now, with a queer self-deception, he tried to attribute his indecision to the fact that she was gone. He wavered away from the booking-office and stood before the bookstall, studying a placard. *Big Push Begins.* He liked the crowd about him, the bustle, movement, obscurity. As a girl brushed past him he remembered Hicks's remark again: Little bit of skirt to-night, Cuthbert ?

He reddened and turned away. To put off time he went into the refreshment-room and ordered a mug of tea and a roll. Why disguise the fact ? He wanted to see Hetty. He was so weak, so tired, so sick with pain and longing, he wanted to be with her, to fall on his knees before her, put his arms about her. Hetty really loved him. She would understand, pity and console him. A melting tenderness consumed him, nothing else mattered, tears filled his eyes. He must, he must see Hetty.

Towards one o'clock he left the station and started to walk towards College Row. He took the slight incline slowly, partly because he was quite exhausted, but chiefly because he was afraid. The mere thought of seeing Hetty again drove the blood from his heart. When he reached No. 17 he was in a pale anguish of expectation. He stood on the opposite side of the street staring across at the Todds' house. Now that he was here he shrank from going in, a host of unhappy thoughts deterred him. How pleased they would be to see him, walking in unexpectedly like this, straight from prison. No, he had not the courage to walk up these steps and ring the bell.

He hung about in an agony of indecision, longing with all his soul to see Hetty, hoping he might have the luck to find her leaving or entering the house. But there was no sign of Hetty. Towards three o'clock the faintness came over him again and he felt he must sit down. He turned towards the Town Moor, which lay at the top of College Row, making for one of the benches under the lime trees, telling himself he would return later and resume his watch. He crossed the road, his feet dragging languidly, and, at the corner, he walked straight into Laura Millington.

The unexpectedness of the meeting was quite startling; it made him catch his breath. At first Laura did not recognise him. Her face, wearing a look of preoccupation, almost of apathy, remained unchanged. She made to pass on. And then she knew him.

" Why, Arthur! " she gasped, " it's you."

His eyes remained upon the pavement.

" Yes," he stammered, " it's me."

She gazed at him intently, her expression altered, shocked from its fixed melancholy.

" Have you been to see my father ? "

He shook his head dumbly with eyes still averted. The hopelessness in his attitude gave her a renewed pang. Deeply touched, she came up to him and took his arm.

" You must come in," she said. " I'm going there now. You look quite ill."

" No," he muttered, drawing away childishly, " they don't want me."

" But you must," she insisted. And like a child he yielded and allowed her to lead him towards the house. He had the awful feeling that at any moment he might burst into tears.

She took a key from her bag, opened the door, and they went into the back sitting-room which he knew so well. The sight of his shaven head forced a gasp of pity from Laura's lips. She took him by the shoulders and put him in a chair by the fire. He sat there with his prison pallor upon him and his clothes hanging on his drooping prison-shrunken frame while she hurried into the kitchen. There she said nothing to Minnie, the maid, but herself quickly brought him a tray with tea and hot buttered toast. She watched him with concern while he drank the tea and ate some of the toast.

" Finish it," she said gently.

He obeyed. His intuition told him immediately that neither Hetty nor her father was in the house. Momentarily his mind detached itself from Hetty. He raised his head and for the first time looked at Laura.

" Thanks, Laura," he said humbly.

She did not answer, but once again that quick sympathy flashed into her pale face as though a sudden gleam from the fire had illumined it. He could not help thinking how much older she looked; there were shadows under her eyes, she was dressed indifferently, her hair quite carelessly arranged. Through his daze, the change in her reached and astounded him.

" Is anything wrong, Laura ? Why are you here, alone ? "

This time a deep and painful emotion broke through the surface of her eyes.

" Nothing's wrong." She bent and stirred up the fire. " I'm staying with father this week. You see, I'm closing up the house at Hilltop, in the meantime."

" Closing your house ? "

She nodded, then added in a low voice:

" Stanley's gone down to Bournemouth to a rest home; you probably didn't know he'd been shell-shocked. I shall join him when I have settled things up here."

He looked at her helplessly; his brain refused to operate.

" But the works, Laura ? " he exclaimed at last.

" That's been arranged," she answered in a flat voice. " That's the least of it, Arthur."

He continued to look at her in a kind of wonder. This was not the Laura he had known. The fixed sadness in her face was quite startling, that droop to her mouth, ironic yet pained. A deep, mysterious instinct, born of his own suffering, made him sense a wounded spirit, behind this outer, indifferent crust. But he could not work it out just now, the insufferable fatigue bore down on him again. A long silence came between them.

" I'm sorry to be a trouble to you, Laura," he said eventually.

" You're no trouble."

He hesitated, feeling she might now wish him to go.

" But now that I'm here, I thought—I thought I might as well wait and see Hetty."

Another silence. He could feel her looking at him. Then she rose from the hearthrug where she had been kneeling, staring into the fire, and stood before him.

" Hetty isn't here any more," she said.

" What ? "

" No," she shook her head. " She's down at Farnborough now—you see——" A pause. " You see, Arthur, that's where Dick Purves is."

" But what——" He broke off, a barb twisting in his heart.

" You don't know," Laura said in that same flat voice. " She married him in January." Her eyes slipped from his, she put her hand on his shoulder. " It was a sudden affair; when they gave him the V.C., it was just immediately after your mother died, after the inquest. He got the V.C. for bringing down the Zeppelin. We never thought, Arthur . . . But Hetty just seemed to make up her mind. The wedding was in all the papers."

He sat perfectly still, in a kind of graven stolidity.

" So Hetty's married."

" Yes, Arthur."

" I never thought of that." He swallowed and the spasm seemed to pass over his entire body. " I don't suppose she'd have had anything to do with me in any case."

Wisely, she made no attempt to console him. He made an effort in the chair.

" Well, I ought to be going now," he said in an unsteady voice.

" No, don't go yet, Arthur. You still look seedy."

" The worst of it is . . . I feel it." He got shakily to his feet. " O Lord, I do feel queer. My head's full of feathers. How do I get to the station ? " He raised his hand stupidly to his brow.

Laura took a step forward, intercepting him on his way to the door.

" You're not going, Arthur. I can't let you go. You're not fit. You ought to be in bed."

" You mean well, Laura," he said thickly, swaying on his feet. " I mean well, too. We both mean well." He laughed. " Only we can't *do* anything."

Resolution formed in her. She put her arm round him determinedly.

" Listen to me, Arthur, I refuse to send you out in such a state. You're going to bed . . . here . . . now. Don't say another word. I'll explain to father whenever he comes in." Supporting him she assisted him into the hall and up the stairs. She lit the gas fire in her bedroom, quietly but firmly helped him out of his clothes and into bed. When this was done she filled a hot bottle and put it to his feet. She considered him anxiously: " How do you feel now ? "

" Better," he answered, without meaning it.

He lay curled up on his side, realising that he was in Hetty's room, in Hetty's bed. How amusing!—he was actually in dear little Hetty's dear little bed. Nice bit of skirt to-night, eh, Cuthbert ? He wanted to laugh but could not. Recollection twisted the barb in his heart again.

It was about five o'clock in the afternoon. The sun, breaking through the low clouds, came slantingly into the room, making the wallpaper glow. In the small back garden some young thrushes were whistling. It was very still and unreal, and the softness of Hetty's bed was unreal, and Laura must have gone away and the unknown longing in his breast hurt him.

" Take this, Arthur. It'll help you to sleep."

Laura had returned. How good she was to him. Resting on his elbow he drank the bowl of hot soup she had brought him. She sat beside him on the edge of the bed, filling the silent room with her real presence. Her hands, holding the tray for him, were white and soft. He had never thought much about Laura before, never cared much for her; but now her kindness overwhelmed him. Out of sheer gratitude he cried: " Why do you bother about me, Laura ? "

" I shouldn't worry, Arthur, if I were you," she said; " everything'll come all right."

She took the empty bowl and placed it upon the tray. She made to get up.

But he reached out and stayed her, like a child fearful of being left alone.

" Don't leave me, Laura."

" Very well."

She sat down again, placed the tray on the bedside table. She began gently to stroke his forehead.

He sobbed, then started to cry brokenly. In complete abandonment he lay against her, his face pressed against her, against her soft body. The comfort of his face against her softness was unbelievable, an ease flowed like warm milk through his being.

" Laura," he whispered, " Laura."

A fire of indulgence blazed in her suddenly. His attitude, his need of comfort, the pressure of his head against the lower part of her body raised a wild tension in her. Staring rigidly across the room she saw her own face in the mirror. A quick revulsion took her. Not that, she thought fiercely, no, not that gift. She gazed down at Arthur again. Worn out, his sobs had stopped, he was already on the edge of sleep. His lips were open, his expression undefended, helpless, exposed. She saw the wounds plainly. There was something infinitely sad and wistful in the flaccid closure of his eyelids, the narrow foreshortening of his chin.

Outside, the thrushes ceased to sing and the dark beginnings of the night crept into the room. She still sat there, though he was asleep, supporting his head. The expression on her face was pathetic and beautiful.

XXI

For a fortnight Arthur lay ill at Todd's, unable to get up. The doctor whom Laura brought had an alarming suspicion of aplastic anæmia. He was Dr. Dobbie from 1 College Row, an intimate of the Todd family, who knew Arthur's history, and he behaved with kindness and discretion. He made several blood counts and treated Arthur with intramuscular injections of manganese. But it was Laura rather than Dr. Dobbie who got Arthur well. There was some rare quality, a passionate selflessness, in the attention she gave him. She had closed the house at Hilltop and all her time she spent looking after Arthur, preparing his food, reading to him, or merely sitting in silent companionship by his bed. Strange behaviour for a woman naturally so indifferent, so apparently self-absorbed. It was perhaps an atonement, a clutching at this chance straw of expiation in the throbbing desire to prove that there was something of good in her. Because of this every step made by Arthur towards recovery, every single word of gratitude he spoke, made her happy. In tending his wounds she healed her own.

Her father did not interfere. It was not Todd's nature to interfere. Besides, he was sorry for Arthur who had, so disastrously, swum against the stream. Twice a day he came into the room and stood awkwardly making conversation, pausing, clearing his throat, and, in an attempt at ease, balancing himself beside the bed first on one leg then on the other, like an elderly, rather dilapidated robin. The obviousness with which he sheered away from topics of danger: the Neptune, the war, Hetty, from anything which might be painful to Arthur, was touching and comic. And he always concluded, edging towards the door:

"There's no hurry, my boy. Stop here as long as it suits you."

Gradually Arthur improved, he left his room, then began to take short walks with Laura. They avoided the crowded places and went usually across the Town Moor, that high sweep of open park from which on a clear day the Otterburne Hills were visible. Though he was not yet aware of how much he owed to Laura, occasionally he would turn to her spontaneously.

"You're decent to me, Laura."

"It's nothing," she would invariably reply.

It was a fresh bright morning and they had seated themselves for a few minutes on a bench upon the highest part of the Moor.

"I don't know what I'd have done without you," he sighed; "slipped right under, I suppose. I mean morally, of course. You don't know the temptation, Laura, just to let everything go."

She did not reply.

"But somehow it feels as if you'd put me together again, made me something like a man. Now I feel I can face things. It isn't fair though. I've had all the benefit. You get nothing."

"You'd wonder," she answered in a strange voice.

While the wind blew cleanly about him he studied her pale, chastely cut profile, the passive immobility of her figure.

"Do you know what you remind me of, Laura?" he said suddenly. "In a book at home, one of Raphael's Madonnas."

She coloured painfully, violently, her face suddenly distorted.

"Don't be a fool," she said harshly and, rising, she walked rapidly away. He stared after her, completely taken aback, then he got up and followed her.

As his strength came back he was able to think of his father, of Sleescale, and of his return. He must return, his manhood demanded it. Although procrastination and timidity were in his blood he had a serious intensity which gave him strength. Besides, prison had hardened him, increased that sense of injury and injustice which now activated his life.

One evening, towards the end of the third week, they were playing bezique together, as they often did after supper. He picked up his cards and, without warning, declared:

"I must get back to Sleescale soon, Laura."

Nothing more was said. Now that he had announced his intention, he was tempted to delay the actual date of his departure. But on the morning of May 16th when he came down to breakfast, after Todd had left for the office, a paragraph in the *Courier* caught his eye. He stood by the table with the paper in his hand, his attitude arrested and motionless. The paragraph was quite small, six bare lines, lost in a mass of shrieking war news. But Arthur seemed to find it important. He sat down with his eyes still fixed upon these six bare lines.

"Is anything the matter?" Laura asked, watching his face.

There was a silence; then Arthur said:

"They've driven the new roadway into the Paradise. They went through to the dead-end three days ago. They've found the ten men and the inquest is to-morrow."

The whole force of the disaster rushed over him again like a wave which has momentarily receded only to return with greater strength. His mind contracted under the impact. He said slowly, his eyes on the paper:

" They've even brought some of the relatives from France . . . for formal identification. I must go back, too. I'll go to-day . . . this morning."

Laura did not answer. She handed him his coffee. He drank it mechanically, confronted once again by the situation which had altered, and ruined, his life. The thing from which there was no escape. Now he must go back, must, must go back.

When he had finished breakfast he looked across at Laura. She interpreted that glance, the fixed idea which compelled him, and she nodded imperceptibly. He rose from the table, went into the hall and put on his hat and coat. He had nothing to pack. Laura accompanied him to the door.

" Promise me, Arthur," she said in her unemotional voice, " you won't do anything stupid."

He shook his head. A silence. Then, impulsively, he took both her hands.

" I'm no good at thanking you, Laura. But you know how I feel. I'll see you again. One day soon. Perhaps I can do something for you then."

" Perhaps," she agreed.

Her unresponsive manner left him rather helpless; he stood in the narrow hall as though he did not quite know what to do. He released her hands.

" Good-bye then, Laura."

" Good-bye."

He turned and walked into the street. A gusty wind holding a spatter of rain blew against him all the way down College Row, but he reached the station by twenty minutes past ten and took his ticket for Sleescale.

The 10.15 local was almost empty and he had a third-class compartment to himself. As the train puffed its way out of Tynecastle, through the interminable sequence of stations, past familiar landmarks, across the Canal Bridge, through Brent Tunnel and finally drew near to Sleescale, Arthur had a strange sense of at last returning to consciousness.

It was half-past eleven when he stepped out on the Sleescale platform. Another passenger was at that moment in the act of alighting from the rear end of the train, and as they both converged upon the ticket collector Arthur saw with a sudden constriction of his heart that it was David Fenwick. David recognised Arthur instantly, but he gave no sign, nor did he try to avoid him. They met and passed through the narrow passage to the street.

" You've come back about the inquest," Arthur said, in a low voice. He had to speak.

David nodded silently. He walked along Freehold Street in his faded uniform and Arthur walked with him. A thin rain, driving in from the sea, met them at the corner. Together they began to climb Cowpen Street.

Arthur took a startled side glance at David, intimidated by his silence, the stern composure of his face. But in a moment David spoke, as if forcing himself to be tranquil and at ease.

" I've been back two days," he said quietly. " My wife is living in Tynecastle with her own people. My little boy, too."

" Yes," Arthur murmured. He knew now why David was on the train. But he could find nothing more to say.

Again silence, until opposite Inkerman Terrace and his old home, David abruptly paused. Fighting that secret bitterness in his voice, he said:

" Come in here a minute, will you ? There's something I must show you."

Mastered by an unknown emotion, overwhelming and intense, Arthur followed David along the broken pavement and into No. 23. They entered the front room. The blinds were drawn but in the dim light Arthur saw two coffins, still open, laid upon boards in the centre of the room. Arthur's senses seethed within him like waves battling in a narrow sea. With a thudding heart he advanced towards the first coffin and his eyes met the dead eyes of Robert Fenwick. Robert's body was four years old: the face perfectly saponified, waxy white in colour, the skin moulded on the shrunken bones, like an effigy. Recoiling, Arthur covered his eyes. He could not meet those dead eyes, the eyes of the victim, blank yet accusing. He wanted to retreat, shuddering, and yet he could not; he was numbed, helpless.

David spoke again, still fighting the bitterness in his tone.

" I found this," he said, " on my father's body. No one else has seen it."

Slowly, Arthur uncovered his face. He stared at the paper in David's hand, then with a sudden movement he took it, held it close to him. It was Robert's letter; and Arthur read the letter. For one second he thought he was going to die.

" You see," David exclaimed in a strained voice. " This makes things clear at last."

Arthur kept staring at the letter. He had turned an earthy grey, he looked as if he might fall down.

" I don't intend to take this any further," David said in a tone of dead finality. " But it's only right you ought to know."

Arthur lifted his eyes from the letter and stared away through David. He put out his hand, supporting himself against the wall. The interior of the room spun round him. It was as though the cumulation of all his sufferings, his suspicions and his fears had struck him at one tremendous blow. He seemed at last to discover David. He folded the letter and handed it back to him. David restored the letter to his inside pocket. Then, in a cracked voice, Arthur said: " You can leave this to me. I'll let my father know." A shiver ran over him. Feeling that he must reach the outer air, he turned blindly and went out of the house.

He walked up to the Law through the heavy shower sweeping the bleak Avenue. But the rain pelted against him without effect. He walked in a kind of trance. The folded slip of paper which had lain for four years against the dead heart of Robert Fenwick had made everything plain to Arthur, everything which he had suspected and feared. Now he neither suspected nor feared. He knew.

An overwhelming surge of conviction broke over him: it was preordained that he should see this letter. The meaning of the letter enlarged and magnified itself and took upon itself many and unfathomable meanings, each diverse and beyond his present understanding but all leading to one common end. His father's guilt. A sick rage blazed up in Arthur; he wanted to see his father.

He went to the steps of the Law and tugged at the bell. Aunt Carrie opened the door herself. She stood motionless, framed in the doorway, gazing at him with wide and startled eyes, then with a cry of thankfulness and pity she flung her arms round his neck.

" Oh, Arthur, my dear," she sobbed. " I'm so glad to see you. I wondered . . . I didn't know . . . oh, you're not looking well, my poor boy, you're looking simply dreadful, but oh, it's wonderful you've come back." Controlling herself with difficulty, she shepherded him into the hall, helped him out of his coat, took possession of his dripping hat. Little phrases of affection and pity kept breaking from her lips. Her delight that he should be home again was pathetic. She fluttered about him, her hands agitated, her pinched lips tremulous.

" You'll take something now, Arthur dear, at once. A glass of milk, a biscuit, something, dear . . ."

" No thank you, Aunt Carrie."

Outside the dining-room towards which she guided him, he paused: " Is my father back yet ? "

" Why no, Arthur," Aunt Carrie stammered, discomposed by the strangeness of his manner.

" Will he be home for lunch ? "

Aunt Carrie gave another little gasp. Her mouth pinched closer and turned down nervously at the corners.

" Yes, Arthur, of course. About one, he said. I know he's got a great many arrangements to make this afternoon. About the funeral. Everything's to be done most handsomely."

He made no attempt to reply. He glanced about him, observing all the changes which had taken place since he had been away: the new furniture, the new carpets and curtains, the new electric fittings in the hall. He remembered his cell, his sufferings in prison, and a shudder of revulsion passed over him at this luxury, a hatred of his father which made him tremble in all his limbs. A nervous excitement, a kind of ecstasy such as he had never known took possession of him. He felt himself strong. He became aware of what he wanted to do and of an almost painful longing to do it. He turned to Aunt Carrie.

"I'll go upstairs for a bit."

"Yes, Arthur, yes," she fluttered even more agitatedly. "Lunch is at one, such a nice lunch." She hesitated, her voice a whisper of distress. "You won't . . . you won't upset your father, dear. He's got so much on his hands, he's . . . he's a little irritable these days."

"Irritable," Arthur repeated. He seemed to try to fathom the meaning of the word. Then he moved away and went steadily upstairs. He did not go to his own room but to his father's study, the room which, since his childhood days, had been sealed with a taboo, making it a sacred, forbidden room. Exactly in the centre of the room stood his father's desk, a solid richly grained mahogany desk with beaded edges, heavy brass locks and handles, more sacred, more forbidden than the room. Hostility burned in Arthur's face as he studied this desk. It stood there large and solid, impregnated with the personality of Barras, a thing hateful to Arthur, the symbol of everything which had destroyed him.

With a sudden gesture he picked up the poker which lay beside the fireplace and advanced on the desk. With deliberate violence he smashed open the lock and examined the contents of the top drawer. Then the next lock, the next drawer; one after another he went through the entire desk, rifling it systematically.

The desk was crammed with the evidence of his father's wealth. Stock receipts, bills of exchange, a list of outstanding mortgages. The leather-bound book, written in his father's precise hand, enumerating properties and rentals. That other book with a tiny pasted label: *My Pictures*, the prices of each purchase marked plainly against the date. A third book holding the record of investments. Quickly, Arthur scanned the columns: everything sound, redeemable and in small parcels, at least two hundred thousand pounds in gilt-edged securities. In a fury Arthur hurled the book from him. Two hundred thousand pounds: the magnitude of the total, the loving neatness, the smug complacency that ran through the rows and rows of figures, maddened him. Money, money, money; money sweated and bled from the bodies of men. Men didn't matter; it was money that mattered, money, money, money. Death, destruction, famine, war—all were as nothing so long as these sleek money bags were safe.

Arthur wrenched at another drawer. An avenging spirit worked within him now. He wanted more, more than the evidence of money. He had the fatal conviction that the plan, the Old Neptune plan, lay here. He knew his father: ingrained with the stigmata of acquisitiveness. Why had he never thought of this before? His father never destroyed documents or papers; it was a physical impossibility, an agony, to destroy documents or papers. If Robert Fenwick's letter did not lie, the plan existed and the plan was here.

Drawer after drawer lay rifled on the floor. Then, in the last bottom drawer, a thin roll of parchment, very soiled and unimportant. Perfectly unimportant. A loud cry broke from Arthur's lips. With a nervous flush he unrolled the plan, and, kneeling, examined it upon the floor. The plan demonstrated instantly that the old waste was clearly indicated, running parallel to the Dyke in its lower levels and approaching within a bare two feet of the Dyke. Arthur peered closer with his prison-dulled eyes. He made out tracings and calculations in his father's hand. It was the final proof, the last iniquity.

He got up from his knees, slowly rolling up the plan. The whole structure of the colossal deceit arose before his tormented sight. He stood in the middle of the sacred room with the plan clenched tight in his hands, his eyes burning, his face still bearing the ingrained pallor of the prison. And as though conscious of himself, the prisoner, holding this evidence of his father's guilt, as though amused by this paradox of human equity, his pale lips parted in a smile. A paroxysm of hysterical laughter convulsed him. He wanted to smash, burn, destroy; he wanted to wreck the room, tear down the pictures, kick out the windows. He wanted punishment, recompense, justice.

With a great effort he controlled himself, turned and went downstairs. In the hall he stood waiting, his eyes upon the front door. From time to time he looked towards the long case clock, hearing the slow inexorable rhythm of the passing seconds in a fever of impatience. But at last he started. At twenty-five minutes to one the car drove up from the station and there was the sound of bustling steps. The door swung open and his father entered the hall. An instant of complete immobility. The eyes of Arthur met his father's eyes.

Arthur drew a quick sobbing breath. He hardly recognised his father. The change in Barras was incredible. Much heavier and stouter, the hard outlines of his figure softened and become flaccid, a pouching of the cheeks, a sagging of the abdomen, a roll of fat behind his collar, the old static immobility supplanted by a bustling activity. The hands were active, fumbling and fussing with a sheaf of newspapers; the eyes were active, darting hither and thither to see what could be seen; the mind was active, responding eagerly to all the diversions of life which were trivial and worthless. In one devastating flash it struck Arthur that the whole trend of this spurious activity was to acknowledge the present, to repudiate the past, to ignore the future; the end of a process of disintegration. He remained standing with his back to the staircase as his father came into the hall. There was a silence.

" So you've come back," Barras said. " It's an unexpected treat."

Arthur did not speak. He watched Barras advance to the table and lay down his papers and a few small parcels which dangled from his fingers. Barras continued, shuffling and arranging the things upon the table:

" You know, of course, that the war is still on. My views have not changed. You know I don't want any slackers here."

In a suppressed tone Arthur said:

" I haven't been slacking. I've been in prison."

Barras gave a short exclamation, moving and re-moving the things upon the table.

" You chose to go there, didn't you ? And if you don't alter your mind you're liable to go back again. You see that, don't you ? "

Arthur answered:

" I've seen a great many things. Prison is a good place for seeing things."

Barras gave over his arranging and darted a furtive glance at Arthur. He began to walk up and down the hall. He took out his beautiful gold watch and looked at that. He said with a flickering animosity:

" I've got an appointment after lunch. I have two meetings to-night. This is an extremely heavy day for me. I really have no time to waste on you, I'm far too busy."

" Too busy winning the war, father ? Is that what you mean ? "

Barras's face became suffused. The arteries in his temple stood out suddenly.

" Yes! since you choose to put it like that, I have been doing my best to win the war."

Arthur's compressed lips twitched bitterly. A great wave of uncontrolled feeling rushed over him.

" No wonder you're proud of yourself. You're a patriot. Everyone admires you. You're on committees, your name gets in the paper, you make speeches about glorious victories when thousands of men are lying butchered in the trenches. And all the time you're coining money, thousands and thousands of pounds, sweating your men in the Neptune, shouting that it's for King and Country when it's really for yourself. That's it, that's it." His voice climbed higher. " You don't care about life or death. You only care about yourself."

" At least I keep out of prison," shouted Barras.

" Don't be sure." Arthur's breath came chokingly. " It looks as if you might soon be there. I'm not going to serve any more of your sentence for you."

Barras stopped his rapid pacing. His mouth dropped open.

"What's that?" he exclaimed in a tone of utter amazement. "Are you mad?"

"No," Arthur answered passionately, "I'm not mad, but I ought to be."

Barras stared at Arthur, then with a shrug of his shoulders abandoned him as hopeless. He pulled out his watch again, using that restless gesture, and looked at it with his small injected eyes.

"I really must go," he said, slurring his words together. "I have an important appointment after lunch."

"Don't go, father," Arthur said. He stood there in a white heat of intensity, consumed by the terrible knowledge within him.

"What——" Barras drew up, red-faced, half-way to the stairs.

"Listen to me, father," Arthur said in a burning voice. "I know all about the disaster now. Robert Fenwick wrote out a message before he died. I have that message. I know that you were to blame."

Barras gave a very perceptible start. A sudden dread seemed to fall on him.

"What do you say?"

"You heard what I said."

For the first time a look of guilt crept into Barras's eyes.

"It's a lie. I absolutely deny it."

"You may deny it. But I have found the Old Neptune plan."

Barras's face became completely congested with blood, the vessels of his neck stood out duskily and thickly. He swayed for a moment and leaned instinctively against the hall table. He stammered:

"You're mad. You've gone out of your mind. I won't listen to you."

"You should have destroyed the plan, father."

All at once Barras lost control of himself. He shouted:

"What do you know about it? Why should I destroy anything? I'm not a criminal. I acted for the best. I won't be bothered with it. It's all finished. There's a war on. I've got an appointment at two . . . a meeting." He clutched at the banisters, breathing desperately, with that suffused and dusky face, trying to push past Arthur.

Arthur did not move.

"Go to your meeting then. But I know that you killed those men. And I'm going to see that they get justice."

In that same panting, flushed voice, Barras went on:

"I have to pay the wages. I have to make the pit pay. I have to take chances just as they do. We're all human. We all make mistakes. I acted for the best. It's finished and done with. They can't reopen the inquiry. I've got to have my lunch and get to my meeting at two." He made that hasty, bustling gesture, feeling for his watch; he missed the pocket and forgot about it; he stared at Arthur, crumbling within himself.

Arthur's soul sickened. This was his father and he had loved him. His voice was impersonal and devoid of feeling.

" In that case I shall forward the plan to the proper quarter. You can't object to my doing that."

Barras compressed his forehead with his hands, as though to still the pounding of his blood.

" I really don't know what you're talking about," he groaned with utter incoherence. " You forget that I have a meeting. An important meeting. I have got to wash, to lunch. At two." He stared at Arthur in a bewildered, childish way. He made a convulsive gesture and found the watch. He considered the watch with that dusky querulous face, then he took a few rapid steps which carried him past Arthur and up the stairs.

Arthur remained standing in the hall, his features contracted, drawn. He felt empty and hopeless. He had come nerved for a fight, a desperate struggle to assert himself, to demand justice. And there had been no fight, no struggle, no justice. Now there would never be justice. He would not send the plan. It was too pitiful, this shell of what had once been a man, his father. Hunched against the banisters he felt crushed by the hypocrisy and ruthlessness of life. He sighed deeply, a sound wrung from his heart. Upstairs, he heard his father moving about: rapid and uneven movements, thumping footsteps. He heard water running. Then, as he turned to leave the house, all at once he heard a heavy fall.

He swung round, listening. No more sounds. Absolute stillness. He ran upstairs, Aunt Carrie was running too. They ran to the bathroom door and hammered on the door. There was no answer. Aunt Carrie let out a terrified shriek. Then Arthur took a rush and burst in the door.

Richard Barras lay on the floor, his face half covered in lather, the soap still clutched in his hand. He was conscious and breathing deeply. It was a stroke.

END OF BCOK TWO

BOOK III

I

THE twenty-fifth of November 1918 and a bright and sunny day. The headgear of the Neptune lay bathed in a clear brightness, the outlines of the headstocks softened, the pulleys whirling in a sparkling iridescence. Puffs of woolly steam broke from the engine house and hung like little halos above the shaft.

As Arthur Barras walked briskly down Cowpen Street he saw the clear brightness upon the pit and the iridescent pulleys and the puffs of smoke which hung like halos. He felt the radiance of the day flooding the Neptune and the future and himself. He smiled.

Unbelievable that he should be happy again, that the fixed and sinister influence of the pit should be dissolved, changed, transmuted into something wonderful and fine. How he had doubted and feared and suffered during these war years, yes, how he had suffered! He had felt his life ruined. But now the future was before him, clear and shining, the result of all his suffering, the reward.

He walked through open gates and crossed the asphalt yard with an alert step. He was well but quietly dressed in a grey tweed suit, wing collar, blue and white bow tie. Though he looked older than his age of twenty-six his expression held a queer eagerness.

Armstrong and Hudspeth were waiting for him in the office, both standing. He nodded to them, hung up his hat behind the door, smoothed his fine fair hair, already thin on the top, and took his place at the desk.

" It's all settled, then," he said. " Bannerman completed the final papers yesterday."

Armstrong cleared his throat.

" I'm sure I'm very pleased," he said obsequiously. " And I wish you every success, sir. I don't see why not. We've done pretty well at the Neptune in the past."

" Nothing to what we're going to do in the future, Armstrong."

" Yes, sir." Armstrong paused, stealing a quick glance at Arthur.

A short silence followed, then Arthur sat back in his chair.

" I want to say one or two things, so that we can start off with everything clearly understood. You've been used to my father giving orders down here and now that he's laid up you've got to get used to me. That's the first change, but it's only the first. We'll have other changes and plenty of them. It's the right time for changes. The war's over and there's going to be no more war. Whatever our difference of principles during the war we're all agreed about the peace. We've got peace and we're going to keep it. We've stopped destroying; thank God, we're going to start reconstructing for a change. That's exactly what we're going to do here. We're going to have a safe pit with no possible chance of another disaster. Do you understand? A safe pit. There's going to be fair play for everybody. And to show that I mean it——" he broke off. "How much have you been getting, Armstrong? Four hundred, isn't it?"

Armstrong coloured and let his eyes drop.

"Yes, that's the figure," he said. "If you think it's too much . . ."

"And you, Hudspeth?" Arthur asked.

Hudspeth gave his short stolid laugh.

"I've been standin' at two-fifty these last three years," he said. "I never seem to move up, nohow."

"Well, you're up now," Arthur said. "You'll take five hundred, Armstrong, as from the first of last month, and you three-fifty, Hudspeth, as from the same date."

Armstrong's flush deepened. He stammered gratefully:

"That's uncommon handsome of you, I must say."

"Ay, it is that," Hudspeth added, his dull eye bright at last.

"That's settled, then." Arthur got up briskly. "Both of you stand by this morning. I have Mr. Todd of Tynecastle coming at eleven. We shall want to make a complete inspection. You understand?"

"Why certainly, Mr. Barras." Armstrong nodded effusively and went out with Hudspeth. Arthur remained alone in the office. He crossed to the window and stood there for a moment watching the sunny pit yard: men crossing and recrossing, tubs moving down the track, an engine shunting perkily. His eye dilated, exulting to the emotion within him. He thought, I haven't suffered for nothing. I'll show them now. It's my chance at last.

He returned to his desk, sat down and took a file of bills and invoices from the top left drawer. These invoices were not new to him, he had most of them by heart, but they had not ceased to shock him. Bad timber, cheap bricks, weak props, dud roofing bars, odd lots and job-lots bought anywhere so long as it was cheap. Material on costs cut to the vanishing point. A subtle skating behind the regulations at every turn—even the spare winding cable was ten years old and had been bought second hand at a bankrupt sale. His father's work; all his father's work; all work which he must rectify.

He was still sitting at his desk, working and figuring, when Saul Pickings, seventy-four, and still going strong, poked his head round the door and announced Adam Todd. Arthur jumped up at once and shook hands with Todd, genuinely glad to see him. Todd had changed very little, still taciturn and vaguely seedy and yellow about the eyes, still smelling of cloves. He sat down beside the desk in answer to Arthur's invitation; he had no personality or presence; he was just there.

A short silence; then Arthur slid the file across to Todd.

" Take a look at these."

Todd took a look at them, wetting his forefinger, slow and exact.

" There's been a few bargains," he said at length.

" Bargains," Arthur said. " It isn't a case of bargains. That stuff is junk."

Old man Todd did not speak, but Arthur saw that he agreed and, lowering his voice carefully, Arthur said:

" Look here, Mr. Todd, I'm going to be quite frank with you. After all you know everything. You warned my father. But you don't have to warn me. I'm out to put things right at last. I'm going to make the Neptune *safe!* "

" Yes, Arthur," said old man Todd with his yellow eyes fixed on the desk. " You're empowered, I suppose? "

" Bannerman has seen to everything. I've sworn the affidavit, I'm in control," Arthur said, his voice low and burning. " You're coming round with me this morning. And you're coming inbye. You're going to make suggestions to me as you did to my father. The difference is that I'm going to take them."

" Yes, Arthur."

" I'm going to replace this junk. I'm going to take out every rotten prop in this rotten pit, burn the timber, strip the brickwork. I'm going to steel girder the new road, cement the roof, put in new haulage."

" That'll cost you a lot of money."

" Money! " Arthur gave a short laugh. " Money has been pouring into this pit during the war . . . like the water that poured into it at the disaster. I'm going to spend some of that money, all of it if need be. I'm going to make a new Neptune. I'm not just stopping at safety. I'm going to show how to get real good out of the men. I'm putting in pit-head baths, drying rooms, locker rooms, everything."

" Yes, Arthur," said Todd, " I see."

Arthur rose abruptly:

" Come on," he said. " We'll go."

They went round the pit bank, engine house and pump room. Then they went inbye. Accompanied by Armstrong and Hudspeth they made a complete inspection above surface and below. They talked and discussed and tested. Arthur had his way every time and his way was the best way.

It was one o'clock when they came back to the office and Todd looked a little tired. At his own suggestion he had a slight refreshment and after the refreshment he looked less tired. Chewing a clove, he figured for a long time with his pencil on a pad. At last he looked up.

" Do you know round about what this is going to cost ? " he inquired slowly.

" No," Arthur spoke indifferently.

" Something in the neighbourhood of one hundred thousand pounds," Todd said.

" That shows how rotten we were! " Arthur clenched his fist in a sudden access of feeling. " We can stand that outlay. I don't care if it was double. I've got to do it."

" Yes, Arthur," old man Todd said again. " Mind you, we'll have a bit of difficulty in getting the stuff. All the plant works have been out of production during the war and it's only the wise ones that have converted back already." He hesitated. " I did hear they'd restarted in Platt Land though."

" At Millington's ? "

" Millington's that was," Todd sighed. " You know Stanley has sold out to Mawson and Gowlan." He placed the papers in his bag and closed it gently, without acrimony.

Arthur took Todd's arm. " You're tired." He smiled, his sensitive, charming smile. " You need some lunch. We're expecting you at the Law. Hilda's home. And Grace and Dan are staying for a day or two. You must come."

They drove up to the Law through the warm sunshine and Todd, reflecting in the warm sunshine, felt less his usual pessimism: it was a fine thing Arthur was doing, a very fine thing, the like of which his father would not have done. This made him meditate:

" It's odd, you know, not seeing your father at the Neptune, Arthur."

Arthur shook his head decisively. " He'll never be there again, I'm afraid." Then quickly: " Mind you, he's better really, a great deal better. He may go on for years, Dr. Lewis says. But the right side is quite paralysed. And the speech, that has suffered. Something has severed, a line of nerve fibres in the brain. To be quite frank, Todd, he's not quite . . . not quite right in his head." There was a silence, then Arthur added in a low voice: " My one hope is that he may go on long enough to see the end of what I'm doing at the Neptune."

A sudden warmth came over Todd: the day, the whisky and a real admiration for Arthur's purpose.

" By God, Arthur," he said, " I hope he does see it."

They entered the Law with this spirit of cheerfulness and enthusiasm between them. It was half-past one and lunch-time. They went straight into the dining-room, where they all sat in together: Arthur at the head of the table, Aunt Carrie at the foot, Todd and Hilda on one side, Grace and Dan on the other.

Everyone was cheerful, a note of optimism vibrated in the air, the ecstasy, the miracle of this new enduring peace. Todd reflected that he had never in all his life seen such a cheerful table at the Law. There was, of course, the sense of something missing. The real presence was not there, the presence was hidden upstairs, speechless and paralysed, yet, even in absence, strangely significant.

Todd wondered for a moment. He turned to Hilda:

" You're looking after your father I suppose, Hilda? Your nursing experience will be useful."

Hilda shook her head.

" Aunt Carrie is the nurse."

Arthur's new buoyant laugh rang out.

" You'll never guess what Hilda's up to. She's going in for medicine. She goes up to London next month."

" Medicine! " Todd echoed. He concealed his amazement under a preoccupation with his mutton.

" Hilda's very pleased," Arthur said. He was in extraordinary spirits. He darted a smile towards Dan, " That's what makes her so agreeable to us all."

Dan reddened, conscious of Hilda's chilly tolerance, and of his own rather awkward position at the Law. He had come only to please Grace; even now he felt Grace's hand seeking his hand under the table. He gave a warm and reassuring pressure to Grace's hand, thinking of Grace and the baby upstairs and the future and not minding a bit that Hilda should snub him. He glanced up, still rather red, to find Todd's eye upon him.

" You'll be starting in at the Neptune again now the war's over? " Todd said.

Dan swallowed a piece of potato the wrong way.

" No," he said. " I'm going farming."

Grace spoke up, squeezing Dan's hand under the table:

" I won't let Dan go back to the pit, Mr. Todd. We're going down to Sussex. We've bought a little place there at Winrush. We bought it with Dan's gratuity," she added swiftly.

" They're a stubborn pair," Arthur explained. " I've done my level best to make Dan see I want him in with me at the pit. But they'll have none of it. Independent as the devil—won't take a penny either. All Grace's doing of course. Grace found Winrush so successful for babies she's trying it on with chickens and piglets."

Grace said, quite untroubled:

" You must come and see us, Mr. Todd, I'm going to take paying guests."

Todd gave Grace his rare, quiet smile, marvelling at her enthusiasm, her resolution. He thought it strange and fine and rather pathetic. It made him feel very old.

Here Aunt Carrie rose, with her head inclined, and noiselessly slipped out. There was no Harriet now, but another invalid to see to. Aunt Carrie's dexterity in turning dirty linen and removing chamber pots was still required at the Law—but in another and more sacred cause.

The recognition of that stricken figure, helpless and imprisoned in his room, brought a sudden silence upon the table. Lunch broke up quickly. Arthur took Todd's arm, escorting him to the car which would carry him to the station. Todd had decided not to go up and see Barras—it might upset him, he wisely observed. For a moment Arthur and Todd stood beside the car.

" I'll let you know about that equipment then," Todd paused. " It's a fine thing you're doing, Arthur. You'll have a model pit if you go ahead with it."

The words thrilled in Arthur's ears: a model pit!

" That's what I've dreamed about," he said in a low voice. " A model pit."

There was a silence, then Todd shook hands and got into the car, which drove off, leaving Arthur standing in the drive. Instinctively he lifted his eyes towards the sky. The sun shone upon him, the world embraced him with its warmth, the awful past was buried and forgotten. He had arisen, miraculously, and his ideal lay before him. Oh, glorious resurrection!

He went upstairs slowly, happily, to make the daily visit which he paid his father. He entered the room and advanced towards the bed.

Barras lay upon his back, a flaccid hulk, inert and helpless and immobile. His right hand was contracted, the fingers of a purplish deadness. One side of his face was stiff and a little trickle of saliva ran down the furrow of his right cheek. He seemed wholly inanimate; only his eyes were alive, rolling towards Arthur as Arthur came into the room with a pitiful and almost animal recognition.

Arthur sat down beside the bed. All the hatred and bitterness he had felt for his father were dead. He felt a calm patience now. He began to talk to his father, to explain to his father a little of what was happening. The doctor had said this might assist his faculties. And, indeed, Arthur could see that Barras understood.

He went on speaking patiently, watching these dull, rolling eyes, the eyes of a pinioned beast. Then he stopped. He saw that his father was trying to speak. A word tried to get through those sealed lips. There were two words really, but the flaccid lips refused to let them through. Arthur bent down to listen to the words but the words would not come. He could not hear them. Not yet.

II

At six o'clock on the evening of Saturday, December 17th, the glorious peace brought David back again. The instant the train drew into Tynecastle Central he jumped out and hurried down the platform, looking expectantly towards the barrier, eager and excited for the sight of Jenny and Robert. The first person he saw was Sally Sunley. He waved; he saw that they had got his wire all right, and she waved back in a careful way. But he hardly noticed; he was busy explaining his voucher to the ticket collector. At last he was through, breathless, smiling.

" Hello, Sally! Where's all the family ? "

Under the vigour of his welcome she smiled too—but in that same difficult manner.

" It's fine to see you back, David. I want to speak to you for a minute. How late your train was! I've been waiting so long I must have a cup of coffee."

" Well," he smiled, " if you want coffee let's hurry along to Scottswood Road."

" No," Sally said. " I must have it now. Come in here."

Uncomprehendingly, he followed her into the refreshment room. Sally bought two cups of coffee at the counter and carried them over to one of the round cold marble-topped tables. David watched her. He protested:

" I don't want any coffee, Sally. I've just had tea on the train."

She did not appear to hear him. She sat down at the table, which was ringed with wet where somebody had lifted and laid a dripping beer glass. He sat down too, bewildered.

She said:

" I want to talk to you, David."

" Well, yes, but can't we talk when we get there ? "

" It isn't convenient." She took up her spoon and stirred her coffee but she did not drink the coffee. Her eyes remained fixed upon his—there was a tragic pity in these eyes but he did not see it. As he gazed at her heavy unattractive face, with its high cheek-bones and rather full chin, he began to feel that something was wrong with Sally.

She drank her coffee very slowly: she seemed to want to spin out her coffee; but at last she had nearly finished. And struggling with his impatience he reached for his haversack.

" Let's get along, then! Do you realise it's nine months since my last leave. I'm dying to see Jenny and the baby. How is the kid—Robert, my boy ? "

She lifted her dark eyes to his once more with sudden decision.

" David, it wasn't really Jenny's fault."

" What ? "

" It wasn't because she was doing war-work or anything like that."

She paused. " You knew the baby was never very strong, David. I want you to understand it wasn't really Jenny's fault."

He sat looking at her in the smoky refreshment room across the wet-ringed marble-topped table. Outside there came a noise of people cheering, welcoming the brave boys back. An engine shrieked derisively.

He did not have to say a single word. He knew why Sally was gazing at him that way. He understood that, although he had looked forward to seeing him so much, he would not see Robert after all.

While, low-voiced, she told him about it—an attack of enteritis in August, a bare two days' illness, Jenny's dread of letting him know—he listened in silence, gritting his teeth together. In the war he had at least learned to keep himself under control. When she had finished he remained curiously still for quite a long time.

" You won't be hard on Jenny," she pleaded. " She asked me specially . . ."

" No, I won't say anything." He rose, flung his pack over his shoulder and held the door open for her. They walked out of the station and along Scottswood Road. Outside No. 117 she halted.

" I'll not come in now, David. I've got something to do."

He stood looking after her, as she went on along the street, conscious, through the pain ringing in his heart, of her kindness in meeting him. What a decent little soul Sally was! Perhaps she knew he hadn't wanted Jenny to take that job at Wirtley, to bring Robert from the clean sea air of Sleescale, to this congested city district. He swung away from the thought. Forcing the darkness from his face he went into the house.

Jenny was alone in the living-room, curled up on the old horsehair sofa, with her shoes off, penitentially caressing her small silk-stockinged toes. The sight of Jenny paying this familiar tribute to her crushed toes touched a throbbing chord of memory. From the doorway he said:

" Jenny! "

She looked up with a gasp, then held out her arms emotionally.

" Oh, David," she cried. " At last! "

He walked over slowly. In a kind of paroxysm she flung her arms round him and, burrowing her cheek into his coat, she began to weep:

" Don't look at me like that, oh, don't be cross with me, David dear. I couldn't help it, I couldn't really. He was running about, the poor little mite, and I was at work, and I never thought to get the doctor, and then his sweet little face all seemed to shrink and he didn't know me, and then—oh, David, how I suffered when the angels took him, oh dear, oh dear . . ."

Sobbing pitifully, she expatiated on the misery she had endured, unconsciously disclosing the details of the death of her unwanted child. He listened, with a set face, in silence. Then with a little rush she cried:

" My heart would really be broken if you wasn't back, David. Oh, it's so wonderful. You don't know how—oh dear, oh dear—all these months—say you understand, David, please, please, it wasn't my fault. I couldn't bear it, I've suffered so much." A big gulp. " But everything's all right now that you're back, my big brave man back from the war. Oh, I haven't been able to sleep or eat——"

He soothed her as best he could. Then, while she sobbed on the sofa, detailing her sufferings, her agonies at the loss of Robert, her pitiful waiting for his return, a cushion slid to the floor, disclosing a large box of chocolates, half finished, and a snappy magazine. Still trying to quieten her he silently replaced the cushion.

She lifted her head at last, a smile breaking through her tears.

" You are glad to be back to me ? Say you are, David ? "

" Yes, it's glorious to be back, Jenny." He paused. " The war's over and we're going to start straight away and get down to a new beginning."

" Oh, we will, David," she agreed, with a little quaver in her voice. " I want to. Oh, you're the best husband that ever was! You're going to take your B.A. and be a head master in no time."

" No, Jenny," he said queerly. " No more teaching. That's a blind alley. Finished. I should have chucked it long ago."

" What then, David ? " she asked almost tearfully. There were new lines round David's eyes and a new hardness about his face which almost startled Jenny.

" Harry Nugent has given me a letter to Heddon at the Federation Offices in Tynecastle. It's pretty well a certainty my getting a job there, Jenny. It won't be much, to be sure; clerical work for a start, but it will be a start. It's the beginning, Jenny." A passionate eagerness crept into the flatness of his voice. " This is going to be the real thing at last."

" But, David . . ."

" Oh, I know the money will be small," he interposed. " Two pounds a week if I'm lucky. But it'll be enough for us to get along on. You'll start out for Sleescale to-morrow, Jenny dear, and open up the house while I go over and fix things with Heddon."

" But David," she gasped again in dismay. " Two pounds a week and I've . . . I've been earning four."

He gazed at her fixedly.

" The money doesn't matter a hang, Jenny. I'm not out for money. There's no compromise this time."

" But couldn't I——" she pleaded, twiddling in the old way with the lapel of his tunic. " Couldn't I just go on with my job a little longer, David; it's such good money ? "

His lips drew together firmly and his brows drew down:

" Jenny darling," he said quietly, " we must understand each other once and for all——"

" Oh, but we do understand each other, David," she gulped with sudden meekness, once again pressing her head into his coat. " And oh, you know I do love you! "

" And I love you, Jenny," he said slowly. " So we pack up and leave for Sleescale and our own home to-morrow."

" Yes, David."

He stared straight ahead as though into the future.

" I've got real work to do this time. Harry Nugent's my friend. I start in with the Federation and I stand for the Town Council, see! If I make good . . ."

" Oh yes, David . . . the *Town Council,* that would be wonderful, David "—lifting moist, admiring eyes.

Already, she saw herself a town-councillor's wife. A pleased look came into her face and instinctively she smoothed her dress. She really was tastefully, quite beautifully dressed: a heavy silk jumper, smart skirt tight to the hips, a couple of rather pretty rings. Her attractiveness was beyond doubt. Perhaps she had been working a little too hard lately. Under the faint layer of powder on her cheeks he saw just the finest little threading of reddish veins. It was like a bloom, a queer exotic bloom under the powder, almost pretty.

She looked up at him, head on one side, her full lips parted, conscious of her charm.

" Well? " she inquired. " Do you still like me? " She gave a little suggestive smile. " Pa and ma have gone down to Whitley Bay. Sally got them tickets for the entertainers there. They won't be in till late."

Abruptly, he got up and moved towards the window, where he stood staring out into the yard. He did not answer.

Jenny's lip drooped. She had to admit to herself that David had changed in some subtle way; he was harder, more resistant and sure, his old boyish stubbornness turned to a firm determination.

Later, when Alfred and Ada came in she saw the change in David more plainly. David was perfectly pleasant about it, yet he established the fact beyond doubt, in the face of Ada's aggrieved air, that Jenny and he were leaving for their own home in Lamb Lane on the following day.

And Jenny, if she had hoped to do so, could not shake him from his resolution. Next morning she departed for Sleescale by the nine forty-five train while David set out to have his interview with Heddon.

The local offices of the Federation were in Rudd Street quite near to Central Station: two simple rooms, an outer office where a grey-haired man with the blue pitted face and hands of the old miner was standing filing cards at a big cabinet, and a small inner room marked Private. There was no linoleum or carpet, merely the bare and very dusty boards; nothing on the walls but a couple of charts and a map of the district, and a notice *Don't spit on the floor.* When Tom Heddon came out of his inner office he took a short pipe from his mouth and, though his intention was towards the empty fireplace, he disobeyed the notice immediately.

" So you're Fenwick," he said. " I remember you before the war at the Inquiry. I knew your father too." He shook hands with a quick grip and waved away David's letter of introduction. " Harry Nugent wrote me himself," he added sourly. " Don't show me that unless there's money in it."

He gave David a dour smile. He was a dour man, Tom Heddon, a short black fiery man with a shock of thick black hair and thick black eyebrows and a sallow dirty skin. He had a tremendous vitality. He sweated, spat and swore. He had a ferocious capacity for food, drink, work and profanity. His favourite was " bloddy." He was a grand stump speaker, full of clichés and a terrific gift of repartee. He had very little brain, a trifling defect which had kept him, a disappointed man, at the local branch in Sleescale for fifteen years. He would never go further and he knew it. He did not wash very often. He looked as though he slept in his underwear. In fact, he did.

" So you've been out with Harry in the bloddy war ? " Heddon inquired sarcastically. " Don't tell me how you liked it. Come ben and crook your hough."

They went ben into the little office. They talked. It was true that Heddon had lost his clerk in the war—combed out by the bloddy Derby Scheme and shot through the bloddy head at Sampreux Wood. He would give David a try out to oblige Harry Nugent. It all depended on David—he would have to step lively to deal with Claims, Benefit and Correspondence at one and the same time. Moreover, David had overestimated the salary, which would be a bare thirty-five shillings a week.

" You'll get to know my style," grunted Heddon. " Here, have a look at this."

With a show of indifference, he opened a drawer and tossed over a newspaper to David—a labour paper—*The Weekly Worker*—some years old. On one of the yellowish sheets, bearing the indefinable staleness of treasured print, an article was marked in blue pencil.

" That's me," Heddon said. " Go on, read it. I wrote the bloddy thing."

While Heddon pretended not to watch him, David read the article. It was headed *Courts and Courts*, and it had a certain savage pungency. It contrasted the court held in Buckingham Palace with another court—Bloggs Court—which the writer knew. The wording was clumsy and brutal but the contrasts were violently effective. " Young Lady de Fallington wore a dress of white satin and a train embroidered with sequins. A string of priceless pearls adorned her patrician neck and her feathers were held in place by a band of diamanté "; and immediately below: " Old Mrs. Slaney is a charwoman. She wears no feathers but a bit of old sacking shaped like a skirt. She lives in one room in Bloggs Buildings, earns twelve shillings a week and has consumption."

David read the article through, carried away despite himself by its earnestness and vigour. The article epitomised Heddon, sincere, fanatical, imbued with a savage class hatred.

"It's good," David said at length and he meant it.

Heddon smiled, touched in his weakest spot, acknowledging David as a friend. He took back the article and replaced it carefully in a drawer. He said:

"That shows what I think of them. I hate them, the whole bloddy lot. I've got my knife in a few of them round about here. I make them dance to my tune all right. Take your bloddy Sleescale, for instance. We're going to have a bit of fun down there, one of these days soon."

David looked interested.

"Ay," Heddon said grimly, "you just watch what I'm telling you. Old Barras has got knocked out and the son thinks he's goin' to run the show. He's spreading hisself on pithead baths and the usual hygienic eyewash, spending some of the money his old man bled out the men, dodging the excess profits, see, an' the super tax, see, makin' us believe a bloddy new Jerusalem is rising out the Neptune. But you wait, just you wait, we haven't forgotten what they done to us at the disaster. They got out of that too easy. I been waiting on the war to finish so as I could get after them. They're goin' to sit up and know some more about it before I'm bloddy well finished with them!" Heddon broke off suddenly, staring in front of him. For a minute he looked hard and dark and grim. Then he relit his pipe which had gone out, pulled a tray of unanswered correspondence towards him. "Start Monday, then," he said to David, terminating the interview with a dreadful jocosity. "Go on! Don't keep your Rolls waiting outside any longer or the footman will be handing in his bloddy notice."

David caught the next train for Sleescale and in the train he turned over his plans deeply and seriously in his mind. The first step in the course he had mapped out for himself had been taken. It was not a thrilling step, but an obscure and very humble rebeginning. It had nothing to commend it except its necessity—not the necessity of money, but the necessity of purpose. His purpose lay clearly defined before him; he had made up his mind that there must be no half measures; it was all or nothing now.

He found Jenny in the middle of re-opening the house, taken out of herself by the novelty of the occasion, intermingling little thrills of discovery with little ejaculations of dismay.

"Look, David, I'd forgotten all about these lovely china candlesticks." Then: "Oh, goodness! will you look at the way the cake stand has peeled and after the way the young man swore to me it was pure nickel-plated," and " I am a house-proud little wife, amn't I, David dear ? "

David took off his coat and rolled up his sleeves and began to move furniture. Then he took bath brick and paraffin and went down on his knees and had it out with the rusty grate. He did a bit of quiet floor scrubbing, and afterwards weeded the overgrown little patch Jenny had once sweetly promised would be a garden. He helped in this way until three o'clock when they had a scratch meal. Then he had a wash, tidied himself up and went out.

It was very wonderful to be back in his own town again with the filth and misery and horror of the war behind him. He walked slowly down Lamb Street, feeling the life of Sleescale re-enfold him, seeing the black headstocks above him, above the town and the harbour and the sea. On his way towards the Terraces several of the men stopped him and shook hands with him and congratulated him on getting back safe. Their friendliness warmed David's heart, encouraged the hope which burned there.

He went first to his mother's and spent an hour with her. Sammy's death had left its mark on Martha, and the knowledge of his marriage had affected her most strangely. For Martha ignored Sammy's marriage; she blotted it completely from her consciousness. The whole town knew of Sammy's marriage: Annie's boy was eleven months old now and christened in the name of Samuel Fenwick. But for Martha the marriage was not; she walled herself in against it and hugged the delusion that Sammy had never belonged to anyone but her.

It was five o'clock when David left his mother and went along Inkerman to Harry Ogle's house. Harry Ogle was the eldest of the Ogle sons, brother of Bob Ogle who lost his life in the disaster, a man of forty-five who had followed and admired Robert Fenwick in his time, a pale wiry man with a curiously husky and ineffectual voice. But though he had no voice Harry had a reputation amongst the men for " a headpiece "; he was Lodge secretary, treasurer of the medical aid and labour member of the Sleescale Town Council.

Harry Ogle was glad to see David and after they had exchanged their news in the little back kitchen David leaned forward intently in his chair.

" Harry! I've come to ask you to do something for me. I want you to help me to get nominated for the Council Election next month."

Harry seldom asked questions and never showed surprise. But now he was silent for a longish time.

" The nomination is easy enough, David, but I'm feared you'd never have a chance. Murchison would be up against you in your ward. He's been in ten years running."

" I know! And he goes to one meeting in six."

David's reply seemed to amuse Harry.

" Maybe that's what keeps him in."

" I want to try, Harry," David said, something of his old impetuousness breaking through. " There's no harm in trying."

Another silence fell.

" Well," Harry said. " Seeing you're so set on it . . . I'll do what I can."

David went home that night feeling, deep within himself, that he had taken the second step. He said nothing to Jenny until, ten days later, his nomination was actually secured. Then he told her.

The Council—David standing for the Council! Oh, Jenny was wildly excited, why hadn't he told her before?—she had thought he was only kidding when he talked that night at Scottswood Road; why, it was wonderful, simply wonderful, David dear!

Delightedly, Jenny flung herself into the campaign. She went canvassing, sewed herself a beautiful " favour," made " little suggestions "—Clarry had a boy friend in the motor line who might lend them a car, she would herself accompany him round the division in the car, or why shouldn't the manager of the new Picturedrome be persuaded to " flash something about David on the screen " ? In every window of the house she stuck a bill head, VOTE FOR FENWICK, in bright red letters. These bill heads sent Jenny into an ecstasy; she would go out and gaze upon them several times a day.

" Why, David, you're going to be famous at last! " she declared airily; and she did not understand why this remark made David close his lips unhappily and turn away.

Naturally, she took it for granted that David would get " in," she visualised in advance little tea parties with the wives of his fellow councillors, she saw herself calling upon Mrs. Ramage at the big new Ramage house on the top of Sluice Dene, she felt vaguely that something would come out of all this for their real advancement. There was no *money* in the Town Council, really, but it might *lead* to something, she reasoned brightly. She did not understand. She was physically incapable of understanding the motive behind David's action.

The day of the election arrived. David, in his heart, was dubious of his prospects. His name was a good name in Sleescale, his father had died in the pit, his brother had died in the war and he himself had served at the front for three years. There was a useful romantic flavour—which he despised—in his returning from the war to stand for the Council. But he was untried and inexperienced, and Murchison had a way of extending credit in his shop about election time, a habit of slipping a box of scented soap or a tin of sardines into the baskets of his customers, which was not good for Murchison's opponent. On the afternoon of that Saturday, as he walked up the town, David met Annie coming down from New Bethel Street School where the polling was taking place. Annie stopped.

" I've just been up voting for you," she said quite simply. " I made sure I'd get finished up in time."

A real glow came over David at the way Annie said it, at the thought that she had troubled to go up and vote for him.

" Thanks, Annie."

They stood opposite each other in silence. Annie never had much to say, no confidences, no rapturous certainty in his success, but he could feel her good wishes coming out towards him. He felt suddenly that he had a great deal to say to her. He wanted to console her about Sammy; to ask about her boy; he had an uncontrollable impulse to speak to her about Robert. But the noisy, crowded street deterred him. Instead, he said:

" I'll never get in."

" Well," she said with her faint smile. " You might and you mightn't, Davey. And there's nothing like having a shot at it." Then, nodding in her own style, she went back home to see to her baby.

It struck David after his meeting with Annie how wisely and encouragingly she had summed up his chances. When the results were declared he had beaten Murchison by a bare forty-seven votes. But he was in.

Jenny, a little dashed at the slenderness of the margin, was nevertheless enchanted that David should be elected.

" Didn't I tell you! " She began to look forward to the first meeting of the new Council with as much sprightliness as if she were the new member herself.

David had hardly the same gaiety. David, with access to minutes and records and agenda, had been inquiring into the petty turmoil of local politics, discovering the usual brew of social, religious and personal interests, the ubiquitous policy of " you do this for me and I'll do that for you." Ramage, of course, was the dominant factor. Ramage had run the Council for the last four years. From the start David saw clearly that Ramage was the man he would be up against.

On the evening of November 2nd the new Council met: Ramage in the chair. The others were Harry Ogle, David, the Rev. Enoch Low of Bethel Street Chapel, Strother, head master of the school, Bates the draper, Connolly of the Gas Company and Rutter the clerk. At the start an exchange of bluff greetings took place in the ante-room between Ramage, Bates and Connolly; there was loud laughter and back slapping and jovial small-talk, while the Rev. Low, just out of earshot of the lewder jokes, was deferential to Connolly and obsequious to Ramage. No one took any notice of David and Harry Ogle. But as they moved into the council chamber Ramage gave David one cold look.

" I'm sorry our old friend Murchison isn't with us," he remarked in his loud blustering voice. " It don't seem proper like with a stranger here."

" Don't worry, lad," Harry whispered to David, " you'll soon get used to his line of gab."

They sat down and Rutter began to read the minutes of the last meeting of the old Council. He read quickly in a dry, sing-song, uninterested voice, then almost without stopping and in the same voice he announced:

" The first business is the passing of the meat and clothing contracts. I suppose, gentlemen, you wish to regard them as passed."

" That's right," yawned Ramage. He sat back in his chair at the head of the table, his big red face directed towards the ceiling, his hands belted round his enormous paunch.

" Ay, they're passed," Bates agreed, twiddling his thumbs and staring hard at the table.

" Passed, gentlemen," said Rutter and he reached for the minute book.

David interposed quietly.

" Just a minute, please! "

There was a silence, a very odd silence.

" I haven't seen these contracts," David remarked in a perfectly calm and reasonable voice.

" You don't have to see them," Ramage sneered. " They're passed by a majority."

" Oh! " exclaimed David in a tone of surprise. " I wasn't aware that we had voted."

Rutter the clerk had turned solemn and uncomfortable, examining the nib of his pen, as if it had made a most surprising blot. He realised that David was looking at him and he had at last to meet that inquiring eye.

" May I see the contracts ? " David asked. He knew all about the contracts; he wished merely to delay the entry in the minute book. These contracts were a long-standing scandal in Sleescale. The clothing contract was not important: it related to the supplying of uniforms to the sanitary inspector, health visitor and sundry local officials, and though Bates the draper took a scandalous profit on the transaction the amount involved was not material. But the meat contract was different. The meat contract, which gave Ramage the contract to supply all meat for the local hospital, was an iniquity in the face of God and man. The prices charged were for the best meat: Ramage supplied shin, neck and buff.

David took the meat contract from Rutter's nervous fingers. David examined the meat contract: the amount was large, the total came to £300. Deliberately he protracted his examination of the blue-grey document, holding up the meeting, feeling their eyes upon him.

" Is this a competitive contract ? " he inquired at length.

Unable to hold himself in any longer Ramage leaned forward across the table, his red face malignant with indignation and rage.

" I've had that contract for over fifteen years. Have ye any objections ? "

David looked across at Ramage: it had come, the first moment, the first test. He felt composed, master of himself. He said coolly:

" I imagine there are a number of people who object."

" The hell you do! " Ramage flared.

" Mr. Ramage, Mr. Ramage," bleated the Rev. Low sympathetically. In and out of the Council Low always toadied to Ramage, his pet parishioner, the man who had laid the foundation-stone of the Bethel Street Chapel, the golden calf amongst his thin-fleeced flock. And now he turned to David, peevishly reproving.

" You are new here, Mr.—er—Fenwick. You are a little over-zealous perhaps. You forget that these contracts are advertised for."

David answered:

" One quarter of an inch stuffed away in the local paper. An advertisement that nobody ever sees."

" Why should they see it ? " Ramage bawled from the end of the table. " And why the hell should you go shovin' in your neck ? The contract's been mine for fifteen year now. And nobody's never said a blasted word."

" Except the people who eat your rotten meat," David said in a level voice.

There was a dead silence. Harry Ogle darted an alarmed glance at David. Rutter the clerk was pale with fright. Ramage, bloated with fury, thumped his big fist on the table.

" That's slander," he shouted. " There's a law agin that sort of thing. Bates, Rutter, you're all witnesses—he's slandered me! "

Rutter lifted his meek face protestingly. The Rev. Low prepared to bleat. But Ramage bawled again:

" He's got to take it back, he's got to bloody well take it back."

Rutter said:

" I must ask you to withdraw, Mr. Fenwick."

A strange ardour suffused David. Without removing his eyes from Ramage's face he felt in his inside pocket and pulled out a packet of papers. He said:

" I need not withdraw if I can prove my statement. I have taken the trouble to collect my evidence. I have here signed statements from fifteen patients in the Cottage Hospital, from the three nurses and from the matron herself. These are the people who eat your meat, Mr. Ramage, and in the words of the matron it isn't fit for a dog. Let me read them to you, gentlemen. Mr. Ramage may regard them in the light of testimonials."

In a mortal stillness David read out the testimonials to Ramage's meat. Tough, full of gristle and sometimes tainted: these were the recommendations of the meat. Jane Lowry, one of the ward maids in the hospital, testified that she had suffered severe colic after eating a piece of rank mutton, Nurse Gibbings at the hospital had contracted an internal parasite which could only have come from polluted meat.

The air was petrified when David finished. As he folded his papers calmly, he could see Harry Ogle beside him, his face working with a grim delight, Ramage opposite, apoplectic with hate and fury.

" It's a pack of lies," Ramage stuttered at last. " The meat I supply is prime."

Ogle spoke up for the first time.

" Then God help prime meat," he growled.

The Rev. Low raised a pearly, propitiating hand. He bleated:

" Perhaps some bad pieces, once in a while; we can never be sure."

Harry Ogle muttered:

" Fifteen years it's been going on—that's your blessed once in a while."

Connolly thrust his hands in his pockets impatiently.

" What a song about nothing! Take a vote." He knew the way to settle the thing for good and all. He repeated loudly: " Vote on it."

" They'll beat you, David," said Harry Ogle in a feverish undertone. Bates, Connolly, Ramage and Low always hung together in their mutual self-interests.

David turned to the Rev. Low.

" I appeal to you as a minister of the gospel. Do you want these sick people in the hospital to go on eating inferior meat ? "

The Rev. Low flushed weakly and a look of obstinacy came in his face.

" I am yet to be convinced."

David relinquished the Rev. Low. He fastened his eye upon Ramage again. He said slowly:

" Let me make it quite clear. If this meeting refuses to sanction a new and adequate advertisement asking for tenders for meat I shall forward these statements to the County Medical Officer of Health and ask for a complete investigation of the entire question."

A duel ensued between the eyes of Ramage and David. But Ramage's eyes fell first. He was afraid. He had been swindling the Council for the past fifteen years, selling bad meat and selling underweight; he was afraid, horribly afraid of what an inquiry might reveal. Damn him, he thought, I'll have to climb down this time, damn the rotten interfering swine. I'll get even with him one day if it kills me. Aloud, he said in a surly voice:

" There's no need to vote. Advertise and be damned. My tender'll be as good as the rest."

A glorious wave of triumph swept over David. I've won, he thought,

I've won. The first step on the long road had been taken. He could do it. And he would.

The business of the meeting proceeded.

III

BUT, alas, the results of David's election to the Town Council proved sadly disappointing to Jenny. Jenny's ardours were invariably so sprightly that the afterglow was always a little tarnished at the edges. And Jenny's enthusiasm for the election went up like a rocket, burst with a beautiful display of stars and then fizzled out.

She had hoped for social advancement through the election, in particular she longed to " know " Mrs. Ramage. The afternoon tea parties which Mrs. Ramage gave were the *haut ton* of Sleescale: Mrs. Strother, the head master's wife, was usually there, and Mrs. Armstrong, and Mrs. Dr. Proctor and Mrs. Bates the draper's wife. Now if Mrs. Bates, why not Mrs. Fenwick ?—that was the question which Jenny asked herself with quite a breathless eagerness. They often had music at these tea parties, and who could sing more nicely than Jenny ? *Passing By* was such a beautiful song—quite *classical* in a manner of speaking: Jenny burned to sing that song before all the ladies of Sleescale in Mrs. Ramage's elegant drawing-room in the big new red sandstone house on Sluice Dene. Oh dear, oh dear, chafed Jenny, if only I could get *in* with Mrs. Ramage.

But no recognition came from Mrs. Ramage, not even the faintest shadow of a cross-street bow. And then, at the beginning of December a dreadful incident occurred. One Tuesday afternoon Jenny went into Bates's shop to buy a short length of muslin—Cousin Mayrianne writing in *Mab's Journal* had just hinted that muslin would soon be the *dernier cri* for smart women's undies—and there, at the counter of the drapery, examining some fine lace, stood Mrs. Ramage. Caught in this unguarded situation she looked quite amiable, did Mrs. Ramage. She was a big hard-boned bleak-faced woman who gave the queer impression of having been knocked about a bit and of having stood up to it with remarkable determination. But on this afternoon, fingering the pieces of lace, she had less determination and more pleasantness in her face. And as Jenny edged close to Mrs. Ramage and thought of both their husbands on the same council, so to speak, Jenny's social aspirations went completely to her head. She came right forward beside the counter and, smiling in her best company manner to Mrs. Ramage and showing all her nice teeth, Jenny said prettily:

" Good afternoon, Mrs. Ramage. Isn't it a beautiful afternoon for the time of year ? "

Mrs. Ramage turned slowly, She looked at Jenny. The horrible thing was that she recognised Jenny, then ceased to recognise her. For, in one deadly second, her face closed up like an oyster. She said very patronisingly and formally:

" I don't think we've met before."

But poor Jenny, flustered and misguided, rushed on to her doom.

"I'm Mrs. Fenwick," she murmured. " My husband is on the Town Council with your husband, Mrs. Ramage."

Mrs. Ramage looked Jenny up and down cruelly:

" Oh, *that*," she said. and raising the shoulder nearest Jenny she went back to the lace, saying in the sweetest manner to Bates' young lady assistant:

" I think after all I'll have the most expensive piece, my dear, and of course you'll send it and charge it to my account."

Jenny blushed scarlet. She could have died with shame. Such an affront, and before the nice young lady in the millinery! She spun round and fled from the shop.

That evening she whimpered out the story to David. He listened with a set face, his lips drawn into a fine line, then he said patiently:

" You can hardly expect the woman to fall on your bosom, Jenny, when Ramage and I are at each other's throats. In these last three months I've blocked his rotten meat contract. I'm trying to hold up the grant of £500 he was calmly asking the town to whack out on the new road past his new house in Sluice Dene. A new road useless for everybody but him! At the last meeting I suggested he was contravening six different regulations in his filthy private slaughter-house. You can imagine he doesn't exactly love me! "

She gazed at him resentfully, with scalding tears in her eyes

" Why must you go against people like that ? " she sobbed. " You're so queer. It would have been so useful for you to be on the right side of Mr. Ramage. I want you to get on."

He answered compassionately:

" But Jenny dear, I've told you getting on in that particular sense doesn't exist for me now. Perhaps I *am* queer. But I've been through some queer experiences in these last years. The pit disaster—and the war! Don't you think, Jenny, that it's high time some of us set ourselves to fight the abuses that produce disasters like the Neptune disaster and wars like the last war ? "

" But David," she wailed with unanswerable logic, " you're only getting thirty-five shillings a week! "

His breast heaved suddenly. He stopped arguing, gave her a quiet look, then rose and went into the other room.

This impressed her with the sense of his neglect, and the hot tears of self-pity trickled afresh. Then she brooded, became sulky and ill-tempered. David was different, completely different; her cajoling went for nothing, she seemed to have no grip upon him at all. She tried with a certain pique to make him passionate towards her, but in that way too he had turned curiously austere. She could feel that the physical side of love, unsupported by tenderness, was repugnant to him. She felt it as an insult. She could feel passionate in a minute, come right out of a violent quarrel to be violently passionate, to want a quick and urgent satisfaction —she called it modestly " making things up." But not David. It was, she told herself, *unnatural*!

Jenny, of course, was not the one, in her own phrase, " to stand being slighted," and she got her own back in many ways. She completely relaxed her efforts to please: David began to come home at nights to an out fire and no supper at all. The fact that he never complained now and never quarrelled exasperated her worst of all. On these nights she tried everything she knew to provoke him to a quarrel and when she failed she started to taunt him:

" Do you know that I was earning four pounds a week during the war ?—that's more than twice what you're earning now! "

" I'm not in this job for the money, Jenny."

" I don't care for money and you know it. I'm not mean. I'm generous. Remember the suit I gave you to go on our honeymoon. Oh, that was a scream that was!—me giving you your trousseau like. Even in those days you hadn't no gumption. I wouldn't call myself a man at all if I couldn't bring home decent money at the end of the week."

" We all have our standards, Jenny."

" Of course," with supreme spitefulness, " I could get a position any time I wanted. I went through the paper this morning and there was half a dozen posts I could have applied for easy. Why! I could get to be a buyer in the millinery any day."

" Be patient, Jenny! Perhaps I'm not going to be such a dud as you imagine."

If Jenny had grasped the situation she might, by construing it to her own standards, have been reconciled to patience. David was proving a success with Heddon—he accompanied him to all the Lodge meetings in the district and he was usually asked to speak. At Seghill he had addressed fifteen hundred men in the local Institute over the question of the Southport Resolutions. Heddon had been fogged by the findings of the January Conference and he had allowed David to handle the whole affair. The speech was a triumph for David: lucid, vital and alive with a passionate sincerity. At the end of the meeting, as he came off the platform, he was surrounded by a mass of men, who, to his amazement, wanted to shake him by the hand. Old Jack Briggs, seventy-six, beer- and case-hardened, the doyen of Seghill, pumped his arm till it ached.

" By Gor," croaked old Jack in the dialect, " tha wor a bloddy gud speech, lad. Aw've heerd mony a one but aw diddent niver hear better nor tha. Ye'll go fawr, hinny! "

And Heddon echoed that historic sentiment. The incredible fact stood established that Heddon, a bitter and unlettered man, was not jealous of David. Heddon had few friends, his violent nature repulsed all but the most persevering of his acquaintances, but from the first Heddon had taken to David. Heddon saw in David a rare and disinterested spirit and he knew so much of the dross of humanity that despite himself Heddon came to love David. He felt instinctively, here is a man who has found his natural bent, a born speaker, unruffled, penetrating and sincere, a clever and passionately earnest man, a man who might do much for his fellow men. And it was as if Heddon had said fiercely to himself: for God's sake don't let me be bitter and mean and envious but let me do my damnedest to help him on!

It was Heddon who read with delight the reports of the Sleescale Town Council meetings which were finding their way into the Tynecastle papers. The Tynecastle papers had discovered David, and his attacks upon the excellent and well-established abuses of Sleescale were manna to them in a dull season. From time to time the Tynecastle papers gaily captioned David and his doings: " Rumpus in Sleescale Council Chamber," and " Sleescale Trouble Maker at Work Again! "

Heddon dissolved in bitter laughter over the report of David's repartees. Peering over the paper's edge:

" Did ye really say that to the ucker, David? "

" Nothing like so good, Tom! "

" I'd have liked to see that Ramage's face when ye told him his bloddy slaughter-house wasn't fit to *kill* pigs in! "

David's inveterate modesty helped him all the more with Tom Heddon. If he had displayed the first signs of swelled head he would have killed himself stone dead with Heddon. But he did not, which made Tom cut out the choicest columns from the Tynecastle *Argus* and forward them to his old friend Harry Nugent with a significant blue pencil scrawl.

Jenny knew nothing of all this. And Jenny was not patient, construing David's absorption into neglect and being maddened by that supposed neglect. Jenny was so mad she had an excellent excuse for finding vicarious consolation in Murchison's invalid port. By the spring of 1919 Jenny was drinking regularly again. And about this time, an event of considerable psychological importance occurred.

On Sunday the 5th of May old Charley Gowlan died. Charley had been ill for six months with Bright's disease and finally, despite repeated tappings of his shiny, swollen abdomen, Charley went to God. It was a grim paradox that Charley, who had never cared for water much, should be water-logged at the end. But paradox or no, Charley did die, in mean, neglected circumstances. And two days later Joe arrived in Sleescale.

Joe's coming to Sleescale fell nothing short of a sensation. He came on the morning of that Tuesday in a glittering Sunbeam motor-car, a new twenty-five green Sunbeam driven by a man in dark green uniform. Immediately Joe stepped out of the car at his old home in Alma Terrace the car was surrounded by a gaping crowd. Harry Ogle, Jake Wicks, the new checkweigher, and a few of the Neptune overmen were at the house—it was almost time for the funeral—and although rumours of Joe's prosperity had reached the Terraces they were frankly dazzled by the change in Joe. Indeed, Frank Walmsley, who had once been his chargeman, straightaway addressed him as sir. Joe was discreetly but handsomely dressed, he wore spats, his cuff links were of dull gold and his watch-chain of fine platinum. He was shaved and manicured and polished. He shone with a bluff and enterprising opulence.

Harry shifted his feet awkwardly before Joe's opulence, struggling with the memory of that young Joe who had been hand-putter in the Paradise.

"I'm glad you've come like, Joe, we clubbed together, a few of us officials, to get the money like, we diddent want your dad to have a guardian's funeral."

"Good God, Harry," Joe blew up dramatically. "Are you talking about the workhouse? D'you mean to say it was as bad as that?"

His eye swept round the low, dirty kitchen where he had once licked pot pie from the blade of his knife, and fell upon the wretched black coffin where the dropsical corpse of his father lay.

"My God," he raved, "why didn't somebody tell me. Why didn't you write to me. You all *know* me, where I am, and *what* I am. Is this a Christian country or what is it? You ought to be damned well ashamed of yourselves, letting the poor old man conk out this way. Too much trouble I suppose to even '*phone* me at my works . . ."

He was equally affected at the funeral. At the graveside he broke down and blubbered into a big silk handkerchief. Everyone agreed it did him the greatest credit. And he drove straight from the cemetery to Pickings in Lamb Street and ordered a magnificent headstone.

"Send the bill to me, Tom," he declared eloquently. "Expense is no object!" Later, Tom did send the bill: he sent the bill a great many times.

After the funeral Joe made a short sentimental tour of the town, evincing all the successful man's emotion at visiting his old haunts. He impressed Harry Ogle with the need for getting him a photograph of the house in Alma Terrace. Joe wanted a photograph, a big enlarged photograph; he must have a photograph of the humble home where he was born. Let Harry get Blair the photographer to do it and send the bill and the photograph to Joe!

Towards the end of the day, about six o'clock, Joe dropped in to see his old friend David. The news of Joe's visit to Sleescale had preceded him, and Jenny, besides informing David, had prepared lavishly and excitedly for Joe.

But Joe declined Jenny's hospitality point blank; he had a dinner engagement at the Central, Tynecastle. Jenny flinched; but she persevered. Then Joe took one calm and competent look at Jenny, up and down, like that, and Jenny saw that it was no go now—no go at all. The gladness went right out of her eye, the coquettishness vanished and she sat silent—quivering and envious.

Yet she was all ears, and, hanging on every word of Joe's account of himself, she could not help comparing the two men and what they had achieved: the glittering success of Joe, and the dismal failure of David.

Joe spoke very openly—there was always a magnificent frankness about Joe. It was clear he had regarded the end of the war as premature—it hadn't been such a bad old war after all. Yet things were looking great even now. Pulling out his gold cigarette case Joe lit up, breathed a Turkish aroma down his nostrils, then, leaning forward, tapped David confidentially on the knee.

"You knew we'd bought out Millington at the foundry—Jim Mawsor and me. God, I'm sorry for poor Stanley. He's living down at Bourne mouth for good now, him and the wife, he couldn't get out Platt Lan quick enough. A nice chap, mind you, but no stability at all. He's a wreck, they tell me, a nervous wreck. Oh well, maybe it was the best thing that could happen to him, us taking the works off his hands; he got a price too, oh yes, he got a price." Joe paused, inhaled cigarette smoke and smiled guilelessly at David. His bragging had acquired subtlety now, he covered it with a bland indifference. "You knew we'd got the order for the new Neptune equipment? What? Yes, sure enough, we turned over again the minute the war went west. While all the mugs sat on their dumps of whizz-bang castings and wondered what was happenin' we got back to tools and shackle bolts and roofing-bars and haulage. You see," Joe became more confidential, more expansive than ever, "while the war was on it was all production at the collieries; not a red one of them had time to recondition their plant, even supposin' they could get the equipment—an' they couldn't. Now Jim and me figured it out they'd be yellin' for stuff when peace come on, and there wouldn't be nobody to answer the yell, except maybe the early birds like Jim and me." Joe sighed gently. "Well, that's how we got the Neptune order. Ah-ha, fifty thousand pounds of stuff we'll sell them at the Neptune before the year's out."

The tremendous, the almost fabulous sum, fifty thousand pounds, resounded in the small room filled with pinchbeck furniture and the smoke of Joe's Turkish cigarette and almost burst poor Jenny's eardrums. To think that Joe was handling such colossal business! She shrank down into her seat, consumed with envy.

Joe saw the effect he was creating, the famished stare in Jenny's eyes, the cold hostility in David's, and it all went a little to his head. With patronising fluency he ran on.

"Mind you, although we're busy at the works—Mawson and Gowlan I ought to say, it's a good name, don't you think?—Excuse me, I can't help being a bit struck on the firm. Well, as I was sayin', Jim and me has all sorts of side lines. Take this, for instance. You've heard of the Disposals Board. No?" Joe shook his head regretfully. "Well, you surely ought to have heard of that. You might have made a bit of money if you'd heard of that, although, mind you, there's got to be capital behind you to do anything. You see the Government, more power to them, has bought and ordered and commandeered a whole pack of things they don't need now, everything from gum elastic boots to a fleet of merchant ships. An' seein' the Government don't need these things naturally the Government wants to be rid of them!" Joe, loyal subject of the Crown, lolled back in his chair, permitting himself a gentle grin at his manner of helping the Government, in his own small way, to be rid of them. "You see that little car of mine outside?"

"Oh yes, Joe," Jenny gulped. "It's a beauty."

"Not so bad, not so bad," Joe admitted. "Just a month old. You might like to know how it happened." He paused, his small brown eyes glistening. "Six weeks ago Jim and myself went up to look at some Government stuff beyond Morpeth. In a timber plantation we come across a couple of traction engines what they'd used to drive the saw-mills and forgot about in their hurry. The engines were standing there among the rotten timber logs, covered with rust and nettles up to their fly-wheels. To look at them, ordinary like, the engines was junk, but to look at them prop'ly they was goers, good as new and worth a couple of thousand apiece." Joe paused blandly. "Well, Jim and me submitted a junk price and got away with it. We had the engines drove down to Tynecastle under their own power, cleaned and painted and sold handsome. We split even on the profit—and the little bus outside"—Joe waved his hand to the window—"is the result!"

Silence. Then, wrenched from Jenny's pale lips, a gasp of unwilling admiration. That wonderful, *wonderful* car shining outside there: bought and paid for and *made* by a single stroke of business. Such cleverness! Oh, it was too much, too much for her to endure.

Joe left it at that. Joe knew when he had put it over all right. He switched his eye towards the cheap blue enamel clock on the mantel-piece and with an exclamation he corroborated the time upon his thin gold watch. He jumped up. "Good God! It's time I was on my way. I'll be late for Jim if I don't look out. Sorry to have to leave so soon, but I'm due at the Central seven o'clock!"

He shook hands and made for the door, voluble and genial, laughing and talking, full of gusto, good-nature and himself! The door banged, the car purred, he was off!

David looked at Jenny with that faint ironic smile upon his lips:

"That was Joe," he said.

Jenny gazed back at him wickedly.

"I know it was Joe," she flared sullenly. "What are you talking about?"

"Oh, nothing, Jenny. But now that he's gone it's just struck me that he still owes me three pounds!"

A perfect demon of temper rose in Jenny's breast, urged and goaded by envy and the knowledge that Joe had so positively finished with her for good. Her lip curled.

"Three pounds," she sneered. "That's what Joe would fling to a waiter. He's worth a fortune, Joe is, he could buy and sell you a thousand times. He's a man, Joe is. He can do things, get out and make some money. Why don't you take a lesson from him? Look at his car, and his clothes, and his jewellery and the cigarettes he smokes. Look at him, I tell you, and think shame of yourself." Her voice rose to a scream. "Joe's the sort of man who would give his wife a good time, take her to restaurants and dances and places, he'd give her society and refinement and that. Take a look at him, I say, and then look at yourself. You're not fit to lick Joe's boots, you aren't. You're not a man at all. You're a washout, that's what you are, that's what Joe's thinkin' about you now. As he's driving away in his lovely big car, Joe's lying back and laughing at you. He's laughing himself silly at you. Washout, he's saying, washout, washout, washout!"

Her voice shrilled and cracked, there was a spume of mucus on her lips and hatred in her eyes.

He stood with clenched hands facing her. With a great effort he controlled himself, realising that the only way to get her out of the paroxysm was to leave her alone. He turned. He went out of the room and into the kitchen.

Jenny remained in the parlour, her breath coming in quick hot gasps. She stifled an impulse to follow David into the kitchen and have it out with him; she saved the taunts and all the wounding insults that still lay on her tongue. She knew a better way than that. She swallowed dryly. The scent of the expensive cigarette smoke still lingering in the air maddened her beyond endurance. She rushed from the room, put on her hat and went out.

It was late when she came home. Nearly eleven o'clock. But David had not gone to bed. He sat by the deal table in the kitchen immersed in a first copy of the new Coal Industry Commission Act which had just come into law. As she came into the kitchen he raised his eyes. She stood in the doorway, hat slightly atilt, eyes glassy, cheeks shot with tiny threads of blood. She was hopelessly drunk.

"Hello," she sneered. "Still busy makin' money?" Her words were all slurred together, but the expression on her face was unmistakable. He jumped up in horror: he had never seen her drunk before.

"Lemme alone," she struck at him and nearly fell. "I don't wan' you playin' 'bout me. Keep y'r han's 'way. You don't deserve nothin' like that! "

His soul sickened within him.

" Jenny! " he implored.

" Shenny! " she mimicked, making a drunken face at him. She wavered towards him, placed her arms drunkenly akimbo. " Y're a fine fellow, makin' me waste th' bes' of my life here. I had plenty o' fun in th' war when y'were 'way. I wan'a have plen'y fun *now*! "

" Please, Jenny," he begged her, frozen with pain. " You'd better lie down."

" I won' lie down! " she cackled. " I won' lie down f'r you . . ."

Watching her, he thought suddenly of the child she had borne him, and the pain of her present degradation became unsupportable.

" For God's sake, Jenny, pull yourself together. Even if I don't mean anything to you now, think of our child, think of Robert. I haven't talked about it. I don't want to hurt you. But doesn't his memory mean anything at all ? "

She burst out laughing, she laughed and laughed drunkenly, until the saliva drooled from her mouth.

" I've been meanin' to tell you 'bout that," she jeered. " Meanin' for long time. *Our* chil'. Y' flatter yourself, m' lord. How d'you know he was yours ? "

Uncomprehending, he looked at her with disgust upon his face. It maddened her.

" You fool," she shrieked suddenly. " It was Joe's! "

He understood. He went dead white. He caught her fiercely by the shoulder and pinned her against the lintel of the door.

" Is that true ? "

Staring back at him glassily, sobered by the shock, she saw that she had gone too far; she had never meant to let out the truth to David. Terrified, she began to cry. She collapsed. Sagging against him she wept herself into hysteria.

" Oh dear, oh dear! I'm sorry, David. I'm bad, I'm bad. I'm bad. I want no more to do with men, never, never, never, never. I want to be good. I want to be good. I'm not well, that's the trouble, I'm not really well, I've got to take a little glass to keep my strength up." She howled and howled.

With that set cold face he dragged her to the sofa, supporting her sagging head with the palm of his hand. She began to drum her heels in the frenzy of her hysteria. She went on:

" Give me another chance, David, oh, for God's sake give me another chance. I'm not bad, really I'm not; he just came round me like and it's all finished and done with years ago; you could see that to-night, you'd have thought I was dirt beneath his feet. And you're the best man living, David, the best man breathing. And I'm sick, David, oh, I'm awfully ill. I haven't had a holiday for ages, I'm not really well. Oh! if only you'll give me another chance, David, David, David . . ."

He stared darkly away from her, letting her race on, letting her work off all the agony of her remorse. A heavy pain pressed upon his breast; it was a frightful blow she had given him. He had loved the memory of little Robert, treasured it in his heart. And she had besmirched even that!

At last she stopped whining, the nervous beating of her heels was still. There was silence. He took a long breath. Then in a still voice he said:

" Let's not talk about it any more, Jenny. It's perfectly true, what you say. You're not well. I think it might do you good if you went away for a little. How would you like to go down to Dan Teasdale's farm in Sussex ? I could easily arrange it. I'm in touch with Dan."

" To the farm ? " Jenny gasped, then lifted agonised, enraptured eyes. " Down in Sussex."

" Yes! "

" Oh, David." Jenny began to weep again; the sudden prospect was so wonderful, and David's kindness so wonderful, and everything so wonderful. " You're so good to me, David, just hold me in your arms and say you still love me."

" Will you promise me not to touch drink down there ? "

" I do, David, I do, I do." Sobbing, she swore it in a passion of goodness and devotion.

" All right, I'll arrange it, Jenny."

" Oh, David," sobbing and choking and clutching at him," you're the best man that ever breathed."

IV

ONE morning early in June, the following month, David saw Jenny off at the Central Station, Tynecastle. It had been a simple matter to arrange with Grace Teasdale for Jenny to go to Winrush—Grace was delighted. The weekly sum which David could pay was small enough, but from Grace's frank and unassuming letter, David had the feeling that it would be welcome.

Jenny was thrilled, the excitement of the holiday had risen to her head and flushed her cheeks and made her eyes bright. She was warm and tender and penitent. She saw herself feeding the chickens, caressing the sweet little lambs and returning to David at the end of the three weeks purified and sanctified and prettier than ever. Oh, it was *nice*!

She stood with David by the open door of her compartment, her corner seat facing the engine reserved by a little pile of papers and a magazine. She thought it good of David to have bought her the magazine—not that she approved much of his choice but it was the correct thing for a lady to set out on a journey with a magazine. And Jenny was never happier than when doing *the correct thing.* She chatted away to David, darting tenderly pathetic glances at him from time to time, indicating her contrition and a sincere desire for amendment. He was very silent. She often wondered what he thought about . . . well . . . what she had so foolishly " let out." Sometimes she felt vaguely that he had forgotten about the whole thing, or that he disbelieved it entirely, for he had never once referred to it. At any rate, she was sure he had forgiven her, and that flattered her vanity. She had no conception of the frightful blow which her disclosure had been to David. He had believed her entirely faithful to him. He had cherished the memory of little Robert with a great tenderness. And in one drunken sentence she had smashed it all. He suffered abominably, but because he did not accuse her, cross-examine her, wrest every sordid detail from her and then beat her within an inch of her life, Jenny felt that he did not suffer. She did not really know David. She could not appreciate the strength and fineness of character which kept him silent. And in her secret heart she was puzzled, pleased. perhaps a little scornful.

She looked at the big clock at the end of the station.

" Well! " she said, " it's nearly time! " She got into the compartment and he shut the door. The whistle blew. She gave him a big hug. Her last words were:

" You'll miss me, David, won't you ? "

Then she settled herself with a pleased sigh. It was a long journey but it passed quickly between her magazine and the sandwiches and an interesting examination of her fellow passengers. Jenny took great pride in her ability to *place* people: at one shrewd glance she could tell what they had on, what the hat cost, whether that diamond was real or false, whether or not " they were real class."

At two o'clock Jenny changed trains, at three she went along the corridor and had a cup of tea and a refined conversation with a nice fair young man at the same table. Really at the next table, he was, but he came over and sat down. Funny he should be a commercial traveller!—with a little inward giggle she remembered the bald-headed commercial she had created for David's benefit on the honeymoon at Cullercoats. Dear David! She was really quite distant to the nice fair young man, only politely interested when he told her he travelled for surgical appliances—oh, she was extremely as she should be, shaking hands ever so ladylike when he said good-bye.

At half-past four she reached Barnham Junction and Dan met her at the station. Dan looked big and healthy and happy—he wore an old army shirt open at the neck, leggings and corduroy breeches. Dan had a little Ford runabout shaped like a lorry at the back, and swinging her suit-case up as if it had been a feather, he drove down to Winrush and the farm.

The farm delighted Jenny and Grace's welcome delighted her even more than the farm. Grace had a splendid tea ready with new-laid eggs and a sponge cake and lots of little short-cakes which were lovely and which Grace said were Sussex griddle cakes. They all sat in together, Jenny, Grace, Dan, little Caroline Ann and Thomas the new baby—who answered to the name of Dickery Dock—perched in his high chair to the right of Grace. They they sat, in the big stone-flagged kitchen, and Jenny went into raptures over the griddle cakes and the new-laid eggs and Dickery Dock. Jenny went into raptures about everything. Everything was so nice, Jenny said.

After tea Grace took Jenny round the farm, explaining to Jenny that it was a very small place, only forty acres, which they had rented from old Mr. Purcell. Grace made no concealment of what shrewd little Jenny had already clearly seen. Grace said with perfect simplicity that Dan and she were extremely hard up. Chicken-farming, which was what Dan chiefly went in for, was hard work and small profit. But they would have a number of paying guests in the summer and paying guests, Grace smiled, did pay. Grace smiled often: she was extremely happy with Dan, Caroline Ann and Dickery Dock; she had to work like a nigger but she was happy. She had got Dan out of the Neptune, far, far away from the wretched pit, and that was what counted. As for money, Grace added, money doesn't matter a dump!

Touched by Grace's confidences Jenny warmly agreed. Why, she simpered, with a little thrill at being able to cap Grace's argument, why, that's exactly what *my* David says about money.

Tired out by her journey, Jenny went to bed early that night. She slept like a top and wakened to bright sunshine and green trees waving in the breeze and the sound of a mooing cow. Oh, it's nice, thought Jenny, lying luxuriously. A knock came to the door.

"Come in," Jenny sang out, feeling wonderful.

A roly poly of a girl—Grace's one maid, a daily from the village—entered, bringing Jenny her tea. The girl's name was Peg. Her cheeks were as red as cherries and her short trotters massive as piano legs. Jenny knew she would get a lot of fun out of Peg's legs—Peg's legs were a scream!

After she had sipped her tea Jenny got up, slipped on her dressing-gown and her green mules with the pretty marabout trimming. Fluffy, like her dressing-gown, and *nice*. She pattered to the bathroom. It was an old house with big bare polished boards and no paper on the walls but Grace had been busy with her paint-brush. The vivid painted walls were extremely effective against the old dark wood. The bathroom was pleasant, too, very plain and enamelled. Jenny took her bath. At home, Jenny never bathed in the morning but when one was staying with people, of course . . . well . . . naturally.

After breakfast Jenny wandered round the farm by herself, discovering fresh enchantments at every turn. The cute little chickens, the lovely smell of the barn, dear Grace's rock garden full of sweet saxifrage, the darlingest school of piglets which fled before her, flicking their tails and leaping, leaping like a pack of miniature hounds. Oh, isn't the country too wonderful, Jenny breathed in an ecstasy of romance.

At eleven Grace asked Jenny if she wanted a swim. Grace said that in the summer Dan and she and " the family " went for a dip every day, no matter how completely or infernally busy they might be. Smiling, she said that Dan and she had solemnly taken an oath to this effect. Jenny couldn't swim but she went gaily with them to the beach—a short strip of sandy beach bordering their land.

Jenny stood watching on the beach while Grace and Dan and " the family " went in. Dan carried Caroline Ann and Grace carried six-months-old Dickery Dock. There was enormous fun in the shallow water; then while the two infants lay sprawling on the warm soft sand Grace and Dan swam out. They swam far out, quite a wonderful swim, and when they came back they looked exactly like the picture on the front cover of Jenny's magazine. A queer catch took Jenny by the throat. Grace's strong slender figure was tanned and upright and careless. She was playing a game with Dan now, tossing Dickery Dock between them like a ball, and didn't Dickery Dock like it! Caroline Ann ran about in the buff, shrieking with delight, imploring her mummy and daddy to let Dickery Dock fall. But mummy and daddy wouldn't and finally Dan pulled Caroline Ann's legs away from her, and there was a glorious mix up on the sand.

Then Dan's half-hour was up and he dashed back to drive the Ford into Fittlehampton. Jenny returned with Grace thoughtfully. What did money matter to these happy people? They had wonderful health, fresh air to breathe, the sea to bathe in and the sun to shine on them.

Jenny sat down straight away after lunch and wrote a four-page tear-stained letter to David, exalting the beauties of the simple life and the pleasures of the country. She walked all the way to Barnham Junction to post it and felt rarefied and pure. She knew that she was *finding* herself. She could be like Grace, too, if she wanted—why, indeed, not? She smiled. Tenderly she tried to pat a tiny lamb which poked its nose at her through the hedge of the lane, but the lamb ran away and stood in the middle of the field doing duties at an adjacent haystack. Never mind, never mind, it was all too wonderful for words.

Next day came bright and sunny and the next and the next, and it was still wonderful. Perhaps . . . well, on reflection . . . perhaps not so completely wonderful. Jenny understood that one got used to things in time and that was why, though still fond of the farm, she was not quite so fond of the farm as she had been. Funny! Jenny smiled to herself as, on the following Saturday, she sat on the beach enjoying a cigarette by herself. It was not that Dan and Grace were not still nice to her. Dan and Grace were perfect. But it was just the tiniest bit dull down here, she had to confess; not a single soul on this beach, let alone a band and a promenade, and as for feeding the chickens she was frankly sick of feeding the chickens! And these pigs—she hated the very sight of the dirty little brutes.

She got up from the beach and, feeling that she must do something, she decided to walk into Barnham. At Barnham she bought another packet of cigarettes and a morning paper, then she called in at the Merrythought and had a glass of port. What a hole! Did they really have the nerve to call it a hotel? And she was looking her best, too, she saw from a mirror advertising Bass on the opposite wall. Looking her best and no one to see her but the gnarled old woman in the Merrythought who glanced at her suspiciously and almost refused to serve her. The old woman had been feeding her hens. O Lord, thought Jenny, amn't I ever to get away from these blessed hens?

She walked back in quite a paddy and went straight up to her room and began to read the paper. It was a London paper. Jenny adored London, she had been to London four times in her life and had loved it every time. She read all the London society news, then she read the advertisements. The advertisements were really interesting, really they were, especially those referring to experienced saleswomen wanted. Jenny went to bed thoughtfully that night.

Next day it was raining.

"O Lord," said Jenny, staring blankly at the rain. "A wet Sunday!" She refused to go to church, mooned about the place and was snappy to Caroline Ann. In the afternoon Grace lay down and Dan went into the barn to trim some hay. Five minutes later Jenny wandered into the barn.

"Hello, you!" she called up brightly to Dan, flashing a sprightly glance at him, her feet planted coquettishly apart.

Dan looked down at her, very simple and unsmiling.

"Hello," he said without enthusiasm, and turning his back he re-engaged himself vigorously with the hay.

Jenny's face fell. She stood for a minute saving her pride. She might have known that Dan had no eyes for anyone but Grace, he was nothing but a turnip. Then she wandered out into the rain. Turnip, she muttered, blessed turnip.

Next day was again wet. Jenny's discontent grew. How long had she to endure it here in this rotten beastly hole? Twelve more days; she'd never do it, never. She wanted a bit of life, a bit of fun, she wasn't cut out for this mangel-wurzel misery. She began to blame David for sending her here, even to hate him for it. Yes! it was all very well for him. He was having a gay time no doubt in Tynecastle; she knew what men were when their wives were away from them, having a rare old time while she was stuck here, here in this hole.

And in her own way Jenny began to turn the whole question of her relations with David over in her mind. She wasn't going to stand it. Why should she? She could earn four pounds a week off her own bat and enjoy London into the bargain. She didn't really love David in any case.

Next day the sun came out, a glorious sun, but it brought no answering warmth to Jenny's face. The doors and windows of the farm were wide open, the lovely breeze blew in. Grace was making cherry jam, lovely cherry jam with cherries from her own orchard. Flushed and happy she moved about the big kitchen. She thought Jenny looked a little down and when she milked the one Guernsey cow she put a glass of the rich foaming milk on the table for Jenny.

" I don't like milk," Jenny said and walked out sulkily into the sunny yard. The bees hummed about the flowers, down in the corner Dan was chopping firewood—the axe made a lovely flashing arc—and across the fields cattle lay chewing in the shade. It was beautiful.

But not to Jenny. She hated it now, hated it and hated it. She longed for London, she had set her heart on London, she yearned for the noise and bustle and glamour of the streets. With her head in the air she marched down to Barnham and bought a paper. She stood outside the shop reading the advertisements, ever and ever so many advertisements; she was positive she could land one of them. Just for fun, she walked to the station and she inquired about the trains to London. An express left at four o'clock. In a flash Jenny's decision was taken. That afternoon while Grace was busy making tea Jenny packed her bag and slipped out. She caught the four o'clock for London.

When Grace went to call Jenny and found out that she had taken her things and gone she was dreadfully upset. She ran down to the kitchen.

" Dan! " she said, " Jenny has gone. What have we done ? "

Dan paused in spreading some of the new cherry jam upon a large slice of bread.

" So she's gone, eh ? "

" Yes, Dan! Have we offended her ? I'm vexed."

Dan resumed his interest in the bread and jam. He took an enormous bite; then, munching slowly:

" I wouldn't be vexed, Grace dear. I don't think she was much good, that one." This indicated perhaps that Dan was less of a turnip than Jenny had believed.

That evening Dan squared his shoulders over a letter to David. He regretted very much, he wrote, that Jenny had been obliged to cut short her stay at Winrush and trusted that she would get home safely.

David received that letter on the evening of the following day and it caused him a definite uneasiness. Jenny had not arrived. He looked across at his mother who had come down to keep house for him. But he said nothing. He felt that Jenny must arrive next day. In spite of everything he still loved Jenny; surely she would come.

But Jenny did not come.

V

GENTLY and tenderly Aunt Carrie wheeled Richard in the Bath chair right up to the laburnum tree on the lawn. The day was warm and sunny, and the yellow blossom dangled thick on the laburnum, turning the tree to a great yellow flower which cast a pleasant shade upon the shorn turf. In this shade, with many fussings, Aunt Carrie began to settle Richard. First there was the little plank she had made Bartley saw specially for his feet, and the hot-water bottle, an aluminium bottle since that kept the heat longest, then the Jaeger rug tucked in carefully the whole way round. Aunt Carrie understood exactly what Richard liked and it was joy for her to humour him in every whim, especially as she knew that he was " getting on " at last.

Aunt Carrie would never forget the first real indication that Richard was getting on, that day, three months and a week ago precisely, when he had spoken to her. In bed, like a great log, dumb and heavy, his eye rolling in his head as it followed her movements about the room, that dull yet living eye, a basilisk, he had mumbled:

" It's you . . . Caroline."

In the inexpressible rapture of it she almost fainted, like a mother with the first speech of her first-born.

" Yes, Richard "—clutching her breast—" it's Caroline . . . Caroline."

He mumbled:

" What did I say ? " Then he lost interest. But after that it did not matter. He had spoken.

Intoxicated by this auspicious sign, she had redoubled her attentions upon him, washing him all over carefully twice a day and rubbing his back with methylated spirits every night before dusting him with talcum. It had been difficult to prevent bedsores, changing the wet sheets sometimes four times in the day, but she had done it. She was getting Richard right. His movements started to return slightly, the movements of the paralysed side, and she would rub the right arm for an hour on end just as she had brushed Harriet's hair. While she rubbed him, his dull eye would roll up and down her figure, not without a certain slyness, and often he mumbled:

" You're a fine woman, Caroline. . . . But they are tampering with me . . . electricity. . . ."

It was one of his delusions that they were sending electrical currents through his body. At night now he always asked Caroline to pull his bed away from the wall so that they could not send electricity through from the adjoining room. He asked her slyly, slurring and mumbling the syllables, mixing up his consonants, sometimes missing out words altogether.

There might be something in these electrical notions, or there might not—Aunt Carrie would not commit herself. She could not dream of questioning Richard's judgment. Her idea was to interest him, take him out of himself, and this made her think of Mrs. Humphry Ward, her favourite author whom in times of spiritual stress she had found to be a true healer. So she began, every forenoon, and every evening, to read aloud to Richard, commencing with *Lady Rose's Daughter*, perhaps a little selfishly, as this was her own favourite, and when she came to the great moment of renunciation tears dropped down Aunt Carrie's cheeks. And Richard would stare at the ceiling or pick at his clothes or put his finger into his mouth and at the end of a chapter he would remark:

" They're tampering with me," and then in a low voice, " Electricity! "

With the coming of the fine weather she had wheeled Richard into the good fresh air, and as he sat upon the lawn she advanced one stage further, putting the open book into his left hand and letting him have the pleasure of reading Mrs. Ward for himself. He seemed to enjoy Mrs. Ward very much. He began by placing *Lady Rose's Daughter* on his knee, pulling out his watch, looking at his watch and putting back his watch. Next he took a pencil and very clumsily, and with great effort, wrote with his left hand on the margin of the book: *Start* 11.15. Then he counted four pages forward and wrote at the foot of the page: 12.15 × 4 *End of the shift*. And after that he stared at the shaky, almost indecipherable writing with an air of childish triumph.

But this bright May morning, whenever he was settled, before he could ask for his book, Aunt Carrie seated herself on the stool beside him and remarked:

" I have a letter from Hilda this morning, Richard. She has passed another of her examinations. Would you like to hear what she says ? "

He reflected vacantly towards the great yellow blossom of the laburnum tree.

" Hilda is a fine woman . . . you are a fine woman yourself, Caroline." He added, " Harriet was a fine woman."

Aunt Carrie, adept at glossing over such little eccentricities, went on pleasantly:

" Hilda's progress has really been splendid, Richard. She writes that she is extremely happy in her work. Listen, Richard." She read out Hilda's letter, dated May 14th, 1920, and written from an address in Chelsea, reading slowly and distinctly, trying her gentle best to keep Richard interested and informed. But the moment she had finished he whimpered:

" Why don't I get letters? . . . never any letters. Where is Arthur? He is the worst offender . . . What is he doing at the Neptune? Where is my book? . . . I want my book."

" Yes, Richard." She soothed him hurriedly and handed him his writing book. " There now."

With the book on his knee he watched her slyly until she had picked up and was busy with her needlework, then he shielded the book against spying eyes with his curved, paralysed hand. Left-handed he wrote:

In defence of the Neptune, notes further to those composed Memorandum—a stumbling secret look at his watch—12.22 × 3.14 *and considered thereafter . . .*

But here a sound disturbed him and in a perfect panic of suspicion he broke off and clumsily shut the book. Ann was coming across the lawn with his milk. He watched Ann approaching and gradually his face cleared, his eye brightened until he was smiling and nodding at her—Ann was a fine woman too. Ann seemed conscious of his smile and the bobbings of his head for she gave the tray to Aunt Carrie, carefully avoiding Richard altogether, and went quickly away.

His face fell ridiculously; he became angry; he refused to drink his milk.

" Why does she go away? Why doesn't Arthur come? What is he doing? Where is he? " The questions tumbled incoherently from his lips.

" Yes, Richard, yes," she murmured. " He's at the pit, of course. You know he'll be here for lunch presently."

" What is he doing? " he repeated. " What is he hiding from me? "

" Nothing, Richard, absolutely nothing. You know he talks to you and tells you. Do drink your milk. Oh, look, you're spilling it all. There now! Shall I give you your book again? That's right."

" No, no, it isn't right. He doesn't understand. No head at all . . . and tampering with things. He's trying to keep me here. Electricity . . . through the walls. If he's not careful," the dull eye rolled cunningly towards her, " if he's not careful he'll be landing himself in trouble. An accident . . . a disaster . . . an inquiry. Extremely foolish! "

" Yes, Richard."

" I must speak to him again . . . I must insist . . . no time like the present."

" No, Richard."

" Take this glass then and stop talking. You talk and talk. It keeps me from my work."

Here another sound disturbed him and this time it was Arthur coming up the drive. With the same furtive haste he handed Aunt Carrie his empty glass, then he waited upon Arthur with a great pretence of unconcern. But underneath he was trembling, shivering with resentment and distrust.

Arthur crossed the lawn towards the laburnum tree. He wore his knickerbockers and heavy pit boots and his shoulders drooped as though he had been working hard. He had, indeed, for more than a year, been pushing forward at full pressure, conscious of his own nervous tension, yet determined not to relax until he had seen it all through. At last, however, the improvements at the Neptune were near completion, the new pithead baths finished, while the combined drying and locker rooms, modelled on the latest type instituted by the Sandstrüm Obergamt, would be ready by the end of June. The entire bank stood reorganised, the old Pierce-Goff ventilators scrapped and modern air pumps substituted, the closing apparatus and winding ropes renewed, the headstocks bedded in concrete cones and fed from the new powerhouse. Impossible almost to recognise this new Neptune—it had lost the old slovenliness, it looked trim, efficient and secure.

What effort he had put into it! And what money! But the splendour of his creation more than repaid him; sustained him when he got worried and depressed. There had been difficulties occasionally. The men were dubious of his intentions; his war record made him an object of suspicion. Besides, his temperament often betrayed him into bouts of causeless melancholy when he felt unsupported and alone.

Such a mood hovered above his shoulder as he drew up beside Barras. It made his tone gentler, more tolerant than was usual.

"Well, father," he said.

Barras peered up at him, with a grotesque assumption of authority.

"What have you been doing?"

"I've been inbye in Globe, this morning," Arthur explained mildly, almost glad to have a word with his father. "That's where we're cutting now."

"In Globe?"

"That's right, father. There's not a big demand for our coal at the moment, father. We're getting out parrot chiefly—at fifty-five shillings a ton."

"Fifty-five shillings." A momentary gleam of intelligence came into Barras's eye: he looked outraged, the old quality of injured probity. "I got eighty shillings for that coal. It's wrong . . . wrong. You're up to something . . . hiding something from me."

"No, father. You must remember that prices have fallen." He paused. "Pithead coal dropped another ten shillings last week."

The light died out of Barras's face but he continued to stare at Arthur suspiciously while the struggling of his crippled mind went on. He mumbled at last:

"What was I saying?" And then, "Tell me . . . tell me . . . tell me what you're doing."

Arthur sighed.

"I've tried to explain before, father. I'm doing my best for the

Neptune. Safety and efficiency—a decent policy of co-operation. Don't you see, father, if you give the men a fair deal they'll give you one. It's the first principle of reason."

Barras's reaction was violent. His hands began to shake, he seemed about to burst into tears.

" You're spending money. You've spent far too much money."

" I have only spent what ought to have been spent years ago. You surely know that, father! "

Barras pretended not to hear. " I'm angry," he whined. " I'm angry with you for spending all that money. you have spent all that money wrong."

" Please, father, don't upset yourself. Please, you can't stand it."

" I can't stand it! " The blood rushed to Barras's face. He stammered, " What do you mean ? You're a fool. Wait till I get back to the pit next week. You wait and I'll show you next week."

" Yes, father," Arthur said gently. Back in the house the gong sounded for luncheon. He turned away.

Barras waited, trembling with exasperation, until Arthur disappeared through the front porch. Then his expression changed back to one of childish cunning. He fumbled beneath his rug and with a covert look towards Aunt Carrie he took out his book and wrote:

In defence of the Neptune. Inquire next week as to money spent against my wishes. It is essential to remember I am in command. Memorandum. During temporary absence from pit keep close watch upon chief offender.

When he had finished he stared at what he had written, childishly pleased. Then, with furtive innocence, he signed Aunt Carrie to wheel him towards the house.

VI

David awoke that morning to the pleasant thought that he was meeting Harry Nugent. Usually his first waking thought was of Jenny—the strange recollection that she was gone, dissevered from him, vanished into the unknown. But this morning it was Harry. He lay for a minute thinking of his friendship with Nugent, of those days in France, Nugent and himself bent at the double, linked by the flopping stretcher, then plodding back with the stretcher heavy and sagging between them. How many of these silent journeys he had made with Harry Nugent!

The sound of his mother moving downstairs and the smell of crisping bacon recalled him. He jumped up and shaved and washed and dressed and ran down the stairs into the kitchen. Though it was not yet eight o'clock, Martha had been up an hour and more, the fire was lit, the grate blackleaded, the fender freshly emeried; the white cloth was on the table, his breakfast of egg and rashers—dished from the pan that minute—waiting for him.

"Morning, mother," he said, sitting in and lifting the *Herald* from beside his plate.

She nodded without speaking—she had no habit of good morning or good night; all Martha's words were useful words and never wasted. She took up his shoes and began to brush them silently.

He went on with the paper for a minute: the day before Harry Nugent with Jim Dudgeon and Clement Bebbington had been opening the new Institute at Edgeley; there was a picture of Harry with Bebbington stuck well in the foreground beside him. Suddenly he looked up and saw Martha brushing his shoes. He coloured and remonstrated:

"Didn't I tell you not to do that?"

Calmly, Martha went on brushing the shoes.

"I've always brushed them," she said, "ay, when they was five pair instead of one. There's no cause like for me to be stoppin' now."

"Why don't you leave them for me to do?" he persisted. "Why don't you sit in and have your breakfast with me properly?"

"There's some folks not that easy to change," she said, brushing away defiantly at the shoes. "And I'm one of them."

He stared at her in perplexity. Now that she had come to keep his house for him she was never done working for him. Everything. He had never been looked after better in his life. And yet he felt that she was withholding something from him; he felt a dark brooding, like a satire, under every action she directed towards his comfort. Watching her, he tested her, out of curiosity:

"I'm lunching with Harry Nugent to-day, mother."

She picked up the second shoe, her strong and masterful figure outlined against the window and her face darkly inscrutable. Breathing on the leather, she said scornfully:

"Lunching, you say?"

He smiled into himself: yes, that was it, she gave herself away. Deliberately, he continued:

"Having a bit of snap with Harry, then, mother, if you like that better. You've surely heard of Nugent. Harry Nugent, M.P. He's a particular friend of mine. He's a man worth hanging in with."

"So it would appear." Her lips drew down.

He smiled more than ever into himself, leading her on with his pretence of boasting.

"Ay! not everybody has the chance to lunch with Harry Nugent, M.P.—a big man in the Federation like him, it's an honour, don't you see, mother."

She looked up with the dark scorn in her face and a bitterness on her tongue, then she saw that he was laughing at her. She reddened to think how he had trapped her and, trying to cover it, she stooped quickly to set his shoes to warm by the fire. Then a grim smile twisted her lips.

" Brag away," she said. " Ye'll not take me in."

" But it's true, mother. I'm a regular time-server. I'm worse even than you think. You'll see me in a boiled shirt before you're done with me."

" I'll not iron it for you," she said, her lips twitching. It was a triumph for his strategy. He had made her smile.

A pause. Then, taking advantage of her humour, he said with sudden seriousness:

" Don't be so set against me in everything I do, then, mother. I'm not doing it for nothing."

" I'm not against you," she retorted, still stooping by the fire to hide her face. " I'm just not over-fond of what you're doing. All this council work and politics and that like. This Nationalisation business you're always on for—and that like foolery. I don't hold with that at all. No, no, it's never been my style or the style of any of my forebears. In my time and their time there's always been mester and man in the pit and it's fair unnatural to think of anything else."

There was a silence. In spite of the harshness of her words he could feel that she was softer, better disposed towards him. And on an impulse he turned the subject. He exclaimed:

" Another thing, mother."

" Well," she said suspiciously.

" About Annie, mother," he said, " and little Sammy. He's a grand little chap now and Annie's doing for him a treat. I've wanted to speak to you about it for a long time. I wish you'd forget all the old bitterness, mother, and have them to the house. I do wish you'd do it, mother."

Her face froze instantly.

" And why should I ? "

" Sammy's your grandson, mother," he answered. " I'm surprised you haven't been thrilled about that before, you would if you knew him the way I do. And Annie, well, she's one of the best, mother. Old Macer is laid up in bed now, he's a regular grumbler, moaning and groaning all the time, and Pug's keeping bad time at the pit, they've hardly enough to rub along with. But the way Annie keeps that place together is nothing short of marvellous."

" What has that to do with me ? " she said, tight-lipped and bitter. His generous praise of Annie had cut her to the quick. He saw that suddenly, saw he had made a mistake.

" Tell me," she repeated in a rising tone, " what has it got to do with me, the wild, bad lot that they always were ? "

" Oh, nothing," he said quietly and went back to his paper.

A minute later, while he was reading she put more bacon on his plate. It was her way of showing that she was not unreasonable, but kind, according to her lights. He took no notice. He thought her wildly unreasonable, but he knew that talking was no good. Talking was never any good with Martha.

At quarter to nine he folded his paper and rose from the table. She helped him on with his coat.

" You'll not be late," she said. " In spite of this grand lunch."

" No."

He smiled at her before he went out the door. It was no good being angry with Martha either.

On the way to the station he walked smartly. The morning was cold, the road already ringing with an early frost. Several of the lads walking from the Terraces to the Neptune saluted him—if he was inclined to be conceited, here, he thought ironically, was the chance. He realised that he had become a prominent figure in the town, yes, in the district, but he realised it without vanity. The greeting which Strother gave him outside New Bethel Street really amused him—a quick half-scared glance of recognition, full of unwilling admiration. Strother was terrified to death of Ramage, chairman of the Board. He had suffered misery from his bullying, and all that he, David, had done to Ramage delighted and frightened Strother and made him long to shake David by the hand. It was funny—in the old days Strother had looked down upon him with such contempt!

Half-way along Freehold Street he saw the new line of half-erected miners' houses stretching off the Hedley Road. In the distance he saw men carrying hods of bricks, mixing mortar, building, building . . . it excited him . . . the queer symbolism behind it, the note of promise, of victory. If only he could raze the Terraces with their broken stone floors, ladder staircases, bug-infested walls and outside privies, make ten new rows like this, plant them—he thought with a smile—in full view of the Ramage mansion on Sluice Dene.

He got into the train absently, forgetting to read his paper. At Tynecastle he walked to Rudd Street in the same thoughtful mood. At the corner of Rudd Street outside a newspaper shop one of the placards made an enormous shriek: *Mines for the Miners*. It was a Labour paper. The placard next made another enormous shriek: *Peeress Rides Pony at Park Lane Party*. It was not a Labour paper. I wonder, reflected David with a sudden glow, and he was not thinking about the peeress.

In the office Heddon had not appeared. David hung up his coat and hat, had a word with old Jack Hetherington, the caretaker, then went into the inner room. He worked all morning. At half-past twelve Heddon came in, apparently in a bad temper for, as was usual in such circumstances, his manner was uncommunicative and brusque.

" You been to Edgeley, Tom ? " David inquired.

" No! " Heddon kept flinging about the papers on his desk looking for something, and when he found it he did not seem to want it. " What have you done with these Seghill returns ? " he barked a minute later.

" I've entered them and filed them."

" The hell you have," Heddon grunted. " You're one of them conscientious b——s! " He looked quickly at David, then away again in a queer mixture of discomfiture and affection. He tilted his hat back on his ears and spat violently towards the fireplace.

" What's wrong, Tom ? " David asked.

" Oh, shut up," Heddon said. " And come on. It's time for the bloddy banquet. I've been wi' Nugent all morning and he said we wassent to be late. Jim Dudgeon and Lord God Almighty Bebbington'll be there too."

Heddon remained silent as they went along Grainger Street towards the North-Eastern Hotel. It was only quarter to one and much too early when they reached the hotel. But they sat down at one of the wicker tables in the lounge and Heddon, as he had probably intended, had a couple of drinks and after that he seemed better. He looked at David with a kind of gloomy cheerfulness.

" As a matter of fact, I'm damned glad about it," he said. " Only it'll be a wrench."

" What in the name of heaven are you talking about ? "

" Nothing, sweet b—— a——, as Shakespeare said. Hello, here are the toffs."

He got up as Harry Nugent, Dudgeon and Clement Bebbington came in. David, rising to his feet, shook hands warmly with Harry and was introduced to Dudgeon and Bebbington. Dudgeon pumped his hand like an old friend but Bebbington's grip was cool and distant. Heddon finished his whisky at a gulp, and although Dudgeon proposed drinks all round Nugent simply shook his head and they all went into the restaurant.

The long cream-coloured room, with windows opening on one side to the quiet Eldon Square and on the other to the bustle of the North-Eastern Station, was almost full, but the head waiter met them and showed them to a table, bowing considerably to Bebbington. It was clear he recognised Bebbington. Clement Bebbington had been in the public eye a good deal lately—tall, cool, inconspicuously well-dressed, with a superior air, a restless eye, suave courtesy and an unpleasant smile, he had a way of magnetising attention towards himself, of making himself news. There was about him a tempered look that came from a hectic ambition studiously concealed beneath that outer shell of rather bored indifference. Essentially he was an aristocrat, product of Winchester and Oxford, he went about socially in London quite a bit and fenced every morning at Bertrand's for exercise. Whether he was attracted towards the Labour galley from conviction or for reasons of health Bebbington did not disclose, but at the last election he had fought Chalworth

Borough, a Conservative stronghold, and handsomely won the seat. He was not yet on the Executive Council but his eyes were on it. David detested him on sight.

Dudgeon was quite different. Jim Dudgeon, like Nugent, had been on the Miners' Executive for years, small and burly and genial, careless of his h's, a raconteur and singer of jovial songs. For nearly twenty-five years he had been returned unopposed from Seghill. He called everybody by their Christian names. His horn-rimmed glasses gave him the look of an old owl as he blinked up at the waiter and, using his hands to indicate size and thickness, ordered a large chump chop accompanied by a tankard of beer.

They were all ordering: Heddon the same as Dudgeon, Nugent and David roast beef and baked potato, Bebbington a grilled sole, toast Melba and Vichy.

" It's good to see you again," Nugent said to David with his friendly, reassuring smile. There was a great friendliness about Harry Nugent, a sincerity which came straight from his candid, unwavering personality. He did not, like Bebbington, strive to be convincing; his manner was unforced, he was perfectly natural, simply himself. Yet to-day David sensed some purpose behind Nugent's encouragement. He felt Bebbington and Dudgeon taking stock of him too. It was curious.

" Not a bad place this," Dudgeon said, chewing roll, gazing round and rubbing his hands.

" You like the mirrors, don't you." Bebbington's unpleasant smile flickered. " With a little careful straining at the collar you can have the incalculable satisfaction of observing six Dudgeons at one and the same time."

" That's right, Clem, that's right," Dudgeon agreed, rubbing his hands more genially than ever. Though Jim could laugh and weep from sheer emotion at moments of political crisis, he was as insensitive to ridicule and personal abuse as a hippopotamus. " A nice-lookin' girl that over there with the blue in her *shapoh*."

" Our little Don Juan! "

" Ah, I've always had a soft side to the fair ones, Clem, lad."

" Why don't you step over and make an assignation for this evening ? "

" No, Clem, no, on second thoughts I won't. A good idee though, if we wasn't catching the three o'clock for London! "

At this Heddon laughed, and Bebbington with a cold astonishment seemed to discover him all at once and then immediately to forget him.

Nugent turned to David:

" You've been busy stirring up Sleescale, I hear."

" I don't know about that, Harry," David answered with a smile.

" Don't you believe it," Heddon interposed bluntly. Heddon was smarting under Bebbington's arrogance, determined not to be put under by any half-baked politician from London. He had downed a pint of bitter on top of two doubles of Scotch and was just in the mood to throw his weight about. " Haven't you read the papers? He's just put a new housing scheme through that's the best in the country. He's got an ante-natal clinic opened, and free milk for necessitous kids. They've always been a set of grafters down there; local government has been one long sweet laugh, but now there's an honest man got in amonst the back-scratchers and they're all sitting up with the fear of God in them askin' to be let join the Band of Hope." Heddon took a dogged pull at his bitter. " Ah, if you want to know, he's bloddy well wiped the floor with them."

A silence followed. Nugent looked pleased. Dudgeon dosed his chump chop with ketchup and said with a grin:

" I wish we could do that with our lot, Harry. We'd knock off Duckham and water pretty quick."

At the mention of the recent Report David leaned forward with sudden interest.

" Is there any immediate prospect of nationalisation ? "

Bebbington and Nugent interchanged a glance, while Dudgeon retired in amusement behind the horn-rimmed spectacles. He put one nobby forefinger on the table-cloth before David.

" You know what Sir John Sankey submitted in his Report. All coal measures and colliery undertakings to be acquired by the Government. You know what Mr. Lloyd George said in the House of Commons on the 18th August. That the Government accepts the policy of State purchase of mineral rights in coal, on which subjects all the reports of the Royal Commission were perfectly unanimous. Well! What more do you want ? Don't ye see it's as good as done! " And, with every evidence of enjoyment, Jim Dudgeon began to laugh.

" I see," David said quietly.

" It was pretty funny, the Commission." Dudgeon laughed even more jovially. " You should have heard Bob Smillie arguing the toss with the Duke of Northumberland and Frank goin' after the Marquess of Bute on the origin of his claim to royalties and wayleaves. All coming from the signature of a boy of ten, Edward the Sixth. Oh, we had a rare bit o' fun. But God! that's nothing. I'd have gave my hat to have had the scalpin' of Lord Kell. *His* great, great, great grandfather got all the coal lands through doin' a pretty bit of pimping for Charles II. Can you beat it ? Millions in royalties for a successful week-end's pimping for 'is Majesty." Dudgeon lay back and relished the joke until the cutlery rattled.

" It doesn't strike me as amusing," David said bitterly. " The Government pledged themselves to the Commission. The whole thing is a gigantic swindle."

" That's exactly what Harry said on the floor of the House of Commons. But, my God, that don't make no difference. Here, waiter, bring me another lot of chips."

While Dudgeon talked, Nugent studied David, remembering long discussions squatting behind the sandbags of the front-line station while a white moon sailed round a misery of wire and mud and shell-holes.

" You still feel pretty strongly about nationalisation ? " he asked.

David nodded without speaking; in this company no answer could have been more effective.

There was a short pause. Silently, Nugent interrogated Dudgeon who, with his mouth full of potato, made an emphatic sound in his throat, then he looked at Bebbington who gave a faint and non-committal acquiescence. Finally Nugent turned to David.

" Listen to me, David," he said authoritatively. " The Council have decided to amalgamate the three local areas here and create a complete new district. The new institute at Edgeley is to be the headquarters. And we want a new organising secretary who'll not only be District Treasurer but Compensation Secretary for the Northern Miners' Association. We're looking for a young man and a live man. I mentioned it to Heddon this morning but it's official now. We've asked you to meet us here to offer you the post."

David stared at Harry Nugent, completely taken aback, overwhelmed by the offer. He coloured deeply.

" You mean you'd like me to apply ? "

Nugent shook his head.

" Your name and three others were submitted to the committee last week. This is the committee and you're the new secretary." He held out his hand.

Mechanically David took it, while the full force of the appointment struck home.

" But, Heddon . . ." He swung round suddenly, facing Tom Heddon, to whom he had been so obviously preferred, and his eyes clouded with dismay.

" Heddon gave you a fine testimonial," Nugent said quietly.

Heddon's eyes met David's in one swift interchange when the hurt yet courageous soul of the man lay exposed; then he forced out his chin with vehemence.

" I wouldn't have the job for love nor money. They want a young man, diddent you hear. I'm glued to Rudd Street. I wouldn't leave it for nobody." His smile, though rather strained about the edges, was almost successful. He thrust his hand upon David.

Bebbington surveyed his wrist watch, fatigued by this emotionalism.

" The train," he said, " leaves at three."

They rose and went by the side door into the station. As they crossed to the crowded platform Nugent lagged a little behind. He pressed David's arm.

" It's a chance for you at last," he said. " A real chance. I've wanted you to have it. We'll be watching to see what you can do with it."

Beside the train a Press photographer was waiting. And at the welcome sight Jim Dudgeon put on his glasses and looked official: he adored being photographed.

" Business is lookin' up," he remarked to David. " This is the second time they've caught me to-day."

Overhearing, Bebbington smiled coldly; he carefully took the foreground.

" It's not surprising," he said, " considering that I arranged it both times."

Harry Nugent said nothing, but when the train steamed out David's last impression, as he stood there with Heddon beside him, was the quiet serenity of his face.

VII

TOWARDS the beginning of the following February when Arthur secured the contract with Mawson, Gowlan & Co. he felt it was the turn of the tide at last. Business at the pit had been deplorable for the past twelve months. Reparations, in wringing coal from Germany, had damaged the export trade on which, at the Neptune, they very considerably depended. France naturally preferred cheap or free coal from Germany to Arthur's beautiful but expensive coal. And as if that were not enough, America had most unkindly entered the European field, a powerful and relentless competitor for Britain's exclusive war-time markets.

Arthur was not a fool. He saw clearly that the pre-existing coal famine in Europe had produced an artificial inflation of the export price of British coal. He felt acutely the general illusion of prosperity, and his efforts were most sensibly directed towards making contact with local consumers and re-establishing himself by selling Neptune coal at home.

This return contract with Mawson Gowlans had been implied when the Neptune order for equipment was placed as far back as 1918. But Mawson Gowlan were keen customers and it was only now that Arthur had persuaded them to implement their word: even so he had been forced to shave his prices to the bone.

Nevertheless his mood that morning was one of natural elation as, with the draft contract in his hand, he rose from his desk and went into Armstrong's office.

" Have a look," he said. " Full time and double shift for the next four months."

With a pleased expression, Armstrong pulled his glasses out of his breast pocket—his sight was not what it had been—and slowly surveyed the contract.

" Mawson Gowlan," he exclaimed. " Well, well! Wouldn't it beat the band, sir, when you think that this fellow Gowlan worked hand-putting under your father and me in this very pit! "

Pacing up and down the office Arthur laughed rather mirthlessly.

" Better not remind him of it, Armstrong. He's coming down at ten. By the way, I shall want you to witness our signatures."

" Ay, he's a big noise in Tynecastle now, by all accounts." Armstrong meditated. " Mawson and he have got their fingers in half a dozen pies. I heard they've taken over Youngs—you know, the brass-finishers in Tynecastle that went burst last month."

" Yes," Arthur said shortly, as if the reminder of yet another local bankruptcy annoyed him, " Gowlan is expanding. That's why we get this contract."

Armstrong gazed at Arthur over the gold rims of his spectacles, then he went back to the contract. He read the contract meticulously, his lips moving over the words. Then, not looking at Arthur, he said:

" I see there's a penalty clause."

" Naturally."

" Your father never held with the penalty clause," Armstrong murmured.

It always irritated Arthur to have his father cast reprovingly in his teeth. He paced up and down the room a little faster with his hands clasped behind his back, and declared with nervous vehemence:

" You can't pick and choose these days. You've got to meet people half-way. If you don't, then somebody else will. And besides, we can fulfil this contract all ends up. We'll have no trouble with the men. We're still under control and the Government have definitely promised no decontrol until August 31st. We have more than six months' guaranteed control to complete a four months' contract. What more do you want? And damn it all, Armstrong, we do need the work."

" That's true," Armstrong agreed slowly, " I was only thinking. But you know what you're doing, sir."

The sound of a car in the yard cut off Arthur's quick reply. He stopped his pacing and stood by the window. There was a silence.

" Here's Gowlan," he said, watching the yard, " and he doesn't look like he was going hand-putting now."

A minute later Joe walked into the office. He advanced impressively, in double-breasted blue, with his hand outstretched and an electric cordiality in his eye. He shook hands vigorously with Arthur and Armstrong, beaming round the office as though it rejoiced him:

" You know it does my heart good to walk into this pit again. You remember I worked here when I was a lad, Mr. Armstrong." Despite Arthur's fears there was no mock modesty about Joe, oh dear, no! his big-hearted frankness was human and edifying. " Yes, it was under you, Mr. Armstrong, I got my first groundings. And from your father, Mr. Barras, I drew the first money I ever earned in my life. Well, well! It's not so long ago either when you come to think of it." He sat down, pulled up his smartly creased trousers, genial and triumphant. " Yes, I will say," he mused, " I was absolutely delighted to think of fixing up this contract. A bit of sentiment maybe, but who can help that? I like this pit and I like the way you do things, Mr. Barras. You've got a magnificent place here, magnificent. That's my exact words to my partner, Jim Mawson. Some folks say there's no feeling in business. Well, well, they're a long way off *beginning* to understand the meaning of business, eh, Mr. Barras? "

Arthur smiled; it was impossible to resist Joe's joyous charm.

" Naturally we're very glad on our side to have this contract."

Joe nodded graciously. " Business not so good as it might be, eh, Mr. Barras? Oh, I know, I know, you don't have to bother to tell me. It's a regular toss upwhen you've got all your eggs in the one basket. That's why Jim and myself keep spreadin'." He paused, helped himself absently to a cigarette from the box on Arthur's desk; then, rather solemnly: " Did you know we were floating ourselves next month? "

" You mean a company? "

" Certainly, I do. A public company. The time's ripe for it. Things is absolutely boomin' on the market."

" But surely you're not relinquishing your interests."

Joe laughed heartily. " What do you take us for, Mr. Barras? We'll take two hundred thousand for the goodwill, a packet of shares and a controlling interest on the board."

" I see." Arthur blenched slightly. For one second, thinking of his own discouragements at the Neptune, he hungered for an equal success, to lay his hands on such a staggering profit.

A silence; then Arthur moved towards the desk.

" What about the contract, then? "

" Certainly, Mr. Barras, sir. I'm ready when you are. Always ready to do business. Ah, ha! good clean honest business."

" There's just one point I'd like to raise. The question of this penalty cause."

" Yes? "

" There isn't the slightest doubt about our fulfilling the contract."

Joe smiled blandly.

" Then why worry about the clause? "

" I'm not worrying, but as we've cut our price so close and included delivery at Yarrow, I thought we might agree to delete it? "

Joe's smile persisted, bland and friendly still, yet tinged with a kind of virtuous regret.

" Ah, now, we've got to protect ourselves, Mr. Barras. If we give you the contract for coking coal we've got to make sure that we get the coal. It's only fair play after all. We're doing our bit and we're only making sure that you do yours. If you don't like it, of course, well, we must just——"

"No," Arthur said quickly. "It's quite all right, really. If you insist I agree."

Arthur above everything did not want to lose the contract. And there was no doubt that the clause was perfectly just; it was simply a very tight piece of business which any firm might well demand at this troubled time. Joe produced a large gold-encased fountain pen to sign the contract. He signed with an enormous flourish and Armstrong, who had once cursed Joe over half a mile of ropeway for letting a tub run amain, witnessed Joe's signature neatly and humbly. Then Joe beamed and pump-handled his way into his car, which whisked him away triumphantly to Tynecastle.

When Joe had gone Arthur sat at his desk worrying a little—as he always did after taking a decision—and wondering if he had not allowed Gowlan to get the better of him. And it struck him that he might insure against the remote contingency of his failure to complete the contract. On an impulse he took the telephone and rang up the Eagle Alliance Offices with whom he usually did business. But the rate quoted was too high, ridiculously high, it would swallow up his small margin of profit. He hung up the receiver and put the matter out of his head.

Indeed, when the men started in full time and double shift on the 10th February, Arthur forgot his worries in the glorious activity and liveliness and bustle about the pit. After the long spell of slackness he felt the pulse of it like his own pulse. It was worth living for, the throbbing, magnificent vigour of the Neptune. This was what he wanted—work for everyone, fair work, fair pay and fair profit. He was happier than he had been for months. That night on his return to the Law he went triumphantly to his father.

"We're working full time on both shifts now. I thought you'd like to know, father. It's full steam ahead at the pit again."

A silence, quivering with suspicion, while Barras peered up at Arthur from the couch in his room where, driven by the cold weather, he kept vigil by the fire. The room was intolerably hot, doors and windows tightly sealed, with Aunt Carrie's aid, against the electricity. A sheaf of scribbled papers lay half-concealed beneath his rug, and beside him a stick, for with its help he could hobble a little, dragging his right foot.

"And why not?" he muttered at last. "Isn't that the way it ought to . . . ought to be?"

Arthur flushed slightly.

"I daresay, father. But it isn't so easy these days."

"These days!" The eyebrows, now grey, twitched with venom. "These days—ha! You don't know the meaning of days. It took me years and years . . . but I'm waiting, oh, waiting. . ."

With a dubious smile towards the prostrate figure: " I only thought you'd like to know, father . . ."

" You're a fool. I do know, I know everything but what you say. That's right, laugh . . . laugh like a fool. But mark my words . . . the pit will never be right till I come back."

" Yes, father," Arthur said, humouring him. " You must hurry up and come back."

He waited in the room a moment longer, then excusing himself he went quite cheerfully in to tea. He was very cheerful for the next few days. He enjoyed his meals, enjoyed his work, enjoyed his leisure. It struck him with a kind of wonder how little leisure he had lately had; for months and months he had been bound, body and soul, to the Neptune. Now in the evenings he was able to relax and take up a book instead of sitting bowed in his chair tensely pondering on where business might be found. He wrote to Hilda and to Grace. He felt himself refreshed and reinvigorated.

All went swimmingly until the morning of the 16th of February when he came down to breakfast and picked up the paper with a sense of well-being and ease. He breakfasted alone, as his father had done in the old days, and he began his grape-fruit with a good appetite, when all at once a middle-page heading in the news arrested his eye. He stared at the heading as though transfixed. He put down his spoon and read the whole column. Then with no thought of breakfast he flung down his napkin, shoved back his chair and rushed to the telephone in the hall. Snatching up the instrument he called Probert of Amalgamated Collieries, who was also a leading member of the Northern Mining Association.

" Mr. Probert," he stammered. " Have you seen *The Times* ? They're going to decontrol. In the King's speech. On March 31st. They're introducing legislation immediately."

Probert's voice came back: " Yes, I've seen it, Arthur. Yes, yes, I know . . . it's much sooner——"

" But March 31st," Arthur cut in desperately. " Next month! It's unbelievable. They pledged themselves not to decontrol till August."

Probert's voice answered, very round and comfortable:

" You're no more staggered than I am, Arthur. We're precipitated into trouble. It's a bombshell! "

" I've got to see you," Arthur cried. " I must run over and see you, Mr. Probert, I must. I'll come straight away."

Taking no time for a possible denial, Arthur snapped up the receiver. Flinging on a coat he ran round to the garage and started up the light two-seater which now replaced the big saloon. He drove in a kind of fury to Probert's house at Hedlington four miles up the coast. He arrived in seven minutes and was shown immediately to the morning-room, where, in a deep leather chair beside the blazing fire, Probert sat at leisure, smoking an after-breakfast cigar, with the paper on his knees. It was a charming picture: the warm, deep-carpeted room, the dignified old man, adequately fed, bathed in a lingering perfume of coffee and Havana, snatching a moment before the labours of the day.

" Mr. Probert," Arthur burst out, " they can't do this."

Edgar Probert rose and took Arthur's hand with a suave gravity.

" I am equally concerned, my dear boy," he said, still holding Arthur's hand. " Upon my soul, I am." He was tall and stately and about sixty-five, with a mane of perfectly white hair, very black eyebrows and a magnificent presence which, as a member of the Northern Mining Association, he used with wonderful effect. He was extremely rich and much respected, and he contributed largely to all local charities which published their lists of subscribers. Every winter his photograph appeared, noble and leonine, on the posters appealing for the Tynecastle Oddfellows Hospital and beneath it, in large type: Mr. Edgar Probert, who has so generously supported our cause, asks you once again to join with him. . . . For thirty years on end he had bled his men white. He was a perfectly charming old scoundrel.

" Be seated, Arthur, my boy," he said, waving the cigar gently.

But Arthur was too agitated to sit down.

" What does it mean ? " he cried. " That's what I want to know. I'm absolutely at a loss."

" I am afraid it means trouble," Probert answered, planting his feet apart on the hearthrug and gazing abstractedly towards the ceiling.

" Yes, but why have they done it ? "

" The Government, Arthur," Probert murmured, " have been taking a big share of our profits but they have no desire to take any share in our losses. In plain language they are getting out while the going is good. But frankly, I'm not sorry. Strictly between ourselves, I've had a private communication from Westminster. It's time we put our house in order. There's a been a storm brewing between ourselves and the men ever since the war. We must dig ourselves in, stand together as one man and fight."

" Fight ? "

Probert nodded through the balmy incense of cigar smoke. He looked very noble; he looked like the Silver King and Dr. Barnardo rolled into one, only kinder. He declared gently:

" I shall propose a cut of 40 per cent. in wages."

" Forty per cent.," Arthur gasped. " Why, that'll bring the standard below pre-war level. The men will never stand that. No, never on your life. They'll strike."

" They may not get the chance to strike." No animosity behind the words, merely that same benign abstraction. " If they don't come to their senses promptly we shall lock them out."

" A lock-out! " Arthur echoed. " That's ruinous."

Probert smiled calmly, removed his gaze from the ceiling and fixed it rather patronisingly upon Arthur.

" I imagine most of us have a little nest-egg from the war tucked away somewhere. We must just nibble at that until the men see reason. Yes, yes, we must just nibble at it."

A little nest-egg! Arthur thought of the capital laid out upon equipment and improvements at the Neptune; he thought of his present full-time contract; and a sudden hot rage came over him.

" I won't lock out my men," he said, " I won't do it. We're working double shift and full time at the Neptune. A 40 per cent. cut is madness. I'm prepared to pay reasonable wages. I'm not going to close down a going pit. I'm not going to cut my own throat for anybody."

Probert patted Arthur on the back, more patronising than ever, remembering Arthur's scandalous war record, despising him as an unbalanced, cowardly young fool, and masking it all with that priestly benevolence.

" There, there, my boy," he said soothingly. " Don't magnify the situation. I know you are naturally impetuous. You'll get over it. We shall have a full meeting of the Association in a week's time. You'll be all right by then. You'll stand in with the rest of us. There's no other course open to you."

Arthur stared at Probert with a strained look in his eyes. A nerve in his cheek began to twitch. No other course open to him! It was true, absolutely true; he was tied to the Association in a hundred different ways, bound hand and foot. He groaned.

" This is going to come hard on me."

Probert patted him a little more tenderly.

" The men must be taught their place, Arthur," he murmured. " Have you had breakfast ? Let me ring for some coffee ? "

" No thanks," Arthur muttered with his head down. " I've got to get back."

" How is your dear father ? " Probert inquired sweetly. " You must miss him sadly at the Neptune, aha, yes, indeed. Yet I hear he is making marvellous headway. He is my oldest colleague on the Association. I hope we shall see him there soon, the dear man. You'll give him my warmest regards! "

" Yes." Arthur nodded jerkily, making for the door.

" You're sure you won't have some coffee ? "

" No."

Arthur had the stinging conviction that the old hypocrite was laughing at him. He got out of Probert's house somehow and tumbled into his car. He drove very slowly to the Neptune, then he entered his office and sat down at his desk. With his head buried in his hands he thought out the situation fully. He had a going pit wonderfully equipped and working full time on a reasonable contract. He was willing and ready to pay his men an adequate wage. Probert's wage offer was derisory. With a choking heart Arthur picked up a pencil and worked it out. Yes. Balanced against the cost of living, the real value of Probert's offer was a pre-war wage of under £1 a week; for the pump-men alone it came to pre-war equivalent of sixteen shillings and ninepence per five-shift week. Sixteen shillings and ninepence—rent, clothes, food for a family out of that! Oh, it was insanity to expect the men to accept it; it was no offer, merely a gage thrown out to promote the struggle. And he was bound to the Association; it was financial suicide even to think of breaking away. He would have to shut down his pit, throw his men out of work, sacrifice his contract. The grim irony of it all made him want to laugh.

At that moment Armstrong came into the office. Arthur looked up with nervous intensity.

"I want you to start overtime immediately on that coking coal, Armstrong. Take as much out as you can and stack it on the bank. Do you understand?—as much as you can manage. Make every effort, use every man."

"Why, yes, Mr. Barras," Armstrong answered in a startled voice.

Arthur had not the heart to enlighten Armstrong then. He made a few more calculations on his pad, threw down the pencil and stared away in front of him. The date was the 16th of February.

On the following day the Association met. As a result a secret circular was dispatched to all district mine owners discreetly indicating the approaching lock-out and urging that reserves of coal should be built up. When Arthur received this confidential document he smiled bitterly. How could he build up four months' output in a bare six weeks!

On March 24th the Coal Decontrol Act became law. Arthur served notices upon his men to terminate the contracts. And on March 31st, with half his contract obligation unfulfilled, the stoppage began.

It was a wet, sad day. In the afternoon, as Arthur stood in his office staring gloomily at the last tubs coming outbye in the pouring rain, the door opened and, quite unannounced, Tom Heddon walked in. There was something almost sinister in Heddon's silent entry. He stood, grim and formidable, with his back to the shut door, facing Arthur, his compact figure slightly bent as if already burdened with the load of the approaching lock-out. He said:

"I want a word with you." He paused. "You've served notices on every man in this pit."

"What about it?" Arthur said heavily. "I'm no different from the rest."

Heddon gave a short, bitterly sarcastic laugh.

"You're this different. You're the wettest pit in the district and you've served notices on your safety men and pumpers."

Striving to keep control of himself, Arthur replied:

" I feel too badly about this to quarrel with you, Heddon. You know my obligations compel me to serve notices on all grades."

" Are you looking for another flooding ? " Heddon asked, with a curious inflection to his voice.

Arthur was very near the end of his resistance; he was not to blame; he would stand no bullying from Heddon. A wave of nervous indignation broke over him. He said:

" The safety men will carry on."

" Oh, will they ? " Heddon sneered. He paused, then rasped with bitter emphasis, " I want you to understand that the safety men are carryin' on simply because I tell them to. If it wasn't for me and the men behind me your bloddy pit would be flooded in twenty-four hours. D'you savvy that—flooded and finished! The miners you're tryin' to starve into the muck heap are goin' on pumpin' to keep you fat and cushy in your bloddy parlour. Just bite on that, will you, for the love of Christ, and see how it tastes."

With a sudden wild gesture as though he could trust himself no longer Heddon swung round and banged his way out. Arthur sat down by the desk. He sat there a long time until darkness came stealing into the office and all but the safety men had left the pit. Then he rose and silently walked home.

The lock-out began. And through the long dreary weeks it drearily dragged on. With the safety of the mines assured there remained only to stand aside and contemplate the struggle between the men and the spectre of want. Day in, day out, with a heavy heart Arthur saw the limits to which this unequal conflict could be pushed—the gaunt cheeks of the men, the women, yes, even the children, the darkness that lay on every face, the streets without laughter, without play. His heart turned within him in a cold pain. Could man inflict this cruelty upon man ? The war to end war, to bring great and lasting peace, a new and glorious era in our civilisation. And now this! Take your pittance, slaves, and toil in the underworld in sweat and dirt and danger, yes, take it or starve. A woman died in childbirth in Inkerman Terrace—Dr. Scott, when pressed by the coroner, used a word, tempered officially to malnutrition. Margarine and bread; bread and margarine; sometimes not that. To raise a sturdy son to sing the song of Empire.

Thoughts like these burned incoherently in Arthur's mind. He could not, would not stand it. At the end of the first month he started soup-kitchens in the town, organised a private relief scheme for the utter destitution in the Terraces. His efforts were met, not with gratitude, but with hatred. He did not blame the men. He understood their bitterness. With a quick pang he felt his inability to turn the tide of sentiment towards himself; he had no gift for spectacular publicity, no winning personality to utilise. Right from the start the men had distrusted him at the Neptune and now outside his soup-kitchen the words were scrawled: *To Hell with the Conchy.* Rubbed off, the phrase, or one more obnoxious, was rechalked at night ready to meet his eye on the following morning. A body of the younger men were most hostile to him; headed by Jack Reedy and Cha Leeming, they comprised many who had lost brothers or fathers in the Neptune disaster. Now, for no reason he could imagine, their hatred expended itself on him.

On and on went the ghastly farce. With a strange disgust Arthur read of the formation of the Defence Force, a fully armed and uniformed body of 80,000 men. The Defence Force—in defence of what? In May trouble began round the Amalgamated Collieries and troops were drafted to the district. There were a great many Royal Proclamations and Mr. Probert took himself and his family for a well-earned and most enjoyable holiday at Bournemouth.

But Arthur remained in Sleescale—through April, May, June. It was in June that the postcards began to arrive—anonymous postcards which were childishly defamatory, even scurrilous. Every day one came, written in a sprawling, unformed hand, which Arthur thought at first to be disguised. At the outset he ignored them, but gradually they came to cause him pain. Who could pursue him with such malice? He could not guess. And then towards the end of the month, the culprit stood revealed, caught in the act of handing a freshly scribbled card to one of the message-boys who came about the Law. It was Barras.

But the old man's ceaseless scrutiny was even worse to bear, watching, watching Arthur all the time, noting his comings and goings, gloating at his dejection, rejoicing in the manifest evidence of trouble. It fell on Arthur like a scourge, that peering, bloodshot, senile orb, sapping away his energy, depleting him.

On July 1st an exhaustion like that of death brought the struggle to an end. The men were beaten, humiliated, crushed. But Arthur had not won. The loss on his defaulted contract was a heavy one. Yet as he saw the men stream slowly and silently across the pit yard once more and saw the wheels revolve again above the headgear, he shook his discouragement away. Reverses must occur. This, though no fault of his own, was one of them. He would not let himself go under. Now, from this minute, he would begin again.

VIII

A SUMMER Sunday of 1925 and David, returning from his afternoon stroll along the Dunes, met Annie and little Sammy at the east end of Lamb Street. At the sight of David, Sammy ran forward with a triumphant shout—he was " a great one " for David, Sammy was, and he chanted:

" Aw've got my holidays Satturday. Isn't that gud ? "

"It's grand, Sammy,man." David smiled at Sammy, reflecting behind his smile that Sammy, outgrowing his strength, looked as if he needed a holiday. Sammy was eight years old now with a pale face and a nobby forehead and cheerful blue eyes that disappeared every time he laughed, like his father's had done before him. He was dressed very neat and clean for his Sunday walk with his mother in a suit which Annie had made for him out of a grey serge remnant bought at Bates'. He was shooting up fast, and his boots, bought less for beauty than to keep out the wet, looked enormous at the end of his thin growing shanks.

" You'll have your hands full, Annie." David turned to Sammy's mother who had come quietly up beside them. " I know these holidays! "

" I'm cross with Sammy," Annie said in a voice that was not cross. " He would climb the gate at Sluice Dene and he's cracked his new celluloid collar."

" Ah, it was to get some oak nuts," Sammy declared earnestly. " Aw wanted th' oak nuts, Davey."

" *Uncle* David," protested Annie reproachfully. " How *can* you, Sammy! "

" Never mind, Annie, lass," said David. " We're old friends together. Aren't we, Sammy ? "

" Ay! " Sammy grinned; and David smiled again. But as he looked at Annie he stopped smiling. Annie really seemed quite done up with the heat; she had a dark line under her eyes and she was quite as pale as Sammy who, as his dad had been, was naturally pale. She held her hand against the side of the wall, supporting herself a little as she stood there. He knew that Annie was continually hard put to it, with old man Macer now completely crippled by rheumatism and Pug not working steady at the Neptune, and Sammy to look after. Annie had been doing washing, he knew, and going out days cleaning to keep things going. He had offered to help Annie a dozen times, but Annie would not look at money, she was very independent. On an impulse he asked:

" Come to think of it, when did you last have a holiday yourself, Annie ? "

Her calm eyes widened slightly in surprise.

" Well, I had my holidays when I was at the school," she said. " Like Sammy has the now."

That was Annie's idea of a holiday—she had no other, no notion of change of scene and air, of white esplanades, gay beaches, music mingling with the waves. The unintentioned pathos of her answer caught David by the throat. He took a quick and most unexpected decision. He said casually:

" How about you and Sammy coming for a week to Whitley Bay ? "

She stood very still with her eyes on the hot pavement. Sammy let out a whoop, then fell into a kind of awe.

"Whitley Bay," he echoed. "By gosh, aw'd like te go te Whitley Bay."

David kept his gaze on Annie.

"Harry Nugent has written me and asked me to meet him there on the 26th." Then he lied: "I'd made up my mind to take a week there beforehand."

She still remained motionless with her eyes on the hot pavement, and she was paler than before.

"Oh no, David," she said. "I don't think so."

"Ah, *mother*," Sammy cried appealingly.

"You could do with a change, Annie, and Sammy too."

"It *has* been sort of hot to-day," she agreed. The thought of a week at Whitley Bay for Sammy and herself was dazzling, but her head was full of the difficulties, oh, half a hundred obstacles; she had no clothes, she would "show up" David, she had the house and her father to look after, Pug might go on the drink if she left him to himself. Then a brilliant idea struck her. She exclaimed: "Take Sammy!"

He said grimly:

"Sammy doesn't go an inch without his mother."

"Now, *mother*," Sammy cried again, his little white face filled with a warning desperation.

There was a silence, then she lifted her eyes and smiled her quiet smile at him.

"Very well, David," she said. "If you're so good as to take us."

It was settled. All at once David felt glad, immensely and surprisingly glad. It was like a sudden glow within him. He watched Annie and Sammy go down the road towards Quay Street with Sammy capering about his mother, big boots and broken collar and all, capering and talking about Whitley Bay. Then he walked home along Lamb Lane to his house. Now there was no chickweed on the path, the little garden was trim and neat at last, and bright yellow nasturtiums grew up white strings on the wall where Martha had trained them. The doorstep was very whitely pipe-clayed and scalloped by Martha, and the window-blinds had a full twelve inches of wonderful crochet-edging worked as only Martha's hands could work it. All the best colliers' houses had crochet-edged blinds—the sign of a tidy collier!—but none in Sleescale were finer than these.

He hung up his hat in the hall and went into the kitchen where Martha was on her feet preparing some watercress for his tea. Martha was always busy in his service, a perfect demi-urge of house-proud service beat beneath her sober bodice. The kitchen was so clean he could have taken his tea off the floor—as they say in these parts. The woodwork of the furniture shone, the china on the dresser gleamed. The fine marble clock, won by Martha's father for pot-stour bowling, and brought down from Inkerman Terrace when she gave up her home, ticked solemnly, a sacred heirloom, on the high mantelpiece. The high clear stillness of Sunday was in the house.

He studied Martha. He said:

"Why don't you come to Whitley Bay for a week, mother? I'm going there on the 19th."

She did not look round but went on scrupulously examining the watercress: she could not bear a speck upon lettuce or watercress. When he began to feel she had not heard him, she said:

"What would I do with Whitley Bay?"

"I thought you might like it, mother. Annie and the boy are coming," he made his tone coaxing. "You better come too!"

Her back was towards him and she did not speak for a minute. But finally, in a bleached voice, she answered:

"No. I'm as well here!" When she turned with the plate of watercress her face was stiff.

He knew better than to press her. Sitting down on the sofa by the window he picked up the current number of the *Workers' Independent*. His weekly article, a series he had been contributing for the past twelve months, was on the front page, and a speech he had made at Seghill on Tuesday was given verbatim on the middle sheet. He read neither. He was thirty-five years of age. For the last four years he had worked like a nigger, organising, speaking, getting about the district, not sparing himself. He had increased the Edgeley membership by over four thousand. He had the name for tenacity and strength and ability. Three monographs of his had been published by the Anvil Press, and his paper *The Nation and the Mines* had won him the Russell medal. The medal was upstairs, lost somewhere, behind a drawer. He felt a momentary sadness come over him. Down in the Dunes this afternoon he had listened to the lark, and the sound of the lark had reminded him of the boy who used to come to the Dunes nearly twenty years before. Then he had fallen to thinking of Jenny. Where in the name of God was Jenny? Dear Jenny—in spite of everything he still loved her and missed her and thought of her. And the thought of her striking through the sunshine and the song of the lark had saddened him. Meeting Annie and Sammy had lifted up his spirits, it is true, but now the sadness was come on him again. Perhaps Martha was responsible—her attitude! Was it not futile for him to keep striving to change the movements of great masses of humanity when the secret heart of each human unit remained secret and unassailable and unchanging? She was very unforgiving, Martha.

He felt better after his tea—the watercress in spite of Martha's unforgiving heart was good—and he sat down to write to Harry. Dudgeon and Bebbington and Harry had all kept their seats in the election that year. A very near thing it had been for Bebbington; there had been some scandal over divorce proceedings brought by Sir Peter Outram, when Bebbington had been named, but the affair had been hurried over, and Bebbington had just managed to come through. David wrote a long letter to Harry. Then he took up Erich Flitner's *Experiments in State Control*. He had been interested in Flitner lately and in Max Sering too, especially *Assault on the Community*, but to-night Flitner rather dodged him. He kept thinking about the coming assault on Whitley Bay and he decided that it would be uncommonly good fun to take Sammy for a swim. There would be ice-cream too; he must on no account forget the ice-cream. It was just possible that Annie might have a secret weakness for ice-cream, the real Italian stuff, a slider. Would Annie remain immutable if confronted with a slider? He lay back and laughed out loud.

In fact, for the whole of the next ten days he couldn't get Whitley Bay and the swimming and Annie and Sammy out of his head. On the morning of the 19th when he arrived at Central Station, Tynecastle, where he had arranged to meet Annie and Sammy, he was genuinely excited. He had been detained by a last-minute compensation case and he came in with a rush to the booking-hall where Annie and Sammy stood waiting.

"I thought I'd be late," he exclaimed, smiling and breathless, and decided it was good still to be young enough to feel excited and breathless.

"There's plenty of time," Annie said in her practical way.

Sammy said nothing, his instructions were to say nothing, but his shining blue eyes in his beautifully washed face expressed a whole philosophy.

They got into the train for Whitley Bay, David carrying the suit-cases. Annie did not like that; she wanted to carry her own suit-case, or rather the suit-case she had borrowed from Pug—it was heavy, and too shabby for David to be seen with. Annie looked distressed, as though it were the most improper thing in the world for David to be carrying the suit-case when she had often carried a fish creel three times the weight herself, but she thought it not her place to protest. Then they were in their compartment, the whistle blew and they were off.

Sammy sat in the corner seat next to David and Annie sat opposite. As they rolled through the suburbs into the flat countryside Sammy's enthusiasm was enormous and, forgetting that he had been vowed to silence, he shared it generously with David.

"See that engine, an' the waggons, and that crane!" he cried. "Oh, and look at the size of that chimney. By gosh, I've never seed a chimney bigger nor that afore."

The chimney led to profound and exciting talk of steeple-jacks and how wonderful it must be to stand on the top of a chimney "that high" with nothing between you and the earth two hundred feet below.

" Perhaps you'd like to be a steeple-jack when you grow up, Sammy ? " David said, smiling at Annie.

Sammy shook his head.

" No," he said with a certain reticence. " I'm going to be like my father."

" A miner ? " David asked.

" Ay! That's what I'm going to be," Sammy said sturdily. Sammy's air was so solemn that David had to laugh.

" You've plenty of time to change your mind," he said.

It was a pleasant journey, though not a long one, and quite soon they were at Whitley Bay. David had taken rooms in Tarrant Street, a small quiet street leading off the promenade near the Waverley Hotel. The rooms had been recommended to him by Dickie, his clerk at the Institute, who said that Mrs. Leslie the landlady often took Federation delegates when the district conferences were on. Mrs. Leslie was the widow of a doctor who had lost his life in a colliery accident at Hedlington about twenty years before. A timberman had been pinned by a fall of roof and it had been impossible to free his forearm which was caught and mangled between two masses of whinstone. Dr. Leslie had gone down to amputate the timberman's forearm and get him out. He had almost got through with the amputation which he had heroically performed on the equally heroic timberman without an anæsthetic, lying on his belly in coal muck, squeezed under the fall, in a sweat of blood and dirt, when quietly and suddenly the whole roof caved in on them, and the doctor and the timberman were both crushed to death. Everyone had forgotten about the incident now, but it was because of that fall of roof that Mrs. Leslie kept lodgings in the downtrodden little road with its row of red-brick houses each having four square yards of front garden, Nottingham lace curtains, glass overmantels and a much-abused piano.

Mrs. Leslie was a tall, dark, reserved woman; she was neither comic nor ill-tempered: she presented none of those features which are traditionally associated with the seaside landlady. She made David and Annie and Sammy quietly welcome and showed them to their rooms. But here Mrs. Leslie made an unexpectedly awkward mistake. She turned to Annie and said:

" I thought you and your husband could have this nice front room and the little boy would take the small room at the back."

Annie did not blush; if anything she paled; and without the slightest trace of awkwardness she answered:

" This is my brother-in-law, Mrs. Leslie. My husband was killed in the war."

It was Mrs. Leslie who blushed, the difficult blush of a reserved woman; she coloured to the roots of her hair.

" That was very stupid of me. I ought to have understood from the letter." So Annie and Sammy had the front room and David the small room at the back. But Mrs. Leslie felt in some odd way that she had wounded Annie and she took a deal of trouble to be nice to Annie. In no time at all Mrs. Leslie and Annie became friends.

The holiday went well. Sammy galvanised the holiday; he was like an electric needle pricking David on, though David did not need pricking—he was having just as lovely a time with Sammy as Sammy was with him. The weather was warm, but the fresh breeze which always blows at Whitley Bay prevented the warmth from being oppressive. They bathed every morning and played French cricket on the sands. They ate unbelievably of ice-cream and fruit and went for walks to Cullercoats to the queer old-fashioned crab-parlour kept by the old woman in Brown's Buildings. David had inward remorse that the crab was not exactly good for Sammy's stomach, but Sammy loved it and with a guilty air they would sneak into the little front parlour in the two-roomed house that smelled of tar and nets and sit down on the horse-hair sofa and eat the fresh crab out of the rough shell while the old woman of the establishment watched them and called Sammy " hinny " and sucked at her clay pipe. The crab tasted marvellous; indeed, it tasted so good David felt it could not possibly do Sammy any harm. On the way back from Cullercoats, Sammy would take David's hand as they walked home along the promenade. That was question-time. David allowed Sammy to ask him any question under the sun and Sammy, trotting alongside, simply bombarded him with questions. David answered correctly when he could and when he couldn't he invented. But Sammy always knew when he was inventing. He would look up at David with those twinkling, disappearing eyes and laugh.

" Eh, yor coddin' now, Uncle Davey ? " But Sammy liked the codding even better than the answers.

David and Sammy had many such wonderful excursions together. Annie seemed to feel that they enjoyed being together and kept herself a good deal in the background. She was naturally self-effacing and she usually had something to do when David and Sammy wanted her to come out—the shopping, or some darning, or she had promised to take a cup of tea with Mrs. Leslie! Annie in collaboration with Mrs. Leslie was always devising some fresh turn on the menu and trying to find out what David liked. Annie's gratitude was enormous, but her fear of obtruding herself on David was more enormous still, and at last David had it out with her. On the Thursday afternoon he came in out of the sunshine and found Annie going upstairs with his grey flannel trousers folded over her arm—she had been pressing them in the kitchen with an iron borrowed from Mrs. Leslie. He saw this and a sudden exasperation took hold of him.

" Good Lord, Annie," he cried. " What do you want to do ironing for! Stopping indoors a fine day like this. Why aren't you down on the beach with Sammy and me ? "

Her eyes dropped; she was furious with herself for letting herself be caught. She said, as in excuse:

" I'll be down later, David."

" Later! " he raged. " It's always later, or in a minute, or when I've had a word with Mrs. Leslie. Good heavens, woman, don't you want to get any good of your holiday; what do you think I brought you for ? "

" Well," she said, " I thought to look after you and Sammy."

" What nonsense! I want you to have a good time, to come out and enjoy yourself, to give us your company, Annie."

" Well," smiling again faintly, " if I'll not be a nuisance to you, but I thought you wouldn't want to be bothered."

She put on her hat and came down to the beach with him and they sat with Sammy on the soft sand and were happy. From time to time he glanced at her as she leaned back her head with her eyes closed towards the bright sun. She puzzled him. She was a great girl, Annie, had always been a great girl—plucky, competent, quiet, modest. There was no flaunting of sex with Annie. Yet she was a fine strapping figure of a woman, with fine limbs and fine firm breasts and a fine smooth curve to her throat. Her calm face now upturned to the sun had a regular, composed, slightly sad beauty. Yes, though she took no care of herself whatever she had an almost classic beauty of which any woman might have been proud. And yet Annie had no pride, that was the queer thing, she had a sturdy independence, but neither vanity nor conceit. She had so little conceit of herself she was afraid of being a nuisance to him, of being in the way, a " bother." What infernally exalted notion had Annie got of him now, he wondered; she used not to be like that at all. But now, if only from the increasing respect of Mrs. Leslie—that plain reflection of Annie's awe—he could almost feel that Annie was afraid of him. And suddenly, as he lay on his elbow on the sand—Sammy was playing with his bucket at the water's edge—he said:

" What's come between you and me, lately, Annie ? We used to be the best of friends."

Still keeping her eyes closed towards the sun she answered:

" You are the best friend I have, David."

He frowned at her, streaming soft sand between his fingers.

" I'd like to know what's going on inside that head of yours. I'd like to shake you, Annie. I'd like to knock a real opinion out of you. You've become a kind of Mona Lisa, Annie. Heavens alive, I believe I'd like to beat you."

" I wouldn't try that if I were you," she said, with her faint smile. " I'm pretty strong."

" Listen," he answered after a minute. " I know what I'm going to do with you! " He looked at her shut eyes with a comic grimness. " When Sammy's in bed to-night I'm going to take you to the Fun

Fair. I'm going to push you into every mad, wild, atrocious side-show that exists. I'm going to jam you on to the cake-walk, the electric motors and the scenic railway. And when you're whirling through the air at eighty miles an hour I'm going to take a good close look at you and find out if the old Annie is still there."

" I'd like to go on the scenic railway," she said with that smiling, that baffling imperturbability. " But it's pretty expensive, isn't it ? "

He lay back and roared with laughter.

" Annie, Annie, you're unbeatable. We'll go on that scenic railway if it costs a million and kills us both! "

They went. After the unsuspecting Sammy had been decoyed with peppermint rock and put early to bed, David and Annie strolled over to the Fun Fair at Tynemouth. The wind had fallen and it was a calm, sweet evening. For no reason he could explain David was reminded suddenly and vividly of the evenings he had spent here with Jenny on their honeymoon at Cullercoats. And as they strolled past Cullercoats he was induced to speak of Jenny. He remarked to Annie:

" You knew I came here once with Jenny ? "

" Well, yes, I did know," Annie said, giving him a queer, involuntary glance.

" It seems a long time ago."

" It's not so very long."

There was a pause, then immersed in his own thoughts, overtaken by a sudden tenderness towards Jenny, David continued:

" I miss Jenny a lot, Annie. Sometimes I miss her terribly. I haven't stopped hoping she'll come back to me."

There was another silence, quite a long silence, then Annie said:

" I hope so, too, David. I've always known you were set on her."

They walked on without speaking after that, and when they entered the Fun Fair it looked almost as if the Fun Fair was not going to be a success, for Annie was not only silent but strangely subdued as well. But David was determined to shake Annie out of her perfectly causeless melancholy. Throwing off his own mood, he really exerted himself. He took Annie everywhere, beginning in the Hall of Mirrors, then passing on to the Helter Skelter. As they came tearing down the Helter Skelter on the same mat, Annie gave a palpitating smile.

" That's better," he said approvingly and dragged her to the Scenic Railway.

The Scenic Railway was better still. They switchbacked and bored through Stygian tunnels on the Scenic Railway and Annie simply could not get her breath. But the Giant Racer was the best of any. They found the Giant Racer about nine o'clock and they swooped and soared and dived from giddy heights on the Giant Racer until the whole glittering Fun Fair spun around them in one glorious daze. There was nothing like the Giant Racer, nothing in heaven, hell, limbo, purgatory or all the dimensions of this present universe. Upon the Giant Racer you climbed to an impossible altitude while all the panorama of the fair-ground lights lay beautiful and glittering and remote beneath. You climbed slowly with a wickedly deceptive slowness, enjoying the cool tranquillity, securely admiring the view. You crawled, simply, to the top. And then, while you still sedately admired the view, the car poised itself upon the brink and without warning hurled into the depths below. Down, down, down you fell into an unknown, shrieking darkness. Your stomach left you, your being dissolved, you died and were reborn again in that terrible ecstatic flight. But one flight was nothing; the car leaped to another summit and fell with you again, down, down, down; you had to die and be reborn all over again.

David helped Annie from the car. She stood uncertainly, holding his arm, with her cheeks flushed and her hat awry and a look in her eyes as if she was glad to be holding his arm.

" Oh, Davey," she gasped, " never take me on that thing again." Then she began to laugh. She laughed and laughed very quietly into herself. And again she gasped: " But it was wonderful."

He looked down at her, smiling.

" It did make you laugh," he said. " And that's what I wanted."

They sauntered about the Fair Ground, companionably interested in everything they saw. The music cascaded, the cheap-jacks shouted, the lights flared, the crowds went round and round. All the people were common and hilarious and poor. Coalies from Tyneside, riveters from Shiphead, moulders and puddlers from Yarrow, hewers from Seghill and Hedlington and Edgeley. Caps on back of the head, mufflers streaming, fag behind the ear. Their women folk were with them, red-faced and happy and eating out of paper bags. When the bags were empty they blew up the bags and burst them. They had teasers too, which blew out and hit you as you passed. It was a saturnalia of the humble and the unknown and the obscure. And suddenly David said to Annie:

" This is where I belong, Annie. These are my people. I'm happy among them."

But she would not admit it. She shook her head vehemently.

" You're going to the top, Davey," she declared, in her slow, straightforward way. " Everybody says it. You're going into Parliament at the next election."

" Who says that ? "

" All the lads say it at the Neptune. Pug was telling me. They say you're the one what'll do things for them."

" If I could," he said, and took a long deep breath.

As they walked home to Tarrant Street along the front a great moon came out of the water and looked at them. The noise and glitter of the Fun Fair died away behind. And he told Annie of what he wanted to do. He was hardly conscious of her stepping steadily beside him, she said so little and listened so well, but all the aspirations of his soul were laid before her. He had no ambition for himself. None.

He wanted justice for the miner, his own people, a class long and bitterly oppressed.

"Justice and safety, Annie," he concluded in a low voice. "Mining isn't like any other industry. It demands Nationalisation. The lives of the men depend on it. So long as you have private enterprise looking for a big profit you'll find the safety factor cut. Once in a while. And then the thing happens. That's the way it was at the Neptune."

Silence came between them as they went up Tarrant Street. With a change of tone he asked:

"Aren't you sick of listening to all my tub-thumping?"

"No," she said. "It isn't tub-thumping . . . it's too real for that."

"I want you to meet Harry Nugent when he comes to-morrow," he said. "Harry's the man who really can be convincing. You'll like him, Annie."

She shook her head quickly.

"Oh no! I'd rather not meet him."

"But why?" he asked, surprised.

"I just don't want to," she said firmly, and with unexpected finality.

Unaccountably, he felt hurt; her incomprehensible withdrawal, coming on top of his friendliness, his effort to take her out of herself, wounded him. He dropped the subject completely and withdrew into himself. When they entered the house, refusing her offer to get him some supper, he said good night at once, and went straight to his room.

Harry Nugent arrived next day. Nugent was fond of Whitley Bay; he swore there was no air in the world like Whitley air; whenever he could snatch a week-end he came to get a lungful of the wonderful air. He put up at the Waverley and David met him there at three o'clock.

Although it was so early in the afternoon, they had tea in the lounge without delay. Nugent was responsible; he was a great tea drinker, he drank endless cups of tea, he would make anything an excuse for a cup of tea. It didn't suit him either, aggravating the dyspepsia from which he habitually suffered. Nugent was physically a delicate man: his bony, ungainly figure and sallow, emaciated face bespoke a constitution ill-adapted to a life of strain. He suffered greatly and often from minor, unromantic maladies—once, for instance, he had endured six months' agony from fistula. But he never complained, never coddled himself, never gave up. He was so absurdly and humanly grateful, too, for the lesser joys of life—a cigarette, a cup of tea, a week-end at Whitley Bay or an afternoon at Kennington Oval. Nugent was above everything a human man; his smile expressed it, quietly forming on his ugly face, a smile which always seemed boyish because of the slight gap between his front teeth. He smiled now, at David, over this third cup.

"Well, I suppose I may as well go straight to the point."

" You usually do," David said.

Nugent lit a cigarette, and held it between his nicotine-stained fingers, tapping in the loose tobacco with a sudden seriousness.

" You did know, David, that Chris Stapleton was ill," he said at length. " Ay, and he turns out to be worse, poor fellow, than any of us thought. He went under an operation at the Freemasons' Hospital last week, internal trouble—you can guess what that means. I saw him yesterday. He's unconscious and sinking fast." He contemplated the glowing end of his cigarette. There was a long silence, then Nugent added: " There'll be a bye-election at Sleescale next month."

A sudden wild emotion rose in David's breast and leaped, like a pang of fear, into his eyes. There was another silence.

Nugent gazed across at him and nodded.

" That's right, David," he said. " I've been in touch with the local executive. There's no question as to who they want. You'll be nominated in the usual way."

David could not believe it. He stared back at Nugent, inarticulate, overcome. Then his eyes clouded suddenly and he could not see Nugent any more.

IX

The first person David met on his return to Sleescale was James Ramage. That Monday morning he had come up from Whitley Bay to Tynecastle with Annie and Sammy and seen them on the train for home. Then he had hurried to Edgeley to put in a full day's work at the Institute. It was seven o'clock in the evening when he came out of Sleescale Station and almost collided with Ramage, who was walking towards the news-stall for a late edition.

Ramage stopped dead in the middle of the passage-way and David saw from his face that he knew. On the Sunday night Stapleton had died in the Freemasons' Hospital and there had been a significant paragraph in this morning's *Tynecastle Herald.*

" Well, well," Ramage said, very sneering, pretending to be highly amused. " So we're goin' to have a try for parleyment, I hear ? "

With the most exasperating amiability he could command David answered:

" That's right, Mr. Ramage! "

" Huh! And you think you'll get in ? "

" Yes, I hope so," David agreed, maddeningly.

Ramage stopped trying to appear amused. His big red face turned redder than before. He clenched one hand and banged it vehemently into the palm of the other.

" Not if I can help it. No, by God, no, not if I can help it. We don't want no blasted agitators to represent this borough."

David watched Ramage's distorted face almost with curiosity, the hatred there was so openly displayed. He had forced Ramage to supply sound meat to the hospital, fought him over his abominable slaughter-house, his insanitary tenements behind Quay Street. He had, altogether, tried to induce James Ramage to do a great deal of good. And James Ramage could have killed him for it. Very curious.

He said quietly, without rancour:

" Naturally you'll support your own candidate."

" You bet your life, I will," Ramage exploded. " We'll swamp you at the polls, we'll wipe you out, we'll make you the laughin' stock of Tyneside . . ." He choked, seeking more violent expletives, then with a final incoherence in his throat he swung round and walked furiously away.

David went down Freehold Street thoughtfully. He knew that Ramage's was not the general opinion. Yet he fully appreciated what he was up against. Sleescale Borough was normally a safe enough Labour seat, but Stapleton, who had held it for the last four years, had been an oldish man, a man stricken in advance with the dreadful infirmity of cancer. At the last election which had sent in the Baldwin Government, Sleescale had wavered slightly, and Laurence Roscoe, the Conservative candidate, had reduced Stapleton's majority to a bare 1,200. Roscoe was certain to stand again, and he was a dangerous opponent. Young, good-looking and rich, David had met him several times, a big lanky-shouldered man of thirty-four with a high forehead, extremely white teeth and an odd habit of straightening his shoulders with a jerk, correcting a tendency to stoop. He was the son of Lynton Roscoe, K.C.—now Sir Lynton and a director of Tynecastle Main Collieries. Following the family tradition, young Roscoe was a barrister on the north-eastern circuit with a fine practice; work simply flowed in to him through his father's position and his own ability. He had got his blue for cricket at Cambridge, and in the war he had served quite romantically in the R.A.F. In fact, he was still interested in flying; he had his pilot's licence and often flew from Heston at the week-end to his father's country place at Morpeth. David felt it as strangely significant that the son of the man who had clashed with him so fiercely at the Inquiry should now oppose him at the polls. Oh well, David thought with a sombre smile, the bigger they are the harder they fall.

He went into his house. Martha was at the table peering over the evening newspaper, wearing the steel-rimmed spectacles which, disdaining his suggestion of an oculist, she had recently purchased for herself at the new Woolworths. Usually Martha did not bother over the evening newspaper but Hannah Brace had flown round upon the wind to gabble out to Martha the election paragraph and Martha for once in her life had gone out and bought the paper. She stood up with a guilty air. He could see that she was astounded, confused, almost stunned. But she would not be stunned, she would not. In her dark and masterful face he could see her struggling not to be impressed. Concealing the paper she said accusingly: " You're early back, I didn't expect you before nine."

But he would not let her off.

" What do you think of it, mother ? "

She paused; then she said dourly:

" I don't like it." She went to get his supper; that was all she said.

As he ate his supper he planned ahead. A vigorous campaign—that's what they called it, but it was not so easy to be vigorous when you were poor. Nugent had been brutally frank on the question of money: it was concession enough for David to secure the nomination. Still, he was not dismayed. His expenses could be cut; old Peter Wilson was a reasonable agent. He would hire one of the Co-operative light lorries and speak a good deal in the open, with the Town Hall for a final meeting. He smiled at Martha as she handed him a plate of stewed prunes. He knew that she knew he had never liked prunes.

" Prunes," he said, " for a member of parliament! "

" Time enough to talk," she answered cryptically.

Nomination took place on the 24th of August. There were only two candidates; the issue lay between David and Roscoe—a straight fight. It was a very wet day, the 24th, the rain came down in bucketfuls which meant, Roscoe jokingly remarked, that the omens were unfavourable for one of the candidates. David hoped it wasn't him. He found Roscoe's brimming confidence a trifle depressing. As far as he could see, the Conservative organisation was three times more efficient than his own. Peter Wilson, the scrubby little Sleescale solicitor, made an insignificant figure beside the morning-coated Bannerman, Roscoe's agent, imported from Tynecastle. And all this apart, the lashing rain made it very unfavourable for light-lorry eloquence. So David, feeling acutely inferior, was obliged to postpone his start. He went home and changed his damp boots.

But the next day was a day of blue sky and sunshine and David flung himself body and soul into the battle. He was at the Neptune gates when the foreshift came out, bareheaded and ready with Harry Ogle, Wicks, the checkweigher, and Bill Snow upon the lorry beside him—Cha Leeming being the volunteer driver. He made a strong, incisive speech and he made it deliberately short. He knew that the men were hungry for their dinner and he didn't keep them long. Roscoe, who had never come out the pit hungry for his snap, might make that mistake, but he wouldn't. The speech was a success.

David's plank was a plain and banal plank, but it gave substantial footing none the less. Justice for the miners. They knew that short of Nationalisation justice would never come. He was fighting on that issue and nothing else. He was competent to fight on that issue. It was the expression of his life-long faith.

At the end of the first week Tom Heddon came down from Tynecastle to " say a word " for David. All David's speeches had been studiously impersonal, for Roscoe was fighting cleanly and the air was clear of mud-slinging. But Heddon was Heddon, and although David had begged him before the meeting to be careful, Tom refused to keep the party clean. With a sour grin on his dark face he began:

" Lissen to me, you lads. There's two candidates in this bloddy election, Roscoe and Davey Fenwick. Now lissen to me a minnit, will ye. When this Roscoe was knockin' a ball about on a cricket-pitch at Eton and Harrow all la-de-dah in his flannelettes, with his ma and his pa and his sister standing by and clapping pretty under their bloomin' parasols, Davey Fenwick was inbye in the Neptune, stripped to the waist, muckin' and sweatin', catchin' and pushin' bloddy tubs of coal like we've all done in our bloddy time. Now answer me, lads, which of the two of them do you want to plump your bloddy vote for ? The one what caught the bloddy tubs or the one what missed the bloddy ball ? "

There was half an hour of this. It was rich and satisfying and highly seasoned and it went over big. Tom Heddon said quietly to David afterwards:

" It's poor stuff, Davey; I'm sick of it myself, but if it's done ye any good I'm sure you're welcome." If Tom Heddon had been a brilliant man he might well have been contesting the seat and Tom Heddon knew that he might have been contesting the seat. Since Tom was not brilliant he could only be unselfish. But his unselfishness did not save him from moments of terrible bitterness, of private self-torture worse than the torture of the damned.

Saturday, September 21st, was the day of the election and at six o'clock on Friday the night of the 20th David addressed his final meeting in the Sleescale Town Hall. The hall was full; they were standing three deep in the passages, and around the doors, wide open for the hot night, a crowd had gathered. All David's supporters were on the platform: Tom Heddon, Harry Ogle, Wicks, Kinch, young Brace, old Tom Ogle, Peter Wilson and Carmichael, who had come specially from Wallington to spend the week-end with David.

As David came forward to speak there was a dead silence. He stood behind the small table and the fly-blown water-bottle that no one ever drank from, and the air was so still he could hear the faint sounds of the waves lapping on the Snook. Before him were rows and rows of faces, all upturned towards him. Beyond the bright glare of the platform they had a massed, symbolic pallor, a look vaguely beseeching. Yet he could distinguish individual faces, all of them faces that he knew. In the very front row he saw Annie with still intent eyes upon him, and Pug beside her and Ned Sinclair and Tom Townley, Cha Leeming with Jack Reedy, very brooding and bitter, Woods, Slattery, and dozens and dozens more, men from the Neptune pit. He knew them, the miners, his own kind. He felt a great humility come over him, his heart filled, swelled towards them. He dropped the clichés, the political casuistry, the tub-thumping rhetoric. Dear God, help me, he thought, help me, help me. He spoke to them simply, from his very soul.

" I know most of you who are here," he said, and his voice trembled with emotion. " Many of you worked in the Neptune pit when I worked there myself. And to-night, somehow, even if I could, I don't feel like going into flights of oratory before you. I look on you as my friends. I want to talk to you as friends."

Here a voice from the back called out encouragingly:

" Go on, Davey lad, wor aal lissenin'! " There were loud cheers; then silence. He went on:

" When you think of it, the life of every man and woman in this hall is tied up in some way with the pit. You're all miners, or the wives or sons or daughters of miners; you're all bound to the mines. And it's on this question of the mines, surely a very vital question to you all, that I want to talk to you to-night . . ."

David's voice, rising in a passion of earnestness, echoed in the steamy hall. He felt strong, suddenly, able to hold, to convince them. He began to lay his arguments before them. He took the system of private ownership, with its frequent disregard to safety, its basis of sheer profiteering whereby the shareholder in the Company came first and the miner last of all. He passed to the question of royalties, that intolerable and immoral principle, allowing enormous sums to be taken out of a district, not because of services rendered to the community but solely on account of a monopoly given hundreds of years ago. Then quickly he placed before them the alternative system. Nationalisation! A word cried in the wilderness for years. He begged them to consider what Nationalisation meant. It meant, firstly, a unification of collieries, of management, and improved methods of production which would in turn be followed by a reorganisation of the system of coal distribution to the consumers. It meant, secondly, safe working at the pits. There were hundreds of pits all over the country, antiquated and badly equipped, where under private ownership the miner had to think of keeping his job first, and of reporting dangers or improper working last. And wages ? Nationalisation meant a better wage, because the lean years in the industry would be balanced by the better years; it meant at least a *living* wage. It meant better housing, too. The State could never allow the deplorable conditions of miners' houses which existed at present in so many districts; it could not for its own honour. This legacy of wretched housing was the result of years of greed, selfishness and apathy. The men who worked in the pits performed a public service, a dangerous public service, they should be looked upon as public servants. They only asked for human justice, the justice that had been denied them for centuries. They asked to be the servants of the State, not the Slaves of Money . . .

For half an hour he held them, hypnotised to silence, hanging upon his words, his arguments. His conviction swept everything before it. He moved them with the history of their own order, iniquity heaped upon iniquity, betrayal following betrayal. He made them glow with the record of their own solidarity, their comradeship in the face of every hardship, their courage in the face of danger. "Help me," he cried finally, with his hands outstretched in impassioned appeal. "Help me to fight for you, to win justice for you at last." He stood, silent, almost blinded by his own emotion. Then, quite abruptly, he sat down. For a moment there was dead stillness, then the cheering began, a perfect roar of cheering. Harry Ogle jumped up and shook David by the hand. Kinch was there, Wilson, Carmichael and Heddon too.

"You held them," Heddon had to shout above the noise. "Every bloddy one of them!"

Wicks was slapping David on the back, a mass of clamouring people swarming forward, surrounding him, wanting to shake hands, all trying to speak at once, overwhelming him. In the body of the hall the din was terrific, stamping, clapping and tinpanning. The sound of it rose echoing into the night.

Next day David polled 12,424 votes. Roscoe polled 3,691. It was a triumph, a victory unthought of, the biggest majority in Sleescale for fourteen years. As David stood bare-headed in front of the Town Hall while the tight-packed exultant crowd cheered and swayed and cheered again he felt dizzily a new elation rise in him and a new power. He had somehow stumbled through. He was there.

Roscoe shook him by the hand and the crowds cheered more thunderously. Roscoe was a good loser, he smiled through his crushing disappointment. But Ramage did not smile. Ramage was there with Bates and Murchison. Nor did Ramage shake hands. He stood with his brows drawn down, sullen and scowling, and on his face, mingled with lingering incredulity, was that look of unforgiving hostility.

David made a short glowing speech. He did not know what he said or how he said it. He thanked them, thanked them from the bottom of his heart. He would work for them, fight for them. He would serve them. A telegram was handed to him; it was from Nugent, a telegram of congratulation. It meant a lot to David, Harry Nugent's telegram. He read it, hastily, thrust it in his breast pocket. More people congratulating him, more handshaking, more cheers. The crowd began suddenly to sing, *For he's a Jolly Good Fellow*. They were singing it for him. A reporter, butting through the crowd, edging up to him. "Any message, Mr.

Fenwick, just a couple of words, sir, for the *Argus* ? " Photographers, inside the passage a big flash. More cheering, then a swaying, a slow dispersal of the crowds. Faint cheering from different parts of the town. Peter Wilson his agent, chuckling and joking, seeing him down the steps. It was over. It was all over. And he had won!

He got to his house at last and came rather dazedly into the kitchen. He stood there pale and finely drawn, looking at his mother. Suddenly he felt tired and terrifically hungry. He said sluggishly:

" I've got in, mother; did you know that I've got in ? "

" I know," she said dryly. " And I know you've had no breakfast. Are you above eating a pit pot-pie ? "

X

THE inevitable reaction came with David's introduction to the House when he felt unimportant, insignificant and friendless. He fought this down stubbornly. It was almost comic, but on that first day, his main encouragement appeared to come from the London police force. He was early and made the usual mistake of attempting to get in through the public entrance. A policeman, intercepting him, amicably indicated the whereabouts of the special private door. Through the yard David went, round the Oliver Cromwell statue, past rows of parked cars and strutting pigeons, and through the private door. Here another friendly policeman directed him to the cloak-room—a long room bristling with pegs, some of which bore bows of curious pink tape. As David divested himself of hat and coat yet another policeman affably took him in hand, explaining the geography of the House, waxing mildly historical, even elucidating the mystery of the pale pink bows.

" It goes back to when they wore swords, sir. They hung them on there afore they went into the House."

" I'd have thought they'd be worn out by now," David answered.

" Lord bless you, no, sir. When one gets to look shabby they takes no end of trouble to put up a new one."

At three o'clock Nugent and Bebbington arrived. He went with them along a vast corridor filled with pale blue books—Hansards, Bills, Parliamentary Procedure—books which conveyed the vague impression of never being read. He had a confused impression of the long high chamber, lounging figures, the Speaker with the Mace before him; of a mumbled prayer, his own name called out, his own figure walking quickly towards the back benches. He had a mingled sense of humility and high purpose—the conviction that his real work had at last begun.

He had taken rooms in Blount Street, Battersea. Actually the rooms made a small upper flat—a bed-sitting-room, kitchenette with gas cooker and bathroom—but the flat was not self-contained and was reached through the ordinary passage and staircase of the house. He paid £1 a week for the small uncontained flat on the understanding that Mrs. Tucker, the landlady, would make his bed and keep the place tidy. Beyond that David wanted to look after himself; he was going even to make his own breakfast, which moved Mrs. Tucker to considerable surprise.

Blount Street was not distinguished, a drab and smoky artery passing between two rows of grimy houses. On the paper-littered pavements a great many pallid children played curious, noisy games and climbed the spiked railings and sat companionably—especially the little girls—on the kerb, with their feet resting in the gutter. But it was within a mile of Battersea Park and No. 33, the Tucker house, had an extra storey which enabled David to get a glimpse of green trees and open sky beyond the fringe of smoking chimney-pots. He had taken an immediate liking to Battersea Park. It was not so pretty as Hyde Park or the Green Park or Kensington Gardens, but it lay altogether nearer to his heart. There he watched the young workmen who practised running and jumping on the cinder track, and the council schoolboys who played strenuous, skilful football, and the pale and adenoidal typists who struggled after the ball on the gritty courts, wielding their rackets in a style never dreamed of at Wimbledon. There were no smart nannies and no well-dressed children frisking behind monogrammed coach-built perambulators. Peter Pan, being a nicely brought up child, would never have looked twice at Battersea Park. But David, mingling with the raw humanity relaxing there, found comfort and a powerful inspiration.

His first real inspection of the park was on that Saturday afternoon when he lunched with Bebbington. David's performance at the election and his largely increased majority had impressed Bebbington, for Bebbington was that kind of man, always eager to cultivate the right people, to attach himself to success—which explained why Bebbington had come forward with Nugent to introduce David to the House. Later Bebbington strolled up.

"Going out of town this week-end?"

"No," David answered.

"I had made arrangements," Bebbington continued impressively, studying the effect sideways. "A house party at Larchwood Park—you know, Lady Outram's place—but at the last minute I've got landed to speak at the Democratic Union on Sunday evening. Beastly, isn't it? How I loathe the week-end in town! Lunch with me on Saturday if you've nothing better to do."

"Very well," David agreed, after a second's hesitation. He did not care much for Bebbington but it seemed boorish to refuse.

They lunched in the green and gold restaurant of the Adalia at a window table with a glorious view of the river. It was immediately clear that in this famous and exclusive place Bebbington knew everybody. And a great many people knew Bebbington. Conscious of the eyes directed towards his erect yet supple figure, Bebbington was pleasant to David in a patronising style, explaining the ropes, whom to run with and whom to avoid. But mainly he talked about himself.

" It was a toss up with me, really," he remarked, " whether to decorate the F.O. or go labour, I'm ambitious, you know. But I think I've been wise. Don't you think there's more scope with the party ? "

" What kind of scope ? " David asked bluntly.

Bebbington raised his eyebrows slightly and looked away as though the question were not in the best of taste.

" Aren't we all ? " he murmured gently.

This time it was David who looked away. Already Bebbington nauseated him with his vanity, his self-seeking, his steely, unwavering egoism. He let his gaze wander round the restaurant, noting the swift service, the flowers, iced wine, rich food and elegant women. The women especially—they blossomed in this warm perfumed air like exotic flowers. They were not like the women of the Terraces, with calloused hands and faces puckered by the eternal struggle to live. They wore costly furs, pearls, precious stones. Their finger nails were crimson, as if delicately dipped in blood. They ate caviar from Russia, *pâté* from Strasbourg, early strawberries forced under glass and carried by aeroplane from Southern France. At an adjoining table a young and pretty woman sat with an old man, He was fat, hook-nosed, bald. His pendulous cheeks shone with gross living; his paunch, protruding against the table, was obscene. She languished towards him. An enormous diamond, large as a bean, was on her forefinger. He ordered a magnum of champagne, explaining that they always put the best wine in the magnums. Though he wanted only a glass he always demanded a magnum. When presently his bill was brought, presented with a genuflection before him, David saw six pounds placed by his fat hand upon the plate. They had trifled with food and drink, these two, for a bare half-hour, and the cost would have kept a family in the Terraces for a month.

A sense of unreality came over David. It was not, it could not be true, this enormity of injustice. A social order which permitted such inequality was surely rotten to the core.

He was very silent for the rest of the meal, and his appetite was gone. He remembered the days of his boyhood, of the strike, when he had gone to the fields and eaten a raw turnip to stave the pangs of hunger. His spirit revolted at this pandering luxury; he breathed with relief when at last he got away. It felt like getting out of a hothouse, where deadly and voluptuous odours intoxicated the senses and destroyed the soul.

Striding back home to his lodgings, it was then that Battersea Park seemed open and undefiled.

The reaction to that inaugural luncheon with Bebbington was an almost passionate strengthening of his resolution to live simply. He had come across a strange book: *The Life of the Curé d'Ars.* The curé was a religious, naturally, a simple village priest in a country district of France, but the austerity of his life and the bare frugality of his diet deeply impressed David. After the wallowing he had witnessed at the Adalia, David felt a new respect for the simple man of Ars whose single daily meal was made up of two cold potatoes washed down with a glass of water from the well.

Mrs. Tucker was distressed by David's intentions upon the Spartan life. She was an elderly voluble Irishwoman—her maiden name she proudly declared to have been Shanahan!—with green eyes and a freckled face and fiery red hair. Her husband was a collector for the Gas Company and she had two grown-up unmarried sons clerking in the City. She had none of the natural indolence of her race, her fiery hair precluded that, and she was used, in her own phrase, to arranging the men. David's refusal to allow her to cook breakfast and supper for him struck at the roots of the Shanahan pride and set her talking freely. She was a great talker, Nora Shanahan that was, and her talking brought mortifying results.

On the last Saturday afternoon of January David went shopping in Bull Street, which was a main thoroughfare just round the corner from Blount Street. He often bought fruit in Bull Street or biscuits or a piece of cheese—there were shops in Bull Street that were both cheap and good. But this afternoon David bought himself a frying-pan. For a long time he had coveted a frying-pan as being simple, and quick in the mornings, and not gaudy then or any other time. And now he had the frying-pan. The girl in the ironmongery found the frying-pan an awkward article to wrap up and after splitting several newspapers and causing David and herself a good deal of amusement she gave over the attempt and asked David if he would take it like that. So David took the new and naked pan and carried it unashamedly to 33 Blount Street.

But at the door of 33 Blount Street something happened. A young man in plus fours and a rain-coat and a soft hat, whom David had seen hanging about at odd times lately, suddenly unslung a camera and took a shot at David. Then he raised the soft hat and walked rapidly away.

Next morning, in the middle of the *Daily Gazette,* the photograph appeared under the caption: The Frying-pan M.P., while below a good half a column extolled the asceticism of the new miners' member from the North. A short but snappy interview with Mrs. Tucker was appended, full of brogue and bunkum.

David's face coloured with anger and dismay. He jumped up from the table and hurried to the telephone on the half-landing. He rang the editor of the *Gazette* and protested indignantly. The editor was sorry, extremely sorry, yet he could not see what harm had been done. It was a good puff, wasn't it?—a really top-notch puff? Mrs. Tucker was equally unable to understand his annoyance; she was highly delighted to have got her name in the papers—respectably, she added.

But David went up to the House that morning feeling resentful and small, hoping the incident had been overlooked. But it was a vain hope. A mild derisive cheer greeted him as he entered. His first recognition—ridicule! He reddened and hung his head, burning that they should think he had courted such a cheap advertisement.

"Just laugh it off," Nugent suggested mildly. "That's the best way. Laugh it off." Nugent understood. But Bebbington did not. Bebbington was coldly satirical and aloof; he saw the incident as carefully pre-arranged and he did not hesitate to say so. Perhaps he grudged David the publicity.

That night Nugent came up to David's flat. He sat down, feeling for his pipe, searching the room with his quiet, contemplative eyes. His face looked more cadaverous than ever and the strands of hair streaked across his brow were few and thin but his boyish and impenetrable cheerfulness prevailed. He lit his pipe, then he said:

"I've been meaning to come up for some time. It's a snug little place you have here."

"Not so bad for a pound a week," David answered shortly. "It isn't all here, of course. The blasted frying-pan is in the kitchen."

Nugent's eyes lit up with amusement.

"You mustn't bother about that sort of nonsense," he said kindly. "It'll probably do you a bit of good with the lads up North."

"I want to do them a bit of good," David chafed.

"That'll all come," Nugent said. "We can't do much at the moment beyond marking time. We're up against a solid Tory wall, 419 seats to our 151. What can you do in the face of that? Nothing but sit tight and wait till our turn comes. Mind you, I know how you feel. You want to get into something. And you can't do it. You want to be done with formality and red tape and divisions and the whole smug procedure. You want results. Well, you just wait, David. One of these days you'll have plenty of chance to cut loose."

David was silent; then he said slowly:

"It's the damned procrastination that seems so senseless. There's trouble brewing in the mines. You can see it a mile away. When the settlement runs out the owners will come up in a body for longer hours and lower wages. In the meantime things are allowed to drift."

"They keep playing about with the idea of another subsidy." Nugent smiled gently. "In 1921 ten million pounds were evaporated in a subsidy. Then they had the great idea—a commission, always a brainwave. But before the commission brings out its findings, the Government pays another subsidy. Then the commission brings out its findings and condemns all subsidies. It's highly instructive. It's even amusing."

"When in the name of God are we going to get Nationalisation?" David asked in a burning voice. "It's the only solution. Have we got to wait till they offer it to us on a plate?"

"We've got to wait till a Labour Government gets it," Nugent said quietly. He smiled. "In the meantime carry on with your blue books and your frying-pan."

There came another silence. And Nugent went on:

"The personal equation is important. There's so many damned distractions and side issues to the game that you're apt to get lost in them unless you're careful. There's nothing like public life for searching out a man's private weaknesses. Personal ambition and social ambition and damned selfishness and self-interest, that's the curse of it, Davey. Take our friend Bebbington, for instance. Do you think he cares about the twenty-odd thousand Durham miners that returned him? Not one twopenny curse! All he cares about is Bebbington. Man, it would break your heart. Take Chalmers for another. Bob Chalmers was a perfect zealot when he came up four years ago. He swore to me with tears in his eyes that he would get a seven-hour day for the spinners or kill himself in the attempt. Well! the seven-hour day hasn't come to Lancashire yet and Bob isn't dead. He's very much alive. He's been bitten by the gold bug. He's in with the Clinton lot, passing on useful information, and making money hand over fist in the City. Cleghorn is another. Only it's the social side with him. He married a society wife. See! And now he'd miss any committee under the sun for a West End first night with the lady wife. I try to be generous, but I'm telling you, David, it would drive a man to despair. I'm no saint, but I hope to God I'm sincere. That's why I'm glad to my very roots to see you dug in here and trying to live a plain and honest kind of life. Stick to it man, for God's sake, stick to it!"

David had never seen Nugent so overwrought. But it was only for a moment. He took command of himself again, the habitual serenity flowed back into his face.

"Sooner or later you'll be up against it. You'll run into corruption like a pitman runs into styfe. The place is thick with it, David. Watch the bar of the House of Commons. Watch who you drink with. Watch Bebbington, Chalmers and Dickson. I know I'm talking like a good templar's tract, but it's God's truth none the less. If you can only be straight with yourself it doesn't matter a damn what else happens." He knocked out his pipe: "That's the end of the sermon. I had to get rid of it. And after that, if I ever walk in here and find your mantelpiece cluttered up with trashy invitations I'll kick you good and hard. If you want to amuse yourself, come round and watch the cricket with me at the Oval, when the good weather comes in. I'm a member. And I'm fond of it."

David smiled:

"That's your form of corruption."

"Exactly! It costs me two guineas a year. And I wouldn't give it up if they offered me the party leadership." With a look at the clock he rose quietly and stretched himself. "I must be going now." He moved to the door. "By the by, I haven't forgotten about your maiden speech. There'll be a grand chance for you in about a fortnight when Clarke proposes the amendment to the Miners' Safety Bill. That's an opportunity to get something off your chest. Good night."

David sat down when Nugent had gone. He felt better, soothed within himself. Nugent always exerted that influence upon him. It was perfectly true that he had been restless—the inertia of parliamentary routine was a dull anticlimax to the fierce encounter of the election and the burning enthusiasm of his beliefs. He resented the slowness, the waste of time, the pointless talking, the absurd questions, the suave answers, the polite insincerity—all dust in the eyes. Instead of a swift whirring of wheels he heard only the ponderous clanking of the machine. But Nugent made him feel his resentment as both natural and absurd. He must cultivate patience. He considered eagerly and with a certain apprehension his maiden speech—it was decidedly important that his speech should be arresting and good; he must make certain about that speech. It was a wonderful opportunity, the Amendment to the Miners' Safety Bill. He saw already, quite clearly, how he would deal with it, the points he would make, what he must emphasise and avoid. The speech began to form beautifully and strongly, to create itself like a living thing, within his mind. He was lifted right out of the room by the force of his own thought; the pit absorbed him and he was once again in the dark tunnels where men worked in constant danger of mutilation and death. It was so easy not to worry about these things if one did not know. But he did know. And he would force the living image of his knowledge into the minds and hearts of those who did not know. It would be different then.

As he sat by the fire, very still and tense, there was a knock at the door and Mrs. Tucker entered the room.

"There's a lady to see you," she announced.

He came back to himself with a start.

"A lady?" he repeated, and all at once a wild hope entered his head. He had always felt that Jenny was in London. Was it possible, could it possibly be that Jenny had come back to him?

"She's downstairs. Shall I show her up?"

"Yes," he whispered.

He stood up, facing the door, with a queer turning of his heart. Then his expression changed, his heart ceased to turn, the swift hope passed as soon as it had risen. It was not Jenny but Hilda Barras.

"Yes, it's only me," she declared, with her usual directness, seeing the sudden alteration in his face. "I got an idea of your whereabouts from the paper this morning and I determined to thrust my congratulations upon you. If you're too busy say so and I'll clear out."

"Don't be absurd, Hilda," he protested. It was an amazing surprise to see Hilda Barras but after his first disappointment he was pleased to see her. She wore a plain grey costume and a plain but good fox fur. Her dark severe face struck a familiar chord of memory; he suddenly remembered their flaming arguments in the old days. He smiled. And the strange thing was that she smiled too; she had never smiled when he knew her before—not much.

"Sit down," he said. "This really is an event."

She sat down and peeled off her gloves; her hands were very white and strong and supple.

"What are you doing in London?" he inquired.

"That's rather good from you," she said calmly. "Considering that you've been here about a month. That's the worst of you provincials."

"Provincial yourself."

"Are we going to start an argument?"

So she remembered the arguments too! He answered:

"Not without hot milk and biscuits."

She actually laughed. When she laughed she was quite pleasant: she had very good teeth. She was much less forbidding than she had been; her contracted, sullen frown was gone, she looked happier and sure of herself. She said:

"It's quite obvious that while I've been following your career with interest you've completely forgotten my existence."

"Oh no," he contradicted. "I knew you had qualified, about four years ago, as a doctor."

"A doctor," she echoed sardonically. "What kind of thing is that? You're not mixing me up with the Luke Fildes picture by any chance? No, there's no ipecacuanha and squills about me. I'm a surgeon—thank God. I took my M.S. with distinction. It probably doesn't interest you, but I'm an honorary at the St. Elizabeth's Women's Hospital, just across the river from you here—Clifford Street, Chelsea."

"That's fine, Hilda," he said, pleased.

"Yes, isn't it?" There was no satire in her voice now, she spoke simply and sincerely.

"You like it, then?"

"I love it," she said with a sudden intensity. "I couldn't live without my work."

So that's what has changed her, he thought instinctively. Just then, she glanced up, and with almost uncanny perception she read his mind.

"I was a beast, wasn't I?" she said calmly. "A beast to Grace and Aunt Carrie and everybody—including myself. Don't contradict me, please, even for the sake of argument. This visit is really an act of reparation."

"I hope you'll repeat it."

"Now that is nice of you," she flushed slightly, grateful. "I'll be quite frank. I've terribly few friends in London, terribly and pathetically few. I'm too stiff. I'm no good at meeting people. I don't make friends easily. But I always did like you. Don't misunderstand that, please. There's no silly nonsense about me. Not one particle. So I only thought that if you were willing we might sharpen our wits against each other occasionally."

"Wits!" he exclaimed. "You haven't any!"

"That's the spirit," she said enthusiastically. "I knew you wouldn't misunderstand me."

He stood with his hands in his pockets and his back to the fire watching her.

"I'm going to have my supper. Cocoa and biscuits. Will you have some?"

"I will," she agreed. "Do you make the cocoa in the frying-pan?"

"All square," he admitted; and went into the kitchen.

While he was in the kitchen she heard him coughing and when he came back she said:

"What's that cough?"

"Smoker's cough. Plus a little German gas."

"You ought to have it seen to."

"I thought you said you were a surgeon."

They had cocoa and biscuits. They talked and they argued. She told him of her work, of the operating theatre, the women who came under her knife. In a sense he envied her; this real outlet, a tangible succouring of suffering humanity.

But here she smiled:

"I'm no humanitarian. It's all technique. Applied mathematics. Cold and deliberate." She added: "All the same it has made *me* human."

"That's a debatable point," he said. And they went at it again. Then they talked of his coming speech. She was interested and excited. He outlined his scheme on which she violently disagreed. It was all very pleasant and like old times.

Ten o'clock came. And she rose to go.

"You must come and see me," she said. "I make much better cocoa than you."

"I will," he said. "But you don't."

In her walk back to Chelsea, Hilda reflected with an inward glow that the evening had been a success. It had taken a strong effort of will on her part to make the visit. She had been afraid, knowing that it was a visit liable to be misunderstood. But David had not misunderstood. He was much too wise, altogether too sensible. Hilda was pleased. Hilda was a fine surgeon. But she was not very strong on psychology.

On the night of his speech she bought a late paper eagerly. It was noticed, and noticed favourably. The morning papers were more favourable still. The *Daily Herald* gave it a column and a half, even *The Times* referred in gracious terms to the sincere and moving eloquence of the new member for Sleescale.

Hilda was delighted. She thought, I will, I must ring him up. Before Hilda went into the wards she rang up David and congratulated him warmly. She came away from the telephone satisfied. Perhaps she had been a little too glowing. But the speech had been wonderful. And naturally, it was the speech which concerned her!

XI

Arthur stood at the window of the office of the Neptune, staring out at the men who filled the pit yard, reminded painfully of the lock-out he had experienced in 1921, the first of a series of industrial disputes into which he had been dragged, all leading towards and culminating in the General Strike of 1926. He passed his hand across his brow, anxious to forget the whole senseless conflict. Sufficient that it was over, the strike broken and the men back, filling the pit yard, pressing forward, pressing and pressing towards the timekeeper's shed. They did not ask for work. They clamoured for work. It was written upon their silent faces. Work! Work! At any price! To look upon these silent faces was to see how glorious had been the victory for the mine owners. The men were not beaten, they were crushed; in their eyes was the panic fear of a winter of starvation. Any conditions, any terms, but work, work at any price! They pressed forward, elbowing and struggling towards the timekeeper's shed where Hudspeth stood with old Pettit, behind the bar, checking and entering the sheet.

Arthur's eyes remained bound to the scene. As each man came forward Hudspeth scrutinised him, weighed him up, looked at Pettit and nodded. If he nodded it was all right, the man got work and the man took his check and walked past the bar like a soul admitted into heaven past the judgment seat. The look upon the silent faces of the men who were admitted was strange: a sudden lightening, a great spasm of relief, of thanksgiving almost unbelievable at being readmitted to the black underworld of the Paradise. But not all the men were admitted, oh no, there was not work for all the men. With a six-hour shift there would have been work for all the men, but there had been a glorious victory for the forces of Law and Order, directed by an exultant, pro-Strike Cabinet, and backed by the British People, so the shift was an eight-hour shift. Never mind, though, never mind, don't bother about that now, any terms, any conditions, only give us work, for God's sake work!

Arthur tried to tear himself away from the window but he could not. The faces of the men held him, the face of one man in particular fascinated him. It was Pug Macer. Arthur knew Pug perfectly well; he knew Pug was an indifferent workman who kept bad time, was absent on Monday mornings, who drank. And Arthur saw that Pug knew this too. The recognition of his own unworthiness was written upon Pug's face alongside his desire to get work, and the conflict of these two emotions made an uncertainty, a suspense that was horrible to watch. It gave Pug Macer the look of a dog grovelling for a bone.

Arthur waited, hypnotised. It came near Pug's turn. Four of the men in front of Pug were taken on, and every man taken lessened Pug's chances of being taken—that was reflected in Pug's face too. Then Pug came before the bar, panting a little from the crush, and from the struggle between his eagerness and fear.

Hudspeth took one look at Pug, one short look, then he looked away. He did not nod, he did not trouble, even, to turn to Pettit, he simply looked away. Pug was not wanted. He was out. Arthur saw Pug's lips moving, he could hear nothing, but he saw Pug's lips moving and moving in a kind of desperate entreaty. No use. Pug was out, one of the four hundred who were out. The expression on Pug's face, on these four hundred faces, drove Arthur frantic. He turned abruptly, wrenched himself away from the window; he wanted to keep these four hundred in work at his pit and he could not. He could not, damn it, he could not. He stared at the calendar which showed the day to be October 15th, 1926. He went up to the calendar and tore off the slip violently. His nerves demanded some outlet. He wanted the day to be over.

Beyond the gates, Pug Macer walked away from the pit yard, down Cowpen Street; he shuffled rather than walked, with his hands in his pockets and his eyes on the ground, his shoulders drooping slightly, feeling the eyes of the women on him, watching him from the doorways of the Terraces—one of the four hundred, not wanted, out.

He turned down the Scut, into Quay Street, and home.

" Where's Annie ? " he asked, on the threshold of the bare, stone-flagged room.

" Out," his father answered from the kitchen bed. Old Macer was quite bedridden now, crippled by rheumatoid arthritis, and since he had always been an active man, his inability even to get up made him difficult and querulous. His complaint gave him constant pain in his back which made him believe he had kidney disease. He swore it was his kidneys and he scraped and saved up everything he could and spent it all on Dr. Poupart's Kidney-pills, a proprietary nostrum manufactured in Whitechapel by a plutocrat named Lorberg at the cost of a penny farthing per box, retailed at three and six, and composed entirely of soap, bad sugar and methylene blue. The pills made old Macer's water blue, and since the advertisement thoughtfully explained that the blueness was due to the impurities coming away, old Macer was very pleased. He felt he would be perfectly well if only he could get the impurities out of his kidneys. The trouble was that old Macer could not get enough of the pills. As the advertisement further explained the pills were expensive to make, the ingredients consisting of expensive Indian herbs gathered on the slopes of the Himalayas at the season of Karma Shalia from a recipe given to the late Dr. Poupart by an Indian sage.

Old Macer had no pills now and he looked across at Pug querulously, a little anxiously.

" What way hev ye not gan te the pit ? "

" Because I haven't," Pug said sullenly.

" Ye man go te work, Pug, lad."

" Oh, man I ? " Pug gritted out. " I'm goin' a bloody yacht cruise te Spain."

Old Macer's head began to shake.

" Ye canna stop off work on yer old fethur, Pug."

Pug did not speak, he stood burning, helpless, sick.

" Aw hev no pills, Pug, aw've got te hev my pills."

" To hell with your pills," Pug said and he flung himself into a chair and there he sat with his greasy cap on his head and his hands in his pockets staring at the spark of fire in the big grate.

Annie had been out taking back some sewing she had done for Mrs. Proctor and at the same time seeing Sammy up the road to the school. She was soon back.

She saw Pug brooding in the chair the instant she came in the door and she knew. The old familiar pang of worry stabbed at her. But she said nothing. She took off her hat and coat and began to clear the dishes from the table and to wash them.

Pug spoke first.

" I'm out, Annie," he said.

" Well, we'll manage, Pug," Annie said, going on with the dishes.

But the ignominy of his dismissal was rankling deep in Pug, hurting him.

" I'm not gud enough for them," he said, speaking with his teeth together. " Not gud enough, see! Me that can do two men's work when I'm put to it."

" I know, Pug," Annie said consolingly. Her fondness for Pug made her feel his hurt. " Don't you trouble, lad."

" They want to see me on the dole," Pug snarled. " Me that wants to work. The dole."

Silence. Old Macer in the bed, following the conversation in a sweat of self-pity, glancing from one to the other with a startled eye, now broke out:

" You'll need te write te Davey Fenwick, Annie. Ye'll need to let him help ye now."

" We'll manage, father," Annie said. She would never take money from David, never. " We always *have* managed."

Annie's idea was to get more work herself. And when she had finished her housework that morning, she went out to see what she could get. Housework was what she wanted, to go out as a daily, but housework, even plain charing, was difficult to come by. She tried at Dr. Scott's, at Mrs. Armstrong's. She even pocketed the last of her pride and tried with Mrs. Ramage. She was not successful. She got the promise of more sewing from Mrs. Proctor, and Mrs. Low, the wife of the New Bethel Street minister, grudgingly bespoke her to come for a day's washing on Monday. That, at least, made sure of half-a-crown though Mrs. Low always paid with an air of dispensing charity. But try as she might Annie got no more work than that. She tried the next day and the day after with the same result. Work was at a discount in Sleescale; and Annie had nothing else to sell.

Meanwhile Pug went up to see about his dole. He did not want to go on the dole but when his rankling sense of injustice became dulled he walked up to the Labour Exchange to apply for the dole. In Sleescale among the lads the Labour Exchange was known as the Buroo. Outside the Buroo a long queue stood waiting. There was no struggling or crushing in this queue like there had been at the pit and no hurry at all; everyone waited. It was an understood thing that one had to wait to get the dole. Pug silently took his place at the end of the queue beside Len Woods and Slattery and Cha Leeming. He did not speak to any of them, nor they to him. It was raining now, not raining heavily which would have given them something to curse, but raining softly, a fine, wet rain. Pug turned up the collar of his jacket and stood. He did not think. He waited.

Five minutes later Jack Reedy came along. Jack did not immediately take up his place. He was in this respect different from the others; he walked up and down the line as though the line infuriated him. Then he went up to the head of the line, slowly buttoned up his jacket, and began to harangue the men. Jack was the brother of Tom and Pat Reedy, both killed in the disaster. Once a fine, well-set lad, Jack was now shrunken by hatred and misfortune, a thin, hollow-chested man with extreme and bitter views. There had been the disaster, first, then Jack—in a mood to fight anybody—had fought in the war and been shot through the thigh at Passchendaele. He was lame as the result of the wound. Hudspeth had just refused to take him back at the Neptune.

Pug lifted his head and listened dully to what Jack was saying, though he knew beforehand what it would be.

"That's what we was, lads, when they wanted us to fight," Jack was saying and there was mutiny in his black, embittered voice, mutiny against life, destiny and the system which had brought him to this. "We was the nation's f—— heroes, and what are we now? Shiftless lazy scum. That's what they call us now. Now lissen, lads, till I put it to ye plain. Who made the bloody aeroplanes and the battleships and the guns and the blasted shells? Labour! Who fired the blasted shells out the blasted guns in the blasted war? Labour! And what has labour got out of it? This what we've got, lads. This! The chance to stand in the blasted rain with our hands held out for charity. We was told to fight for England—our own beloved soil. Christ! we fought for it, diddent we? And we've f—— well got it. We're standin' in it now. And what is it? Muck! Plain muck! But ye cannot eat muck, lads. Muck won't keep your wife and kids." Jack paused, pale as bone, and drew the back of his hand across his lips. He went on, his voice rising, his face contorted as with pain. "When you and me was fightin' and workin' during the blasted war there was millions of pounds of profits come out the pits. It's down in black and white, lads. A hundred and forty million pounds of profits. That's what tided the owners bye the strike. Why wassent they used to tide us bye? Now, lissen, lads——" A hand fell on Jack's shoulder. Jack stopped dead, remained quite motionless, then slowly looked round.

"We can't have none of that," Roddam said. "Get back in the queue there and shut your gob."

Roddam was the station sergeant now, fat, important and fifty.

"Let me be," Jack said in a low, poisonous voice, his eyes glittering in his bone-white face. "I fought in the f—— war, I did. I'm not used to bein' handled by the likes of you."

The queue was alive with interest now, much greater interest than had been displayed in Jack's speech.

Roddam reddened violently.

"You shut your gob, Reedy, or I'll run you to the station."

"I've as much right to talk as you," said Jack sullenly.

"Go back in the queue," Roddam blustered, pushing Jack down the line. "Back to the end there. Go on, back you go!"

"I don't have to go to the end," Jack cried, resisting, jerking his head. "That's my place there, beside Pug Macer."

"Go back where I tell you," Roddam ordered. "Right back to the hin' end." And he gave Jack a final push.

Jack turned, his chest heaving, his gaze fastened on Roddam as though he could have killed him. Then all at once his eyes fell, he seemed to gather himself up, to save himself for a future occasion. He limped quietly back to the end of the queue. A sigh went up from the watching men, a quiet sigh of disappointment. Their bodies relaxed, their attention wandered back to their own miseries. Roddam walked up and down the line officiously, rather grandly, in his big oilskin cape with the fine buckle and chain. The men stood and waited. The rain fell softly.

Sometimes it was dry when they waited for the dole. But it was a bad winter and mostly the rain fell—often it fell heavily. Once or twice it snowed. But they were always there, they had to be there, they waited. And Pug waited with the rest. Sammy did not like Pug being on the dole. As he came back from school he always went past the queue looking the other way, pretending not to see Pug, and Pug, who had his own humiliation from Sammy's passing, never attempted to recognise him either. The matter was not raised between Pug and Sammy but Sammy felt it deeply nevertheless. And in all sorts of other ways besides. For instance, Pug couldn't give him any cigarette cards now, and he missed the Saturday penny that Pug used to slip him on the sly. And worst of all he didn't ever get taken to the Sleescale football matches by Pug, though the unemployed got in for threepence now—yes, that was perhaps the worst of all.

Well, in a way, hardly the worst. The food kept getting plainer and plainer at home and sometimes there wasn't as much of it as Sammy would have liked. During the big stoppage it had been summer time and you didn't feel half so hungry in the summer. But the winter was different. Once when Pug broke out and had a blind on his dole money there hadn't been a bit of cake in the house the whole blessed week. And his mother made such champion cake. All that week it had been porridge and soup, and soup and porridge—his grandad had made a regular fuss. If it hadn't been for his mother going out washing and mending they wouldn't have had anything at all. Sammy wished that he were a little older. He would be working then, helping his mother. In spite of the depression Sammy was confident he could get a job; they always wanted boys for trappers at the Neptune.

Week after week Sammy saw Pug standing in that dole queue and pretended not to see him and the queue got longer every week. It preyed so much on Sammy that he took to running past the queue. Whenever he came near the Buroo he would discover something of immense interest at the foot of New Bethel Street, right down there at the very foot, and, with his eyes glued forwards, he would go clattering down towards it. Of course, when he got to the foot of New Bethel Street there wasn't anything there after all.

However, on the last Friday afternoon of January, when the queue was longer and later than ever, and Sammy went clattering down to the foot of the street, something did occur at last. Tearing down New Bethel Street, and round the corner of Lamb Street, Sammy ran straight into his grandmother Martha.

Sammy got the worst of the collision; he slid on the steel toe-caps of his boots, wobbled, stumbled and fell. He wasn't hurt, but scared to think of what he had done. Awkwardly, he picked himself up and gathered up his cap and his school books and prepared with a very red face to go on.

Then he discovered that Martha was looking at him. She was Martha Fenwick, his grandmother, he knew that well. But she had never looked at him before; she had always walked by him in the street the way he walked by Pug in the queue, not seeing him; he might not have existed at all.

Yet now she stood looking at him—looking and looking, ever so oddly. Then she actually spoke. In a queer voice she said:

" Did you hurt yourself? "

" No, mam." He shook his head confusedly.

A silence.

" What's your name? " It was the stupidest thing to say, and her voice seemed to crack in the stupidest manner.

" Sammy Fenwick," he answered.

She repeated it:

" Sammy Fenwick." Her eyes devoured him, his pale face and nobby forehead, and bright blue eyes, his growing figure in the home-made, patched suit, his thin legs ending in the heavy boots. Though Sammy could not guess it, for months and months now Martha had watched him, every day she watched him as he went to school, watched him surreptitiously from behind the curtains of the side window of the house in Lamb Lane. He was growing so like her own Sammy; he was ten years old now. It was agony for Martha not to have him near her. Would nothing ever break her icy pride? Cautiously, she said:

" Do you know who I am? "

" You're my grandma," he said at once.

She coloured deeply, and with pleasure. Sammy had broken the ice at last, shivered the frozen covering of the old woman's heart.

" Come here, Sammy."

He came and she took his hand in hers. Sammy felt it awfully strange and he was inclined to be scared, but he walked with her to the house in the lane. They went in together.

" Sit down, Sammy," Martha said. It gave her an exquisite, an unbearable pleasure to speak the name of Sammy once again.

Sammy sat down, looking round the kitchen. It was a good kitchen, absolutely clean and as it should be, like his own kitchen, but the furniture was better and there was more of it. Then Sammy's eye lit up; he saw that Martha was cutting a cake, cutting an enormous wedge of plum cake.

" Thanks," he said, accepting the cake, balancing his books and his cap on his knees, then filling his mouth with the cake.

Her hard dark eyes dwelt absorbedly upon his young face. It was her own Sammy's face.

" Is it a good cake? " she asked intensely.

" Yes, mam," he said, wiring into it, " it's fair champion."

" Is it the best cake you ever tasted? "

" Well! " He hesitated, troubled, afraid to wound her feelings; but he had to speak the truth. " My mother makes as good a cake when she has the stuff. But she hasn't had the stuff, not lately."

But even this could not break the spell of Martha's rapture.

" Your uncle's on the dole ? " she asked. " Pug Macer ? "

His thin young face flushed.

" Well, yes, Pug is now, but only for the time being like."

" Your father would never have been on the dole," she declared with pride.

" I know," he said.

" He was the best hewer in the Neptune."

" I know," he said again. " My mother told me."

Silence. She watched him finish, then she cut him another piece of cake. He took it with a shy smile, her own Sammy's smile.

" What are ye goin' to be when you grow up, Sammy ? "

He reflected, while she hung upon his answer.

" I'd like to be like my father," he said.

" You would," she whispered. " Ay, ye would, Sammy."

" Ay."

She stood quite motionless. She felt weak, ravaged, overcome. Her own Sammy come back to her, to carry on the brave tradition; she would see it yet, Sammy Fenwick again the best hewer in the Neptune. She could not speak.

He finished the last crumb of cake, recovered his cap and books from off his knees and rose.

" Don't go yet, Sammy," she protested.

" My mother'll be wondering," he replied.

" Take this in your pocket then, Sammy, take this for your bait, Sammy." Feverishly she cut him another wedge of cake, wrapped it in greased paper, picked a red apple from the dresser, made him stow cake and apple in his pocket. At the door she paused: " Come and see me to-morrow, Sammy." And her voice was pleading . . . pleading . . .

" Righto," he said and darted like a little trout down the path.

She stood watching, watching until he was long gone. Then she turned and went back into the kitchen. She moved slowly, as if with difficulty. In the kitchen she caught sight of the cut cake. She stood there silent and immobile while across the screen of her impassive sight a flood of memory poured. All at once her face broke. She sat down at the kitchen table, put her head upon her arms, and sobbed bitterly.

XII

DAVID's political development came like the development of the human body—it was a slow growth, imperceptible from day to day, yet apparent when balanced against his stature of five years before. Though his purpose was so definite and strong he advanced towards it by long and difficult roads. The political meteor flashes only through the imagination of the novelist. David experienced the reality. He worked; he worked unbelievably hard; and he waited. He learned many things; but chiefly to cultivate the faculty of patience. His maiden address was followed, some months later, by another speech on the distress in mining areas. The comment which this occasioned caused him to be approached by several of the party leaders for data on this subject. Several admirable orations bearing on the distressed areas were made thereafter in the House for which David received no credit although the speeches were almost entirely his. Later, however, by way of recognition, he was invited to sit on a departmental committee investigating the question of industrial disability in mines. During the next twelve months he worked with this committee on nystagmus, beat knee and the incidence of silicosis in non-metalliferous mines. Before the end of that session he was co-opted to a board pursuing an inquiry into the qualifications of mine officials under the existing legislature. In the following year Nugent, billed to speak at the mass demonstration held by the T.U.C. in the Albert Hall, fell ill with influenza, and at his urgent request David was called upon to deputise. Addressing an audience of five thousand, he made the speech of the evening, a speech of flaming ardour, humane feeling and trenchant style. Paradoxically enough, the glamour of this one evening focused more attention upon him than all his hard work of the previous two years. He became noticed at the conferences. It was he who prepared the memorandum for the T.U.C. on Nationalisation of the Mines, and the proposed Power and Transport Commission. His paper, Electric Power and National Progress, was read at the American Labour Conference. Thereafter he became chief miners' representative on the board reviewing the question of water dangers in mines. By the autumn of 1928 he was a member of the Parliamentary Labour Party Committee and finally, at the beginning of the following year, he reached the peak of his achievement. He was appointed to the executive of the Miners' Federation.

David's hopes ran high. In himself he felt extremely well, clear-headed, able to cope with any amount of work. And more than ever he sensed the favourable turn of events. The present Government was moribund, sadly preparing to die. The country, sick of stale policies, reiterated platitudes and the old die-hard administration, was raising eyes of conjecture towards a fresh horizon. At last, through their constitutional hidebound apathy, people were beginning to question the soundness of a political and economic system which left want, misery and unemployment unrelieved. New and bold ideas went into circulation. Men no longer retreated in terror from the suggestion that capitalism, as a system of life, had failed. Recognition grew that the world would never be reconstructed by the violence and suppression of economic nationalism. Workers on the dole were not now designated shiftless scum. The factitious explanation of " world conditions " became a hypocritical echo, a music-hall joke.

David felt with all his soul that Labour's chance must come. There would be an election this year, an election which must be fought on the question of the Mines. The party stood pledged to it. And what a glorious platform it made: this great national constructive scheme to benefit the miner and bring prosperity to the community.

That bright April morning, David's spirits were high as he sat by the window in his rooms, glancing through the paper. It was Saturday. He was looking forward to a morning spent on the new Low-Temperature Report, a recent process it was proposed to incorporate in the Power section of the scheme, when, unexpectedly, a diversion occurred. The telephone rang.

He did not immediately answer it, for usually Mrs. Tucker went first, but as the raining continued he dropped his paper and descended to the half-landing where he picked up the receiver. Straightaway Sally's shrill, throaty voice came over the wire—he recognised it at once.

" Hello, hello," she said, " you must be awful busy. I've been trying to get you for the last five minutes."

Smiling into the receiver he exclaimed:

" Sally! "

" So you knew me ? "

" You're unmistakable."

They both laughed and he said:

" Where are you ? "

" I'm at Stanton's Hotel, you know, near the British Museum, and Alf is along with me."

" But what in all the world are you doing up here ? "

" Well, as a matter of fact, Davey," she answered, " I'm going to be married. So I thought I'd take dad for a bit of a trip to London before I got hitched up. The Pigeon Show's on at the Crystal Palace and dad did want to see it."

" Why, that's great news, Sally," he declared, both surprised and pleased. " Who is he ? Have I met him ? "

" I don't know, David." Her voice was happy, a shade self-conscious. " He's Dick Jobey, of Tynecastle."

" Dick Jobey," he exclaimed. " Why, Sally, that's a great match."

A silence ; he could feel that she was gratified ; then she said :

" I want to see you, David. And Alf does too. Will you have a bite with us to-day ? Listen. We've arranged to go to the Crystal Palace this afternoon, but come along and have an early lunch with us at the hotel. Come now, David."

He reflected: Saturday and the Report could wait.

" All right," he cried. " I'm with you. I'll be along shortly after twelve. Yes, I know Stanton's, Sally. I'll be there."

He came away from the telephone still smiling—there was something incorrigibly light-hearted about Sally which never failed to cheer him.

At half-past eleven he took the underground for Museum Station and walked along Thackeray Street towards Stanton's, a quiet, unostentatious hotel in Woburn Square. It was a bright morning; a sense of spring was in the air, the trees of the Square were already in leaf and a gay chirruping of sparrows came from in front of a seat within the Square Gardens where an old man sat feeding them with crumbs. The passing taxicabs had a gay note, too, as though they rejoiced in the fineness of the day. He arrived at the hotel a few minutes before noon but Alf and Sally were waiting for him in the lounge. They greeted him affectionately.

It was some years since David had seen Alf Sunley but Alf was not greatly changed. His moustache was perhaps more tobacco stained and ragged, and his face more sallow, and the crick in his neck more pronounced, but he was still the same friendly, common, doggedly unassertive little man. He wore a new black suit for the occasion, very stiff and new and rather big for him, and a new made-up tie, and his boots were probably new for they squeaked whenever he moved.

But Sally had changed. Taking after her mother, perhaps, she had turned round as a barrel, little bracelets of plumpness were on her wrists and her face was frankly fat. She smiled at David's hastily concealed surprise.

" Yes, I've put on a bit, haven't I ? But never mind. Let's go and have some lunch."

They had lunch. They sat at one of the tables in the quiet restaurant while the sun shone in on them and they had cold meat and salad. The cold meat and salad tasted good and the rhubarb tart which came afterwards was good too. Sally ate a hearty lunch and enjoyed it. She had a bottle of Guinness all to herself. Her plump little face flushed, and her figure seemed almost to expand with the excellence of the meal. When she had finished she drew a satisfied breath and shamelessly eased her waistbelt. David smiled across at her.

" So you're getting married. I thought something like that would happen one day ? "

" Dick's a good chap," Sally sighed contentedly. " Not much to say, but one of the best. I can tell you I'm lucky. You see, David, I'm getting a bit sick of the road. I've been goin' round the Payne-Gould circuit till I'm giddy. I'm sick of summer pierrots and winter pantos. And besides, I'm putting on weight something terrible. In a couple of years I'd only be fit for the fairy queen. An' I'd a sight rather have Dick than the demon king. I want to settle down and be comfortable."

He gazed at her quizzically, remembering the terrible strivings of her early youth, the passionate desire for fame upon the boards.

" But what about that great ambition, Sally ? "

She smiled comfortably.

" That's got a bit of fat on it too, lad. You'd 've liked me how they make them in the story books. With my name in big lights in Piccadilly." She stopped laughing and shook her head; then lifting her eyes she looked at him steadily. " It's one in a million does that, David. I'm not her. I've got a bit of talent maybe, but that's the end of it. Don't you think I haven't found that out by now. Put me against the real thing and I don't exist."

" Oh, I don't know, Sally . . ." he remonstrated.

" You don't," she answered with something of her old fierceness. " Well, I do. I've tried it and I know where I get off. We all start out with great ideas as to where we're going, Davey, but it's precious few that gets there. I'm lucky to have found a half-way stop that suits me."

There was a silence. Sally recovered herself immediately, yet, though the fire died out of her eyes, she remained unusually serious. She began to play with her spoon, abstractedly, drawing circles with the handle upon the tablecloth. Her face was overcast as if something had recurred to her and now lay upon her mind. Suddenly, as though taking a decision, she glanced at Alf, who lay back in his chair, bowler hat over his eyes, sleepily using the wooden toothpick he had just shaped from a match.

" Alf," she remarked meditatively, " I want to have a word with David. Take a stroll round the Square for a couple of minutes."

" Eh ? " Alf sat up, taken by surprise. He stared at her.

" You'll find David and me here when you come back," insisted Sally.

Alf nodded. Sally's word was always law. He rose and readjusted his hat. As she watched him go Sally reflected:

" He's a good sort, Alf, a regular treat. Thank God, I can get him away from his white lead now. I'm buying him a bungalow at Gosforth. Dick's told me to go ahead. I'm settling Alf there and letting him breed homers to his heart's content."

David had an odd sense of warmth within his breast. It was his nature always to be moved by the evidence of generosity or kindness in others. And he felt these qualities shining in Sally's affection for her father, the little man in the black misfitting suit and squeaky boots and made-up tie.

" You're a brick, Sally," he said. " You've never hurt anyone in all your life."

" I don't know about that." She was still unsmiling. " I think perhaps I'm going to hurt you now."

" Why, what's the matter ? " he inquired in surprise.

" Well," she paused, opened her bag and slowly drew out a letter. " I've got something to tell you. I hate to, David. But I must, you'd hate me if I didn't." Another pause. " I've heard from Jenny."

" Jenny ? " he gasped.

" That's right," she answered in a low voice. " She sent me this letter." And saying no more, she handed it to him.

Mechanically he took the letter. It was on thick violet notepaper with deckled edges, heavily scented, and written in Jenny's round, childish hand. The envelope had a deep violet lining. The address was: The Excelsior Hotel, Cheltenham, and the date a few weeks before.

" My dearest Sally," the letter ran, " I feel I must take up my pen to bridge the long silence chiefly due to me being *abroad*. What you must have thought I really cannot imagine. But wait, Sally, till I tell you. When I was in Barnham I saw an advertisement in the paper for an old lady needing a companion. Well, just for fun like I applied and to my supprise I received a most polite answer enclosing railway fare to London. So I went to see her and oh my dear she would not take no. She was going abroad to Spain and Italy and Venice and Paris. She had white hair and the loveliest lace and a mauve dress and the most beautiful kind eyes. Such a fancy she took for me you could not believe. My dear, she kep saying your sweet, I cannot let you go, so to cut a long story short I just had to Sally. Oh I know I done wrong, but there I could not resist the travel. My dear we been *everywhere*—Spain and Italy and Venice and Paris, oh, and Egypt too. And *such* style! The best hotels everywhere, servants bowing and scraping, the opera in foreign places, a box mind you, with counts in uniform. Oh, Mrs. Vansittar cannot bear me out her sight, she *dotes* on me. She says I am like a daughter to her. I am in her will too. I only read to her and go for drives and out to tea and that. Oh, and arrange the flowers. I must say I am lucky don't you think so Sally. Oh, I would not make you jealous for untold gold Sally but if you could only see the style we keep your eyes would drop out your head. I meant to plan so we could meet but we are only hear a few days just to drink the waters then we are off again. Dear, dear life is very gay for me Sally I wish you was as lucky as me. Give my love to mar and Clarice and Phyllis and pa and of course your self. If you see David tell him I think about him sometimes. There is nobody in my life now, Sally, tell him that too. I think men is beasts. He was good to me though. Now I must close as it is time for me to dress for dinner, I have a new one black, with sequins, think on me in it Sally oh it's a dream. Goodbye and God bless you then Yours for ever and a day Jenny."

Silence. Then a long sigh came from David. He stared and stared at the grotesque effusion, every line of which breathed a memory of Jenny, painful and pitiful, yet somehow tender.

"Why didn't you let me know before?" he asked heavily at length.

"What was the use?" Sally answered in a quiet voice. She hesitated. "You see, I went to Cheltenham, to the Excelsior Hotel. Jenny had been there all right for a couple of days during the race week. But not with Mrs. what's her name."

"So I can gather," he said grimly.

"Don't let it upset you, David." She reached across the table and touched his hand. "Cheer up now, there's a good lad. It's something to know she's alive and well."

"Yes, I suppose that's something."

"Did I do right showing you?" she persisted anxiously.

He folded the letter and slipped it in the envelope, then placed it in his pocket.

"I'm glad you did, Sally," he said. "Surely I'm the one who ought to know."

"Yes. That's what I thought."

Another silence fell, during which Alf rejoined them. He glanced quickly from one to the other but he asked no questions. Alf's taciturnity sometimes revealed itself as a gift greater than many tongues.

They left the hotel half an hour later, and David walked down with Alf and Sally to their bus. He forced himself to appear unconcerned, even to smile. Sally was happy—he had no wish to spoil her happiness with his private sorrow nor to make her feel that in showing him the letter—so obviously her duty—she had reopened a deep and painful wound. He knew the letter to be cheap and vulgar and untrue. With unerring vision he drew the picture: Jenny, alone for an hour in this cheap hotel while her companion visited the races or an adjoining pub; a momentary impulse to kill her boredom, utilise the visit to Cheltenham—such a refined resort!—to impress her family, appease the insatiable cravings of her romantic mind. He sighed. The scent from the cheap notepaper nauseated him. *Tell David I sometimes think about him.* Why should that touch him? But did she ever think about him? He wondered sadly. Yes, perhaps she did; even as he thought of her. For in spite of everything he could not forget her. He still felt tenderness towards Jenny; her memory lived with him, lay like a light shadow across his heart. He knew he might despise her, he might even hate her. But he could never wipe that shadow, that secret tenderness away.

That night he sat brooding by the fire with the Report lying on the table untouched. He could not settle to it. A strange restlessness had seized him. Late at night he went out and took a long walk through the empty streets.

For days his restlessness continued, and he made no attempt to work. He walked. He revisited the Tate Gallery, standing silently before the small Degas, *Lecture de la Letter*, which had always fascinated him. He sought distraction and enlightenment in Tolstoi, whose nervous impressionism seemed to vibrate in sympathy with his present mood. Rapidly he re-read *Anna Karenina*, *Three Sons*, *Resurrection* and *The Power of Darkness*. He, too, saw human society as crossed by fateful and contrary tendencies, earthbound by a sordid self-interest, yet soaring occasionally with a gesture of nobility, of sacrifice, towards the sublime.

He was able, at last, to concentrate upon work. April passed into May. Then events came tumbling rapidly one upon another. It became more and more evident that the Government was about to die. Immersed in the preparation for the great campaign David had no opportunity for brooding. He found time to dash up to Tynecastle to attend Sally's wedding. But for the rest he had not a moment to himself.

On May 10th Parliament dissolved, nominations were in by the 20th of the same month and on May 30th the General Election took place. The policy of Nationalisation was the main plank in the Labour Programme. Labour appealed to the nation in the great manifesto:

The state of the coal-mining industry is so tragic that measures would be immediately undertaken to alleviate the distress in the coal-fields, reorganise the industry from top to bottom, both on its productve and marketing sides, and shorten the hours of labour. A Labour majority would Nationalise the Mines and Minerals as the only condition for satisfactory working. It would develop the scientific utilisation of coal and its valuable by-products, now largely wasted.

The manifesto was signed J. Ramsay Macdonald.
J. R. Clynes.
Herbert Morrison.
Arthur Henderson.

On that manifesto and its policy of Nationalisation Labour went into office. David increased his majority by almost two thousand. Nugent, Bebbington, Dudgeon, Chalmers, Cleghorn polled more votes than ever before. With a sense of exultation mingled with expectation, David returned to London. He visualised the Coal Mines Bill so long projected by the party, presented, pressed in the face of all protests and triumphantly debated. The thought mounted to his head like wine. At last, he thought, at last! On July 2nd, 1929, the Session formally opened.

XIII

On a foggy evening early that autumn David and Harry Nugent came out of the House and stood for a moment on the low steps in conversation. Ten weeks ago the King had made his speech from the throne. The Labour ministers had kissed hands. Jim Dudgeon, clothed in knee-breeches and resplendent cocked hat, had stood in supreme affability before a dozen press photographers. The Prime Minister, hurrying through a visit to the United States, had flashed a message to the Labour Party Conference: *We have to raise the coal industry from the depths into which long years of drifting and blind policy have plunged it.*

But David's face, seen indistinctly through the curling swathes of fog, wore an expression curiously at variance with so commendable a beginning. With hands in his pockets and head sunk into the upturned collar of his overcoat he had an air both troubled and restive.

" Shall we see the Bill this year ? " he asked of Nugent. " That's what I'd like to know."

Tucking his scarf around his neck, Nugent answered in his quiet voice:

" Yes, by December, if what I'm told is correct."

David stared out into the blank uncertainty of the fog which somehow seemed to symbolise his mood.

" Well, we must wait until we see the text of it," he said with a sigh. " But I can't understand this procrastination. It bothers me. It strikes me we're all so busy trying to appear constitutional and respectable that no one has the time to show any initiative."

" It isn't just the question of time," Nugent replied slowly. " It's rather significant the Government keeps asking us to remember we're in office and not in power."

" I've heard that so often, Harry, I feel one day it'll be on my tombstone."

" You'll hardly be in office then." Nugent's lips twitched slightly but immediately he was serious again. " Still, you're right when you say we must wait for the Bill. And in the meantime hope for the best."

" I am," David answered grimly. There was a pause, during which a long dark car drew up silently opposite the entrance. Both men stared at it in silence. And presently, from the lobby behind, Bebbington appeared. He glanced at Nugent and David with his usual superficial air.

" Wretched evening," he remarked suavely. " Can I give you a lift up west ? "

David shook his head without speaking and Nugent answered:

" No, thanks. We're waiting on Ralston."

Bebbington smiled, rather aloof and condescending, then with a faint nod he descended the steps and briskly entered the car. The chauffeur placed a fur rug about his knees, and sprang into the driving-seat. The car purred into the fog.

" It's extremely strange," David reflected in an odd voice. " That car of Bebbington's. It's a Minerva, isn't it ? I wonder how exactly it came along ? "

Harry Nugent glanced sideways at David, his eyes gently satirical beneath the bony ridges of his brow.

" Perhaps it's for his services to the State," he suggested.

" No, but seriously, Harry," David persisted, unsmiling. " Bebbington's perpetual wail is that he has no private means. And now that car and chauffeur."

" Is it worth while being serious ? " Nugent's mouth twisted with unusual cynicism. " If you must know the truth, our friend Bebbington has just joined the board of Amalgamated Collieries. Now, don't look so desperate. There's plenty of precedent. It's all perfectly in order and neither you nor I nor anyone else dare say a word! "

" Amalgamated Collieries! " In spite of himself David's tone was bitter. He glanced across at Nugent, stung by a swift resentment. Nugent's passive acceptance of the fact added to his troubled restlessness. Nugent had been a tired man lately, rather jaded in his manner, slower, even, in his walk, accepting his failure to secure inclusion in the Cabinet almost with resignation. There was little doubt that Nugent's health had failed greatly, his old vitality seemed spent. For that reason alone David did not pursue the subject. When Ralston arrived he switched the conversation to the meeting which they had all three promised to attend at the League of Democratic Control, and together they set out towards Victoria Street through the fog.

But David was not happy in his mind. The session, begun with such elation, continued strangely ineffectual, strangely like those sessions which had preceded it. Often, during the weeks which followed, his thoughts returned to Sleescale, to the men whom he had promised justice. He had pledged himself. The party as a whole had pledged itself. That pledge had won them the election. It must be implemented, even if it meant throwing themselves upon the country once again. The conditions in Sleescale were so appalling now—the town stricken with destitution, the men harbouring a hidden mutiny against the social order which condoned such misery—that he felt the growing urgency for action. He was in touch with the men, with Heddon, Ogle and the local officials. He *knew*. The situation was not imaginary but existed in grim reality. It was desperate.

In the face of the crisis David built all his hopes upon the new Coal Mines Bill. He saw it as the sole solution of the problem, the one logical means to achieve the vindication of his party and the salvation of the men. From time to time he had news of the Bill which was in the process of being drafted by a Cabinet Committee consulting with a special committee of the Miners' Federation. But neither Nugent nor he was on this committee and information was of the scantiest. The internal administration of the party had become universally stringent and members of committee resented any form of approach. It was, in fact, impossible to discover the shape or context of the Bill. Nevertheless, the Bill was coming forward, this much was assured. And, as December drew near, David told himself that his premonitions had been absurd, merely the echo of his own impatience. He waited with a growing expectancy.

Quite suddenly, on December 11th, the Bill was introduced. Sponsored by the President of the Board of Trade, supported by the Attorney-General and the Minister for Mines, it was formally presented for the first time. The House was not particularly full, nor was there any sense of the momentous in the air. The whole thing passed undramatically, even hurriedly. The title of the Bill was short, generalised and elusive. A bare ten lines quickly read out; a bare ten minutes from first to last, and the thing was over. David listened with a rising apprehension. He could not fully understand. There was, as yet, no indication of the scope of the Bill; yet, even at this early stage, its limited application was borne in on him. Rising hurriedly, he went into the lobby and made representations to several members of committee, urgently requesting a draft copy of the Bill. He even approached Bebbington in his anxiety to secure the draft. By that same night the full text of the draft was in his hands. Only then did he appreciate the significance of the new measure. His reaction was indescribable. He was not only stunned. He was appalled.

It so happened that on the 11th Nugent had been called up to Edgeley and David spent the evening alone, studying the draft. Even yet he could not believe the evidence before his eyes. It was incredible, staggering—a shattering blow.

He sat late into the night, thinking, trying to define his own line of action. Resolution firmed within him. He saw all that he could do, all that he must do.

On the next day he attended early at the meeting of the Parliamentary Labour Party Committee. It was a small meeting, perhaps half the normal size. As he surveyed the meagre gathering, David's heart sank. Lately, ministers had been irregular in attendance, but this to-day was especially significant, the more so as the Minister for Mines was absent. Only Dudgeon, Bebbington, Nugent, Ralston, Chalmers and some twenty-odd members of committee were in the room. An after-luncheon feeling hung about the air—Chalmers had the two bottom buttons of his waistcoat loose, while Cleghorn, with a half-shut drowsy eye, settled himself to snatch a comfortable nap.

Jim Dudgeon was in the chair. He glanced at the papers in his blotter, swept the table with his owl-like gaze, then read rapidly:

" The programme of the House this week will include discussion on unemployment, debate on housing and the second reading of the Coal Mines Bill . . ."

David jumped to his feet.

" Mr. Chairman," he exclaimed, " on a point of order may I ask whether this Bill is intended to represent the policy of the Labour Party ? "

" Hear, hear! " called out several members from the committee left wing.

Dudgeon did not look in the least put out. He eyed David affably, up and down.

" Have you any reason to believe that it does not represent the policy of the party ? "

David struggled for calm, yet he could not restrain a biting sarcasm from his tone.

" It would appear that this Bill, in its present form, is slightly inadequate. We were returned to this House pledged to Nationalisation. We bound ourselves in a signed manifesto to alleviate the tragic distress in the coalfields, and to reorganise the industry on national lines from top to bottom. And how are we proposing to do it ? I am not aware if all the members of this committee have seen the full text of this Bill. But I have seen it. And I can assure them that it outrages every promise that was given."

There was a silence. Dudgeon rubbed his chin reflectively, peering at David from behind his big horn rims.

" The point you forget is that we're in office here, we're not in power. We must make shift the best way we can. The Government is bound to compromise."

" Compromise! This isn't a compromise. It's sheer cowardice. The Opposition could not have produced a Bill which panders more to the owners. This Bill is all coalowner. Retaining the quota system, throwing out the minimum wage proposals, blinking at the ' spread over '—it is a Tory Bill and every member of the House will shortly be aware of it."

" Just a minute," Dudgeon murmured blandly. " I'm a practical man. At least, I've got a reputation for bein' a practical man. I believe in goin' to the point. Now what exactly is your objection ? "

" My objection! " David broke out. " You know that this Bill offers no fundamental solution to our difficulties. Its essential purpose is to market coal. It is a ridiculous attempt to reconcile two definitely irreconcilable principles. The quota system is a positive injury to the miners and can never be anything else. When you compare what we pledged ourselves to do and what the Government now proposes to do, the thing becomes a crying outrage."

" And even so, what is the alternative ? " protested Dudgeon. " Remember our position."

" That's exactly what I do remember," David declared in a white heat of indignation, " our position and our honour."

" For God's sake! " Chalmers interposed coarsely, with his eyes on the ceiling. " What does this member want ? "

" What I want is to see this Bill amended to the form when it implements our pledge and satisfies the conscience of every man inside the party. Then take it to the House. If we're defeated we go to the country on our Bill. Then the men know that we fought for them. We could not have a better case."

Another cry of " Hear, hear," from the far end of the room; but in the main a murmur of disapproval went up from around the table. Chalmers bent slowly forward.

" I've been put here," he said, prodding the table with one forefinger to emphasise his words, " and I'm going to stay put."

" Don't you realise," Dudgeon resumed affably, " we've got to show the country our ability to govern. We're winnin' golden opinions for the way we're handlin' affairs."

" Don't delude yourself," David returned bitterly. " They're laughing at us. Read the Tory papers! The lower class aping their betters. The tame menagerie. According to them we're not governing, we're performing. And if we run away from them over this Bill they'll have nothing but contempt for us! "

" Order, order," Dudgeon sighed reproachfully. " We don't want any hard words inside the party." He blinked at David in a kind of genial exasperation. " Haven't we made it clear to you that we've got to go slow ? "

" Slow! " echoed David savagely. " At this rate we'll still be preparing to nationalise in another two thousand years."

For the first time Nugent spoke.

" Fenwick is right," he said slowly. " On point of principle there's no question but what we ought to fight. We may keep ourselves here for another twelve months playing at power, keeping up the sham, simply deluding ourselves. But we'll go out on our necks in the end. Why not go out with flying colours ? And, besides, as Fenwick says, we've got the men to consider. They're pretty well at the end of their tether on Tyneside. I'm telling you and I know."

Cleghorn said acidly:

" If you're asking us to resign from office because of a few Tynecastle malcontents you're walking in the wrong street."

" Did you call them malcontents when you asked for their votes ? " David cried. " It's enough to drive the men to revolution."

Chalmers banged irritably on the table.

" You're making a damned nuisance of yourself, Fenwick. Revolution be damned! We don't want any Russian ideas brought up at a time like this."

" Most uncomfortable for the middle classes! " Bebbington agreed in a sneering undertone.

" You see," Dudgeon went on smoothly, " we all admit there ought to be a complete revaluation of human effort. But we can't go and repudiate the present system offhand like we were thowing away an old boot. We've got to be careful. We've got to be constitutional. Damn it all, I'm too popular to do anything against the British Constitution."

" You prefer to do nothing." A flood of anger rushed over David. " To sit and draw a Cabinet minister's salary while thousands of miners starve on the dole."

There was an outcry at this and cries of " Order, order! Withdraw! "

" I'm not going to commit political suicide for nobody," Dudgeon muttered, reddening.

" Is that the opinion of this committee ? " David asked, looking round intensely. " What do you propose to do ? To keep your word or break it ? "

" I propose to keep my reputation for sanity," Bebbington said icily.

" Hear, hear! " shouted several; then Cleghorn's voice: " I move next business, Mr. Chairman." The cry was taken up.

" I ask you to reconsider the form of this Bill," David intervened desperately. " I can't believe that you refuse to amend it. Leave the issue of Nationalisation alone. I appeal to you at least to consider the insertion of a minimum wages clause."

Chalmers, this time moving irritably in his chair:

" Mr. Chairman, there is no time obviously to take this discussion further. Surely the member can keep his theories to himself and trust the Government to do all that is possible in the present circumstances."

Several voices then cried:

" Next business, Mr. Chairman."

" I'm not talking to you in terms of theories," David shouted. " I am talking to you in terms of men and women. I warn the committee that the Bill will drive the miners to despair, to rioting. . . ."

" You will have an opportunity of amending it at the proper time," Dudgeon countered shortly. Then aloud: " What is your pleasure ? "

A loud shout from his supporters:

" Next business."

Despairingly, David attempted to carry on a cross-bench argument. It was no use. Dudgeon's voice monotonously took up the thread of the interrupted meeting. The business of the Committee proceeded.

XIV

THAT cold December morning, Arthur walked down to the Neptune and entered his office. He was early. He hung up his hat and coat, stood for a moment staring at the calendar, then he went forward quickly and tore off the date. Another day. Surely that was something. He had survived another day. He sat down at his desk. Although he had just risen from bed he had slept badly and felt tired already, tired of the endless struggle, of this endless battering against the economic forces which threatened to destroy him. His face was thin and lined, he had the appearance of a man consumed by worry.

He pressed the bell upon his desk and immediately Pettit, his clerk and timekeeper, brought in the morning mail—the letters arranged methodically, the largest beneath, the smallest upon the top. Pettit was always very neat.

" Morning, Pettit," Arthur said automatically. He felt his voice artificial though he tried to make it cordial and encouraging.

" Morning, Mr. Barras. Heavy ground frost last night, sir."

" Yes, it's cold, Pettit."

" Perishing, sir. Shall I put more coal on the fire ? "

" No thanks, Pettit."

Almost before Pettit was out the door Arthur reached for the top letter, the letter he had been expecting, the letter from his bankers in Tynecastle.

Slitting the stiff envelope he read the formal communication quickly, not surprised, in a sense not even dismayed. The present policy of the bank was opposed to further short-term loans, they deeply regretted their inability. . . . Arthur let the letter drop. Regret, of course, was a fine word; everybody had the deepest feeling of regret when compelled from the highest motives to refuse a request for money. He sighed. Yet he had anticipated this answer even before he wrote. He had reached the limit of his overdraft, borrowed the last farthing upon his equipment and headgear; he had the advantage at least of knowing where he stood.

He remained seated at his desk—though he was tired it cost him an effort to keep still, his nerves demanded some violent outlet. And with a certain feverish intentness, he reviewed the situation. The strain of it was visible upon his brow.

It was a long road he had travelled since the days of the disaster. And now there was no road but merely a kind of bog, an industrial morass, the slump. Coal had fallen a further fifteen shillings per ton; and even so he could not sell it. The combines, the big amalgamations were selling coal. But he, the small private producer, was powerless. Yet his overhead kept up: his pumps must be maintained, his royalties paid—6*d.* on every ton which he took out of his pit. And the men ? Here he sighed again. By his policy of conciliation and safety he had hoped to carry them with him. But all along he had been sadly disillusioned. They seemed actually to resent his attempt to reorganise them, to suspect the motive behind his sweeping reforms. To many his wonderful pithead baths were still a source of irritation and ribald comment. He knew he was a bad leader. Often he wavered in his decisions, was persuasive when he should have been firm, stubborn when a stronger man would have laughed and yielded. The men saw his weakness and played upon it. Old Barras's bullying they understood; they had feared, even admired it. But Arthur's altruism and high ideals they mistrusted and despised.

The pitiless paradox stung Arthur to the quick. He lifted his head in a hot wave of exasperation. He refused, yes, refused to admit it.

He was not beaten. At a low ebb merely. He would go on, win through. The tide must flow again; it was not far off flowing now. He applied himself to the problem with renewed intensity. In the fever of his concentration the position clarified, the fact became lucid, the figures marshalled themselves before his mind's eye. The pit was mortgaged, his credit exhausted, his output the lowest in twenty years. But he had a strong conviction that trade would presently mend. The slump must end, it must end soon. He would hang on, hang on until the end of the slump, then all would be well. He could keep going for another twelve months at least, this he knew with certainty. He had considered it, in anticipation of the bank's refusal, worked it all out to the last detail. There was nothing he had not foreseen. A case of cutting down, further economy, of holding on, yes, sitting tight and holding on. He could do it, he knew that he could do it.

He drew a sharp nervous breath. The cutting down was the worst, but it simply had to be. Another fifty men must go to-day; he would take them out Five Quarter Seam and close the headings there till trade improved. It broke his heart to give these fifty their time, to send them to join the six hundred men from the Neptune already on the dole. But he had no option. He would take them back the moment, the instant, he was able.

With a jerky movement he looked at the clock. He must let Armstrong know at once. He flung open the door and went quickly along the corridor towards Armstrong's room.

He spent half an hour with Armstrong deciding which of the men must go. It had come to that now. Arthur himself insisted on weighing and considering each individual case before striking out the name. Nothing could have been more painful for him; some of the men were old hands, experienced and skilful men who had been getting coal in the Neptune for twenty years and more. But they had to go. They had to go to join the six hundred men upon the dole, to swell the destitution and discontent that seethed in Sleescale.

At last it was done. Arthur watched Armstrong cross the yard to the timekeeper's box with the white sheet fluttering in his hand. A strange sense of having slain these men worked within his breast, hurting him. He raised his hand to his forehead and pressed his forehead regardless of the trembling of his hand. Then he turned and walked back into his own office.

The office was not empty. Just inside the door Hudspeth was waiting for him, waiting with a red and angry face. Hudspeth had a lad with him, a big lump of a youngster who stood sulkily with one hand in his pocket and the other holding his cap. The lad was Bert Wicks, Arthur saw, the son of Jake Wicks, the men's checkweigher. He worked in Globe

Coal. One look at the pair showed Arthur it was trouble, and his nerves vibrated through his body.

' What is it ? " he said, trying to remain calm.

Hudspeth said:

" Look." And he held out a packet of cigarettes and a box of matches.

They all stared at the cigarettes and the box of matches, even Bert Wicks stared, and the effect of these trivial articles was clearly enormous.

Hudspeth said:

" In the stables, too. In the new Globe roadway, sitting there smoking in the stables, among the straw—excuse me, Mr. Barras, but you wouldn't believe it. Forbes, the deputy, just brought him outbye! "

Arthur kept staring at the cigarettes and the matches; he seemed unable to withdraw his eyes from the matches especially. Little waves kept bursting over him, over his nerves. He had to keep his whole body clenched to suppress the waves which broke over him and over his nerves. There was firedamp in the new Globe headings, recent inspections had revealed firedamp in explosive concentration. He was afraid to look at young Wicks for fear everything inside him would break loose.

" What have you to say ? "

" I didn't do nowt," Bert Wicks said.

" You were smoking."

" I wore only hevin' a puff in the stable. I diddent do nowt."

A little shiver went through Arthur.

" You took matches inbye. You were smoking."

Wicks said nothing.

" In spite of the regulations," Arthur went on with set lips, " and all my warnings about naked lights in Globe."

Bert Wicks twisted the peak of his cap. He knew what the men thought about Arthur, what they said about him too, cursing everything he did from his coddling to his blasted safety regulations. He was tough, Bert was, he was not going to let himself be put down. Half frightened and half sullen, he said:

" My fethur says there's niver been no firedamp in the Neptune. He says the order agin matches is all b—s."

Arthur's nerves broke, everything inside him broke loose. The ignorance, the stupidity, the insolence. He had sacrificed himself, nearly ruined himself, yes, half killed himself with work and worry to make the Neptune safe, to give the men a decent deal. And this was the answer. He lost himself. He took a step forward and hit Wicks in the face.

" You fool," he said; his breath came panting like he was running. " You cursed ignorant fool. Do you want to blow the pit to bits ? Do you want us with another disaster ? Do you want that ? Do you want it, I say ? Here am I throwing decent workmen out the pit with you skulking about in a corner, loafing, smoking, ready to blow us all to damnation.

Get out, for God's sake. Get out of my sight. You're sacked. Take your matches and your filthy cigarettes. Go on, get out before I kick you out."

He caught Wicks by the shoulders, spun him round and fired him through the door. Wicks went sprawling his full length on the corridor outside, and hit his leg against the step. Arthur banged the door.

Silence in the office. Arthur leaned back against his desk, still breathing like he had been running; he seemed scarcely able to breathe. Hudspeth gave him one quick perturbed glance. It was instinctive that glance and Arthur saw it.

" He deserved it," he cried. " I had to sack him ? "

" Ay, you wouldn't want to keep a lad like him," Hudspeth said, staring awkwardly at the floor.

" I can't sit down under that sort of thing ? "

" No, you wouldn't want to do that," Hudspeth said, still staring uncomfortably at the floor. He paused. " He'll go straight and tell his father, of course—Jake Wicks, the checkweigher."

Arthur struggled for control.

" I didn't hit him hard."

" He'll be making out you near killed him. They're rare ones for trouble that Wicks lot." He broke off, turned to the door. " I better go over," he said. He went out.

Arthur remained supporting himself against the desk. It was a mistake he had made, a horrible mistake, the cumulation of his anxiety and strain had made him make this horrible mistake, striking Bert Wicks.

Hudspeth had gone over to smooth out the mistake. He hoped it would be all right. He straightened himself and entered his little changing room that opened off the office. He had arranged to inspect New Paradise this morning and he got into his pit clothes. As he stepped into the cage to go inbye he still hoped it would be all right.

But it was not all right. When Bert Wicks picked himself up he made for the bank where his father stood checking tubs as they came rolling down the track. His leg hurt him where it had hit against the step and the more he thought about his leg the more his leg hurt him. He became afraid to put any weight upon his leg.

His father, Jake Wicks, saw him coming like that, afraid to put weight on his leg. Jake stopped the tubs.

" What's up, Bert ? " he asked.

In a high blubbering voice Bert told him, and when Jake had heard everything he said:

" He can't do a thing like that."

" He did it," Bert answered. " He knocked us down and kicked us, he did. He kicked us when I wor down."

Jake rammed the book he kept for checking tubs into the inside of his jacket and hitched his leather belt tight.

" He can't do it," he said again. " He can't get away with that sort of thing on us." Frowning, he reflected. All because poor Bert had forgotten to take a couple of matches out his pocket before he went inbye. All because of that and these blasted new regulations. Would anybody stand it?—let alone him, the men's checkweigher at the pit. He said suddenly: " Come on, Bert."

He left the tubs altogether and he walked Bert the whole way up to the hospital. Dr. Webber, the young resident house surgeon, newly qualified and not long appointed to the hospital, was on duty and Jake, with the peremptory manner of a man who knew his own position, asked Dr. Webber to examine Bert's leg. Jake Wicks, besides being checkweigher to the men, the post which Charlie Gowlan had once held, was treasurer to the Medical Aid Committee. It was quite important for Dr. Webber to be pleasant to Jake Wicks and he was most pleasant and obliging, making a long and grave examination of Bert's leg.

" Is the leg broke ? " Jake asked.

Dr. Webber did not think so. In fact he was practically certain that the leg was not broken, but you could never be sure and in any case it was not wise to be sure. The medical journals were always turning up with fracture cases, nasty cases of damages too, damages against the doctor. And Jake Wicks was an unpleasant customer. Dr. Webber, not to put too fine a point on it, was afraid of Jake, and he said:

" We ought to have an X-ray."

Jake Wicks thought an X-ray would be a good idea.

" Suppose we keep him in for twenty-four hours," Dr. Webber suggested pleasantly. " Twenty-four hours in bed won't hurt you, Bert, just to be safe, have a proper diagnosis. How does that strike you ? "

It struck Jake and Bert as being quite the best course under the circumstances. Bert was put to bed in the men's ward and Jake went straight down to the Institute and rang up Heddon at the Lodge offices in Tynecastle.

" Hello, hello," he said cautiously. " Is that Tom Heddon ? This is Jake Wicks, Tom. You know, Tom, the Neptune checkweigher." Jake's tone with Heddon was rather different from his tone with Dr. Webber.

" What is it ? " Heddon's voice came curtly over the wire. " And cut it short, for God's sake. I haven't all day to listen to you. What *is* it ? "

" It's my lad, Bert," Jake said very propitiatingly. " It's assault and victimisation. You've got to listen, Tom."

For a full five minutes Heddon listened. He sat at the other end of the wire with the receiver clapped to his ear, listening darkly, intently biting his thumb nail and spitting the tiny pieces on to the blotter before him.

" All right," he said at the end of it. " All *right*, I tell you I'll be along."

Two hours later when Arthur rode to bank from the Paradise and came out of the cage and across the yard Heddon was seated in the office, waiting on him. The sight of Heddon gave Arthur a shock; he went cold suddenly. Heddon did not get up, but sat squarely in his chair as though planted there. And he did not speak.

Arthur did not speak for a minute either. He walked through to the bathroom and washed his hands and face. Then he came out, drying himself, but he had not washed himself properly, for his hands left a dark smudge on the towel. He stood with his back to the window, wiping his hands on the towel. He found it easier to keep doing something. He was not so nervous if he kept on wiping his hands. Trying to speak casually he said:

" What is it this time, Heddon ? "

Heddon lifted a ruler from the desk and began to play with it.

" You know what it is," he said.

" If it's Wicks you've come about," Arthur said, " I can't do anything. I discharged him for rank disobedience."

" Is that so ? "

" He was caught smoking inbye in Globe. You know we've found firedamp there. I've spent a lot of money making this pit safe, Heddon. I don't want any worse trouble than what we've had."

Heddon crossed his legs easily, still holding the ruler. He was in no hurry. But at last he said:

" Bert Wicks is in hospital." He told it to the ruler.

Arthur's inside turned over and went hollow. He felt sick. He stopped wringing his hands upon the towel:

" In hospital! " After a minute: " What's happened to him ? "

" You should know."

" I don't know."

" They think his leg's broken."

" I don't believe it," Arthur cried. " I didn't do anything. Mr. Hudspeth was there. He'll tell you it was nothing."

" Wicks has got to be X-rayed to-morrow—that'll show you if it's nothing. Dr. Webber's orders. I've just come from the hospital."

Arthur was very pale now; he felt weak. He had to sit down on the window sill. He remembered that young Wicks had fallen heavily outside the door.

" For God's sake, Heddon," he said in a low voice. " What are you getting at ? "

Heddon dropped the ruler. There was no sweetness or brotherly love about Heddon; his job was to be violent and arbitrary and he intended to do his job.

" Look here, Barras. I'll speak plain. You lost your temper to-day and assaulted a man. Don't deny it. Never mind what the man did. You assaulted him with violence. You've as good as broke his leg. That's a serious matter. It isn't a question of reinstatement. It's criminal. Don't interrupt. I'm talking. I represent every man that's left in your bloddy pit and if I lift my finger they'll walk out on you."

" What good will that do them ? " Arthur said. " They want to work, they don't want to walk out."

"The men have got to stand together. What affects one affects all. I don't like this Neptune pit. It stinks with me this pit ever since that time back when you had the flooding. I'm not going to stand no nonsense."

The violence in Heddon's voice knocked the heart right out of Arthur.

"Do you know how I've slaved at this pit?" he protested weakly. "What are you getting after?"

"You'll find out in plenty of time," Heddon answered. "We've called a meeting at the Institute for six o'clock. There's a strong feeling about it. I'm only warning you. It's no good your doing anything now. It's done. You're in a mess. You're in one hell of a mess."

Arthur did not speak. He was limp, sick of Heddon and Heddon's threats. These threats were part of Heddon's business. Heddon was trying to bully him and probably succeeding. But in his heart he could not believe that Heddon would bring the men out, the men who were at the Neptune were too glad to be in work to come out. The destitution in the district was terrible, the town festering with unemployed; the men in work were the lucky ones. He stood up listlessly.

"Have it your own way," he said. "I know you don't want trouble."

Heddon stood up, too. Heddon was used to men who banged the desk with their fists and snarled at him and told him to get to hell out of here. He was used to bluster and counterbluster, oaths, threats and blasphemy. He was paid to fight and he fought. Arthur's lethargy brought a vague pity to his eyes.

"That's everything," he said. "You'll hear from us later." And with a short nod he walked out.

Arthur remained motionless. He was still holding the half-folded towel and he completed folding the towel. He went into the bathroom and hung the towel up on the hot pipe. Then he saw that the towel was not very clean. He picked if off the rail and dropped it in the empty bath to be removed.

He changed into his ordinary clothes. He could not be bothered to take a bath to-night. He was still tired and listless and sick. Everything was a little unreal; he felt light inside his clothes, as if he did not belong to them. He was so sensitive he could feel acutely, but once his feeling had traversed a certain point of acuity he became numb. He was numb now. He caught sight of himself suddenly in the small square of mirror hung on the white enamel wall. No wonder he felt done up. He looked ten years more than his age of thirty-six, there were lines round his eyes, his hair was lustreless, almost gone upon the top. Why was he wasting his life like this, making an old man of himself before his time, chasing insane ideals, embracing the mad illusion of justice? Other men were enjoying their lives, making the most of their money, while he stuck here at this joyless pit working the treadmill thanklessly. For the first time he thought, God, what a fool I've been!

Back in the office he looked at the clock. Almost six o'clock. He took his hat and went out. He walked out of the empty pit yard and along Cowpen Street. He ought, of course, to go to the hospital to inquire about young Wicks, but he decided to put it off until later. It was very typical, this procrastination. As he walked up the Avenue he heard a loud sound of voices from the Miners' Institute. The voices came distantly, they seemed to him futile and remote. He knew there could be no trouble, it was too silly to think of trouble at a time like this.

XV

But Arthur was wrong. Fact, once in a while, does violence to logic. And the events of the evening of December 14th do not necessarily discredit Arthur's judgment. They merely took place.

The meeting at the Institute was held at six. It was short. Heddon saw to it that the meeting was short. Heddon's policy was quite clear; he wanted no trouble, no trouble at all. The sadly depleted funds of the Union would not stand trouble. His policy was to intimidate Arthur, leave Arthur uncertain and worrying for twenty-four hours, then come down on the following day to drive a hard bargain with Arthur. Re-instatement for Bert Wicks and compensation and a something extra thrown in to make good measure. But above all Heddon's policy was to get home, change his socks which were damp because his feet sweated badly, sit down to his tea in dry socks and slippers and then get into a chair by the fireside with his pipe. Heddon was not so young as he had been, his ambitions were dead, the hatreds of his youth merely smouldering. His policy was still vigorous enough, but it was governed less by Heddon's head and more by Heddon's feet.

He rushed the proceedings at the meeting, snubbed Jake Wicks, endorsed Harry Ogle's briefly expressed views, then hurried out to catch the 6.45 for Tynecastle.

On the steps of the Institute he paused, rather taken aback by the size of the crowd outside. Hell, he thought, what's taken them like, down here! There were perhaps as many as five hundred men, standing there, hanging about, waiting and talking amongst themselves. They were mostly men who were on the dole.

Confronted by this gathering Heddon felt an obligation to address it. He put his hands in his pockets, thrust forward his head and declared briefly:

"Listen, lads. We've just held a meeting to discuss the case that happened to-day. We can't allow any member of our Union to be victimised. I'll not stand for an unjust dismissal. But in the meantime we've adjourned on a point of order. I'll be here again to-morrow for further negotiations. That's all, lads." With his usual abrupt gesture, Heddon went down the steps and towards the station.

The men cheered Tom Heddon as he walked up Freehold Street. Heddon represented the hope of these men, a vague and faintly illusory hope they were well aware, but still a hope. He represented tobacco, beer, a good bed, warm clothing and work. That was partly why they cheered him. But it was not a loud cheer and in it there could be detected a flatness, a basic note of dissatisfaction and unrest.

When Jake Wicks came out of the Institute five minutes after Heddon had gone it was apparent that he, too, was far from satisfied. He came down the steps slowly, wearing an injured look, and he was at once surrounded by the waiting men who wanted to know more about it. Everybody wanted to know, and in particular Jack Reedy and Jack's crowd wanted to know. Jack's crowd was part of the waiting men and yet it was not, it was perhaps a little different. They were mostly youngish men and they did not talk much, but they all had cigarettes. Their faces were curiously alike, each had a kind of hardness as though the owner of the face did not care any more. Jack's face was exactly like that as if at one time he had cared but now did not care any more. The lines of Jack's face all sloped downwards and the lines were twisted and set. The face was sucked in about the cheeks and temples and was very pale except for a yellow stain of nicotine at the corner of the upper lip. But the setness of the face was its most remarkable quality; the face was so set you saw at once it could not smile. You had the queer impression that if Jack's face tried to smile it would break.

"What happened?" Jack demanded, shouldering forward.

Jake Wicks looked at Jack Reedy and Wood and Slattery and Cha Leeming who stood close to him.

"Just imagine!" he snorted. "He's gone an' bitched up everything." In a heated voice he told them what had happened at the meeting.

"Did he say nowt about benefit?" Harry Kinch called out from the edge of the crowd.

"B—— all," answered Jake.

There was a bitter silence amongst the men. The dole had been reduced at the beginning of the month and transitional benefit cut.

Jack stared at Wicks with his set face; there was something formidable in that impassive face. He asked, in his hard, offensive tone:

"What about him bringing out the men?"

"That's the last thing he's after," Jake frothed with indignation. "He's lost his nerve. He won't do nothing."

"He won't do nothing?" Jack echoed almost into himself. "Well, we've got to do something."

"We ought to have another demonstration," Wood said.

" A demonstration ! " Jack said bitterly, and that finished the demonstration. There had been one demonstration already that week, a demonstration of the unemployed, a procession to the Snook with the red flag and mounted police and speeches. It had been nice, the police riding along companionably, and everything had passed off splendidly with nobody a bit the worse. Oh, Jack's thoughts were bitter, bitter. That sort of thing was no use. It was *no use*. He wanted, he must have action, his whole being craved action.

On the pretext of young Wick's dismissal Jack had hoped wildly that Heddon would declare a strike. A strike was mass action and mass action was the only way. A few men out, a few hundreds out, meant nothing, but every man out meant something: it meant the bust up of the Neptune, it meant showing them, it meant action, action. But there was to be no strike after all.

Jack's forehead was knitted as if in pain. He seemed like some dumb creature working out the incomprehensible. He muttered:

" The meetin' you had wassent no good. We got to have another meeting. We got to do something. For Christ's sake give us a fag."

A cigarette was offered at once by Wood. The cigarette came with the other cigarettes from an automatic machine that Wood could *work*. A match shielded by one cupped hand was offered by Slattery. Jack merely inclined his bone-pale head and inhaled deeply. Then he looked at the men round about and raised his voice.

" Lissen, lads," he said. " A mass meeting at eight. D'ye understand ? Pass the word. Eight o'clock mass meeting."

The word passed, but Jake Wicks protested, half alarmed, half ingratiating:

" You'll have to watch out for yourself, Jack."

" Ah, what the hell! " Jack said in that uncaring voice. " Stop home if you want. Or go way up in the hospitle wi' Bert."

Jake's heavy face flushed, but he did not answer. It was always better not to answer Jack back.

" Come on," Jack said to the others. " Do you want to stick here all night ? "

He led the way, limping, down Cowpen Street towards the Salutation and into the Salutation. Jack did not use his hand to push the swing door of the Salutation, he walked at the door with his shoulder and went through. The others did the same.

The bar of the Salutation was full and Bert Amour was behind the bar. Bert had been behind the bar a good many years now; he seemed to grow there with his brassy face and his hair flattened and his forelock wetted and smoothly turned as though a cow had licked it back.

" Hello, Bert," Jack said with a dreadful friendliness. " What'll you have, lads ? "

The others said what they would have and Bert filled out the drinks.

Nobody paid and Bert smiled as if it hurt him.

" Fill them up, Bert," Jack said, and Bert winced and his face got brassier than ever. But he filled them up again. It was because Bert Amour had been so many years behind the bar of the Salutation that he knew when to fill them up and smile and say nothing. The spirit trade was a queer trade and it was better for Bert to be in with Jack Reedy and his crowd, much better.

" That's a bad business, Jack," Bert said, attempting a conversation. " About young Bert Wicks."

Jack pretended not to hear, but Cha Leeming leaned politely across the bar.

" What the hell do you know about it ? "

Bert looked at Cha Leeming and thought it wiser not to take any notice. Cha was exactly like his father, Slogger Leeming, except that Cha had been in the war and that made Cha more up to date. Cha had won the military medal in the war and last week after the demonstration on the Snook, Cha had tied his military medal to the tail of a stray mongrel dog. The mongrel dog had run all through the town trailing the beautiful military medal in the muck and Cha had called the dog *War Hero*. A man should get prison for that. Cha would some day, only too true, Bert thought.

Bert reached out his hand to reclaim the bottle of whisky, but before he could do so Jack lifted the bottle off the bar and crossed over to a table in the corner. They all went over to the table. A number of men were already there but they made way at once. Jack and his crowd sat down and began talking. Bert watched them talking; wiping the top of the bar, he watched them.

They sat at the corner table talking and drinking and finishing the bottle. The longer they sat there, the more men crowded round them, listening and talking and drinking. The noise became terrific until it seemed they all spoke at once, all violently debating—Wicks's case, Heddon's lack of action, the cut in benefit, their hopes of the new Mines Bill. All but Jack Reedy. Jack sat at the table with his dead eyes fixed before him. He was not drunk, no amount could ever make Jack drunk, that was the worst of it. His lips were drawn in tight and narrow and he kept pressing his teeth against them as though he bit against his own bitterness. Jack's life had shaped him into this mould of bitterness; he was all pain inside and his pained eyes looked upon a world of pain. The disaster had shaped Jack, and the war, and the peace—the degradation and misery of the dole, the pinchings and shifts and pawnings, the brutality of want, the desolation of the soul that is worse than hunger.

All this talk drove him to despair; it was all big mouth and wind. It would be the same at the meeting at eight—words and still more words, which meant nothing, did nothing, and led nowhere. A great hopelessness came over him.

And then, as he sat there, the door swung open and Harry Kinch burst into the bar. Harry was the nephew of that same Will Kinch who had rushed into the Salutation all those years before when Ramage refused him the " end of hough " for his little Alice. But there was this difference. Harry was a greater student of politics than ever Will had been. And Harry had a late *Argus* in his hand. He stood for a moment facing the others, then he cried:

" It's in the paper, lads. It's out at last." His voice broke. " They've sold us . . . they've swindled us . . ."

Every eye was turned on Kinch.

" How, then?" Slattery said thickly. " What's like the matter, Harry?"

Harry pushed back the hair from his brow.

" It's in the paper . . . the new Bill . . . it's the biggest swindle in years. They've gi'en us nothing, lads. Not one damned thing. . . ." Again words failed him.

Dead silence had come upon the company. They all knew what had been promised them. Subconsciously the hopes of every man within that room had centred on the Bill. Jack Reedy moved first.

" By God," he said. " Show us that paper." He seized the paper and looked at it. They all bent over crowding and craning, looking at the paper where, in a double‸spread, the terms of their betrayal lay revealed.

" By God," Jack said again. " So it is! "

Then Cha Leeming jumped to his feet, half-tight and furious.

" It's too much," he shouted, " we'll not put up with it."

Everybody started talking at once, an uproar. The paper was passed from hand to hand. Jack Reedy was on his feet now, cold and contained. In the midst of the chaos he saw his opportunity. His eyes were not dead now, but burning.

" Give us another whisky," he said. " Quick." He tossed down the whisky. He looked round the men. Then he shouted: " I'm goin' to the Institute. Them that wants can come after us."

An answering shout went up. They all came after him. They crowded out of the pub into the squally darkness of Cowpen Street, crowding towards the Institute with Jack slightly in the lead.

Outside the Institute more men had collected—most of the younger Neptune men who were out, all of the men who had been discharged at the beginning, and every one of them brought to a pitch of desperation by this news flashed through the Terraces, the final extinction of their hopes.

Jack raced up the steps of the Institute and stood facing the men. Above the door of the Institute an electric globe stuck out like a yellow pear on the end of a stiff branch and the light from the electric pear fell upon Jack's unbroken face. It was almost dark in the street; the street lamps cast only a flickering pallor in little pools.

Jack stood for a minute facing the men in the darkness. The whisky in him concentrated his bitterness to a kind of venom; his whole body pulsed with that envenomed bitterness. He felt that his moment was approaching, the moment for which he had suffered, for which he had been born.

"Comrades," he cried, "we've just got the news. We've been swindled. They've give us the go-bye, like Heddon did; they've twisted us, like they always do. And in spite of everything they promised!" He drew a panting, tortured breath, his eyes glittering towards them. "They're not going to help us! Nobody's goin' to help us. Nobody! D'y hear me. Nobody! We've got to help ourselves. If we don't we'll never get out the bloody gutter where Capitalism has shoved us. Christ Almighty, can't you see it, lads, the whole economic system's rotten as dung. They've got the money, the motor-cars, fine houses, carpets on the floor, an' it's all bled out the likes of us. We do the slavin' and sweatin' for them. An' what do we get? We don't even get food, lads, nor fire, nor proper clothes, nor boots for our kids. The minnit things go wrong we're chucked out on our necks! Chucked on to bread and margarine, and not enough of it to feed the missus and kids! Don't tell me it's because there's no money. The country's choked with money, the banks is burstin' with it, millions and millions of money. Don't tell me it's because there's no food. They're throwin' fish back into the sea, burnin' coffee and wheat, slaughterin' pigs to let them rot, and us here goin' half-starvin'. If that's a proper system, lads, then God Almighty strike me dead." Another sobbing breath. Then in a rising voice: "We didn't see it when they had the disaster in this bloody Neptune pit and murdered a hundred men. We didn't see it in the war when they murdered millions of men. But by Christ we see it now! We can't stand it, lads. We've got to do something. We've got to show them, lads. We've got to do somethin'. We've got to, I tell you, we've got to. If we don't we can rot in hell for all our days." His voice rose to a shriek now, wild and mad. "I'm goin' to do somethin', lads, and them that wants to can come along. I'm goin' to make a start this minnit. I'm goin' to show them at the Neptune pit where my two brothers was done in. Now I'm goin' to wreck the pit, lads. I'm goin' to do a bit of payin' back on my own. Are you comin' with me or are you not?"

A loud yell went up from the mob. Inflamed by Reedy's words they pressed round him as he ran down the steps, escorted him in a body down the street. Some, terrified, melted back towards the Terraces. But at least a hundred men joined up with Jack. They all began to move to the Neptune pit, exactly as the crowd had moved towards Ramage's shop over twenty years before. But there were more men in the movement, a great many more. The pit was a greater attraction than Ramage's shop. The pit was the focus, the centre wherein the sound and the fury of their souls were concentrated. The pit was the arena, the amphitheatre. Life and death and work and wages and sweat and blood were mingled in the black dust of that arena, of that dark amphitheatre.

The men poured into the pit yard with Jack Reedy leading them. The pit yard was silent and the offices were closed and the shaft gaped empty like the entrance to a great empty tomb. There was no person underground, no night shift now, not a soul inbye. Even the pit bank seemed deserted, though the safety men were there, the pump-men. The two pump-men were in the engine house behind the locker room; their names were Joe Davis and Hugh Galton. The crowd streamed towards the engine house where Davis and Galton were, and Galton heard them coming first. One of the windows of the engine house was half open to let out the heat and the hot smell of oil, and Galton, an oldish man with a short grey beard, popped his head through the window.

The crowd were around the engine house now, a crowd of one hundred men, their faces all upturned to Galton in the high window of the engine house.

" What is it ? " Galton called down.

With his face upturned Jack Reedy said:

" Come out here. We want you out here."

" What for ? " Galton said.

Jack repeated in a deadly tone:

" Come out here. Come out and you'll not get hurt."

In answer Galton drew his head back and banged down the window shut. There was a pause of about ten seconds filled by the slow thumping of the pumping engines, then Cha Leeming let out a yell and threw a brick. The window shivered, and the sound of shivering glass came above the thumping and thudding of the pumping engines. That did it. Jack Reedy ran up the steps of the engine house and Leeming and a dozen others ran after him. They burst through the door of the engine house.

The engine house was very hot and bright and full of oily heat and vibrating noise.

" What the hell," Joe Davis said. He was a man of forty in blue dungarees with his sleeves rolled up and a coil of waste wrapped round his neck. He had been cleaning brasses with bath brick and a tin of paraffin.

Jack Reedy looked at Joe Davis from under the peak of his cap. He said rapidly:

" We don't mean you no harm, none of the two of you. We only want you out. Out, see."

" I'll be damned," Joe Davis said.

Jack came a step forward. He said, carefully watching Joe Davis:

" You'll get out, see; the men want you out."

" What men ? " Joe Davis said.

Then Jack rushed at Joe Davis and caught him round the waist. They caught each other round the waist and wrestled like that. They wrestled and struggled for a minute with everybody looking on, and as they wrestled they knocked over the tin of paraffin. It was a big tin of paraffin and it ran out over the grating and poured into the box of cleaning rags; Slattery was the only one who saw the paraffin pour into the waste rags, they were all watching the fight, and with a kind of reflex Slattery took the cigarette end out his mouth and flicked it at the waste rags. The lighted cigarette end fell right in the middle of the box of waste rags. No one but Slattery saw it fall, for at that moment Davis slipped and went down with Jack on the top of him. The crowd rushed forward. They got hold of Davis, then rushed at Galton, and bundled them out of the engine house.

After that it all happened quickly. No one did it. They all did it, throwing loose tools, spanners and common rods, a heavy sledge, even the can of bath brick, into the mesh of slow, gleaming pistons. The sledge actually caused the damage. The sledge hit the crosshead, danced off and fell upon the main cylinder, cracked the main cylinder, then fell smash into the bearings. There was a horrible grinding and a hiss of steam. The smooth machinery twisted and shivered and locked itself abominably. The whole engine house shuddered to its foundation and was still.

Then Slattery shouted as if he had made a great discovery:

" It's on fire. Jesus Christ! Look! It's on fire there."

They looked at the waste box from which flames were leaping and they looked at the still dead engines of the pumps. Then they made for the door. They squeezed through the door in a kind of panic. Jack Reedy stayed behind. Jack always was resourceful. He walked over to the oil drum and turned on the spigot. For a minute he watched the oil flow darkly. His gaze was pale and cold and bitterly triumphant. He had done something, done something. He walked quickly out and slammed the door.

Outside they stood packed in the yard. There were no flames at first, only thick coils of smoke, but soon the flames sprang, great tongues of flame.

They retreated a little before the flames which lit their upturned faces in the dark amphitheatre of the pit bank. Wafts of heat reached towards them through the coldness of the night. Then, as the flames sprang towards the power-house roof the slates began to pop. It was amazing how the slates popped. They popped off the roof like peas bouncing from a drum, one, two, three, a perfect hail of slates came pelting down, each making a lovely blazing curve, then crashing on the concrete yard.

The crowd retreated further, pressing back against the walls of the offices, back through the yard gates, back into Cowpen Street. They released Galton and Joe Davis. It was all right, all right now. Galton ran into the main office, ran to the telephone. They let him go. It was all right, all right now; another fusillade of slates came down and the lamp-room was alight and crackling. Galton began to telephone furiously. He telephoned Arthur, Armstrong and the fire-station. He telephoned the Lodge offices in Tynecastle. He left word at the Exchange to inform everyone in the district who might be of service in the emergency. Then he sprinted out of the office to do what he could do. As he came through the door into the yard a red-hot slate whizzed past his skull and missed splitting it by inches. The slate shattered on the office floor and the fragments scattered joyfully. One sizzled straight into the wastepaper basket. That set the offices on fire.

Everything was happening very fast. More men were entering the pit yard, Forbes the deputy, Harry Ogle, some of the officials and older colliers. Then the police came, Roddam, the sergeant, and a dozen men at the double. Galton joined the police, the deputy and the officials and ran with them to the safety room where Joe Davis had already uncoiled the hoses. They led the hoses out and coupled them to the hydrant, then Davis threw on the pressure. The hoses jerked and kicked and spouted water from a dozen slits. Someone had gashed the hoses. They were useless.

Arthur and Armstrong arrived simultaneously. Arthur had been reading in his room when Galton telephoned, Armstrong on the point of going to bed. They dashed up to the knot of men outside the safety room. While the leaping flames cast light and shadow across them they stood for a moment in rapid consultation, then Arthur rushed over to the offices to telephone. He found the offices on fire.

The Sleescale fire engine arrived at last and Camhow coupled up the hose line. A thin jet of water went hissing into the flames. Another hose was coupled and a second jet went up. But the jets were thin and feeble. And these two hoses were the only hoses that they had.

Things were happening faster now and there was more confusion. Men darted about the yard with their heads ducked down. Beams were falling and red-hot bricks. The flames ate everything, wood, rubble, stone and metal; the flames consumed them. Loud reports went off from time to time and the sound went booming through the town like gunfire from the sea. Cowpen Street was solid with the people, all watching, watching.

Half of the bank was razed when Heddon reached the pit. He raced from the station in the day-bright glare, fighting his way forward through the crowds. As he struggled to reach the yard two fire engines from Amalgamated Collieries came clanging down the street. He swung himself up on the tail of the last engine. He entered the Neptune yard.

The power house was gone now, the safety room, lamp room and pumping station. The wind, a freshening forced draught, was fanning the blaze under the broken gables of the offices. The heat was torrid.

Heddon threw off his coat and joined with the firemen from Amalgamated. Hose after hose sent its powerful stream hoisting upon the flaming bank: steam boiled amongst the smoke and raised a pall that hung and drifted sluggishly. Ladders went scaling up. Men ran, climbed, hacked and sweated. And the night passed.

When the dawn broke there was no fire, only a smouldering. The grey cold light of the morning showed that; and all the desolation of the wreckage.

Arthur, supporting himself against a ladder, gazed upon the wrecked pit-surface. A sigh broke from his chest. He knew there was worse below. Suddenly he heard someone shouting. It was Heddon.

" Here, Armstrong," Heddon shouted. " You'll need to rig new pumps quick."

Armstrong looked at Heddon and walked on. He walked up to the charred headstocks where Arthur stood beside the empty cage. In a cracked voice Armstrong said:

" We'd better see about new pumping gear. We'd better ring Tynecastle immediately if it's to be any use."

Arthur raised his head slowly. His brow was blacked, his eyes inflamed by smoke, his whole face empty.

" For God's sake," he whispered. " For God's sake let me be."

XVI

Despite the new and spirited memoranda in his diary beginning *Further defence of Neptune Schedule P*, and some complex figures multiplied determinedly in the margins of *Robert Elsmere*, Richard could not wholly understand. Every day at the hour of noon he struggled down to the foot of the lawn past the bare laburnum tree and balanced himself against the clean white gate of the paddock. This viewpoint, from which he could just see, and no more, the tops of the Neptune headstocks, he had named *Observation Post No.* 1. Strange, very strange: no signs of activity about the headstocks, neither steam nor smoke visible. Were the wheels spinning, the wheels of the winding headgear ? Impossible to tell, even when the ringed eyes were shielded by both tremulous hands, telescope fashion, as befitted *Observation Post No.* 1. Strange, oh, very strange.

On this early January day he returned from *Observation Post No.* 1 with an air both baffled and triumphant: dimly aware that there was trouble, the trouble he had predicted. He was, indeed, triumphant solely because he had predicted trouble. They would call him in soon, presently, immediately!—to correct the trouble. They!

But for all his triumph he looked a shaky and ill old man. He walked very badly, even Aunt Carrie admitted that there was not much improvement with poor Richard lately, and as he came back across the lawn he staggered and almost fell. His walk was like a stuttering speech, made up of little runs and halts, a quick rush of steps, quicker and quicker, until suddenly the steps tripped themselves up and there was a stagger, then the steps had to wait and start again as though fumbling for the right syllable. But in spite of every difficulty Richard would take his walk alone, refusing Aunt Carrie's arm with abruptness and even suspicion. It was quite natural; the man was interfered with, watched and threatened. He had his own interests to safeguard. A man must look after himself.

Having crossed the lawn he avoided Aunt Carrie's sad and tender eye as she stood awaiting him by the portico and stuttered and stammered his way round to the French window of the drawing-room. He let himself in by the French window, lifting his feet with great care over the narrow bottom ledge. He went into the smoking-room and composed himself in a chair to write. His way of composing himself was to adjust himself accurately with his back to the chair and then allow himself to fall.

He wrote shakily: *Memorandum from Observation Post No.* 1 12.15 × 3.14. *No smoke again to-day, a bad sign. The chief offender has not appeared but am convinced of trouble. Am daily expecting to be called in defence of Neptune. Query. Am still concerned over the presence here of my daughter Hilda and the man Teasdale. Why? The answer to this may reveal the clue. But there are many comings and goings against me especially since the disappearance of Ann. Above all I must protect myself and hold myself in complete readiness.*

A sound disturbed him and he looked up peevishly. Aunt Carrie had come in—Caroline was always coming in; why couldn't she leave him alone? He shut his writing-book jealously and crouched in the chair very shrunken and angry and suspicious.

"You haven't taken your rest, Richard."

"I don't want my rest."

"Very well, Richard." Aunt Carrie did not insist; she looked at Richard with that sad and tender gaze, her eyes red around the rims and swollen about the lids. Aunt Carrie's heart gushed towards Richard; poor dear Richard, it was dreadful that he should not know and yet it might be worse, even, if he did. Aunt Carrie could not bear to think of it.

"I want to ask you, Caroline." The dull suspicious eye became shot with a coaxing playfulness. "Tell me, Caroline, what are they doing at the Neptune?"

"Why, nothing, Richard," she stammered.

"I've got my interests to safeguard," Richard said with great cunning. "A man must look after himself. A man who is tampered with like me. You understand, Caroline."

A painful silence. Aunt Carrie said again, pleadingly:

"Don't you think you should rest a little now, Richard?" Dr. Lewis was always insisting that Richard should have more rest but Richard would not rest more. Aunt Carrie was sure it would help Richard's poor head if Richard rested more.

Richard said:

" Why is Hilda here ? "

Aunt Carrie smiled with a watery brightness.

" Why, she's come up to see you, Richard, and to see Arthur. Grace might have come too . . . only she's going to have another baby. . . . You remember, Richard dear, I told you."

" Why do all these people keep coming about the house ? "

" Why." Aunt Carrie's watery smile was brave; not wild horses would have dragged the truth from her. If Richard must know he would not know from her. " Why, what people, Richard ? Now do come and rest. I beg of you."

He glared at her, his irritation mounting to a fever heat, then leaving him suddenly; and when his irritation left him he felt quite bewildered. His pale ringed eyes fell and he discovered his own hand that held the diary shaking violently. Often his hands would twitch this way and his legs too. It was the electricity. All at once he wanted to cry.

" Very well." Drooping, and with a childish desire for sympathy, he explained: " It's the current that makes me . . . the electricity."

Aunt Carrie helped him from his chair and helped him upstairs and helped him partially to undress and to stretch himself out upon his bed. He looked an old exhausted man and his face was very flushed. He fell asleep instantly and slept for two hours. He snored heavily.

When he awoke he felt splendid, completely refreshed and full of vigour and intelligence. He ate his bread and milk greedily, a lovely big bowl of bread and milk. It tasted sweet and pulpy and it was not burning in his mouth and his hand did not twitch with electricity any longer. He looked to see that Aunt Carrie had gone out of the room; then he licked up the last of the bowlful with his tongue. It always tasted better that way.

Afterwards he lay staring at the ceiling clasping the warmth in his stomach and hearing the buzz of a blue-bottle on the window-pane and letting warm thoughts buzz through his head and being conscious of his own prodigious capabilities. All sorts of projects and conjectures flashed through his prodigiously capable mind. There was even a marriage ceremony at the back of it all, dim and warm, with music, great swelling organ music and a slender virgin of unsurpassable beauty who adored him.

He was lying like this when the noise of cars arriving disturbed him. He raised himself on his elbow, listening, and with great quickness he understood that people were coming. A look of delighted cunning flashed into his face. This was his chance, a great chance while the electricity was off.

He got up. It was not easy for him to get up, the movements were complicated and numerous, but with such prodigious capabilities nothing was impossible. He worked himself sideways upon his elbow and rolled off the bed. He fell with a bump in the kneeling position. He waited for a minute, listening to see if anybody had heard the bump. Good! No one had heard the bump. He crawled on his knees to the window and looked out of the window. One car, two cars; it was exciting now, he was enjoying himself, he wanted to laugh.

Supporting himself on the window ledge he raised himself slowly—this was the worst of all but it was done at last—then he got into his dressing-gown. It took him quite five minutes to get into his dressing-gown; the arms were so difficult and he began by putting it on back to front, but eventually the dressing-gown was on and corded over his underwear. He did not put on shoes for shoes make a noise. He stood triumphant in his dressing-gown and underwear and socks, then very cautiously he went out of his room and started to descend the stairs.

There was only one way to descend the stairs. The banister was useless, the banister held and hindered. No! The only way to descend the stairs was to stand accurately on the top stair of all and look straight ahead like a diver and then suddenly let the feet go. The feet went down the stairs with quite a rush that way, but it was important not to look at the feet nor to think about them either.

Richard got down to the hall in this manner and he stood in the hall very pleased with himself and listening. They were in the dining-room; he could hear the voices plainly, and he advanced slyly to the door of the dining-room. Yes, they were in there, he could hear them talking and he was listening. Good, very good! Richard got down, and sprawled on the tiled floor with his eye to the keyhole. *Observation Post No.* 2, Richard thought, oh, very, very good—Richard saw and heard everything.

They were all seated round the dining-room table with Mr. Bannerman, the lawyer, at the head and Arthur at the foot. Aunt Carrie was there and Hilda and Adam Todd and the man Teasdale. Mr. Bannerman had a great many papers and Arthur had papers too, and Adam Todd had one single paper but Hilda and Aunt Carrie and Teasdale had no papers at all. Mr. Bannerman was speaking.

" It is an offer," Mr. Bannerman said. " That's how I regard it. It is an offer."

Arthur answered:

" It's not an offer; it's contemptible, it's an insult."

Richard heard the trouble in Arthur's voice and he was pleased. Arthur looked bowed and hopeless, he spoke with his forehead resting in one hand. Richard chuckled within himself.

Mr. Bannerman scrutinised a paper he did not need to scrutinise. He looked lean and dried up and tight about the collar. He balanced his monocle which had a broad black ribbon and said smoothly:

" I repeat that it is an offer, the only offer we have received, and it is tangible."

Silence. Then Adam Todd said:

" Is it impossible to arrange to dewater the pit ? To rebuild the bank ? Is it quite impossible ? "

" Who is going to put up the money ? " Arthur exclaimed.

" We've been over all this before," Mr. Bannerman said, pretending not to look at Arthur yet looking at him all the time.

" It seems a pity," Todd murmured dejectedly. " A great pity." He raised his head suddenly. " What about the pictures, your father's pictures? Can't you raise the money on them?"

" They're worthless," Arthur answered. " I had young Vincent out to value them. He just laughed. The Goodalls and Copes you couldn't give away. Nobody wants them now."

Another silence. Then Hilda spoke decisively.

" Arthur must have no more worry. That's all I have to say. In his present state he's not fit to stand it."

Arthur's shoulders sagged, and he shielded his face more with his hand. He said heavily :

" You're decent, Hilda. But I know what you're all thinking, what a hopeless mess I've made of it. I did what I thought was right and best. I couldn't help anything. It just came. But you're all thinking this would never have happened if my father had been here."

Outside the door Richard's face became suffused with satisfaction. He did not really understand, of course, but he saw that there was trouble and they wanted him to set the trouble right. They would call him in.

Arthur was talking again. Arthur said dully:

" I was always moaning about justice. And now I've got it! We squeezed the men and flooded the mine and finished the men. And now when I try to do everything for them the men turn round and flood the mine and finish me."

" Oh, Arthur, my dear, don't talk that way," Aunt Carrie whimpered, putting her hand tremulously towards Arthur's hand.

" I'm sorry," Arthur said. " But that's the way I see it."

" Suppose we confine ourselves to business," Mr. Bannerman said very drily.

" Go on, then," Arthur said heavily. " Go on and settle the damned thing and let's be done with it."

" Please! " Mr. Bannerman said.

Hilda intervened.

" What is this offer then, Mr. Bannerman ? How does it work out ? "

Mr. Bannerman adjusted his monocle and looked at Hilda.

" The position is precisely this. We are faced on the one side with a dislocated pit, flooded workings and burnt-out gear. On the other side you may place this offer to take over the Neptune, purchase the whole non-producing concern, lock, stock and barrel, and if I may respectfully say so, flood water as well."

"They know very well they can get rid of the water," Arthur said bitterly. "I've spent thousands on these underground roads. It's the finest pit in the district and they know it. They're offering not one-tenth of the value of the pit. It's sheer insanity to take it."

"Times," Mr. Bannerman said, "are difficult, Arthur. And the particular circumstances are more difficult still."

Hilda said:

"Suppose we accepted this offer?"

Mr. Bannerman hesitated. He removed his monocle, studied it.

"Well," he said, "we should be clear of our liabilities." He paused. "Arthur, if I may venture to say so, was reckless in his expenditure. We must remember the liabilities in which we are involved."

Hilda looked at Mr. Bannerman darkly. That *we* particularly exasperated Hilda for Mr. Bannerman was not involved and Mr. Bannerman had no liabilities whatever. Rather sharply Hilda said:

"Can't you get an increase on the offer?"

"They are keen people these," Mr. Bannerman answered. "Very keen people indeed. This offer is their final offer."

"It's sheer robbery," Arthur groaned.

"Who are they?" Hilda asked.

Mr. Bannerman fitted back his monocle delicately:

"They are Mawson & Gowlan," he said. "Yes! Mr. Joseph Gowlan is the negotiating party."

There was a silence. Arthur lifted his head slowly and looked across at Hilda. His voice was savagely ironic.

"You know the fellow, don't you?" he said. "These new offices in Grainger Street. All black and marble. The site alone cost them forty thousand. He's the Joe Gowlan who worked as a hand-putter in the Neptune."

"He does not work there now," Mr. Bannerman said precisely. Inspecting the heading of the notepaper before him he declared: "Messrs. Mawson & Gowlan have now the controlling interest in Northern Steel Industries Ltd., in United Brassfounders Ltd., in the Tyneside Commercial Corporation, in Corporation and Northern Securities Ltd., and in the Rusford Aeroplane Co."

There was another silence. Adam Todd seemed very unhappy and he chewed a clove as if the flavour of the clove was not good.

"Is there no other way?" he said, shifting restlessly on his seat. "I know the stuff that's in the Neptune. Wonderful stuff. It's always been Barras's Neptune. Isn't there any other way?"

"Have you any suggestion?" Mr. Bannerman inquired politely. "If so be kind enough to let us have it."

"Why don't you go to this Gowlan," said Todd suddenly, turning to Arthur, " and try to get in with him? . . . Bargain with him. Tell him you don't want to sell for cash. You want to amalgamate with him. You want a seat on the board, shares, just to be *in* with him, Arthur. If only you get in with Gowlan you'd be absolutely made! "

Arthur reddened slowly. " That's a grand idea, Todd. But unfortunately it's no use. You see, I've tried it." He faced them all and with a sudden outburst of bitter cynicism he cried: " I went up to Gowlan two days ago, up to his damned new offices. God! You ought to see them—solid bronze doors, Carrara marble, teak and tapestry elevator. I tried to sell myself to him. You know what he is. He began by swindling Millington out of the foundry. He swindled his shareholders in the boom. He's never done an honest day's work in his life. Everything he's got has come crookedly—from sweating his workmen, corruption on contracts, that big munitions ramp. But I swallowed all that, tried to sell my soul." Trembling, he paused. " It would have made you laugh. He played with me like a cat with a mouse. He began by telling me how honoured he was but that our ideas seemed to be slightly different. He went on about the new aeroplane works at Rusford where he's turning out military aeroplanes by the hundred and selling them to every country in Europe. He enlarged on the prospects of the Rusford 'plane because it has what he called greater killing power than any other line. He took me on bit by bit, putting out a hint here and a promise there, until I'd sworn away everything I'd ever believed in. And when he'd got me stripped naked he laughed at me and offered me a job as underviewer at the Neptune."

Yet another silence, a long silence. Dan Teasdale moved restively, and for the first time spoke.

" It's a damned shame." His ruddy face was alive with indignation. " Why don't you chuck the whole thing up, Arthur, and come down with us? We don't make money. But we don't want it. And we're perfectly happy without it. There's better things—that's what Grace has taught me. Health, and working in the fresh air, and seeing your children grow up strong. You come down, Arthur, and start fresh with us."

" I should look well," Arthur said in an agony of dejection, " among the chickens."

Bannerman made another gesture of impatience. " Might I ask what your instructions are, then? "

" Haven't I told you to sell? " The words came with a terrible disillusionment, and Arthur rose abruptly as though to terminate the whole affair. " Sell the Law too. Gowlan wants that as well. Let him take the whole damned lot. He can have me as underviewer too, for all I care."

Outside the door, sprawling on his knees, Richard Barras gaped and stared. Richard's face was very red now and terribly confused. He did not fully gauge what was happening within. But he grasped with his poor muddled brain that there was trouble at the Neptune which he alone could readjust. Moreover, they had all forgotten about him and his power to achieve the impossible. It was splendid. He sat back on his haunches on the tiled floor of the hall. They were not talking any more inside now and he was a little tired from sprawling and he wanted greater comfort to enable him to think.

Suddenly, as he squatted there, the door of the dining-room opened and they all came out. The unexpectedness of it slumped Richard over upon his back. His dressing-gown flew up exposing his lean shanks, his underwear, his very person. The whole pitiful travesty of the man was there, shrunken yet distorted, cunning yet inane. But Richard did not mind. He sat there, as he was, on the cold tiles of the vestibule, and he looked very sly and he laughed. He sniggered.

Every face expressed concern and Hilda ran forward crying:

" My poor father! "

Teasdale and Hilda helped him to his feet and assisted him upstairs to his room. Bannerman, one eyebrow lifted, shrugged his shoulders and took a formal good-bye of Arthur.

Arthur remained standing in the hall, his eyes fixed on the yellowish eyes of Adam Todd who, all those years before, had implored him not to swim against the stream. He said suddenly:

" Let's go into Tynecastle, Todd. I think I want to get drunk."

XVII

FOR the next few days Richard lay very low. After the incident entered in his writing-book as *Discovery at Observation No.* 2, Hilda had spoken gravely upon the advisability of keeping him in bed. He was so feeble now and so uncertain upon his legs that Hilda insisted, before she left for London, he must at least remain in his bedroom. That alarmed Richard for Richard was aware that he could not conduct operations from his bedroom. So he feigned most exemplary behaviour, was good and docile and did whatever Aunt Carrie told him.

All his thoughts were now concentrated upon his great new idea for regenerating his Neptune pit. The whole of that Friday forenoon he was so excited by his idea he could not contain himself. As he sat in his room a hammer kept beating in his head, and his scalp was tight like the skin of a drum. Once he almost thought the electricity had got him but he lay back and closed his eyes until at last they turned it off.

When he came round he found Arthur in the room standing before him.

" Are you all right, father? " Arthur asked and he looked at his father with sadness filmed over the fixity of his face. Arthur could not behold this poor shrunken silly old man, nor feel that sly and bloodshot eye wavering across his, without sadness. He said:

" I thought I'd come up and have a word with you, father. Can you understand what I say ? "

Could he understand!—the insolence sent the blood bursting again through Richard's head. He drew within himself at once.

" Not now."

" I'd like to straighten things out for you, father," Arthur said. " It might make it easier for you. You're restless and so excited. You do not realise that you're not well."

" I am well," Richard said angrily. " I was never better in my life."

" It struck me, father," Arthur went on, wishing to break as gently as he could the impending disruption, " that it mightn't be a bad thing if we gave up the Law and took a smaller place. You see——"

" Not now," Richard interrupted. " To-morrow, perhaps. I won't listen. Some other time. I simply won't listen. Not now." He lay back again in his chair with closed eyes and would not listen to Arthur until Arthur at last gave up and went out of the room. It was not his intention to talk to Arthur yet. No, indeed! He would dictate his terms to Arthur later, when the regeneration of the Neptune was complete. Here he opened his eyes with a start, his remote yet feverish stare transfixing the blank ceiling vacantly. What was it ? Ah, he remembered. The vacancy left his face, the dull eye watered and gleamed; why had he not thought of it before, why not, why ? The pit, of course, his Neptune pit! It was superb, his terrible yet brilliant idea. He must defy them all by going to the Neptune in person.

Tremulous with agitation and excitement, he rose and went downstairs. So far so good. There was no one about; everyone was occupied and worried and distressed. He slunk into the hall, where, hurriedly, he took his hard hat and pressed it upon his head. His hair had not been cut for some time and it stuck out behind his hard hat in a tangled fringe. But Richard did not mind. With great secrecy he let himself out by the front door and stood balancing upon the steps. The drive lay before him with the gate open and unguarded beyond. It was all forbidden ground, dangerous ground, far away from the lawn and the laburnum tree. Both Hilda and Dr. Lewis had made it seriously forbidden and dangerous. The whole thing was a terrible undertaking. But Richard did not mind that either. He compassed the steps and the drive in one stuttering rush and was out, at last, and free. He staggered, it is true, and almost fell ; but what did that matter, his staggering, when he was so soon to be rid of it, staggering, hammering, electricity, the whole horrible conspiracy against him?

He walked up the drive towards the top of Sluice Dene. He was much too clever to take the ordinary road to the Neptune, for that road would certainly be watched and he would be intercepted. No, no! he knew better than that. He took the long way round, the way which went behind the woods of Sluice Dene and across the fields and the Snook and into the Neptune from the back. He exulted in the brilliance of his counterstroke. Wonderful, wonderful!

But it had been raining heavily and the road he took was muddy and bad. The heavy rain had left big puddles in the ruts and Richard could not lift his feet. Soon he was splashed with water and mud. He floundered along through the water and the mud with his little starts and staggers until he reached the stile at the top of Sluice Dene.

At the stile he drew up. The stile presented an unconsidered difficulty. Richard saw that he would have to climb the stile. But Richard could not raise his foot more than six inches at the utmost and the height of the step upon the stile was at least eighteen. Richard could not climb the stile and tears came trembling into his old dazed eyes.

Tears and fury; oh, a terrible fury. He was not defeated, he was not. The stile was merely part of the conspiracy; he must defeat it too, the stile, the conspiring stile. Trembling with rage Richard raised his arms and fell upon the stile. His belly hit the top bar of the stile, for a second he was balanced, as though swimming, upon the top bar of the stile, then he toppled and was over. Wonderful, wonderful, he was over! He fell heavily on his face and head into a puddle of slush and he lay panting and stunned and slobbering while the hammer and electricity worked at him through the slush and the mud.

He lay quite a long time there, for the big hammer seemed to have burst something inside his head, and the mud was cool against the outside of the burst place in his head. But he got up at last, oh yes, he got up, elbow, knees and a dreadful clamber to his feet. The earth swayed slightly and he had lost his hat and his face and clothes and hands were terribly daubed with mud. But never mind, never mind all that. He was up again and walking. He was walking to the Neptune.

Walking was not so easy now. The hammer had hit so hard, his right leg was dull and dead, he had to drag it along with him like a sort of supercargo. That was peculiar, for usually both hammer and electricity worked upon his left leg, but now they had got his right leg and his right arm too. His whole right side was paralysed.

On he went, behind the wood and along the path towards the Snook, staggering and dragging the leg, bareheaded and bedaubed with mud, his red-injected eye fixed feverishly upon the headstock of the Neptune which showed above the last row of houses that bordered the Snook. Although he wished to go quickly he went very slowly; he was all bound and clogged; he knew that he was going slowly and this infuriated him. He tried to make himself go quicker and could not; he had the idea that something was happening at the Neptune, a conspiracy or a catastrophe, and that he would not get there in time. This drove him frantic.

Then the rain came on, a heavy lashing shower. The rain streamed upon him and upon his old bare head. The rain flattened the long grey hair upon his old bare head, washed the mud into his eyes, battered and soaked and blinded him.

He stopped, all the fury washed out of him, and he stood quite still under the hissing rain. He was frightened. And suddenly he began to cry. His tears mingled with the rain and wetted him the more. He moved blindly forward. He wanted shelter.

At the end of the row of houses which bordered the Snook stood a small public-house, known as The Hewer's Rest, a poor and wretched place which was kept by a widow named Susan Mitchell. Nobody went there except the poorest workers from around the Snook. But Richard went there, into the public-house known as The Hewer's Rest.

He came in as though blown by a gust of wind and rain and he stood on the stone floor, dripping wet and swaying upon his feet like an old drunk tramp. Only two men were in the bar, two labouring men in moleskins, who were playing dominoes, their empty beer mugs beside them on the one trestle table. They stared at Richard and they laughed. They did not know Richard. They thought Richard was an old tramp who had certainly had his gill. One winked at the other and spoke to Richard.

" How, hinny ? " he said. " Ye've been to a weddin' I see."

Richard looked at him and something in Richard's look, as Richard swayed there, made both of the men laugh. They shook with laughter. Then the second man said:

" Niver mind, man. We've all been glee-eyed in our time."

And he took Richard by the shoulders and steered him to the wooden settle at the window. Richard fell into the settle. He did not know where he was and he did not know who were these two men who both stared at him. He fumbled in his pocket with his numb hand for his handkerchief and as he pulled it out a coin came with it and rolled on the stone floor. It was a half-crown.

The second man picked up the coin and spat on it and grinned.

" Eh, mon," he said. " You're a champion, right enough. Is it a half-gill, hinny, a half-gill the piece ? "

Richard did not understand, so the second man rapped on the counter hard:

" Three half-gills," he called out.

A woman came out of the back, a thin dark woman with a pale face. She filled three measures of whisky but as she filled the third she looked doubtfully at Richard.

" He'd do better without it," she said.

The first man said:

" A drop more'll do him no harm."

The second man came over to Richard.

" Here, hinny," he said. " Drink this."

Richard took the glass the man gave him and drank what was in the glass. It was whisky and the whisky took his breath and warmed him inside and started the hammer beating inside his head. The whisky made him remember the Neptune too. He thought it had stopped raining. The men were staring at him, too, until at last he became frightened of the men. He remembered himself as Richard Barras, owner of the Neptune, a man of dignity and substance. He wanted to be out, away from here and at the Neptune. He rose with an effort from the settle and staggered to the door. The laughter of the men followed him.

When Richard came out of The Hewer's Rest the rain had ceased and the sky broken. The bright sun, striking across the steaming waste of the Snook, glittered into his eyes and hurt them, but through the blinding brightness he made out the headstocks of the Neptune rising in a kind of celestial glory. The Neptune, his Neptune, the Neptune of Richard Barras. He struck across the Snook.

The journey across the Snook was a strange and dreadful journey. Richard Barras was not conscious of the journey. His feet stumbled amongst the sodden hummocks and slushy runnels of the troubled land. His feet betrayed him and threw him mercilessly. He crawled and climbed. He floundered like a strange amphibian. But he knew nothing. He did not feel it when he fell, nor when he got up and fell again. His body was dead, his mind was dead, but his spirit soared in a great live purpose. The Neptune, the Neptune pit, the glory of those rising headstocks of the Neptune drew his spirit and held it. The rest was a mere vague nightmare.

But he did not reach the Neptune pit. Half-way across the Snook he fell and did not rise. His face beneath its crust of mud was ashen, his lips dry and blue, his breath coming in a quick stertor. There was no electricity now. The electricity was gone, leaving his body flaccid; but the hammering was bad again, the hammering was worse. It beat and beat inside his head and tried to burst again. Feebly he tried to rise. Then the hammer in Richard's head struck one final blow. He fell forward and did not move. The last rays of the setting sun, striking across the charred headstocks of the pit, lit up the troubled land and found him there, quite dead. His lifeless hand, stretched forwards, grasped a handful of dirt.

XVIII

It was the day of the Third Reading of the Mines Bill, which had now reached the Report Stage, skilfully whittled away and studded with Opposition Amendments. At this moment an amendment in the name of the hon. member for Keston, Mr. St. Clair Boone, was under consideration. Mr. St. Clair Boone, with admirable legal precision, had formally begged to move that in line 3 of clause 7 before the word " appointed " there should be inserted the word " duly." For over three hours a bland discussion had resulted on this quibble, affording ample opportunity for the Government and its adherents in the Opposition to eulogise the Bill.

Seated with folded arms and expressionless face David listened to the debate. One after another the Government henchmen rose to enumerate the difficulties with which the Government was faced and the extraordinary efforts the Government were making, and would continue to make, to overcome them. Burning with indignation, David listened—speeches by Dudgeon, Bebbington, Hume and Cleghorn, every word an expression of compromise, of procrastination. His ear, trained by experience and attuned by his present emotion, caught the inflection in every phrase—the latent apology, the sedulous intention to make the best of a bad job. Seated there, cold yet burning, David waited to catch the Speaker's eye. He must speak. Impossible to sit passively under this betrayal. Was it for this he had worked, fought, dedicated his life? As he waited, all his exertion in those last years came before him: his humble beginning in the Federation office, his struggle through the welter of local politics, his long and unremitting effort through these last years—striving, drudging, putting all his soul into the work. And to what purpose if this futile measure, this repudiation of every pledge, this travesty of justice, marked the consummation of it all!

He raised his head abruptly, filled with a fury of determination, fixing the present speaker with a dilated eye. It was Stone who now stood on his feet, old Eustace Stone who had begun as a Radical, switched to the Liberal ticket and then, in the war, blossomed once and for all in true Tory colours. Stone, master of political casuistry, cunning as an old fox, was extolling the Bill in the hope of a peerage in the next honours list. All his life Stone had hungered for a peerage, and now he sniffed it like a luxurious bunch of grapes lowered inch by inch until it hung almost within reach of his snapping jaws. In an effort to extend his popularity, he flung bouquets right and left, striking a flowery and declamatory note. His thesis was the nobility of the miner, which he artfully developed to discredit all arguments that the Bill might provoke further disaffection amongst the men. " Who in this House," he proclaimed sonorously, " will dare to declare that the veriest shadow of disloyalty lurks in the heart of the British miner? In this connection no fitter words were ever spoken than those so poetically uttered by the Rt. Hon. Member for Carnarvon Boroughs. Indeed I crave the indulgence of this House to quote the memorable lines." He pursed his lips roundly and recited: " ' I have seen the miner as a worker and there is none better. I have seen him as a politician and there is none sounder. I have seen him as a singer and there is no sweeter. I have seen him as a footballer and he is a terror. But in all capacities he is loyal and earnest and courageous . . .' "

O God, groaned David, how long must this go on? He thought of the burning of the Neptune, an act of sabotage, in itself an inexcusable madness, yet solely expressive of the mutiny of the miners against their fate. His very soul flamed with passionate resentment as one hypocritical phrase after another dripped from the lips of the wily Stone. He glanced swiftly at Nugent who sat beside him, his face covered with his hand. Nugent felt this as deeply as he; but Nugent had greater resignation, a sort of fatalism which caused him to bow more easily before the inevitable. He could not bend like that. Never, never. He must speak, he must. In an agony of purpose he strove for calmness, for composure, for courage. As Stone at last meandered to the end of his peroration, beaming upon the House, and sat down, David sprang to his feet.

He waited, tense, immobile; he caught the Speaker's eye. He drew a long breath that entered his chest slowly, painfully, and seemed to flow through all his body in a great wave of resolution. At that instant he determined to make one great despairing effort, to pit the strength of his lifelong purpose against the Bill. Another breath. Command came to him, command and courage. He began slowly, almost impersonally, with such a deadly sincerity that, after the bombast of the previous speaker, the attention of the House was immediately riveted upon him.

" I have been listening to the Debate for the entire afternoon. I wish with all my heart I could share the admiration of my hon. Friends for this Bill." A silence. " But while I have been listening to their polished phrases I could not refrain from thinking of the men to whom the hon. Member who has preceded me has so poetically referred. This House knows that on several occasions I have directed its attention towards the distress in the mining areas of this country. I have on more than one occasion invited the hon. Member to accompany me to my own constituency to see with his own eyes the terrible and hopeless despair which stalks the streets there. To see the derelict men, women whose hearts are broken, little children with starvation written on their faces. If the hon. Member had accepted my invitation I imagine he would have gasped in a kind of wonder: ' How on earth do these people live? ' The answer is that they do not live. They exist. They exist in a broken and demoralised condition, bearing a burden which is the more insufferable because it falls heaviest upon the weak and the young. Hon. Members will no doubt rise and tell me that I am wallowing in exaggerated sentiment. Let me refer them to the reports of school medical officers in these districts, in my own district, where they will find full and ample confirmation of the facts. Children suffering from lack of clothing, children without boots, children far under average weight, children certified as sub-normal because of lack of nourishment. Lack of nourishment!

Perhaps hon. Members have sufficient intelligence to understand the meaning of that polite euphemism. Recently, at the opening of this parliament, we had again the opportunity of witnessing all the splendour, pomp and pageantry which, my hon. Friends will assure me, bespeaks the greatness of our nation. Did any of my hon. Friends contrast it, for one second, with the beggary, poverty, misery and penury which exists within the greatness of that nation? Perhaps I do this House a grave injustice." A note of bitter indignation now crept into the voice. "On two occasions I have heard an hon. Member rise with the suggestion that the House 'put round the hat' to alleviate the suffering in these mining areas. Could anything be more infamous? Worn to the point of exhaustion as they are, these people do not want your charity. They want justice! This Bill gives them no justice. It is lip service, it is hypocrisy. Does not this House realise that the coal-mining industry by its very nature is different from all other industries? It is unique. It is not merely the process of getting coal. It is the basic industry which provides the raw material for half the prosperous industries of this country. And the men who produce this unique and vital commodity at the risk of their lives are kept in penury and misery, employed at a wage which would be insufficient to pay the cigar bills of certain hon. Members of this House. Does any Member of this House honestly believe that this inadequate and hypocritical Bill will finally save the industry? If so I challenge him to come forward. Our present mining system has grown haphazard—not as the result of economic causes—but because of historic and personal causes. As has been said, it is planned not for geological, but for genealogical reasons. Do my hon. Friends realise that we are the only important coal-producing country in the world where there is no national communal control over the mineral itself? Two Royal Commissions have emphatically recommended the Nationalisation of minerals in order that the State might reorganise the coalfields on modern scientific lines. This present Government, before it came into office, pledged itself to nationalise the mines. And how does it now redeem that pledge? By continuing the chaos, seeking blindly for an outlet through the old competitive system, applying the stranglehold of restricted production, reducing output instead of widening markets, subsidising discarded mines to keep them closed, turning the working class, the wealth producers of this country, on to the streets in hundreds and thousands. I warn this House that you may continue for a short time in that way but the end inevitably is the degradation of the workman and the ruin of the nation as a whole." His voice rose. "You cannot get more blood from the veins of the miners to revitalise the industry. Their veins are shrunken white. Wages of beggary and conditions of famine have existed in the mining districts ever since the war, when the hon. Member who preceded me kept telling the country we had only to kill sufficient Germans to live in peace and prosperity till the end of our days. Let this House take heed. It cannot condemn the mining community to further years of misery." He paused again, and his tone turned persuasive, almost pleading. "This proposed Bill by its very nature admits the failure of the individual pit in the face of competition by the great combines. Does not this, of itself, state conclusively the case for a nationally owned industry? The House cannot be blind to the fact that there has been prepared a great nationally owned scheme to eliminate waste, work at the highest efficiency, reduce costs and prices, and to stimulate high-power consumption. Why has the Labour Government of this country ignored this integration in favour of a shadowy capitalistic amalgamation? Why has not the Government boldly said: 'We are going once and for all to clean up the mess left by our predecessors. We are going to end for ever the system which has landed us into this chaos. We are going to take over on behalf of the nation the mining industry and run it for the welfare of this country'?" A final silence, then David's voice rose to his highest pitch of passionate entreaty. "I appeal to the House in the name of honour and conscience to examine the case I have put before it. And before the House divides I appeal especially to my colleagues in this Government. I implore them not to betray the men and the movement which put them here. I implore them to reconsider their position, to throw out this palliative measure, to implement their pledge and bring in a straight Bill of Nationalisation. If and when we are defeated on the floor of this House we will go to the country for a mandate. In the name of humanity, I beg you, I entreat you to seek this mandate armed with that glorious defeat."

There was a dead silence when David sat down, a silence which was at once undecided and intense. The House, in spite of itself, was impressed. Then Bebbington, in a voice of cool detachment, threw out the words:

"The hon. Member for Sleescale Borough evidently believes that this Government can nationalise the mines with the same facility as he takes out a dog licence."

A ripple went over the House, uncomfortable, uncertain. Then came the Hon. Basil Eastman's historic sally. The hon. Member, a young Tory back-bencher from the Shires, who spent his rare visits to the House in a state of hereditary coma, had one rare parliamentary qualification which endeared him to his party. He could make animal noises to perfection. And now, roused from his habitual lethargy by the mention of the word dog, he sat up in his seat and yelped suddenly in imitation of a startled hound. The House started, held its breath, then tittered. The titter grew, swelled to a laugh. The House roared with delighted laughter. Several Members rose, the question was put, the Committee divided. It was a happy ending to a crisis. As the members poured into the division lobby, quite unnoticed David passed out of the House.

XIX

He walked into St. James's Park. He walked rapidly as though towards some fixed destination with his head slightly advanced and his eyes staring a long way in front of him. He was quite unconscious of being in the Park, he was conscious only of his defeat.

He felt neither humiliation nor mortification in his defeat, but simply a great sadness which pressed upon him like a weight and bore him down. Bebbington's final sneer gave him no pain, Eastman's derision and the laughter of the House left no rancour. His thoughts were projected out with himself as though towards some point at a far distance where they centralised and fused in a light of sadness, and the sadness was not for himself.

He came out of the Park at the Admiralty Arch for he had, unconsciously, walked round by the Mall, and here the noise of traffic broke through his far, fixed sadness. He stood for a moment staring at the rush of life, men and women hurrying and hurrying, taxis and omnibuses and cars streaming before his eyes, streaming in the one-way traffic, racing and accelerating and hooting, as though each one amongst them were trying desperately to be first. They cut in and squeezed past one another, and took to the last inch every advantage they could take, and they all went the same way. In a circle.

He gazed and the pain deepened in his sad eyes. The mad swift rush became for him the symbol of the life of men, the one-way traffic of man's life. On and on; on and on; always in the same direction; and each man for himself.

He studied the faces of the hurrying men and women and it seemed that each wore a queer intentness, as if each face were absorbed by the intimate and special life behind the face and by nothing else. This man was absorbed by money, this other by food, and the next by women. The first had taken fifty pounds from some other man on the Stock Exchange that afternoon and he was pleased, the second reviewed the mental images of lobster and *pâté* and asparagus and puzzled his brain as to which would gratify him the most, while the third balanced in his mind his chances of seducing his partner's wife, who had smiled at him in a significant manner at dinner on the previous night.

The terrible thought struck David that each man in this vast hurrying stream of life was living for his own interest, for his own satisfaction, for his own welfare, for himself. Each man was conscious only of himself, and the lives of other men stood merely as the adjuncts of his own existence—they did not matter, it was he who mattered, he, the man himself. The lives of all other men mattered only in so far as they affected the man's own happiness, and the man would sacrifice the happiness and the lives of other men, cheat and swindle, exterminate and annihilate, for the sake of his own welfare, his own interest, for the sake of himself.

The thought crushed David; he turned from it and from the mad circling rush of the traffic. Abruptly he walked away. He went up the Haymarket. In the Haymarket at the corner of Panton Street some men were singing in the street, a group of four men, he could see that they were miners. They stood facing each other, all young men, and all bent together with their foreheads nearly touching. They sang a song in Welsh. They were young Welsh miners and they were destitute—singing in the streets while all the wealth and luxury of London rolled past them.

The song finished, and one of the men held out a box. Yes, he was a miner, David saw. He was well shaved and his clothing though poor and ill assorted was clean—as though he wanted to keep himself up and not let himself go down into those depths which waited for him. David could see the tiny blue pit scars on his clean well-shaven face. David put a shilling in the box. The man thanked him without obsequiousness and with an even greater sadness. David thought, has that shilling helped more than all my work and striving and speaking in the last five years ?

He walked on slowly towards the Piccadilly tube.

He crossed over to the tube, took his ticket and got into the next train. Sitting opposite was a workman reading the evening paper, reading an account of David's speech which was already in the late editions. The man read slowly with the paper folded very small while the train thundered through the dark reverberating tunnels of the underground. David had a great impulse to ask the man what he thought about the speech. But he did not ask.

At Battersea Station David left the train and walked towards Blount Street. He felt tired as he let himself into No. 33, and he ascended the worn carpeted stairs with a certain relief. But Mrs. Tucker stopped him before he had gone half-way up. He turned to face her as she spoke from the open door of her sitting-room below.

" Dr. Barras was on the telephone," she said. " She rang up several times but wouldn't leave a message."

" Thank you, Mrs. Tucker," he said.

" She said to ring up whenever you came in."

" Very well."

He imagined Hilda had rung up to condole with him, and while he was grateful he was not yet in the mood for her condolences. But Mrs. Tucker persisted:

" I promised Dr. Barras you'd ring up the minute you came in."

" Oh, very well," he said again and he turned to the telephone which was on the half landing behind him. As he called Hilda's number he heard the satisfied click of Mrs. Tucker's door.

He was some time in getting Hilda's number but the moment he got through Hilda answered. There was one second of ringing tone and then Hilda's voice. Hilda had been sitting at the 'phone, waiting.

" Hello, Hilda, is that you ? " He could not help his voice being dull and tired.

" David," she said, " I've been trying to get you all the afternoon."

" Yes ? "

" I want to see you, now, at once."

He hesitated.

" I'm sorry, Hilda, I'm rather tired just now; would you mind very much . . ."

" You must," she broke in. " It's important. Now."

There was a silence.

" What is it ? " he asked.

" I can't say, oh, I can't say over the wire." A pause. " But it's your wife."

" What! "

" Yes."

He stood with the receiver in his hand galvanised out of his tiredness, his inertia, everything.

" Jenny," he said, as if to himself.

" Yes," she repeated.

There was another momentary silence, then speaking rapidly, almost incoherently:

" You've seen Jenny. Where is she ? Tell me, Hilda. Do you know where Jenny is ? "

" Yes, I know." Hilda's voice came back and stirred him anew.

" Tell me, then. Why can't you tell me ? "

" You must come over," she answered flatly. " Or if you wish I'll come over to you. We can't go on talking over the 'phone."

" All right, all right," he agreed quickly. " I'll be over with you now."

He hung up the receiver and ran down the stairs which he had ascended so slowly. He hailed a passing taxi-cab in Bull Street and drove in a great hurry to Hilda's flat. Within seven minutes he was ringing the bell of Hilda's door.

The maid was out and Hilda let him in herself. He looked at Hilda eagerly, feeling his heart thumping from eagerness and hurry; he searched Hilda's face.

" Well," he said quickly. He almost hoped that Jenny might be at Hilda's flat; perhaps that was Hilda's reason for asking him to come to the flat.

But Hilda shook her head. Her face was pale and sad as she took him into the room which overlooked the river and she sat down without looking at him.

" What is it, Hilda ? " he said. " There's nothing wrong ? "

She sat very still and upright in her severe dark dress with her black hair drawn back from her pale brow and her beautiful pale hands resting in her dark lap. She looked afraid to speak and she was afraid. She said:

"Jenny came to my clinic to-day."

"She's ill?" Concern flooded his face.

"Yes, she's ill."

"In hospital?"

"Yes, in hospital."

A silence. All the quick gladness in him changed to quick pain. A lump came in his throat.

"What is it?" he said. "Is Jenny very ill?"

"Yes, she's rather ill, David, I'm afraid." And still she did not look at him. "She came to my out-patients' this afternoon. She doesn't know how ill she is. But she just came in, asking for me, because she knew of me . . ."

"But is it serious?" he said anxiously.

"Well, yes . . . internal trouble. . . . I suppose in a way it is."

He stared at Hilda not seeing Hilda but seeing Jenny, poor little Jenny, and there was trouble and a great tenderness in his eyes.

He made an instinctive gesture, exclaiming:

"I'll go to the hospital now. Don't let's waste another minute. Shall you come with me or shall I go myself?"

"Wait," she said.

He paused half-way to the door. Even her lips were pale now; she was dreadfully distressed. She said:

"I couldn't get Jenny admitted to St. Elizabeth's. I did my very utmost, but I couldn't; there's something behind it, you see, the cause —— Oh! I had to arrange, I had to send her . . . I had to get her into another hospital . . . first."

"What hospital?" he asked.

She looked at him at last. He had to know, some time he had to know, and so she said:

"The Lock Hospital in Canon Street."

At first he did not understand and he stared at Hilda's distressed face in a kind of wonder; but only for a few seconds did he stare like that. A cry of pain came out of him, inarticulately.

"I could not help myself," Hilda said; and she withdrew her eyes because it hurt her to see him suffer. She stared out of the window towards the river which flowed in full stream beneath her. The river flowed silently and there was silence in the room. The silence in the room lasted a long time, lasted until he spoke.

"Will they let me see her?"

"Yes. I can arrange that. I'll ring up now." She hesitated, eyes still averted. "Or would you like me to come?"

"No, Hilda," he muttered. "I'll go myself."

He stood there while she used the telephone and spoke to the house surgeon and when she said it was all right he thanked her hurriedly and went out. He felt faint. He thought for a moment that he was going to faint and he hung on to the spiked railings round the block of flats. It was hateful to do this; he was afraid Hilda would be watching from the window and see him, but he could not help himself. A gramophone was playing in one of the bottom flats; it was playing *You are my heart's delight.* Everyone was playing and singing that song just now—it was the rage of London. He remembered he had eaten nothing since lunch-time. He thought, I'd better eat something or I shall make a scene at the hospital.

He let go of the cold iron spikes and went along the Embankment to a coffee-stall which was there. The coffee-stall was really a cabmen's shelter, but the man in charge of the shelter must have seen that he was ill for he gave him hot coffee and a sandwich.

" How much ? " David said.

" Fivepence," the man said.

While David drank the coffee and ate the sandwich the gramophone tune kept going in his head.

The Lock Hospital. It was not so far from the coffee-stall and a taxi took him there quickly. He sat hunched up in the taxi, which was clean and new with a bunch of yellow paper flowers stuck in a chromium vase. There was a faint lingering of scent in the taxi, scent and cigarette smoke. The yellow paper flowers seemed to exhale a perfume of scent and smoke.

The doorkeeper of the Canon Street Lock Hospital was an old man with spectacles; he was old and slow and in spite of Hilda's having 'phoned there was some delay. David waited outside the old man's box while the old man spoke to the ward upon the house telephone. The mosaic floor had a pattern of red and blue and the edges of the floor were curved towards the walls to prevent the accumulation of dust.

The lift whined up slowly and he stood outside the ward. Jenny, his wife, was inside that ward. His heart began to beat with suffocating rapidity. He followed the sister into the ward.

The ward was long and cool and white and on either side were the narrow white beds. Everything was beautifully white and in each beautifully white bed was a woman. *You are my heart's delight* the gramophone kept playing, on and on, inside his head.

Jenny. At last it was Jenny, his wife Jenny in the end bed, in the last beautifully white bed of all, behind a beautiful white screen. The known and loved face of his wife Jenny came into his sight among the beautiful and strange imposing whiteness of the ward. His heart turned over inside of him and beat more suffocatingly. He trembled in every part of his body.

"Jenny," he whispered.

The ward sister took one look at him and left him. The ward sister's lips were pursed and her hips swaggered.

" Jenny," he whispered again.

" I thought you'd come," she said, and she smiled at him faintly with the old questioning and propitiating smile.

His heart broke within him, he could say nothing, he sank into the seat beside the bed. Her eyes hurt him the most, they were like the eyes of a beaten dog. Her cheeks were netted with fine red veins. Her lips were pale. She was still pretty and she did not seem old, but her prettiness was faintly bloated. She had the tragic look of one who has been used.

" Yes," she said, " I thought you'd come. It was funny like me going in to see Dr. Barras, but when I got sick I didn't want a stranger. And I'd heard of Hilda Barras. And us being friendly in Sleescale with her and that . . . Oh, well, there it was! And oh, I thought you'd come."

He saw that she was pleased to see him. Nothing of the terrible emotion which consumed him. Faintly, apologetically pleased to see him. He struggled to speak.

" Are you comfortable here ? " he asked.

She flushed, a little ashamed of what in the old days she would have called her position. She said awkwardly:

" Oh yes, ever so comfortable. I know it's the public ward, but sister's ever so nice. Quite the lady." Her voice was slightly husky. One of the pupils of her beaten eyes was wide and black and larger than the other.

" I'm glad you're comfortable."

" Yes," she said. " I never was one for hospitals though. I remember when dad broke his leg." She smiled at him again and her smile lancinated him—again the cringing of the beaten dog. In a low voice he said:

" If you'd only written to me, Jenny ! "

" I read about you," she said. " I read about you ever so much in the papers. Do you know, David "—her voice took on a sudden animation—" do you know once you passed me in the street ? In the Strand it was; you passed me close as close."

" Why didn't you speak to me ? "

" Well—I thought I would, then I thought I wouldn't." She coloured slightly again. " I was with a friend, you see."

" I see," he said.

A silence came.

" You've been in London," he said at last.

" That's right," she agreed humbly. " I got to like London something terrible. The restrongs and the shops and that like. I've been getting along all right, very well in fact. I wouldn't like you to think I've been down on my luck all the time. I've had a lot of good times." She paused. She stretched out her hand for the drinking-cup that stood beside her bed. He reached quickly for the cup and gave it to her.

" Funny," she said. " Like a little tea-pot."

" Are you thirsty ? "

" Well, no, it's just in my stomach. It oughtn't to take long to put right. Dr. Barras is going to operate on me when I'm strong enough." She said it almost proudly.

" Yes, Jenny," he agreed.

She handed him back the drinking-cup and looked at him. Something in his eyes made her own eyes fall. There was a silence.

" I'm sorry, David," she said at last. " I'm sorry if I didn't treat you right."

Tears started into his eyes. He could not speak for a moment, then he whispered:

" You get better, Jenny, that's all I want you to do."

She said dully:

" You know what this ward is ? "

" Yes," he said.

There was a silence. She said:

" They'll give me treatment before my operation."

" Yes, Jenny."

Another silence, then all at once she began to cry. She cried silently into her pillow. Out of her eyes, that were like the eyes of a beaten dog, the tears welled silently.

" Oh, David," she gasped, " I'm ashamed to look at you."

The sister came up.

" Come, come now," she said. " I think that should be all for to-night." And she stood there, dispassionate, formidable.

David said:

" I'll come again, Jenny. To-morrow."

She smiled through her tears:

" Yes, come to-morrow, David, do."

He rose. He bent forward and kissed her.

The sister saw him to the swing doors. She said coldly:

" You ought to know, it's hardly wise to kiss anyone in this ward."

He did not answer. He went out of the hospital. In Canon Street outside a barrel organ was playing *You are my heart's delight.*

XX

TOWARDS ten o'clock Aunt Caroline looked out at the fine October day from the window of her room in Linden Place and decided pleasurably that she would take " a little walk." Twice a day now, forenoon and afternoon, when the weather was favourable, Aunt Caroline took a little walk. Foremost amongst the pleasures of being in London were these little walks which Aunt Caroline so quietly and gently took.

Yes, Aunt Carrie was in London. Strange indeed to find herself in that mighty hub of Empire which had always puzzled and intimidated her from afar! Yet was it so strange? Richard was dead, the Neptune sold, reclaimed and restarted by Mawson, Gowlan & Co. The Law, alas, was gone too, for Mr. Gowlan had himself taken up residence in the house and was reported to be spending enormous sums upon its reconstruction and its gardens. Oh dear, oh dear! Aunt Carrie winced at the thought of rude hands laid upon her asparagus bed. How could she have borne these changes and have still remained in Sleescale? Nor had she been invited to remain. Arthur, turned sullen and morose, engaged as underviewer at the pit, had not invited her to share the small house he had rented in Hedley Road. Indeed, she would never forget that dreadful night when he returned from Tynecastle the worse for drink and harshly told her she must now " shift for herself." Poor fellow! He little knew how his words had cut her. Not, mind you, that she would have dreamed of dragging on, the victim of odious sympathy, within the ambit of her former dignity. She was only sixty-four. She had £120 a year. It was independence—and London, city of intellect and culture, lay waiting. Gasping at her audacity, she had nevertheless reasoned it out in her own careful fashion. In London she would be near Hilda, who had lately been kind to her, and not far distant from Grace, who had always been kind to her. Dear Grace—thought Aunt Carrie—still simple and unassuming and poor, living a carefree life with her husband and her brood of children, careless of money and all material things, but happy, healthy and happy. Yes, she would certainly spend a month or two at Barnham every year. And there was Laura, too, Laura Millington, settled through all those years with her invalid husband at Bournemouth. She must certainly took Laura up. Altogether prospects in the South of England looked bright for Aunt Carrie. The last thirty years of her life she had lived chiefly in the sick-rooms of Harriet and Richard. Perhaps in her secret heart Aunt Carrie was a little tired of sick-rooms and the turning of dirty linen therein.

Bayswater, naturally, was the district towards which she was drawn. No one knew better than Aunt Carrie that Bayswater had " come down "—but then she had a certain proud consciousness of having come down herself. The remnants of gentility in Bayswater awoke a sentimental echo in her heart and made her head incline with not unhappy resignation. And Linden Place was so very suitable, the green of the trees in spring was delicate and charming against the faded yellowish paint upon the old stuccoed houses and there was a church at the end of the street which afforded both atmosphere and solace. Lately Aunt Carrie had turned even more devout and, in St. Philip's, matins and evensong, which she regularly attended, often drew tears of voluptuous tenderness from her eyes. From the spire of St. Philip's a high clear bell rang occasionally, and the milkman called pleasantly in the street and the smell of roasting mutton came from many basements. Mrs. Gittins's house, No. 104C, where after full investigation Aunt Carrie had selected her room, was of an eminent respectability and the bath, though cracked and flaking its enamel, was always clean. The twopence in the slot geyser gave excellent hot water and, most properly, the washing of clothes in the bathroom was strictly prohibited. All Mrs. Gittins's people were elderly ladies except for one young Indian gentleman, a law student, but even he, though coloured, kept the bath meticulously clean.

Conscious of her manifold advantages, Aunt Carrie turned from the window, and surveyed her room. Here she was in comfort, surrounded by her own things, her treasures—what a blessing that in all her life she had never thrown anything out!—the room was furnished practically with her precious and valued possessions. On the table stood the model of the Swiss chalet which Harriet had brought her forty years ago from Lucerne; the carving was really delightful and there were models of little cows inside—and to think that once she had almost sent it to the St. James's Jumble Sale! There, too, hanging from the black bell-handle by the marble mantelpiece were the three postcards which Arthur had once sent her from Boulogne and which she herself had framed a long time ago in *passe-partout.* She had always liked these postcards, the colouring was cheerful and of course the foreign stamps, still upon the back, might, in time, be valuable. And there, on the other wall, was the poker-work memorial she had done for dear Harriet fourteen years before. The poetry, beginning *Auspicious day when first you breathed,* was quite beautiful and the poker work!—well, she had been considered an *adept* at poker work in her time.

They were all here, all her things, her photographs, her album on the table, her set of Goss china, the yellowish globe of the world preserved from the schoolroom, the big cowrie shell that always stood beside it, the game of solitaire with one glass ball lost by Arthur at the age of seven—oh, her panic, then, that Arthur might have swallowed it!—the pen wiper and blotter combined, the court guide and gazetteer of 1907, everything, she had even saved the wicker fly-whisk which she had bought for Richard towards the end.

This single room held the record of Aunt Carrie's life and in it Aunt Carrie could not bemoan her lot. No, she counted her blessings here and counted them gratefully. But meanwhile she was going for her little walk—ah yes. She advanced to the small square of mirror and put on her hat. She had bought her hat seven years ago and it was rather faded now perhaps, with a feather that was slightly emasculate. But still a perfectly good hat—black " went " with almost anything. Pulling on her gloves, she took her tightly rolled umbrella under her arm as though it were a gun. She swept her room with a final look: the half loaf of bread and the little jug of milk neatly stowed on the shelf, the tomato left over from yesterday beside them, the lid on the cocoa tin to keep out the damp, the gas ring safely turned out, the window open just enough to let in the air, no matches left lying about, everything tidy and in order. Satisfied, with her head in the air, Aunt Carrie went out.

She strolled along Linden Place into Westbourne Grove looking into the windows and admiring many of the articles in the shops. Then at the end of Westbourne Grove she turned into Merrett's with an air of familiarity and purpose. Merrett's was a delightful place, quite the best of the large department stores where it was possible to inspect and admire everything, simply everything. For half an hour Aunt Carrie moved about the aisles of Merrett's, head to one side under the antique black hat, gazing at everything, even stopping once or twice to inquire the price. The assistants were civil to a degree—particularly gratifying since Aunt Carrie's purchases in Merrett's could never be extensive. Her financial position, on one hundred and twenty pounds a year, was perfectly secure, yet the fact remained that she could not be reckless. But this morning she was reckless. For some weeks she had kept her eye upon a letter opener, indistinguishable from real ivory and fashioned incredibly into a parrot's beak at one end—how on earth do they do it? Aunt Carrie marvelled—oh, a gem of a letter opener, the price of which was ninepence. But this morning Aunt Carrie's eyes widened with delight. The letter opener bore a little card marked *Reduced to* 6½*d.* Good gracious!—such an opportunity, such a bargain! Aunt Carrie bought the letter opener, and saw it wrapped in green paper and tied with green string. There and then she decided she would give the letter opener to Hilda.

Pleased with her purchase, for it was a point of honour with her to buy something in Merrett's once in a while, Aunt Carrie advanced to the lift. In the lift the girl attendant was dressed like a jockey and by pressing a button she went swishing up with Aunt Carrie to the top floor. " Reading, writing and rest-room," called out the lift girl smartly. It was a beautiful room with cedar panelling and mirrors and agreeable chairs, full of newspapers and periodicals and ladies in the act of resting. And it was free, too, absolutely and unbelievably free.

As Aunt Carrie stepped out of the lift her umbrella, which she still carried like a gun, prodded the lift girl in the buttocks.

" Oh, pardon me," Aunt Carrie cried, her feather quivering with apology. " Quite a mistake I assure you."

" It's quite all right, madam," the lift girl answered.

Such civility!

An hour passed while Aunt Carrie read the papers. A number of ladies like Aunt Carrie seemed to be reading the papers. Perhaps the mirrors created an optical illusion, so many of the ladies were elderly, and a little pinched and clothed in faded black and eager to make the most of the free newspapers. In point of fact the papers were full of news this morning. The country was in a whirl of excitement. Mr. MacDonald had been to see the King again, the National Cabinet was making splendid statements and there was great talk of the coming election. Aunt Carrie was all for a National Government—it was so *secure.* There was an excellent article in the *Tribune* entitled, *Don't Let the Socialists Squander YOUR Money*, and another in the *Meteor*, *Bolshevism Gone Mad.* Aunt Carrie read them both. She went through all the papers with great enjoyment—with the exception of one dreadful Labour rag which was full of distorted reports of destitution in the South Wales valleys. She had always had so little time for reading at the Law. She appreciated her leisure now.

The same lift took her down again and the same lift girl smiled at her. She was a pleasant girl that, indeed she was, Aunt Carrie hoped sincerely she would have promotion.

Outside Merrett's, Aunt Carrie set her course towards Hilda's flat, with the intention of delivering her present. She went, as usual, by Kensington Gardens. It was a pleasant road to the Gardens but it held a great temptation in the shape of Ye Apple Blossom Pantry. Aunt Carrie could seldom resist the delightful home-made cakes and biscuits and in spite of her unusual extravagance at Merrett's she entered Ye Apple Blossom Pantry. The young lady knew her, smiled, went to the wire basket and took a twopenny iced coffee cake which she placed in a paper bag.

" It looks like rain," the young lady remarked, handing Aunt Carrie the bag.

" Oh, I hope not, my dear," Aunt Carrie said handing the girl twopence. She now had the letter opener and the twopenny cake which, nibbled delicately, would make her tea a joy. Quite a morning's shopping.

The Gardens were beautiful, the children in particular by the Round Pond were always adorable. To-day there was one, just a toddler, Aunt Carrie thought to herself, just a little toddler in a tiny red tailor-made coat who toddled and toddled and nearly toddled away from his nannie into the pond. The little love.

There were the sea-gulls, too, which swooped and screamed for bread and bacon rind, oh, Aunt Carrie was thrilled by the sea-gulls. So much bread had been thrown to the sea-gulls that the edges of the Round Pond were fringed with floating bread, hundreds of pieces of floating bread. Cast your bread upon the waters, Aunt Carrie thought, but it was strange nevertheless to see all that bread gone to waste when, if that dreadful paper she had read in Merrett's was to be believed, so many children went in want of it. But it could not be; it was a gross exaggeration; besides there was always charity.

Comforted, she walked down Exhibition Road. South Kensington was delightful, and Chelsea too, Carlyle and the mulberry-tree—or was it bush? Aunt Carrie neared Hilda's flat. She greatly enjoyed visiting Hilda. Indeed, at the back of Aunt Carrie's mind a vague hope lingered that Hilda might one day ask her to keep house for her. She saw herself in high-necked black admitting seriously ill and important people to Hilda's consulting-room—the more gravely ill and important the better. Although Aunt Carrie had emanciated herself from the sick-room, sickness still retained a certain morbid fascination for her.

Hilda was in, the maid declared, and Aunt Carrie, smiling her special smile towards Hilda's maid, the faintly ingratiating smile she had towards the servants at the Law for thirty years, followed her into the flat.

But here a shock awaited Aunt Carrie. Hilda was not alone and it sent Aunt Carrie into a perfect flutter to see that Hilda's visitor was David Fenwick. She came to a full stop inside the door of Hilda's room and her peaked face flushed.

"I'm sorry, Hilda," she breathed. "I had no idea. I thought you were alone."

Hilda rose. She had been sitting in silence, and she seemed not entirely pleased to see Aunt Carrie. But she said:

"Come in, Aunt Carrie. You know David Fenwick."

In a greater flutter than ever Aunt Carrie shook hands with David. She was aware that Hilda and David were friends. But the sight of him in the flesh, her nice young man who had once tutored Arthur and who now made such terrible inflammatory speeches in Parliament, almost overcame her. She subsided in a chair by the window.

David glanced at his watch.

"I'm afraid I must be going," he said to Hilda, "if I'm to be at the hospital this afternoon."

"Oh, don't let me drive you away," Aunt Carrie cried hastily. She thought him pale and worn. His eyes were worried, too, dreadfully worried; they had a look of pained expectancy.

"It's a beautiful day outside," she went on quickly. "I thought it might rain, but it hasn't."

"I don't think it'll rain," Hilda said after an awkward pause.

Aunt Carrie said:

"Indeed, I hope not."

Another pause.

"I came across the Gardens," Aunt Carrie persisted. "They're very beautiful just now."

"Are they?" Hilda said. "Yes, I suppose they are just now."

"There was the dearest little mite by the Round Pond," Aunt Carrie continued, smiling. "In a tiny red coat. I do wish you could have seen him. He was *sweet*."

Despite her good intentions Aunt Carrie had the confused feeling that Hilda was not really attending to her. Vaguely taken aback she gazed at David, who stood silent and preoccupied by the window.

Aunt Carrie smelled trouble in the air—she had a nose for trouble like a fox for a hunting morning. Curiosity rose within her. But David looked at his watch again, then glanced towards Hilda.

" Now I really must go," he said. " I'll see you again at three." He shook hands with Aunt Carrie and went out. Pricking up her ears, Aunt Carrie could hear him talking to Hilda in the hall, but to her disappointment could not make out what he said. For once curiosity mastered timidity. When Hilda returned she exclaimed:

" What's the matter, Hilda dear ? He seemed so upset. And what did he mean by hospital ? "

For a moment Hilda gave no appearance of having heard. Then her answer came unwillingly as if once and for all she wished to cut short Aunt Carrie's curiosity.

" It's his wife. She's in hospital. Being operated on this afternoon."

" Oh dear, oh dear! " gasped Aunt Carrie, and her eyes went wide in a spasm of satisfied sensation. " But——"

" There's aren't any buts," Hilda cut in shortly. " I'm doing the operation and I prefer not to discuss it."

Aunt Carrie's eyes went wider than ever. There was a silence, then she murmured, humbly:

" Shall you make her better, Hilda dear ? "

" What do you expect ? " Hilda retorted rudely.

Aunt Carrie's face fell. Oh dear, oh dear, Hilda could still be very abrupt when she chose. She wanted terribly to ask Hilda what was wrong with David's wife, but Hilda's expression forbade it. Crestfallen and subdued she sighed deeply and was again silent for a minute. Then, remembering suddenly, her face lit up. She smiled:

" Oh, by the way, Hilda, I've brought you the sweetest little present. At least "—modestly—" I *think* it's rather sweet." And, beaming towards the sombre Hilda, she gaily produced the letter opener.

XXI

At half-past one that afternoon David set out for St. Elizabeth's Hospital —where, following a satisfactory blood-test, Jenny had now been transferred. He was aware that he was much too early, but he could not bear to sit still in his rooms thinking of Jenny under the operation. Jenny, his wife, being operated on to-day!

Often during these months of treatment which had been necessary to fit her for the operation he had asked himself about his feeling for

Jenny. It was not love. No, it could not be love, that was dead a long time ago. But it was a great and overwhelming feeling nevertheless. And it was something more than pity.

Her story was quite clear to him now; she had told him snatches here and there, lying occasionally and embroidering always, but failing pitifully to make fiction out of fact. When she first came to London she took a post at one of the big department stores. But the work was hard, much harder than at Slattery's, and the pay small, much smaller than her optimism had allowed her to imagine. Soon Jenny had a friend. Then she had another friend. Jenny's friends had all been perfect gentlemen at the start and had shown themselves in the end to be perfect beasts. The lady-companion story was of course a myth—she had never been out of England. He found it strange that Jenny should have so little sense of her own position. She had still the same childish facility for excusing herself, the same childish capacity for tearful self-compassion. She was hurt and she was down, but it was not she who was to blame. "Men, David," she wept. "You wouldn't believe. I never want to see another man, not as long as I live."

Still the same Jenny. When he brought her flowers she was deeply gratified, not because she cared much for flowers, but because it would show sister she was "a cut above" the others in the ward. He suspected Jenny had elaborated a little tale for sister, no doubt a polite, romantic tale. It was the same when, on her transference to St. Elizabeth's, he had arranged for her to have a side-room—it indicated to the new sister how highly he "thought of her." Even in hospital she was romantic. It was incredible, but it was true. When she had condemned the bestiality of man she asked him please to hand her the tube of lipstick from her bag which she had smuggled into the locker beside her bed. She kept a tiny mirror hidden under her bedside table so that she might arrange herself before his visits. The mirror was forbidden, but Jenny kept it; she wanted to be *nice* for him, she said.

David sighed as he turned from the Embankment towards the hospital. He hoped things would all turn out right in the end—he hoped this with all his soul.

He looked at the clock above the hospital archway. He was still too early, far too early, but he felt he must go into the hospital. He could not wait outside, hang about in the street, he must go inside. He went past the porter's box and walked upstairs. He came to the second floor where Jenny was and he stood in the cool, high vestibule.

A great many doors opened off the vestibule—the door of Hilda's room, sister's room, the waiting-room. But one pair of glass doors drew his eyes, the doors of the operating theatre. He stared at the doors of the operating theatre, two white-frosted glass doors, and it hurt him to think what was going on behind these doors.

The sister in charge, Sister Clegg, came out of the ward. She was not the theatre sister. She looked at him with a mild reproof. She said: " You're much too early. They have only just begun."

" Yes, I know," he answered. " But I had to come."

She walked away without asking him to go into the waiting-room. She simply left him there, and there he stood, with his back against the wall, making himself unobtrusive so that he might not be asked to go away, watching the white-frosted doors of the operating theatre.

As he watched the doors they became transparent and he could see what was taking place inside. He had often assisted at operations in the base hospital, he saw it all clearly and exactly as though he were in the theatre himself.

Exactly in the centre of the theatre there was a metal table which was less like a table than a shining machine with shining levers and wheels to enable it to be contorted into strange and wonderful positions. No! it was not like a machine either. It was like a flower, a great shining metallic flower which grew on a shining stem from the floor of the theatre. And yet it was neither machine nor flower, but a table on which something was laid. Hilda was on one side of this shining table, and Hilda's assistant upon the other, and round about, clustered closely as though they were pressing in upon the table and trying to see what was laid upon the table, were a number of nurses. They were all in white with white caps, and white masks, but they all had black and shiny hands. Their hands were dripping and rubbery and smooth.

The theatre was very hot and it was full of a hot bubbling and hissing. At the head of the table the anæsthetist sat on a round white stool with metal cylinders near and red tubes and an enormous red bag. The anæsthetist was a woman, too, and she was very calm and bored.

Great coloured bottles of antiseptic solution stood near the table and trays of instruments which came hot from the steaming sterilisers. The instruments were handed to Hilda. Hilda did not look at the instruments, she simply held out her black rubbery hand and an instrument was placed there, and Hilda used it.

Hilda bent over the table slightly to use the instruments. It was almost impossible to see what was on the table because the nurses pressed round closely as though looking and trying to screen what was on the table. It was Jenny, though, the body of Jenny. And yet it was not Jenny, nor Jenny's body. Everything was covered up and swathed in white as with a great secrecy, white towels clipped everywhere, covering white towels.

Only one neat square of Jenny's body remained uncovered and the neat square showed up distinctly against the white clipped towels because the square was coloured a fine bright yellow. The picric acid did that. It was inside this square that everything was taking place, inside the square that Hilda used her instruments, her smooth rubbery hands.

First there came the incision, yes, the incision came first. The warm shining lancet drew a slow firm line across the bright yellow skin and the skin took lips and smiled in a wide red smile. Little jets of red spouted from the smiling red lips and Hilda's black hands moved and moved and a ring of shiny forceps lay all round the wound.

Another incision, deeper and deeper inside the red mouth of the wound, which was not smiling now, but laughing, the lips were so wide.

Then Hilda's hand went right inside the wound. Hilda's black shiny hand drew small and pointed like the black shiny head of a snake and penetrated deep within the wound. It was as though the laughing red mouth swallowed the head of the snake.

After that more instruments were used and the forceps in the ring lay thickly one upon another. The confusion of instruments seemed inextricable, but it was not inextricable, it was all necessary and mathematical. It was impossible to see Hilda's face behind the white gauze mask, but Hilda's dark eyes showed above the white mask and the eyes were steeled. Hilda's hands became the projection of Hilda's eyes. They too were inexorable and steeled.

It was necessary to be steeled. In the operating theatre the healthy body was a disenchantment, but in disease the body was obscene. Men should be brought to the operating theatre to view the last extremity of the painted smile. Useless, quite useless. Forgetfulness was too easy Even now the wound itself was losing its horror and its instruments and forgetting and becoming again a warm smiling wound, a painted smile.

The lips of the painted smiling wound drew together as the sutures quickly went in. Hilda put in the sutures with a beautiful precision and the lips of the wound puckered together thinly. It was nearly over now, sealed up and finished, and forgotten. The hissing and bubbling faded a little and the room did not seem to be so hot. The nurses did not press so closely round the table. One coughed into her mask and ended the long silence. Another began to count the bloodied swabs.

In the cool high vestibule David stood motionless with his eyes upon the frosted doors. And at last the doors swung open and the wheeled stretcher came out. Two nurses wheeled the stretcher which moved without sound on its rubber tyres. The nurses did not see him as he pressed back against the wall, but he saw Jenny upon the stretcher. Jenny's face was twisted sideways towards him, flushed and swollen; the eyelids and cheeks especially were very swollen and suffused as though Jenny were in a deep and beautiful drunken sleep. The cheeks puffed in and out as Jenny snored. The hair had fallen out of Jenny's white cap and was tangled as if someone had tried to tug it out. Jenny did not look romantic now.

He watched the swing doors of the ward close upon the wheeled stretcher as they took Jenny to her room at the end of the ward. Then he turned and saw Hilda coming down the incline from the theatre. She advanced towards him. She looked cold and remote and contemptuous. She said abruptly:

" Well, it's over, and she ought to be all right."

He was grateful for her hardness; he could not have borne anything else. He asked:

" When can I see her ? "

" Some time this evening. It was not a long anæsthetic." She paused. " By eight o'clock she should be receiving visitors."

He felt her coldness and again he was glad; kindness would have been odious, too abominable for words. Something of the hardness and cold brilliance of the theatre still clung to her and her words cut sharply like a knife. She would not stand in the vestibule. Almost impatiently, she flung open the door of her room and went in. The door remained open and although she appeared to have forgotten him he followed her into the room. He said in a low voice:

" I want you to know that I'm grateful, Hilda."

" Grateful! " She moved about the room picking up reports and laying them down. Under her cold hardness she was deeply upset. Her whole purpose had been the success of the operation, she had willed herself fiercely to succeed, to demonstrate before him her skill, her brilliance. And now that it was done she hated it. She saw her exquisite handiwork as brutal and crude, adjusting only the relations of the body and leaving the adjustments of the mind and soul untouched. What was the use! She patched up the carcass of the animal and that was about all. This worthless woman would return to him, sound only in body, still morbid in her soul. It rankled more deeply with Hilda because of her own feeling for David. This was not love—oh no, it was subtler far than that. He was the one man who had ever attracted her. At one time indeed she had almost willed herself to fall in love with him. Impossible! She could not love any man. The sense of her failure, that she could like but never love him, made it harder than ever to restore this woman, this Jenny, to him. She swung round. " I shall be here at eight this evening," she said. " I'll leave word then if you may see her."

" Very well."

She went to the tap and ran the water hard, filled a tumbler and, masking her emotion, drank it.

" I must go round the ward now."

" Very well," he said again.

He went away. He went down the stairs and out of the hospital. At the end of John Street he jumped on to a bus going towards Battersea Bridge and in the bus his thoughts ran deeply. No matter what Jenny had done to him or to herself he was glad that she had come through. He could never dissever himself completely from Jenny, she was like a light shadow which had always lain across his heart. Through all these years of her absence she had still lived with him dimly, he had never forgotten her, and now that he had found her and everything was dead between them his curious sense of being bound and obligated to her persisted.

He saw, perfectly, that Jenny was cheap and common and vulgar. He knew that she had been on the streets. His attitude should normally have been one of horror and disgust. But, no, he could not. Strange. All that was best in Jenny presented itself to him, he remembered her moments of unselfishness, her sudden kind impulses, her generosity with money, especially he remembered the honeymoon at Cullercoats and how Jenny had insisted that he take the money to buy himself a suit.

He descended from the bus and walked along Blount Street and into his room. The house was very quiet. He sat down by the window and stared at the tree-tops of the park which showed above the opposite roofs, at the sky which showed beyond the tree-tops. The silence of the room sank into him, the tick of the clock took on a slow and measured rhythm, it was like the tramp of marching feet, of men marching slowly forward.

He straightened himself unconsciously and his eye kindled towards the distant sky. He did not feel himself defeated now. The old stubborn impulse to fight and fight again was resurrected in his soul. Defeat was only contemptible when it brought submission in its train. He would abandon nothing. Nothing. He still had his faith and the faith of the men behind him. The future remained to him. Hope came back to him with a great rush.

Rising abruptly, he went over to the table and wrote three letters. He wrote to Nugent, to Heddon and to Wilson his agent in Sleescale. The letter to Wilson was important. He assured Wilson he would be in Sleescale on the next day but one to address the meeting of the local divisional executive. There was a vigorous optimism in the letter. He felt it himself as he read the letter and he was pleased. These last few days, while the appoach of Jenny's operation had banished all other thoughts from his head, the political situation had rapidly approached a head. In August, as he had predicted, forces in finance and politics had forced the vacillating Government out of office. The previous week, on October 6th, the temporary coalition had voluntarily dissolved. Nomination day for the new election was on the 16th October. David's lips came together firmly. He would fight that election as never before. The proposed National policy he regarded as a determined attack upon the worker's standard of living, instituted to meet a situation caused by the great banking interests. Drastic cuts in unemployment benefit were justified under the grotesque phrase "equality of sacrifice." Sacrifices by the workers were intended to be certain, sacrifices by other sections of the community less so. Meanwhile four thousand millions of British capital were invested abroad. Labour was faced with the greatest crisis in its history. And it did not help Labour that certain of her leaders had thrown in their lot with the Coalition.

Half-past six. A glance at the clock showed David it was later than he had imagined. He made himself a cup of cocoa and drank it slowly, reading the evening paper which Mrs. Tucker had just brought in. The paper was full of garbled propaganda. Keep Industry safe from Nationalisation. Bolshevism gone mad. The Nightmare of Labour Control—these phrases struck his eye. There was a cartoon indicating a valiant John Bull in the act of stamping on a loathsome viper. The viper was plainly labelled: Socialism. Several of Bebbington's choicer sayings were prominently reported. Bebbington was now a hero in the National Cause. The day before he had declared: " Peace in Industry is threatened by doctrines of class warfare. We are safeguarding the worker from himself! "

David smiled grimly and let the paper fall upon the table. When he got back to Sleescale he would have something to say upon that same point. Something a little different perhaps.

By now it was after seven o'clock and he rose, washed his face and hands, took his hat and went out. The strange lightness persisted within him and was heightened by the beauty of the evening. As he crossed Battersea Bridge the sky was red and gold and the river held the coloured brightness of the sky. He reached the hospital in a mood very different from his despondency of the afternoon. Everything was easy if one had courage.

At the top of the stairs he ran straight into Hilda. She had just made her evening visit and was standing with Sister Clegg in the vestibule talking for a moment before she went away. He stopped.

" Is it all right for me to go in now ? " he asked.

" Yes, it is quite all right," Hilda said. She was more composed than she had been in the afternoon. Perhaps, like him, she had reasoned herself into this composure. Her manner was remote and formal, but it was above everything composed. " I think you will find her extremely comfortable," she added. " The anæsthetic has not upset her ; she has come through it all remarkably well."

He could find nothing to say. He was conscious of them both studying him. Sister Clegg in particular seemed always to have a feminine unconquerable curiosity towards him.

" I told her you were coming," Hilda said calmly. " She seemed very pleased."

Sister Clegg looked at Hilda and smiled her cold smile. Aside, she said:

" She actually asked me if her hair was all right."

David flushed slightly. There was something inhuman in Sister Clegg's frigid exposure of Jenny's vanity. A quick reply rose to his lips. But he did not make that reply. As he raised his eyes to Sister Clegg a young nurse rushed out of the ward. She was a junior nurse or she would not have rushed like that. Her face was flour white. She looked frightened. When she saw Sister Clegg she gave a little gasp of relief.

" Come, Sister," she said. " Come! "

Sister Clegg did not ask any question. She knew what that look meant on a junior nurse's face. It meant an emergency. She turned without a word and walked back into the ward. Hilda stood for a moment; then she too turned and walked into the ward.

David remained alone in the vestibule. The incident had happened so suddenly it left him at a loss. He did not know whether he ought to pass through the ward if there was some trouble in the ward. But before he decided Hilda was back again. Hilda was back with an almost unbelievable urgency.

" Go into the waiting-room," Hilda said.

He stared at Hilda. Two nurses came out of the ward and walked rapidly towards the operating theatre; they walked abreast, vaguely unreal, like the advance of a forthcoming procession. Then the lights of the theatre clicked on and the frosted glass doors of the theatre showed bright and white like an illumined cinema screen.

" Go into the waiting-room," Hilda repeated. The urgency was in her voice now, in her eyes, her harsh commanding face. There was nothing else to do. He obeyed; he went into the waiting-room. The door closed behind him and he heard the quick sound of Hilda's steps.

The emergency was Jenny, he knew that with a sudden chilling certainty. He stood in the bare waiting-room listening to the sound of feet crossing and recrossing the vestibule. He heard the whine of the lift. He heard more steps. A period of silence followed, then he heard a sound which absolutely horrified him: it was the sound of someone running. Someone ran from the theatre to Hilda's room and then ran back again. His heart contracted. When discipline yielded itself to such haste the emergency must be serious, oh, desperately serious. The thought caused him to stand motionless as though frozen.

A long time passed, a very long time. He did not know how long. Half an hour, perhaps an hour, he simply did not know. Immobilised, strained to an attitude of listening, his muscles refused to allow him to look at his watch.

Suddenly the door opened and Hilda entered the room. He could not believe it was Hilda, the change in her was so great; she seemed exhausted and spiritually spent. She said almost wearily:

" You had better go to see her now."

He came forward hurriedly.

" What has happened ? "

She looked at him.

" Hæmorrhage."

He repeated the word.

Her lips contracted. She said very distinctly and bitterly:

" The moment Sister came out of the room she raised herself in bed. She reached for a mirror. To see if she was pretty." The bitterness, the defeatedness in Hilda's voice was terrible. " To see if she was pretty, if her hair was straight, to use her lipstick. Can you think of it? Reaching for a mirror, after all I'd done." Hilda broke off, wholly overcome, her hardness of that afternoon forgotten, her sole thought the destruction of her handiwork. It prostrated her. She flung the door wide with a helpless gesture. " You'd better go now if you wish to see her."

He went out of the waiting-room and through the ward and into Jenny's room. Jenny lay flat on her back with the end of the bed raised high on blocks. Sister Clegg was giving Jenny an injection into her arm. The room was in confusion, basins everywhere and ice and towels. The pieces of a smashed hand mirror were lying on the floor.

Jenny's face was the colour of clay. She breathed in little shallow gasps. Her eyes were upon the ceiling. They were terrified, the eyes; they seemed to cling to the ceiling as though afraid to let the ceiling go.

His heart melted and flooded through him. He fell on his knees beside the bed.

"Jenny," he said. " Oh, Jenny, Jenny."

The eyes removed themselves from the ceiling and wavered towards him. Excusingly, the white lips whispered:

" I wanted to be nice for you."

Tears ran down his face. He took her bloodless hand and held it.

"Jenny," he said. " Oh, Jenny, Jenny, my dear."

She whispered, as though it were a lesson:

" I wanted to be nice for you."

Tears choked him; he could not speak. He pressed the white hand against his cheek.

" I'm thirsty," she gasped feebly. " Can I have a drink? "

He took the drinking-cup—funny, like a little tea-pot!—and held it to her white lips. She raised her hand weakly and took the drinking-cup. Then a faint shiver went through all her body. The liquid in the drinking-cup spilled all over her nightgown.

Everything had turned out for the best for Jenny in the end. The little finger of her hand which still held the drinking-cup was politely curved. That would have pleased Jenny if she had known. Jenny had died polite.

XXII

At half-past eight on the morning after Jenny's funeral David stepped on to the platform of Sleescale Station and was met by Peter Wilson. The whole of the previous day, October 15th, had been a swift unreality of sadness, completing the last pitiful arrangements, following all that remained of Jenny to the cemetery, placing a wreath of flowers upon her grave. He had travelled from London by the night train and he had not slept much. Yet he did not feel tired; the keen wind blowing from the sea struck along the platform and braced him with a tense energy. He had a curious sense of physical resistance as he put down his suit-case and shook hands with Wilson.

" Here you are," Wilson said, " and not before time." Wilson's slow, good-natured smile was absent. His little pointed beard made those restless jerks which always indicated some disturbance in his mind. " It's a great pity you missed your meeting yesterday, the Committee was extremely put about. You can't know what we're up against."

" I imagine it's going to be a hard fight," David answered quietly.

" Perhaps harder," Wilson declared. " Have you heard who they're putting up against you ? " He paused, searching David's eyes with a perturbed inquiry; then he threw out violently: " It's Gowlan."

David's heart seemed to stand still, his body to contract, ice-like, at the sound of the name.

" Joe Gowlan! " he repeated, tonelessly.

There was a strained silence. Wilson smiled grimly.

" It only came out last night. He's at the Law now—living in style. Since he's opened the Neptune he's become the local swell. He's got Ramage in tow, and Connolly and Low. He's got most of the Conservative Executive eating out of his hand. There's been a big push from Tynecastle, too. Yes, he's been nominated; it's all arranged and settled."

A heavy bewilderment mingled with a kind of terror came over David—he could not believe it, no, the thing was too wildly, too madly impossible. He asked mechanically:

" Are you serious ? "

" I was never more serious in my life."

Another silence. It was true, then, this staggering and brutal news. With a set face, David picked up the suit-case and started off with Wilson. They came out of the station and down Cowpen Street without exchanging a word. Joe, Joe Gowlan, turning over and over, relentlessly, in David's brain. There was no doubt about Joe's qualifications—he had money, success, influence. He was like Lennard, for instance, who, with a fortune made from gimcrack furniture, had nonchalantly bought Clipton at the last election—Lennard, who had never made a speech in his life, who spent his rare visits to the House standing treat in the bar and doing cross-word puzzles in the smoke-room. One of the nation's legislators. And yet, thought David bitterly, the easy-going Lennard was hardly the exemplar. Joe would use the House for more than cross-word puzzles. There was no knowing to what diverse and interesting uses Joe might turn his position if he won the seat.

Abruptly David turned away from his bitterness. That was no help. The only answer to the situation was that Joe must not get in. O God, he thought, walking into the keen sea wind, O God, if I only do one thing more let me beat Joe Gowlan at this election.

Filled more than ever with the sense of his obligations, he had breakfast with Wilson at Wilson's house and they went over the position intensively. Wilson did not spare his facts. David's unforeseen delay in returning to Sleescale had created an unfavourable feeling. Moreover, as David already knew, the executive of the Labour Party had not favoured his re-nomination; ever since his speech on the Mines Bill he had been marked down as a rebel, treated with hostility and suspicion. But the party, indebted to the Miners' Federation for affiliation fees, had been unwilling to block the Federation nominee. Yet this had not prevented them sending an agent from Transport House in an effort to influence the miners towards another candidate.

"He came up like a confounded spy," Wilson growled in conclusion. "But he didn't get any change out of us. The Lodge wanted you. They pressed the matter with the Divisional Executive. And that was the end of it."

After that, Wilson insisted that David go home to get some sleep before the committee meeting at three. David felt no need of sleep, but he went home; he wanted to think things out by himself.

Martha was expecting him—he had wired her the night before—and her eyes flew to his black tie. Her eyes revealed nothing as they took in that black tie and she asked no question.

"You're late, surely," she said. "Your breakfast's been waiting this hour past."

He sat down by the table.

"I've had breakfast with Wilson, mother."

She did not like that, she persisted:

"Will you not even have a cup of tea?"

He nodded.

"Very well."

He watched her as she infused fresh tea, first pouring hot water in the brown teapot, then measuring the tea exactly from the brass canister that had been her mother's, he watched her sure and firm movements and he thought with a kind of wonder how little she had changed. Not far off seventy now, still vigorous and dark and unyielding, she was indomitable. He said suddenly:

"Jenny died three days ago."

Her features remained impenetrable, slightly formidable.

"I thought that must be the way of it," she said, putting the tea before him.

A silence fell. Was that all she could say? It struck him as insufferably cruel that she could hear of Jenny's death without speaking one word of regret. But while he despaired of her vindictiveness, she declared, almost brusquely:

"I'm sorry it has grieved ye, David." The words seemed wrung from her. Then, following something like embarrassment, she looked at him covertly. " And what's like going to happen with you now ? "

" Another election . . . another start."

" Ye're not tired of it, yet ? "

" No, mother."

When he had drunk his tea, he went upstairs to lie down for a few hours. He closed his eyes, but for a long time sleep eluded him. The thought remained hammering in his head, insistent, and agitating, like a prayer—O God, let me keep Joe Gowlan out, let me keep him out. Everything he had battled against all his life was concentrated in this man who now opposed him. He must win. He must. Willing that with all his strength, a drowsiness came over him, he fell asleep at last.

The next day, October 16th, was the official nomination day, and at eleven o'clock in the forenoon, at the very outset of the campaign, David encountered Joe. The meeting took place outside the Town Hall. David, accompanied by Wilson, was advancing up the steps to hand in his papers, when at that moment Joe, escorted by Ramage, Connolly and the Rev. Low, all members of his executive, together with a number of his supporters, swung through the doorway and began to come down. At the sight of David, Joe stopped short dramatically, and faced him with a manly recognition. He stood two steps above David, a fine expansive figure, his chest thrown out impressively, his double-breasted jacket open, a large bunch of blue cornflowers in his buttonhole. Towering in rough-hewn grandeur, he held out his meaty hand. He smiled—his hearty, man-to-man smile.

" Well met, Fenwick," he cried. " Better early than late, eh ? I hope this is going to be a clean contest. It will be on my side. Fair play and no favour. And may the best man win."

There was a murmur of approval from Joe's partisans, while David went cold outside and sick within.

" Mind you," went on Joe, " there's going to be no kid gloves about it though, no gloves at all; it's going to be bare fists all the time. I consider I'm fighting for the Constitution, Fenwick, the British Constitution. Don't make any mistake about that, I warn you. All the same we'll fight clean. British sportsmanship, see, that's what I mean, British sportsmanship."

Again there was a cheer from the rapidly accumulating crowd of Joe's supporters, and in the enthusiasm of the moment several pressed forward and shook hands with him. David turned away in a cold disgust. Without a word he went into the Town Hall. But Joe, quite undismayed by the incivility of his opponent, continued shaking hands. Joe was not proud, he would shake any man's hand, by God, provided the man was decent and British and a sportsman. Standing there on the steps of the Town Hall, Joe was moved to express that sentiment to the assembly now before him. He declared:

" I'm proud and willing to shake the hand of any decent man." A pause of deep feeling. " Provided he'll shake hands with me. But don't let the Bolshies come up and try it on. No, by God, no! " Joe threw out his chest pugnaciously. He felt lusty, powerful, he was glorying in it now. " I want you lads to know that I'm against the Bolshies and the Reds and all the other scrimshankers. I'm for the British Constitution and the British Flag and the British Pound. We didn't do our bit in the war at home and abroad for nothing. I'm for law and order and sport and sociability. That's what I'm fighting the election for, and that's what you're voting for. No man has the right to leave the world as bad as he finds it. We've got to do what we can to make the world better, see. We've got to stand by ethics and education and the ten commandments. Yes, by God, the ten commandments! We're not going to stand any antichristian Bolshie anarchism against the ten commandments! And no anarchism against the British Flag and the British Constitution and the British Pound. That's why I'm asking you to vote for me, lads. And if you want to keep yourselves in work don't you forget it! "

Led by Ramage, cheers were raised and raised again. The cheers intoxicated Joe; he felt himself a born orator, elevated by the approval of his own conscience and of his fellow men. He beamed and shook hands with everyone near him, then he marched down the steps.

As he reached the pavement, a little boy got entangled with his legs and fell. Stooping in an excess of kindliness, Joe picked him up and set him on his bare feet.

" There," he laughed paternally. " There ! "

Joe's laugh seemed to startle the boy, who was a very ragged little boy of about six, with a pallid underfed face and uncut hair falling over big frightened eyes, and all at once he began to cry. His mother, holding a baby to her with one arm, came forward to pluck him out of Joe's way with the other.

" He's a fine little lad, missus," Joe beamed. " A regular champion. What's his name ? "

The young woman flushed nervously at finding herself the object of the great man's attention. She tightened the skimpy shawl which bound the baby to her and ventured timidly:

" His name's Joey Townley, Mr. Gowlan. His father's brother, that's to say his uncle, Tom Townley, worked in the heading next yours in the Paradise, when you used to work inbye yourself. Before you became . . . like you are now . . . like."

" Well, well," Joe rejoined, beaming. " Would you believe it! And does your husband work in the Neptune an' all, Mrs. Townley ? "

Mrs. Townley blushed more deeply, confused, ashamed, terrified at her own boldness.

" No, Mr. Gowlan, sir, he's on the dole. But, oh sir, if he could just get back in work . . ."

Joe nodded his head with sudden gravity.

" You leave it to me, missus. That's why I'm fightin' this election," he announced fervently. " Yes, by God, I'm goin' to change things for the better here." He patted little Joe Townley's head and smiled again, facing the crowd with magnificent modesty. " A fine little lad. And Joe too! Well, well, who knows, he might turn out to be another Joe Gowlan hisself! "

Still beaming, he moved away towards his waiting car. The effect was superb. News spread up and down the Terraces that Joe Gowlan was going to take back Sarah Townley's man and give him a first-class job inbye, the best heading in the pit. There were a few like Sarah Townley in Sleescale. It all did Joe a vast amount of good.

Joe's power as a speaker developed. He had good lungs, absolute assurance and a throat of brass. He blared at them. He was virile. He developed slogans. Huge posters appeared and spread across every hoarding in the town.

Down with Idleness, Tribulation, Sickness,
Poverty and Sin!
Up with Law, Order, Sport and the British
Constitution ! !
VOTE FOR JOE GOWLAN ! ! !

He was a bulwark of morality; but, of course, intensely human, a man's man, a regular sport. At his first meeting in New Bethel Street School, after exhorting his listeners to support the Flag, he beamed upon them slyly:

" And put your shirt on *Radio* at the next Gosforth Park Races." *Radio* was his own horse. The tip sent his stock booming.

Often, too, his dignity as a man of substance and position would yield, dissolve, melt down to the bones of god-fearing humility .

" I'm one of yourselves, lads," he cried. " I wassent born with a silver spoon in my mouth. I was brought up hard and proper. I fought my way up. It's my policy to give every one of you the chance to do the same! "

But his trump card, never thrown down openly, but skilfully displayed up his sleeve, was his power to afford them employment. Though he was human, one of themselves, a man who had been ground through the mill, he was nevertheless the Boss. Behind all his brag and bluster he exhibited himself as their benefactor, who had taken over the derelict Neptune, who now proposed to find honest work for every man jack of them. That would come, naturally, after the Election.

His campaign grew in flamboyance and power. Ramage, who had once kicked the youthful Joe's backside for stealing a pig's bladder, was now his most devoted toady. At Ramage's behest, the Rev. Low preached a fervid sermon from New Bethel Street pulpit, extolling the virtues of law and order and Mr. Joseph Gowlan, and condemning to the everlasting outer darkness those who dared to vote for Fenwick. Connolly, at the gas-works, had declared openly that any employee who did not support Gowlan was a b—— Red and would be sacked on the spot. The Tynecastle Press was solid for Joe. Jim Mawson, enigmatically in the background, pulled several strings in the high cause of humanity. Every day two aeroplanes flew over from the Rusford works and gambolled in advertisement above Sleescale. On fine afternoons there was even some accidental sky writing. Money talked in many devious ways. Strange men were seen in Sleescale, mingling with the workers, making groups at the street corners, standing treat in the Salutation. As for promises—Joe promised everything.

David saw the forces marshalled against him, and he fought back with a desperate courage. But how pitiful his weapons were against Joe's armoury! Everywhere he turned he felt an insidious grip upon him, limiting his activities, crushing him. Unsparingly, he redoubled his efforts, using all his physical resources, all the training and experience of his political career. The more he battled, the more Joe countered. The heckling, which from the outset had interrupted David's meetings, now became unmerciful. Ordinary interruptions he could deal with and often turn to his own advantage. But this heckling was not legitimate. It came from a gang of Tynecastle rowdies who turned up at every meeting organised under Pete Bannon, ex-middle weight and bartender from the Malmo Wharf, ready and willing for trouble. Free fights regularly took place; it became the rule for all David's outdoor meetings to be broken up in wild disorder. Wilson, the agent, protested furiously to the police and demanded adequate protection. His protest was apathetically received.

" It's none of our business," Roddam told him impudently. " This Bannon has nothing to do with us. You can find your own b—— stewards."

The clean campaign continued, developing along subtler lines. On the morning of the following Tuesday, on the way to his committee rooms, David was met by a notice, roughly splashed in white paint on the wall at the end of Lamb Lane: *Ask Fenwick about his wife.* His face paled, he took a step forward as if to wipe out the indignity. Useless, quite useless. The notice shrieked all over the town, every prominent wall and house-end, even the railway sidings, bore the brutal and unanswerable words. In a mist of pain and horror, David went along Lamb Street and entered his rooms. Wilson and Harry Ogle were waiting on him. Both had seen the notice. Ogle's face worked with indignation.

" It's too bad, David," he groaned. " It's too damnable. We've got to go to him . . . lodge a protest."

" He'll only deny it," David answered in a steely voice. " Nothing would please him better than for us to go whining to him."

"Then by God we'll get our own back somehow," Harry answered passionately. "I'll have something to say about him when I speak for you at the Snook to-night."

"No, Harry." David shook his head with sudden determination. "I'll have no retaliation."

Lately in the face of this organised persecution he had felt neither anger nor hatred, but an extraordinary intensification of his inward life. He saw this inward life as the real explanation of man's existence, independent of the forms of religion, inseparably detached from the material plane. Purity of motive was the only standard, the real expression of the soul. Nothing else mattered. And the fullness of this spiritual interpretation of his own purpose left no room for malice or hatred.

But Harry Ogle felt otherwise. Harry was on fire with indignation, his simple soul demanded fair play, or at least the plain justice of measure for measure. At the Snook that night, where, at eight o'clock, he was holding a supporters' open-air meeting on his own, Harry was carried away and so far forgot himself as to criticise Joe's tactics. David had been up at Hedley Road End, the new miners' rows, and he did not reach home until late. It was a darkish, windy night. Several times a sound outside caused him to look up in anticipation, for he expected Harry to look in to let him know how the Snook meeting had gone. At ten o'clock he rose to lock the front door. It was then Harry stumbled in upon him, his face white and bloodied, half-fainting, bleeding profusely from a gash above his eye.

Lying flat on the couch with a cold compress laid on the gaping wound, while David sent Jack Kinch tearing for Dr. Scott, Harry gasped shakily:

"Coming back over the Snook they set about us, Davey—Bannon and his hooligans. I'd happened to say about Gowlan sweatin' his employees like, an' about him makin' fightin' aeroplanes an' munitions. I'd have held my own, lad, but one o' them had a bit o' lead pipe . . ." Harry smiled weakly and fainted altogether.

Harry took ten stitches in his forehead, then Harry was carried to his bed. Naturally, Joe flamed with righteous wrath. Could such a thing happen on British soil! From the platform of the Town Hall he denounced the Red Fiends, the Bolshies, who could turn, even, and assault their own leaders. He sent Harry Ogle messages of sympathy. Great prominence was given to Joe's solicitude; his most magnanimous trumpetings were printed verbatim in the newspapers. Altogether, the incident redounded highly to his credit.

But the loss of Harry's personal support was a serious blow for David. Harry, a respected figure, carried weight in Sleescale with the cautious element, and now the older men, mystified and slightly intimidated, began to think better of attending David's meetings. At that moment, too, the wave of hysteria sweeping the country against Labour reached its climax. Terror was driven into the hearts of the people by wild predictions of financial ruin. Frenzied pictures were drawn of the worker, paid in handfuls of worthless paper, desperately seeking to purchase food. And far from attributing the impending cataclysm to the end results of the existing economic system, everything was laid upon the shoulders of Labour. Don't let them take your money, was the cry. The issue was Money. We must keep our Money, at all costs keep it, preserve it, this sacred thing. Money . . . Money!

With almost superhuman endurance, David threw himself into a final effort. On October 26th he toured the town in the old light lorry which had borne him to his original success. He was in the open all day, snatching a mouthful of food between times. He spoke till his voice was almost gone. At eleven o'clock, after a last naphtha-flare meeting outside the Institute, he returned to Lamb Lane, and flung himself upon his bed, exhausted. He fell asleep instantly. The next day was polling day.

Early reports indicated a heavy poll. David remained indoors all the forenoon. He had done his best, given of his utmost; for the present he could give no more. Consciously, he did not anticipate the result, nor preconsider the verdict to be delivered upon him by his own people. Yet beneath the surface, his mind struggled between hope and fear. Sleescale had always been a safe seat for Labour, a stronghold of the miners. The men knew he had worked and fought for them. If he had failed it was not his fault. Surely they would give him the chance to work and fight for them again. He did not underrate Gowlan, nor the strategic advantage of Gowlan's position as owner of the Neptune. He was aware that Joe's unscrupulous methods had undoubtedly split the solidarity of the men; cast doubts and suspicion on his own reputation. Remembering that hateful reference to Jenny, which had damaged him more than all Joe's misrepresentation, David's heart contracted. He had a quick vision of Jenny lying in the grave. And at that a surge of pity and aspiration came over him, the old familiar feeling, intensified and strengthened. He wanted with all his soul to win, to prove the good in humanity rather than the bad. They had accused him of preaching Revolution. But the only Revolution he demanded was in the heart of man, an escape from meanness, cruelty and self-interest towards that devotion and nobility of which the human heart was capable. Without that, all other change was futile.

Towards six o'clock David went out to visit Harry Ogle and while he walked slowly up Cowpen Street he observed a figure advancing along Freehold Street. It was Arthur Barras. As they approached each other David kept his eyes straight ahead, thinking that Arthur might not wish to recognise him. But Arthur stopped.

" I've been up to vote for you," he said, quite abruptly. His voice was flat, almost harsh, his cheek sallow and inclined to twitch. The odour of spirits came from his breath.

" I'm obliged to you, Arthur," David answered.

A silence.

" I'd been underground this afternoon. But when I came outbye, I suddenly remembered."

David's eyes were troubled and full of pity. He said awkwardly:

" I hardly expected your support."

" Why not ? " Arthur said. " I'm nothing now, neither red nor blue nor anything else." Then with sudden bitterness: " What does it matter, anyhow ? "

Another silence, through which the words he had just spoken seemed to wrench at Arthur. He raised his heavy eyes to David's helplessly.

" Funny, isn't it ? " he said. " Ending up like this." With an expressionless nod he turned and made his way down the street.

David continued on his way to Ogle's, touched and profoundly troubled by this encounter, where so little had been said and everything implied. It was like a warning: how terrible defeat could be. Arthur's ideals were shattered, he had stepped away from life, shrinking, with every fibre crying: " I have suffered enough. I will suffer no more." The battle was over, the flame had gone out. David sighed as he turned into Ogle's house.

He spent the evening with Harry, who was considerably better and in bright spirits. Though both their minds were concentrated on the coming result, they talked little of the election. Harry, however, in his gentle, thoughtful manner, predicted victory—anything else was unthinkable. After supper they played cribbage, to which game Harry was an addict, until nearly eleven o'clock. But David's eyes kept straying towards the clock. Now that he must know so soon, an intolerable sense of strain possessed him. Twice he suggested it was time for him to go, that the counting at the Town Hall must be well upon the way. But Ogle, aware, perhaps, of David's anxiety, insisted that he remain a little longer. The result could not be known before two o'clock. In the meantime here was a comfortable fire and a chair. So David acquiesced, curbing his restlessness, expectation and uneasiness. But finally, just after one o'clock, he rose. Before he left the room Harry shook him by the hand.

" Since I can't be there, I'm going to congratulate you now. But I'm sorry to miss the sight of Gowlan's face when he hears you've licked him."

The night had turned still now, and there was a bright half moon. As David neared the Town Hall he was amazed at the crowds in the streets. He had some difficulty in forcing himself towards the steps of the Hall. But he got in at last and joined Wilson in the lobby. Inside the

Council Chamber the open count was taking place. Wilson turned enigmatically and made room for David beside him. He looked tired.

"Another half-hour and we'll know."

The lobby was filling up with people. Then, from outside, came the slow hooting of a car. A minute later Gowlan entered at the head of his party—Snagg, his agent, Ramage, Connolly, Bostock, several of his Tynecastle associates, and in honour of this final occasion, Jim Mawson in person. Joe wore a coat with an astrakhan fur collar which hung open, displaying his evening clothes beneath. His face was full and slightly flushed. He had been dining late with his friends; and after dinner there had been old brandy and cigars. He swaggered down the lobby, through the crowd which parted before him, then outside the council room door he drew up with his back towards David and was immediately surrounded by his partisans. Loud laughter and conversation immediately engaged the group.

About ten minutes later old Rutter, Clerk to the Council and Recording Officer, came out of the room with a paper in his hand. Immediately there was a hush. Rutter looked immensely important; and he was smiling. When David saw that smile on Rutter's face his heart gave a thud, then sank within him. Still smiling, peering over his gold-rimmed glasses. Rutter searched the crowded lobby, then, holding his importance, he called out the names of the two candidates.

Immediately Joe's group pressed through the double doors after Rutter. At the same time Wilson rose.

"Come on," he said to David; and his voice held a note of anxiety.

David rose and crowded with the others through the council room. There was no order, no sense of precedence, merely a flood of tense and unrestrained excitement.

"Please, gentlemen, please," Rutter kept repeating, "allow the candidates to come through."

Up the familiar iron staircase, through the small committee room and at last out upon the balcony. The cool night air came gratefully after the heat and lights within. Below an enormous gathering of people filled the street in front of the Hall. The pale half moon sailed high above the headstocks of the Neptune and laid faint silver scales upon the sea. A mutter of anticipation kept rising from the waiting crowd.

The balcony was very full. David was squeezed forward to the extreme corner. Beside him, carried away from Gowlan by the press, was Ramage. The fat butcher stared at David, his big hands twitching, his deep-set eyes lit, beneath their bushy grey brows, by excitement and spite. The frantic desire to see David beaten was written on his face.

Rutter was in the middle of the balcony now, facing the hushed crowd, the paper in his hand. One moment of deadly stillness, electric, agonising. Never in all his life had David known a moment so painful, so agitating as this. His heart beat wildly within his breast. Then Rutter's shrill high voice rang out:

Mr. Joseph Gowlan	.. ..	8,852
Mr. David Fenwick	.. ..	7,490

A great shout went up and it was Ramage who led it. "Hurrah, hurrah!" Ramage bellowed like a bull, waving his arms, ecstatic with delight. Cheer after cheer split the air. Joe's supporters were mobbing him on the balcony, overwhelming him with congratulations. David gripped the cold iron rail, striving for control, for strength. Beaten, beaten, beaten! He raised his eyes, saw Ramage bending towards him, lips working with outrageous delight.

"You're beat, damn you," gloated Ramage. "You've lost. You've lost everything."

"Not everything," David answered in a low voice.

More cheers, shouts, persistent calls for Joe. He was in the direct centre of the balcony now, against the railing, drinking in the adulation of the dense, excited crowd. He towered above them, a massive, dominant figure, black against the moonlight, unbelievably enlarged and menacing. Below, the pale faces of the people lay before him. They were his—all his, they belonged to him, for his use, to his purpose. The earth was his, and the heavens. A faint hum came distantly—a night flight of his Rusford planes. He was a king, he was divine, power illimitable was his. He was only beginning. He would go on, on. The fools beneath his feet would help him. He would mount to the heights, crack the world with his bare hands, split the sky with his lightning. Peace and War answered to his call. Money belonged to him. Money, money, money . . . and the slaves of money. Raising both his arms towards the sky in a gesture of supreme hypocrisy he began:

"My dear friends . . ."

XXIII

FIVE o'clock on this cold September morning. It was not yet light and the wind, pouring out of the sea darkness, rushed across the arches of the sky and polished the stars to a high glitter. Silence lay upon the Terraces.

And then, breaking fitfully through the silence and the darkness, a gleam appeared in Hannah Brace's window. The gleam lingered and ten minutes later the door opened and old Hannah came out of her house catching her breath as the icy wind took her. She wore a shawl, hobnailed boots and a huddle of petticoats lined with brown paper for warmth. A man's cap was pulled upon her head hiding her thin straggle of grizzled hair, and bound longwise about her old jaws and ears was a swathe of red flannel. In her hand she carried a long pole. Since old Tom Calder had died of pleurisy, Hannah was now the caller of the Terraces, and glad enough these hard times for " the extra little bit " the work brought in. Waddling slightly because of her rupture, she made her way slowly along Inkerman, a poor old bundle, scarcely human, tapping the windows with her pole, calling the men due on the foreshift of the pit.

But outside No. 23 she spared her knocking. Never any need to call up No. 23, then or now, never, never, thought Hannah with a flicker of approval. Past the illumined window Hannah went, shivering her way along, lifting her pole, knocking and calling, calling and knocking, disappearing into the raw dimness of Sebastopol beneath.

Inside No. 23 Martha moved about the bright kitchen briskly. The fire was already ablaze, her bed in the alcove made, the kettle steaming, sausages sizzling in the pan. Deftly she spread a blue-checked cover on the table and laid a place for one. She wore her seventy years with lightness, even with alacrity. On her face there lay a look of indomitable satisfaction. Ever since she had come back to her own house in Inkerman, her old place, her own home, that deep-set satisfaction had burned in her eyes, easing the sombre furrow on her brow, making her expression strangely gay.

A survey of her arrangements showed everything in order, and a glance towards the clock—that famous marbled pot-stour trophy—indicated half-past five. Moving lightly on her felt slippers she took three brisk steps upwards on the open ladder and called to the room above :

" David! Half-past five, David."

And listening, one ear tilted, she waited until she heard him stirring overhead—firm footsteps, the sound of water splashing from the ewer, his cough several times repeated.

Ten minutes later David came down, stood for a moment holding his cold hands to the fire, then sat in at the table. He wore pit clothes.

Martha served him his breakfast without delay, the sausages, her home-made bread and a pot of scalding tea. Real tenderness was in her face as she watched him eat.

" I've put some cinnamon in the tea," she remarked. " It'll cut that cough of yours in no time."

" Thanks, mother."

" I mind it used to help your father. He swore by my cinnamon tea."

" Yes, mother." He did not immediately glance up, but in a moment, lifting his head suddenly, he caught her unawares. Her expression, quite unguarded, was startling in its devotion. Quickly, almost with embarrassment, he averted his eyes: for the first time in all his recollection he had seen open love for him in her face. To cover his feelings he went on eating, bending over the table, sipping the steaming tea. He knew, of course, the reason of this new demonstrativeness—it was because he was back in the pit at last. Through all those years of study, of schoolmastering, of the Federation, yes, even of Parliament, she had sealed her heart against him. But now that he had been driven to return to the Neptune she saw him truly her son, following the tradition of his father, a reality, a man at last.

It was not an instinct of bravado which had forced him to the pit again but the plain and bitter fact of sheer necessity. He had been obliged to find work, and to find it quickly, and it was amazing how difficult the task had been. There was no room now in the Federation office; the antagonism of Transport House had shut him out there; in his half-qualified state teaching was absolutely closed to him; he had been compelled to turn inbye—standing in the line before Arthur in the underviewer's office, begging to go underground again. Misfortune had not come to him alone—his shift in this predicament was far from being unique. Labour's annihilation at the Election had placed many unseated candidates in a desperate position. Ralston was clerking in a Liverpool ship-broker's office, Bond assisting a photographer in Leeds, and Davis, good old Jack Davis, was playing the piano in a Rhondda cinema. How different from the position of the apostates! He smiled grimly, thinking of Dudgeon, Chalmers, Bebbington and the rest, basking in national popularity, tranquilly subscribing to a policy which cut at the very heart of Labour conviction. Bebbington in particular, featured and photographed in every paper, broadcasting on all stations the week before—a noble speech, resounding with platitudes and pietic jingoism—was hailed as the saviour of the nation.

Abruptly, David scraped back his chair and reached for his muffler which lay on the rails above the range. With his back to the fire he swathed it about his neck, then laced on his heavy boots, stamping them comfortable on the stone floor. Martha had his bait-poke ready, all neatly stowed in greased paper, his can filled with tea and safely corked. She stood polishing a big red apple on her skirt, polishing until it shone. As she put in in his poke with the rest she smiled.

" You were always set on an apple, Davey. I minded when I was in the co-operative yesterday."

" Ay, mother." He smiled back at her, both touched and amused by her obvious solicitude. " Only I didn't get so many in those days."

A slight reproving shake of her head. Then:

" You'll not forget to bring Sammy up to-night, like. I'm bakin' currant cake this mornin'."

" But mother," he protested, " you'll have Annie after you, if you keep stealing Sammy every meal-time."

Her gaze wandered from his; there was no rancour in her face, only a vague embarrassment.

" Oh well," she mumbled, at length, " if she feels that way she better come up herself like, too. I cannot have my Sammy work his first shift in the pit without I gie him currant cake." She paused, masking her softness with a pretence of severity. " D'ye hear me, man. Ask the woman to come up too."

" Right, mother," he answered, moving towards the door.

But she had to see him off, and with her own hands to open the door for him. She always did that for him now, it was the highest sign of her regard. Facing the keen darkness she answered his final nod with a slow movement of her head, then stood with one hand on her hip, watching his figure step out along Inkerman. Only when it had vanished did she close the door to return to the warmth of the kitchen. And immediately, although it was so early, she began with a kind of secretive joy to lay out her baking things—flour and currants and peel—laying them out eagerly, tenderly, to make the cake for Sammy. She tried to hide it, but she could not, the look of happiness that dwelt triumphantly upon her proud dark face.

Along the Terraces David went, his footfalls ringing and echoing amongst the other footfalls of the early frigid twilight. Dim shapes moved with him in comradeship, the shapes of the twilight men. A muffled word of greeting: " How, Ned "; " How, Tom "; " How, Davey." But for the most part silence. Heavy-footed, bent of head, breath coming whitely from the frost, a faint pipe glow here and there, massing forward in shadowy formation, the march of the twilight men.

Ever since his return to the Neptune, David felt this moment deeply. He had failed, perhaps, to lead the van in battle, but at least he was marching with the men. He had not betrayed himself or them. Their lot remained bound to his lot, their future to his future. Courage came to him from the thought. Perhaps one day he would rise again from the pit, one day, perhaps, help this plodding army towards a new freedom. Instinctively he lifted his head.

Opposite Quay Street he crossed the road and knocked at the door of one of the houses. Without waiting for an answer he turned the handle, ducked his head and entered. This kitchen, too, was full of firelight. And Sammy, ready to the last bootlace, stood waiting impatiently in the middle of the floor while Annie, his mother, considered him silently from the shadow of the hearth.

" You're in good time, Sammy lad," David cried cheerily. " I was afraid I'd have to pull you out of bed."

Sammy grinned, his blue eyes disappearing from sheer excitement. He was not very tall for fourteen years, but he made up for it in spirit, thrilling to the great adventure of his first day underground.

" He could hardly get to sleep last night for thinking about it," Annie said, coming forward. " He's had me up this last hour."

" Eh, he looks a regular pitman," David smiled. " I'm pretty lucky to have him for my trapper, Annie."

" You'll be careful with him, Davey," Annie murmured, in a quiet aside.

" Oh, mother," protested Sammy, colouring.

" I'll watch out for him, Annie," David said reassuringly. " Don't you worry." He glanced towards Annie who now stood with her fine pale face warmed by the fire glow, the top button of her blouse, unfastened, revealing her smooth straight throat. Her figure, erect even in repose, had both strength and softness. Her faint anxiety for Sammy, only half concealed, caused her to seem curiously young and untried. All at once, his heart moved in affection towards her. How brave she was, how honest and unselfish!—she had real nobility. " By the by, Annie," he remarked, making his words offhand, " you and Sammy are invited up to-night. There's going to be a regular spread."

A silence.

" Am I really asked ? " she said.

He nodded emphatically, quizzically.

" My mother's own words."

The trace of wistfulness left her; her eyes fell; he could see that she was deeply gratified at this recognition, at last, from the old woman.

" I'll be glad to come, Davey," she said.

Sammy, already at the door, was chafing to be away. He turned the handle suggestively. And David, with a quick good-bye to Annie, followed him outside. Down the street they went, side by side, towards the pit. David was silent at first; he had his own thoughts. That look in Annie's eyes as they lingered upon Sammy had strangely inspired him. Courage and hope, he thought, courage and hope.

They passed Ramage's shop. When they came out of the Neptune at the end of the shift the shutters would be down, the door open, a Ramage planted there, waiting to gloat upon David's humiliation. Every day of those four weeks, Ramage had waited, wickedly jubilant, exacting the last ounce of triumph from his victory.

And now David and Sammy drew near to the pit yard. They made a little detour to avoid some trucks on which, printed large in white, was the name MAWSON & GOWLAN. On they went, part of the slowly moving stream of men. Above them, looming in the darkness, rose the new headstocks of the Neptune, higher than before, dominating the town, the harbour and the sea. David stole a sidelong glance at Sammy whose face had now lost a trifle of its exuberance, intimidated by the nearness of the great event. And, drawing closer to the boy, David began to talk to him, diverting his attention towards other things.

" We'll go fishing, Saturday, you and I, Sammy. September's always a good month up the Wansbeck. We'll get some brandlings at Middlerig and up we'll go. Are you game, Sammy ? "

" Ay, Uncle Davey." With eager yet doubtful eyes upon the headstocks.

" And when we come back, Sammy, hanged if I don't stand you a pie and lemonade in old Mrs. Wept's."

" Ay, Uncle Davey." Eyes still fascinated upon the headstocks. And then, with a little rush. " It's pretty dark when you get down, like, isn't it ? "

David smiled encouragingly.

" Not on your life, man. And in any case you'll soon get used to it."

Together they crossed the pit yard and, with the others, climbed the steps towards the cage. And sheltering Sammy, David guided him safely through the crush into the great steel pen. Sammy pressed very close to David now and in the confines of the cage his hand sought out David's hand.

" Does it drop quick ? " he whispered, with a catch in his throat.

" Not so quick," David whispered back. " Just hold your breath the first time, Sammy lad, and it's not so bad."

A silence. The bar clanged. Another silence. The sound of a distant bell. They stood there, the men, massed together in the cage, massed together in the silence and the dimness of the dawn. Above them towered the headstocks of the pit, dominating the town, the harbour and the sea. Beneath them, like a tomb, lay the hidden darkness of the earth. The cage dropped. It dropped suddenly, swiftly, into the hidden darkness. And the sound of its falling rose out of that darkness like a great sigh which mounted towards the furthermost stars.

THE END